D0882684

EVERYMAN, I will go with thee,

and be thy guide,

In thy most need to go by thy side

HENRY WADSWORTH LONGFELLOW

Born in 1807 at Portland, Maine, the son of a lawyer. Travelled in Europe before accepting Chair of Modern Languages, first at Bowdoin College and later at Harvard. Died in 1882.

Longfellow's Poems

INTRODUCTION BY
THOMAS BYROM
M.A., B.LITT.(Oxon.), A.M.(Harvard)

DENT: LONDON
EVERYMAN'S LIBRARY
DUTTON: NEW YORK

© Introduction, J. M. Dent & Sons Ltd, 1970
Made in Great Britain
at the
Aldine Press · Letchworth · Herts
for
J. M. DENT & SONS LTD
Alaine House · Bedford Street · London
First included in Everyman's Library 1969
Enlarged edition 1960
Last reprinted 1970

NO. 382

ISBN: 0 460 00382 8

INTRODUCTION

WE USED to apologize for Longfellow, angrily or coyly. When we were in the schoolroom our first ideas of poetry were formed, at least partly, by *Hiawatha*, *Evangeline* and *The Wreck of the Hesperus*. When we grew up we saw that there is some difference between popular and good poetry, and we learned to speak scornfully of a poet who allowed billows to froth like yeast. How embarrassing to have enjoyed the trochees of a man who wore his heart so much upon his sleeve! Valuing as we do the recondite and the suggestive, how could we have been stirred by such homely and sententious stuff! And having in this way caught ourselves napping, we talked in an alert manner not of Longfellow's poems but only of his reputation—how he outsold even the Tennyson of *Enoch Arden*—as if embarrassment were on behalf of our grandfathers. *We* had never really liked Longfellow. But of course we were about as alert as the Dormouse, and history (especially in the form of a fine essay written ten years ago by Howard Nemerov) has poured on our nose such hot tea that we shall not drop off again soon. We are awake to the fact that we do after all like Longfellow, that his reputation is not more interesting than his poems, that we have no lasting reason to feel sorry for enjoying a large number of them.

Longfellow was born in 1807 in Portland, Maine, of comfortable English stock, tolerant in their puritanism and prosperous. His childhood was calm and cheerful. When he graduated from Bowdoin College he was offered a professorship in Modern Languages there, and travelled in Europe from 1826 to 1829 to prepare himself. He married happily in 1831, in 1834 succeeded Ticknor in the Smith Professorship at Harvard, but first went to Europe again to brush up his languages. His wife died on this trip. From 1836 to 1854 he taught at Harvard, and published in 1839 *Hyperion* and his first really original and important book of verse, *Voices of the Night*; in 1842 *Poems on Slavery*; in 1843 an anthology with some of his own translations, *Poets and Poetry of Europe*. In 1843 he married Fanny Appleton, a beautiful, wealthy and independently minded woman, whose father presented the couple with the grand Craigie House in Cambridge, where Longfellow lived for the rest of his life.

Fanny burned to death when her clothes caught fire, in the summer of 1861. Longfellow consoled himself by working away on his translation of Dante. Meanwhile he had published *Evangeline*, *Hiawatha* and *The Courtship of Miles Standish*. In 1868 he went a third time to Europe, where Oxford and Cambridge conferred honorary degrees upon him and where Queen Victoria, Tennyson and Dickens all received him warmly. He published the first part of his *Tales of a Wayside Inn* in 1863, and the third part in 1873; his translation of Dante in 1867; in 1878 *Kéramos* and in 1880 *Ultima Thule*. He died in 1882, greatly venerated and read more widely, as one of his correspondents had told him, than any poet had ever been read in his own lifetime.

Except for the deaths of his two wives and an infant daughter, there were few outward checks to a life of long and easy success, of calm industry, happy friendships and prosperity. Yet the modern biographers have revealed, after close study of his rather stoical correspondence and diaries, that gentle Longfellow was often inwardly tormented—an insomniac, the victim of savage headaches, nervous depression, melancholia and lethargy. He was buffeted by a private storm which his art was unable to express; neither could he find to comfort him, in metaphysics or psychology, a name for what troubled him.

We shall not understand him, I think, if we do not bear in mind that he was afraid, and that his fears remained nameless, inexpressible. His poetry is limited by his fright, and the beauty of his words is apprehended only if we strain to hear the words he dared not utter. I feel sure that poetry was for him a kind of fastness. where he could find and impart consolation. He wrote as if he wanted poetry to be above all else 'helpful to the mass of men' (as Charles Eliot Norton put it); it must be of sound social service by promoting an ethic of 'charity, gentleness and faith'. He made a small but strong fort of verse in order to comfort and cheer the 'mankind' for whom he felt a broad simple Unitarian compassion. Here I am making a crucial claim out of conjecture. But when a poet is so bland, guesses may be all we have to work with. And after all it is not credible that in such times a quietist is strong and certain because of inner assurances.

The three great poets of the age, Emily Dickinson, Poe and Whitman, all wrote out of a pressing sense of the darkness and the silence of their country, and if the dark was wholly personal

for them, it must have been felt personally also by a sensitive man like Longfellow, who fights as they all do a rearguard action against a national history barren of a national art. Longfellow's public role of bard needs to be seen more as a role of withdrawal and reticence than of self-assertion and self-possession: he was hiding easily in the crowd. And what makes him of minor stature compared with his three contemporaries is that from the fastness he rarely sallied forth to brave, as Emily Dickinson did in rural Amherst, the dark places of the soul; to outface as Poe did a suspicion of grossness in the heart; to shout down as Whitman did the overwhelming silence. In a queer way, Longfellow knew his limits—he was not a pioneer like these others, but one who stayed put half way into the wilds and rallied the timorous.

This is doubtless too bold a way of saying it. I mean neither to make a melodrama of a guess nor to suggest that Longfellow's achievement is mainly negative nor indeed to cast him as a glamorous poet of dereliction and deprivation. He was after all a parlour poet and his tone is that of domestic evangelicalism. He builds his poems securely out of present comforts, not out of the nameless fears with which Robert Frost and Robert Lowell frame their verse. Yet these two New England poets, his local though unwilling heirs, demonstrate in the themes and attitudes they share with Longfellow how in a central if restricted way the parlour poet, for all 'the grizzled silver' of his beard (as Lowell has remarked in a poem preferring Hawthorne), wrote about the right, the important, things. It is not so distant a step from the novel *Kavanagh* to *The Mills of the Kavanaughs*, from *By The Seaside* to *Near the Ocean*, or from 'The Jewish Cemetery at Newport' to 'The Quaker Graveyard in Nantucket'. The anti-war protestor who wrote 'The Arsenal at Springfield' is an ancestor of the poet of 'Fall 1961'. And in his view of New England ways, Longfellow is like Frost—chaste, stoical, denying all complacency. 'The Fire of Drift-Wood' and 'The Ropewalk', beautiful neglected poems, seal this bond. So do some of the famous neglected pieces, especially *Hiawatha*, a much tougher poem than most of us remember. Again, like Lowell, Longfellow is a magpie of history. Both have a strong, romantic and somewhat undiscriminating sense of history, both self-appointed salvagers of a foreign past and its literary artefacts. While Longfellow's too placid translations are obviously different from Lowell's rowdier 'imitations', the purpose is identical, local, of the same

culture. Distant wars, country ways, the unreclaimable past, the failure of community in the present new world, or the small successes of friendship and love, the vanity within the heart— these are the themes all three poets share; biblical, Horatian and New England themes.

But here it is as well to be wary of special pleading. Between Longfellow and the great New England poets of his own and of our century there is one crucial difference. It is what critics and biographers call Longfellow's gentleness. By this they usually mean placidity or docility. The criticism is only hinted at, so the problem may be avoided. I have deliberately put Longfellow against a harsh background in order to throw his excessive sweetness into relief, not to justify it but only to explain it sympathetically. He is too docile, partly of course because of the writers who influenced him most strongly— dignified Bryant, sentimental Tom Moore, Campbell and Samuel Rogers, daydreaming Washington Irving. A very soft stable! No wonder he clung to the (for him) disabling belief that 'life, like French poetry, is imperfect without the feminine rhyme'. His Indian poems (except for *Hiawatha*) hardly get beyond the pathetic and elegiac vogue of Freneau.

But other influences, seeming as soft, are more telling, especially Cowper's. I imagine Longfellow felt great kinship with a mind which, like his, turned continually from the terrors of the dark to domestic comforts, holding fast to the frail objects of civilized life. It is easy to hear the despair of crazy Cowper under Longfellow's fireside meditations on the Devereux farm near Marblehead. He and his friends sit and listen to the wind and the sea, and watch the flames of driftwood. They speak of:

> The first slight swerving of the heart,
> That words are powerless to express,
> And leave it still unsaid in part,
> Or say it in too great excess.
>
> Oft died the words upon our lips,
> As suddenly, from out the fire
> Built of the wreck of stranded ships,
> The flames would leap and then expire.
>
> And, as their splendour flashed and failed,
> We thought of wrecks upon the main,—
> Of ships dismasted, that were hailed
> And sent no answer back again.

As the poet speaks openly of the namelessness of the troubles which saddened him, we think of Cowper's 'The Castaway' and

we understand the nature of the 'gentleness' characteristic of both. We think of the world Longfellow felt unable to face, beyond the parlour and the palisade. And we are reminded that for all his idealism ('this world is only the *negative* of the world to come') he felt something despairing about nature, about what is given to man, as Frost and Lowell have felt. It is not hope or assurance which moves him to remark that man must spiritualize the laws of nature 'by a gloss—by a voluptuous commentary'. It is rather a bleak and faltering view of our condition, as if the best we can hope to do is patch up a bad job, 'till the deformed seems beautiful, and the sensual is clothed upon with the ideal'. Here the puritan, weary of the vain shows and delusions of the world, nearly unburdens his heart.

But he was never really able to speak his heart. There was to be no revelation for him, no facing up to the wretched facts, no lasting consolation—not in the fashionable transcendentalism, nor at the spiritualist's table which he occasionally visited, certainly not in his latitudinarian puritanism, not in success, long life, prosperity and love. He hoped, secretly, only for what he might shore against the ruins. And only in his poetry, his fastness, was he able to find and give solace. His best verse provides, as he most wanted it to, a voluptuous commentary, a gloss helpful to the mass of men—still urgent in its counsel of charity, gentleness and faith, still helpful and cheering.

THOMAS BYROM.

Harvard,
   January, 1970.

SELECT BIBLIOGRAPHY

POETRY. *Voices of the Night*, 1839; *Ballads and Other Poems*, 1842; *Poems on Slavery*, 1842; *The Spanish Student*, 1843; *The Belfry of Bruges and Other Poems*, 1845; *Evangeline*, 1847; *The Seaside and the Fireside*, 1849; *The Golden Legend*, 1851; *Hiawatha*, 1855; *The Courtship of Miles Standish*, 1858; *Tales of a Wayside Inn*, 1863-74, 1886; *The Divine Comedy* (translation), 1867; *Christus*, 1872; *The Masque of Pandora*, 1875; *Kéramos*, 1878; *Ultima Thule*, 1880; *In the Harbor*, 1882.

COLLECTED EDITIONS. Edited R. Buchanan, 1868; with critical Memoir by W. M. Rossetti, 1870, 1880, 1881; Chandos Poets, 1880; Newbery Classics, 1891; Complete Poetical Works (Oxford), 6 vols., 1893; Cambridge Edition, 1895; Oxford Miniature Edition, 1902; World's Classics, 1903; Oxford Complete Copyright Edition, 1904; New Century Library, 1907.

PROSE. *Outre-Mer: A Pilgrimage Beyond the Sea*, 1834-5; *Hyperion*, 1839; *Kavanagh*, 1849; collected edition in the Chandos Classics, 1887.

COLLECTED WORKS. Riverside edition, 11 vols., 1886; with Life by R. Cochrane, 1888.

BIOGRAPHY AND CRITICISM. G. L. Austin, *Henry Wadsworth Longfellow: His Life, His Works, His Friendships*, Boston, 1883; S. Longfellow, *Life of Henry Wadsworth Longfellow*, Boston, 1886; E. S. Robertson, *Life of Longfellow*, 1887; W. D. Howells, *Literary Friends and Acquaintance*, 1900; T. W. Higginson, *Henry Wadsworth Longfellow*, Boston and New York, 1902; E. Norton, *Henry Wadsworth Longfellow: A Sketch of his Life*, Boston and New York, 1907; O. Smeaton, *Longfellow and his Poetry*, 1919; E. W. Longfellow, *Random Memories*, Boston and New York, 1922; E. Goggio, *Longfellow and Dante*, Cambridge, Mass., 1924; H. S. Gorman, *Henry Wadsworth Longfellow*, New York, 1926; J. T. Hatfield, *New Light on Longfellow*, Boston and New York, 1933; L. Thompson, *Young Longfellow, 1809-1843*, 1938; C. L. Johnson, *Professor Longfellow of Harvard*, Oregon, 1944; E. Wagenknecht, *Longfellow: A Full-Length Portrait*, New York, 1955 and (ed.), *Mrs Longfellow: Selected Letters and Journals of Fanny Appleton Longfellow*, New York, 1956; N. Arvin, *Longfellow: His Life and Work*, Boston, 1963; E. Wagenknecht, *Henry Wadsworth Longfellow: Portrait of an American Humourist*, 1966.

CONTENTS

Contents

LONGFELLOW'S POEMS

VOICES OF THE NIGHT

Πότνια, πότνια νύξ,
ὑπνοδότειρα τῶν πολυπόνων βροτῶν,
Ἐρεβόθεν ἴθι· μόλε μόλε κατάπτερος
Ἀγαμεμνόνιον ἐπὶ δόμον·
ὑπὸ γὰρ ἀλγέων, ὑπό τε συμφορᾶς
διοιχόμεθ', οἰχόμεθα.

EURIPIDES.

PRELUDE

PLEASANT it was, when woods were
    green
And winds were soft and low,
To lie amid some sylvan scene,
Where, the long drooping boughs
    between,
Shadows dark and sunlight sheen
    Alternate come and go;

Or where the denser grove receives
    No sunlight from above,
But the dark foliage interweaves
In one unbroken roof of leaves,
Underneath whose sloping eaves
    The shadows hardly move.

Beneath some patriarchal tree
    I lay upon the ground;
His hoary arms uplifted he,
And all the broad leaves over me
Clapped their little hands in glee,
    With one continuous sound;—

A slumberous sound, a sound that
    brings
    The feelings of a dream,
As of innumerable wings,
As, when a bell no longer swings,
Faint the hollow murmur rings
    O'er meadow, lake, and stream.

And dreams of that which cannot
    die,
    Bright visions, came to me,

As lapped in thought I used to lie,
And gaze into the summer sky,
Where the sailing clouds went by,
    Like ships upon the sea;

Dreams that the soul of youth
    engage
    Ere Fancy has been quelled;
Old legends of the monkish page,
Traditions of the saint and sage,
Tales that have the rime of age,
    And chronicles of eld.

And, loving still these quaint old
    themes,
    Even in the city's throng
I feel the freshness of the streams,
That, crossed by shades and sunny
    gleams,
Water the green land of dreams,
    The holy land of song.

Therefore, at Pentecost, which
    brings
    The Spring, clothed like a
    bride,
When nestling buds unfold their
    wings,
And bishop's-caps have golden
    rings,
Musing upon many things,
    I sought the woodlands wide.

The green trees whispered low and
    mild;
    It was a sound of joy!

3

They were my playmates when a
   child,
And rocked me in their arms so
   wild!
Still they looked at me and smiled,
   As if I were a boy;

And even whispered, mild and low,
   "Come, be a child once more!"
And waved their long arms to and
   fro,
And beckoned solemnly and slow;
Oh, I could not choose but go
   Into the woodlands hoar,—

Into the blithe and breathing air,
   Into the solemn wood,
Solemn and silent everywhere!
Nature with folded hands seemed
   there,
Kneeling at her evening prayer!
   Like one in prayer I stood.

Before me rose an avenue
   Of tall and sombrous pines;
Abroad their fan-like branches
   grew,
And, where the sunshine darted
   through,
Spread a vapour soft and blue,
   In long and sloping lines.

And, falling on my weary brain,
   Like a fast-falling shower,
The dreams of youth came back
   again,—
Low lispings of the summer rain,
Dropping on the ripened grain,
   As once upon the flower.

Visions of childhood! Stay, oh,
   stay!
   Ye were so sweet and wild!
And distant voices seemed to say,
   "It cannot be! They pass away!
Other themes demand thy lay;
   Thou art no more a child!

"The land of Song within thee lies,
   Watered by living springs;

The lids of Fancy's sleepless eyes
Are gates unto that Paradise;
Holy thoughts, like stars, arise;
   Its clouds are angels' wings.

"Learn, that henceforth thy song
   shall be,
   Not mountains capped with
    snow,
Nor forests sounding like the sea,
Nor rivers flowing ceaselessly,
Where the woodlands bend to see
   The bending heavens below.

"There is a forest where the din
   Of iron branches sounds!
A mighty river roars between,
And whosoever looks therein
Sees the heavens all black with sin,
   Sees not its depths, nor bounds.

"Athwart the swinging branches
   cast,
   Soft rays of sunshine pour;
Then comes the fearful wintry
   blast;
Our hopes, like withered leaves,
   fall fast;
Pallid lips say, 'It is past!
   We can return no more!'

"Look, then, into thine heart,
   and write!
   Yes, into Life's deep stream!
All forms of sorrow and delight,
All solemn Voices of the Night,
That can soothe thee, or affright,—
   Be these henceforth thy theme."

HYMN TO THE NIGHT

Ασπασίη, τρίλλιστος

I heard the trailing garments of
   the Night
   Sweep through her marble halls!
I saw her sable skirts all fringed
   with light
   From the celestial walls!

I felt her presence, by its spell of
 might,
  Stoop o'er me from above;
The calm, majestic presence of the
 Night,
  As of the one I love.

I heard the sounds of sorrow and
 delight,
  The manifold, soft chimes,
That fill the haunted chambers of
 the Night,
  Like some old poet's rhymes.

From the cool cisterns of the mid-
 night air
  My spirit drank repose;
The fountain of perpetual peace
 flows there,—
  From those deep cisterns flows.

O holy Night! from thee I learn to
 bear
  What man has borne before!
Thou layest thy finger on the lips
 of Care,
  And they complain no more.

Peace! Peace! Orestes-like I
 breathe this prayer!
Descend with broad-winged flight,
The welcome, the thrice-prayed
 for, the most fair,
  The best-beloved Night!

A PSALM OF LIFE

WHAT THE HEART OF THE YOUNG
MAN SAID TO THE PSALMIST

Tell me not, in mournful numbers,
 " Life is but an empty dream! "
For the soul is dead that slumbers,
 And things are not what they
  seem.

Life is real! Life is earnest!
 And the grave is not its goal;
" Dust thou art, to dust returnest,"
 Was not spoken of the soul.

Not enjoyment, and not sorrow,
 Is our destined end or way;
But to act, that each to-morrow
 Finds us farther than to-day.

Art is long, and Time is fleeting,
 And our hearts, though stout
  and brave,
Still, like muffled drums, are beat-
 ing
  Funeral marches to the grave.

In the world's broad field of battle,
 In the bivouac of Life,
Be not like dumb, driven cattle!
 Be a hero in the strife!

Trust no Future, howe'er pleasant!
 Let the dead Past bury its dead!
Act,—act in the living Present!
 Heart within, and God o'erhead!

Lives of great men all remind us
 We can make our lives sublime,
And, departing, leave behind us
 Footprints on the sands of time;

Footprints, that perhaps another,
 Sailing o'er life's solemn main,
A forlorn and shipwrecked brother,
 Seeing, shall take heart again.

Let us, then, be up and doing,
 With a heart for any fate;
Still achieving, still pursuing,
 Learn to labour and to wait.

THE REAPER AND THE FLOWERS

There is a Reaper, whose name is
 Death,
  And, with his sickle keen,
He reaps the bearded grain at a
 breath,
  And the flowers that grow
  between.

"Shall I have nought that is
    fair?" saith he,
  "Have nought but the bearded
    grain?
Though the breath of these flowers
    is sweet to me,
  I will give them all back again."

He gazed at the flowers with tear-
    ful eyes,
  He kissed their drooping leaves;
It was for the Lord of Paradise
  He bound them in his sheaves.

"My Lord has need of these
    flowerets gay,"
  The Reaper said, and smiled;
"Dear tokens of the earth are they,
  Where he was once a child.

"They shall all bloom in fields of
    light,
  Transplanted by my care,
And saints, upon their garments
    white,
  These sacred blossoms wear."

And the mother gave, in tears and
    pain,
  The flowers she most did love;
She knew she should find them all
    again
  In the fields of light above.

O, not in cruelty, not in wrath,
  The Reaper came that day;
'Twas an angel visited the green
    earth,
  And took the flowers away.

THE LIGHT OF STARS

The night is come, but not too soon;
  And sinking silently,
All silently, the little moon
  Drops down behind the sky.

There is no light in earth or heaven,
  But the cold light of stars;

And the first watch of night is
    given
To the red planet Mars.

Is it the tender star of love?
  The star of love and dreams?
O no! from that blue tent above,
  A hero's armour gleams.

And earnest thoughts within me
    rise,
  When I behold afar,
Suspended in the evening skies,
  The shield of that red star.

O star of strength! I see thee
    stand
  And smile upon my pain;
Thou beckonest with thy mailed
    hand,
  And I am strong again.

Within my breast there is no light,
  But the cold light of stars;
I give the first watch of the night
  To the red planet Mars.

The star of the unconquered will,
  He rises in my breast,
Serene, and resolute, and still,
  And calm, and self-possessed.

And thou, too, whosoe'er thou art,
  That readest this brief psalm,
As one by one thy hopes depart,
  Be resolute and calm.

O fear not in a world like this,
  And thou shalt know ere long,
Know how sublime a thing it is
  To suffer and be strong.

FOOTSTEPS OF ANGELS

When the hours of Day are
    numbered,
  And the voices of the Night
Wake the better soul, that
    slumbered,
  To a holy, calm delight;

Ere the evening lamps are lighted,
  And, like phantoms grim and
    tall,
Shadows from the fitful firelight
  Dance upon the parlour wall;

Then the forms of the departed
  Enter at the open door;
The beloved, the true-hearted,
  Come to visit me once more;

He, the young and strong, who
    cherished
  Noble longings for the strife,
By the roadside fell and perished,
  Weary with the march of life!

They, the holy ones and weakly,
  Who the cross of suffering bore,
Folded their pale hands so meekly,
  Spake with us on earth no more!

And with them the Being
    Beauteous,
  Who unto my youth was given,
More than all things else to love me,
  And is now a saint in heaven.

With a slow and noiseless footstep
  Comes that messenger divine,
Takes the vacant chair beside me,
  Lays her gentle hand in mine.

And she sits and gazes at me
  With those deep and tender eyes,
Like the stars, so still and saint-like,
  Looking downward from the
    skies.

Uttered not, yet comprehended,
  Is the spirit's voiceless prayer,
Soft rebukes, in blessings ended,
  Breathing from her lips of air.

O, though oft depressed and lonely,
  All my fears are laid aside,
If I but remember only
  Such as these have lived and
    died!

FLOWERS

Spake full well, in language quaint
    and olden,
  One who dwelleth by the castled
    Rhine,
When he called the flowers, so blue
    and golden,
  Stars, that in earth's firmament
    do shine.

Stars they are, wherein we read
    our history,
  As astrologers and seers of eld;
Yet not wrapped about with awful
    mystery,
  Like the burning stars, which
    they beheld.

Wondrous truths, and manifold as
    wondrous,
  God hath written in those stars
    above;
But not less in the bright flowerets
    under us
  Stands the revelation of his love.

Bright and glorious is that revela-
    tion,
  Written all over this great world
    of ours;
Making evident our own creation,
  In these stars of earth,—these
    golden flowers.

And the Poet, faithful and far-
    seeing,
  Sees, alike in stars and flowers, a
    part
Of the self-same, universal being,
  Which is throbbing in his brain
    and heart.

Gorgeous flowerets in the sunlight
    shining,
  Blossoms flaunting in the eye of
    day,

Tremulous leaves, with soft and
　silver lining,
　　Buds that open only to decay;

Brilliant hopes, all woven in gor-
　geous tissues,
Flaunting gayly in the golden light;
Large desires, with most uncertain
　issues,
　　Tender wishes, blossoming at
　　night!

These in flowers and men are more
　than seeming;
　　Workings are they of the self-
　　same powers,
Which the Poet, in no idle dream-
　ing,
　　Seeth in himself and in the
　　flowers.

Everywhere about us are they
　glowing,
　　Some like stars, to tell us Spring
　　is born;
Others, their blue eyes with tears
　o'erflowing,
　　Stand like Ruth amid the golden
　　corn;

Not alone in Spring's armorial
　bearing,
　　And in Summer's green - em-
　　blazoned field,
But in arms of brave old Autumn's
　wearing,
　　In the centre of his brazen shield;

Not alone in meadows and green
　alleys,
　　On the mountain-top, and by
　　the brink
Of sequestered pools in woodland
　valleys,
　　Where the slaves of Nature
　　stoop to drink;

Not alone in her vast dome of glory,
　　Not on graves of bird and beast
　　alone,

But in old cathedrals, high and
　hoary,
　　On the tombs of heroes, carved
　　in stone;

In the cottage of the rudest
　peasant,
　　In ancestral homes, whose
　　crumbling towers,
Speaking of the Past unto the
　Present,
　　Tell us of the ancient Games of
　　Flowers;

In all places, then, and in all
　seasons,
　　Flowers expand their light and
　　soul-like wings,
Teaching us, by most persuasive
　reasons,
　　How akin they are to human
　　things.

And with childlike, credulous affec-
　tion
　　We behold their tender buds
　　expand;
Emblems of our own great resur-
　rection,
　　Emblems of the bright and
　　better land.

THE BELEAGUERED CITY

I have read, in some old marvel-
　lous tale,
　　Some legend strange and vague,
That a midnight host of spectres
　pale
　　Beleaguered the walls of Prague.

Beside the Moldau's rushing
　stream,
　　With the wan moon overhead,
There stood, as in an awful dream,
　　The army of the dead.

White as a sea-fog, landward
bound,
  The spectral camp was seen,
And, with a sorrowful, deep sound,
  The river flowed between.

No other voice nor sound was there,
  No drum, nor sentry's pace;
The mist-like banners clasped the
  air,
    As clouds with clouds embrace.

But, when the old cathedral bell
  Proclaimed the morning prayer,
The white pavilions rose and fell
  On the alarmed air.

Down the broad valley fast and far
  The troubled army fled;
Up rose the glorious morning star,
  The ghastly host was dead.

I have read, in the marvellous
  heart of man,
  That strange and mystic scroll,
That an army of phantoms vast
  and wan
    Beleaguer the human soul.

Encamped beside Life's rushing
  stream,
  In Fancy's misty light,
Gigantic shapes and shadows gleam
  Portentous through the night.

Upon its midnight battle-ground
  The spectral camp is seen,
And, with a sorrowful, deep sound,
  Flows the River of Life between.

No other voice, nor sound is there,
  In the army of the grave;
No other challenge breaks the air,
  But the rushing of Life's wave.

And, when the solemn and deep
  church-bell
  Entreats the soul to pray,
The midnight phantoms feel the
  spell
    The shadows sweep away.

Down the broad Vale of Tears afar
  The spectral camp is fled;
Faith shineth as a morning star,
  Our ghastly fears are dead.

MIDNIGHT MASS FOR THE DYING YEAR

Yes, the Year is growing old,
  And his eye is pale and bleared!
Death, with frosty hand and cold,
  Plucks the old man by the beard,
    Sorely,—sorely!

The leaves are falling, falling,
  Solemnly and slow;
Caw! caw! the rooks are calling,
  It is a sound of woe,
    A sound of woe!

Through woods and mountain
  passes
  The winds, like anthems, roll;
They are chanting solemn masses,
  Singing; "Pray for this poor
    soul,
      Pray,—pray!"

And the hooded clouds, like friars,
  Tell their beads in drops of rain,
And patter their doleful prayers:—
  But their prayers are all in vain,
    All in vain!

There he stands in the foul
  weather,
  The foolish, fond Old Year,
Crowned with wild flowers and
  with heather,
  Like weak, despised Lear,
    A king,—a king!

Then comes the summer-like day,
  Bids the old man rejoice!
His joy! his last! O, the old man
  gray,
  Loveth that ever-soft voice,
    Gentle and low.

To the crimson woods he saith,—
　To the voice gentle and low
Of the soft air, like a daughter's
　　breath,—
　　" Pray do not mock me so!
　　　Do not laugh at me! "

And now the sweet day is dead;
　Cold in his arms it lies;
No stain from its breath is spread
　Over the glassy skies,
　　No mist or stain!

Then, too, the Old Year dieth,
　And the forests utter a moan,
Like the voice of one who crieth
　In the wilderness alone,
　　" Vex not his ghost! "

Then comes, with an awful roar,
　Gathering and sounding on,

The storm-wind from Labrador,
　The wind Euroclydon,
　　The storm-wind!

Howl! howl! and from the forest
　Sweep the red leaves away!
Would the sins that thou thus
　　abhorrest,
　O Soul! could thus decay
　　And be swept away!

For there shall come a mightier
　　blast,
　There shall be a darker day;
And the stars from heaven down-
　　cast,
　Like red leaves be swept away!
　　Kyrie, eleyson!
　　Christe, eleyson!

EARLIER POEMS

[These poems were written for the most part during my college life, and all of them before the age of nineteen. Some have found their way into schools, and seem to be successful. Others lead a vagabond and precarious existence in the corners of newspapers; or have changed their names and run away to seek their fortunes beyond the sea. I say, with the Bishop of Avranches, on a similar occasion: " I cannot be displeased to see these children of mine, which I have neglected, and almost exposed, brought from their wanderings in lanes and alleys, and safely lodged, in order to go forth into the world together in a more decorous garb."]

AN APRIL DAY

WHEN the warm sun, that brings
Seed-time and harvest, has re-
　　turned again,

'Tis sweet to visit the still wood,
　where springs
　The first flower of the plain.

I love the season well,
When forest glades are teeming
　with bright forms,
Nor dark and many-folded clouds
　foretell
　The coming-on of storms.

From the earth's loosened
　mould
The sapling draws its sustenance,
　and thrives;
Though stricken to the heart with
　winter's cold,
　The drooping tree revives.

The softly-warbled song
Comes from the pleasant woods,
　and coloured wings
Glance quick in the bright sun,
　that moves along
　The forest openings.

When the bright sunset fills
The silver woods with light, the
green slope throws
Its shadows in the hollows of the
hills,
And wide the upland glows.

And, when the eve is born,
In the blue lake the sky, o'er-
reaching far,
Is hollowed out, and the moon dips
her horn,
And twinkles many a star.

Inverted in the tide,
Stand the gray rocks, and trem-
bling shadows throw,
And the fair trees look over, side
by side,
And see themselves below.

Sweet April!—many a thought
Is wedded unto thee, as hearts are
wed;
Nor shall they fail, till, to its
autumn brought,
Life's golden fruit is shed.

AUTUMN

With what glory comes and goes
the year!
The buds of spring, those beautiful
harbingers
Of sunny skies and cloudless times,
enjoy
Life's newness, and earth's garni-
ture spread out;
And when the silver habit of the
clouds
Comes down upon the autumn sun,
and with
A sober gladness the old year takes
up
His bright inheritance of golden
fruits,
A pomp and pageant fill the
splendid scene.

There is a beautiful spirit
breathing now
Its mellow richness on the clus-
tered trees,
And, from a beaker full of richest
dyes,
Pouring new glory on the autumn
woods,
And dipping in warm light the
pillared clouds,
Morn on the mountain, like a
summer bird,
Lifts up her purple wing, and in
the vales
The gentle wind, a sweet and pas-
sionate wooer,
Kisses the blushing leaf, and stirs
up life
Within the solemn woods of ash
deep-crimsoned,
And silver beech, and maple
yellow-leaved,
Where autumn, like a faint old
man, sits down
By the wayside a-weary. Through
the trees
The golden robin moves. The
purple finch,
That on wild cherry and red cedar
feeds,
A winter bird, comes with its
plaintive whistle,
And pecks by the witch-hazel,
whilst aloud,
From cottage roofs the warbling
bluebird sings,
And merrily, with oft-repeated
stroke,
Sounds from the threshing-floor
the busy flail.

O what a glory doth this world
put on
From him who, with a fervent
heart, goes forth
Under the bright and glorious sky,
and looks
On duties well performed, and
days well spent!

For him the wind, ay, and the yellow leaves
Shall have a voice, and give him eloquent teachings;
He shall so hear the solemn hymn, that Death
Has lifted up for all, that he shall go
To his long resting-place without a tear.

WOODS IN WINTER

When winter winds are piercing chill,
    And through the hawthorn blows the gale,
With solemn feet I tread the hill,
    That overbrows the lonely vale.

O'er the bare upland, and away
    Through the long reach of desert woods,
The embracing sunbeams chastely play,
    And gladden these deep solitudes.

Where, twisted round the barren oak,
    The summer vine in beauty clung,
And summer winds the stillness broke,
    The crystal icicle is hung.

Where, from their frozen urns, mute springs
    Pour out the river's gradual tide,
Shrilly the skater's iron rings,
    And voices fill the woodland side.

Alas! how changed from the fair scene,
    When birds sang out their mellow lay,
And winds were soft, and woods were green,
    And the song ceased not with the day.

But still wild music is abroad,
    Pale, desert woods! within your crowd;
And gathering winds, in hoarse accord,
    Amid the vocal reeds pipe loud.

Chill airs and wintry winds! my ear
    Has grown familiar with your song;
I hear it in the opening year,—
    I listen and it cheers me long.

HYMN OF THE MORAVIAN NUNS OF BETHLEHEM,

AT THE CONSECRATION OF PULASKI'S BANNER

When the dying flame of day
Through the chancel shot its ray,
Far the glimmering tapers shed
Faint light on the cowled head;
And the censer burning swung,
Where, before the altar, hung
The blood-red banner, that with prayer
Had been consecrated there.
And the nun's sweet hymn was heard the while,
Sung low in the dim, mysterious aisle.

    "Take thy banner! May it wave
    Proudly o'er the good and brave;
    When the battle's distant wail
    Breaks the sabbath of our vale,
    When the clarion's music thrills
    To the hearts of these lone hills,

When the spear in conflict
shakes,
And the strong lance shiver-
ing breaks.

"Take thy banner! and, be-
neath
The battle-cloud's encircling
wreath,
Guard it!—till our homes are
free!
Guard it!—God will prosper
thee!
In the dark and trying hour,
In the breaking forth of
power,
In the rush of steeds and men,
His right hand will shield thee
then.

"Take thy banner! But,
when night
Closes round the ghastly fight,
If the vanquished warrior
bow,
Spare him!—By our holy
vow,
By our prayers and many
tears,
By the mercy that endears,
Spare him!—he our love hath
shared!
Spare him!—as thou wouldst
be spared!
"Take thy banner!—and if
e'er
Thou shouldst press the
soldier's bier,
And the muffled drum should
beat
To the tread of mournful feet,
Then this crimson flag shall be
Martial cloak and shroud for
thee."

The warrior took that banner
proud,
And it was his martial cloak and
shroud!

SUNRISE ON THE HILLS

I stood upon the hills, when
heaven's wide arch
Was glorious with the sun's return-
ing march,
And woods were brightened, and
soft gales
Went forth to kiss the sun-clad
vales.
The clouds were far beneath me;—
bathed in light,
They gathered mid-way round the
wooded height,
And, in their fading glory, shone
Like hosts in battle overthrown,
As many a pinnacle, with shifting
glance,
Through the gray mist thrust up
its shattered lance,
And rocking on the cliff was left
The dark pine blasted, bare, and
cleft.
The veil of cloud was lifted, and
below
Glowed the rich valley, and the
river's flow
Was darkened by the forest's
shade,
Or glistened in the white cascade;
Where upward, in the mellow
blush of day,
The noisy bittern wheeled his
spiral way.

I heard the distant waters dash,
I saw the current whirl and flash,
And richly, by the blue lake's
silver beach,
The woods were bending with a
silent reach,
Then o'er the vale, with gentle
swell,
The music of the village bell
Came sweetly to the echo-giving
hills;
And the wild horn, whose voice the
woodland fills,

Was ringing to the merry shout,
That faint and far the glen sent out,
Where, answering to the sudden
    shot, thin smoke,
Through thick-leaved branches,
    from the dingle broke.

If thou art worn and hard beset
With sorrows, that thou wouldst
    forget,
If thou wouldst read a lesson, that
    will keep
Thy heart from fainting and thy
    soul from sleep,
Go to the woods and hills!—no
    tears
Dim the sweet look that Nature
    wears.

THE SPIRIT OF POETRY

There is a quiet spirit in these
    woods,
That dwells where'er the gentle
    south wind blows;
Where, underneath the white-
    thorn, in the glade,
The wild flowers bloom, or, kissing
    the soft air,
The leaves above their sunny
    palms outspread.
With what a tender and impas-
    sioned voice
It fills the nice and delicate ear of
    thought,
When the fast-ushering star of
    morning comes
O'er-riding the gray hills with
    golden scarf;
Or when the cowled and dusky-
    sandalled Eve,
In mourning weeds, from out the
    western gate,
Departs with silent pace! That
    spirit moves
In the green valley, where the
    silver brook,

From its full laver, pours the
    white cascade;
And, babbling low amid the
    tangled woods,
Slips down through moss-grown
    stones with endless laughter.
And frequent, on the everlasting
    hills,
Its feet go forth, when it doth wrap
    itself
In all the dark embroidery of the
    storm,
And shouts the stern, strong wind.
    And here, amid
The silent majesty of these deep
    woods,
Its presence shall uplift thy
    thoughts from earth,
As to the sunshine and the pure,
    bright air
Their tops the green trees lift.
    Hence gifted bards
Have ever loved the calm and
    quiet shades.
For them there was an eloquent
    voice in all
The sylvan pomp of woods, the
    golden sun,
The flowers, the leaves, the river
    on its way,
Blue skies, and silver clouds, and
    gentle winds,—
The swelling upland, where the
    sidelong sun
Aslant the wooded slope, at even-
    ing, goes,—
Groves, through whose broken roof
    the sky looks in,
Mountain, and shattered cliff, and
    sunny vale,
The distant lake, fountains,—and
    mighty trees,
In many a lazy syllable, repeating
Their old poetic legends to the
    wind.

And this is the sweet spirit, that
    doth fill
The world; and, in these wayward
    days of youth,

My busy fancy oft embodies it,
As a bright image of the light and
  beauty
That dwell in nature,—of the
  heavenly forms
We worship in our dreams, and the
  soft hues
That stain the wild bird's wing,
  and flush the clouds
When the sun sets. Within her
  eye
The heaven of April, with its
  changing light,
And when it wears the blue of May,
  is hung,
And on her lip the rich, red rose.
  Her hair
Is like the summer tresses of the
  trees,
When twilight makes them brown,
  and on her cheek
Blushes the richness of an autumn
  sky,
With ever-shifting beauty. Then
  her breath,
It is so like the gentle air of Spring,
As, from the morning's dewy
  flowers, it comes
Full of their fragrance, that it is a
  joy
To have it round us,—and her
  silver voice
Is the rich music of a summer bird,
Heard in the still night, with its
  passionate cadence.

BURIAL OF THE MINNISINK

On sunny slope and beechen
  swell,
The shadowed light of evening fell;
And, where the maple's leaf was
  brown,
With soft and silent lapse came
  down
The glory, that the wood receives,
At sunset, in its brazen leaves.

Far upward in the mellow light
Rose the blue hills. One cloud of
  white,
Around a far uplifted cone,
In the warm blush of evening
  shone;
An image of the silver lakes,
By which the Indian's soul awakes.

But soon a funeral hymn was
  heard
Where the soft breath of evening
  stirred
The tall, gray forest; and a band
Of stern in heart, and strong in
  hand,
Came winding down beside the
  wave,
To lay the red chief in his grave.

They sang, that by his native
  bowers
He stood, in the last moon of
  flowers,
And thirty snows had not yet shed
Their glory on the warrior's head;
But, as the summer fruit decays,
So died he in those naked days.

A dark cloak of the roebuck's
  skin
Covered the warrior, and within
Its heavy folds the weapons, made
For the hard toils of war, were
  laid;
The cuirass, woven of plaited reeds,
And the broad belt of shells and
  beads.

Before, a dark-haired virgin
  train
Chanted the death dirge of the
  slain;
Behind, the long procession came
Of hoary men and chiefs of fame,
With heavy hearts, and eyes of
  grief,
Leading the war-horse of their
  chief.

Stripped of his proud and mar-
tial dress,
Uncurbed, unreined, and riderless,
With darting eye, and nostril
spread,
And heavy and impatient tread,
He came; and oft that eye so
proud
Asked for his rider in the crowd.

They buried the dark chief, they
freed
Beside the grave his battle steed;
And swift an arrow cleaved its way
To his stern heart! One piercing
neigh
Arose,—and, on the dead man's
plain,
The rider grasps his steed again.

THE INDIAN HUNTER

When the summer harvest was
gather'd in,
And the sheaf of the gleaner grew
white and thin,
And the ploughshare was in its
furrow left,
Where the stubble land had been
lately cleft,
An Indian hunter, with unstrung
bow,
Look'd down where the valley lay
stretch'd below.

He was a stranger there, and all
that day,
Had been out on the hills, a
perilous way,
But the foot of the deer was far
and fleet,
And the wolf kept aloof from the
hunter's feet,
And bitter feelings pass'd o'er
him then,

As he stood by the populous
haunts of men.

The winds of autumn came over
the woods
As the sun stole out from their
solitudes,
The moss was white on the maple's
trunk,
And dead from its arms the pale
vine shrunk,
And ripen'd the mellow fruit
hung, and red
Were the tree's wither'd leaves
round it shed.

The foot of the reaper moved slow
on the lawn,
And the sickle cut down the yellow
corn,—
The mower sung loud by the
meadow-side,
Where the mists of evening were
spreading wide,
And the voice of the herdsman
came up the lea,
And the dance went round by the
greenwood tree.

Then the hunter turn'd away from
that scene,
Where the home of his fathers once
had been,
And heard by the distant and
measured stroke,
That the woodman hew'd down
the giant oak,
And burning thoughts flash'd over
his mind
Of the white man's faith, and love
unkind.

The moon of the harvest grew high
and bright,
As her golden horn pierced the
cloud of white,—
A footstep was heard in the rust-
ling brake,
Where the beech overshadow'd
the misty lake,

And a mourning voice, and a
   plunge from shore;—
And the hunter was seen on the
   hills no more.

When years had pass'd on, by
   that still lake-side
The fisher look'd down through
   the silver tide,
And there on the smooth yellow
   sand display'd,
A skeleton wasted and white was
   laid,
And 'twas seen, as the waters
   moved deep and slow,
That the hand was still grasping a
   hunter's bow.

JECKOYVA

The Indian chief, Jeckoyva, as
tradition says, perished alone on the
mountain which now bears his name.
Night overtook him whilst hunting
among the cliffs, and he was not
heard of till after a long time, when
his half-decayed corpse was found at
the foot of a high rock, over which
he must have fallen. Mount Jeckoyva
is near the White Hills.

They made the warrior's grave
   beside
The dashing of his native tide:
And there was mourning in the
   glen—
The strong wail of a thousand
   men—
  O'er him thus fallen in his pride,
Ere mist of age—or blight or blast
Had o'er his mighty spirit past.

They made the warrior's grave
   beneath
The bending of the wild-elm's
   wreath,
When the dark hunter's piercing
   eye

Had found that mountain rest on
   high,
  Where, scatter'd by the sharp
    wind's breath,
Beneath the rugged cliff were
   thrown
The strong belt and the moulder-
   ing bone.

Where was the warrior's foot, when
   first
The red sun on the mountain
   burst?—
Where—when the sultry noon-
   time came
On the green vales with scorching
   flame,
  And made the woodlands faint
    with thirst?
'Twas where the wind is keen and
   loud,
And the gray eagle breasts the
   cloud.

Where was the warrior's foot,
   when night
Veil'd in thick cloud the moun-
   tain height?
None heard the loud and sudden
   crash,—
None saw the fallen warrior
   dash
  Down the bare rock so high and
    white!—
But he that droop'd not in the
   chase
Made on the hills his burial-place.

They found him there, when the
   long day
Of cold desertion pass'd away,
And traces on that barren cleft
Of struggling hard with death
   were left—
  Deep marks and footprints in
    the clay!
And they have laid this feathery
   helm
By the dark river and green elm.

Don Jorge Manrique, the author of the following poem, flourished in the last half of the fifteenth century. He followed the profession of arms, and died on the field of battle. Mariana, in his History of Spain, makes honourable mention of him, as being present at the siege of Uclés; and speaks of him as "a youth of estimable qualities, who in this war gave brilliant proofs of his valour. He died young; and was thus cut off from long exercising his great virtues, and exhibiting to the world the light of his genius, which was already known to fame." He was mortally wounded in a skirmish near Cañavete, in the year 1479.

The name of Rodrigo Manrique, the father of the poet, Conde de Paredes and Maestre de Santiago, is well known in Spanish history and song. He died in 1476; according to Mariana, in the town of Uclés; but, according to the poem of his son, in Ocaña. It was his death that called forth the poem upon which rests the literary reputation of the younger Manrique. In the language of his historian, "Don Jorge Manrique, in an elegant Ode, full of poetic beauties, rich embellishments of genius, and high moral reflections, mourned the death of his father as with a funeral hymn." This praise is not exaggerated. The poem is a model in its kind. Its conception is solemn and beautiful; and, in accordance with it, the style moves on—calm, dignified, and majestic.]

COPLAS DE MANRIQUE

FROM THE SPANISH

O LET the soul her slumbers break,
Let thought be quickened, and
    awake;
Awake to see
How soon this life is past and gone,
And death comes softly stealing on,
How silently!

Swiftly our pleasures glide away,
Our hearts recall the distant day
With many sighs;
The moments that are speeding
    fast
We heed not, but the past,—the
    past,—
More highly prize.
Onward its course the present
    keeps,
Onward the constant current
    sweeps,
Till life is done;
And, did we judge of time aright,
The past and future in their flight
Would be as one.

Let no one fondly dream again,
That Hope and all her shadowy
    train
Will not decay;
Fleeting as were the dreams of old,
Remembered like a tale that's
    told,
They pass away.

Our lives are rivers, gliding free
To that unfathomed, boundless
    sea,
The silent grave!
Thither all earthly pomp and
    boast
Roll, to be swallowed up and lost
In one dark wave.

Thither the mighty torrents stray,
Thither the brook pursues its way,
And tinkling rill

There all are equal.   Side by side
The poor man and the son of pride
Lie calm and still.

I will not here invoke the throng
Of orators and sons of song,
The deathless few;
Fiction entices and deceives,
And, sprinkled o'er her fragrant
leaves,
Lies poisonous dew.

To One alone my thoughts arise,
The Eternal Truth,—the Good
and Wise,—
To Him I cry,
Who shared on earth our common
lot,
But the world comprehended not
His deity.

This world is but the rugged road
Which leads us to the bright abode
Of peace above;
So let us choose that narrow way,
Which leads no traveller's foot
astray
From realms of love.

Our cradle is the starting-place,
In life we run the onward race,
And reach the goal;
When, in the mansions of the blest,
Death leaves to its eternal rest
The weary soul.

Did we but use it as we ought,
This world would school each
wandering thought
To its high state.
Faith wings the soul beyond the
sky,
Up to that better world on high,
For which we wait.

Yes,—the glad messenger of love,
To guide us to our home above,
The Saviour came;
Born amid mortal cares and fears,

He suffered in this vale of tears
A death of shame.

Behold of what delusive worth
The bubbles we pursue on earth,
The shapes we chase,
Amid a world of treachery!
They vanish ere death shuts the
eye,
And leave no trace.

Time steals them from us,—
chances strange,
Disastrous accidents, and change,
That come to all;
Even in the most exalted state,
Relentless sweeps the stroke of
fate;
The strongest fall.

Tell me,—the charms that lovers
seek
In the clear eye and blushing
cheek,
The hues that play
O'er rosy lip and brow of snow,
When hoary age approaches slow,
Ah, where are they?

The cunning skill, the curious arts,
The glorious strength that youth
imparts
In life's first stage;
These shall become a heavy weight,
When Time swings wide his out-
ward gate
To weary age.

The noble blood of Gothic name,
Heroes emblazoned high to fame,
In long array;
How, in the onward course of time,
The landmarks of that race
sublime
Were swept away!

Some, the degraded slaves of lust,
Prostrate and trampled in the dust,
Shall rise no more;

Others, by guilt and crime, maintain
The scutcheon, that, without a stain,
Their fathers bore.

Wealth and the high estate of pride,
With what untimely speed they glide,
How soon depart!
Bid not the shadowy phantoms stay,
The vassals of a mistress they,
Of fickle heart.

These gifts in Fortune's hands are found;
Her swift revolving wheel turns round,
And they are gone!
No rest the inconstant goddess knows,
But changing, and without repose,
Still hurries on.

Even could the hand of avarice save
Its gilded baubles, till the grave
Reclaimed its prey,
Let none on such poor hopes rely;
Life, like an empty dream, flits by,
And where are they?

Earthly desires and sensual lust
Are passions springing from the dust,—
They fade and die;
But, in the life beyond the tomb,
They seal the immortal spirit's doom
Eternally!

The pleasures and delights, which mask
In treacherous smiles life's serious task,
What are they, all,
But the fleet coursers of the chase,
And death an ambush in the race,
Wherein we fall?

No foe, no dangerous pass, we heed,
Brook no delay,—but onward speed
With loosened rein;
And, when the fatal snare is near,
We strive to check our mad career,
But strive in vain.

Could we new charms to age impart
And fashion with a cunning art
The human face,
As we can clothe the soul with light,
And make the glorious spirit bright
With heavenly grace,—

How busily each passing hour
Should we exert that magic power!
What ardour show,
To deck the sensual slave of sin,
Yet leave the freeborn soul within,
In weeds of woe!

Monarchs, the powerful and the strong,
Famous in history and in song
Of olden time,
Saw, by the stern decrees of fate,
Their kingdoms lost, and desolate
Their race sublime.

Who is the champion? who the strong?
Pontiff and priest, and sceptred throng?
On these shall fall
As heavily the hand of Death,
As when it stays the shepherd's breath
Beside his stall.

I speak not of the Trojan name,
Neither its glory nor its shame

Has met our eyes;
Nor of Rome's great and glorious
  dead,
Though we have heard so oft, and
  read,
Their histories.

Little avails it now to know
Of ages passed so long ago,
Nor how they rolled;
Our theme shall be of yester-
  day,
Which to oblivion sweeps away,
Like days of old.

Where is the King, Don Juan?
  Where
Each royal prince and noble heir
Of Aragon?
Where are the courtly gallantries?
The deeds of love and high em-
  prise
In battle done?

Tourney and joust, that charmed
  the eye,
And scarf, and gorgeous panoply,
And nodding plume,—
What were they but a pageant
  scene?
What but the garlands, gay and
  green
That deck the tomb?

Where are the high-born dames,
  and where
Their gay attire and jewelled hair,
And odours sweet?
Where are the gentle knights, that
  came
To kneel, and breathe love's ardent
  flame,
Low at their feet?

Where is the song of Troubadour?
Where are the lute and gay tam-
  bour
They loved of yore?
Where is the mazy dance of old,

The flowing robes, inwrought with
  gold,
The dancers wore?

And he who next the sceptre
  swayed,
Henry, whose royal court dis-
  played
Such power and pride;
O, in what winning smiles arrayed,
The world its various pleasures
  laid
His throne beside!

But O! how false and full of guile
That world, which wore so soft a
  smile
But to betray!
She, that had been his friend
  before,
Now from the fated monarch tore
Her charms away.

The countless gifts,—the stately
  walls,
The royal palaces, and halls
All filled with gold;
Plate with armorial bearings
  wrought,
Chambers with ample treasures
  fraught
Of wealth untold;

The noble steeds, and harness
  bright,
And gallant lord, and stalwart
  knight,
In rich array,—
Where shall we seek them now?
  Alas!
Like the bright dewdrops on the
  grass,
They passed away.

His brother, too, whose factious
  zeal
Usurped the sceptre of Castile,
Unskilled to reign;
What a gay, brilliant court had he,

When all the flower of chivalry
Was in his train!

But he was mortal; and the breath,
That flamed from the hot forge of
　　Death,
Blasted his years;
Judgment of God! that flame by
　　thee,
When raging fierce and fearfully,
Was quenched in tears!

Spain's haughty Constable,—the
　　true
And gallant Master, whom we
　　knew
Most loved of all,
Breathe not a whisper of his
　　pride,—
He on the gloomy scaffold died,
Ignoble fall!

The countless treasures of his
　　care,
His hamlets green, and cities fair,
His mighty power,—
What were they all but grief and
　　shame,
Tears and a broken heart, when
　　came
The parting hour?

His other brothers, proud and
　　high,
Masters, who, in prosperity,
Might rival kings;
Who made the bravest and the
　　best
The bondsmen of their high behest,
Their underlings;

What was their prosperous estate,
When high exalted and elate
With power and pride?
What, but a transient gleam of
　　light,
A flame, which, glaring at its
　　height,
Grew dim and died?

So many a duke of royal name,
Marquis and count of spotless fame,
And baron brave,
That might the sword of empire
　　wield,
All these, O Death, hast thou con-
　　cealed
In the dark grave!

Their deeds of mercy and of arms,
In peaceful days, or war's alarms,
When thou dost show,
O Death, thy stern and angry face,
One stroke of thy all-powerful
　　mace
Can overthrow.

Unnumbered hosts, that threaten
　　nigh,
Pennon and standard flaunting
　　high,
And flag displayed;
High battlements intrenched
　　around,
Bastion, and moated wall, and
　　mound,
And palisade,

And covered trench, secure and
　　deep,—
All these cannot one victim keep,
O Death, from thee,
When thou dost battle in thy
　　wrath,
And thy strong shafts pursue their
　　path
Unerringly.

O World! so few the years we live,
Would that the life which thou
　　dost give
Were life indeed!
Alas! thy sorrows fall so fast,
Our happiest hour is when at last
The soul is freed.

Our days are covered o'er with
　　grief,
And sorrows neither few nor brief

Veil all in gloom;
Left desolate of real good,
Within this cheerless solitude
No pleasures bloom.

Thy pilgrimage begins in tears,
And ends in bitter doubts and
fears,
Or dark despair;
Midway so many toils appear,
That he who lingers longest here
Knows most of care.

Thy goods are brought with many
a groan,
By the hot sweat of toil alone,
And weary hearts;
Fleet-footed is the approach of
woe,
But with a lingering step and slow
Its form departs.

And he, the good man's shield and
shade,
To whom all hearts their homage
paid,
As Virtue's son,—
Roderic Manrique, — he whose
name
Is written on the scroll of Fame,
Spain's champion;

His signal deeds and prowess
high
Demand no pompous eulogy,—
Ye saw his deeds!
Why should their praise in verse
be sung?
The name, that dwells on every
tongue,
No minstrel needs.

To friends a friend;—how kind to
all
The vassals of this ancient hall
And feudal fief!
To foes how stern a foe was he!
And to the valiant and the free
How brave a chief!

What prudence with the old and
wise:
What grace in youthful gayeties;
In all how sage!
Benignant to the serf and slave,
He showed the base and falsely
brave
A lion's rage.

His was Octavian's prosperous
star,
The rush of Cæsar's conquering car
At battle's call;
His, Scipio's virtue; his, the skill
And the indomitable will
Of Hannibal.

His was a Trajan's goodness,—his
A Titus' noble charities
And righteous laws;
The arm of Hector, and the might
Of Tully, to maintain the right
In truth's just cause;

The clemency of Antonine,
Aurelius' countenance divine,
Firm, gentle, still;
The eloquence of Adrian,
And Theodosius' love to man,
And generous will;

In tented field and bloody fray,
An Alexander's vigorous sway
And stern command;
The faith of Constantine; ay,
more,
The fervent love Camillus bore
His native land.

He left no well-filled treasury,
He heaped no pile of riches high,
Nor massive plate;
He fought the Moors, and, in their
fall,
City and tower and castled wall
Were his estate.

Upon the hard-fought battle-
ground,

Brave steeds and gallant riders
found
A common grave;
And there the warrior's hand did
gain
The rents, and the long vassal train,
That conquest gave.

And if, of old, his halls displayed
The honoured and exalted grade
His worth had gained,
So, in the dark, disastrous hour,
Brothers and bondsmen of his
power
His hand sustained.

After high deeds, not left untold,
In the stern warfare, which of old
'Twas his to share,
Such noble leagues he made, that
more
And fairer regions, than before,
His guerdon were.

These are the records, half effaced,
Which, with the hand of youth, he
traced
On history's page;
But with fresh victories he drew
Each fading character anew
In his old age.

By his unrivalled skill, by great
And veteran service to the state,
By worth adored,
He stood, in his high dignity,
The proudest knight of chivalry,
Knight of the Sword.

He found his cities and domains
Beneath a tyrant's galling chains
And cruel power;
But, by fierce battle and blockade,
Soon his own banner was dis-
played
From every tower.

By the tried valour of his hand,
His monarch and his native land

Were nobly served;
Let Portugal repeat the story,
And proud Castile, who shared the
glory
His arms deserved.

And when so oft, for weal or woe,
His life upon the fatal throw
Had been cast down;
When he had served, with patriot
zeal,
Beneath the banner of Castile,
His sovereign's crown;

And done such deeds of valour
strong,
That neither history nor song
Can count them all;
Then, on Ocaña's castled rock,
Death at his portal came to knock,
With sudden call,—

Saying, " Good Cavalier, prepare
To leave this world of toil and care
With joyful mien;
Let thy strong heart of steel this
day
Put on its armour for the fray,—
The closing scene.

" Since thou hast been, in battle-
strife,
So prodigal of health and life,
For earthly fame,
Let virtue nerve thy heart again;
Loud on the last stern battle-plain
They call thy name.

" Think not the struggle that
draws near
Too terrible for man,—nor fear
To meet the foe;
Nor let thy noble spirit grieve,
Its life of glorious fame to leave
On earth below.

" A life of honour and of worth
Has no eternity on earth,—
'Tis but a name;

And yet its glory far exceeds
That base and sensual life, which
    leads
To want and shame.

" The eternal life, beyond the sky,
Wealth cannot purchase, nor the
    high
And proud estate;
The soul in dalliance laid,—the
    spirit
Corrupt with sin,—shall not inherit
A joy so great.

" But the good monk, in cloistered
    cell,
Shall gain it by his book and bell,
His prayers and tears;
And the brave knight, whose arm
    endures
Fierce battle, and against the
    Moors
His standard rears.

" And thou, brave knight, whose
    hand has poured
The life-blood of the Pagan horde
O'er all the land,
In heaven shalt thou receive, at
    length,
The guerdon of thine earthly
    strength
And dauntless hand.

" Cheered onward by this promise
    sure,
Strong in the faith entire and pure
Thou dost profess,
Depart,—thy hope is certainty,—
The third—the better life on high
Shalt thou possess."

" O Death, no more, no more delay:
My spirit longs to flee away,
And be at rest;
The will of Heaven my will shall
    be,—
I bow to the divine decree,
To God's behest.

" My soul is ready to depart,
No thought rebels, the obedient
    heart
Breathes forth no sigh;
The wish on earth to linger still
Were vain, when 'tis God's
    sovereign will
That we shall die.

" O thou, that for our sins didst
    take
A human form, and humbly make
Thy home on earth;
Thou, that to thy divinity
A human nature didst ally
By mortal birth,

" And in that form didst suffer here
Torment, and agony, and fear,
So patiently;
By thy redeeming grace alone,
And not for merits of my own,
O, pardon me!"

As thus the dying warrior prayed,
Without one gathering mist or
    shade
Upon his mind;
Encircled by his family,
Watched by affection's gentle eye,
So soft and kind;

His soul to Him, who gave it, rose;
God lead it to its long repose.
Its glorious rest!
And, though the warrior's sun has
    set,
Its light shall linger round us yet,
Bright, radiant, blest.[1]

[1] This poem of Manrique is a great favourite in Spain. No less than four poetic Glosses, or running commentaries, upon it have been published, no one of which, however, possesses great poetic merit. That of the Carthusian monk, Rodrigo de Valddepeñas, is the best. It is known as the *Glosa del Cartujo*. There is also a prose Commentary by Luis de Aranda.

The following stanzas of the poem

THE GOOD SHEPHERD

FROM THE SPANISH OF LOPE DE VEGA

Shepherd! that with thine amorous, sylvan song
Hast broken the slumber which encompassed me,—
That mad'st thy crook from the accursed tree,
On which thy powerful arms were stretched so long!
Lead me to mercy's ever-flowing fountains;
For thou my shepherd . guard, and guide shalt be;
I will obey thy voice, and wait to see
Thy feet all beautiful upon the mountains.

Here, Shepherd!—thou who for thy flock art dying,
O, wash away these scarlet sins, for thou
Rejoicest at the contrite sinner's vow.
O, wait!—to thee my weary soul is crying,—
Wait for me!—Yet why ask it, when I see,
With feet nailed to the cross, thou'rt waiting still for me!

TO-MORROW

FROM THE SPANISH OF LOPE DE VEGA

Lord, what am I, that, with unceasing care,
Thou didst seek after me,—that thou didst wait,
Wet with unhealthy dews, before my gate,
And pass the gloomy nights of winter there?
O strange delusion!—that I did not greet
Thy blest approach, and O, to Heaven how lost,
If my ingratitude's unkindly frost
Has chilled the bleeding wounds upon thy feet.
How oft my guardian angel gently cried,
"Soul, from thy casement look, and thou shalt see
How he persists to knock and wait for thee!"
And, O! how often to that voice of sorrow,
"To-morrow we will open," I replied,
And when the morrow came I answered still, "To-morrow."

---

were found in the author's pocket, after his death on the field of battle:—

"O World! so few the years we live,
Would that the life which thou dost give
Were life indeed!
Alas! thy sorrows fall so fast,
Our happiest hour is when at last
The soul is freed.

"Our days are covered o'er with grief,
And sorrows neither few nor brief
Veil all in gloom;
Left desolate of real good.
Within this cheerless solitude
No pleasures bloom.

"Thy pilgrimage begins in tears,
And ends in bitter doubts and fears,
Or dark despair;
Midway so many toils appear,
That he who lingers longest here
Knows most of care.

"Thy goods are bought with many a groan,
By the hot sweat of toil alone,
And weary hearts;
Fleet-footed is the approach of woe,
But with a lingering step and slow
Its form departs."

THE NATIVE LAND

FROM THE SPANISH OF FRANCISCO
DE ALDANA

Clear fount of light! my native
  land on high,
Bright with a glory that shall never
  fade!
Mansion of truth! without a veil
  or shade,
Thy holy quiet meets the spirit's
  eye.
There dwells the soul in its ethereal
  essence,
Gasping no longer for life's feeble
  breath;
But, sentinelled in heaven, its
  glorious presence
With pitying eye beholds, yet
  fears not, death.
Beloved country! banished from
  thy shore,
A stranger in this prison-house of
  clay,
The exiled spirit weeps and sighs
  for thee!
Heavenward the bright perfections
  I adore
Direct, and the sure promise cheers
  the way,
That, whither love aspires, there
  shall my dwelling be.

THE IMAGE OF GOD

FROM THE SPANISH OF FRANCISCO
DE ALDANA

O Lord! that seest, from yon
  starry height
Centred in one the future and the
  past,
Fashioned in thine own image, see
  how fast
The world obscures in me what
  once was bright!
Eternal Sun! the warmth which
  thou hast given,

To cheer life's flowery April, fast
  decays;
Yet, in the hoary winter of my
  days,
Forever green shall be my trust in
  Heaven.
Celestial King! O let thy presence
  pass
Before my spirit, and an image fair
Shall meet that look of mercy from
  on high,
As the reflected image in a glass
Doth meet the look of him who
  seeks it there,
And owes its being to the gazer's
  eye.

THE BROOK

FROM THE SPANISH

Laugh of the mountain!—lyre of
  bird and tree!
Pomp of the meadow! mirror of
  the morn!
The soul of April, unto whom are
  born
The rose and jessamine, leaps wild
  in thee!
Although, where'er thy devious
  current strays,
The lap of earth with gold and
  silver teems
To me thy clear proceeding
  brighter seems
Than golden sands, that charm
  each shepherd's gaze.
How without guile thy bosom, all
  transparent
As the pure crystal, lets the
  curious eye
Thy secrets scan, thy smooth,
  round pebbles count!
How, without malice murmuring,
  glides thy current!
O sweet simplicity of days gone by!
Thou shun'st the haunts of man,
  to dwell in limpid fount!

THE CELESTIAL PILOT

FROM DANTE. PURGATORIO, II.

And now, behold! as at the approach of morning,
Through the gross vapours, Mars grows fiery red
Down in the west upon the ocean floor,

Appeared to me,—may I again behold it!—
A light along the sea, so swiftly coming.
Its motion by no flight of wing is equalled.

And when therefrom I had withdrawn a little
Mine eyes, that I might question my conductor,
Again I saw it brighter grown and larger.

Thereafter, on all sides of it appeared
I knew not what of white, and underneath,
Little by little, there came forth another.

My master yet had uttered not a word,
While the first brightness into wings unfolded;
But, when he clearly recognised the pilot,

He cried aloud: " Quick, quick, and bow the knee!
Behold the Angel of God! fold up thy hands!
Henceforward shalt thou see such officers!

" See, how he scorns all human arguments,
So that no oar he wants, nor other sail
Than his own wings, between so distant shores!

" See, how he holds them, pointed straight to heaven,
Fanning the air with the eternal pinions,
That do not moult themselves like mortal hair! "

And then, as nearer and more near us came
The Bird of Heaven, more glorious he appeared,
So that the eye could not sustain his presence,

But down I cast it; and he came to shore
With a small vessel, gliding swift and light,
So that the water swallowed naught thereof.

Upon the stern stood the Celestial Pilot!
Beatitude seemed written in his face!
And more than a hundred spirits sat within.

" *In exitu Israel* out of Egypt! "
Thus sang they all together in one voice,
With whatso in that Psalm is after written.

Then made he sign of holy rood upon them,
Whereat all cast themselves upon the shore,
And he departed swiftly as he came.

THE TERRESTRIAL PARADISE

FROM DANTE. PURGATORIO, XXVIII.

Longing already to search in and round
The heavenly forest, dense and living-green,
Which to the eyes tempered the new-born day,

Withouten more delay I left the bank,

Crossing the level country slowly, slowly,

Over the soil, that everywhere breathed fragrance,

A gently-breathing air, that no mutation

Had in itself, smote me upon the forehead,

No heavier blow, than of a pleasant breeze.

Whereat the tremulous branches readily

Did all of them bow downward towards that side

Where its first shadow casts the Holy Mountain;

Yet not from their upright direction bent

So that the little birds upon their tops

Should cease the practice of their tuneful art;

But, with full-throated joy, the hours of prime

Singing received they in the midst of foliage

That made monotonous burden to their rhymes,

Even as from branch to branch it gathering swells,

Through the pine forests on the shore of Chiassi,

When Æolus unlooses the Sirocco.

Already my slow steps had led me on

Into the ancient wood so far, that I
Could see no more the place where I had entered.

And lo! my farther course cut off a river,

Which, towards the left hand, with its little waves,

Bent down the grass, that on its margin sprang.

All waters that on earth most limpid are,

Would seem to have within themselves some mixture,

Compared with that, which nothing doth conceal,

Although it moves on with a brown, brown current,

Under the shade perpetual, that never

Ray of the sun lets in, nor of the moon.

BEATRICE

FROM DANTE. PURGATORIO, XXX., XXXI.

Even as the Blessed, in the new covenant,

Shall rise up quickened, each one from his grave,

Wearing again the garments of the flesh,

So, upon that celestial chariot,

A hundred rose *ad vocem tanti senis,*

Ministers and messengers of life eternal.

They all were saying: " *Bene-dictus qui venis,*"

And scattering flowers above and round about,

" *Manibus o date lilia plenis.*"

I once beheld, at the approach of day

The orient sky all stained with roseate hues,

And the other heaven with light serene adorned,

And the sun's face uprising, over-
shadowed,
So that, by temperate influence of
vapours,
The eye sustained his aspect for
long while;

Thus in the bosom of a cloud of
flowers,
Which from those hands angelic
were thrown up
And down descended inside and
without,

With crown of olive o'er a snow-
white veil,
Appeared a lady, under a green
mantle,
Vested in colours of the living
flame.

.   .   .   .   .   .

Even as the snow, among the
living rafters
Upon the back of Italy, congeals,
Blown on and beaten by Scla-
vonian winds,

And then, dissolving, filters through
itself,
Whene'er the land, that loses
shadow, breathes,
Like as a taper melts before a fire,

Even such I was, without a sigh or
tear,
Before the song of those who chime
forever
After the chiming of the eternal
spheres;

But, when I heard in those sweet
melodies
Compassion for me, more than had
they said,
" O wherefore, lady, dost thou
thus consume him ? "

The ice, that was about my heart
congealed,

To air and water changed, and, in
my anguish,
Through lips and eyes came gush-
ing from my breast.

.   .   .   .   .   .

Confusion and dismay, together
mingled,
Forced such a feeble " Yes ! " out
of my mouth,
To understand it one had need of
sight.

Even as a cross-bow breaks, when
'tis discharged,
Too tensely drawn the bow-string
and the bow,
And with less force the arrow hits
the mark;
So I gave way under this heavy
burden,
Gushing forth into bitter tears and
sighs,
And the voice, fainting, flagged
upon its passage.

SPRING

FROM THE FRENCH OF CHARLES
D'ORLEANS

XV. CENTURY

Gentle Spring!—in sunshine clad,
   Well dost thou thy power dis-
      play!
For Winter maketh the light heart
   sad,
   And thou,—thou makest the sad
      heart gay.
He sees thee, and calls to his
   gloomy train,
The sleet, and the snow, and the
   wind, and the rain;
And they shrink away, and they
   flee in fear,
   When thy merry step draws
      near.

Winter giveth the fields and the trees, so old,
Their beards of icicles and snow;
And the rain, it raineth so fast and cold,
We must cower over the embers low;
And, snugly housed from the wind and weather,
Mope like birds that are changing feather.
But the storm retires, and the sky grows clear,
When thy merry step draws near.

Winter maketh the sun in the gloomy sky
Wrap him round with a mantle of cloud;
But, Heaven be praised, thy step is nigh;
Thou tearest away the mournful shroud,
And the earth looks bright, and Winter surly,
Who has toiled for naught both late and early,
Is banished afar by the new-born year,
When thy merry step draws near.

THE CHILD ASLEEP

FROM THE FRENCH

Sweet babe! true portrait of thy father's face,
Sleep on the bosom, that thy lips have pressed!
Sleep, little one; and closely, gently place
Thy drowsy eyelid on thy mother's breast.

Upon that tender eye, my little friend,
Soft sleep shall come, that cometh not to me!

I watch to see thee, nourish thee, defend;—
'Tis sweet to watch for thee,— alone for thee!

His arms fall down; sleep sits upon his brow;
His eye is closed; he sleeps, nor dreams of harm.
Wore not his cheek the apple's ruddy glow,
Would you not say he slept on Death's cold arm?

Awake, my boy!—I tremble with affright!
Awake, and chase this fatal thought!—Unclose
Thine eye but for one moment on the light!
Even at the price of thine, give me repose!

Sweet error! — he but slept, — I breathe again;—
Come, gentle dreams, the hour of sleep beguile!
O! when shall he, for whom I sigh in vain,
Beside me watch to see thy waking smile?

THE GRAVE

FROM THE ANGLO-SAXON

For thee was a house built
Ere thou wast born,
For thee was a mould meant
Ere thou of mother camest.
But it is not made ready,
Nor its depth measured,
Nor is it seen
How long it shall be.
Now I bring thee
Where thou shalt be;
Now I shall measure thee,
And the mould afterwards.

Thy house is not
Highly timbered,
It is unhigh and low;
When thou art therein
The heel-ways are low,
The side-ways unhigh.
The roof is built
Thy breast full nigh,
So thou shalt in mould
Dwell full cold,
Dimly and dark.

Doorless is that house,
And dark it is within;
There thou art fast detained
And Death hath the key.
Loathsome is that earth-house,
And grim within to dwell.
There thou shalt dwell,
And worms shall divide thee.

Thus thou art laid,
And leavest thy friends;
Thou hast no friend,
Who will come to thee,
Who will ever see
How that house pleaseth thee;
Who will ever open
The door for thee,
And descend after thee,
For soon thou art loathsome
And hateful to see.

KING CHRISTIAN

A NATIONAL SONG OF DENMARK

FROM THE DANISH OF JOHANNES
EVALD

King Christian stood by the lofty
　　mast
　　In mist and smoke;
His sword was hammering so fast,
Through Gothic helm and brain it
　　past;

Then sank each hostile hulk and
　　mast,
　　In mist and smoke.
"Fly!" shouted they, "fly, he
　　who can!
Who braves of Denmark's Chris-
　　tian
　　The stroke?"

Nils Juel gave heed to the tem-
　　pest's roar,
　　Now is the hour!
He hoisted his blood-red flag once
　　more,
And smote upon the foe full
　　sore,
And shouted loud, through the
　　tempest's roar,
　　"Now is the hour!"
"Fly!" shouted they, "for shelter
　　fly!
Of Denmark's Juel who can defy
　　The power?"

North Sea! a glimpse of Wessel
　　rent
　　Thy murky sky!
Then champions to thine arms
　　were sent;
Terror and Death glared where he
　　went;
From the waves was heard a wail,
　　that rent
　　Thy murky sky!
From Denmark, thunders Torden-
　　skiol',
Let each to Heaven commend his
　　soul,
　　And fly!

Path of the Dane to fame and
　　might!
　　Dark-rolling wave!
Receive thy friend, who, scorning
　　flight,
Goes to meet danger with despite,
Proudly as thou the tempest's
　　might,
　　Dark-rolling wave!

And amid pleasures and alarms,
And war and victory, be thine
    arms
  My grave! [1]

THE HAPPIEST LAND

FRAGMENT OF A MODERN BALLAD

FROM THE GERMAN

There sat one day in quiet,
  By an alehouse on the Rhine,
Four hale and hearty fellows,
  And drank the precious wine.

The landlord's daughter filled
    their cups,
  Around the rustic board;
Then sat they all so calm and still,
  And spake not one rude word.

But, when the maid departed,
  A Swabian raised his hand,
And cried, all hot and flushed with
    wine,
  "Long live the Swabian land!

"The greatest kingdom upon
    earth
  Cannot with that compare;
With all the stout and hardy men
    And the nut-brown maidens
    there."

"Ha!" cried a Saxon, laughing,—
  And dashed his beard with wine;
"I had rather live in Lapland,
  Than that Swabian land of thine!

"The goodliest land on all this
    earth,
  It is the Saxon land!

[1] Nils Juel was a celebrated Danish Admiral, and Peder Wessel a Vice-Admiral, who for his great prowess received the popular title of Torden-skiold, or *Thunder shield*. In childhood he was a tailor's apprentice, and rose to his high rank before the age of twenty-eight, when he was killed in a duel.

There have I as many maidens
  As fingers on this hand!"

"Hold your tongues! both Swabian
    and Saxon!"
  A bold Bohemian cries;
"If there's a heaven upon this
    earth,
  In Bohemia it lies.

"There the tailor blows the lute,
  And the cobbler blows the horn,
And the miner blows the bugle,
  Over mountain gorge and
    bourn."

.   .   .   .   .   .

And then the landlord's daughter
  Up to heaven raised her hand,
And said, "Ye may no more con-
    tend,—
  There lies the happiest land!"

THE WAVE

FROM THE GERMAN OF TIEDGE

"Whither, thou turbid wave?
Whither, with so much haste,
As if a thief wert thou?"

"I am the Wave of Life,
Stained with my margin's dust,
From the struggle and the strife
Of the narrow stream I fly
To the Sea's immensity,
To wash from me the slime
Of the muddy banks of Time."

THE DEAD

FROM THE GERMAN OF KLOPSTOCK

How they so softly rest,
All, all the holy dead,
Unto whose dwelling-place
Now doth my soul draw near!

How they so softly rest,
All in their silent graves,
Deep to corruption
Slowly down-sinking!

And they no longer weep,
Here, where complaint is still!
And they no longer feel,
Here, where all gladness flies?
And, by the cypresses
Softly o'ershadowed,
Until the Angel calls them, they
    slumber!

THE BIRD AND THE SHIP

FROM THE GERMAN OF MÜLLER

" The rivers rush into the sea,
    By castle and town they go;
The winds behind them merrily
    Their noisy trumpets blow.

" The clouds are passing far and
    high,
    We little birds in them play;
And everything, that can sing and
    fly,
    Goes with us, and far away.

" I   greet   thee,   bonny   boat!
    Whither, or whence,
    With thy fluttering golden
        band?"—
" I greet thee, little bird!   To the
    wide sea
    I haste from the narrow land.

" Full and swollen is every sail;
    I see no longer a hill,
I have trusted all to the sounding
    gale,
    And it will not let me stand still.

" And wilt thou, little bird, go
    with us?
    Thou mayest stand on the main-
        mast tall,

For full to sinking is my house
    With merry companions all."—

" I need not and seek not com-
    pany,
    Bonny boat, I can sing all alone;
For the mainmast tall too heavy
    am I,
    Bonny boat, I have wings of my
        own.

" High over the sails, high over
    the mast,
    Who shall gainsay these joys?
When thy merry companions are
    still, at last,
    Thou shalt hear the sound of
        my voice.

" Who neither may rest, nor listen
    may,
    God bless them every one!
I dart away, in the bright blue day,
    And the golden fields of the sun.

" Thus do I sing my weary song,
    Wherever the four winds blow;
And this same song, my whole life
    long,
Neither Poet nor Printer may
    know."

WHITHER?

FROM THE GERMAN OF MÜLLER

I heard a brooklet gushing
    From its rocky fountain near,
Down into the valley rushing,
    So fresh and wondrous clear.

I know not what came o'er me,
    Nor who the counsel gave;
But I must hasten downward,
    All with my pilgrim-stave;

Downward, and ever farther,
    And ever the brook beside;

And ever fresher murmured,
  And ever clearer, the tide.

Is this the way I was going?
  Whither, O brooklet, say!
Thou hast, with thy soft murmur,
  Murmured my senses away.

What do I say of a murmur?
  That can no murmur be;
'Tis the water-nymphs, that are
    singing
  Their roundelays under me.

Let them sing, my friend, let them
    murmur,
  And wander merrily near;
The wheels of a mill are going
  In every brooklet clear.

BEWARE!

FROM THE GERMAN

I know a maiden fair to see,
  Take care!
She can both false and friendly be,
  Beware! Beware!
  Trust her not,
She is fooling thee!

She has two eyes, so soft and
    brown,
  Take care!
She gives a side-glance and looks
    down,
  Beware! Beware!
  Trust her not,
She is fooling thee!

And she has hair of a golden hue,
  Take care!
And what she says, it is not true,
  Beware! Beware!
  Trust her not,
She is fooling thee!

She has a bosom as white as snow,
  Take care!
She knows how much it is best to
    show,
  Beware! Beware!
  Trust her not,
She is fooling thee!

She gives thee a garland woven
    fair,
  Take care!
It is a fool's-cap for thee to wear,
  Beware! Beware!
  Trust her not,
She is fooling thee!

SONG OF THE BELL

FROM THE GERMAN

Bell! thou soundest merrily,
When the bridal party
  To the church doth hie!
Bell! thou soundest solemnly,
When, on Sabbath morning,
  Fields deserted lie!

Bell! thou soundest merrily;
Tellest thou at evening,
  Bed-time draweth nigh!
Bell! thou soundest mournfully
Tellest thou the bitter
  Parting hath gone by!

Say! how canst thou mourn?
How canst thou rejoice?
  Thou art but metal dull!
And yet all our sorrowings,
And all our rejoicings,
  Thou dost feel them all!

God hath wonders many,
Which we cannot fathom,
  Placed within thy form!
When the heart is sinking,
Thou alone canst raise it,
  Trembling in the storm!

THE CASTLE BY THE SEA

FROM THE GERMAN OF UHLAND

" Hast thou seen that lordly castle,
　　That Castle by the Sea?
Golden and red above it
　　The clouds float gorgeously.

" And fain it would stoop down-
　　　ward
　　To the mirrored wave below;
And fain it would soar upward
　　In the evening's crimson glow."

" Well have I seen that castle,
　　That Castle by the Sea,
And the moon above it standing,
　　And the mist rise solemnly."

" The winds and the waves of
　　　ocean,
　　Had they a merry chime?
Didst thou hear, from those lofty
　　　chambers,
　　The harp and the minstrel's
　　　rhyme?

" The winds and the waves of
　　　ocean,
　　They rested quietly,
But I heard on the gale a sound of
　　　wail,
　　And tears came to mine eye."

" And sawest thou on the turrets
　　The King and his royal bride?
And the wave of their crimson
　　　mantles?
　　And the golden crown of pride?

" Led they not forth, in rapture,
　　A beauteous maiden there?
Resplendent as the morning sun,
　　Beaming with golden hair?"

" Well saw I the ancient parents,
　　Without the crown of pride;
They were moving slow, in weeds
　　　of woe,
　　No maiden was by their side!"

THE BLACK KNIGHT

FROM THE GERMAN OF UHLAND

'Twas Pentecost, the Feast of
　　Gladness,
When woods and fields put off all
　　sadness.
　　Thus began the King and spake;
" So from the halls
Of ancient Holfburg's walls,
　　A luxuriant Spring shall break."

Drums and trumpets echo loudly,
Wave the crimson banners proudly,
　　From balcony the King looked
　　　on;
In the play of spears,
Fell all the cavaliers,
　　Before the monarch's stalwart
　　　son.

To the barrier of the fight
Rode at last a sable Knight.
　　" Sir Knight! your name and
　　　scutcheon, say!"
" Should I speak it here,
Ye would stand aghast with fear;
　　I am a Prince of mighty sway!"

When he rode into the lists,
The arch of heaven grew black
　　with mists,
　　And the castle 'gan to rock,
At the first blow,
Fell the youth from saddle-bow,
　　Hardly rises from the shock.

Pipe and viol call the dances,
Torch-light through the high halls
　　glances;
　　Waves a mighty shadow in;
With manner bland
Doth ask the maiden's hand,
　　Doth with her the dance begin;

Danced in sable iron sark,
Danced a measure weird and dark,
　　Coldly clasped her limbs around,

From breast and hair
Down fall from her the fair
  Flowerets, faded, to the ground.

To the sumptuous banquet came
Every Knight and every Dame.
  'Twixt son and daughter all distraught,
With mournful mind
The ancient King reclined,
  Gazed at them in silent thought.

Pale the children both did look,
But the guest a beaker took;
  "Golden wine will make you whole!"
The children drank,
Gave many a courteous thank;
  "O that draught was very cool!"

Each the father's breast embraces,
Son and daughter; and their faces
Colourless grow utterly.
Whichever way
Looks the fear-struck father gray,
  He beholds his children die.

"Woe! the blessed children both
Takest thou in the joy of youth;
  Take me, too, the joyless father!"
Spake the grim Guest,
From his hollow, cavernous breast,
  "Roses in the spring I gather!"

SONG OF THE SILENT LAND

FROM THE GERMAN OF SALIS

Into the Silent Land!
Ah! who shall lead us thither?
Clouds in the evening sky more darkly gather,
And shattered wrecks lie thicker on the strand.
Who leads us with a gentle hand
Thither, O thither,
Into the Silent Land?

Into the Silent Land!
To you, ye boundless regions
Of all perfection! Tender morning visions
Of beauteous souls! The Future's pledge and band!
Who in Life's battle firm doth stand,
Shall bear Hope's tender blossoms
Into the Silent Land!

O Land! O Land!
For all the broken-hearted
The mildest herald by our fate allotted,
Beckons, and with inverted torch doth stand
To lead us with a gentle hand
Into the land of the great Departed,
Into the Silent Land!

L'ENVOI

Ye voices, that arose,
After the Evening's close,
And whispered to my restless heart repose!

Go, breathe it in the ear
Of all who doubt and fear,
And say to them, "Be of good cheer!"

Ye sounds, so low and calm,
That in the groves of balm
Seemed to me like an angel's psalm!

Go, mingle yet once more
With the perpetual roar
Of the pine forest dark and hoar!

Tongues of the dead, not lost,
But speaking from death's frost,
Like fiery tongues at Pentecost!

Glimmer, as funeral lamps,
Amid the chills and damps
Of the vast plain where Death encamps.

BALLADS AND OTHER POEMS

1841

THE SKELETON IN ARMOUR

[The following Ballad was suggested to me while riding on the seashore at Newport. A year or two previous a skeleton had been dug up at Fall River, clad in broken and corroded armour; and the idea occurred to me of connecting it with the Round Tower at Newport, generally known hitherto as the Old Wind-Mill, though now claimed by the Danes as a work of their early ancestors.]

"Speak! speak! thou fearful
      guest!
Who, with thy hollow breast
Still in rude armour drest,
      Comest to daunt me!
Wrapt not in Eastern balms,
But with thy fleshless palms
Stretched, as if asking alms,
      Why dost thou haunt me?"

Then, from those cavernous eyes
Pale flashes seemed to rise,
As when the Northern skies
      Gleam in December;
And, like the water's flow
Under December's snow,
Came a dull voice of woe
      From the heart's chamber.

"I was a Viking old!
My deeds, though manifold,
No Skald in song has told,
      No Saga taught thee!
Take heed, that in thy verse
Thou dost the tale rehearse,
Else dread a dead man's curse;
      For this I sought thee.

"Far in the Northern Land,
By the wild Baltic's strand,
I, with my childish hand,

Tamed the gerfalcon;
And, with my skates fast-bound,
Skimmed the half-frozen Sound,
That the poor whimpering hound
      Trembled to walk on.

"Oft to his frozen lair
Tracked I the grisly bear,
While from my path the hare
      Fled like a shadow;
Oft through the forest dark
Followed the were-wolf's bark,
Until the soaring lark
      Sang from the meadow.

"But when I older grew,
Joining a corsair's crew,
O'er the dark sea I flew
      With the marauders.
Wild was the life we led;
Many the souls that sped,
Many the hearts that bled,
      By our stern orders.

"Many a wassail-bout
Wore the long Winter out;
Often our midnight shout
      Set the cocks crowing,
As we the Berserk's tale
Measured in cups of ale,
Draining the oaken pail,
      Filled to o'erflowing.

"Once as I told in glee
Tales of the stormy sea,
Soft eyes did gaze on me,
      Burning yet tender;
And as the white stars shine
On the dark Norway pine,
On that dark heart of mine
      Fell their soft splendour.

"I wooed the blue-eyed maid,
Yielding, yet half afraid,

38

And in the forest's shade
   Our vows were plighted.
Under its loosened vest
Fluttered her little breast,
Like birds within their nest
   By the hawk frighted.

" Bright in her father's hall
Shields gleamed upon the wall,
Loud sang the minstrels all,
   Chaunting his glory;
When of old Hildebrand
I asked his daughter's hand,
Mute did the minstrels stand
   To hear my story.

" While the brown ale he quaffed,
Loud then the champion laughed.
And as the wind gusts waft
   The sea-foam brightly,
So the loud laugh of scorn,
Out of those lips unshorn,
From the deep drinking-horn
   Blew the foam lightly.

" She was a Prince's child,
I but a Viking wild,
And though she blushed and
   smiled,
   I was discarded!
Should not the dove so white
Follow the sea-mew's flight,
Why did they leave that night
   Her nest unguarded?

" Scarce had I put to sea,
Bearing the maid with me,—
Fairest of all was she
   Among the Norsemen!—
When on the white sea-strand,
Waving his armèd hand,
Saw we old Hildebrand,
   With twenty horsemen.

" Then launched they to the blast,
Bent like a reed each mast,
Yet we were gaining fast,
   When the wind failed us;
And with a sudden flaw

Came round the gusty Skaw,
So that our foe we saw
   Laugh as he hailed us.

" And as to catch the gale
Round veered the flapping sail,
Death! was the helmsman's hail,
   Death without quarter!
Mid-ships with iron keel
Struck we her ribs of steel;
Down her black hulk did reel
   Through the black water!

" As with his wings aslant,
Sails the fierce cormorant,
Seeking some rocky haunt,
   With his prey laden,
So toward the open main,
Beating to sea again,
Through the wild hurricane
   Bore I the maiden.

" Three weeks we westward bore,
And when the storm was o'er,
Cloud-like we saw the shore
   Stretching to lee-ward;
There for my lady's bower
Built I the lofty tower,
Which, to this very hour,
   Stands looking seaward.

" There lived we many years;
Time dried the maiden's tears;
She had forgot her fears,
   She was a mother;
Death closed her mild blue
   eyes,
Under that tower she lies;
Ne'er shall the sun arise
   On such another!

" Still grew my bosom then,
Still as a stagnant fen!
Hateful to me were men,
   The sunlight hateful!
In the vast forest here,
Clad in my warlike gear,
Fell I upon my spear,
   O, death was grateful!

" Thus, seamed with many scars
Bursting these prison bars,
Up to its native stars
　My soul ascended!
There from the flowing bowl
Deep drinks the warrior's soul,
Skoal ! [1] to the Northland! *skoal !* "
—Thus the tale ended.

THE WRECK OF THE
HESPERUS

It was the schooner Hesperus,
　That sailed the wintry sea;
And the skipper had taken his little
　　daughtèr,
　To bear him company.

Blue were her eyes as the fairy-
　　flax,
　Her cheeks like the dawn of
　　day,
And her bosom white as the haw-
　　thorn buds
　That ope in the month of May.

The skipper he stood beside the
　　helm,
　His pipe was in his mouth,
And he watched how the veering
　　flaw did blow
　The smoke now West, now
　　South.

Then up and spake an old Sailòr,
　Had sailed the Spanish Main,
" I pray thee, put into yonder
　　port,
　For I fear a hurricane.

" Last night the moon had a
　　golden ring,
　And to-night no moon we
　　see!"

[1] In Scandinavia this is the custom-
ary salutation when drinking a health.
I have slightly changed the ortho-
graphy of the word, in order to pre-
serve the correct pronunciation.

The skipper he blew a whiff from
　　his pipe,
　And a scornful laugh laughed
　　he.

Colder and colder blew the wind,
　A gale from the North-east;
The snow fell hissing in the brine,
　And the billows frothed like
　　yeast.

Down came the storm, and smote
　　amain,
　The vessel in its strength;
She shuddered and paused, like a
　　frightened steed,
　Then leaped her cable's length.

" Come hither! come hither! my
　　little daughtèr,
　And do not tremble so;
For I can weather the roughest
　　gale,
　That ever wind did blow."

He wrapped her warm in his sea-
　　man's coat
　Against the stinging blast;
He cut a rope from a broken spar,
　And bound her to the mast.

" O father! I hear the church-
　　bells ring,
　O say, what may it be?"
" 'Tis a fog-bell on a rock-bound
　　coast!"—
　And he steered for the open
　　sea.

" O father! I hear the sound of
　　guns,
　O say, what may it be?"
" Some ship in distress, that
　　cannot live
　In such an angry sea!"

" O father! I see a gleaming light,
　O say, what may it be?"
But the father answered never a
　　word,
　A frozen corpse was he.

Lashed to the helm, all stiff and
    stark,
    With his face turned to the
      skies,
The lantern gleamed through the
    gleaming snow
On his fixed and glassy eyes.

Then the maiden clasped her hands
    and prayed
    That savèd she might be;
And she thought of Christ, who
    stilled the wave,
    On the Lake of Galilee.

And fast through the midnight dark
    and drear,
    Through the whistling sleet
      and snow,
Like a sheeted ghost, the vessel
    swept
    Towards the reef of Norman's
      Woe.

And ever the fitful gusts between
    A sound came from the land;
It was the sound of the trampling
    surf,
    On the rocks and the hard sea-
      sand.

The breakers were right beneath
    her bows,
    She drifted a dreary wreck,
And a whooping billow swept the
    crew
    Like icicles from her deck.

She struck where the white and
    fleecy waves
    Looked soft as carded wool,
But the cruel rocks, they gored her
    side
    Like the horns of an angry bull.

Her rattling shrouds, all sheathed
    in ice,
    With the masts went by the
      board;

Like a vessel of glass, she stove
    and sank,
    Ho! ho! the breakers roared!

At daybreak, on the bleak sea-
    beach,
    A fisherman stood aghast,
To see the form of a maiden fair,
    Lashed close to a drifting
      mast.

The salt sea was frozen on her
    breast,
    The salt tears in her eyes;
And he saw her hair, like the
    brown sea-weed,
    On the billows fall and rise.

Such was the wreck of the
    Hesperus,
    In the midnight and the snow!
Christ save us all from a death like
    this
    On the reef of Norman's Woe!

THE LUCK OF EDENHALL

FROM THE GERMAN OF UHLAND

[The tradition, upon which this ballad
is founded, and the " shards of the
Luck of Edenhall," still exists in
England. The goblet is in the
possession of Sir Christopher Mus-
grave, Bart., of Eden Hall, Cumber-
land; and is not so entirely shattered
as the ballad leaves it.]

Of Edenhall, the youthful Lord
Bids sound the festal trumpet's
    call;
He rises at the banquet board,
And cries, 'mid the drunken
    revellers all,
" Now bring me the Luck of Eden-
    hall! "

The butler hears the words with
    pain,
The house's oldest seneschal,

Takes slow from its silken cloth
again
The drinking glass of crystal tall;
They call it The Luck of Edenhall.

Then said the Lord, " This glass to
praise,
Fill with red wine from Portugal! "
The gray-beard with trembling
hand obeys;
A purple light shines over all,
It beams from the Luck of Eden-
hall.

Then speaks the Lord, and waves
it light,
" This glass of flashing crystal tall
Gave to my sires the Fountain-
Sprite;
She wrote in it, *If this glass doth
fall,
Farewell then, O Luck of Edenhall !*

" 'Twas right a goblet the Fate
should be
Of the joyous race of Edenhall!
Deep draughts drink we right
willingly;
And willingly ring, with merry call,
Kling! klang! to the Luck of
Edenhall! "

First rings it deep, and full, and
mild,
Like to the song of a nightingale;
Then like the roar of a torrent
wild;
Then mutters at last like the
thunder's fall,
The glorious Luck of Edenhall.

" For its keeper takes a race of
might,
The fragile goblet of crystal tall;
It has lasted longer than is right;
Kling! klang!—with a harder
blow than all
Will I try the Luck of Edenhall! "

As the goblet ringing flies apart,
Suddenly cracks the vaulted hall;

And through the rift, the wild
flames start;
The guests in dust are scattered all,
With the breaking Luck of Eden-
hall!

In storms the foe, with fire and
sword;
He in the night had scaled the
wall,
Slain by the sword lies the youth-
ful Lord,
But holds in his hand the crystal
tall,
The shattered Luck of Edenhall.

On the morrow the butler gropes
alone,
The gray-beard in the desert hall,
He seeks his Lord's burnt skeleton,
He seeks in the dismal ruin's fall
The shards of the Luck of Eden-
hall.

" The stone wall," saith he, " doth
fall aside,
Down must the stately columns
fall;
Glass is this earth's Luck and
Pride;
In atoms shall fall this earthly ball
One day like the Luck of Eden-
hall! "

THE ELECTED KNIGHT

FROM THE DANISH

[The following strange and somewhat
mystical ballad is from Nyerup and
Rahbek's *Danske Viser* of the
Middle Ages. It seems to refer
to the first preaching of Christi-
anity in the North, and to the in-
stitution of Knight-Errantry. The
three maidens I suppose to be
Faith, Hope, and Charity. The
irregularities of the original have
been carefully preserved in the
translation.]

Sir Oluf he rideth over the plain.
   Full seven miles broad and seven
      miles wide,

But never, ah never can meet with
the man
A tilt with him dare ride.

He saw under the hillside
A Knight full well equipped;
His steed was black, his helm was
barred;
He was riding at full speed.

He wore upon his spurs
Twelve little golden birds;
Anon he spurred his steed with a
clang,
And there sat all the birds and
sang.

He wore upon his spurs
Twelve little golden wheels;
Anon in eddies the wild wind blew,
And round and round the wheels
they flew.

He wore before his breast
A lance that was poised in rest;
And it was sharper than diamond-
stone,
It made Sir Oluf's heart to groan.

He wore upon his helm,
A wreath of ruddy gold;
And that gave him the Maidens
three.
The youngest was fair to behold.

Sir Oluf questioned the Knight
eftsoon
If he were come from heaven
down;
" Art thou Christ of Heaven,"
quoth he,
" So will I yield me unto thee."

" I am not Christ the Great,
Thou shalt not yield thee yet;
I am an Unknown Knight,
Three modest Maidens have me
bedight."

" Art thou a Knight elected,
And have three Maidens thee be-
dight;
So shalt thou ride a tilt this day,
For all the Maidens' honour! "

The first tilt they together rode
They put their steeds to the test;
The second tilt they together rode,
They proved their manhood best.

The third tilt they together rode,
Neither of them would yield;
The fourth tilt they together rode,
They both fell on the field.

Now lie the lords upon the plain,
And their blood runs unto death:
Now sit the Maidens in the high
tower,
The youngest sorrows till death.

THE CHILDREN OF THE LORD'S SUPPER

FROM THE SWEDISH OF BISHOP TEGNÈR

PENTECOST, day of rejoicing, had come. The church of the village
Gleaming stood in the morning's sheen. On the spire of the belfry,
Tipped with a vane of metal, the friendly flames of the Spring-sun
Glanced like the tongues of fire, beheld by Apostles aforetime.
Clear was the heaven and blue, and May, with her cap crowned with
  roses,
Stood in her holiday dress in the fields, and the wind and the brooklet
Murmured gladness and peace. God's-peace! with lips rosy-tinted
Whispered the race of the flowers, and merry on balancing branches
Birds were singing their carol, a jubilant hymn to the Highest.
Swept and clean was the churchyard. Adorned like a leaf-woven
  arbour
Stood its old-fashioned gate; and within upon each cross of iron
Hung was a fragrant garland, new twined by the hands of affection.
Even the dial, that stood on a hillock among the departed,
(There full a hundred years had it stood), was embellished with
  blossoms.
Like to the patriarch hoary, the sage of his kith and the hamlet,
Who on his birthday is crowned by children and children's children,
So stood the ancient prophet, and mute with his pencil of iron
Marked on the tablet of stone, and measured the time and its changes,
While all around at his feet, an eternity slumbered in quiet.
Also the church within was adorned, for this was the season
When the young, their parents' hope, and the loved-ones of heaven,
Should at the foot of the altar renew the vows of their baptism.
Therefore each nook and corner was swept and cleaned, and the dust
  was
Blown from the walls and ceilings, and from the oil-painted benches
There stood the church like a garden; the Feast of the Leafy Pavilions [1]
Saw we in living presentment. From noble arms on the church wall
Grew forth a cluster of leaves, and the preacher's pulpit of oak-wood
Budded once more anew, as aforetime the rod before Aaron.
Wreathed thereon was the Bible with leaves, and the dove, washed
  with silver,
Under its canopy fastened, had on it a necklace of wind-flowers.
But in front of the choir, round the altar-piece painted by Hörberg, [2]
Crept a garland gigantic; and bright-curling tresses of angels

[1] The Feast of the Tabernacles; in Swedish, *Löfhydaohögtiden*, the Leaf huts'-high-tide.
[2] The peasant-painter of Sweden. He is known chiefly by his altar-pieces in the village churches.

Peeped, like the sun from a cloud, from out of the Shadowy leaf-work.
Likewise the lustre of brass, new-polished, blinked from the ceiling,
And for lights there were lilies of Pentecost set in the sockets.

Loud rang the bells already; the thronging crowd was assembled
Far from valleys and hills, to list to the holy preaching.
Hark! then roll forth at once the mighty tones from the organ,
Hover like voices from God, aloft like invisible spirits.
Like as Elias in heaven, when he cast off from him his mantle,
Even so cast off the soul its garments of earth; and with one voice
Chimed in the congregation, and sang an anthem immortal
Of the sublime Wallin,[1] of David's harp in the North-land
Tuned to the choral of Luther; the song on its powerful pinions
Took every living soul, and lifted it gently to heaven,
And every face did shine like the Holy One's face upon Tabor.
Lo! there entered then into the church the Reverend Teacher.
Father he hight and he was in the parish; a christianly plainness
Clothed from his head to his feet the old man of seventy winters.
Friendly was he to behold, and glad as the heralding angel
Walked he among the crowds, but still a contemplative grandeur
Lay on his forehead as clear, as on moss-covered gravestone a sunbeam.
As in his inspiration (an evening twilight that faintly
Gleams in the human soul, even now, from the day of creation)
Th' Artist, the friend of heaven, imagines Saint John when in Patmos,
Gray, with his eyes uplifted to heaven, so seemed then the old man;
Such was the glance of his eye, and such were his tresses of silver.
All the congregation arose in the pews that were numbered.
But with a cordial look, to the right and the left hand, the old man,
Nodding all hail and peace, disappeared in the innermost chancel.

Simply and solemnly now proceeded the Christian service,
Singing and prayer, and at last an ardent discourse from the old man.
Many a moving word and warning, that out of the heart came,
Fell the dew of the morning, like manna on those in the desert.
Afterwards, when all was finished, the Teacher re-entered the chancel,
Followed therein by the young. On the right hand the boys had
    their places,
Delicate figures, with close-curling hair and cheeks rosy-blooming.
But on the left hand of these, there stood the tremulous lilies,
Tinged with the blushing light of the morning, the diffident maidens,—
Folding their hands in prayer, and their eyes cast down on the pave-
    ment.
Now came, with question and answer, the catechism. In the beginning
Answered the children with troubled and faltering voice, but the old
    man's
Glances of kindness encouraged them soon, and the doctrines eternal
Flowed, like the waters of fountains, so clear from lips unpolluted.

[1] A distinguished pulpit-orator and poet. He is particularly remarkable
for the beauty and sublimity of his psalms.

Whene'er the answer was closed, and as oft as they named the
    Redeemer,
Lowly louted the boys, and lowly the maidens all courtesied.
Friendly the Teacher stood, like an angel of light there among them,
And to the children explained he the holy, the highest, in few words,
Thorough, yet simple and clear, for sublimity always is simple,
Both in sermon and song, a child can seize on its meaning.
Even as the green-growing bud is unfolded when Springtide approaches,
Leaf by leaf is developed, and warmed by the radiant sunshine,
Blushes with purple and gold, till at last the perfected blossom
Opens its odorous chalice, and rocks with its crown in the breezes,
So was unfolded here the Christian lore of salvation,
Line by line from the soul of childhood. The fathers and mothers
Stood behind them in tears, and were glad at each well-worded answer.

Now went the old man up to the altar;—and straightway trans-
    figured
(So did it seem unto me) was then the affectionate Teacher.
Like the Lord's Prophet sublime, and awful as Death and as Judgment
Stood he, the God-commissioned, the soul-searcher, earthward
    descending.
Glances, sharp as a sword, into hearts, that to him were transparent
Shot he; his voice was deep, was low like the thunder afar off.
So on a sudden transfigured he stood there, he spake and he questioned.

" This is the faith of the Fathers, the faith the Apostles delivered,
This is moreover the faith whereunto I baptised you, while still ye
Lay on your mothers' breasts, and nearer the portals of heaven.
Slumbering received you then the Holy Church in its bosom;
Wakened from sleep are ye now, and the light in its radiant splendour
Rains from the heaven downward;—to-day on the threshold of
    childhood
Kindly she frees you again, to examine and make your election,
For she knows nought of compulsion, and only conviction desireth.
This is the hour of your trial, the turning-point of existence,
Seed for the coming days; without revocation departeth
Now from your lips the confession; Bethink ye, before ye make answer!
Think not, O think not with guile to deceive the questioning Teacher.
Sharp is his eye to-day, and a curse ever rests upon falsehood.
Enter not with a lie on Life's journey; the multitude hears you,
Brothers and sisters and parents, what dear upon earth is and holy
Standeth before your sight as a witness; the Judge everlasting
Looks from the sun down upon you, and angels in waiting beside him
Grave your confession in letters of fire, upon tablets eternal.
Thus then,—believe ye in God, in the Father who this world created?
Him who redeemed it, the Son, and the Spirit where both are united?
Will ye promise me here, (a holy promise!) to cherish
God more than all things earthly, and every man as a brother?
Will ye promise me here, to confirm your faith by your living,

Th' heavenly faith of affection! to hope, to forgive, and to suffer,
Be what it may your condition, and walk before God in uprightness?
Will ye promise me this before God and man?"—With a clear voice
Answered the young men Yes! and Yes! with lips softly-breathing
Answered the maidens eke. Then dissolved from the brow of the
    Teacher
Clouds with the thunders therein, and he spake in accents more gentle,
Soft as the evening's breath, as harps by Babylon's rivers.

"Hail, then, hail to you all! To the heirdom of heaven be ye
    welcome!
Children no more from this day, but by covenant brothers and sisters!
Yet,—for what reason not children? Of such is the kingdom of
    heaven.
Here upon earth an assemblage of children, in heaven one Father,
Ruling them all as his household,—forgiving in turn and chastising,
That is of human life a picture, as Scripture has taught us.
Blessed are the pure before God! Upon purity and upon virtue
Resteth the Christian Faith; she herself from on high is descended.
Strong as a man and pure as a child, is the sum of the doctrine,
Which the Divine One taught, and suffered and died on the cross for.
O! as ye wander this day from childhood's sacred asylum
Downward and ever downward, and deeper in Age's chill valley,
O! how soon will ye come,—too soon!—and long to turn backward
Up to its hill-tops again, to the sun-illumined, where Judgment
Stood like a father before you, and Pardon, clad like a mother,
Gave you her hand to kiss, and the loving heart was forgiven,
Life was a play and your hands grasped after the roses of heaven!
Seventy years have I lived already; the Father eternal
Gave me gladness and care; but the loveliest hours of existence,
When I have steadfastly gazed in their eyes, I have instantly known
    them,
Known them all again;—they were my childhood's acquaintance.
Therefore take from henceforth, as guides in the paths of existence,
Prayer, with her eyes raised to heaven, and Innocence, bride of a
    man's childhood.
Innocence, child beloved, is a guest from the world of the blessed,
Beautiful, and in her hand a lily; on life's roaring billows
Swings she in safety, she heedeth them not, in the ship she is sleeping.
Calmly she gazes around in the turmoil of men; in the desert
Angels descend and minister unto her; she herself knoweth
Naught of her glorious attendance; but follows faithful and humble,
Follows so long as she may her friend; O do not reject her,
For she cometh from God and she holdeth the keys of the heavens.—
Prayer is Innocence' friend; and willingly flyeth incessant
'Twixt the earth and the sky, the carrier-pigeon of heaven.
Son of Eternity, fettered in Time, and an exile, The Spirit
Tugs at his chains evermore, and struggles like flames ever upward.
Still he recalls with emotion his Father's manifold mansions,

Thinks of the land of his fathers, where blossomed more freshly the
　　flowers,
Shone a more beautiful sun, and he played with the wingèd angels.
Then grows the earth too narrow, too close; and homesick for heaven
Longs the wanderer again; and the Spirit's longings are worship;
Worship is called his most beautiful hour, and its tongue is entreaty.
Ah! when the infinite burden of life descendeth upon us,
Crushes to earth our hope, and, under the earth, in the graveyard,—
Then it is good to pray unto God; for his sorrowing children
Turns he ne'er from his door, but he heals and helps and consoles them.
Yet is it better to pray when all things are prosperous with us,
Pray in fortunate days, for life's most beautiful Fortune
Kneels down before the Eternal's throne; and, with hands interfolded,
Praises, thankful and moved, the only giver of blessings.
Or do ye know, ye children, one blessing that comes not from Heaven?
What has mankind forsooth, the poor! that it has not received?
Therefore, fall in the dust and pray! The seraphs adoring
Cover with pinions six their face in the glory of him who
Hung his masonry pendant on naught, when the world he created.
Earth declareth his might, and the firmament uttereth his glory.
Races blossom and die, and stars fall downward from heaven,
Downward like withered leaves; at the last stroke of midnight,
　　millenniums
Lay themselves down at his feet, and he sees them, but counts them
　　as nothing,
Who shall stand in his presence? The wrath of the judge is terrific,
Casting the insolent down at a glance. When he speaks in his anger
Hillocks skip like the kid, and mountains leap like the roebuck.
Yet,—why are ye afraid, ye children? This awful avenger,
Ah! is a merciful God! God's voice was not in the earthquake,
Not in the fire, nor the storm, but it was in the whispering breezes.
Love is the root of creation; God's essence; worlds without number
Lie in his bosom like children; he made them for this purpose only.
Only to love and to be loved again, he breathed forth his spirit
Into the slumbering dust, and upright standing, it laid its
Hand on its heart, and felt it was warm with a flame out of heaven.
Quench, O quench not that flame! It is the breath of your being.
Love is life, but hatred is death! Not father, nor mother
Loved you, as God has loved you; for 'twas that you may be happy
Gave he his only Son. When he bowed down his head in the death-
　　hour
Solemnised Love its triumph; the sacrifice then was completed.
Lo! then was rent on a sudden the vail of the temple, dividing
Earth and heaven apart, and the dead from their sepulchres rising
Whispered with pallid lips and low in the ears of each other
Th' answer, but dreamed of before, to creation's enigma,—Atonement!
Depths of Love are Atonement's depths, for Love is Atonement.
Therefore, child of mortality, love thou the merciful Father;
Wish what the Holy One wishes, and not from fear, but affection;

Fear is the virtue of slaves; but the heart that loveth is willing;
Perfect was before God, and perfect is Love, and Love only.
Lovest thou God as thou oughtest, then lovest thou likewise thy
    brethren;
One is the sun in heaven, and one, only one, is Love also.
Bears not each human figure the godlike stamp on his forehead?
Readest thou not in his face thine origin? Is he not sailing
Lost like thyself on an ocean unknown, and is he not guided
By the same stars that guide thee? Why shouldst thou hate then
    thy brother?
Hateth he thee, forgive! For 'tis sweet to stammer one letter
Of the Eternal's language;—on earth it is called Forgiveness!
Knowest thou Him, who forgave, with the crown of thorns round his
    temples?
Earnestly prayed for his foes, for his murderers? Say, dost thou know
    him?
Ah! thou confessest his name, so follow likewise his example,
Think of thy brother no ill, but throw a veil over his failings,
Guide the erring aright; for the good, the heavenly shepherd
Took the lost lamb in his arms, and bore it back to its mother.
This is the fruit of Love, and it is by its fruits that we know it.
Love is the creature's welfare, with God; but Love among mortals
Is but an endless sigh! He longs, and endures, and stands waiting,
Suffers and yet rejoices, and smiles with tears on his eyelids.
Hope,—so is called upon earth, his recompense,—Hope, the be-
    friending,
Does what she can, for she points evermore up to heaven, and faithful
Plunges her anchor's peak in the depths of the grave, and beneath it
Paints a more beautiful world, a dim, but a sweet play of shadows!
Races, better than we, have leaned on her wavering promise,
Having naught else but Hope. Then praise we our Father in heaven,
Him, who has given us more; for to us has Hope been transfigured,
Groping no longer in night; she is Faith, she is living assurance.
Faith is enlightened Hope; she is light, is the eye of affection,
Dreams of the longing interprets, and carves their visions in marble.
Faith is the son of life; and her countenance shines like the Hebrew's,
For she has looked upon God; the heaven on its stable foundation
Draws she with chains down to earth, and the New Jerusalem sinketh
Splendid with portals twelve in golden vapours descending.
There enraptured she wanders, and looks at the figure majestic,
Fears not the wingèd crowd, in the midst of them all is her homestead.
Therefore love and believe; for works will follow spontaneous
Even as day does the sun; the Right from the Good is an offspring,
Love in a bodily shape; and Christian works are no more than
Animate Love and faith, as flowers are the animate springtide.
Works do follow us all unto God; there stand and bear witness
Not what they seemed,—but what they were only. Blessed is he who
Hears their confession secure; they are mute upon earth until death's
    hand

Opens the mouth of the silent.　Ye children, does Death e'er alarm
　　you?
Death is the brother of Love, twin-brother is he, and is only
More austere to behold.　With a kiss upon lips that are fading
Takes he the soul and departs, and rocked in the arms of affection,
Places the ransomed child, new born, 'fore the face of its father.
Sounds of his coming already I hear,—see dimly his pinions,
Swart as the night, but with stars strewn upon them!　I fear not
　　before him.
Death is only released, and in mercy is mute.　On his bosom
Freer breathes, in its coolness, my breast; and face to face standing
Look I on God as he is, a sun unpolluted by vapours;
Look on the light of the ages I loved, the spirits majestic,
Nobler, better than I; they stand by the throne all transfigured,
Vested in white, and with harps of gold, and are singing an anthem,
Writ in the climate of heaven, in the language spoken by angels.
You, in like manner, ye children beloved, he one day shall gather,
Never forgets he the weary;—then welcome, ye loved ones, hereafter!
Meanwhile forget not the keeping of vows, forget not the promise,
Wander from holiness onward to holiness; earth shall ye heed not;
Earth is but dust and heaven is light; I have pledged you to heaven.
God of the Universe, hear me! thou fountain of Love everlasting,
Hark to the voice of thy servant!　I send up my prayer to thy
　　heaven!
Let me hereafter not miss at thy throne one spirit of all these,
Whom thou hast given me here!　I have loved them all like a father.
May they bear witness for me, that I taught them the way of salvation,
Faithful, so far as I knew of thy word; again may they know me,
Fall on their Teacher's breast, and before thy face may I place them,
Pure as they now are, but only more tried, and exclaiming with
　　gladness,
Father, lo!　I am here, and the children, whom thou hast given me! "

　Weeping he spake in these words; and now at the beck of the old
　　man
Knee against knee they knitted a wreath round the altar's enclosure.
Kneeling he read them the prayers of the consecration, and softly
With him the children read; at the close, with tremulous accents,
Asked he the peace of heaven, a benediction upon them.
Now should have ended his task for the day; the following Sunday
Was for the young appointed to eat of the Lord's holy Supper.
Sudden, as struck from the clouds, stood the Teacher silent and laid
　　his
Hand on his forehead, and cast his looks upward; while thoughts
　　high and holy
Flew through the midst of his soul, and his eyes glanced with wonder-
　　ful brightness.
" On the next Sunday, who knows! perhaps I shall rest in the grave-
　　yard!

Some one perhaps of yourselves, a lily broken untimely,
Bow down his head to the earth; why delay I? the hour is accomplished.
Warm is the heart;—I will so! for to-day grows the harvest of heaven.
What I began accomplish I now; for what failing therein is
I, the old man, will answer to God and the reverend father.
Say to me only, ye children, ye denizens new-come in heaven,
Are ye ready this day to eat of the bread of Atonement?
What it denoteth, that know ye full well, I have told it you often.
Of the new covenant a symbol it is, of Atonement a token,
'Stablished between earth and heaven. Man by his sins and transgressions
Far hath wandered from God, from his essence. 'Twas in the beginning
Fast by the Tree of Knowledge he fell, and it hangs its crown o'er the
Fall to this day; in the Thought is the Fall; in the Heart the Atonement.
Infinite is the Fall, the Atonement infinite likewise.
See! behind me, as far as the old man remembers, and forward,
Far as Hope in her flight can reach with her wearied pinions,
Sin and Atonement incessant go through the lifetime of mortals.
Brought forth is sin full-grown; but Atonement sleeps in our bosoms
Still as the cradled babe; and dreams of heavens and of angels,
Cannot awake to sensation; is like the tones in the harp's strings,
Spirits imprisoned, that wait evermore the deliverer's finger.
Therefore, ye children beloved, descended the Prince of Atonement,
Woke the slumberer from sleep, and she stands now with eyes all resplendent,
Bright as the vault of the sky, and battles with Sin and o'ercomes her,
Downward to earth he came and transfigured, thence reascended,
Not from the heart in like wise, for there he still lives in the Spirit,
Loves and atones evermore. So long as Time is, is Atonement.
Therefore with reverence receive this day her visible token.
Tokens are dead if the things do not live. The light everlasting
Unto the blind man is not, but is born of the eye that has vision.
Neither in bread nor in wine, but in the heart that is hallowed
Lieth forgiveness enshrined; the intention alone of amendment
Fruits of the earth ennobles to heavenly things, and removes all
Sin and the guerdon of sin. Only Love with his arms wide extended,
Penitence weeping and praying: the Will that is tried, and whose gold flows
Purified forth from the flame; in a word, mankind by Atonement
Breaketh Atonement's bread, and drinketh Atonement's wine-cup.
But he who cometh up hither, unworthy, with hate in his bosom,
Scoffing at men and at God, is guilty of Christ's blessed body,
And the Redeemer's blood! To himself he eateth and drinketh
Death and doom! And from this, preserve us, thou Heavenly Father!
Are ye ready, ye children, to eat of the bread of Atonement?"
Thus with emotion he asked, and together answered the children

Yes! with deep sobs interrupted.   Then read he the due supplications,
Read the Form of Communion, and in chimed the organ and anthem;
O! Holy Lamb of God, who takest away our transgressions,
Hear us! give us thy peace! have mercy, have mercy upon us!
Th' old man, with trembling hand, and heavenly pearls on his eyelids,
Filled now the chalice and paten, and dealt round the mystical
    symbols.
O! then seemed it to me as if God, with the broad eye of midday,
Clearer looked in at the windows, and all the trees in the churchyard
Bowed down their summits of green, and the grass on the graves 'gan
    to shiver.
But in the children, (I noted it well; I knew it) there ran a
Tremor of holy rapture along through their icy cold members.
Decked like an altar before them, there stood the green earth, and
    above it
Heaven opened itself, as of old, before Stephen; they saw there
Radiant in glory the Father, and on his right hand the Redeemer.
Under them hear they the clang of harpstrings, and angels from gold
    clouds
Beckon to them like brothers, and fan with their pinions of purple.

  Closed was the Teacher's task, and with heaven in their hearts and
      their faces,
Up rose the children all, and each bowed him, weeping full sorely,
Downward to kiss that reverend hand, but all of them pressed he
Moved to his bosom, and laid, with a prayer, his hands full of blessings,
Now on the holy breast, and now on the innocent tresses.

EVANGELINE

A TALE OF ACADIE

1847

THIS is the forest primeval. The murmuring pines and the hemlocks,
Bearded with moss, and in garments green, indistinct in the twilight,
Stand like Druids of old, with voices sad and prophetic,
Stand like harpers hoar, with beards that rest on their bosoms.
Loud from its rocky caverns, the deep-voiced neighbouring ocean
Speaks, and in accents disconsolate answers the wail of the forest.

This is the forest primeval; but where are the hearts that beneath it
Leaped like the roe, when he hears in the woodland the voice of the
 huntsman?
Where is the thatch-roofed village, the home of Acadian farmers,—
Men whose lives glided on like rivers that water the woodlands,

Darkened by shadows of earth, but reflecting an image of heaven?
Waste are those pleasant farms, and the farmers forever departed!
Scattered like dust and leaves, when the mighty blasts of October
Seize them, and whirl them aloft, and sprinkle them far o'er the ocean.
Naught but tradition remains of the beautiful village of Grand-Pré.

Ye who believe in affection that hopes, and endures, and is patient,
Ye who believe in the beauty and strength of woman's devotion,
List to the mournful tradition still sung by the pines of the forest;
List to a Tale of Love in Acadie, home of the happy.

PART THE FIRST

I.

In the Acadian land, on the shores of the Basin of Minas
Distant, secluded, still, the little village of Grand-Pré
Lay in the fruitful valley. Vast meadows stretched to the eastward,
Giving the village its name, and pasture to flocks without number.
Dikes, that the hands of the farmers had raised with labour incessant,
Shut out the turbulent tides; but at stated seasons the flood-gates
Opened, and welcomed the sea to wander at will o'er the meadows.
West and south there were fields of flax, and orchards and corn-fields
Spreading afar and unfenced o'er the plain; and away to the north-
 ward

Blomidon rose, and the forests old, and aloft on the mountains
Sea-fogs pitched their tents, and mists from the mighty Atlantic
Looked on the happy valley, but ne'er from their station descended.
There, in the midst of its farms, reposed the Acadian village.
Strongly built were the houses, with frames of oak and of chestnut,
Such as the peasants of Normandy built in the reign of the Henries.
Thatched were the roofs, with dormer-windows; and gables projecting
Over the basement below protected and shaded the door-way.
There in the tranquil evenings of summer, when brightly the sunset
Lighted the village street, and gilded the vanes on the chimneys,
Matrons and maidens sat in snow-white caps and in kirtles
Scarlet and blue and green, with distaffs spinning the golden
Flax for the gossiping looms, whose noisy shuttles within doors
Mingled their sound with the whir of the wheels and the songs of the
     maidens.
Solemnly down the street came the parish priest, and the children
Paused in their play to kiss the hand he extended to bless them.
Reverend walked he among them; and up rose matrons and maidens,
Hailing his slow approach with words of affectionate welcome.
Then came the labourers home from the field, and serenely the sun sank
Down to his rest, and twilight prevailed.   Anon from the belfry
Softly the Angelus sounded, and over the roofs of the village
Columns of pale blue smoke, like clouds of incense ascending,
Rose from a hundred hearths, the homes of peace and contentment.
Thus dwelt together in love these simple Acadian farmers,—
Dwelt in the love of God and of man.   Alike were they free from
Fear, that reigns with the tyrant, and envy, the vice of republics.
Neither locks had they to their doors, nor bars to their windows;
But their dwellings were open as day and the hearts of the owners;
There the richest was poor, and the poorest lived in abundance.

    Somewhat apart from the village, and nearer the Basin of Minas,
Benedict Bellefontaine, the wealthiest farmer of Grand-Pré,
Dwelt on his goodly acres; and with him, directing his household,
Gentle Evangeline lived, his child, and the pride of the village.
Stalworth and stately in form was the man of seventy winters;
Hearty and hale was he, an oak that is covered with snowflakes;
White as the snow were his locks, and his cheeks as brown as the
     oak-leaves.
Fair was she to behold, that maiden of seventeen summers.
Black were her eyes as the berry that grows on the thorn by the
     wayside,
Black, yet how softly they gleamed beneath the brown shade of her
     tresses!
Sweet was her breath as the breath of kine that feed in the meadows.
When in the harvest heat she bore to the reapers at noontide
Flagons of home-brewed ale, ah! fair in sooth was the maiden!
Fairer was she when, on Sunday morn, while the bell from its turret
Sprinkled with holy sounds the air, as the priest with his hyssop

Sprinkles the congregation, and scatters blessings upon them.
Down the long street she passed, with her chaplet of beads and her
missal,
Wearing her Norman cap, and her kirtle of blue, and the ear-rings,
Brought in the olden time from France, and since, as an heirloom,
Handed down from mother to child, through long generations.
But a celestial brightness—a more ethereal beauty—
Shone on her face and encircled her form, when, after confession,
Homeward serenely she walked with God's benediction upon her.
When she had passed, it seemed like the ceasing of exquisite music.

Firmly builded with rafters of oak, the house of the farmer
Stood on the side of a hill commanding the sea; and a shady
Sycamore grew by the door, with a woodbine wreathing around it.
Rudely carved was the porch, with seats beneath; and a footpath
Led through an orchard wide, and disappeared in the meadow.
Under the Sycamore-tree were hives overhung by a penthouse,
Such as the traveller sees in regions remote by the roadside,
Built o'er a box for the poor, or the blessed image of Mary.
Farther down, on the slope of the hill, was the well with its moss-
grown
Bucket, fastened with iron, and near it a trough for the horses.
Shielding the house from storms, on the north, were the barns and
the farmyard.
There stood the broad-wheeled wains and the antique ploughs and
the harrows;
There were the folds for the sheep; and there, in his feathered seraglio,
Strutted the lordly turkey, and crowed the cock, with the selfsame
Voice that in ages of old had startled the penitent Peter.
Bursting with hay were the barns, themselves a village. In each one
Far o'er the gable projected a roof of thatch; and a staircase,
Under the sheltering eaves, led up to the odorous corn-loft.
There too the dove-cot stood, with its meek and innocent inmates
Murmuring ever of love; while above in the variant breezes
Numberless noisy weathercocks rattled and sang of mutation.

Thus, at peace with God and the world, the farmer of Grand-Pré
Lived on his sunny farm, and Evangeline governed his household.
Many a youth, as he knelt in the church and opened his missal,
Fixed his eyes upon her, as the saint of his deepest devotion;
Happy was he who might touch her hand or the hem of her garment!
Many a suitor came to her door, by the darkness befriended,
And as he knocked and waited to hear the sound of her footsteps,
Knew not which beat the louder, his heart or the knocker of iron;
Or at the joyous feast of the Patron Saint of the village,
Bolder grew, and pressed her hand in the dance as he whispered
Hurried words of love, that seemed a part of the music.
But, among all who came, young Gabriel only was welcome;
Gabriel Lajeunesse, the son of Basil the blacksmith,

Who was a mighty man in the village, and honoured of all men;
For since the birth of time, throughout all ages and nations,
Has the craft of the smith been held in repute by the people.
Basil was Benedict's friend. Their children from earliest childhood
Grew up together as brother and sister; and Father Felician,
Priest and pedagogue both in the village, had taught them their
    letters
Out of the selfsame book, with the hymns of the church and the
    plain-song.
But when the hymn was sung, and the daily lesson completed,
Swiftly they hurried away to the forge of Basil the blacksmith.
There at the door they stood, with wondering eyes to behold him
Take in his leathern lap the hoof of the horse as a plaything,
Nailing the shoe in its place; while near him the tire of the cart-wheel
Lay like a fiery snake, coiled round in a circle of cinders.
Oft on autumnal eves, when without in the gathering darkness
Bursting with light seemed the smithy, through every cranny and
    crevice,
Warm by the forge within they watched the labouring bellows,
And as its panting ceased, and the sparks expired in the ashes,
Merrily laughed, and said they were nuns going into the chapel.
Oft on sledges in winter, as swift as the swoop of the eagle,
Down the hillside bounding, they glided away o'er the meadow.
Oft in the barns they climbed to the populous nests on the rafters,
Seeking with eager eyes that wondrous stone, which the swallow
Brings from the shore of the sea to restore the sight of its fledglings;
Lucky was he who found that stone in the nest of the swallow!
Thus passed a few swift years, and they no longer were children.
He was a valiant youth, and his face, like the face of the morning,
Gladdened the earth with its light, and ripened thought into action.
She was a woman now, with the heart and hopes of a woman.
" Sunshine of Saint Eulalie " was she called; for that was the sunshine
Which, as the farmers believed, would load their orchards with apples;
She, too, would bring to her husband's house delight and abundance,
Filling it full of love and the ruddy faces of children.

II.

Now had the season returned, when the nights grow colder and longer,
And the retreating sun the sign of the Scorpion enters.
Birds of passage sailed through the leaden air from the ice-bound,
Desolate northern bays to the shores of tropical islands.
Harvests were gathered in; and wild with the winds of September
Wrestled the trees of the forest, as Jacob of old with the angel.
All the signs foretold a winter long and inclement.
Bees, with prophetic instinct of want, had hoarded their honey
Till the hives overflowed; and the Indian hunters asserted
Cold would the winter be, for thick was the fur of the foxes.

Such was the advent of autumn. Then followed that beautiful season,
Called by the pious Acadian peasants the Summer of All-Saints!
Filled was the air with a dreamy and magical light; and the landscape
Lay as if new-created in all the freshness of childhood.
Peace seemed to reign upon earth, and the restless heart of the ocean
Was for a moment consoled. All sounds were in harmony blended.
Voices of children at play, the crowing of cocks in the farmyards,
Whir of wings in the drowsy air, and the cooing of pigeons,
All were subdued and low as the murmurs of love, and the great sun
Looked with the eye of love through the golden vapours around him;
While arrayed in its robes of russet and scarlet and yellow,
Bright with the sheen of the dew, each glittering tree of the forest
Flashed like the plane-tree the Persian adorned with mantles and jewels.

Now recommenced the reign of rest and affection and stillness.
Day with its burden and heat had departed, and twilight descending
Brought back the evening star to the sky, and the herds to the homestead.
Pawing the ground they came, and resting their necks on each other,
And with their nostrils distended inhaling the freshness of evening.
Foremost, bearing the bell, Evangeline's beautiful heifer,
Proud of her snow-white hide, and the ribbon that waved from her collar,
Quietly paced and slow, as if conscious of human affection.
Then came the shepherd back with his bleating flock from the seaside,
Where was their favourite pasture. Behind them followed the watch-dog,
Patient, full of importance, and grand in the pride of his instinct,
Walking from side to side with a lordly air, and superbly
Waving his bushy tail, and urging forward the stragglers;
Regent of flocks was he when the shepherd slept; their protector,
When from the forest at night, through the starry silence the wolves howled.
Late, with the rising moon, returned the wains from the marshes,
Laden with briny hay, that filled the air with its odour.
Cheerily neighed the steeds, with dew on their manes and their fetlocks,
While aloft on their shoulders the wooden and ponderous saddles,
Painted with brilliant dyes, and adorned with tassels of crimson,
Nodded in bright array, like hollyhocks heavy with blossoms.
Patiently stood the cows meanwhile, and yielded their udders
Unto the milkmaid's hand; whilst loud and in regular cadence
Into the sounding pails the foaming streamlets descended.
Lowing of cattle and peals of laughter were heard in the farmyard,
Echoed back by the barns. Anon they sank into stillness;
Heavily closed, with a jarring sound, the valves of the barn-doors,
Rattled the wooden bars, and all for a season was silent.

Indoors, warm by the wide-mouthed fireplace, idly the farmer

Sat in his elbow-chair, and watched how the flames and the smoke wreaths
Struggled together like foes in a burning city.   Behind him,
Nodding and mocking along the wall, with gestures fantastic,
Darted his own huge shadow, and vanished away into darkness.
Faces, clumsily carved in oak, on the back of his arm-chair
Laughed in the flickering light, and the pewter plates on the dresser
Caught and reflected the flame, as shields of armies the sunshine.
Fragments of song the old man sang, and carols of Christmas,
Such as at home, in the olden time, his fathers before him
Sang in their Norman orchards and bright Burgundian vineyards.
Close at her father's side was the gentle Evangeline seated,
Spinning flax for the loom, that stood in the corner behind her.
Silent awhile were its treadles, at rest was its diligent shuttle,
While the monotonous drone of the wheel, like the drone of a bagpipe,
Followed the old man's song, and united the fragments together.
As in a church, when the chant of the choir at intervals ceases,
Footfalls are heard in the aisles, or words of the priest at the altar,
So, in each pause of the song, with measured motion the clock clicked.

Thus as they sat, there were footsteps heard, and, suddenly lifted,
Sounded the wooden latch, and the door swung back on its hinges.
Benedict knew by the hob-nailed shoes it was Basil the blacksmith,
And by her beating heart Evangeline knew who was with him.
" Welcome! " the farmer exclaimed, as their footsteps paused on the
        threshold,
" Welcome, Basil, my friend!   Come, take thy place on the settle
Close by the chimney-side, which is always empty without thee;
Take from the shelf overhead thy pipe and the box of tobacco;
Never so much thyself art thou as when through the curling
Smoke of the pipe or the forge thy friendly and jovial face gleams
Round and red as the harvest moon through the mist of the marshes."
Then, with a smile of content, thus answered Basil the blacksmith,
Taking with easy air the accustomed seat by the fireside:—
" Benedict Bellefontaine, thou hast ever thy jest and thy ballad!
Ever in cheerfullest mood art thou, when others are filled with
Gloomy forebodings of ill, and see only ruin before them.
Happy art thou, as if every day thou hadst picked up a horse-shoe."
Pausing a moment, to take the pipe that Evangeline brought him,
And with a coal from the embers had lighted, he slowly continued:—
" Four days now are passed since the English ships at their anchors
Ride in the Gaspereau's mouth, with their cannon pointed against us.
What their design may be is unknown; but all are commanded
On the morrow to meet in the church, where his Majesty's mandate
Will be proclaimed as law in the land.   Alas! in the mean time
Many surmises of evil alarm the hearts of the people."
Then made answer the farmer:—" Perhaps some friendlier purpose
Brings these ships to our shores.   Perhaps the harvests in England
By the untimely rains or untimelier heat have been blighted,

And from our bursting barns they would feed their cattle and children."
" Not so thinketh the folk in the village," said, warmly, the black-
    smith,
Shaking his head, as in doubt; then, heaving a sigh, he continued:—
" Louisburg is not forgotten, nor Beau Séjour, nor Port Royal.
Many already have fled to the forest, and lurk on its outskirts,
Waiting with anxious hearts the dubious fate of to-morrow.
Arms have been taken from us, and warlike weapons of all kinds;
Nothing is left but the blacksmith's sledge and the scythe of the
    mower."
Then with a pleasant smile made answer the jovial farmer:—
" Safer are we unarmed, in the midst of our flocks and our corn-fields,
Safer within these peaceful dikes, besieged by the ocean,
Than were our fathers in forts, besieged by the enemy's cannon.
Fear no evil, my friend, and to-night may no shadow of sorrow
Fall on this house and hearth; for this is the night of the contract.
Built are the house and the barn. The merry lads of the village
Strongly have built them and well; and, breaking the glebe round
    about them,
Filled the barn with hay, and the house with food for a twelvemonth.
René Leblanc will be here anon, with his papers and inkhorn.
Shall we not then be glad, and rejoice in the joy of our children? "
As apart by the window she stood, with her hand in her lover's,
Blushing Evangeline heard the words that her father had spoken,
And as they died on his lips the worthy notary entered.

III.

Bent like a labouring oar, that toils in the surf of the ocean,
Bent, but not broken, by age was the form of the notary public;
Shocks of yellow hair, like the silken floss of the maize, hung
Over his shoulders; his forehead was high; and glasses with horn
    bows
Sat astride on his nose, with a look of wisdom supernal.
Father of twenty children was he, and more than a hundred
Children's children rode on his knee, and heard his great watch tick.
Four long years in the times of the war had he languished a captive,
Suffering much in an old French fort as the friend of the English.
Now, though warier grown, without all guile or suspicion,
Ripe in wisdom was he, but patient, and simple, and childlike.
He was beloved by all, and most of all by the children;
For he told them tales of the Loup-garou in the forest,
And of the goblin that came in the night to water the horses,
And of the white Létiche, the ghost of a child who unchristened
Died, and was doomed to haunt unseen the chambers of children;
And how on Christmas eve the oxen talked in the stable,
And how the fever was cured by a spider shut up in a nutshell,

And of the marvellous powers of four-leaved clover and horse-shoes,
With whatsoever else was writ in the lore of the village.
Then up rose from his seat by the fireside Basil the blacksmith,
Knocked from his pipe the ashes, and slowly extending his right hand,
"Father Leblanc," he exclaimed, "thou hast heard the talk in the
     village,
And, perchance, canst tell us some news of these ships and their
     errand."
     Then with modest demeanour made answer the notary public,—
"Gossip enough have I heard, in sooth, yet am never the wiser;
And what their errand may be I know not better than others.
Yet am I not of those who imagine some evil intention
Brings them here, for we are at peace; and why then molest us?"
"God's name!" shouted the hasty and somewhat irascible blacksmith;
"Must we in all things look for the how, and the why, and the
     wherefore?
Daily injustice is done, and might is the right of the strongest!"
But, without heeding his warmth, continued the notary public,—
"Man is unjust, but God is just; and finally justice
Triumphs; and well I remember a story, that often consoled me,
When as a captive I lay in the old French fort at Port Royal."
This was the old man's favourite tale, and he loved to repeat it
When his neighbours complained that any injustice was done them.
"Once in an ancient city, whose name I no longer remember,
Raised aloft on a column, a brazen statue of Justice
Stood in the public square, upholding the scales in its left hand,
And in its right a sword, as an emblem that justice presided
Over the laws of the land, and the hearts and homes of the people.
Even the birds had built their nests in the scales of the balance,
Having no fear of the sword that flashed in the sunshine above them.
But in the course of time the laws of the land were corrupted;
Might took the place of right, and the weak were oppressed, and the
     mighty
Ruled with an iron rod.   Then it chanced in a nobleman's palace
That a necklace of pearls was lost, and ere long a suspicion
Fell on an orphan girl who lived as maid in the household.
She, after form of trial condemned to die on the scaffold,
Patiently met her doom at the foot of the statue of Justice.
As to her Father in heaven her innocent spirit ascended,
Lo! o'er the city a tempest rose; and the bolts of the thunder
Smote the statue of bronze, and hurled in wrath from its left hand
Down on the pavement below the clattering scales of the balance,
And in the hollow thereof was found the nest of a magpie,
Into whose clay-built walls the necklace of pearls was inwoven."
Silenced, but not convinced, when the story was ended, the black-
     smith
Stood like a man who fain would speak, but findeth no language;
All his thoughts were congealed into lines on his face, as the vapours
Freeze in fantastic shapes on the window-panes in the winter.

Then Evangeline lighted the brazen lamp on the table,
Filled, till it overflowed, the pewter tankard with home-brewed
Nut-brown ale, that was famed for its strength in the village of
    Grand-Pré;
While from his pocket the notary drew his papers and inkhorn,
Wrote with a steady hand the date and the age of the parties,
Naming the dower of the bride in flocks of sheep and in cattle.
Orderly all things proceeded, and duly and well were completed,
And the great seal of the law was set like a sun on the margin.
Then from his leathern pouch the farmer threw on the table
Three times the old man's fee in solid pieces of silver;
And the notary rising, and blessing the bride and the bridegroom,
Lifted aloft the tankard of ale and drank to their welfare.
Wiping the foam from his lip, he solemnly bowed and departed,
While in silence the others sat and mused by the fireside,
Till Evangeline brought the draught-board out of its corner.
Soon was the game begun.   In friendly contention the old men
Laughed at each lucky hit, or unsuccessful manœuvre,
Laughed when a man was crowned, or a breach was made in the
    king-row.
Meanwhile apart, in the twilight gloom of a window's embrasure,
Sat the lovers, and whispered together, beholding the moon rise
Over the pallid sea and the silvery mist of the meadows.
Silently, one by one, in the infinite meadows of heaven,
Blossomed the lovely stars, the forget-me-nots of the angels.

Thus passed the evening away.   Anon the bell from the belfry
Rang out the hour of nine, the village curfew, and straightway
Rose the guests and departed; and silence reigned in the household.
Many a farewell word and sweet good-night on the door-step
Lingered long in Evangeline's heart, and filled it with gladness.
Carefully then were covered the embers that glowed on the hearth-
    stone,
And on the oaken stairs resounded the tread of the farmer.
Soon with a soundless step the foot of Evangeline followed.
Up the staircase moved a luminous space in the darkness,
Lighted less by the lamp than the shining face of the maiden.
Silent she passed through the hall, and entered the door of her
    chamber.
Simple that chamber was, with its curtains of white, and its clothes-
    press
Ample and high, on whose spacious shelves were carefully folded
Linen and woollen stuffs, by the hand of Evangeline woven.
This was the precious dower she would bring to her husband in
    marriage,
Better than flocks and herds, being proofs of her skill as a housewife.
Soon she extinguished her lamp, for the mellow and radiant moonlight
Streamed through the windows, and lighted the room, till the heart
    of the maiden

Swelled and obeyed its power, like the tremulous tides of the ocean.
Ah! she was fair, exceeding fair to behold, as she stood with
Naked snow-white feet on the gleaming floor of her chamber!
Little she dreamed that below, among the trees of the orchard,
Waited her lover and watched for the gleam of her lamp and her
    shadow.
Yet were her thoughts of him, and at times a feeling of sadness
Passed o'er her soul, as the sailing shade of clouds in the moonlight
Flitted across the floor and darkened the room for a moment.
And as she gazed from the window she saw serenely the moon pass
Forth from the folds of a cloud, and one star follow her footsteps,
As out of Abraham's tent young Ishmael wandered with Hagar!

IV.

Pleasantly rose next morn the sun on the village of Grand-Pré.
Pleasantly gleamed in the soft, sweet air the Basin of Minas,
Where the ships, with their wavering shadows, were riding at anchor.
Life had long been astir in the village, and clamorous labour
Knocked with its hundred hands at the golden gates of the morning.
Now from the country around, from the farms and the neighbouring
    hamlets,
Came in their holiday dresses the blithe Acadian peasants.
Many a glad good-morrow and jocund laugh from the young folk
Made the bright air brighter, as up from the numerous meadows,
Where no path could be seen but the track of wheels in the greensward,
Group after group appeared, and joined, or passed on the highway.
Long ere noon, in the village all sounds of labour were silenced.
Thronged were the streets with people; and noisy groups at the
    house-doors
Sat in the cheerful sun, and rejoiced and gossiped together.
Every house was an inn, where all were welcomed and feasted;
For with this simple people, who lived like brothers together,
All things were held in common, and what one had was another's.
Yet under Benedict's roof hospitality seemed more abundant:
For Evangeline stood among the guests of her father;
Bright was her face with smiles, and words of welcome and gladness
Fell from her beautiful lips, and blessed the cup as she gave it.

Under the open sky, in the odorous air of the orchard,
Bending with golden fruit, was spread the feast of betrothal.
There in the shade of the porch were the priest and the notary seated;
There good Benedict sat, and sturdy Basil the blacksmith.
Not far withdrawn from these, by the cider-press and the bee-hives,
Michael the fiddler was placed, with the gayest of hearts and of
    waistcoats.
Shadow and light from the leaves alternately played on his snow-white

Hair, as it waved in the wind, and the jolly face of the fiddler
Glowed like a living coal when the ashes are blown from the embers
Gayly the old man sang to the vibrant sound of his fiddle,
Tous les Bourgeois de Chartres, and *Le Carillon de Dunkerque*,
And anon with his wooden shoes beat time to the music.
Merrily, merrily whirled the wheels of the dizzying dances
Under the orchard-trees and down the path to the meadows;
Old folk and young together, and children mingled among them.
Fairest of all the maids was Evangeline, Benedict's daughter!
Noblest of all the youths was Gabriel, son of the blacksmith!

So passed the morning away. And lo! with a summons sonorous
Sounded the bell from its tower, and over the meadows a drum beat,
Thronged ere long was the church with men. Without, in the churchyard,
Waited the women. They stood by the graves, and hung on the headstones
Garlands of autumn leaves and evergreens fresh from the forest.
Then came the guard from the ships, and marching proudly among them
Entered the sacred portal. With loud and dissonant clangour
Echoed the sound of their brazen drums from ceiling and casement,—
Echoed a moment only, and slowly the ponderous portal
Closed, and in silence the crowd awaited the will of the soldiers.
Then up rose their commander, and spake from the steps of the altar,
Holding aloft in his hands, with its seals, the royal commission,
"You are convened this day," he said, "by his Majesty's orders.
Clement and kind has he been; but how you have answered his kindness,
Let your own hearts reply! To my natural make and my temper
Painful the task is I do, which to you I know must be grievous.
Yet must I bow and obey, and deliver the will of our monarch;
Namely, that all your lands, and dwellings, and cattle of all kinds
Forfeited be to the crown; and that you yourselves from this province
Be transported to other lands. God grant you may dwell there
Ever as faithful subjects, a happy and peaceable people!
Prisoners now I declare you; for such is his Majesty's pleasure!"
As, when the air is serene in the sultry solstice of summer,
Suddenly gathers a storm, and the deadly sling of the hailstones
Beats down the farmer's corn in the field and shatters his windows,
Hiding the sun, and strewing the ground with thatch from the house-roofs,
Bellowing fly the herds, and seek to break their inclosures;
So on the hearts of the people descended the words of the speaker.
Silent a moment they stood in speechless wonder, and then rose
Louder and ever louder a wail of sorrow and anger,
And, by one impulse moved, they madly rushed to the doorway.
Vain was the hope of escape; and cries and fierce imprecations
Rang through the house of prayer; and high o'er the heads of the others

Rose, with his arms uplifted, the figure of Basil the blacksmith,
As, on a stormy sea, a spar is tossed by the billows.
Flushed was his face and distorted with passion; and wildly he
    shouted,—
" Down with the tyrants of England! we never have sworn them
    allegiance!
Death to these foreign soldiers, who seize on our homes and our
    harvests! "
More he fain would have said, but the merciless hand of a soldier
Smote him upon the mouth, and dragged him down to the pavement.

    In the midst of the strife and tumult of angry contention,
Lo! the door of the chancel opened, and Father Felician
Entered, with serious mien, and ascended the steps of the altar.
Raising his reverend hand, with a gesture he awed into silence
All that clamorous throng; and thus he spake to his people;
Deep were his tones and solemn; in accents measured and mournful
Spake he, as, after the tocsin's alarum, distinctly the clock strikes.
" What is this that ye do, my children? what madness has seized you?
Forty years of my life have I laboured among you, and taught you,
Not in word alone, but in deed, to love one another!
Is this the fruits of my toils, of my vigils and prayers and privations?
Have you so soon forgotten all lessons of love and forgiveness?
This is the house of the Prince of Peace, and would you profane it
Thus with violent deeds and hearts overflowing with hatred?
Lo! where the crucified Christ from his cross is gazing upon you!
See! in those sorrowful eyes what meekness and holy compassion!
Hark! how those lips still repeat the prayer, ' O Father, forgive
    them! '
Let us repeat that prayer in the hour when the wicked assail us,
Let us repeat it now, and say, ' O Father, forgive them! ' "
Few were his words of rebuke, but deep in the hearts of his people
Sank they, and sobs of contrition succeeded that passionate outbreak;
And they repeated his prayer, and said, " O Father, forgive them! "

    Then came the evening service. The tapers gleamed from the altar.
Fervent and deep was the voice of the priest, and the people responded,
Not with their lips alone, but their hearts; and the Ave Maria
Sang they, and fell on their knees, and their souls, with devotion
    translated,
Rose on the ardour of prayer, like Elijah ascending to heaven.

    Meanwhile had spread in the village the tidings of ill, and on all sides
Wandered, wailing, from house to house the women and children.
Long at her father's door Evangeline stood, with her right hand
Shielding her eyes from the level rays of the sun, that, descending,
Lighted the village street with mysterious splendour, and roofed each
Peasant's cottage with golden thatch, and emblazoned its windows.
Long within had been spread the snow-white cloth on the table;

There stood the wheaten loaf, and the honey fragrant with wild flowers;
There stood the tankard of ale, and the cheese fresh brought from
the dairy,
And at the head of the board the great armchair of the farmer.
Thus did Evangeline wait at her father's door, as the sunset
Threw the long shadows of trees o'er the broad ambrosial meadows.
Ah! on her spirit within a deeper shadow had fallen,
And from the fields of her soul a fragrance celestial ascended,—
Charity, meekness, love, and hope, and forgiveness, and patience!
Then, all-forgetful of self, she wandered into the village,
Cheering with looks and words the disconsolate hearts of the women
As o'er the darkening fields with lingering steps they departed,
Urged by their household cares, and the weary feet of their children.
Down sank the great red sun, and in golden, glimmering vapours
Veiled the light of his face, like the Prophet descending from Sinai.
Sweetly over the village the bell of the Angelus sounded.

Meanwhile, amid the gloom, by the church Evangeline lingered.
All was silent within; and in vain at the door and the windows
Stood she, and listened and looked, until, overcome by emotion
" Gabriel! " cried she aloud with tremulous voice; but no answer
Came from the graves of the dead, nor the gloomier grave of the living.
Slowly at length she returned to the tenantless house of her father.
Smouldered the fire on the hearth, on the board stood the supper
untasted,
Empty and drear was each room, and haunted with phantoms of terror.
Sadly echoed her step on the stair and the floor of her chamber.
In the dead of the night she heard the whispering rain fall
Loud on the withered leaves of the Sycamore-tree by the window.
Keenly the lightning flashed; and the voice of the echoing thunder
Told her that God was in heaven, and governed the world he created!
Then she remembered the tale she had heard of the justice of heaven;
Soothed was her troubled soul, and she peacefully slumbered till
morning.

V.

Four times the sun had risen and set; and now on the fifth day
Cheerily called the cock to the sleeping maids of the farmhouse.
Soon o'er the yellow fields, in silent and mournful procession,
Came from the neighbouring hamlets and farms the Acadian women,
Driving in ponderous wains their household goods to the sea-shore,
Pausing and looking back to gaze once more on their dwellings,
Ere they were shut from sight by the winding road and the woodland.
Close at their sides their children ran, and urged on the oxen,
While in their little hands they clasped some fragments of playthings.

Thus to the Gaspereau's mouth they hurried; there on the sea-beach
Piled in confusion lay the household goods of the peasants.

All day long between the shore and the ships did the boats ply;
All day long the wains came labouring down from the village.
Late in the afternoon, when the sun was near to his setting,
Echoing far o'er the fields came the roll of drums from the churchyard.
Thither the women and children thronged.   On a sudden the church-
    doors
Opened, and forth came the guard, and marching in gloomy procession
Followed the long-prisoned, but patient Acadian farmers.
Even as pilgrims, who journey afar from their homes and their country,
Sing as they go, and in singing forget they are weary and wayworn,
So with songs on their lips the Acadian peasants descended
Down from the church to the shore, amid their wives and their
    daughters.
Foremost the young men came; and, raising together their voices,
Sang they with tremulous lips a chant of the Catholic Missions:—
" Sacred heart of the Saviour!   O inexhaustible fountain!
Fill our hearts this day with strength and submission and patience! "
Then the old men, as they marched, and the women that stood by
    the wayside
Joined in the sacred psalm, and the birds in the sunshine above them
Mingled their notes therewith, like voices of spirits departed.

Half-way down to the shore Evangeline waited in silence,
Not overcome with grief, but strong in the hour of affliction,—
Calmly and sadly waited, until the procession approached her,
And she beheld the face of Gabriel pale with emotion.
Tears then filled her eyes, and eagerly running to meet him,
Clasped she his hands, and laid her head on his shoulder, and
    whispered,—
" Gabriel! be of good cheer! for if we love one another,
Nothing, in truth, can harm us, whatever mischances may happen! "
Smiling she spake these words; then suddenly paused, for her father
Saw she slowly advancing.   Alas! how changed was his aspect!
Gone was the glow from his cheek, and the fire from his eye, and his
    footstep
Heavier seemed with the weight of the weary heart in his bosom.
But with a smile and a sigh, she clasped his neck and embraced him,
Speaking words of endearment where words of comfort availed not.
Thus to the Gaspereau's mouth moved on that mournful procession.

There disorder prevailed, and the tumult and stir of embarking.
Busily plied the freighted boats; and in the confusion
Wives were torn from their husbands, and mothers, too late, saw
    their children
Left on the land, extending their arms, with wildest entreaties.
So unto separate ships were Basil and Gabriel carried,
While in despair on the shore Evangeline stood with her father.
Half the task was not done when the sun went down, and the twilight
Deepened and darkened around; and in haste the refluent ocean

Fled away from the shore, and left the line of the sand-beach
Covered with waifs of the tide, with kelp and the slippery seaweed.
Farther back in the midst of the household goods and the wagons,
Like to a gypsy camp, or a leaguer after a battle,
All escape cut off by the sea, and the sentinels near them,
Lay encamped for the night the houseless Acadian farmers.
Back to its nethermost caves retreated the bellowing ocean,
Dragging adown the beach the rattling pebbles, and leaving
Inland and far up the shore the stranded boats of the sailors.
Then, as the night descended, the herds returned from their pastures;
Sweet was the moist still air with the odour of milk from their udders;
Lowing they waited, and long, at the well-known bars of the farmyard,—
Waited and looked in vain for the voice and the hand of the milkmaid.
Silence reigned in the streets; from the church no Angelus sounded,
Rose no smoke from the roofs, and gleamed no lights from the windows.

But on the shores meanwhile the evening fires had been kindled,
Built of the drift-wood thrown on the sands from wrecks in the tempest.
Round them shapes of gloom and sorrowful faces were gathered,
Voices of women were heard, and of men, and the crying of children.
Onward from fire to fire, as from hearth to hearth in his parish,
Wandered the faithful priest, consoling and blessing and cheering,
Like unto shipwrecked Paul on Melita's desolate seashore.
Thus he approached the place where Evangeline sat with her father,
And in the flickering light beheld the face of the old man,
Haggard and hollow and wan, and without either thought or emotion,
E'en as the face of a clock from which the hands have been taken.
Vainly Evangeline strove with words and caresses to cheer him,
Vainly offered him food; yet he moved not, he looked not, he spake not,
But, with a vacant stare, ever gazed at the flickering fire-light.
" *Benedicite !* " murmured the priest, in tones of compassion.
More he fain would have said, but his heart was full, and his accents
Faltered and paused on his lips, as the feet of a child on a threshold,
Hushed by the scene he beholds, and the awful presence of sorrow.
Silently, therefore, he laid his hand on the head of the maiden,
Raising his eyes, full of tears, to the silent stars that above them
Moved on their way, unperturbed by the wrongs and sorrows of
     mortals,
Then sat he down at her side, and they wept together in silence.

Suddenly rose from the south a light, as in autumn the blood-red
Moon climbs the crystal walls of heaven, and o'er the horizon
Titan-like stretches its hundred hands upon mountain and meadow,
Seizing the rocks and the rivers, and piling huge shadows together.
Broader and ever broader it gleamed on the roofs of the village,
Gleamed on the sky and the sea, and the ships that lay in the roadstead.
Columns of shining smoke uprose, and flashes of flame were
Thrust through their folds and withdrawn, like the quivering hands
     of a martyr.

Then as the wind seized the gleeds and the burning thatch, and, uplifting,
Whirled them aloft through the air, at once from a hundred house-tops
Started the sheeted smoke with flashes of flame intermingled.

These things beheld in dismay the crowd on the shore and on shipboard.
Speechless at first they stood, then cried aloud in their anguish,
" We shall behold no more our homes in the village of Grand-Pré! "
Loud on a sudden the cocks began to crow in the farmyards,
Thinking the day had dawned; and anon the lowing of cattle
Came on the evening breeze, by the barking of dogs interrupted.
Then rose a sound of dread, such as startles the sleeping encampments
Far in the western prairies or forests that skirt the Nebraska,
When the wild horses affrighted sweep by with the speed of the whirl-
wind,
Or the loud bellowing herds of buffaloes rush to the river.
Such was the sound that arose on the night, as the herds and the horses
Broke through their folds and fences, and madly rushed o'er the meadows.

Overwhelmed with the sight, yet speechless, the priest and the maiden
Gazed on the scene of terror that reddened and widened before them;
And as they turned at length to speak to their silent companion,
Lo! from his seat he had fallen, and stretched abroad on the seashore
Motionless lay his form, from which the soul had departed.
Slowly the priest uplifted the lifeless head, and the maiden
Knelt at her father's side, and wailed aloud in her terror.
Then in a swoon she sank, and lay with her head on his bosom.
Through the long night she lay in deep, oblivious slumber;
And when she woke from the trance, she beheld a multitude near her.
Faces of friends she beheld, that were mournfully gazing upon her,
Pallid, with tearful eyes, and looks of saddest compassion.
Still the blaze of the burning village illumined the landscape,
Reddened the sky overhead, and gleamed on the faces around her,
And like the day of doom it seemed to her wavering senses.
Then a familiar voice she heard, as it said to the people,—
" Let us bury him here by the sea.   When a happier season
Brings us again to our homes from the unknown land of our exile,
Then shall his sacred dust be piously laid in the churchyard."
Such were the words of the priest.   And there in haste by the seaside,
Having the glare of the burning village for funeral torches,
But without bell or book, they buried the farmer of Grand-Pré.
And as the voice of the priest repeated the service of sorrow,
Lo! with a mournful sound, like the voice of a vast congregation,
Solemnly answered the sea, and mingled its roar with the dirges.
'Twas the returning tide, that afar from the waste of the ocean,
With the first dawn of the day, came heaving and hurrying landward.
Then recommenced once more the stir and noise of embarking;
And with the ebb of that tide the ships sailed out of the harbour,
Leaving behind them the dead on the shore, and the village in ruins.

PART THE SECOND

I.

Many a weary year had passed since the burning of Grand-Pré,
When on the falling tide the freighted vessels departed,
Bearing a nation, with all its household gods, into exile,
Exile without an end, and without an example in story.
Far asunder, on separate coasts, the Acadians landed;
Scattered were they, like flakes of snow, when the wind from the
     northeast
Strikes aslant through the fogs that darken the Banks of Newfound-
     land.
Friendless, homeless, hopeless, they wandered from city to city,
From the cold lakes of the North to sultry Southern savannas,—
From the bleak shores of the sea to the lands where the Father of
     Waters
Seizes the hills in his hands, and drags them down to the ocean,
Deep in their sands to bury the scattered bones of the mammoth.
Friends they sought and homes; and many, despairing, heartbroken,
Asked of the earth but a grave, and no longer a friend nor a fireside.
Written their history stands on tablets of stone in the churchyards.
Long among them was seen a maiden who waited and wandered,
Lowly and meek in spirit, and patiently suffering all things.
Fair was she and young; but, alas! before her extended,
Dreary and vast and silent, the desert of life, with its pathway
Marked by the graves of those who had sorrowed and suffered before
     her,
Passions long extinguished, and hopes long dead and abandoned,
As the emigrant's way o'er the Western desert is marked by
Camp-fires long consumed, and bones that bleach in the sunshine.
Something there was in her life incomplete, imperfect, unfinished;
As if a morning of June, with all its music and sunshine,
Suddenly paused in the sky, and, fading, slowly descended
Into the east again, from whence it late had arisen.
Sometimes she lingered in towns, till, urged by the fever within her,
Urged by a restless longing, the hunger and thirst of the spirit,
She would commence again her endless search and endeavour;
Sometimes in churchyards strayed, and gazed on the crosses and
     tombstones,
Sat by some nameless grave, and thought that perhaps in its bosom
He was already at rest, and she longed to slumber beside him.
Sometimes a rumour, a hearsay, an inarticulate whisper,
Came with its airy hand to point and beckon her forward.
Sometimes she spake with those who had seen her beloved and known
     him,

But it was long ago, in some far-off place or forgotten.
" Gabriel Lajeunesse! " said they; " O, yes! we have seen him.
He was with Basil the blacksmith, and both have gone to the prairies;
Coureurs-des-Bois are they, and famous hunters and trappers."
" Gabriel Lajeunesse! " said others; " O, yes! we have seen him.
He is a *Voyageur* in the lowlands of Louisiana."
Then would they say,—" Dear child! why dream and wait for him
    longer ?
Are there not other youths as fair as Gabriel ? others
Who have hearts as tender and true, and spirits as loyal ?
Here is Baptiste Leblanc, the notary's son, who has loved thee
Many a tedious year; come, give him thy hand and be happy!
Thou art too fair to be left to braid St. Catherine's tresses."
Then would Evangeline answer, serenely but sadly,—" I cannot!
Whither my heart has gone, there follows my hand, and not elsewhere.
For when the heart goes before, like a lamp, and illumines the pathway,
Many things are made clear, that else lie hidden in darkness."
And thereupon the priest, her friend and father-confessor,
Said, with a smile,—" O daughter! thy God thus speaketh within
    thee!
Talk not of wasted affection, affection never was wasted;
If it enrich not the heart of another, its waters, returning
Back to their springs, like the rain, shall fill them full of refreshment;
That which the fountain sends forth returns again to the fountain.
Patience; accomplish thy labour; accomplish thy work of affection!
Sorrow and silence are strong, and patient endurance is godlike.
Therefore accomplish thy labour of love, till the heart is made godlike,
Purified, strengthened, perfected, and rendered more worthy of
    heaven! "
Cheered by the good man's words, Evangeline laboured and waited.
Still in her heart she heard the funeral dirge of the ocean,
But with its sound there was mingled a voice that whispered, " Despair
    not! "
Thus did that poor soul wander in want and cheerless discomfort,
Bleeding, barefooted, over the shards and thorns of existence.
Let me essay, O Muse! to follow the wanderer's footsteps;—
Not through each devious path, each changeful year of existence;
But as a traveller follows a streamlet's course through the valley:
Far from its margin at times, and seeing the gleam of its water
Here and there, in some open space, and at intervals only;
Then drawing nearer its banks, through sylvan glooms that conceal it,
Though he behold it not, he can hear its continuous murmur;
Happy, at length, if we find the spot where it reaches an outlet.

II.

It was the month of May.   Far down the Beautiful River,
Past the Ohio shore and past the mouth of the Wabash,
Into the golden stream of the broad and swift Mississippi,
Floated a cumbrous boat, that was rowed by Acadian boatmen.
It was a band of exiles: a raft, as it were, from the shipwrecked
Nation, scattered along the coast, now floating together,
Bound by the bonds of a common belief and a common misfortune;
Men and women and children, who, guided by hope or by hearsay,
Sought for their kith and their kin among the few-acred farmers
On the Acadian coast, and the prairies of fair Opelousas.
With them Evangeline went, and her guide, the Father Felician.
Onward o'er sunken sands, through a wilderness sombre with forests,
Day after day they glided adown the turbulent river;
Night after night, by their blazing fires, encamped on its borders.
Now through rushing chutes, among green islands, where plume-like
Cotton-trees nodded their shadowy crests, they swept with the current.
Then emerged into broad lagoons, where silvery sand-bars
Lay in the stream, and along the wimpling waves of their margin,
Shining with snow-white plumes, large flocks of pelicans waded.
Level the landscape grew, and along the shores of the river,
Shaded by china-trees, in the midst of luxuriant gardens,
Stood the houses of planters, with negro-cabins and dove-cots.
They were approaching the region where reigns perpetual summer,
Where through the Golden Coast, and groves of orange and citron,
Sweeps with majestic curve the river away to the eastward.
They, too, swerved from their course; and, entering the Bayou of
     Plaquemine,
Soon were lost in a maze of sluggish and devious waters,
Which, like a network of steel, extended in every direction.
Over their heads the towering and tenebrous boughs of the cypress
Met in a dusky arch, and trailing mosses in mid-air
Waved like banners that hang on the walls of ancient cathedrals.
Deathlike the silence seemed, and unbroken, save by the herons
Home to their roosts in the cedar-trees returning at sunset,
Or by the owl, as he greeted the moon with demoniac laughter.
Lovely the moonlight was as it glanced and gleamed on the water,
Gleamed on the columns of cypress and cedar sustaining the arches,
Down through whose broken vaults it fell as through chinks in a ruin.
Dreamlike, and indistinct, and strange were all things around them;
And o'er their spirits there came a feeling of wonder and sadness,—
Strange forebodings of ill, unseen and that cannot be compassed.
As, at the tramp of a horse's hoof on the turf of the prairies,
Far in advance are closed the leaves of the shrinking mimosa,
So, at the hoof-beats of fate, with sad forebodings of evil,
Shrinks and closes the heart, ere the stroke of doom has attained it.
But Evangeline's heart was sustained by a vision, that faintly

Floated before her eyes, and beckoned her on through the moonlight.
It was the thought of her brain that assumed the shape of a phantom.
Through those shadowy aisles had Gabriel wandered before her,
And every stroke of the oar now brought him nearer and nearer.

Then, in his place, at the prow of the boat, rose one of the oarsmen,
And, as a signal sound, if others like them peradventure
Sailed on those gloomy and midnight streams, blew a blast on his bugle.
Wild through the dark colonnades and corridors leafy the blast rang,
Breaking the seal of silence, and giving tongues to the forest.
Soundless above them the banners of moss just stirred to the music.
Multitudinous echoes awoke and died in the distance,
Over the watery floor, and beneath the reverberant branches;
But not a voice replied; no answer came from the darkness;
And when the echoes had ceased, like a sense of pain was the silence.
Then Evangeline slept; but the boatmen rowed through the midnight,
Silent at times, then singing familiar Canadian boat-songs,
Such as they sang of old on their own Acadian rivers.
And through the night were heard the mysterious sounds of the desert,
Far off, indistinct, as of wave or wind in the forest,
Mixed with the whoop of the crane and the roar of the grim alligator.

Thus ere another noon they emerged from those shades; and before
   them
Lay, in the golden sun, the lakes of the Atchafalaya.
Water-lilies in myriads rocked on the slight undulations
Made by the passing oars, and, resplendent in beauty, the lotus
Lifted her golden crown above the heads of the boatmen.
Faint was the air with the odorous breath of magnolia blossoms,
And with the heat of noon; and numberless sylvan islands,
Fragrant and thickly embowered with blossoming hedges of roses,
Near to whose shores they glided along, invited to slumber.
Soon by the fairest of these their weary oars were suspended.
Under the boughs of Wachita willows, that grew by the margin,
Safely their boat was moored; and scattered about on the greensward,
Tired with their midnight toil, the weary travellers slumbered.
Over them vast and high extended the cope of a cedar.
Swinging from its great arms, the trumpet-flower and the grape-vine
Hung their ladder of ropes aloft like the ladder of Jacob,
On whose pendulous stairs the angels ascending, descending,
Were the swift humming-birds, that flitted from blossom to blossom.
Such was the vision Evangeline saw as she slumbered beneath it.
Filled was her heart with love, and the dawn of an opening heaven
Lighted her soul in sleep with the glory of regions celestial.

Nearer and ever nearer, among the numberless islands,
Darted a light, swift boat, that sped away o'er the water,
Urged on its course by the sinewy arms of hunters and trappers.
Northward its prow was turned, to the land of the bison and beaver.

At the helm sat a youth, with countenance thoughtful and careworn.
Dark and neglected locks overshadowed his brow, and a sadness
Somewhat beyond his years on his face was legibly written.
Gabriel was it, who, weary with waiting, unhappy and restless,
Sought in the Western wilds oblivion of self and of sorrow.
Swiftly they glided along, close under the lee of the island,
But by the opposite bank, and behind a screen of palmettos,
So that they saw not the boat, where it lay concealed in the willows,
And undisturbed by the dash of their oars, and unseen, were the
    sleepers;
Angel of God was there none to awaken the slumbering maiden.
Swiftly they glided away, like the shade of a cloud on the prairie.
After the sound of their oars on the tholes had died in the distance,
As from a magic trance the sleepers awoke, and the maiden
Said with a sigh to the friendly priest,—" O Father Felician!
Something says in my heart that near me Gabriel wanders.
Is it a foolish dream, an idle and vague superstition?
Or has an angel passed, and revealed the truth to my spirit?"
Then, with a blush, she added,—" Alas for my credulous fancy!
Unto ears like thine such words as these have no meaning."
But made answer the reverend man, and he smiled as he answered,—
" Daughter, thy words are not idle; nor are they to me without
    meaning.
Feeling is deep and still; and the word that floats on the surface
Is as the tossing buoy, that betrays where the anchor is hidden.
Therefore trust to thy heart, and to what the world calls illusions.
Gabriel truly is near thee; for not far away to the southward,
On the banks of the Têche, are the towns of St. Maur and St. Martin.
There the long-wandering bride shall be given again to her bridegroom,
There the long-absent pastor regain his flock and his sheepfold.
Beautiful is the land, with its prairies and forests of fruit-trees;
Under the feet a garden of flowers, and the bluest of heavens
Bending above, and resting its dome on the walls of the forest.
They who dwell there have named it the Eden of Louisiana."

And with these words of cheer they arose and continued their journey.
Softly the evening came. The sun from the western horizon
Like a magician extended his golden wand o'er the landscape;
Twinkling vapours arose; and sky and water and forest
Seemed all on fire at the touch, and melted and mingled together.
Hanging between two skies, a cloud with edges of silver,
Floated the boat, with its dripping oars, on the motionless water.
Filled was Evangeline's heart with inexpressible sweetness.
Touched by the magic spell, the sacred fountains of feeling
Glowed with the light of love, as the skies and waters around her.
Then from a neighbouring thicket the mocking-bird, wildest of singers,
Swinging aloft on a willow spray that hung o'er the water,
Shook from his little throat such floods of delirious music,
That the whole air and the woods and the waves seemed silent to listen.

Plaintive at first were the tones and sad; then soaring to madness
Seemed they to follow or guide the revel of frenzied Bacchantes.
Single notes were then heard, in sorrowful, low lamentation;
Till, having gathered them all, he flung them abroad in derision,
As when, after a storm, a gust of wind through the tree-tops
Shakes down the rattling rain in a crystal shower on the branches.
With such a prelude as this, hearts that throbbed with emotion,
Slowly they entered the Tèche, where it flows through the green
     Opelousas,
And through the amber air, above the crest of the woodland,
Saw the column of smoke that arose from a neighbouring dwelling;—
Sounds of a horn they heard, and the distant lowing of cattle.

III.

Near to the bank of the river, o'ershadowed by oaks, from whose
     branches
Garlands of Spanish moss and of mystic mistletoe flaunted,
Such as the Druids cut down with golden hatchets at Yule-tide,
Stood secluded and still, the house of the herdsman. A garden
Girded it round about with a belt of luxuriant blossoms,
Filling the air with fragrance. The house itself was of timbers
Hewn from the cypress-tree, and carefully fitted together.
Large and low was the roof; and on slender columns supported,
Rose-wreathed, vine-encircled, a broad and spacious veranda,
Haunt of the humming-bird and the bee, extended around it.
At each end of the house, amid the flowers of the garden,
Stationed the dove-cots were, as love's perpetual symbol,
Scenes of endless wooing, and endless contentions of rivals.
Silence reigned o'er the place. The line of shadow and sunshine
Ran near the tops of the trees; but the house itself was in shadow,
And from its chimney-top, ascending and slowly expanding
Into the evening air, a thin blue column of smoke rose.
In the rear of the house, from the garden gate, ran a pathway
Through the great groves of oak to the skirts of the limitless prairie,
Into whose sea of flowers the sun was slowly descending.
Full in his track of light, like ships with shadowy canvas
Hanging loose from their spars in a motionless calm in the tropics,
Stood a cluster of trees, with tangled cordage of grape-vines.

Just where the woodlands met the flowery surf of the prairie,
Mounted upon his horse, with Spanish saddle and stirrups,
Sat a herdsman, arrayed in gaiters and doublet of deerskin.
Broad and brown was the face that from under the Spanish sombrero
Gazed on the peaceful scene, with the lordly look of its master.
Round about him were numberless herds of kine, that were grazing
Quietly in the meadows, and breathing the vapoury freshness

That uprose from the river, and spread itself over the landscape.
Slowly lifting the horn that hung at his side, and expanding
Fully his broad, deep chest, he blew a blast, that resounded
Wildly and sweet and far, through the still damp air of the evening.
Suddenly out of the grass the long white horns of the cattle
Rose like flakes of foam on the adverse currents of ocean.
Silent a moment they gazed, then bellowing rushed o'er the prairie,
And the whole mass became a cloud, a shade in the distance.
Then, as the herdsman turned to the house, through the gate of the
    garden
Saw he the forms of the priest and the maiden advancing to meet him.
Suddenly down from his horse he sprang in amazement, and forward
Rushed with extended arms and exclamations of wonder;
When they beheld his face, they recognised Basil the blacksmith.
Hearty his welcome was, as he led his guests to the garden.
There in an arbour of roses with endless question and answer
Gave they vent to their hearts, and renewed their friendly embraces,
Laughing and weeping by turns, or sitting silent and thoughtful.
Thoughtful, for Gabriel came not; and now dark doubts and mis-
    givings
Stole o'er the maiden's heart; and Basil, somewhat embarrassed,
Broke the silence and said,—" If you came by the Atchafalaya,
How have you nowhere encountered my Gabriel's boat on the bayous?"
Over Evangeline's face at the words of Basil a shade passed.
Tears came into her eyes, and she said, with a tremulous accent,—
" Gone? is Gabriel gone?" and, concealing her face on his shoulder,
All her o'erburdened heart gave way and she wept and lamented.
Then the good Basil said,—and his voice grew blithe as he said it,—
" Be of good cheer, my child; it is only to-day he departed.
Foolish boy! he has left me alone with my herds and my horses.
Moody and restless grown, and, tried and troubled, his spirit
Could no longer endure the calm of this quiet existence.
Thinking ever of thee, uncertain and sorrowful ever,
Ever silent, or speaking only of thee and his troubles,
He at length had become so tedious to men and to maidens,
Tedious even to me, that at length I bethought me, and sent him
Unto the town of Adayes to trade for mules with the Spaniards.
Thence he will follow the Indian trails to the Ozark Mountains,
Hunting for furs in the forests, on rivers trapping the beaver.
Therefore be of good cheer; we will follow the fugitive lover;
He is not far on his way, and the Fates and the streams are against
    him.
Up and away to-morrow, and through the red dew of the morning
We will follow him fast, and bring him back to his prison."

Then glad voices were heard, and up from the banks of the river,
Borne aloft on his comrades' arms, came Michael the fiddler.
Long under Basil's roof had he lived like a god on Olympus,
Having no other care than dispensing music to mortals.

Far renowned was he for his silver locks and his fiddle.
" Long live Michael," they cried, " our brave Acadian minstrel! "
As they bore him aloft in triumphal procession; and straightway
Father Felician advanced with Evangeline, greeting the old man
Kindly and oft, and recalling the past, while Basil, enraptured,
Hailed with hilarious joy his old companions and gossips,
Laughing loud and long, and embracing mothers and daughters.
Much they marvelled to see the wealth of the ci-devant blacksmith,
All his domains and his herds, and his patriarchal demeanour;
Much they marvelled to hear his tales of the soil and the climate,
And of the prairies, whose numberless herds were his who would take
    them;
Each one thought in his heart, that he, too, would go and do likewise.
Thus they ascended the steps, and, crossing the airy veranda,
Entered the hall of the house, where already the supper of Basil
Waited his late return; and they rested and feasted together.

  Over the joyous feast the sudden darkness descended.
All was silent without, and, illuming the landscape with silver,
Fair rose the dewy moon and the myriad stars; but within doors,
Brighter than these, shone the faces of friends in the glimmering
    lamplight.
Then from his station aloft, at the head of the table, the herdsman
Poured forth his heart and his wine together in endless profusion.
Lighting his pipe, that was filled with sweet Natchitoches tobacco,
Thus he spake to his guests, who listened, and smiled as they listened:—
" Welcome once more, my friends, who so long have been friendless
    and homeless,
Welcome once more to a home, that is better perchance than the old
    one!
Here no hungry winter congeals our blood like the rivers;
Here no stony ground provokes the wrath of the farmer;
Smoothly the ploughshare runs through the soil as a keel through
    the water.
All the year round the orange-groves are in blossom; and grass grows
More in a single night than a whole Canadian summer.
Here, too, numberless herds run wild and unclaimed in the prairies;
Here, too, lands may be had for the asking, and forests of timber
With a few blows of the axe are hewn and framed into houses.
After your houses are built, and your fields are yellow with harvests,
No King George of England shall drive you away from your home-
    steads,
Burning your dwellings and barns, and stealing your farms and your
    cattle."
Speaking these words, he blew a wrathful cloud from his nostrils,
And his huge, brawny hand came thundering down on the table,
So that the guests all started; and Father Felician, astonished,
Suddenly paused, with a pinch of snuff half-way to his nostrils.
But the brave Basil resumed, and his words were milder and gayer:—

" Only beware of the fever, my friends, beware of the fever!
For it is not like that of our cold Acadian climate,
Cured by wearing a spider hung round one's neck in a nutshell!"
Then there were voices heard at the door, and footsteps approaching
Sounded upon the stairs and floor of the breezy veranda.
It was the neighbouring Creoles and small Acadian planters,
Who had been summoned all to the house of Basil the Herdsman.
Merry the meeting was of ancient comrades and neighbours:
Friend clasped friend in his arms; and they who before were as
    strangers,
Meeting in exile, became straightway as friends to each other,
Drawn by the gentle bond of a common country together.
But in the neighbouring hall a strain of music, proceeding
From the accordant strings of Michael's melodious fiddle,
Broke up all further speech.   Away, like children delighted,
All things forgotten beside, they gave themselves to the maddening
Whirl of the dizzy dance, as it swept and swayed to the music,
Dreamlike, with beaming eyes and the rush of fluttering garments.

Meanwhile, apart, at the head of the hall, the priest and the herds-
    man
Sat, conversing together of past and present and future;
While Evangeline stood like one entranced, for within her
Olden memories rose, and loud in the midst of the music
Heard she the sound of the sea, and an irrepressible sadness
Came o'er her heart, and unseen she stole forth into the garden.
Beautiful was the night.   Behind the black wall of the forest,
Tipping its summit with silver, arose the moon.   On the river
Fell here and there through the branches a tremulous gleam of the
    moonlight,
Like the sweet thoughts of love on a darkened and devious spirit,
Nearer and round about her, the manifold flowers of the garden
Poured out their souls in odours, that were their prayers and confessions
Unto the night, as it went its way, like a silent Carthusian.
Fuller of fragrance than they, and as heavy with shadows and night-
    dews,
Hung the heart of the maiden.   The calm and the magical moonlight
Seemed to inundate her soul with indefinable longings,
As, through the garden gate, beneath the brown shade of the oak-trees,
Passed she along the path to the edge of the measureless prairie.
Silent it lay, with a silvery haze upon it, and fire-flies
Gleaming and floating away in mingled and infinite numbers.
Over her head the stars, the thoughts of God in the heavens,
Shone on the eyes of man, who had ceased to marvel and worship,
Save when a blazing comet was seen on the walls of that temple,
As if a hand had appeared and written upon them, " Upharsin."
And the soul of the maiden, between the stars and the fire-flies,
Wandered alone, and she cried,—" O Gabriel!   O my beloved!
Art thou so near unto me, and yet I cannot behold thee?

Art thou so near unto me, and yet thy voice does not reach me?
Ah! how often thy feet have trod this path to the prairie!
Ah! often thine eyes have looked on the woodlands around me!
Ah! how often beneath this oak, returning from labour,
Thou hast lain down to rest, and to dream of me in thy slumbers.
When shall these eyes behold, these arms be folded about thee?"
Loud and sudden and near the note of a whippoorwill sounded
Like a flute in the woods; and anon, through the neighbouring thickets,
Farther and farther away it floated and dropped into silence.
"Patience!" whispered the oaks from oracular caverns of darkness;
And, from the moonlit meadow, a sigh responded, "To-morrow!"

Bright rose the sun next day; and all the flowers of the garden
Bathed his shining feet with their tears, and anointed his tresses
With the delicious balm that they bore in their vases of crystal.
"Farewell!" said the priest, as he stood at the shadowy threshold;
"See that you bring us the Prodigal Son from his fasting and famine,
And, too, the Foolish Virgin, who slept when the bridegroom was coming."
"Farewell!" answered the maiden, and, smiling, with Basil descended
Down to the river's brink, where the boatmen already were waiting,
Thus beginning their journey with morning, and sunshine, and gladness,
Swiftly they followed the flight of him who was speeding before them,
Blown by the blast of fate like a dead leaf over the desert.
Not that day, nor the next, nor yet the day that succeeded,
Found they trace of his course, in lake or forest or river,
Nor, after many days, had they found him; but vague and uncertain
Rumours alone were their guides through a wild and desolate country;
Till, at the little inn of the Spanish town of Adayes,
Weary and worn, they alighted, and learned from the garrulous landlord
That on the day before, with horses and guides and companions,
Gabriel left the village, and took the road to the prairies.

IV.

Far in the West there lies a desert land, where the mountains
Lift, through perpetual snows, their lofty and luminous summits.
Down from their jagged, deep ravines, where the gorge, like a gateway,
Opens a passage rude to the wheels of the emigrant's wagon,
Westward the Oregon flows and the Walleway and Owyhee.
Eastward, with devious course, among the Wind-river Mountains,
Through the Sweet-water Valley precipitate leaps the Nebraska;
And to the south, from Fontaine-qui-bout and the Spanish sierras,
Fretted with sands and rocks, and swept by the wind of the desert,
Numberless torrents, with ceaseless sound, descend to the ocean,

Like the great chords of a harp, in loud and solemn vibrations.
Spreading between these streams are the wondrous, beautiful prairies,
Billowy bays of grass ever rolling in shadow and sunshine,
Bright with luxuriant clusters of roses and purple amorphas.
Over them wander the buffalo herds, and the elk and the roebuck;
Over them wander the wolves, and herds of riderless horses;
Fires that blast and blight, and winds that are weary with travel;
Over them wander the scattered tribes of Ishmael's children,
Staining the desert with blood; and above their terrible war-trails
Circles and sails aloft, on pinions majestic, the vulture,
Like the implacable soul of a chieftain slaughtered in battle,
By invisible stairs ascending and scaling the heavens.
Here and there rise smokes from the camps of these savage marauders;
Here and there rise groves from the margins of swift-running rivers;
And the grim, taciturn bear, the anchorite monk of the desert,
Climbs down their dark ravines to dig for roots by the brookside,
And over all is the sky, the clear and crystalline heaven,
Like the protecting hand of God inverted above them.

Into this wonderful land, at the base of the Ozark Mountains,
Gabriel far had entered, with hunters and trappers behind him.
Day after day, with their Indian guides, the maiden and Basil
Followed his flying steps, and thought each day to o'ertake him.
Sometimes they saw, or thought they saw, the smoke of his camp-fire
Rise in the morning air from the distant plain; but at nightfall,
When they had reached the place, they found only embers and ashes.
And, though their hearts were sad at times and their bodies were weary,
Hope still guided them on, as the magic Fata Morgana
Showed them her lakes of light, that retreated and vanished before
    them.

Once, as they sat by their evening fire, there silently entered
Into the little camp an Indian woman, whose features
Wore deep traces of sorrow, and patience as great as her sorrow.
She was a Shawnee woman returning home to her people,
From the far-off hunting-grounds of the cruel Camanches,
Where her Canadian husband, a Coureur-des-Bois, had been murdered.
Touched were their hearts at her story, and warmest and friendliest
    welcome
Gave they, with words of cheer, and she sat and feasted among them
On the buffalo-meat and the venison cooked on the embers,
But when their meal was done, and Basil and all his companions,
Worn with the long day's march and the chase of the deer and the
    bison,
Stretched themselves on the ground, and slept where the quivering
    firelight
Flashed on their swarthy cheeks, and their forms wrapped up in their
    blankets,
Then at the door of Evangeline's tent she sat and repeated

Slowly, with soft, low voice, and the charm of her Indian accent.
All the tale of her love, with its pleasures, and pains, and reverses.
Much Evangeline wept at the tale, and to know that another
Hapless heart like her own had loved and had been disappointed.
Moved to the depths of her soul by pity and woman's compassion,
Yet in her sorrow pleased that one who had suffered was near her,
She in turn related her love and all its disasters.
Mute with wonder the Shawnee sat, and when she had ended
Still was mute; but at length, as if a mysterious horror
Passed through her brain, she spake, and repeated the tale of the
    Mowis;
Mowis, the bridegroom of snow, who won and wedded a maiden,
But, when the morning came, arose and passed from the wigwam,
Fading and melting away and dissolving into the sunshine,
Till she beheld him no more, though she followed far into the forest.
Then, in those sweet, low tones, that seemed like a weird incantation,
Told she the tale of the fair Lilinau, who was wooed by a phantom,
That, through the pines o'er her father's lodge, in the hush of the
    twilight,
Breathed like the evening wind, and whispered love to the maiden,
Till she followed his green and waving plume through the forest,
And never more returned, nor was seen again by her people.
Silent with wonder and strange surprise, Evangeline listened
To the soft flow of her magical words, till the region around her
Seemed like enchanted ground, and her swarthy guest the enchantress.
Slowly over the tops of the Ozark Mountains the moon rose,
Lighting the little tent, and with a mysterious splendour
Touching the sombre leaves, and embracing and filling the woodland.
With a delicious sound the brook rushed by, and the branches
Swayed and sighed overhead in scarcely audible whispers.
Filled with the thoughts of love was Evangeline's heart, but a secret,
Subtile sense crept in of pain and indefinite terror,
As the cold, poisonous snake creeps into the nest of the swallow.
It was no earthly fear. A breath from the region of spirits
Seemed to float in the air of night; and she felt for a moment
That, like the Indian maid, she, too, was pursuing a phantom.
And with this thought she slept, and the fear and the phantom had
    vanished.

Early upon the morrow the march was resumed; and the Shawnee
Said, as they journeyed along,—" On the western slope of these
    mountains
Dwells in his little village the Black Robe chief of the Mission.
Much he teaches the people, and tells them of Mary and Jesus;
Loud laugh their hearts with joy, and weep with pain, as they hear
    him."
Then, with a sudden and secret emotion, Evangeline answered,—
" Let us go to the Mission, for there good tidings await us! "
Thither they turned their steeds; and behind a spur of the mountains,

Just as the sun went down, they heard a murmur of voices,
And in a meadow green and broad, by the bank of a river,
Saw the tents of the Christians, the tents of the Jesuit Mission.
Under a towering oak, that stood in the midst of the village,
Knelt the Black Robe chief with his children.   A crucifix fastened
High on the trunk of the tree, and overshadowed by grape-vines,
Looked with its agonised face on the multitude kneeling beneath it.
This was their rural chapel.   Aloft, through the intricate arches
Of its aërial roof, arose the chant of their vespers,
Mingling its notes with the soft susurrus and sighs of the branches.
Silent, with heads uncovered, the travellers, nearer approaching,
Knelt on the swarded floor, and joined in the evening devotions.
But when the service was done, and the benediction had fallen
Forth from the hands of the priest, like seed from the hands of the
     sower,
Slowly the reverend man advanced to the strangers, and bade them
Welcome; and when they replied, he smiled with benignant expression
Hearing the homelike sounds of his mother-tongue in the forest,
And with words of kindness conducted them into his wigwam.
There upon mats and skins they reposed, and on cakes of the maize-ear
Feasted, and slaked their thirst from the water-gourd of the teacher.
Soon was their story told; and the priest with solemnity answered:—
" Not six suns have risen and set since Gabriel, seated
On this mat by my side, where now the maiden reposes,
Told me this same sad tale; then arose and continued his journey! "
Soft was the voice of the priest, and he spake with an accent of
     kindness;
But on Evangeline's heart fell his words as in winter the snow-flakes
Fall into some lone nest from which the birds have departed.
" Far to the north he has gone," continued the priest; " but in
     autumn,
When the chase is done, will return again to the Mission."
Then Evangeline said, and her voice was meek and submissive,—
" Let me remain with thee, for my soul is sad and afflicted."
So seemed it wise and well unto all; and betimes on the morrow,
Mounting his Mexican steed, with his Indian guides and companions,
Homeward Basil returned, and Evangeline stayed at the Mission.

   Slowly, slowly, slowly the days succeeded each other,—
Days and weeks and months; and the fields of maize that were
     springing
Green from the ground when a stranger she came, now waving above
     her,
Lifted their slender shafts, with leaves interlacing, and forming
Cloisters for mendicant crows and granaries pillaged by squirrels.
Then in the golden weather the maize was husked, and the maidens
Blushed at each blood-red ear, for that betokened a lover,
But at the crooked laughed, and called it a thief in the corn-field.
Even the blood-red ear to Evangeline brought not her lover.

" Patience! " the priest would say; " have faith, and thy prayer will
    be answered!
Look at this delicate plant that lifts its head from the meadow,
See how its leaves all point to the north, as true as the magnet;
It is the compass-flower, that the finger of God has suspended
Here on its fragile stalk, to direct the traveller's journey
Over the sea-like, pathless, limitless waste of the desert.
Such in the soul of man is faith.   The blossoms of passion,
Gay and luxuriant flowers, are brighter and fuller of fragrance,
But they beguile us, and lead us astray, and their odour is deadly.
Only this humble plant can guide us here, and hereafter
Crown us with asphodel flowers, that are wet with the dews of
    nepenthe."

So came the autumn, and passed, and the winter,—yet Gabriel
    came not;
Blossomed the opening spring and the notes of the robin and blue-
    bird
Sounded sweet upon wold and in wood, yet Gabriel came not.
But on the breath of the summer winds a rumour was wafted
Sweeter than song of bird, or hue or odour of blossom.
Far to the north and east, it said, in the Michigan forests,
Gabriel had his lodge by the banks of the Saginaw river.
And, with returning guides, that sought the lakes of St. Lawrence
Saying a sad farewell, Evangeline went from the Mission.
When over weary ways, by long and perilous marches,
She had attained at length the depths of the Michigan forests,
Found she the hunter's lodge deserted and fallen to ruin!

Thus did the long sad years glide on, and in seasons and places
Divers and distant far was seen the wandering maiden;—
Now in the tents of grace of the meek Moravian Missions,
Now in the noisy camps and the battle-fields of the army,
Now in secluded hamlets, in towns and populous cities.
Like a phantom she came, and passed away unremembered.
Fair was she and young, when in hope began the long journey;
Faded was she and old, when in disappointment it ended.
Each succeeding year stole something away from her beauty,
Leaving behind it, broader and deeper, the gloom and the shadow.
Then there appeared and spread faint streaks of gray o'er her forehead,
Dawn of another life, that broke o'er her earthly horizon,
As in the eastern sky the first faint streaks of the morning.

V.

In that delightful land which is washed by the Delaware's waters,
Guarding in sylvan shades the name of Penn the apostle,
Stands on the banks of its beautiful stream the city he founded.

There all the air is balm, and the peach is the emblem of beauty,
And the streets still re-echo the names of the trees of the forest,
As if they fain would appease the Dryads whose haunts they molested.
There from the troubled sea had Evangeline landed, an exile,
Finding among the children of Penn a home and a country.
There old René Lablanc had died; and when he departed,
Saw at his side only one of all his hundred descendants.
Something at least there was in the friendly streets of the city,
Something that spake to her heart, and made her no longer a
        stranger;
And her ear was pleased with the Thee and Thou of the Quakers,
For it recalled the past, the old Acadian country,
Where all men were equal, and all were brothers and sisters.
So, when the fruitless search, the disappointed endeavour,
Ended, to recommence no more upon earth, uncomplaining,
Thither, as leaves to the light, were turned her thoughts and her foot-
        steps.
As from a mountain's top the rainy mists of the morning
Roll away, and afar we behold the landscape below us,
Sun-illumined, with shining rivers and cities and hamlets,
So fell the mists from her mind, and she saw the world far below her,
Dark no longer, but all illumined with love; and the pathway
Which she had climbed so far, lying smooth and fair in the distance.
Gabriel was not forgotten.   Within her heart was his image,
Clothed in the beauty of love and youth, as last she beheld him,
Only more beautiful made by his deathlike silence and absence.
Into her thoughts of him time entered not, for it was not.
Over him years had no power; he was not changed, but transfigured;
He had become to her heart as one who is dead, and not absent;
Patience and abnegation of self, and devotion to others,
This was the lesson a life of trial and sorrow had taught her.
So was her love diffused, but, like to some odorous spices,
Suffered no waste nor loss, though filling the air with aroma.
Other hope had she none, nor wish in life, but to follow
Meekly, with reverent steps, the sacred feet of her Saviour.
Thus many years she lived as a Sister of Mercy; frequenting
Lonely and wretched roofs in the crowded lanes of the city,
Where distress and want concealed themselves from the sunlight,
Where disease and sorrow in garrets languished neglected.
Night after night, when the world was asleep, as the watchman
        repeated
Loud, through the gusty streets, that all was well in the city,
High at some lonely window he saw the light of her taper.
Day after day, in the gray of the dawn, as slow through the suburbs
Plodded the German farmer, with flowers and fruits for the market,
Met he that meek, pale face, returning home from its watchings.

Then it came to pass that a pestilence fell on the city,
Presaged by wondrous signs, and mostly by flocks of wild pigeons,

Darkening the sun in their flight, with naught in their craws but an
    acorn.
And, as the tides of the sea arise in the month of September,
Flooding some silver stream, till it spreads to a lake in the meadow,
So death flooded life, and, o'erflowing its natural margin,
Spread to a brackish lake, the silver stream of existence.
Wealth had no power to bribe, nor beauty to charm, the oppressor;
But all perished alike beneath the scourge of his anger;—
Only, alas! the poor, who had neither friends nor attendants,
Crept away to die in the almshouse, home of the homeless.
Then in the suburbs it stood, in the midst of meadows and wood-
    lands;—
Now the city surrounds it; but still, with its gateway and wicket
Meek, in the midst of splendour, its humble walls seem to echo
Softly the words of the Lord:—" The poor ye always have with you."
Thither, by night and by day, came the Sister of Mercy. The dying
Looked up into her face, and thought, indeed, to behold there
Gleams of celestial light encircle her forehead with splendour,
Such as the artist paints o'er the brows of saints and apostles,
Or such as hangs by night o'er a city seen at a distance.
Unto their eyes it seemed the lamps of the city celestial,
Into whose shining gates ere long their spirits would enter.

Thus, on a Sabbath morn, through the streets, deserted and silent,
Wending her quiet way, she entered the door of the almshouse.
Sweet on the summer air was the odour of flowers in the garden;
And she paused on her way to gather the fairest among them,
That the dying once more might rejoice in their fragrance and beauty.
Then, as she mounted the stairs to the corridors, cooled by the east
    wind,
Distant and soft on her ear fell the chimes from the belfry of Christ
    Church,
While, intermingled with these, across the meadows were wafted
Sounds of psalms, that were sung by the Swedes in the church at
    Wicaco.
Soft as descending wings fell the calm of the hour on her spirit;
Something within her said,—" At length thy trials are ended; "
And, with light in her looks, she entered the chambers of sickness.
Noiselessly moved about the assiduous, careful attendants,
Moistening the feverish lip, and the aching brow, and in silence
Closing the sightless eyes of the dead, and concealing their faces,
Where on their pallets they lay, like drifts of snow by the roadside.
Many a languid head, upraised as Evangeline entered,
Turned on its pillow of pain to gaze while she passed, for her presence
Fell on their hearts like a ray of the sun on the walls of a prison.
And, as she looked around, she saw how Death, the consoler,
Laying his hand upon many a heart, had healed it forever.
Many familiar forms had disappeared in the night-time;
Vacant their places were, or filled already by strangers.

Suddenly, as if arrested by fear or a feeling of wonder,
Still she stood, with her colourless lips apart, while a shudder
Ran through her frame, and forgotten, the flowerets dropped from her
    fingers,
And from her eyes and cheeks the light and bloom of the morning.
Then there escaped from her lips a cry of such terrible anguish,
That the dying heard it, and started up from their pillows.
On the pallet before her was stretched the form of an old man.
Long, and thin, and gray were the locks that shaded his temples;
But, as he lay in the morning light, his face for a moment
Seemed to assume once more the forms of its earlier manhood;
So are wont to be changed the faces of those who are dying.
Hot and red on his lips still burned the flush of the fever,
As if life, like the Hebrew, with blood had besprinkled its portals,
That the Angel of Death might see the sign, and pass over.
Motionless, senseless, dying, he lay, and his spirit exhausted
Seemed to be sinking down through infinite depths in the darkness,
Darkness of slumber and death, forever sinking and sinking.
Then through those realms of shade, in multiplied reverberations,
Heard he that cry of pain, and through the hush that succeeded
Whispered a gentle voice, in accents tender and saint like,
" Gabriel! O my beloved! " and died away into silence.
Then he beheld, in a dream, once more the home of his childhood;
Green Acadian meadows, with sylvan rivers among them,
Village, and mountain, and woodlands; and, walking under their shadow,
As in the days of her youth, Evangeline rose in his vision.
Tears came into his eyes; and as slowly he lifted his eyelids,
Vanished the vision away, but Evangeline knelt by his bedside.
Vainly he strove to whisper her name, for the accents unuttered
Died on his lips, and their motion revealed what his tongue would
    have spoken.
Vainly he strove to rise; and Evangeline, kneeling beside him,
Kissed his dying lips, and laid his head on her bosom.
Sweet was the light of his eyes; but it suddenly sank into darkness,
As when a lamp is blown out by a gust of wind at a casement.

All was ended now, the hope, and the fear, and the sorrow,
All the aching of heart, the restless, unsatisfied longing,
All the dull, deep pain, and constant anguish of patience!
And, as she pressed once more the lifeless head to her bosom,
Meekly she bowed her own, and murmured, " Father, I thank thee! "

Still stands the forest primeval; but far away from its shadow,
Side by side, in their nameless graves, the lovers are sleeping.
Under the humble walls of the little Catholic churchyard,
In the heart of the city, they lie, unknown and unnoticed.
Daily the tides of life go ebbing and flowing beside them,
Thousands of throbbing hearts, where theirs are at rest and forever,
Thousands of aching brains, where theirs no longer are busy,

Thousands of toiling hands, where theirs have ceased from their labours,
Thousands of weary feet, where theirs have completed their journey!

Still stands the forest primeval; but under the shade of its branches
Dwells another race, with other customs and language.
Only along the shores of the mournful and misty Atlantic
Linger a few Acadian peasants whose fathers from exile
Wandered back to their native land to die in its bosom.
In the fisherman's cot the wheel and the loom are still busy;
Maidens still wear their Norman caps and their kirtles of homespun,
And by the evening fire repeat Evangeline's story,
While from its rocky caverns the deep-voiced, neighbouring ocean
Speaks, and in accents disconsolate answers the wail of the forest.

NUREMBERG

In the valley of the Pegnitz, where across broad meadow-lands
Rise the blue Franconian mountains, Nuremberg, the ancient, stands.

Quaint old town of toil and traffic, quaint old town of art and song,
Memories haunt thy pointed gables, like the rooks that round them
    throng:

Memories of the Middle Ages, when the emperors, rough and bold,
Had their dwelling in thy castle, time-defying, centuries old;

And thy brave and thrifty burghers boasted, in their uncouth rhyme,
That their great imperial city stretched its hand through every clime.[1]

In the courtyard of the castle, bound with many an iron band,
Stands the mighty linden planted by Queen Cunigunde's hand;

On the square the oriel window, where in old heroic days
Sat the poet Melchior singing Kaiser Maximilian's praise.[2]

---

[1] An old proverb of the town runs:—

> " *Nürnberg's Hand*
> *Geht durch alle Land.*"
>
> Nuremberg's hand
> Goes through every land.

[2] Melchior Pfinzing was one of the most celebrated German poets of the
sixteenth century. The hero of his *Teuerdank* was the reigning emperor,
Maximilian; and the poem was to the Germans of that day what the *Orlando
Furioso* was to the Italians. Maximilian is mentioned before, in the *Belfry
of Bruges*.

Everywhere I see around me rise the wondrous world of Art:
Fountains wrought with richest sculpture standing in the common mart;

And above cathedral doorways saints and bishops carved in stone,
By a former age commissioned as apostles to our own.

In the church of sainted Sebald sleeps enshrined his holy dust,[1]
And in bronze the Twelve Apostles guard from age to age their trust;

In the church of sainted Lawrence stands a pix of sculpture rare,[2]
Like the foamy sheaf of fountains, rising through the painted air.

Here, when Art was still religion, with a simple, reverent heart,
Lived and laboured Albrecht Dürer, the Evangelist of Art;

Hence in silence and in sorrow, toiling still with busy hand,
Like an emigrant he wandered, seeking for the Better Land.

Emigravit is the inscription on the tombstone where he lies;
Dead he is not,—but departed,—for the artist never dies.

Fairer seems the ancient city, and the sunshine seems more fair,
That he once has trod its pavement, that he once has breathed its air!

Through these streets so broad and stately, these obscure and dismal lanes,
Walked of yore the Mastersingers, chanting rude poetic strains.

From remote and sunless suburbs, came they to the friendly guild,
Building nests in Fame's great temple, as in spouts the swallows build.

As the weaver plied the shuttle, wove he too the mystic rhyme,
And the smith his iron measures hammered to the anvil's chime;

Thanking God, whose boundless wisdom makes the flowers of poesy bloom
In the forge's dust and cinders, in the tissues of the loom.

Here Hans Sachs, the cobbler-poet, laureate of the gentle craft,
Wisest of the Twelve Wise Masters,[3] in huge folios sang and laughed.

---

[1] The tomb of Saint Sebald, in the church which bears his name, is one of the richest works of art in Nuremberg. It is of bronze, and was cast by Peter Vischer and his sons, who laboured upon it thirteen years. It is adorned with nearly one hundred figures, among which those of the Twelve Apostles are conspicuous for size and beauty.

[2] This pix, or tabernacle for the vessels of the sacrament, is by the hand of Adam Kraft. It is an exquisite piece of sculpture in white stone, and rises to the height of sixty-four feet. It stands in the choir, whose richly-painted windows cover it with varied colours.

[3] The Twelve Wise Masters was the title of the original corporation of the Mastersingers. Hans Sachs, the cobbler of Nuremberg, though not one of the original Twelve, was the most renowned of the Mastersingers, as well as the most voluminous. He flourished in the sixteenth century; and left behind him thirty-four folio volumes of manuscript, containing two hundred and eight plays, one thousand and seven hundred comic tales, and between four and five thousand lyric poems.

But his house is now an ale-house, with a nicely sanded floor,
And a garland in the window, and his face above the door;

Painted by some humble artist, as in Adam Puschman's song,[1]
As the old man gray and dove-like, with his great beard white and long.

And at night the swart mechanic comes to drown his cark and care,
Quaffing ale from pewter tankards, in the master's antique chair.

Vanished is the ancient splendour, and before my dreamy eye
Wave these mingling shapes and figures, like a faded tapestry.

Not thy Councils, not thy Kaisers, win for thee the world's regard;
But thy painter, Albrecht Dürer, and Hans Sachs, thy cobbler-bard.

Thus, O Nuremberg, a wanderer from a region far away,
As he paced thy streets and court-yards, sang in thought; his careless
　　　lay:

Gathering from the pavement's crevice, as a floweret of the soil,
The nobility of labour,—the long pedigree of toil.

[1] Adam Puschman, in his poem on the death of Hans Sachs, describes him
as he appeared in a vision:—

> " An old man,
> Gray and white, and dove-like,
> Who had, in sooth, a great beard,
> And read in a fair, great book,
> Beautiful, with golden clasps."

THE GOLDEN LEGEND

PROLOGUE

THE SPIRE OF STRASBURG CATHEDRAL

Night and storm. LUCIFER, *with the Powers of the Air, trying to tear down the Cross.*

Lucifer. Hasten! hasten!
O ye spirits!
From its station drag the ponderous
Cross of iron, that to mock us
Is uplifted high in air!
   Voices. O, we cannot!
For around it
All the Saints and Guardian Angels
Throng in legions to protect it;
They defeat us everywhere!

   The Bells.

    Laudo Deum verum!
    Plebem voco!
    Congrego clerum!
Lucifer. Lower! lower!
Hover downward!
Seize the loud, vociferous bells, and
Clashing, clanging, to the pavement
Hurl them from their windy tower!
   Voices. All thy thunders
Here are harmless!
For these bells have been anointed,
And baptized with holy water!
They defy our utmost power.

   The Bells.

    Defunctos ploro.
    Pestem fugo!
    Festa decoro!

Lucifer. Shake the casements!
Break the painted
Panes, that flame with gold and crimson:

Scatter them like leaves of Autumn,
Swept away before the blast!
   Voices. O, we cannot!
The Archangel
Michael flames from every window,
With the sword of fire that drove us
Headlong, out of heaven, aghast!

   The Bells.

    Funera plango!
    Fulgura frango!
    Sabbata pango!
   Lucifer. Aim your lightnings
At the oaken,
Massive, iron-studded portals!
Sack the house of God, and scatter
Wide the ashes of the dead!
   Voices. O, we cannot!
The Apostles
And the Martyrs, wrapped in mantles,
Stand as warders at the entrance,
Stand as sentinels o'erhead!

   The Bells.

    Excito lentos!
    Dissipo ventos!
    Paco cruentos!
Lucifer. Baffled! baffled!
Inefficient,
Craven spirits! leave this labour
Unto Time, the great Destroyer!
Come away, ere night is gone!
   Voices. Onward! onward!
With the night-wind,
Over field and farm and forest,
Lonely homestead, darksome hamlet,
Blighting all we breathe upon!
   (*They sweep away. Organ and Gregorian Chant.*)
   Choir. Nocte surgentes
    Vigilemus omnes!

I.

THE CASTLE OF VAUTSBERG
ON THE RHINE

A chamber in a tower. PRINCE
HENRY, *sitting alone, ill and
restless. Midnight.*

Prince Henry. I cannot sleep!
my fervid brain
Calls up the vanished Past again,
And throws its misty splendours
deep
Into the pallid realms of sleep!
A breath from that far-distant
shore
Comes freshening ever more and
more,
And wafts o'er intervening seas
Sweet odours from the Hesperides!
A wind, that through the corridor
Just stirs the curtain, and no more,
And, touching the æolian strings,
Faints with the burden that it
brings!
Come back! ye friendships long
departed!
That like o'erflowing streamlets
started,
And now are dwindled, one by one,
To stony channels in the sun!
Come back! ye friends, whose lives
are ended,
Come back, with all that light
attended,
Which seemed to darken and
decay
When ye arose and went away!

They come, the shapes of joy and
woe,
The airy crowds of long-ago,
The dreams and fancies known of
yore,
That have been, and shall be no
more.

They change the cloisters of the
night
Into a garden of delight;
They make the dark and dreary
hours
Open and blossom into flowers!
I would not sleep! I love to be
Again in their fair company;
But ere my lips can bid them
stay,
They pass and vanish quite away!
Alas! our memories may retrace
Each circumstance of time and
place,
Season and scene come back again,
And outward things unchanged
remain;
The rest we cannot reinstate;
Ourselves we cannot re-create,
Nor set our souls to the same
key
Of the remembered harmony!

Rest! rest! O, give me rest and
peace!
The thought of life that ne'er shall
cease
Has something in it like despair,
A weight I am too weak to bear!
Sweeter to this afflicted breast
The thought of never-ending rest!
Sweeter the undisturbed and deep
Tranquillity of endless sleep!
    (*A flash of lightning, out of which
    LUCIFER appears, in the garb
    of a travelling Physician.*)
Lucifer. All hail, Prince Henry!
Prince Henry, starting. Who is
it speaks?
Who and what are you?
Lucifer.　　　　One who seeks
A moment's audience with the
Prince.
Prince Henry. When came you
in?
Lucifer.　　　　A moment since.
I found your study door unlocked,
And thought you answered when
I knocked.

Prince Henry. I did not hear you.

Lucifer. You heard the thunder;
It was loud enough to waken the dead.
And it is not a matter of special wonder
That, when God is walking overhead,
You should not hear my feeble tread.

Prince Henry. What may your wish or purpose be?

Lucifer. Nothing or everything, as it pleases
Your Highness. You behold in me
Only a travelling Physician;
One of the few who have a mission
To cure incurable diseases,
Or those that are called so.

Prince Henry. Can you bring
The dead to life?

Lucifer. Yes; very nearly.
And, what is a wiser and better thing,
Can keep the living from ever needing
Such an unnatural, strange proceeding,
By showing conclusively and clearly
That death is a stupid blunder merely,
And not a necessity of our lives.
My being here is accidental;
The storm, that against your casement drives,
In the little village below waylaid me.
And there I heard, with a secret delight,
Of your maladies physical and mental,
Which neither astonished nor dismayed me.
And I hastened hither, though late in the night,
To proffer my aid!

Prince Henry, ironically. For this you came!
Ah, how can I ever hope to requite
This honour from one so erudite?

Lucifer. The honour is mine, or will be when
I have cured your disease.

Prince Henry. But not till then.

Lucifer. What is your illness?

Prince Henry. It has no name.
A smouldering, dull, perpetual flame,
As in a kiln, burns in my veins,
Sending up vapours to the head;
My heart has become a dull lagoon,
Which a kind of leprosy drinks and drains;
I am accounted as one who is dead,
And, indeed, I think that I shall be soon.

Lucifer. And has Gordonius the Divine,
In his famous Lily of Medicine,—
I see the book lies open before you,—
No remedy potent enough to restore you?

Prince Henry. None whatever!

Lucifer. The dead are dead,
And their oracles dumb, when questionèd
Of the new diseases that human life
Evolves in its progress, rank and rife.
Consult the dead upon things that were,
But the living only on things that are.
Have you done this, by the appliance
And aid of doctors?

Prince Henry. Ay, whole schools
Of doctors, with their learned rules;
But the case is quite beyond their science.
Even the doctors of Salern

Send me back word they can discern
No cure for a malady like this,
Save one which in its nature is
Impossible, and cannot be!

Lucifer. That sounds oracular!
Prince Henry. Unendurable!
Lucifer. What is their remedy?
Prince Henry. You shall see;
Writ in this scroll is the mystery.
Lucifer, reading. "Not to be
cured, yet not incurable!
The only remedy that remains
Is the blood that flows from a
maiden's veins,
Who of her own free will shall
die,
And give her life as the price of
yours!"
That is the strangest of all cures,
And one, I think, you will never
try;
The prescription you may well put
by,
As something impossible to find
Before the world itself shall end!
And yet who knows? One cannot
say
That into some maiden's brain that
kind
Of madness will not find its way.
Meanwhile permit me to recommend,
As the matter admits of no delay,
My wonderful Catholicon,
Of very subtile and magical
powers.
Prince Henry. Purge with your
nostrums and drugs infernal
The spouts and gargoyles of these
towers,
Not me. My faith is utterly gone
In every power but the Power
Supernal!
Pray tell me, of what school are
you?
Lucifer. Both of the Old and of
the New!
The school of Hermes Trismegistus,

Who uttered his oracles sublime
Before the Olympiads, in the dew
Of the early dusk and dawn of
Time,
The reign of dateless old
Hephæstus!
As northward, from its Nubian
springs,
The Nile, forever new and old,
Among the living and the dead,
Its mighty, mystic stream has
rolled;
So, starting from its fountain-
head
Under the lotus-leaves of Isis,
From the dead demigods of eld,
Through long, unbroken lines of
kings
Its course the sacred art has
held,
Unchecked, unchanged by man's
devices.
This art the Arabian Geber
taught,
And in alembics, finely wrought,
Distilling herbs and flowers, discovered
The secret that so long had hovered
Upon the misty verge of Truth,
The Elixir of Perpetual Youth,
Called Alcohol, in the Arab speech!
Like him, this wondrous lore I
teach!
Prince Henry. What! an adept?
Lucifer. Nor less, nor more!
Prince Henry. I am a reader of
your books,
A lover of that mystic lore!
With such a piercing glance it
looks
Into great Nature's open eye,
And sees within it trembling lie
The portrait of the Deity!
And yet, alas! with all my pains,
The secret and the mystery
Have baffled and eluded me,
Unseen the grand result remains!
Lucifer, showing a flask. Behold
it here! this little flask

Contains the wonderful quint-
essence,
The perfect flower and efflores-
cence,
Of all the knowledge man can ask!
Hold it up thus against the light!
   Prince Henry. How limpid,
     pure, and crystalline,
How quick, and tremulous, and
   bright
The little wavelets dance and
   shine,
As were it the Water of Life in
   sooth!
   Lucifer. It is! It assuages
     every pain,
Cures all disease, and gives again
To age the swift delights of youth.
Inhale its fragrance.
   Prince Henry. It is sweet.
A thousand different odours meet
And mingle in its rare perfume,
Such as the winds of summer waft
At open windows through a room!
   Lucifer. Will you not taste it?
   Prince Henry. Will one draught
Suffice?
   Lucifer. If not, you can drink
     more.
   Prince Henry. Into this crystal
     goblet pour
So much as safely I may drink.
   Lucifer, pouring. Let not the
     quantity alarm you;
You may drink all; it will not
   harm you.
   Prince Henry. I am as one who
     on the brink
Of a dark river stands and sees
The waters flow, the landscape
   dim
Around him waver, wheel, and
   swim,
And, ere he plunges, stops to think
Into what whirlpools he may sink;
One moment pauses, and no more,
Then madly plunges from the
   shore!
Headlong into the mysteries

Of life and death I boldly leap,
Nor fear the fateful current's
   sweep,
Nor what in ambush lurks below!
For death is better than disease!
   (*An* ANGEL *with an æolian harp*
     hovers in the air.)
   Angel. Woe! woe! eternal woe!
Not only the whispered prayer
Of love,
But the imprecations of hate,
Reverberate
For ever and ever through the air
Above!
This fearful curse
Shakes the great universe!
   Lucifer, disappearing. Drink!
     drink!
And thy soul shall sink
Down into the dark abyss,
Into the infinite abyss,
From which no plummet nor rope
Ever drew up the silver sand of
   hope!
   Prince Henry, drinking. It is
     like a draught of fire!
Through every vein
I feel again
The fever of youth, the soft desire;
A rapture that is almost pain
Throbs in my heart and fills my
   brain.
O joy! O joy! I feel
The band of steel
That so long and heavily has
   pressed
Upon my breast
Uplifted, and the malediction
Of my affliction
Is taken from me, and my weary
   breast
At length finds rest
   The Angel. It is but the rest of
     the fire, from which the air
     has been taken!
It is but the rest of the sand, when
   the hour-glass is not shaken!
It is but the rest of the tide be-
   tween the ebb and the flow!

It is but the rest of the wind be-
tween the flaws that blow!
With fiendish laughter,
Hereafter,
This false physician
Will mock thee in thy perdition.

Prince Henry. Speak! speak!
Who says that I am ill?
I am not ill! I am not weak!
The trance, the swoon, the dream,
is o'er!
I feel the chill of death no more!
At length,
I stand renewed in all my strength!
Beneath me I can feel
The great earth stagger and reel,
As if the feet of a descending God
Upon its surface trod,
And like a pebble it rolled beneath
his heel!
This, O brave physician! this
Is thy great Palingenesis!
     (Drinks again.)

The Angel. Touch the goblet no
more!
It will make thy heart sore
To its very core!
Its perfume is the breath
Of the Angel of Death,
And the light that within it lies
Is the flash of his evil eyes.
Beware! O, beware!
For sickness, sorrow, and care
All are there!

Prince Henry, sinking back. O
thou voice within my breast!
Why entreat me, why upbraid me,
When the steadfast tongues of
truth
And the flattering hopes of youth
Have all deceived me and betrayed
me?
Give me, give me rest, O, rest!
Golden visions wave and hover,
Golden vapours, waters streaming,
Landscapes moving, changing,
gleaming!
I am like a happy lover,
Who illumines life with dreaming!

Brave physician! Rare physi-
cian!
Well hast thou fulfilled thy
mission!
    (His head falls on his book.)
The Angel, receding. Alas! alas!
Like a vapour the golden vision
Shall fade and pass,
And thou wilt find in thy heart
again
Only the blight of pain,
And bitter, bitter, bitter contri-
tion!

COURT-YARD OF THE CASTLE

HUBERT *standing by the gateway.*

   HUBERT. How sad the grand
old castle looks!
O'erhead, the unmolested rooks
Upon the turret's windy top
Sit, talking of the farmer's crop;
Here in the court-yard springs the
grass,
So few are now the feet that pass;
The stately peacocks, bolder
grown,
Come hopping down the steps of
stone,
As if the castle were their own;
And I, the poor old seneschal,
Haunt, like a ghost, the banquet-
hall.
Alas! the merry guests no more
Crowd through the hospitable
door;
No eyes with youth and passion
shine,
No cheeks grow redder than the
wine;
No song, no laugh, no jovial din
Of drinking wassail to the pin;
But all is silent, sad, and drear,
And now the only sounds I hear
Are the hoarse rooks upon the
walls,
And horses stamping in their
stalls!
    (A horn sounds.)

What ho! that merry, sudden
blast
Reminds me of the days long past!
And, as of old resounding, grate
The heavy hinges of the gate,
And, clattering loud, with iron
clank,
Down goes the sounding bridge of
plank,
As if it were in haste to greet
The pressure of a traveller's feet!

Enter WALTER *the Minnesinger.*

Walter. How now, my friend!
This looks quite lonely!
No banner flying from the walls,
No pages and no seneschals,
No warders, and one porter only!
Is it you, Hubert?
    Hubert.   Ah! Master Walter!
    Walter. Alas! how forms and
faces alter!
I did not know you. You look
older!
Your hair has grown much grayer
and thinner,
And you stoop a little in the
shoulder!
    Hubert. Alack! I am a poor old
sinner,
And, like these towers, begin to
moulder;
And you have been absent many a
year!
    Walter. How is the Prince?
    Hubert.   He is not here;
He has been ill: and now has fled.
    Walter. Speak it out frankly:
say he's dead!
Is it not so?
    Hubert.   No; if you please;
A strange, mysterious disease
Fell on him with a sudden blight.
Whole hours together he would
stand
Upon the terrace, in a dream,
Resting his head upon his hand,
Best pleased when he was most
alone,

Like Saint John Nepomuck in
stone,
Looking down into a stream.
In the Round Tower, night after
night,
He sat, and bleared his eyes with
books,
Until one morning we found him
there
Stretched on the floor, as if in a
swoon
He had fallen from his chair.
We hardly recognized his sweet
looks!
    Walter. Poor Prince!
    Hubert. I think he might have
mended;
And he did mend; but very soon
The Priests came flocking in, like
rooks,
With all their crosiers and their
crooks,
And so at last the matter ended.
    Walter. How did it end?
    Hubert.   Why, in Saint Rochus
They made him stand, and wait
his doom;
And, as if he were condemned to
the tomb,
Began to mutter their hocus-
pocus.
First, the Mass for the Dead they
chanted,
Then three times laid upon his
head
A shovelful of church-yard clay,
Saying to him, as he stood un-
daunted,
" This is a sign that thou art dead,
So in thy heart be penitent! "
And forth from the chapel door he
went
Into disgrace and banishment,
Clothed in a cloak of hodden
gray,
And bearing a wallet, and a bell,
Whose sound should be a per-
petual knell
To keep all travellers away.

Walter. O, horrible fate! Outcast, rejected,
As one with pestilence infected!
　Hubert. Then was the family tomb unsealed,
And broken helmet, sword and shield,
Buried together, in common wreck,
As is the custom, when the last
Of any princely house has passed,
And thrice, as with a trumpet-blast,
A herald shouted down the stair
The words of warning and despair,—
" O Hoheneck! O Hoheneck! "
　Walter. Still in my soul that cry goes on,—
Forever gone! forever gone!
Ah, what a cruel sense of loss,
Like a black shadow, would fall across
The hearts of all, if he should die!
His gracious presence upon earth
Was as a fire upon a hearth;
As pleasant songs, at morning sung,
The words that dropped from his sweet tongue
Strengthened our hearts; or, heard at night,
Made all our slumbers soft and light.
Where is he?
　Hubert. 　　In the Odenwald.
Some of his tenants, unappalled
By fear of death, or priestly word,—
A holy family, that make
Each meal a Supper of the Lord,—
Have him beneath their watch and ward,
For love of him, and Jesus' sake!
Pray you come in. For why should I
With out-door hospitality
My prince's friend thus entertain?

Walter. I would a moment here remain.
But you, good Hubert, go before,
Fill me a goblet of May-drink,
As aromatic as the May
From which it steals the breath away,
And which he loved so well of yore;
It is of him that I would think.
You shall attend me, when I call,
In the ancestral banquet-hall.
Unseen companions, guests of air,
You cannot wait on, will be there;
They taste not food, they drink not wine,
But their soft eyes look into mine,
And their lips speak to me, and all
The vast and shadowy banquet-hall
Is full of looks and words divine!
　　　(*Leaning over the parapet.*)
The day is done; and slowly from the scene
The stooping sun upgathers his spent shafts,
And puts them back into his golden quiver!
Below me in the valley, deep and green
As goblets are, from which in thirsty draughts
We drink its wine, the swift and mantling river
Flows on triumphant through these lovely regions,
Etched with the shadows of its sombre margent,
And soft, reflected clouds of gold and argent!
Yes, there it flows, forever, broad and still,
As when the vanguard of the Roman legions
First saw it from the top of yonder hill!
How beautiful it is! Fresh fields of wheat,

Vineyard, and town, and tower
with fluttering flag,
The consecrated chapel on the
crag,
And the white hamlet gathered
round its base,
Like Mary sitting at her Saviour's
feet,
And looking up at his beloved face!
O friend! O best of friends! Thy
absence more
Than the impending night darkens
the landscape o'er!

II.

A FARM IN THE ODENWALD

A garden. Morning. PRINCE
HENRY *seated, with a book.*
ELSIE, *at a distance, gathering
flowers.*

Prince Henry, reading. One
morning, all alone,
Out of his convent of gray stone,
Into the forest older, darker,
grayer,
His lips moving as if in prayer,
His head sunken upon his breast
As in a dream of rest,
Walked the Monk Felix. All
about
The broad, sweet sunshine lay
without,
Filling the summer air;
And within the woodlands as he
trod,
The twilight was like the Truce of
God
With worldly woe and care;
Under him lay the golden moss;
And above him the boughs of
hemlock trees
Waved, and made the sign of the
cross,
And whispered their Benedicites;
And from the ground

Rose an odour sweet and fragrant
Of the wild-flowers and the
vagrant
Vines that wandered,
Seeking the sunshine, round and
round.

These he heeded not, but pondered
On the volume in his hand,
A volume of Saint Augustine,
Wherein he read of the unseen
Splendours of God's great town
In the unknown land,
And, with his eyes cast down
In humility, he said;
" I believe, O God,
What herein I have read,
But alas! I do not understand! "

And lo! he heard
The sudden singing of a bird,
A snow-white bird, that from a
cloud
Dropped down,
And among the branches brown
Sat singing
So sweet, and clear, and loud,
It seemed a thousand harp-strings
ringing,
And the Monk Felix closed his
book,
And long, long,
With rapturous look,
He listened to the song,
And hardly breathed or stirred,
Until he saw, as in a vision,
The land Elysian,
And in the heavenly city heard
Angelic feet
Fall on the golden flagging of the
street.
And he would fain
Have caught the wondrous bird,
But strove in vain;
For it flew away, away,
Far over hill and dell,
And instead of its sweet singing
He heard the convent bell
Suddenly in the silence ringing

For the service of noonday.
And he retraced
His pathway homeward sadly and
　　in haste.

In the convent there was a change!
He looked for each well-known
　　face,
But the faces were new and
　　strange;
New figures sat in the oaken stalls,
New voices chaunted in the choir;
Yet the place was the same place,
The same dusky walls
Of cold, gray stone,
The same cloisters and belfry and
　　spire.

A stranger and alone
Among that brotherhood
The Monk Felix stood.
" Forty years," said a Friar,
" Have I been Prior
Of this convent in the wood,
But for that space
Never have I beheld thy face! "

The heart of the Monk Felix fell:
And he answered, with submissive
　　tone,
" This morning, after the hour of
　　Prime,
I left my cell,
And wandered forth alone,
Listening all the time
To the melodious singing
Of a beautiful white bird,
Until I heard
The bells of the convent ringing
Noon from their noisy towers.
It was as if I dreamed;
For what to me had seemed
Moments only, had been hours! "

" Years! " said a voice close by.
It was an aged monk who spoke,
From a bench of oak
Fastened against the wall:—
He was the oldest monk of all.

For a whole century
Had he been there,
Serving God in prayer,
The meekest and humblest of his
　　creatures.
He remembered well the features
Of Felix, and he said,
Speaking distinct and slow:
" One hundred years ago,
When I was a novice in this place,
There was here a monk, full of
　　God's grace,
Who bore the name
Of Felix, and this man must be
　　the same."

And straightway
They brought forth to the light of
　　day
A volume old and brown,
A huge tome, bound
In brass and wild-boar's hide,
Wherein were written down
The names of all who had died
In the convent, since it was edified.
And there they found,
Just as the old monk said,
That on a certain day and date,
One hundred years before,
Had gone forth from the convent
　　gate
The Monk Felix, and never more
Had entered that sacred door.
He had been counted among the
　　dead!
And they knew, at last,
That, such had been the power
Of that celestial and immortal song,
A hundred years had passed,
And had not seemed so long
As a single hour!
　　(ELSIE *comes in with flowers.*)
　　Elsie. Here are flowers for you,
But they are not all for you.
Some of them are for the Virgin
And for Saint Cecilia.
　　Prince Henry. As thou standest
　　there,
Thou seemest to me like the angel

That brought the immortal roses
To Saint Cecilia's bridal chamber.
   Elsie. But these will fade.
   Prince Henry. Themselves will
    fade,
But not their memory,
And memory has the power
To re-create them from the dust.
They remind me, too,
Of martyred Dorothea,
Who from celestial gardens sent
Flowers as her witnesses
To him who scoffed and doubted.
   Elsie. Do you know the story
Of Christ and the Sultan's
    daughter?
That is the prettiest legend of
    them all.
   Prince Henry. Then tell it to me.
But first come hither.
Lay the flowers down beside me,
And put both thy hands in mine.
Now tell me the story.
   Elsie. Early in the morning
The Sultan's daughter
Walked in her father's garden,
Gathering the bright flowers,
All full of dew.
   Prince Henry. Just as thou hast
    been doing
This morning, dearest Elsie.
   Elsie. And as she gathered
    them
She wondered more and more
Who was the Master of the Flowers,
And made them grow
Out of the cold, dark earth.
" In my heart," she said,
" I love him; and for him
Would leave my father's palace,
To labour in his garden."
   Prince Henry. Dear, innocent
    child!
How sweetly thou recallest
The long-forgotten legend,
That in my early childhood
My mother told me!
Upon my brain
It reappears once more,

As a birth-mark on the forehead
When a hand suddenly
Is laid upon it, and removed!
   Elsie. And at midnight,
As she lay upon her bed,
She heard a voice
Call to her from the garden,
And, looking forth from her
    window,
She saw a beautiful youth
Standing among the flowers.
It was the Lord Jesus;
And she went down to him,
And opened the door for him;
And he said to her, " O maiden!
Thou hast thought of me with love,
And for thy sake
Out of my Father's kingdom
Have I come hither:
I am the Master of the Flowers.
My garden is in Paradise,
And if thou wilt go with me,
Thy bridal garland
Shall be of bright red flowers."
And then He took from his finger
A golden ring,
And asked the Sultan's daughter
If she would be his bride.
And when she answered him with
    love,
His wounds began to bleed,
And she said to him,
" O Love! how red thy heart is,
And thy hands are full of roses."
" For thy sake," answered he,
" For thy sake is my heart so red,
For thee I bring these roses.
I gathered them at the cross
Whereon I died for thee!
Come, for my Father calls.
Thou art my elected bride! "
And the Sultan's daughter
Followed him to his Father's
    garden.
   Prince Henry. Wouldst thou
    have done so, Elsie?
   Elsie. Yes, very gladly.
   Prince Henry. Then the Celes-
    tial Bridegroom

Will come for thee also.
Upon thy forehead he will place,
Not his crown of thorns,
But a crown of roses.
In thy bridal chamber,
Like Saint Cecilia,
Thou shalt hear sweet music,
And breathe the fragrance
Of flowers immortal!
Go now and place these flowers
Before her picture.

A ROOM IN THE FARM-HOUSE

Twilight. URSULA *spinning.*
GOTTLIEB *asleep in his chair.*

Ursula. Darker and darker!
    Hardly a glimmer
Of light comes in at the window-
    pane;
Or is it my eyes are growing
    dimmer?
I cannot disentangle this skein,
Nor wind it rightly upon the reel.
    Elsie!
Gottlieb, starting. The stopping
    of thy wheel
Has wakened me out of a pleasant
    dream.
I thought I was sitting beside a
    stream,
And heard the grinding of a mill,
When suddenly the wheels stood
    still,
And a voice cried " Elsie " in my
    ear!
It startled me, it seemed so near.
    Ursula. I was calling her; I
    want a light.
I cannot see to spin my flax.
Bring the lamp, Elsie. Dost thou
    hear?
    Elsie, within. In a moment!
    Gottlieb. Where are Bertha and
    Max?
    Ursula. They are sitting with
    Elsie at the door.

She is telling them stories of the
    wood,
And the Wolf, and Little Red
    Ridinghood.
    Gottlieb. And where is the
    Prince?
    Ursula. In his room overhead;
I heard him walking across the
    floor,
As he always does, with a heavy
    tread.

    (ELSIE *comes in with a lamp.* MAX
      and BERTHA *follow her; and*
      they all sing the Evening
      Song on the lighting of the
      lamps.)

EVENING SONG

O gladsome light
Of the Father Immortal,
And of the celestial
Sacred and blessed
Jesus, our Saviour!

Now to the sunset
Again hast thou brought us;
And, seeing the evening
Twilight, we bless thee,
Praise thee, adore thee!

Father omnipotent!
Son, the Life-giver!
Spirit, the Comforter!
Worthy at all times
Of worship and wonder!

Prince Henry, at the door.
Amen!
    Ursula. Who was it said Amen?
    Elsie. It was the Prince: he
    stood at the door,
And listened a moment, as we
    chaunted
The evening song. He is gone
    again.
I have often seen him there before.
    Ursula. Poor Prince!
    Gottlieb. I thought the house
    was haunted!

Poor Prince, alas! and yet as mild
And patient as the gentlest child!
    Max. I love him because he is
        so good,
And makes me such fine bows and
    arrows,
To shoot at the robins and the
    sparrows
And the red squirrels in the wood!
    Bertha. I love him, too!
    Gottlieb.   Ah, yes! we all
Love him, from the bottom of our
    hearts;
He gave us the farm, the house,
    and the grange,
He gave us the horses and the
    carts,
And the great oxen in the stall,
The vineyard, and the forest
    range!
We have nothing to give him but
    our love!
    Bertha. Did he give us the
        beautiful stork above
On the chimney-top, with its large,
    round nest?
    Gottlieb. No, not the stork; by
        God in heaven,
As a blessing, the dear, white stork
    was given;
But the Prince has given us all the
    rest.
God bless him, and make him well
    again.
    Elsie. Would I could do some-
        thing for his sake,
Something to cure his sorrow and
    pain!
    Gottlieb. That no one can;
        neither thou nor I,
Nor any one else.
    Elsie.   And must he die?
    Ursula. Yes; if the dear God
        does not take
Pity upon him, in his distress,
And work a miracle!
    Gottlieb.   Or unless
Some maiden, of her own accord,
Offers her life for that of her lord,

And is willing to die in his stead.
    Elsie.   I will!
    Ursula. Prithee, thou foolish
        child, be still!
Thou shouldst not say what thou
    dost not mean!
    Elsie. I mean it truly!
    Max. O father! this morning,
Down by the mill, in the ravine,
Hans killed a wolf, the very same
That in the night to the sheepfold
    came,
And ate up my lamb, that was left
    outside.
    Gottlieb. I am glad he is dead.
        It will be a warning
To the wolves in the forest, far and
    wide.
    Max. And I am going to have
        his hide!
    Bertha. I wonder if this is the
        wolf that ate
Little Red Ridinghood!
    Ursula.   Oh, no!
That wolf was killed a long while
    ago.
Come, children, it is growing late.
    Max. Ah, how I wish I were a
        man,
As stout as Hans is, and as strong!
I would do nothing else, the whole
    day long,
But just kill wolves.
    Gottlieb.   Then go to bed.
And grow as fast as a little boy
    can.
Bertha is half asleep already.
See how she nods her heavy head,
And her sleepy feet are so unsteady
She will hardly be able to creep
    upstairs.
    Ursula. Good night, my chil-
        dren. Here's the light.
And do not forget to say your
    prayers
Before you sleep.
    Gottlieb.   Good night!
    Max and Bertha. Good night!
        (*They go out with* ELSIE.)

Ursula, spinning. She is a strange and wayward child,
That Elsie of ours. She looks so old,
And thoughts and fancies weird and wild
Seem of late to have taken hold
Of her heart, that was once so docile and mild!
Gottlieb. She is like all girls.
Ursula. Ah no, forsooth!
Unlike all I have ever seen.
For she has visions and strange dreams,
And in all her words and ways, she seems
Much older than she is in truth.
Who would think her but fourteen?
And there has been of late such a change!
My heart is heavy with fear and doubt
That she may not live till the year is out.
She is so strange,—so strange,—so strange!
Gottlieb. I am not troubled with any such fear;
She will live and thrive for many a year.

ELSIE'S CHAMBER

Night. ELSIE *praying.*

Elsie. My Redeemer and my Lord,
I beseech thee, I entreat thee,
Guide me in each act and word,
That hereafter I may meet thee,
Watching, waiting, hoping, yearning,
With my lamp well trimmed and burning!

Interceding
With these bleeding
Wounds upon thy hands and side,
For all who have lived and errèd
Thou hast suffered, thou hast died,
Scourged, and mocked, and crucified,
And in the grave hast thou been buried!

If my feeble prayer can reach thee,
O my Saviour, I beseech thee,
Even as thou hast died for me,
More sincerely
Let me follow where thou leadest,
Let me, bleeding as thou bleedest,
Die, if dying I may give
Life to one who asks to live,
And more nearly,
Dying thus, resemble thee!

THE CHAMBER OF GOTTLIEB AND URSULA

Midnight. ELSIE *standing by their bedside, weeping.*

Gottlieb. The wind is roaring; the rushing rain
Is loud upon roof and window-pane,
As if the wild Huntsman of Rodenstein,
Boding evil to me and mine,
Were abroad to-night with his ghostly train!
In the brief lulls of the tempest wild,
The dogs howl in the yard; and hark!
Some one is sobbing in the dark,
Here in the chamber!
Elsie. It is I.
Ursula. Elsie! what ails thee, my poor child?
Elsie. I am disturbed and much distressed,
In thinking our dear Prince must die;
I cannot close mine eyes, nor rest.
Gottlieb. What wouldst thou?
In the Power Divine

His healing lies, not in our own;
It is in the hand of God alone.
 Elsie. Nay, He has put it into
  mine,
And into my heart!
 Gottlieb. Thy words are wild!
 Ursula. What dost thou mean?
  my child! my child!
 Elsie. That for our dear Prince
  Henry's sake
I will myself the offering make,
And give my life to purchase his.
 Ursula. Am I still dreaming, or
  awake?
Thou speakest carelessly of death,
And yet thou knowest not what it
 is.
 Elsie. 'Tis the cessation of our
  breath.
Silent and motionless we lie;
And no one knoweth more than
 this.
I saw our little Gertrude die;
She left off breathing, and no more
I smoothed the pillow beneath her
 head.
She was more beautiful than
 before.
Like violets faded were her eyes;
By this we knew that she was
 dead.
Through the open window looked
 the skies
Into the chamber where she lay,
And the wind was like the sound of
 wings,
As if angels came to bear her away.
Ah! when I saw and felt these
 things,
I found it difficult to stay;
I longed to die, as she had died,
And go forth with her, side by side.
The Saints are dead, the Martyrs
 dead,
And Mary, and our Lord; and I
Would follow in humility
The way by them illuminèd!
 Ursula. My child! my child!
  thou must not die!

 Elsie. Why should I live? Do
  I not know
The life of woman is full of woe?
Toiling on and on and on,
With breaking heart, and tearful
 eyes,
And silent lips, and in the soul
The secret longings that arise,
Which this world never satisfies!
Some more, some less, but of the
 whole
Not one quite happy, no, not
 one!
 Ursula. It is the malediction of
  Eve!
 Elsie. In place of it, let me
  receive
The benediction of Mary, then.
 Gottlieb. Ah, woe is me! Ah,
  woe is me!
Most wretched am I among men!
 Ursula. Alas! that I should live
  to see
Thy death, beloved, and to stand
Above thy grave! Ah, woe the
 day!
 Elsie. Thou wilt not see it. I
  shall lie
Beneath the flowers of another
 land,
For at Salerno, far away
Over the mountains, over the sea,
It is appointed me to die!
And it will seem no more to thee
Than if at the village on market-
 day
I should a little longer stay
Than I am used.
 Ursula. Even as thou sayest!
And how my heart beats, when
 thou stayest!
I cannot rest until my sight
Is satisfied with seeing thee.
What, then, if thou wert dead?
 Gottlieb. Ah me!
Of our old eyes thou art the light!
The joy of our old hearts art thou!
And wilt thou die?
 Ursula. Not now! not now!

Elsie. Christ died for me, and
  shall not I
Be willing for my Prince to die?
You both are silent; you cannot
  speak.
This said I at our Saviour's feast,
After confession, to the priest,
And even he made no reply.
Does he not warn us all to seek
The happier, better land on high,
Where flowers immortal never
  wither;
And could he forbid me to go
  thither?
  Gottlieb. In God's own time, my
    heart's delight!
When he shall call thee, not before!
  Elsie. I heard him call. When
    Christ ascended
Triumphantly, from star to star,
He left the gates of heaven ajar.
I had a vision in the night,
And saw him standing at the door
Of his Father's mansion, vast and
  splendid,
And beckoning to me from afar.
I cannot stay!
  Gottlieb. She speaks almost
As if it were the Holy Ghost
Spake through her lips, and in her
  stead!
What if this were of God?
  Ursula. Ah, then
Gainsay it dare we not.
  Gottlieb. Amen!
Elsie! the words that thou hast
  said
Are strange and new for us to
  hear,
And fill our hearts with doubt and
  fear.
Whether it be a dark temptation
Of the Evil One, or God's inspira-
  tion,
We in our blindness cannot say.
We must think upon it, and pray;
For evil and good it both re-
  sembles.
If it be of God, his will be done!

May He guard us from the Evil
  One!
How hot thy hand is! how it
  trembles!
Go to thy bed, and try to sleep.
  Ursula. Kiss me. Good night;
    and do not weep!
      (*Elsie goes out.*)
Ah, what an awful thing is this!
I almost shuddered at her kiss,
As if a ghost had touched my
  cheek,
I am so childish and so weak!
As soon as I see the earliest gray
Of morning glimmer in the east,
I will go over to the priest,
And hear what the good man has
  to say!

A VILLAGE CHURCH

*A woman kneeling at the
  confessional.*

The Parish Priest, from within.
Go, sin no more! Thy penance o'er,
A new and better life begin!
God maketh thee forever free
From the dominion of thy sin!
Go, sin no more! He will restore
The peace that filled thy heart
  before,
And pardon thine iniquity!
  *The woman goes out. The Priest
    comes forth, and walks slowly
    up and down the church.*
O blessed Lord! how much I need
Thy light to guide me on my way!
So many hands, that, without
  heed,
Still touch thy wounds, and make
  them bleed!
So many feet, that, day by day,
Still wander from thy fold astray!
Unless thou fill me with thy light,
I cannot lead thy flock aright;
Nor, without thy support, can bear
The burden of so great a care,
But am myself a castaway!
    (*A pause.*)

The day is drawing to its close;
And what good deeds, since first it
    rose,
Have I presented, Lord, to thee,
As offerings of my ministry?
What wrong repressed, what right
    maintained,
What struggle passed, what victory
    gained,
What good attempted and at-
    tained?
Feeble, at best, is my endeavour!
I see, but cannot reach, the height
That lies forever in the light,
And yet forever and forever,
When seeming just within my
    grasp,
I feel my feeble hands unclasp,
And sink discouraged into night!
For thine own purpose, thou hast
    sent
The strife and the discouragement!
                (A pause.)
Why stayest thou, Prince of
    Hoheneck?
Why keep me pacing to and fro
Amid these aisles of sacred gloom,
Counting my footsteps as I go,
And marking with each step a
    tomb?
Why should the world for thee
    make room,
And wait thy leisure and thy
    beck?
Thou comest in the hope to hear
Some word of comfort and of
    cheer.
What can I say? I cannot give
The counsel to do this and live;
But rather, firmly to deny
The tempter, though his power be
    strong,
And, inaccessible to wrong,
Still like a martyr live and die!
                (A pause.)
The evening air grows dusk and
    brown;
I must go forth into the town,
To visit beds of pain and death,

Of restless limbs, and quivering
    breath,
And sorrowing hearts, and patient
    eyes
That see, through tears, the sun go
    down,
But never more shall see it rise.
The poor in body and estate,
The sick and the disconsolate,
Must not on man's convenience
    wait.   *(Goes out.)*

    Enter LUCIFER, *as a Priest.*

    *Lucifer, with a genuflexion,
    mocking.* This is the Black
    Pater-noster.
God was my foster,
He fostered me
Under the book of the Palm-tree!
St. Michael was my dame.
He was born at Bethlehem,
He was made of flesh and blood.
God send me my right food,
My right food, and shelter too,
That I may to yon kirk go,
To read upon yon sweet book
Which the mighty God of heaven
    shook.
Open, open, hell's gates!
Shut, shut, heaven's gates!
All the devils in the air
The stronger be, that hear the
    Black Prayer!
      (Looking round the church.)
What a darksome and dismal place!
I wonder that any man has the face
To call such a hole the House of
    the Lord,
And the Gate of Heaven,—yet
    such is the word.
Ceiling, and walls, and windows old,
Covered with cobwebs, blackened
    with mould;
Dust on the pulpit, dust on the
    stairs,
Dust on the benches, and stalls,
    and chairs!
The pulpit, from which such
    ponderous sermons

Have fallen down on the brains of
   the Germans,
With about as much real edifica-
   tion
As if a great Bible, bound in lead,
Had fallen, and struck them on
   the head;
And I ought to remember that
   sensation!
Here stands the holy-water stoup!
Holy-water it may be to many,
But to me, the veriest Liquor
   Gehennæ!
It smells like a filthy fast-day
   soup!
Near it stands the box for the poor;
With its iron padlock, safe and
   sure.
I and the priest of the parish know
Whither all these charities go;
Therefore, to keep up the institu-
   tion,
I will add my little contribution!
           (He puts in money.)
Underneath this mouldering tomb,
With statue of stone, and scut-
   cheon of brass,
Slumbers a great lord of the
   village.
All his life was riot and pillage,
But at length, to escape the
   threatened doom
Of the everlasting, penal fire,
He died in the dress of a mendicant
   friar,
And bartered his wealth for a daily
   mass.
But all that afterwards came to
   pass,
And whether he finds it dull or
   pleasant,
Is kept a secret for the present,
At his own particular desire.

And here, in a corner of the wall,
Shadowy, silent, apart from all,
With its awful portal open wide,
And its latticed windows on either
   side,

And its step well worn by the
   bended knees
Of one or two pious centuries,
Stands the village confessional!
Within it, as an honoured guest,
I will sit me down awhile and rest!
    (Seats himself in the confessional.)
Here sits the priest; and faint
   and low,
Like the sighing of an evening
   breeze,
Comes through these painted
   lattices
The ceaseless sound of human woe;
Here, while her bosom aches and
   throbs
With deep and agonising sobs,
That half are passion, half contri-
   tion,
The luckless daughter of perdition
Slowly confesses her secret shame!
The time, the place, the lover's
   name!
Here the grim murderer, with a
   groan,
From his bruised conscience rolls
   the stone,
Thinking that thus he can atone
For ravages of sword and flame!
Indeed, I marvel, and marvel
   greatly,
How a priest can sit here so
   sedately,
Reading, the whole year out and in,
Naught but the catalogue of sin,
And still keep any faith whatever
In human virtue! Never! never!

I cannot repeat a thousandth part
Of the horrors and crimes and sins
   and woes
That arise, when with palpitating
   throes
The grave-yard in the human heart
Gives up its dead, at the voice of
   the priest,
As if he were an archangel, at
   least.
It makes a peculiar atmosphere,

This odour of earthly passions and
crimes,
Such as I like to breathe, at times,
And such as often brings me here
In the hottest and most pestilential
season.
To-day, I come for another reason;
To foster and ripen an evil thought
In a heart that is almost to mad-
ness wrought,
And to make a murderer out of a
prince,
A sleight of hand I learned long
since!
He comes. In the twilight he will
not see
The difference between his priest
and me!
In the same net was the mother
caught!

Prince Henry, entering and kneel-
ing at the confessional.

Remorseful, penitent, and lowly,
I come to crave, O Father holy,
Thy benediction on my head.
　Lucifer. The benediction shall be
said
After confession, not before!
'Tis a God-speed to the parting
guest,
Who stands already at the door,
Sandalled with holiness, and
dressed
In garments pure from earthly
stain.
Meanwhile, hast thou searched
well thy breast?
Does the same madness fill thy
brain?
Or have thy passion and unrest
Vanished forever from thy mind?
　Prince Henry. By the same
madness still made blind,
By the same passion still possessed,
I come again to the house of
prayer,
A man afflicted and distressed!
As in a cloudy atmosphere,

Through unseen sluices of the air,
A sudden and impetuous wind
Strikes the great forest white with
fear,
And every branch, and bough, and
spray
Points all its quivering leaves one
way,
And meadows of grass, and fields
of grain,
And the clouds above, and the
slanting rain,
And smoke from chimneys of the
town,
Yield themselves to it, and bow
down,
So does this dreadful purpose
press
Onward, with irresistible stress,
And all my thoughts and faculties,
Struck level by the strength of this,
From their true inclination turn,
And all stream forward to Salern!
　Lucifer. Alas! we are but eddies
of dust,
Uplifted by the blast, and whirled
Along the highway of the world
A moment only, then to fall
Back to a common level all,
At the subsiding of the gust!
　Prince Henry. O holy Father!
pardon in me
The oscillation of a mind
Unsteadfast, and that cannot find
Its centre of rest and harmony!
For evermore before mine eyes
This ghastly phantom flits and flies,
And as a madman through a crowd,
With frantic gestures and wild cries,
It hurries onward, and aloud
Repeats its awful phrophecies!
Weakness is wretchedness! To be
strong
Is to be happy! I am weak,
And cannot find the good I seek,
Because I feel and fear the wrong!
　Lucifer. Be not alarmed! The
Church is kind,
And in her mercy and her meekness

She meets half-way her children's
weakness,
Writes their transgressions in the
dust!
Though in the Decalogue we find
The mandate written, " Thou
shalt not kill! "
Yet there are cases when we must.
In war, for instance, or from
scathe
To guard and keep the one true
Faith!
We must look at the Decalogue in
the light
Of an ancient statute, that was
meant
For a mild and general application,
To be understood with the reser-
vation
That, in certain instances, the
Right
Must yield to the Expedient!
Thou art a Prince. If thou
shouldst die,
What hearts and hopes would
prostrate lie!
What noble deeds, what fair re-
nown,
Into the grave with thee go down!
What acts of valour and courtesy
Remain undone, and die with thee!
Thou art the last of all thy race!
With thee a noble name expires,
And vanishes from the earth's face
The glorious memory of thy sires!
She is a peasant. In her veins
Flows common and plebeian blood;
It is such as daily and hourly
stains
The dust and the turf of battle
plains,
By vassals shed, in a crimson flood,
Without reserve, and without
reward,
At the slightest summons of their
lord!
But thine is precious; the fore-
appointed
Blood of kings, of God's anointed!

Moreover, what has the world in
store
For one like her, but tears and toil?
Daughter of sorrow, serf of the
soil,
A peasant's child and a peasant's
wife,
And her soul within her sick and
sore
With the roughness and barren-
ness of life!
I marvel not at the heart's recoil
From a fate like this in one so
tender,
Nor at its eagerness to surrender
All the wretchedness, want, and
woe
That await it in this world below,
Nor the unutterable splendour
Of the world of rest beyond the
skies.
So the Church sanctions the sacri-
fice:
Therefore inhale this healing balm,
And breathe this fresh life into
thine;
Accept the comfort and the calm
She offers, as a gift divine;
Let her fall down and anoint thy
feet
With the ointment costly and
most sweet
Of her young blood, and thou shalt
live.
    Prince Henry. And will the
righteous Heaven forgive?
No action, whether foul or fair,
Is ever done, but it leaves some-
where
A record, written by fingers
ghostly,
As a blessing or a curse, and mostly
In the greater weakness or greater
strength
Of the acts which follow it, till at
length
The wrongs of ages are redressed,
And the justice of God made
manifest!

Lucifer. In ancient records it is
    stated
That, whenever an evil deed is done,
Another devil is created
To scourge and torment the offend-
    ing one!
But evil is only good perverted,
And Lucifer, the Bearer of Light,
But an angel fallen and deserted,
Thrust from his Father's house
    with a curse
Into the black and endless night.
    Prince Henry. If justice rules
    the universe,
From the good actions of good men
Angels of light should be begotten,
And thus the balance restored
    again.
    Lucifer. Yes; if the world were
    not so rotten,
And so given over to the Devil!
    Prince Henry. But this deed, is
    it good or evil?
Have I thine absolution free
To do it, and without restriction?
    Lucifer. Ay; and from whatso-
    ever sin
Lieth around it and within,
From all crimes in which it may
    involve thee,
I now release thee and absolve
    thee!
    Prince Henry. Give me thy
    holy benediction.

*Lucifer, stretching forth his hand
    and muttering.*

    Maledictione perpetua
    Maledicat vos
    Pater eternus!

The Angel, with the aeolian harp.

Take heed! take heed!
Noble art thou in thy birth,
By the good and the great of earth
Hast thou been taught!
Be noble in every thought
And in every deed!
Let not the illusion of thy senses
Betray thee to deadly offences.
Be strong! be good! be pure!
The right only shall endure,
All things else are but false pre-
    tences.
I entreat thee, I implore,
Listen no more
To the suggestions of an evil spirit,
That even now is there,
Making the foul seem fair,
And selfishness itself a virtue and
    a merit!

A ROOM IN THE FARM-HOUSE

    Gottlieb. It is decided!   For
    many days,
And nights as many, we have had
A nameless terror in our breast,
Making us timid, and afraid
Of God, and his mysterious ways!
We have been sorrowful and sad;
Much have we suffered, much have
    prayed
That he would lead us as is best,
And show us what his will required.
It is decided; and we give
Our child, O Prince, that you may
    live!
    Ursula. It is of God.   He has
    inspired
This purpose in her; and through
    pain,
Out of a world of sin and woe,
He takes her to himself again.
The mother's heart resists   no
    longer;
With the Angel of the Lord in
    vain
It wrestled, for he was the stronger.
    Gottlieb. As Abraham offered
    long ago
His son unto the Lord, and even
The Everlasting Father in heaven
Gave his, as a lamb unto the
    slaughter,
So do I offer up my daughter!
                    (URSULA *hides her face.*)

Elsie. My life is little,
Only a cup of water,
But pure and limpid.
Take it, O my Prince!
Let it refresh you,
Let it restore you.
It is given willingly,
It is given freely;
May God bless the gift!
Prince Henry. And the giver!
Gottlieb. Amen!
Prince Henry. I accept it!
Gottlieb. Where are the children?
Ursula. They are already asleep.
Gottlieb. What if they were dead?

IN THE GARDEN

Elsie. I have one thing to ask
of you.
Prince Henry.   What is it?
It is already granted.
Elsie.   Promise me,
When we are gone from here, and
on our way
Are journeying to Salerno, you
will not,
By word or deed, endeavour to
dissuade me
And turn me from my purpose;
but remember
That as a pilgrim to the Holy City
Walks unmolested, and with
thoughts of pardon
Occupied wholly, so would I ap-
proach
The gates of Heaven, in this great
jubilee,
With my petition, putting off from
me
All thoughts of earth, as shoes
from off my feet.
Promise me this.
Prince Henry. Thy words fall
from thy lips
Like roses from the lips of Angelo:
and angels
Might stoop to pick them up!
Elsie.   Will you not promise?

Prince Henry. If ever we depart
upon this journey,
So long to one or both of us, I
promise.
Elsie. Shall we not go, then?
Have you lifted me
Into the air, only to hurl me back
Wounded upon the ground? and
offered me
The waters of eternal life, to bid me
Drink the polluted puddles of this
world?
Prince Henry. O Elsie! what a
lesson thou dost teach me!
The life which is, and that which
is to come,
Suspended hang in such nice
equipoise
A breath disturbs the balance;
and that scale
In which we throw our hearts pre-
ponderates,
And the other, like an empty one,
flies up,
And is accounted vanity and air!
To me the thought of death is
terrible,
Having such hold on life. To
thee it is not
So much even as the lifting of a
latch;
Only a step into the open air
Out of a tent already luminous
With light that shines through its
transparent walls!
O pure in heart! from thy sweet
dust shall grow
Lilies, upon whose petals will be
written
"Ave Maria" in characters of gold!

III.

A STREET IN STRASBURG

Night. PRINCE HENRY *wandering
alone, wrapped in a cloak.*
Prince Henry. Still is the night.
The sound of feet

Has died away from the empty
    street,
And like an artisan, bending down
His head on his anvil, the dark
    town
Sleeps, with a slumber deep and
    sweet.
Sleepless and restless, I alone,
In the dusk and damp of these
    walls of stone,
Wander and weep in my remorse!

Crier of the dead, ringing a bell.

Wake! wake!
All ye that sleep!
Pray for the Dead!
Pray for the Dead!

Prince Henry. Hark! with what
    accents loud and hoarse
This warder on the walls of death
Sends forth the challenge of his
    breath!
I see the dead that sleep in the
    grave!
They rise up and their garments
    wave,
Dimly and spectral, as they rise,
With the light of another world in
    their eyes!

Crier of the dead.

Wake! wake!
All ye that sleep!
Pray for the Dead!
Pray for the Dead!

Prince Henry. Why for the
    dead, who are at rest?
Pray for the living, in whose
    breast
The struggle between right and
    wrong
Is raging terrible and strong,
As when good angels war with
    devils!
This is the Master of the Revels,
Who, at Life's flowing feast, pro-
    poses
The health of absent friends, and
    pledges,

Not in bright goblets crowned
    with roses,
And tinkling as we touch their
    edges,
But with his dismal, tinkling bell,
That mocks and mimics their
    funeral knell!

Crier of the dead.

Wake! wake!
All ye that sleep!
Pray for the Dead!
Pray for the Dead!

Prince Henry. Wake not, be-
    loved! be thy sleep
Silent as night is, and as deep!
There walks a sentinel at thy gate
Whose heart is heavy and desolate,
And the heavings of whose bosom
    number
The respirations of thy slumber,
As if some strange, mysterious fate
Had linked two hearts in one, and
    mine
Went madly wheeling about thine,
Only with wider and wilder sweep!

Crier of the dead, at a distance.

Wake! wake!
All ye that sleep!
Pray for the Dead!
Pray for the Dead!

Prince Henry. Lo! with what
    depth of blackness thrown
Against the clouds, far up the
    skies
The walls of the cathedral rise,
Like a mysterious grove of stone,
With fitful lights and shadows
    blending,
As from behind, the moon, ascend-
    ing,
Lights its dim aisles and paths un-
    known!
The wind is rising; but the boughs
Rise not and fall not with the wind
That through their foliage sobs and
    soughs;
Only the cloudy rack behind,

Drifting onward, wild and ragged,
Gives to each spire and buttress
   jagged
A seeming motion undefined.
Below on the square, an armèd
   knight,
Still as a statue and as white,
Sits on his steed, and the moon-
   beams quiver
Upon the points of his armour
   bright
As on the ripples of a river.
He lifts the visor from his cheek,
And beckons, and makes as he
   would speak.
   Walter the Minnesinger. Friend!
     can you tell me where alight
Thuringia's horsemen for the
   night?
For I have lingered in the rear,
And wander vainly up and down.
   Prince Henry. I am a stranger
     in the town,
As thou art; but the voice I hear
Is not a stranger to mine ear.
Thou art Walter of the Vogelweid!
   Walter. Thou hast guessed
     rightly; and thy name
Is Henry of Hoheneck!
   Prince Henry.   Ay, the same.
   Walter, embracing him. Come
     closer, closer to my side!
What brings thee hither? What
   potent charm
Has drawn thee from thy German
   farm
Into the old Alsatian city?
   Prince Henry. A tale of wonder
     and of pity!
A wretched man, almost by
   stealth
Dragging my body to Salern,
In the vain hope and search for
   health,
And destined never to return.
Already thou hast heard the rest.
But what brings thee, thus armed
   and dight
In the equipments of a knight?

   Walter. Dost thou not see upon
     my breast
The cross of the Crusaders shine?
My pathway leads to Palestine.
   Prince Henry. Ah, would that
     way were also mine!
O noble poet! thou whose heart
Is like a nest of singing-birds
Rocked on the topmost bough of
   life,
Wilt thou, too, from our sky de-
   part,
And in the clanguor of the strife
Mingle the music of thy words?
   Walter. My hopes are high, my
     heart is proud,
And like a trumpet long and loud,
Thither my thoughts all clang and
   ring!
My life is in my hand, and lo!
I grasp and bend it as a bow,
And shoot forth from its trembling
   string
An arrow, that shall be, perchance,
Like the arrow of the Israelite
   king
Shot from the window toward the
   east,
That of the Lord's deliverance!
   Prince Henry. My life, alas! is
     what thou seest!
O enviable fate! to be
Strong, beautiful, and armed like
   thee
With lyre and sword, with song
   and steel;
A hand to smite, a heart to feel!
Thy heart, thy hand, thy lyre, thy
   sword,
Thou givest all unto thy Lord;
While I, so mean and abject grown,
Am thinking of myself alone.
   Walter. Be patient: Time will
     reinstate
Thy health and fortunes.
   Prince Henry.   'Tis too late
I cannot strive against my fate!
   Walter. Come with me; for my
     steed is weary;

Our journey has been long and dreary,
And, dreaming of his stall, he dints
With his impatient hoofs the flints.
Prince Henry, aside. I am ashamed, in my disgrace,
To look into that noble face!
To-morrow, Walter, let it be.
Walter. To-morrow, at the dawn of day,
I shall again be on my way.
Come with me to the hostelry,
For I have many things to say.
Our journey into Italy
Perchance together we may make;
Wilt thou not do it for my sake?
Prince Henry. A sick man's pace would but impede
Thine eager and impatient speed.
Besides, my pathway leads me round
To Hirschau, in the forest's bound,
Where I assemble man and steed,
And all things for my journey's need.

          (They go out.)
Lucifer, flying over the city.
Sleep, sleep, O city! till the light
Wake you to sin and crime again,
Whilst on your dreams, like dismal rain,
I scatter downward through the night
My maledictions dark and deep.
I have more martyrs in your walls
Than God has; and they cannot sleep;
They are my bondsmen and my thralls;
Their wretched lives are full of pain,
Wild agonies of nerve and brain;
And every heart-beat, every breath,
Is a convulsion worse than death!
Sleep, sleep, O city! though within
The circuit of your walls there lies
No habitation free from sin,
And all its nameless miseries;
The aching heart, the aching head,
Grief for the living and the dead,
And foul corruption of the time,
Disease, distress, and want, and woe,
And crimes, and passions that may grow
Until they ripen into crime!

SQUARE IN FRONT OF THE CATHEDRAL

Easter Sunday. FRIAR CUTHBERT *preaching to the crowd from a pulpit in the open air.* PRINCE HENRY *and* ELSIE *crossing the square.*

Prince Henry. This is the day, when from the dead
Our Lord arose; and everywhere,
Out of their darkness and despair,
Triumphant over fears and foes,
The hearts of his disciples rose,
When to the women, standing near,
The Angel in shining vesture said,
"The Lord is risen; he is not here!"
And, mindful that the day is come,
On all the hearths in Christendom
The fires are quenched, to be again
Rekindled from the sun, that high
Is dancing in the cloudless sky.
The churches are all decked with flowers,
The salutations among men
Are but the Angel's words divine,
"Christ is arisen!" and the bells
Catch the glad murmur, as it swells,
And chant together in their towers.
All hearts are glad; and free from care
The faces of the people shine.
See what a crowd is in the square,
Gaily and gallantly arrayed!
    Elsie. Let us go back; I am afraid!

Prince Henry. Nay, let us
mount the church-steps here,
Under the doorway's sacred
shadow;
We can see all things, and be freer
From the crowd that madly heaves
and presses!
　Elsie. What a gay pageant!
what bright dresses!
It looks like a flower-besprinkled
meadow.
What is that yonder on the square?
　Prince Henry. A pulpit in the
open air,
And a Friar, who is preaching to
the crowd
In a voice so deep and clear and
loud,
That, if we listen, and give heed,
His lowest words will reach the ear.
　*Friar Cuthbert, gesticulating and
cracking a postilion's whip.*
What ho! good people! do you
not hear?
Dashing along at the top of his
speed,
Booted and spurred, on his jaded
steed,
A courier comes with words of
cheer.
Courier! what is the news, I pray?
"Christ is arisen!" Whence come
you? "From court."
Then I do not believe it; you say
it in sport.
　　(Cracks his whip again.)
Ah, here comes another, riding
this way;
We soon shall know what he has
to say.
Courier! what are the tidings to-
day?
"Christ is arisen!" Whence come
you? "From town."
Then I do not believe it; away
with you, clown.
　(Cracks his whip more violently.)
And here comes a third, who is
spurring amain;

What news do you bring, with
your loose-hanging rein,
Your spurs wet with blood, and
your bridle with foam?
"Christ is arisen!" Whence come
you? "From Rome."
Ah, now I believe. He is risen,
indeed.
Ride on with the news, at the top
of your speed!
　(Great applause among the crowd.)
To come back to my text! When
the news was first spread
That Christ was arisen indeed
from the dead,
Very great was the joy of the
angels in heaven;
And as great the dispute as to who
should carry
The tidings thereof to the Virgin
Mary,
Pierced to the heart with sorrows
seven.
Old Father Adam was first to
propose,
As being the author of all our woes;
But he was refused, for fear, said
they,
He would stop to eat apples on
the way!
Abel came next, but petitioned in
vain,
Because he might meet with his
brother Cain!
Noah, too, was refused, lest his
weakness for wine
Should delay him at every tavern-
sign;
And John the Baptist could not
get a vote,
On account of his old-fashioned
camel's-hair coat;
And the Penitent Thief, who died
on the cross,
Was reminded that all his bones
were broken!
Till at last, when each in turn had
spoken,
The company being still at loss,

The Angel, who rolled away the stone,
Was sent to the sepulchre, all alone,
And filled with glory that gloomy prison,
And said to the Virgin, "The Lord is arisen!"

(The Cathedral bells ring.)

But hark! the bells are beginning to chime;
And I feel that I am growing hoarse.
I will put an end to my discourse,
And leave the rest for some other time.
For the bells themselves are the best of preachers;
Their brazen lips are learned teachers,
From their pulpits of stone, in the upper air,
Sounding aloft, without crack or flaw,
Shriller than trumpets under the Law,
Now a sermon, and now a prayer.
The clangorous hammer is the tongue,
This way, that way, beaten and swung,
That from mouth of brass, as from Mouth of Gold,
May be taught the Testaments, New and Old.
And above it the great cross-beam of wood
Representeth the Holy Rood,
Upon which, like the bell, our hopes are hung.
And the wheel wherewith it is swayed and rung
Is the mind of man, that round and round
Sways, and maketh the tongue to sound!
And the rope, with its twisted cordage three,
Denoteth the Scriptural Trinity
Of Morals, and Symbols, and History;
And the upward and downward motions show
That we touch upon matters high and low;
And the constant change and transmutation
Of action and of contemplation,
Downward, the Scripture brought from on high,
Upward, exalted again to the sky;
Downward, the literal interpretation,
Upward, the Vision and Mystery!

And now, my hearers, to make an end,
I have only one word more to say;
In the church, in honour of Easter day
Will be presented a Miracle Play;
And I hope you will all have the grace to attend.
Christ bring us at last to his felicity!
Pax vobiscum! et Benedicite!

IN THE CATHEDRAL.

Chant. Kyrie Eleison!
　　　Christe Eleison!
Elsie. I am at home here in my Father's house!
These paintings of the Saints upon the walls
Have all familiar and benignant faces.
Prince Henry. The portraits of the family of God!
Thine own hereafter shall be placed among them.
Elsie. How very grand it is and wonderful!
Never have I beheld a church so splendid!
Such columns, and such arches, and such windows,

So many tombs and statues in the chapels,
And under them so many confessionals.
They must be for the rich. I should not like
To tell my sins in such a church as this.
Who built it?
    Prince Henry. A great master of his craft,
Erwin von Steinbach; but not he alone,
For many generations laboured with him.
Children that came to see these Saints in stone,
As day by day out of the blocks they rose,
Grew old and died, and still the work went on,
And on, and on, and is not yet completed.
The generation that succeeds our own
Perhaps may finish it. The architect
Built his great heart into these sculptured stones,
And with him toiled his children, and their lives
Were builded, with his own, into the walls,
As offerings unto God. You see that statue
Fixing its joyous, but deep-wrinkled eyes
Upon the Pillar of the Angels yonder.
That is the image of the master, carved
By the fair hand of his own child, Sabina.
    Elsie. How beautiful is the column that he looks at!
    Prince Henry. That, too, she sculptured. At the base of it
Stand the Evangelists; above their heads

Four Angels blowing upon marble trumpets,
And over them the blessed Christ, surrounded
By his attendant ministers, upholding
The instruments of his passion.
    Elsie.   O my Lord!
Would I could leave behind me upon earth
Some monument to thy glory, such as this!
    Prince Henry. A greater monument than this thou leavest
In thine own life, all purity and love!
See, too, the Rose, above the western portal
Flamboyant with a thousand gorgeous colours,
The perfect flower of Gothic loveliness!
    Elsie. And, in the gallery, the long line of statues,
Christ with his twelve Apostles watching us!
    (*A Bishop in armour, booted and spurred, passes with his train.*)
    Prince Henry. But come away; we have not time to look.
The crowd already fills the church, and yonder
Upon a stage, a herald with a trumpet,
Clad like the Angel Gabriel, proclaims
The Mystery that will now be represented.

THE NATIVITY

A MIRACLE-PLAY

Introitus

Præco. Come, good people, all and each,
Come and listen to our speech!
In your presence here I stand,

With a trumpet in my hand,
To announce the Easter Play,
Which we represent to-day!
First of all we shall rehearse,
In our action and our verse,
The Nativity of our Lord,
As written in the old record
Of the Protevangelion,
So that he who reads may run!
(*Blows his trumpet.*)

I. HEAVEN

Mercy, at the feet of God. Have
  pity, Lord! be not afraid
To save mankind, whom thou hast
  made,
Nor let the souls that were be-
  trayed
  Perish eternally!
Justice. It cannot be, it must
  not be!
When in the garden placed by thee,
The fruit of the forbidden tree
  He ate, and he must die!
Mercy. Have pity, Lord! let
  penitence
Atone for disobedience,
Nor let the fruit of man's offence
  Be endless misery!
Justice. What penitence pro-
  portionate
Can e'er be felt for sin so great?
Of the forbidden fruit he ate,
  And damned must he be!
God. He shall be saved, if that
  within
The bounds of earth one free from
  sin
Be found, who for his kith and kin
  Will suffer martyrdom.
The Four Virtues. Lord! we have
  searched the world around,
From centre to the utmost bound,
But no such mortal can be found;
  Despairing, back we come.
Wisdom. No mortal, but a God
  made man,
Can ever carry out this plan,

Achieving what none other can,
  Salvation unto all!
God. Go, then, O my beloved
  Son!
It can by thee alone be done;
By thee the victory shall be won
  O'er Satan and the Fall!
(*Here the* ANGEL GABRIEL *shall
  leave Paradise and fly towards
  the earth ; the jaws of Hell
  open below, and the Devils
  walk about, making a great
  noise.*)

II. MARY AT THE WELL

Mary. Along the garden walk,
  and thence
Through the wicket in the garden
  fence,
  I steal with quiet pace,
My pitcher at the well to fill,
That lies so deep and cool and still
  In this sequestered place.
These sycamores keep guard
  around;
I see no face, I hear no sound,
  Save bubblings of the spring,
And my companions, who within
The threads of gold and scarlet
  spin,
  And at their labour sing.
The Angel Gabriel. Hail, Virgin
  Mary, full of grace!
(*Here* MARY *looketh around her,
  trembling, and then saith :*)
Mary. Who is it speaketh in
  this place,
  With such a gentle voice?
Gabriel. The Lord of heaven is
  with thee now!
Blessed among all women thou,
  Who art his holy choice!
Mary, setting down the pitcher.
What can this mean? No one is
  near,
And yet such sacred words I hear,
  I almost fear to stay.

(*Here the* ANGEL, *appearing to her, shall say :*)
Gabriel. Fear not, O Mary! but believe!
For thou, a Virgin, shalt conceive
A child this very day.

Fear not, O Mary! from the sky
The majesty of the Most High
    Shall overshadow thee!
    Mary. Behold the handmaid of the Lord!
According to thy holy word,
    So be it unto me!
(*Here the Devils shall again make a great noise, under the stage.*)

III. THE ANGELS OF THE SEVEN PLANETS, BEARING THE STAR OF BETHLEHEM.

The Angels. The Angels of the Planets Seven,
Across the shining fields of heaven
    The natal star we bring!
Dropping our sevenfold virtues down
As priceless jewels in the crown
    Of Christ, our new-born King.
    Raphael. I am the Angel of the Sun,
Whose flaming wheels began to run
    When God's almighty breath
Said to the darkness and the Night,
Let there be light! and there was light!
    I bring the gift of Faith.
    Gabriel. I am the Angel of the Moon,
Darkened to be rekindled soon
    Beneath the azure cope!
Nearest to earth, it is my ray
That best illumes the midnight way;
    I bring the gift of Hope!
    Anael. The Angel of the Star of Love,
The Evening Star, that shines above

The place where lovers be,
Above all happy hearths and homes,
On roofs of thatch, or golden domes,
    I give him Charity!
    Zobiachel. The Planet Jupiter is mine!
The mightiest star of all that shine,
    Except the sun alone!
He is the High Priest of the Dove,
And sends, from his great throne above,
    Justice, that shall atone!
    Michael. The Planet Mercury, whose place
Is nearest to the sun in space,
    Is my allotted sphere!
And with celestial ardour swift
I bear upon my hands the gift
    Of heavenly Prudence here!
    Uriel. I am the Minister of Mars,
The strongest star among the stars!
My songs of power prelude
The march and battle of man's life,
And for the suffering and the strife,
    I give him Fortitude!
    Orifel. The Angel of the uttermost
Of all the shining, heavenly host,
    From the far-off expanse
Of the Saturnian, endless space
I bring the last, the crowning grace,
    The gift of Temperance!
    (*A sudden light shines from the windows of the stable in the village below.*)

IV. THE WISE MEN OF THE EAST

The stable of the Inn.   The VIRGIN *and* CHILD.   *Three Gipsy Kings,* GASPAR, MELCHIOR, *and* BELSHAZZAR, *shall come in.*

    Gaspar. Hail to thee, Jesus of Nazareth!

Though in a manger thou drawest
   thy breath,
Thou art greater than Life and
   Death,
   Greater than Joy or Woe!
This cross upon the line of life
Portendeth struggle, toil, and
   strife,
And through a region with dangers
   rife
   In darkness shalt thou go!
   Melchior. Hail to thee, King of
   Jerusalem!
Though humbly born in Bethle-
   hem,
A sceptre and a diadem
   Await thy brow and hand!
The sceptre is a simple reed,
The crown will make thy temples
   bleed,
And in thine hour of greatest
   need,
   Abashed thy subjects stand!
   Belshazzar. Hail to thee, Christ
   of Christendom!
O'er all the earth thy kingdom
   come!
From distant Trebizond to Rome
   Thy name shall men adore!
Peace and good-will among all
   men,
The Virgin has returned again,
Returned the old Saturnian reign
   And Golden Age once more.
   The Child Christ. Jesus, the Son
   of God, am I,
Born here to suffer and to die
According to the prophecy,
   That other men may live!
   The Virgin. And now these
   clothes, that wrapped Him,
   take
And keep them precious, for his
   sake;
Our benediction thus we make,
   Naught else have we to give.

(*She gives them swaddling-clothes,
   and they depart.*)

V. THE FLIGHT INTO EGYPT

Here JOSEPH *shall come in, leading
an ass, on which are seated* MARY
and the CHILD.

   Mary. Here will we rest us under
   these
O'erhanging branches of the trees,
   Where robins chant their Litanies
   And canticles of joy.
   Joseph. My saddle-girths have
   given way
With trudging through the heat
   to-day;
To you I think it is but play
   To ride and hold the boy.
   Mary. Hark! how the robins
   shout and sing,
As if to hail their infant King!
I will alight at yonder spring
   To wash his little coat.
   Joseph. And I will hobble well
   the ass,
Lest, being loose upon the grass,
He should escape; for, by the
   mass,
   He is nimble as a goat.
   (*Here* MARY *shall alight and go
   to the spring.*)
   Mary. O Joseph! I am much
   afraid,
For men are sleeping in the shade;
I fear that we shall be waylaid,
   And robbed and beaten sore!
   (*Here a band of robbers shall be seen
   sleeping, two of whom shall
   rise and come forward.*)
   Dumachus. Cock's soul! deliver
   up your gold!
   Joseph. I pray you, Sirs, let go
   your hold!
You see that I am weak and old,
   Of wealth I have no store.
   Dumachus. Give up your
   money!
   Titus.   Prithee cease.
Let these people go in peace.
   Dumachus. First let them pay
   for their release,

And then go on their way.
Titus. These forty groats I give
   in fee,
If thou wilt only silent be.
   Mary. May God be merciful to
      thee
   Upon the Judgment Day!
   Jesus. When thirty years shall
      have gone by,
I at Jerusalem shall die,
By Jewish hands exalted high
   On the accursed tree.
Then on my right and my left side,
These thieves shall both be cruci-
   fied,
And Titus thenceforth shall abide
   In paradise with me.
   (*Here a great rumour of trumpets
      and horses, like the noise of a
      king with his army, and the
      robbers shall take flight.*)

VI.   THE SLAUGHTER OF THE
            INNOCENTS

King Herod. Potz - tausend!
   Himmel-sacrament!
Filled am I with great wonderment
At this unwelcome news!
Am I not Herod? Who shall dare
My crown to take, my sceptre bear,
   As king among the Jews?
   (*Here he shall stride up and down
      and flourish his sword.*)
What ho! I fain would drink a
   can
Of the strong wine of Canaan!
   The wine of Helbon bring,
I purchased at the Fair of Tyre,
As red as blood, as hot as fire,
   And fit for any king!
   (*He quaffs great goblets of wine.*)
Now at the window will I stand,
While in the street the armed band
   The little children slay:
The babe just born in Bethlehem
Will surely slaughtered be with
   them,
   Nor live another day!

   (*Here a voice of lamentation shall
      be heard in the street.*)
   Rachel. O wicked king! O cruel
      speed!
To do this most unrighteous deed!
   My children all are slain!
   Herod. Ho seneschal! another
      cup!
With wine of Sorek fill it up!
   I would a bumper drain!
   Rahab. May maledictions **fall**
      and blast
Thyself and lineage, to the last
   Of all thy kith and kin!
   Herod. Another goblet! quick!
      and stir
Pomegranate juice and drops of
   myrrh
   And calamus therein!
   Soldiers, in the street. Give up
      thy child into our hands!
It is King Herod who commands
   That he should thus be slain!
   The Nurse Medusa. O monstrous
      men! What have ye done!
It is King Herod's only son
   That ye have cleft in twain!
   Herod. Ah, luckless day! What
      words of fear
Are these that smite upon my ear
   With such a doleful sound!
What torments rack my heart and
   head!
Would I were dead! would I were
   dead,
   And buried in the ground!
   (*He falls down and writhes as
      though eaten by worms. Hell
      opens, and* SATAN *and* ASTA-
      ROTH *come forth, and drag
      him down.*)

VII.   JESUS AT PLAY WITH HIS
             SCHOOLMATES

   Jesus. The shower is over. Let
      us play,
And make some sparrows out of
   clay,

Down by the river's side.

Judas. See, how the stream has overflowed

Its banks, and o'er the meadow road

Is spreading far and wide!

(*They draw water out of the river by channels, and form little pools.* JESUS *makes twelve sparrows of clay, and the other boys do the same.*)

Jesus. Look! look! how prettily I make

These little sparrows by the lake

Bend down their necks and drink!

Now will I make them sing and soar

So far, they shall return no more

Unto this river's brink.

Judas. That canst thou not! They are but clay,

They cannot sing, nor fly away

Above the meadow lands!

Jesus. Fly, fly! ye sparrows! you are free!

And while you live, remember me,

Who made you with my hands.

(*Here* JESUS *shall clap his hands, and the sparrows shall fly away, chirruping.*)

Judas. Thou art a sorcerer, I know;

Oft has my mother told me so,

I will not play with thee!

(*He strikes* JESUS *in the right side.*)

Jesus. Ah, Judas! thou hast smote my side,

And when I shall be crucified,

There shall I piercèd be!

(*Here* JOSEPH *shall come in, and say:*)

Joseph. Ye wicked boys! why do ye play,

And break the holy Sabbath day?

What, think ye, will your mothers say

To see you in such plight!

In such a sweat and such a heat,

With all that mud upon your feet!

There's not a beggar in the street

Makes such a sorry sight!

VIII.   THE VILLAGE SCHOOL

The RABBI BEN ISRAEL, *with a long beard, sitting on a high stool, a rod in his hand.*

Rabbi. I am the Rabbi Ben Israel,

Throughout this village known full well,

And, as my scholars all will tell,

Learned in things divine;

The Kabala and Talmud hoar

Than all the prophets prize I more,

But Mishna is strong wine.

My fame extends from West to East,

And always, at the Purim feast,

I am as drunk as any beast

That wallows in his sty;

The wine it so elateth me,

That I no difference can see

Between " Accursed Haman be! "

And " Blessed be Mordecai! "

Come hither, Judas Iscariot.

Say, if thy lesson thou hast got

From the Rabbinical Book or not.

Why howl the dogs at night?

Judas. In the Rabbinical Book, it saith

The dogs howl, when with icy breath

Great Sammaël, the Angel of Death,

Takes through the town his flight!

Rabbi. Well, boy! now say, if thou art wise,

When the Angel of Death, who is full of eyes,

Comes where a sick man dying lies,

What doth he to the wight?

Judas. He stands beside him,
dark and tall,
Holding a sword, from which doth
fall
Into his mouth a drop of gall,
  And so he turneth white.
Rabbi. And now, my Judas, say
to me
What the great Voices Four may
be,
That quite across the world do flee,
  And are not heard by men?
Judas. The Voice of the Sun in
heaven's dome,
The Voice of the Murmuring of
Rome,
The Voice of a Soul that goeth
home,
  And the Angel of the Rain!
Rabbi. Well have ye answered
every one!
Now little Jesus, the carpenter's
son,
Let us see how thy task is done;
  Canst thou thy letters say?
Jesus. Aleph.
Rabbi. What next? Do not
stop yet!
Go on with all the alphabet.
Come, Aleph, Beth; dost thou
forget?
  Cock's soul! thou'dst rather
play!
Jesus. What Aleph means I fain
would know,
  Before I any farther go!
Rabbi. O, by Saint Peter! wouldst
thou so?
  Come hither, boy, to me.
As surely as the letter Jod
Once cried aloud, and spake to
God,
So surely shalt thou feel this rod,
  And punished shalt thou be!

(*Here* RABBI BEN ISRAEL *shall lift
up his rod to strike* JESUS,
*and his right arm shall be
paralysed.*)

IX. CROWNED WITH FLOWERS

JESUS *sitting among his playmates,
crowned with flowers as their King*

Boys. We spread our garments
on the ground!
With fragrant flowers thy head is
crowned,
While like a guard we stand
around,
  And hail thee as our King!
Thou art the new King of the Jews!
Nor let the passers-by refuse
To bring that homage which men
use
  To majesty to bring.
(*Here a traveller shall go by, and
the boys shall lay hold of his
garments and say :*)
Boys. Come hither! and all
reverence pay
Unto our monarch, crowned to
day!
Then go rejoicing on your way,
  In all prosperity!
Traveller. Hail to the King of
Bethlehem,
Who weareth in his diadem
The yellow crocus for the gem
  Of his authority!
(*He passes by ; and others come
in, bearing on a litter a sick
child.*)
Boys. Set down the litter and
draw near!
The King of Bethlehem is here!
What ails the child, who seems to
fear
  That we shall do him harm?
The Bearers. He climbed up to
the robin's nest,
And out there darted, from his
rest,
A serpent with a crimson crest,
  And stung him in the arm.
Jesus. Bring him to me, and let
me feel
The wounded place; my touch can
heal

The sting of serpents, and can steal
    The poison from the bite!
    (*He touches the wound, and the
      boy begins to cry.*)
Cease to lament! I can foresee
That thou hereafter known shalt
    be,
Among the men who follow me,
    As Simon the Canaanite!

EPILOGUE

In the after part of the day
Will be represented another play,
Of the Passion of our Blessed Lord,
Beginning directly after Nones!
At the close of which we shall
    accord,
By way of benison and reward,
The sight of a holy Martyr's bones!

IV.

THE ROAD TO HIRSCHAU

PRINCE HENRY *and* ELSIE, *with
    their attendants, on horseback.*

    Elsie. Onward and onward the
    highway runs to the distant
    city, impatiently bearing
Tidings of human joy and disaster,
    of love and of hate, of doing
    and daring!
    Prince Henry. This life of ours is
    a wild æolian harp of many a
    joyous strain,
But under them all there runs a
    loud perpetual wail, as of
    souls in pain.
    Elsie. Faith alone can interpret
    life, and the heart that aches
    and bleeds with the stigma
Of pain, alone bears the likeness of
    Christ, and can comprehend
    its dark enigma.
    Prince Henry. Man is selfish, and
    seeketh pleasure with little
    care of what may betide;

Else why am I travelling here
    beside thee, a demon that
    rides by an angel's side?
    Elsie. All the hedges are white
    with dust, and the great dog
    under the creaking wain
Hangs his head in the lazy heat,
    while onward the horses toil
    and strain.
    Prince Henry. Now they stop at
    the way-side inn, and the
    wagoner laughs with the
    landlord's daughter,
While out of the dripping trough
    the horses distend their
    leathern sides with water.
    Elsie. All through life there are
    way-side inns, where man may
    refresh his soul with love;
Even the lowest may quench his
    thirst at rivulets fed by
    springs from above.
    Prince Henry. Yonder, where
    rises the cross of stone, our
    journey along the highway
    ends,
And over the fields, by a bridle
    path, down into the broad
    green valley descends.
    Elsie. I am not sorry to leave
    behind the beaten road with
    its dust and heat;
The air will be sweeter far, and
    the turf will be softer under
    our horses' feet.
    (*They turn down a green lane.*)

    Elsie. Sweet is the air with the
    budding haws, and the valley
    stretching for miles below
Is white with blossoming cherry-
    trees, as if just covered with
    lightest snow.
    Prince Henry. Over our heads a
    white cascade is gleaming
    against the distant hill;
We cannot hear it, nor see it move,
    but it hangs like a banner
    when winds are still.

Elsie. Damp and cool is this deep ravine, and cool the sound of the brook by our side!

What is this castle that rises above us, and lords it over a land so wide?

Prince Henry. It is the home of the Counts of Calva; well have I known these scenes of old,

Well I remember each tower and turret, remember the brooklet, the wood, and the wold.

Elsie. Hark! from the little village below us the bells of the church are ringing for rain!

Priests and peasants in long procession come forth and kneel on the arid plain.

Prince Henry. They have not long to wait, for I see in the south uprising a little cloud,

That before the sun shall be set will cover the sky above us as with a shroud.

          (They pass on.)

THE CONVENT OF HIRSCHAU IN THE BLACK FOREST

The Convent cellar. FRIAR CLAUS *comes in with a light and a basket of empty flagons.*

Friar Claus. I always enter this sacred place
With a thoughtful, solemn, and reverent pace,
Pausing long enough on each stair
To breathe an ejaculatory prayer,
And a benediction on the vines
That produce these various sorts of wines!
For my part, I am well content
That we have got through with the tedious Lent!
Fasting is all very well for those
Who have to contend with invisible foes;
But I am quite sure it does not agree
With a quiet, peaceable man like me,
Who am not of that nervous and meagre kind
That are always distressed in body and mind!
And at times it really does me good
To come down among this brotherhood,
Dwelling forever underground,
Silent, contemplative, round and sound;
Each one old, and brown with mould,
But filled to the lips with the ardour of youth,
With the latent power and love of truth,
And with virtues fervent and manifold.

I have heard it said, that at Easter-tide,
When buds are swelling on every side,
And the sap begins to move in the vine,
Then in all the cellars, far and wide,
The oldest, as well as the newest, wine
Begins to stir itself, and ferment,
With a kind of revolt and discontent
At being so long in darkness pent,
And fain would burst from its sombre tun
To bask on the hill-side in the sun;
As in the bosom of us poor friars,
The tumult of half-subdued desires
For the world that we have left behind
Disturbs at times all peace of mind!
And now that we have lived through Lent,

My duty it is, as often before,
To open awhile the prison-door,
And give these restless spirits vent.

Now here is a cask that stands alone,
And has stood a hundred years or more,
Its beard of cobwebs, long and hoar,
Trailing and sweeping along the floor,
Like Barbarossa, who sits in his cave,
Taciturn, sombre, sedate, and grave,
Till his beard has grown through the table of stone!
It is of the quick and not of the dead!
In its veins the blood is hot and red,
And a heart still beats in those ribs of oak
That time may have tamed, but has not broke!
It comes from Bacharach on the Rhine,
Is one of the three best kinds of wine,
And costs some hundred florins the ohm,
But that I do not consider dear,
When I remember that every year
Four butts are sent to the Pope of Rome.
And whenever a goblet thereof I drain,
The old rhyme keeps running in my brain:
  At Bacharach on the Rhine,
  At Hochheim on the Main,
  And at Würzburg on the Stein,
  Grow the three best kinds of wine!

They are all good wines, and better far
Than those of the Neckar, or those of the Ahr.
In particular, Würzburg well may boast
Of its blessed wine of the Holy Ghost,
Which of all wines I like the most.
This I shall draw for the Abbot's drinking,
Who seems to be much of my way of thinking.
                    (*Fills a flagon.*)
Ah! how the streamlet laughs and sings!
What a delicious fragrance springs
From the deep flagon, while it fills,
As of hyacinths and daffodils!
Between this cask and the Abbot's lips
Many have been the sips and slips;
Many have been the draughts of wine,
On their way to his, that have stopped at mine;
And many a time my soul has hankered
For a deep draught out of his silver tankard,
When it should have been busy with other affairs,
Less with its longings and more with its prayers.
But now there is no such awkward condition,
No danger of death and eternal perdition;
So here's to the Abbot and Brothers all,
Who dwell in this convent of Peter and Paul!
                    (*He drinks.*)
O cordial delicious! O soother of pain!
It flashes like sunshine into my brain!
A benison rest on the Bishop who sends
Such a fudder of wine as this to his friends!

And now a flagon for such as may
   ask
A draught from the noble Bacha-
   rach cask,
And I will be gone, though I know
   full well
The cellar's a cheerfuller place
   than the cell.
Behold where he stands, all sound
   and good,
Brown and old in his oaken hood;
Silent he seems externally
As any Carthusian monk may be;
But within, what a spirit of deep
   unrest!
What a seething and simmering in
   his breast!
As if the heaving of his great heart
Would burst his belt of oak apart!
Let me unloose this button of
   wood,
And quiet a little his turbulent
   mood.

(Sets it running.)

See! how its currents gleam and
   shine,
As if they had caught the purple
   hues
Of autumn sunsets on the Rhine,
Descending and mingling with the
   dews;
Or as if the grapes were stained
   with the blood
Of the innocent boy, who, some
   years back,
Was taken and crucified by the
   Jews,
In that ancient town of Bacha-
   rach;
Perdition upon those infidel Jews,
In that ancient town of Bacharach!
The beautiful town, that gives us
   wine
With the fragrant odour of Mus-
   cadine!
I should deem it wrong to let this
   pass
Without first touching my lips to
   the glass,

For here in the midst of the current
   I stand,
Like the stone Pfalz in the midst
   of the river,
Taking toll upon either hand,
And much more grateful to the
   giver.

(He drinks.)

Here, now, is a very inferior kind,
Such as in any town you may find,
Such as one might imagine would
   suit
The rascal who drank wine out of
   a boot.
And, after all, it was not a crime,
For he won thereby Dorf Hüffel-
   sheim.
A jolly old toper! who at a pull
Could drink a postilion's jack-boot
   full,
And ask with a laugh, when that
   was done,
If the fellow had left the other one!
This wine is as good as we can
   afford
To the friars, who sit at the lower
   board,
And cannot distinguish bad from
   good,
And are far better off than if they
   could,
Being rather the rude disciples of
   beer
Than of anything more refined and
   dear!

(Fills the other flagon and departs.)

THE SCRIPTORIUM

FRIAR PACIFICUS *transcribing and
   illuminating.*

Friar Pacificus. It is growing
   dark! Yet one line more,
And then my work for to-day is
   o'er.
I come again to the name of the
   Lord!
Ere I that awful name record,

That is spoken so lightly among
    men,
Let me pause awhile, and wash
    my pen;
Pure from blemish and blot must
    it be
When it writes that word of
    mystery!

Thus have I laboured on and on,
Nearly through the Gospel of John.
Can it be that from the lips
Of this same gentle Evangelist,
That Christ himself perhaps has
    kissed,
Came the dread Apocalypse!
It has a very awful look,
As it stands there at the end of
    the book,
Like the sun in an eclipse.
Ah me! when I think of that
    vision divine,
Think of writing it, line by line,
I stand in awe of the terrible curse,
Like the trump of doom, in the
    closing verse.
God forgive me! if ever I
Take aught from the book of that
    Prophecy,
Lest my part too should be taken
    away
From the Book of Life on the
    Judgment Day.

This is well written, though I say
    it!
I should not be afraid to display it
In open day, on the selfsame shelf
With the writings of St. Thecla
    herself,
Or of Theodosius, who of old
Wrote the Gospels in letters of
    gold!
That goodly folio standing yonder,
Without a single blot or blunder,
Would not bear away the palm
    from mine,
If we should compare them line
    for line.

There, now, is an initial letter!
Saint Ulric himself never made a
    better!
Finished down to the leaf and the
    snail,
Down to the eyes on the peacock's
    tail!
And now, as I turn the volume
    over,
And see what lies between cover
    and cover,
What treasures of art these pages
    hold,
All ablaze with crimson and gold,
God forgive me! I seem to feel
A certain satisfaction steal
Into my heart, and into my brain,
As if my talent had not lain
Wrapped in a napkin, and all in
    vain.
Yes, I might almost say to the
    Lord,
Here is a copy of thy Word,
Written out with much toil and
    pain;
Take it, O Lord, and let it be
As something I have done for thee!
            (*He looks from the window.*)
How sweet the air is! How fair
    the scene!
I wish I had as lovely a green
To paint my landscapes and my
    leaves!
How the swallows twitter under
    the eaves!
There, now, there is one in her
    nest;
I can just catch a glimpse of her
    head and breast,
And will sketch her thus, in her
    quiet nook,
For the margin of my Gospel book.
            (*He makes a sketch.*)
I can see no more.   Through the
    valley yonder
A shower is passing; I hear the
    thunder
Mutter its curses in the air,
The Devil's own and only prayer!

The dusty road is brown with rain,
And, speeding on with might and
  main,
Hitherward rides a gallant train.
They do not parley, they cannot
  wait,
But hurry in at the convent gate.
What a fair lady! and beside her
What a handsome, graceful, noble
  rider!
Now she gives him her hand to
  alight;
They will beg a shelter for the
  night.
I will go down to the corridor,
And try to see that face once more;
It will do for the face of some
  beautiful Saint,
Or for one of the Maries I shall
  paint.

(Goes out.)

THE CLOISTERS

The ABBOT ERNESTUS *pacing to
and fro.*

Abbot. Slowly, slowly up the wall
Steals the sunshine, steals the
  shade;
Evening damps begin to fall,
Evening shadows are displayed.
Round me, o'er me, everywhere,
All the sky is grand with clouds,
And athwart the evening air
Wheel the swallows home in
  crowds.
Shafts of sunshine from the west
Paint the dusky windows red;
Darker shadows, deeper rest,
Underneath and overhead.
Darker, darker, and more wan,
In my breast the shadows fall;
Upward steals the life of man,
As the sunshine from the wall.
From the wall into the sky,
From the roof along the spire;
Ah, the souls of those that die
Are but sunbeams lifted higher.

Enter PRINCE HENRY.

Prince Henry. Christ is arisen!
Abbot.   Amen! He is arisen!
His peace be with you!
  Prince Henry. Here it reigns
    forever!
The peace of God, that passeth
  understanding,
Reigns in these cloisters and these
  corridors.
Are you Ernestus, Abbot of the
  convent?
  Abbot. I am.
  Prince Henry. And I Prince
    Henry of Hoheneck,
Who crave your hospitality to-
  night.
  Abbot. You are thrice welcome
    to our humble walls.
You do us honour; and we shall
  requite it,
I fear, but poorly, entertaining you
With Paschal eggs, and our poor
  convent wine,
The remnants of our Easter
  holidays.
  Prince Henry. How fares it
    with the holy monks of Hir-
    schau?
Are all things well with them?
  Abbot.   All things are well.
  Prince Henry. A noble convent!
    I have known it long
By the report of travellers. I now
  see
Their commendations lag behind
  the truth.
You lie here in the valley of the
  Nagold
As in a nest: and the still river,
  gliding
Along its bed, is like an admoni-
  tion
How all things pass. Your lands
  are rich and ample,
And your revenues large. God's
  benediction
Rests on your convent.

Abbot. By our charities
We strive to merit it. Our Lord
and Master,
When he departed, left us in his
will,
As our best legacy on earth, the
poor!
These we have always with us;
had we not,
Our hearts would grow as hard as
are these stones.
Prince Henry. If I remember
right, the Counts of Calva
Founded your convent.
Abbot. Even as you say.
Prince Henry. And, if I err not,
it is very old.
Abbot. Within these cloisters lie
already buried
Twelve holy Abbots. Underneath
the flags
On which we stand, the Abbot
William lies,
Of blessed memory.
Prince Henry. And whose tomb
is that,
Which bears the brass escutcheon?
Abbot. A benefactor's.
Conrad, a Count of Calva, he who
stood
Godfather to our bells.
Prince Henry. Your monks are
learned
And holy men, I trust.
Abbot. There are among them
Learned and holy men. Yet in
this age
We need another Hildebrand, to
shake
And purify us like a mighty
wind.
The world is wicked, and some-
times I wonder
God does not lose his patience
with it wholly,
And shatter it like glass! Even
here, at times,
Within these walls, where all
should be at peace,

I have my trials. Time has laid
his hand
Upon my heart, gently, not
smiting it,
But as a harper lays his open palm
Upon his harp, to deaden its
vibrations.
Ashes are on my head, and on my
lips
Sackcloth, and in my breast a
heaviness
And weariness of life, that makes
me ready
To say to the dead Abbots under
us,
"Make room for me!" Only I
see the dusk
Of evening twilight coming, and
have not
Completed half my task; and so
at times
The thought of my shortcomings
in this life
Falls like a shadow on the life to
come.
Prince Henry. We must all die,
and not the old alone;
The young have no exemption
from that doom.
Abbot. Ah, yes! the young may
die, but the old must!
That is the difference.
Prince Henry. I have heard
much laud
Of your transcribers. Your Scrip-
torium
Is famous among all, your manu-
scripts
Praised for their beauty and their
excellence.
Abbot. That is indeed our boast.
If you desire it,
You shall behold these treasures.
And meanwhile
Shall the Refectorarius bestow
Your horses and attendants for
the night.

(They go in. The Vesper-bell rings.)

THE CHAPEL

Vespers; after which the monks retire, a chorister leading an old monk who is blind.

Prince Henry. They are all gone, save one who lingers,
Absorbed in deep and silent prayer.
As if his heart could find no rest,
At times he beats his heaving breast
With clenched and convulsive fingers,
Then lifts them trembling in the air.
A chorister, with golden hair,
Guides hitherward his heavy pace.
Can it be so? Or does my sight
Deceive me in the uncertain light?
Ah no! I recognise that face,
Though Time has touched it in his flight,
And changed the auburn hair to white.
It is Count Hugo of the Rhine,
The deadliest foe of all our race,
And hateful unto me and mine!
　　The Blind Monk. Who is it that doth stand so near
His whispered words I almost hear?
　　Prince Henry. I am Prince Henry of Hoheneck,
And you, Count Hugo of the Rhine!
I know you, and I see the scar,
The brand upon your forehead, shine
And redden like a baleful star!
　　The Blind Monk. Count Hugo once, but now the wreck
Of what I was. O Hoheneck!
The passionate will, the pride, the wrath
That bore me headlong on my path,
Stumbled and staggered into fear,
And failed me in my mad career,
As a tired steed some evil-doer,
Alone upon a desolate moor,
Bewildered, lost, deserted, blind,
And hearing loud and close behind
The o'ertaking steps of his pursuer.
Then suddenly from the dark there came
A voice that called me by my name,
And said to me, " Kneel down and pray! "
And so my terror passed away,
Passed utterly away for ever.
Contrition, penitence, remorse,
Came on me, with o'erwhelming force;
A hope, a longing, an endeavour,
By days of penance and nights of prayer,
To frustrate and defeat despair!
Calm, deep, and still is now my heart,
With tranquil waters overflowed;
A lake whose unseen fountains start,
Where once the hot volcano glowed.
And you, O Prince of Hoheneck!
Have known me in that earlier time,
A man of violence and crime,
Whose passions brooked no curb nor check.
Behold me now, in gentler mood,
One of this holy brotherhood.
Give me your hand; here let me kneel;
Make your reproaches sharp as steel;
Spurn me, and smite me on each cheek;
No violence can harm the meek,
There is no wound Christ cannot heal!
Yes; lift your princely hand, and take
Revenge, if 'tis revenge you seek;
Then pardon me, for Jesus' sake!
　　Prince Henry. Arise, Count Hugo! let there be

No farther strife nor enmity
Between us twain; we both have
erred!
Too rash in act, too wroth in word,
From the beginning have we stood
In fierce, defiant attitude,
Each thoughtless of the other's
right,
And each reliant on his might.
But now our souls are more sub-
dued;
The hand of God, and not in vain,
Has touched us with the fire of
pain.
Let us kneel down and side by side
Pray, till our souls are purified,
And pardon will not be denied!
(They kneel.)

THE REFECTORY

Gaudiolum of Monks at midnight.
LUCIFER *disguised as a Friar.*

Friar Paul sings.

Ave! color vini clari,
Dulcis potus, non amari,
Tua nos inebriari
Digneris potentia!

Friar Cuthbert. Not so much
noise, my worthy freres,
You'll disturb the Abbot at his
prayers.

Friar Paul sings.

O! quam placens in colore!
O! quam fragrans in odore!
O! quam sapidum in ore!
Dulce linguæ vinculum!

Friar Cuthbert. I should think
your tongue had broken its
chain!

Friar Paul sings.

Felix venter quem intrabis!
Felix guttur quod rigabis!
Felix os quod tu lavabis!
Et beata labia!

Friar Cuthbert. Peace! I say,
peace!
Will you never cease!

You will rouse up the Abbot, I tell
you again!

Friar John. No danger! to-
night he will let us alone,
As I happen to know he has guests
of his own.

Friar Cuthbert. Who are they?

Friar John. A German Prince
and his train,
Who arrived here just before the
rain.
There is with him a damsel fair to
see,
As slender and graceful as a reed!
When she alighted from her steed,
It seemed like a blossom blown
from a tree.

Friar Cuthbert. None of your
pale-faced girls for me!
None of your damsels of high
degree!

Friar John. Come, old fellow,
drink down to your peg!
But do not drink any farther, I beg!

Friar Paul sings.

In the days of gold,
The days of old,
Crosier of wood
And bishop of gold!

Friar Cuthbert. What an infernal
racket and riot!
Can you not drink your wine in
quiet?
Why fill the convent with such
scandals,
As if we were so many drunken
Vandals?

Friar Paul continues.

Now we have changed
That law so good,
To crosier of gold
And bishop of wood!

Friar Cuthbert. Well, then, since
you are in the mood
To give your noisy humours vent,
Sing and howl to your heart's
content!

Chorus of Monks.
Funde vinum, funde!
Tanquam sint fluminis undæ,
Nec quæras unde,
Sed fundas semper abunde!
Friar John. What is the name of yonder friar,
With an eye that glows like a coal of fire,
And such a black mass of tangled hair?
Friar Paul. He who is sitting there,
With a rollicking,
Devil may care,
Free and easy look and air,
As if he were used to such feasting and frolicking?
Friar John. The same.
Friar Paul. He's a stranger. You had better ask his name,
And where he is going, and whence he came.
Friar John. Hallo! Sir Friar!
Friar Paul. You must raise your voice a little higher,
He does not seem to hear what you say.
Now, try again! He is looking this way.
Friar John. Hallo! Sir Friar, We wish to inquire
Whence you came, and where you are going,
And anything else that is worth the knowing.
So be so good as to open your head.
Lucifer. I am a Frenchman born and bred,
Going on a pilgrimage to Rome.
My home
Is the convent of St. Gildas de Rhuys,
Of which, very like, you never have heard.
Monks. Never a word!
Lucifer. You must know, then, it is in the diocese
Called the Diocese of Vannes,

In the province of Brittany.
From the gray rocks of Morbihan
It overlooks the angry sea;
The very sea-shore where,
In his great despair,
Abbot Abelard walked to and fro,
Filling the night with woe,
And wailing aloud to the merciless seas
The name of his sweet Heloise!
Whilst overhead
The convent windows gleamed as red
As the fiery eyes of the monks within,
Who with jovial din
Gave themselves up to all kinds of sin!
Ha! that is a convent! that is an abbey!
Over the doors,
None of your death-heads carved in wood,
None of your Saints looking pious and good,
None of your Patriarchs old and shabby!
But the heads and tusks of boars,
And the cells
Hung all round with the fells
Of the fallow-deer.
And then what cheer!
What jolly, fat friars,
Sitting round the great, roaring fires,
Roaring louder than they,
With their strong wines,
And their concubines,
And never a bell,
With its swagger and swell,
Calling you up with a start of affright
In the dead of night,
To send you grumbling down dark stairs,
To mumble your prayers.
But the cheery crow
Of cocks in the yard below,
After daybreak, an hour or so,

And the barking of deep-mouthed
    hounds,
These are the sounds
That, instead of bells, salute the
    ear.
And then all day
Up and away
Through the forest, hunting the
    deer!
Ah, my friends! I'm afraid that
    here
You are a little too pious, a little
    too tame,
And the more is the shame.
'Tis the greatest folly
Not to be jolly;
That's what I think!
Come, drink, drink,
Drink, and die game!
    Monks. And your Abbot
      What's-his-name?
    Lucifer. Abelard!
    Monks. Did he drink hard?
    Lucifer. O, no! Not he!
He was a dry old fellow,
Without juice enough to get
    thoroughly mellow.
There he stood,
Lowering at us in sullen mood,
As if he had come into Brittany
Just to reform our brotherhood!
      (A roar of laughter.)
But you see
It never would do!
For some of us knew a thing or
    two,
In the Abbey of St. Gildas de
    Rhuys!
For instance, the great ado
With old Fulbert's niece,
The young and lovely Heloise!
    Friar John. Stop there, if you
      please,
Till we drink to the fair Heloise.
    (All, drinking and shouting.)
Heloise! Heloise!
    (The Chapel-bell tolls.)
    Lucifer, starting. What is that
    bell for? Are you such asses

As to keep up the fashion of mid-
    night masses?
    Friar Cuthbert. It is only a poor,
    unfortunate brother,
Who is gifted with most miracu-
    lous powers
Of getting up at all sorts of hours,
And, by way of penance and
    Christian meekness,
Of creeping silently out of his cell
To take a pull at that hideous bell;
So that all the monks who are
    lying awake
May murmur some kind of prayer
    for his sake,
And adapted to his peculiar weak-
    ness!
    Friar John. From frailty and
      fall—
    All. Good Lord, deliver us all!
    Friar Cuthbert. And before the
      bell for matins sounds,
He takes his lantern, and goes the
    rounds,
Flashing it into our sleepy eyes,
Merely to say it is time to arise.
But enough of that. Go on, if
    you please,
With your story about St. Gildas
    de Rhuys.
    Lucifer. Well, it finally came to
    pass
That, half in fun and half in
    malice,
One Sunday at Mass
We put some poison into the
    chalice.
But, either by accident or design,
Peter Abelard kept away
From the chapel that day,
And a poor young friar, who in his
    stead
Drank the sacramental wine,
Fell on the steps of the altar,
    dead!
But look! do you see at the
    window there
That face, with a look of grief and
    despair,

That ghastly face, as of one in
    pain?
  Monks. Who? where?
  Lucifer. As I spoke, it vanished
    away again.
  Friar Cuthbert. It is that nefari-
    ous
Siebald the Refectorarius.
That fellow is always playing the
    scout,
Creeping and peeping and prowl-
    ing about;
And then he regales
The Abbot with scandalous tales.
  Lucifer. A spy in the convent?
    One of the brothers
Telling scandalous tales of the
    others?
Out upon him, the lazy loon!
I would put a stop to that pretty
    soon,
In a way he should rue it.
  Monks. How shall we do it?
  Lucifer. Do you, brother Paul,
Creep under the window, close to
    the wall,
And open it suddenly when I call.
Then seize the villain by the hair,
And hold him there,
And punish him soundly, once for
    all.
  Friar Cuthbert. As St. Dunstan
    of old,
We are told,
Once caught the Devil by the nose!
  Lucifer. Ha! ha! that story is
    very clever,
But has no foundation whatsoever.
Quick! for I see his face again
Glaring in at the window-pane;
Now! now! and do not spare
    your blows.
    (FRIAR PAUL *opens the window*
    suddenly, and seizes SIEBALD.
    They beat him.)
  Friar Siebald. Help! help! are
    you going to slay me?
  Friar Paul. That will teach you
    again to betray me!

  Friar Siebald. Mercy! mercy!
  Friar Paul, shouting and beating.
    Rumpas bellorum lorum
    Vim confer amorum
    Morum verorum rorum
    Tu plena polorum!
  Lucifer. Who stands in the door-
    way yonder,
Stretching out his trembling
    hand,
Just as Aberlard used to stand,
The flash of his keen, black eyes
Forerunning the thunder?
  The Monks, in confusion. The
    Abbot! the Abbot!
  Friar Cuthbert. And what is the
    wonder!
He seems to have taken you by
    surprise.
  Friar Francis. Hide the great
    flagon
From the eyes of the dragon!
  Friar Cuthbert. Pull the brown
    hood over your face!
This will bring us into disgrace!
  Abbot. What means this revel
    and carouse?
Is this a tavern and drinking-
    house?
Are you Christian monks, or
    heathen devils,
To pollute this convent with your
    revels?
Were Peter Damian still upon
    earth,
To be shocked by such ungodly
    mirth,
He would write your names, with
    pen of gall,
In his Book of Gomorrah, one and
    all!
Away, you drunkards! to your
    cells,
And pray till you hear the matin-
    bells;
You, Brother Francis, and you,
    Brother Paul!
And as a penance mark each
    prayer

With the scourge upon your
    shoulders bare;
Nothing atones for such a sin
But the blood that follows the
    discipline.
And you, Brother Cuthbert, come
    with me
Alone into the sacristy;
You, who should be a guide to
    your brothers,
And are ten times worse than all
    the others,
For you I've a draught that has
    long been brewing,
You shall do a penance worth the
    doing!
Away to your prayers, then, one
    and all!
I wonder the very convent wall
Does not crumble and crush you
    in its fall!

THE NEIGHBOURING NUNNERY

The ABBESS IRMINGARD *sitting
    with* ELSIE *in the moonlight.*

Irmingard. The night is silent,
    the wind is still,
The moon is looking from yonder
    hill
Down upon convent, and grove,
    and garden;
The clouds have passed away
    from her face,
Leaving behind them no sorrowful
    trace,
Only the tender and quiet grace
Of one, whose heart has been
    healed with pardon!

And such am I. My soul within
Was dark with passion and soiled
    with sin.
But now its wounds are healed
    again;
Gone are the anguish, the terror,
    and pain;
For across that desolate land of
    woe,

O'er whose burning sands I was
    forced to go,
A wind from heaven began to
    blow;
And all my being trembled and
    shook,
As the leaves of the tree, or the
    grass of the field,
And I was healed, as the sick are
    healed,
When fanned by the leaves of the
    Holy Book!

As thou sittest in the moonlight
    there,
Its glory flooding thy golden hair,
And the only darkness that which
    lies
In the haunted chambers of thine
    eyes,
I feel my soul drawn unto thee,
Strangely, and strongly, and more
    and more,
As to one I have known and loved
    before;
For every soul is akin to me
That dwells in the land of mystery!
I am the Lady Irmingard,
Born of a noble race and name!
Many a wandering Suabian bard,
Whose life was dreary, and bleak,
    and hard,
Has found through me the way to
    fame.
Brief and bright were those days,
    and the night
Which followed was full of a lurid
    light.
Love, that of every woman's heart
Will have the whole and not a
    part,
That is to her, in Nature's plan,
More than ambition is to man,
Her light, her life, her very breath,
With no alternative but death,
Found me a maiden soft and
    young
Just from the convent's cloistered
    school,

And seated on my lowly stool,
Attentive while the minstrels sung.

Gallant, graceful, gentle, tall,
Fairest, noblest, best of all,
Was Walter of the Vogelweid;
And, whatsoever may betide,
Still I think of him with pride!
His song was of the summer-
     time,
The very birds sang in his rhyme;
The sunshine, the delicious air,
The fragrance of the flowers, were
     there;
And I grew restless as I heard,
Restless and buoyant as a bird,
Down soft, aerial currents sailing,
O'er blossomed orchards, and
     fields in bloom,
And through the momentary
     gloom
Of shadows o'er the landscape
     trailing,
Yielding and borne I knew not
     where,
But feeling resistance unavailing.

And thus, unnoticed and apart,
And more by accident than choice,
I listened to that single voice
Until the chambers of my heart
Were filled with it by night and
     day.
One night,—it was a night in
     May,—
Within the garden, unawares,
Under the blossoms in the gloom,
I heard it utter my own name
With protestations and wild
     prayers;
And it rang through me, and
     became
Like the archangel's trump of
     doom,
Which the soul hears, and must
     obey;
And mine arose as from a tomb.
My former life now seemed to me
Such as hereafter death may be,

When in the great Eternity
We shall awake and find it day.

It was a dream, and would not
     stay;
A dream, that in a single night
Faded and vanished out of sight.
My father's anger followed fast
This passion, as a freshening blast
Seeks out and fans the fire, whose
     rage
It may increase, but not assuage.
And he exclaimed: " No wander-
     ing bard
Shall win thy hand, O Irmingard!
For which Prince Henry of Hohe-
     neck
By messenger and letter sues."

Gently, but firmly, I replied:
" Henry of Hoheneck I discard!
Never the hand of Irmingard
Shall lie in his as the hand of a
     bride! "
This said I, Walter, for thy sake;
This said I, for I could not choose.
After a pause, my father spake
In that cold and deliberate tone
Which turns the hearer into stone,
And seems itself the act to be
That follows with such dread
     certainty;
"This, or the cloister and the veil!"
No other words than these he said,
But they were like a funeral wail;
My life was ended, my heart was
     dead.

That night from the castle-gate
     went down,
With silent, slow, and stealthy
     pace,
Two shadows, mounted on
     shadowy steeds,
Taking the narrow path that leads
Into the forest dense and brown.
In the leafy darkness of the place,
One could not distinguish form nor
     face,

Only a bulk without a shape,
A darker shadow in the shade;
One scarce could say it moved or
stayed.
Thus it was we made our escape!
A foaming brook, with many a
bound,
Followed us like a playful hound;
Then leaped before us, and in the
hollow
Paused, and waited for us to
follow,
And seemed impatient, and
afraid
That our tardy flight should be
betrayed
By the sound our horses' hoof-
beats made.
And when we reached the plain
below,
We paused a moment and drew
rein
To look back at the castle again;
And we saw the windows all
aglow
With lights, that were passing to
and fro;
Our hearts with terror ceased to
beat;
The brook crept silent to our feet;
We knew what most we feared to
know.
Then suddenly horns began to
blow;
And we heard a shout, and a
heavy tramp,
And our horses snorted in the
damp
Night-air of the meadows green
and wide,
And in a moment, side by side,
So close, they must have seemed
but one,
The shadows across the moonlight
run,
And another came, and swept
behind,
Like the shadow of clouds before
the wind!

How I remember that breathless
flight
Across the moors, in the summer
night!
How under our feet the long,
white road
Backward like a river flowed,
Sweeping with it fences and
hedges,
Whilst farther away, and overhead,
Paler than I, with fear and dread,
The moon fled with us, as we fled
Along the forest's jagged edges!

All this I can remember well;
But of what afterwards befell
I nothing farther can recall
Than a blind, desperate, headlong
fall;
The rest is a blank and darkness
all.
When I awoke out of this swoon,
The sun was shining, not the moon,
Making a cross upon the wall
With the bars of my windows
narrow and tall;
And I prayed to it, as I had been
wont to pray,
From early childhood, day by day,
Each morning, as in bed I lay!
I was lying again in my own room!
And I thanked God, in my fever
and pain,
That those shadows on the mid-
night plain
Were gone, and could not come
again!
I struggled no longer with my
doom!

This happened many years ago.
I left my father's home to come
Like Catherine to her martyrdom,
For blindly I esteemed it so.
And when I heard the convent door
Behind me close, to ope no more,
I felt it smite me like a blow.
Through all my limbs a shudder
ran,

And on my bruised spirit fell
The dampness of my narrow cell
As night-air on a wounded man,
Giving intolerable pain.

But now a better life began.
I felt the agony decrease
By slow degrees, then wholly
    cease,
Ending in perfect rest and peace!
It was not apathy, nor dulness,
That weighed and pressed upon
    my brain,
But the same passion I had given
To earth before, now turned to
    heaven
With all its overflowing fulness.

Alas! the world is full of peril!
The path that runs through the
    fairest meads,
On the sunniest side of the valley,
    leads
Into a region bleak and sterile!
Alike in the high-born and the
    lowly,
The will is feeble, and passion
    strong.
We cannot sever right from wrong;
Some falsehood mingles with all
    truth;
Nor is it strange the heart of
    youth
Should waver and comprehend but
    slowly
The things that are holy and un-
    holy!
But in this sacred and calm retreat,
We are all well and safely shielded
From winds that blow, and waves
    that beat,
From the cold, and rain, and
    blighting heat,
To which the strongest hearts have
    yielded.
Here we stand as the Virgins
    Seven,
For our celestial bridegroom yearn-
    ing;

Our hearts are lamps forever burn-
    ing,
With a steady and unwavering
    flame,
Pointing upward, forever the
    same,
Steadily upward toward the
    Heaven!

The moon is hidden behind a
    cloud;
A sudden darkness fills the room,
And thy deep eyes, amid the
    gloom,
Shine like jewels in a shroud.
On the leaves is a sound of falling
    rain;
A bird, awakened in its nest,
Gives a faint twitter of unrest,
Then smooths its plumes and
    sleeps again.
No other sounds than these I hear;
The hour of midnight must be near.
Thou art o'erspent with the day's
    fatigue
Of riding many a dusty league;
Sink, then, gently to thy slumber;
Me so many cares encumber,
So many ghosts, and forms of
    fright,
Have started from their graves to-
    night,
They have driven sleep from mine
    eyes away:
I will go down to the chapel and
    pray.

V.

A COVERED BRIDGE AT LUCERNE

Prince Henry. God's blessing on
    the architects who build
The bridges o'er swift rivers and
    abysses
Before impassable to human feet,
No less than on the builders of
    cathedrals,

Whose massive walls are bridges
thrown across
The dark and terrible abyss of
Death.
Well has the name of Pontifex
been given
Unto the Church's head, as the
chief builder
And architect of the invisible
bridge
That leads from earth to heaven.

Elsie.   How dark it grows!
What are these paintings on the
walls around us?

Prince Henry. The Dance Maca-
ber!

Elsie.   What?

Prince Henry. The Dance of
Death!
All that go to and fro must look
upon it,
Mindful of what they shall be,
while beneath,
Among the wooden piles, the
turbulent river
Rushes, impetuous as the river of
life,
With dimpling eddies, ever green
and bright,
Save where the shadow of this
bridge falls on it.

Elsie. O, yes! I see it now!

Prince Henry. The grim musician
Leads all men through the mazes
of that dance,
To different sounds in different
measures moving;
Sometimes he plays a lute, some-
times a drum,
To tempt or terrify.

Elsie.   What is this picture?

Prince Henry. It is a young
man singing to a nun,
Who kneels at her devotions, but
in kneeling
Turns round to look at him; and
Death, meanwhile,
Is putting out the candles on the
altar!

Elsie. Ah, what a pity 'tis that
she should listen
Unto such songs, when in her
orisons
She might have heard in heaven
the angels singing!

Prince Henry. Here he has
stolen a jester's cap and bells,
And dances with the Queen.

Elsie.   A foolish jest!

Prince Henry. And here the
heart of the new-wedded wife,
Coming from church with her be-
loved lord,
He startles with the rattle of his
drum.

Elsie. Ah, that is sad! And
yet perhaps 'tis best
That she should die, with all the
sunshine on her,
And all the benedictions of the
morning,
Before this affluence of golden light
Shall fade into a cold and clouded
gray,
Then into darkness!

Prince Henry. Under it is
written,
" Nothing but death shall separate
thee and me! "

Elsie. And what is this, that
follows close upon it?

Prince Henry. Death, playing
on a dulcimer. Behind him,
A poor old woman, with a rosary,
Follows the sound, and seems to
wish her feet
Were swifter to o'ertake him.
Underneath,
The inscription reads, " Better is
Death than Life."

Elsie. Better is Death than
Life! Ah yes! to thousands
Death plays upon a dulcimer, and
sings
That song of consolation, till the
air
Rings with it, and they cannot
choose but follow

Whither he leads. And not the
old alone,
But the young also hear it, and
are still.
  Prince Henry. Yes, in their
sadder moments. 'Tis the
sound
Of their own hearts they hear,
half full of tears,
Which are like crystal cups, half
filled with water,
Responding to the pressure of a
finger
With music sweet and low and
melancholy.
Let us go forward, and no longer
stay
In this great picture-gallery of
Death!
I hate it! ay, the very thought of it!
  Elsie. Why is it hateful to you?
  Prince Henry. For the reason
That life, and all that speaks of
life, is lovely,
And death, and all that speaks of
death, is hateful.
  Elsie. The grave itself is but a
covered bridge,
Leading from light to light,
through a brief darkness!
  *Prince Henry, emerging from the
bridge.* I breathe again more
freely! Ah, how pleasant
To come once more into the light
of day,
Out of that shadow of death! To
hear again
The hoof-beats of our horses on
firm ground,
And not upon those hollow planks,
resounding
With a sepulchral echo, like the
clods
On coffins in a churchyard!
Yonder lies
The Lake of the Four Forest-
Towns, apparelled
In light, and lingering, like a
village maiden,

Hid in the bosom of her native
mountains,
Then pouring all her life into
another's,
Changing her name and being!
Overhead,
Shaking his cloudy tresses loose
in air,
Rises Pilatus, with his windy pines.
            (*They pass on.*)

THE DEVIL'S BRIDGE

PRINCE HENRY *and* ELSIE *crossing,
with attendants.*

  Guide. This bridge is called the
Devil's Bridge.
With a single arch, from ridge to
ridge,
It leaps across the terrible chasm
Yawning beneath us, black and
deep,
As if, in some convulsive spasm,
The summits of the hills had
cracked,
And made a road for the cataract,
That raves and rages down the
steep!
  Lucifer, under the bridge. Ha!
ha!
  Guide. Never any bridge but
this
Could stand across the wild abyss;
All the rest, of wood or stone,
By the Devil's hand were over-
thrown.
He toppled crags from the pre-
cipice,
And whatsoe'er was built by day
In the night was swept away;
None could stand but this alone.
  Lucifer, under the bridge. Ha!
ha!
  Guide. I showed you in the
valley a boulder
Marked with the imprint of his
shoulder;
As he was bearing it up this way,

The Golden Legend

A peasant, passing, cried, "Herr
    Jé!"
And the Devil dropped it in his
    fright,
And vanished suddenly out of
    sight!

Lucifer, under the bridge. Ha!
    ha!

Guide. Abbot Giraldus of Ein-
    siedel,
For pilgrims on their way to Rome,
Built this at last, with a single
    arch,
Under which, on its endless march,
Runs the river, white with foam,
Like a thread through the eye of a
    needle,
And the Devil promised to let it
    stand,
Under compact and condition
That the first living thing which
    crossed
Should be surrendered into his
    hand,
And be beyond redemption lost.

Lucifer, under the bridge. Ha!
    ha! perdition!

Guide. At length, the bridge
    being all completed,
The Abbot, standing at its head,
Threw across it a loaf of bread,
Which a hungry dog sprang after,
And the rocks re-echoed with the
    peals of laughter
To see the Devil thus defeated!
                    (*They pass on.*)

Lucifer, under the bridge. Ha!
    ha! defeated!
For journeys and for crimes like
    this
I let the bridge stand o'er the
    abyss!

THE ST. GOTHARD PASS

Prince Henry. This is the highest
    point. Two ways the rivers
Leap down to different seas, and
    as they roll

Grow deep and still, and their
    majestic presence
Becomes a benefaction to the
    towns
They visit, wandering silently
    among them,
Like patriarchs old among their
    shining tents.

Elsie. How bleak and bare it is!
    Nothing but mosses
Grow on these rocks.

Prince Henry. Yet are they not
    forgotten;
Beneficent Nature sends the mists
    to feed them.

Elsie. See yonder little cloud,
    that, borne aloft
So tenderly by the wind, floats
    fast away
Over the snowy peaks! It seems
    to me
The body of St. Catherine, borne
    by angels!

Prince Henry. Thou art St.
    Catherine, and invisible angels
Bear thee across these chasms and
    precipices,
Lest thou shouldst dash thy feet
    against a stone.

Elsie. Would I were borne unto
    my grave, as she was,
Upon angelic shoulders! Even now
I seem uplifted by them, light as
    air!
What sound is that?

Prince Henry. The tumbling
    avalanches!

Elsie. How awful, yet how
    beautiful!

Prince Henry.   These are
The voices of the mountains!
    Thus they ope
Their snowy lips, and speak unto
    each other,
In the primeval language, lost to
    man.

Elsie. What land is this that
    spreads itself beneath us?

Prince Henry. Italy! Italy!

Elsie.   Land of the Madonna!
How beautiful it is! It seems a garden
Of Paradise!
    Prince Henry. Nay, of Gethsemane
To thee and me, of passion and of prayer!
Yet once of Paradise.   Long years ago
I wandered as a youth among its bowers,
And never from my heart has faded quite
Its memory, that, like a summer sunset,
Encircles with a ring of purple light
All the horizon of my youth.
    Guide.   O friends!
The days are short, the way before us long;
We must not linger, if we think to reach
The inn at Belinzona before vespers!

                (They pass on.)

AT THE FOOT OF THE ALPS

A halt under the trees at noon.

    Prince Henry. Here let us pause a moment in the trembling
Shadow and sunshine of the roadside trees,
And, our tired horses in a group assembling,
Inhale long draughts of this delicious breeze.
Our fleeter steeds have distanced our attendants,
They lag behind us with a slower pace;
We will await them under the green pendants
Of the great willows in this shady place.
Ho, Barbarossa! how thy mottled haunches
Sweat with this canter over hill and glade!
Stand still, and let these overhanging branches
Fan thy hot sides and comfort thee with shade!
    Elsie. What a delightful landscape spreads before us,
Marked with a whitewashed cottage here and there!
And, in luxuriant garlands drooping o'er us,
Blossoms of grape-vines scent the sunny air.
    Prince Henry. Hark! what sweet sounds are those, whose accents holy
Fill the warm noon with music sad and sweet!
    Elsie. It is a band of pilgrims, moving slowly
On their long journey, with uncovered feet.
    Pilgrims, chanting the Hymn of St. Hildebert.
        Me receptet Sion illa,
        Sion David, urbs tranquilla,
        Cujus faber auctor lucis,
        Cujus portæ lignum crucis,
        Cujus claves lingua Petri,
        Cujus cives semper læti,
        Cujus muri lapis vivus,
        Cujus custos Rex festivus!
    Lucifer, as a Friar in the procession. Here am I, too, in the pious band,
In the garb of a barefooted Carmelite dressed!
The soles of my feet are as hard and tanned
As the conscience of old Pope Hildebrand,
The Holy Satan, who made the wives
Of the bishops lead such shameful lives.
All day long I beat my breast,
And chant with a most particular zest

The Latin hymns, which I understand
Quite as well, I think, as the rest.
And at night such lodging in barns and sheds,
Such a hurly-burly in country inns,
Such a clatter of tongues in empty heads,
Such a helter-skelter of prayers and sins!
Of all the contrivances of the time
For sowing broadcast the seeds of crime,
There is none so pleasing to me and mine
As a pilgrimage to some far-off shrine!

Prince Henry. If from the outward man we judge the inner,
And cleanliness is godliness, I fear
A hopeless reprobate, a hardened sinner,
Must be that Carmelite now passing near.

Lucifer. There is my German Prince again,
Thus far on his journey to Salern,
And the lovesick girl, whose heated brain
Is sowing the cloud to reap the rain;
But it's a long road that has no turn!
Let them quietly hold their way,
I have also a part in the play,
But first I must act to my heart's content
This mummery and this merriment,
And drive this motley flock of sheep
Into the fold, where drink and sleep
The jolly old friars of Benevent.
Of a truth, it often provokes me to laugh
To see these beggars hobble along,
Lamed and maimed, and fed upon chaff,
Chanting their wonderful piff and paff,
And, to make up for not understanding the song,
Singing it fiercely, and wild, and strong!
Were it not for my magic garters and staff,
And the goblets of goodly wine I quaff,
And the mischief I make in the idle throng,
I should not continue the business long.

Pilgrims, chanting.

In hâc urbe, lux solennis,
Ver æternum, pax perennis;
In hâc odor implens cælos,
In hâc semper festum melos!

Prince Henry. Do you observe that monk among the train,
Who pours from his great throat the roaring bass,
As a cathedral spout pours out the rain,
And this way turns his rubicund, round face?

Elsie. It is the same who, on the Strasburg square,
Preached to the people in the open air.

Prince Henry. And he has crossed o'er mountain, field, and fell,
On that good steed, that seems to bear him well,
The hackney of the Friars of Orders Gray,
His own stout legs! He, too, was in the play,
Both as King Herod and Ben Israel.
Good morrow, Friar!

Friar Cuthbert. Good morrow, noble Sir!

Prince Henry. I speak in German, for, unless I err,
You are a German.

Friar Cuthbert. I cannot gainsay
   you.
But by what instinct, or what
   secret sign,
Meeting me here, do you straight-
   way divine
That northward of the Alps my
   country lies?
   Prince Henry. Your accent, like
   St. Peter's, would betray
   you,
Did not your yellow beard and
   your blue eyes.
Moreover, we have seen your face
   before,
And heard you preach at the
   Cathedral door
On Easter Sunday, in the Stras-
   burg square.
We were among the crowd that
   gathered there,
And saw you play the Rabbi with
   great skill,
As if, by leaning o'er so many
   years
To walk with little children, your
   own will
Had caught a childish attitude
   from theirs,
A kind of stooping in its form and
   gait,
And could no longer stand erect
   and straight.
Whence come you now?
   Friar Cuthbert. From the old
   monastery
Of Hirschau, in the forest; being
   sent
Upon a pilgrimage to Benevent,
To see the image of the Virgin
   Mary,
That moves its holy eyes, and
   sometimes speaks,
And lets the piteous tears run
   down its cheeks.
To touch the hearts of the impeni-
   tent.
   Prince Henry. O, had I faith,
   as in the days gone by,

That knew no doubt, and feared
   no mystery!
   Lucifer, at a distance. Ho,
   Cuthbert! Friar Cuthbert!
   Friar Cuthbert. Farewell, Prince!
I cannot stay to argue and con-
   vince.
   Prince Henry. This is indeed
   the blessed Mary's land,
Virgin and Mother of our dear
   Redeemer!
All hearts are touched and softened
   at her name;
Alike the bandit, with the bloody
   hand,
The priest, the prince, the scholar,
   and the peasant,
The man of deeds, the visionary
   dreamer,
Pay homage to her as one ever
   present!
And even as children, who have
   much offended
A too indulgent father, in great
   shame,
Penitent, and yet not daring un-
   attended
To go into his presence, at the
   gate
Speak with their sister, and con-
   fiding wait
Till she goes in before and inter-
   cedes;
So men, repenting of their evil
   deeds,
And yet not venturing rashly to
   draw near
With their requests an angry
   father's ear,
Offer to her their prayers and their
   confession,
And she for them in heaven makes
   intercession.
And if our Faith had given us
   nothing more
Than this example of all woman-
   hood,
So mild, so merciful, so strong, so
   good,

So patient, peaceful, loyal, loving,
pure,
This were enough to prove it
higher and truer
Than all the creeds the world had
known before.

Pilgrims, chanting afar off.

Urbs cœlestis, urbs beata,
Supra petram collocata,
Urbs in portu satis tuto
De longinquo te saluto,
Te saluto, te suspiro,
Te affecto, te requiro!

THE INN AT GENOA

*A terrace overlooking the sea.
Night.*

Prince Henry. It is the sea, it is
the sea,
In all its vague immensity,
Fading and darkening in the dis-
tance!
Silent, majestical, and slow,
The white ships haunt it to and fro,
With all their ghostly sails un-
furled,
As phantoms from another world
Haunt the dim confines of exist-
ence!
But ah! how few can comprehend
Their signals, or to what good end
From land to land they come and
go!
Upon a sea more vast and dark
The spirits of the dead embark,
All voyaging to unknown coasts.
We wave our farewells from the
shore,
And they depart, and come no
more,
Or come as phantoms and as
ghosts.

Above the darksome sea of death
Looms the great life that is to be,
A land of cloud and mystery,
A dim mirage, with shapes of men

Long dead, and passed beyond our
ken.
Awe-struck we gaze, and hold our
breath
Till the fair pageant vanisheth,
Leaving us in perplexity,
And doubtful whether it has been
A vision of the world unseen,
Or a bright image of our own
Against the sky in vapours thrown.

Lucifer, singing from the sea.

Thou didst not make it, thou
canst not mend it,
But thou hast the power to end
it!
The sea is silent, the sea is dis-
creet,
Deep it lies at thy very feet;
There is no confessor like unto
Death!
Thou canst not see him, but he is
near;
Thou needst not whisper above thy
breath,
And he will hear;
He will answer the questions,
The vague surmises and sugges-
tions,
That fill thy soul with doubt and
fear!

Prince Henry. The fisherman,
who lies afloat,
With shadowy sail, in yonder boat,
Is singing softly to the Night!
But do I comprehend aright
The meaning of the words he sung
So sweetly in his native tongue?
Ah, yes! the sea is still and deep.
All things within its bosom sleep!
A single step, and all is o'er;
A plunge, a bubble, and no more;
And thou, dear Elsie, wilt be free
From martyrdom and agony.

*Elsie, coming from her chamber
upon the terrace.* The night is
calm and cloudless,
And still as still can be,
And the stars come forth to listen
To the music of the sea.

They gather, and gather, and
　　gather,
Until they crowd the sky,
And listen, in breathless silence,
To the solemn litany.
It begins in rocky caverns,
As a voice that chants alone
To the pedals of the organ
In monotonous undertone;
And anon from shelving beaches,
And shallow sands beyond,
In snow-white robes uprising
The ghostly choirs respond.
And sadly and unceasing
The mournful voice sings on,
And the snow-white choirs still
　　answer
Christe eleison!
　　Prince Henry. Angel of God!
　　　thy finer sense perceives
Celestial and perpetual harmonies!
Thy purer soul, that trembles and
　　believes,
Hears the archangel's trumpet in
　　the breeze,
And where the forest rolls, or
　　ocean heaves,
Cecilia's organ sounding in the
　　seas,
And tongues of prophets speaking
　　in the leaves.
But I hear discord only and
　　despair,
And whispers as of demons in the
　　air!

AT SEA

　　Il Padrone. The wind upon our
　　　quarter lies,
And on before the freshening gale,
That fills the snow-white lateen
　　sail,
Swiftly our light felucca flies.
Around, the billows burst and
　　foam;
They lift her o'er the sunken rock,
They beat her sides with many a
　　shock,

And then upon their flowing dome
They poise her, like a weather-
　　cock!
Between us and the western skies
The hills of Corsica arise;
Eastward, in yonder long, blue line,
The summits of the Apennine,
And southward, and still far away,
Salerno, on its sunny bay.
You cannot see it, where it lies.
　　Prince Henry. Ah, would that
　　　never more mine eyes
Might see its towers by night or
　　day!
　　Elsie. Behind us, dark and
　　　awfully,
There comes a cloud out of the sea,
That bears the form of a hunted
　　deer,
With hide of brown, and hoofs of
　　black,
And antlers laid upon its back,
And fleeing fast and wild with
　　fear,
As if the hounds were on its track!
　　Prince Henry. Lo! while we
　　　gaze, it breaks and falls
In shapeless masses, like the walls
Of a burnt city. Broad and red
The fires of the descending sun
Glare through the windows, and
　　o'erhead,
Athwart the vapours, dense and
　　dun,
Long shafts of silvery light arise,
Like rafters that support the skies!
　　Elsie. See! from its summit the
　　　lurid levin
Flashes downward without warn-
　　ing,
As Lucifer, son of the morning,
Fell from the battlements of
　　heaven!
　　Il Padrone. I must entreat you,
　　　friends, below!
The angry storm begins to blow,
For the weather changes with the
　　moon.
All this morning, until noon,

We had baffling winds, and sudden
    flaws
Struck the sea with their cat's-
    paws.
Only a little hour ago
I was whistling to Saint Antonio
For a capful of wind to fill our sail,
And instead of a breeze he has sent
    a gale.
Last night I saw Saint Elmo's
    stars,
With their glimmering lanterns,
    all at play
On the tops of the masts and the
    tips of the spars,
And I knew we should have foul
    weather to-day.
Cheerly, my hearties! yo heave
    ho!
Brail up the mainsail, and let her
    go
As the winds will and Saint
    Antonio!

Do you see that Livornese felucca,
That vessel to the windward
    yonder,
Running with her gunwale under?
I was looking when the wind o'er-
    took her.
She had all sail set, and the only
    wonder
Is, that at once the strength of the
    blast
Did not carry away her mast.
She is a galley of the Gran Duca,
That, through the fear of the
    Algerines,
Convoys those lazy brigantines,
Laden with wine and oil from
    Lucca.
Now all is ready, high and low;
Blow, blow, good Saint Antonio!

Ha! that is the first dash of the
    rain,
With a sprinkle of spray above
    the rails,
Just enough to moisten our sails,

And make them ready for the
    strain.
See how she leaps, as the blasts
    o'ertake her,
And speeds away with a bone in
    her mouth!
Now keep her head toward the
    south,
And there is no danger of bank or
    breaker.
With the breeze behind us, on we
    go;
Not too much, good Saint Antonio!

VI.

THE SCHOOL OF SALERNO

*A travelling Scholastic affixing his
    Thesis to the gate of the College.*

Scholastic. There, that is my
    gauntlet, my banner, my
    shield,
Hung up as a challenge to all the
    field!
One hundred and twenty-five pro-
    positions,
Which I will maintain with the
    sword of the tongue
Against all disputants, old and
    young.
Let us see if doctors or dialecti-
    cians
Will dare to dispute my definitions,
Or attack any one of my learned
    theses.
Here stand I; the end shall be as
    God pleases.
I think I have proved, by pro-
    found researches,
The error of all those doctrines so
    vicious
Of the old Areopagite Dionysius,
That are making such terrible
    work in the churches,
By Michael the Stammerer sent
    from the East,

And done into Latin by that
Scottish beast,
Erigena Johannes, who dares to
maintain,
In the face of the truth, the error
infernal,
That the universe is and must be
eternal;
At first laying down, as a fact
fundamental,
That nothing with God can be
accidental;
Then asserting that God before the
creation
Could not have existed, because it
is plain
That, had he existed, he would
have created;
Which is begging the question
that should be debated,
And moveth me less to anger than
laughter.
All nature, he holds, is a respiration
Of the Spirit of God, who, in
breathing, hereafter
Will inhale it into his bosom again,
So that nothing but God alone will
remain.
And therein he contradicteth himself;
For he opens the whole discussion
by stating,
That God can only exist in creating.
That question I think I have laid
on the shelf!
   (*He goes out. Two Doctors come
in disputing, and followed by
pupils.*)
  Doctor Serafino. I, with the
Doctor Seraphic, maintain,
That a word which is only conceived in the brain
Is a type of eternal Generation;
The spoken word is the Incarnation.
  Doctor Cherubino. What do I
care for the Doctor Seraphic,
With all his wordy chaffer and
traffic?
  Doctor Serafino. You make but
a paltry show of resistance;
Universals have no real existence!
  Doctor Cherubino. Your words
are but idle and empty
chatter;
Ideas are eternally joined to
matter!
  Doctor Serafino. May the Lord
have mercy on your position,
You wretched, wrangling culler of
herbs!
  Doctor Cherubino. May he send
your soul to eternal perdition,
For your Treatise on the Irregular
Verbs!
   *They rush out fighting. Two
Scholars come in.*
  First Scholar. Monte Cassino,
then, is your College.
What think you of ours here at
Salern?
  Second Scholar. To tell the
truth, I arrived so lately,
I hardly yet have had time to discern.
So much, at least, I am bound to
acknowledge:
The air seems healthy, the buildings stately,
And on the whole I like it greatly.
  First Scholar. Yes, the air is
sweet; the Calabrian hills
Send us down puffs of mountain
air;
And in summer-time the seabreeze fills
With its coolness cloister, and
court, and square.
Then at every season of the
year
There are crowds of guests and
travellers here;
Pilgrims, and mendicant friars,
and traders
From the Levant, with figs and
wine,

And bands of wounded and sick
    Crusaders,
Coming back from Palestine.
    Second Scholar. And what are
    the studies you pursue?
What is the course you here go
    through?
    First Scholar. The first three
    years of the college course
Are given to Logic alone, as the
    source
Of all that is noble, and wise, and
    true.
    Second Scholar. That seems
    rather strange, I must confess,
In a Medical School; yet, never-
    theless,
You doubtless have reasons for
    that.
    First Scholar.   O, yes!
For none but a clever dialectician
Can hope to become a great
    physician;
That has been settled long ago.
Logic makes an important part
Of the mystery of the healing art;
For without it how could you hope
    to show
That nobody knows so much as
    you know?
After this there are five years more
Devoted wholly to medicine,
With lectures on chirurgical lore,
And dissections of the bodies of
    swine,
As likest the human form divine.
    Second Scholar. What are the
    books now most in vogue?
    First Scholar. Quite an exten-
    sive catalogue;
Mostly, however, books of our own;
As Gariopontus' Passionarius,
And the writings of Matthew
    Platearius;
And a volume universally known
As the Regimen of the School of
    Salern,
For Robert of Normandy written
    in terse

And very elegant Latin verse.
Each of these writings has its turn.
And when at length we have
    finished these,
Then comes the struggle for
    degrees,
With all the oldest and ablest
    critics;
The public thesis and disputation,
Question, and answer, and ex-
    planation
Of a passage out of Hippocrates,
Or Aristotle's Analytics.
There the triumphant Magister
    stands!
A book is solemnly placed in his
    hands,
On which he swears to follow the
    rule
And ancient forms of the good old
    School;
To report if any confectionarius
Mingles his drugs with matters
    various,
And to visit his patients twice a
    day,
And once in the night, if they live
    in town,
And if they are poor, to take no
    pay.
Having faithfully promised these,
His head is crowned with a laurel
    crown;
A kiss on his cheek, a ring on his
    hand,
The Magister Artium et Physices
Goes forth from the school like a
    lord of the land.
And now, as we have the whole
    morning before us,
Let us go in, if you make no objec-
    tion,
And listen awhile to a learned
    prelection
On Marcus Aurelius Cassiodorus.
    (*They go in. Enter* LUCIFER *as
    a Doctor.*)
    Lucifer. This is the great School
    of Salern!

A land of wrangling and of quarrels,
Of brains that seethe, and hearts
  that burn,
Where every emulous scholar
  hears,
In every breath that comes to his
  ears,
The rustling of another's laurels!
The air of the place is called salu-
  brious;
The neighbourhood of Vesuvius
  lends it
An odour volcanic, that rather
  mends it,
And the buildings have an aspect
  lugubrious,
That inspires a feeling of awe and
  terror
Into the heart of the beholder,
And befits such an ancient home-
  stead of error,
Where the old falsehoods moulder
  and smoulder,
And yearly by many hundred
  hands
Are carried away, in the zeal of
  youth,
And sown like tares in the field of
  truth,
To blossom and ripen in other
  lands.

What have we here, affixed to the
  gate?
The challenge of some scholastic
  wight,
Who wishes to hold a public
  debate
On sundry questions wrong or
  right!
Ah, now this is my great delight!
For I have often observed of late
That such discussions end in a
  fight.
Let us see what the learned wag
  maintains
With such a prodigal waste of
  brains.
                              (*Reads.*)

" Whether angels in moving from
  place to place
Pass through the intermediate
  space.
Whether God himself is the author
  of evil,
Or whether that is the work of the
  Devil.
When, where, and wherefore
  Lucifer fell,
And whether he now is chained in
  hell."

I think I can answer that question
  well!
So long as the boastful human mind
Consents in such mills as this to
  grind,
I sit very firmly upon my throne!
Of a truth it almost makes me
  laugh,
To see men leaving the golden grain
To gather in piles the pitiful chaff
That old Peter Lombard thrashed
  with his brain,
To have it caught up and tossed
  again
On the horns of the Dumb Ox of
  Cologne!

But my guests approach! there is
  in the air
A fragrance, like that of the
  Beautiful Garden
Of Paradise, in the days that were!
An odour of innocence, and of
  prayer,
And of love, and faith that never
  fails,
Such as the fresh young heart
  exhales
Before it begins to wither and
  harden!
I cannot breathe such an atmo-
  sphere!
My soul is filled with a nameless
  fear,
That, after all my trouble and pain,
After all my restless endeavour,

The youngest, fairest soul of the
twain,
The most ethereal, most divine,
Will escape from my hands for
ever and ever.
But the other is already mine!
Let him live to corrupt his race,
Breathing among them, with every
breath,
Weakness, selfishness, and the base
And pusillanimous fear of death.
I know his nature, and I know
That of all who in my ministry
Wander the great earth to and fro,
And on my errands come and go,
The safest and subtlest are such
as he.

Enter PRINCE HENRY *and* ELSIE,
with attendants.

Prince Henry. Can you direct
us to Friar Angelo?
Lucifer. He stands before you.
Prince Henry. Then you know
our purpose.
I am Prince Henry of Hoheneck,
and this
The maiden that I spake of in my
letters.
Lucifer. It is a very grave and
solemn business!
We must not be precipitate. Does
she
Without compulsion, of her own
free will,
Consent to this?
Prince Henry. Against all oppo-
sition,
Against all prayers, entreaties,
protestations.
She will not be persuaded.
Lucifer.   That is strange!
Have you thought well of it?
Elsie.   I come not here
To argue, but to die. Your busi-
ness is not
To question, but to kill me. I am
ready.
I am impatient to be gone from
here

Ere any thoughts of earth disturb
again
The spirit of tranquillity within
me.
Prince Henry. Would I had not
come here! Would I were
dead,
And thou wert in thy cottage in
the forest,
And hadst not known me! Why
have I done this?
Let me go back and die.
Elsie.   It cannot be;
Not if these cold, flat stones on
which we tread
Were coulters heated white, and
yonder gateway
Flamed like a furnace with a
sevenfold heat.
I must fulfil my purpose.
Prince Henry.   I forbid it!
Not one step further. For I only
meant
To put thus far thy courage to the
proof.
It is enough. I, too, have strength
to die,
For thou hast taught me!
Elsie. O my Prince! remember
Your promises. Let me fulfil my
errand.
You do not look on life and death
as I do.
There are two angels, that attend
unseen
Each one of us, and in great books
record
Our good and evil deeds. He who
writes down
The good ones, after every action
closes
His volume, and ascends with it
to God.
The other keeps his dreadful day-
book open
Till sunset, that we may repent;
which doing,
The record of the action fades
away,

And leaves a line of white across
the page.
Now if my act be good, as I believe,
It cannot be recalled. It is
already
Sealed up in heaven, as a good
deed accomplished.
The rest is yours.   Why wait you?
I am ready.
(*To her attendants.*)
Weep not, my friends! rather re-
joice with me.
I shall not feel the pain, but shall
be gone,
And you will have another friend
in heaven.
Then start not at the creaking of
the door
Through which I pass.   I see
what lies beyond it.
(*To* PRINCE HENRY.)
And you, O Prince! bear back my
benison
Unto my father's house, and all
within it.
This morning in the church I
prayed for them,
After confession, after absolution,
When my whole soul was white, I
prayed for them.
God will take care of them, they
need me not.
And in your life let my remem-
brance linger,
As something not to trouble and
disturb it,
But to complete it, adding life to
life.
And if at times beside the evening
fire
You see my face among the other
faces,
Let it not be regarded as a ghost
That haunts your house, but as a
guest that loves you.
Nay, even as one of your own
family,
Without whose presence there
were something wanting.

I have no more to say.   Let us go
in.
Prince Henry. Friar Angelo!   I
charge you on your life,
Believe not what she says, for she
is mad,
And comes here not to die, but to
be healed.
Elsie. Alas! Prince Henry!
Lucifer. Come with me;   this
way.

(ELSIE *goes in with* LUCIFER, *who
thrusts* PRINCE HENRY *back
and closes the door.*)

Prince Henry. Gone! and the
light of all my life gone with
her!
A sudden darkness falls upon the
world!
O, what a vile and abject thing
am I,
That purchase length of days at
such a cost!
Not by her death alone, but by
the death
Of all that's good and true and
noble in me!
All manhood, excellence, and self-
respect,
All love, and faith, and hope, and
heart are dead!
All my divine nobility of nature
By this one act is forfeited forever.
I am a Prince in nothing but in
name!
(*To the attendants.*)
Why did you let this horrible deed
be done?
Why did you not lay hold on her,
and keep her
From self-destruction?   Angelo!
murderer!

(*Struggles at the door, but cannot
open it.*)

Elsie, within. Farewell, dear
Prince! farewell!
Prince Henry. Unbar the door!
Lucifer. It is too late!

Prince Henry. It shall not be too late!

(*They burst the door open and rush in.*)

THE COTTAGE IN THE ODENWALD

URSULA, *spinning. Summer afternoon. A table spread.*

Ursula. I have marked it well,
—it must be true,—
Death never takes one alone, but two!
Whenever he enters in at a door,
Under roof of gold or roof of thatch,
He always leaves it upon the latch,
And comes again ere the year is o'er.
Never one of a household only!
Perhaps it is a mercy of God,
Lest the dead there under the sod,
In the land of strangers, should be lonely!
Ah me! I think I am lonelier here!
It is hard to go,—but harder to stay!
Were it not for the children, I should pray
That Death would take me within the year!
And Gottlieb!—he is at work all day,
In the sunny field, or the forest murk,
But I know that his thoughts are far away,
I know that his heart is not in his work!
And when he comes home to me at night
He is not cheery, but sits and sighs,
And I see the great tears in his eyes,
And try to be cheerful for his sake.
Only the children's hearts are light.

Mine is weary, and ready to break.
God help us! I hope we have done right;
We thought we were acting for the best!

(*Looking through the open door.*)
Who is it coming under the trees?
A man, in the Prince's livery dressed!
He looks about him with doubtful face,
As if uncertain of the place.
He stops at the beehives;—now he sees
The garden gate;—he is going past!
Can he be afraid of the bees?
No; he is coming in at last!
He fills my heart with strange alarm!

(*Enter a Forester.*)

Forester. Is this the tenant Gottlieb's farm?
Ursula. This is his farm, and I his wife.
Pray sit. What may your business be?
Forester. News from the Prince!
Ursula. Of death or life?
Forester. You put your questions eagerly!
Ursula. Answer me, then! How is the Prince?
Forester. I left him only two hours since
Homeward returning down the river,
As strong and well as if God, the Giver,
Had given him back his youth again.
Ursula, despairing. Then Elsie, my poor child, is dead!
Forester. That, my good woman, I have not said,
Don't cross the bridge till you come to it,
Is a proverb old, and of excellent wit.

Ursula. Keep me no longer in this pain!

Forester. It is true your daughter is no more;—
That is, the peasant she was before.

Ursula. Alas! I am simple and lowly bred,
I am poor, distracted, and forlorn.
And it is not well that you of the court
Should mock me thus, and make a sport
Of a joyless mother whose child is dead,
For you, too, were of mother born!

Forester. Your daughter lives, and the Prince is well!
You will learn ere long how it all befell.
Her heart for a moment never failed;
But when they reached Salerno's gate,
The Prince's nobler self prevailed,
And saved her for a noble fate.
And he was healed, in his despair,
By the touch of St. Matthew's sacred bones;
Though I think the long ride in the open air,
That pilgrimage over stocks and stones,
In the miracle must come in for a share!

Ursula. Virgin! who lovest the poor and lowly,
If the loud cry of a mother's heart
Can ever ascend to where thou art,
Into thy blessed hands and holy
Receive my prayer of praise and thanksgiving.
Let the hands that bore our Saviour bear it
Into the awful presence of God;
For thy feet with holiness are shod,
And if thou bearest it he will hear it.
Our child who was dead again is living!

Forester. I did not tell you she was dead;
If you thought so 'twas no fault of mine;
At this very moment, while I speak,
They are sailing homeward down the Rhine,
In a splendid barge, with golden prow,
And decked with banners white and red
As the colours on your daughter's cheek.
They call her the Lady Alicia now;
For the Prince in Salerno made a vow
That Elsie only would he wed.

Ursula. Jesu Maria! what a change!
All seems to me so weird and strange!

Forester. I saw her standing on the deck,
Beneath an awning cool and shady;
Her cap of velvet could not hold
The tresses of her hair of gold,
That flowed and floated like the stream,
And fell in masses down her neck.
As fair and lovely did she seem
As in a story or a dream
Some beautiful and foreign lady.
And the Prince looked so grand and proud,
And waved his hand thus to the crowd
That gazed and shouted from the shore,
All down the river, long and loud.

Ursula. We shall behold our child once more;
She is not dead! She is not dead!
God, listening, must have overheard
The prayers, that, without sound or word,
Our hearts in secrecy have said!
O, bring me to her; for mine eyes
Are hungry to behold her face;

My very soul within me cries;
My very hands seem to caress her,
To see her, gaze at her, and bless
    her;
Dear Elsie, child of God and grace!
    (*Goes out toward the garden.*)

Forester. There goes the good
    woman out of her head;
And Gottlieb's supper is waiting
    here;
A very capacious flagon of beer,
And a very portentous loaf of
    bread.
One would say his grief did not
    much oppress him.
Here's to the health of the Prince,
    God bless him!
                (*He drinks.*)
Ha! it buzzes and stings like a
    hornet!
And what a scene there, through
    the door!
The forest behind and the garden
    before,
And midway an old man of three-
    score,
With a wife and children that
    caress him.
Let me try still further to cheer
    and adorn it
With a merry, echoing blast of my
    cornet!
        (*Goes out blowing his horn.*)

THE CASTLE OF VAUTSBERG
        ON THE RHINE

PRINCE HENRY *and* ELSIE *standing
    on the terrace at evening. The
    sound of bells heard from a
    distance.*

Prince Henry. We are alone.
    The wedding guests
Ride down the hill, with plumes
    and cloaks,
And the descending dark invests
The Niederwald, and all the nests
Among its hoar and haunted oaks.
    Elsie. What bells are those, that
        ring so slow,
So mellow, musical, and low?
    Prince Henry. They are the
        bells of Geisenheim,
That with their melancholy chime
Ring out the curfew of the sun.
    Elsie. Listen, beloved.
    Prince Henry.   They are done!
Dear Elsie! many years ago
Those same soft bells at eventide
Rang in the ears of Charlemagne,
As, seated by Fastrada's side
At Ingelheim, in all his pride
He heard their sound with secret
    pain.
    Elsie. Their voices only speak
        to me
Of peace and deep tranquillity,
And endless confidence in thee!
    Prince Henry. Thou knowest
        the story of her ring,
How, when the court went back
    to Aix,
Fastrada died; and how the king
Sat watching by her night and day,
Till into one of the blue lakes,
Which water that delicious land,
They cast the ring, drawn from
    her hand;
And the great monarch sat serene
And sad beside the fated shore,
Nor left the land for evermore.
    Elsie. That was true love.
    Prince Henry. For him the
        queen
Ne'er did what thou hast done for
    me.
    Elsie. Wilt thou as fond and
        faithful be?
Wilt thou so love me after death?
    Prince Henry. In life's delight,
        in death's dismay,
In storm and sunshine, night and
    day,
In health, in sickness, in decay,
Here and hereafter, I am thine!

Thou hast Fastrada's ring. Beneath
The calm, blue waters of thine eyes,
Deep in thy steadfast soul it lies,
And, undisturbed by this world's breath,
With magic light its jewels shine!
This golden ring, which thou hast worn
Upon thy finger since the morn,
Is but a symbol and a semblance,
An outward fashion, a remembrance,
Of what thou wearest within unseen,
O my Fastrada, O my queen!
Behold! the hill-tops all aglow
With purple and with amethyst;
While the whole valley deep below
Is filled, and seems to overflow,
With a fast-rising tide of mist.
The evening air grows damp and chill;
Let us go in.
 Elsie.   Ah, not so soon.
See yonder fire! It is the moon
Slow rising o'er the eastern hill.
It glimmers on the forest tips,
And through the dewy foliage drips
In little rivulets of light,
And makes the heart in love with night.
 Prince Henry. Oft on this terrace, when the day
Was closing, have I stood and gazed,
And seen the landscape fade away,
And the white vapours rise and drown
Hamlet and vineyard, tower and town,
While far above the hill-tops blazed.
But then another hand than thine
Was gently held and clasped in mine;

Another head upon my breast
Was laid, as thine is now, at rest.
Why dost thou lift those tender eyes
With so much sorrow and surprise?
A minstrel's, not a maiden's hand,
Was that which in my own was pressed.
A manly form usurped thy place,
A beautiful, but bearded face,
That now is in the Holy Land,
Yet in my memory from afar
Is shining on us like a star.
But linger not. For while I speak,
A sheeted spectre white and tall,
The cold mist climbs the castle wall,
And lays his hand upon thy cheek.
      (They go in.)

EPILOGUE

THE TWO RECORDING ANGELS ASCENDING

The Angel of Good Deeds, with closed book. God sent his messenger the rain,
And said unto the mountain brook,
" Rise up, and from thy caverns look
And leap, with naked, snow-white feet,
From the cool hills into the heat
Of the broad, arid plain."

God sent his messenger of faith,
And whispered in the maiden's heart,
" Rise up, and look from where thou art,
And scatter with unselfish hands
Thy freshness on the barren sands
And solitudes of Death."

O beauty of holiness,
Of self-forgetfulness, of lowliness!
O power of meekness,

Whose very gentleness and weakness
Are like the yielding, but irresistible air!
Upon the pages
Of the sealed volume that I bear,
The deed divine
Is written in characters of gold,
That never shall grow old,
But through all ages
Burn and shine,
With soft effulgence!
O God! it is thy indulgence
That fills the world with the bliss
Of a good deed like this!

*The Angel of Evil Deeds, with
open book.* Not yet, not yet
Is the red sun wholly set,
But evermore recedes,
While open still I bear
The Book of Evil Deeds,
To let the breathings of the upper air
Visit its pages and erase
The records from its face!
Fainter and fainter as I gaze
In the broad blaze
The glimmering landscape shines,
And below me the black river
Is hidden by wreaths of vapour!
Fainter and fainter the black lines
Begin to quiver
Along the whitening surface of the paper;
Shade after shade
The terrible words grow faint and fade,
And in their place
Runs a white space!

Down goes the sun!
But the soul of one,
Who by repentance
Hath escaped the dreadful sentence,
Shines bright below me as I look.
It is the end!
With closed Book
To God do I ascend.

Lo! over the mountain steeps
A dark, gigantic shadow sweeps
Beneath my feet;
A blackness inwardly brightening
With sullen heat,
As a storm-cloud lurid with lightning.
And a cry of lamentation,
Repeated and again repeated,
Deep and loud
As the reverberation
Of cloud answering unto cloud,
Swells and rolls away in the distance,
As if the sheeted
Lightning retreated,
Baffled and thwarted by the wind's resistance.

It is Lucifer,
The son of mystery;
And since God suffers him to be,
He, too, is God's minister,
And labours for some good
By us not understood!

THE COURTSHIP OF MILES STANDISH

I.

MILES STANDISH

In the Old Colony days, in Plymouth the land of the Pilgrims,
To and fro in a room of his simple and primitive dwelling,
Clad in doublet and hose, and boots of Cordovan leather,
Strode, with a martial air, Miles Standish the Puritan Captain.
Buried in thought he seemed, with his hands behind him, and pausing
Ever and anon to behold his glittering weapons of warfare,
Hanging in shining array along the walls of the chamber,—
Cutlass and corselet of steel, and his trusty sword of Damascus,
Curved at the point and inscribed with its mystical Arabic sentence,
While underneath, in a corner, were fowling-piece, musket, and match-
lock.
Short of stature he was, but strongly built and athletic,
Broad in the shoulders, deep-chested, with muscles and sinews of iron;
Brown as a nut was his face, but his russet beard was already
Flaked with patches of snow, as hedges sometimes in November.
Near him was seated John Alden, his friend, and household companion,
Writing with diligent speed at a table of pine by the window;
Fair-haired, azure-eyed, with delicate Saxon complexion,
Having the dew of his youth, and the beauty thereof, as the captives
Whom Saint Gregory saw, and exclaimed, "Not Angles but Angels."
Youngest of all was he of the men who came in the May Flower.

Suddenly breaking the silence, the diligent scribe interrupting,
Spake, in the pride of his heart, Miles Standish the Captain of Plymouth.
"Look at these arms," he said, "the warlike weapons that hang here
Burnished and bright and clean, as if for parade or inspection!
This is the sword of Damascus I fought with in Flanders; this breast-
plate,
Well I remember the day! once saved my life in a skirmish;
Here in front you can see the very dint of the bullet
Fired point-blank at my heart by a Spanish arcabucero.
Had it not been of sheer steel, the forgotten bones of Miles Standish
Would at this moment be mould, in their grave in the Flemish
morasses."
Thereupon answered John Alden, but looked not up from his writing:
"Truly the breath of the Lord hath slackened the speed of the bullet;

158

He in his mercy preserved you, to be our shield and our weapon!
Still the Captain continued, unheeding the words of the stripling:
" See, how bright they are burnished, as if in an arsenal hanging;
That is because I have done it myself, and not left it to others.
Serve yourself, would you be well served, is an excellent adage;
So I take care of my arms, as you of your pens and your inkhorn.
Then, too, there are my soldiers, my great, invincible army,
Twelve men, all equipped, having each his rest and his matchlock,
Eighteen shillings a month, together with diet and pillage,
And, like Cæsar, I know the name of each of my soldiers! "
This he said with a smile, that danced in his eyes, as the sunbeams
Dance on the waves of the sea, and vanish again in a moment.
Alden laughed as he wrote, and still the Captain continued:
" Look! you can see from this window my brazen howitzer planted
High on the roof of the church, a preacher who speaks to the purpose,
Steady, straight-forward, and strong, with irresistible logic,
Orthodox, flashing conviction right into the hearts of the heathen.
Now we are ready, I think, for any assault of the Indians;
Let them come, if they like, and the sooner they try it the better,—
Let them come if they like, be it sagamore, sachem, or pow-wow,
Aspinet, Samoset, Corbitant, Squanto, or Tokamahamon! "

Long at the window he stood, and wistfully gazed on the landscape,
Washed with a cold gray mist, the vapoury breath of the east wind,
Forest and meadow and hill, and the steel-blue rim of the ocean,
Lying silent and sad, in the afternoon shadows and sunshine.
Over his countenance flitted a shadow like those on the landscape,
Gloom intermingled with light; and his voice was subdued with emotion,
Tenderness, pity, regret, as after a pause he proceeded:
" Yonder there, on the hill by the sea, lies buried Rose Standish;
Beautiful rose of love, that bloomed for me by the wayside!
She was the first to die of all who came in the May Flower!
Green above her is growing the field of wheat we have sown there,
Better to hide from the Indian scouts the graves of our people,
Lest they should count them and see how many already have perished! "
Sadly his face he averted, and strode up and down, and was thoughtful.

Fixed to the opposite wall was a shelf of books, and among them
Prominent three, distinguished alike for bulk and for binding;
Bariffe's Artillery Guide, and the Commentaries of Cæsar,
Out of the Latin translated by Arthur Goldinge of London,
And, as if guarded by these, between them was standing the Bible.
Musing a moment before them, Miles Standish paused, as if doubtful
Which of the three he should choose for his consolation and comfort,
Whether the wars of the Hebrews, the famous campaigns of the
    Romans,
Or the Artillery practice, designed for belligerent Christians.
Finally down from its shelf he dragged the ponderous Roman,
Seated himself at the window, and opened the book, and in silence

Turned o'er the well-worn leaves, where thumb-marks thick on the margin,
Like the trample of feet, proclaimed the battle was hottest.
Nothing was heard in the room but the hurrying pen of the stripling,
Busily writing epistles important, to go by the May Flower,
Ready to sail on the morrow, or next day at latest, God willing!
Homeward bound with the tidings of all that terrible winter,
Letters written by Alden, and full of the name of Priscilla.
Full of the name and the fame of the Puritan maiden Priscilla!

II.

LOVE AND FRIENDSHIP

Nothing was heard in the room but the hurrying pen of the stripling,
Or an occasional sigh from the labouring heart of the Captain,
Reading the marvellous words and achievements of Julius Cæsar.
After a while he exclaimed, as he smote with his hand, palm downwards,
Heavily on the page: " A wonderful man was this Cæsar!
You are a writer, and I am a fighter, but here is a fellow
Who could both write and fight, and in both was equally skilful! "
Straightway answered and spake John Alden, the comely, the youthful:
" Yes, he was equally skilled, as you say, with his pen and his weapons.
Somewhere have I read, but where I forget, he could dictate
Seven letters at once, at the same time writing his memoirs."
" Truly," continued the Captain, not heeding or hearing the other,
" Truly a wonderful man was Caius Julius Cæsar!
Better be first, he said, in a little Iberian village,
Than be second in Rome, and I think he was right when he said it.
Twice was he married before he was twenty, and many times after;
Battles five hundred he fought, and a thousand cities he conquered;
He, too, fought in Flanders, as he himself has recorded;
Finally he was stabbed by his friend, the orator Brutus!
Now, do you know what he did on a certain occasion in Flanders,
When the rear-guard of his army retreated, the front giving way too,
And the immortal Twelfth Legion was crowded so closely together
There was no room for their swords? Why, he seized a shield from a soldier,
Put himself straight at the head of his troops, and commanded the captains,
Calling on each by his name, to order forward the ensigns;
Then to widen the ranks, and give more room for their weapons;
So he won the day, the battle of something-or-other.
That's what I always say; if you wish a thing to be well done,
You must do it yourself, you must not leave it to others! "

All was silent again; the Captain continued his reading.
Nothing was heard in the room but the hurrying pen of the stripling
Writing epistles important to go next day by the May Flower,

Filled with the name and the fame of the Puritan maiden Priscilla;
Every sentence began or closed with the name of Priscilla,
Till the treacherous pen, to which he confided the secret,
Strove to betray it by singing and shouting the name of Priscilla!
Finally closing his book, with a bang of the ponderous cover,
Sudden and loud as the sound of a soldier grounding his musket.
Thus to the young man spake Miles Standish the Captain of Plymouth:
" When you have finished your work, I have something important to
    tell you.
Be not however in haste; I can wait; I shall not be impatient! "
Straightway Alden replied, as he folded the last of his letters,
Pushing his papers aside, and giving respectful attention:
" Speak; for whenever you speak, I am always ready to listen,
Always ready to hear whatever pertains to Miles Standish."
Thereupon answered the Captain, embarrassed, and culling his phrases:
" 'Tis not good for a man to be alone, say the Scriptures.
This I have said before, and again and again I repeat it;
Every hour in the day, I think it, and feel it, and say it.
Since Rose Standish died, my life has been weary and dreary;
Sick at heart have I been, beyond the healing of friendship.
Oft in my lonely hours have I thought of the maiden Priscilla.
She is alone in the world; her father and mother and brother
Died in the winter together; I saw her going and coming,
Now to the grave of the dead, and now to the bed of the dying,
Patient, courageous, and strong, and said to myself, that if ever
There were angels on earth, as there are angels in heaven,
Two have I seen and known: and the angel whose name is Priscilla
Holds in my desolate life the place which the other abandoned.
Long have I cherished the thought, but never have dared to reveal it,
Being a coward in this, though valiant enough for the most part.
Go to the damsel Priscilla, the loveliest maiden of Plymouth,
Say that a blunt old Captain, a man not of words but of actions,
Offers his hand and his heart, the hand and heart of a solider.
Not in these words, you know, but this in short is my meaning;
I am a maker of war, and not a maker of phrases.
You, who are bred as a scholar, can say it in elegant language,
Such as you read in your books of the pleadings and wooings of lovers,
Such as you think best adapted to win the heart of a maiden."

When he had spoken, John Alden, the fairhaired, taciturn stripling,
All aghast at his words, surprised, embarrassed, bewildered,
Trying to mask his dismay by treating the subject with lightness,
Trying to smile, and yet feeling his heart stand still in his bosom,
Just as a timepiece stops in a house that is stricken by lightning,
Thus made answer and spake, or rather stammered than answered:
" Such a message as that, I am sure I should mangle and mar it;
If you would have it well done,—I am only repeating your maxim,—
You must do it yourself, you must not leave it to others! "
But with the air of a man whom nothing can turn from his purpose,

Gravely shaking his head, made answer the Captain of Plymouth
" Truly the maxim is good, and I do not mean to gainsay it;
But we must use it discreetly, and not waste powder for nothing.
Now, as I said before, I was never a maker of phrases.
I can march up to a fortress and summon the place to surrender,
But march up to a woman with such a proposal, I dare not.
I'm not afraid of bullets, nor shot from the mouth of a cannon,
But of a thundering " No! " point-blank from the mouth of a woman,
That I confess I'm afraid of, nor am I ashamed to confess it!
So you must grant my request, for you are an elegant scholar,
Having the graces of speech, and skill in the turning of phrases."
Taking the hand of his friend, who still was reluctant and doubtful,
Holding it long in his own, and pressing it kindly, he added:
" Though I have spoken thus lightly, yet deep is the feeling that
        prompts me;
Surely you cannot refuse what I ask in the name of our friendship! "
Then made answer John Alden: " The name of friendship is sacred;
What you demand in that name, I have not the power to deny you! "
So the strong will prevailed, subduing and moulding the gentler,
Friendship prevailed over love, and Alden went on his errand.

III.

THE LOVER'S ERRAND

So the strong will prevailed, and Alden went on his errand,
Out of the street of the village, and into the paths of the forest,
Into the tranquil woods, where blue-birds and robins were building
Towns in the populous trees, with hanging gardens of verdure,
Peaceful, aerial cities of joy and affection and freedom.
All around him was calm, but within him commotion and conflict,
Love contending with friendship, and self with each generous impulse
To and fro in his breast his thoughts were heaving and dashing,
As in a foundering ship, with every roll of the vessel,
Washes the bitter sea, the merciless surge of the ocean!
" Must I relinquish it all," he cried with a wild lamentation,
" Must I relinquish it all, the joy, the hope, the illusion?
Was it for this I have loved, and waited, and worshipped in silence?
Was it for this I have followed the flying feet and the shadow
Over the wintry sea, to the desolate shores of New England?
Truly the heart is deceitful, and out of its depths of corruption
Rise, like an exhalation, the misty phantoms of passion;
Angels of light they seem, but are only delusions of Satan.
All is clear to me now; I feel it, I see it distinctly!
This is the hand of the Lord; it is laid upon me in anger,
For I have followed too much the heart's desires and devices,
Worshipping Astaroth blindly, and impious idols of Baal.
This is the cross I must bear; the sin and the swift retribution."

So through the Plymouth woods John Alden went on his errand;
Crossing the brook at the ford, where it brawled over pebble and
    shallow,
Gathering still, as he went, the May-flowers blooming around him,
Fragrant, filling the air with a strange and wonderful sweetness,
Children lost in the woods, and covered with leaves in their slumber.
" Puritan flowers," he said, " and the type of Puritan maidens,
Modest and simple and sweet, the very type of Priscilla!
So I will take them to her; to Priscilla the May-flower of Plymouth,
Modest and simple and sweet, as a parting gift will I take them;
Breathing their silent farewells, as they fade and wither and perish,
Soon to be thrown away as is the heart of the giver."
So through the Plymouth woods John Alden went on his errand;
Came to an open space, and saw the disk of the ocean,
Sailless, sombre and cold with the comfortless breath of the east wind;
Saw the new-built house, and people at work in a meadow;
Heard, as he drew near the door, the musical voice of Priscilla
Singing the hundreth Psalm, the grand old Puritan anthem,
Music that Luther sang to the sacred words of the Psalmist,
Full of the breath of the Lord, consoling and comforting many.
Then, as he opened the door, he beheld the form of the maiden
Seated beside her wheel, and the carded wool like a snow-drift
Piled at her knee, her white hands feeding the ravenous spindle,
While with her foot on the treadle she guided the wheel in its motion.
Open wide on her lap lay the well-worn psalm-book of Ainsworth,
Printed in Amsterdam, the words and the music together,
Rough-hewn, angular notes, like stones in the wall of a churchyard,
Darkened and overhung by the running vine of the verses.
Such was the book from whose pages she sang the old Puritan anthem,
She, the Puritan girl, in the solitude of the forest,
Making the humble house and the modest apparel of home-spun
Beautiful with her beauty, and rich with the wealth of her being!
Over him rushed, like a wind that is keen and cold and relentless,
Thoughts of what might have been, and the weight and woe of his
    errand;
All the dreams that had faded, and all the hopes that had vanished,
All his life henceforth a dreary and tenantless mansion,
Haunted by vain regrets, and pallid, sorrowful faces.
Still he said to himself, and almost fiercely he said it,
" Let not him that putteth his hand to the plough look backwards;
Though the ploughshare cut through the flowers of life to its fountains,
Though it pass o'er the graves of the dead and the hearths of the living,
It is the will of the Lord; and his mercy endureth for ever! "

So he entered the house: and the hum of the wheel and the singing
Suddenly ceased; for Priscilla, aroused by his step on the threshold,
Rose as he entered, and gave him her hand, in signal of welcome,
Saying," I knew it was you, when I heard your step in the passage;
For I was thinking of you, as I sat there singing and spinning."

Awkward and dumb with delight, that a thought of him had been
    mingled
Thus in the sacred psalm, that came from the heart of the maiden,
Silent before her he stood, and gave her the flowers for an answer,
Finding no words for his thought. He remembered that day in the
    winter,
After the first great snow, when he broke a path from the village,
Reeling and plunging along through the drifts that encumbered the
    doorway,
Stamping the snow from his feet as he entered the house, and Priscilla
Laughed at his snowy locks, and gave him a seat by the fireside,
Grateful and pleased to know he had thought of her in the snow-storm.
Had he but spoken then! perhaps not in vain had he spoken;
Now it was all too late; the golden moment had vanished!
So he stood there abashed, and gave her the flowers for an answer.

Then they sat down and talked of the birds and the beautiful Spring-
    time,
Talked of their friends at home, and the May Flower that sailed on
    the morrow.
" I have been thinking all day," said gently the Puritan maiden,
" Dreaming all night, and thinking all day, of the hedgerows of
    England,—
They are in blossom now, and the country is all like a garden;
Thinking of lanes and fields, and the song of the lark and the linnet,
Seeing the village street, and familiar faces of neighbours
Going about as of old, and stopping to gossip together,
And, at the end of the street, the village church, with the ivy
Climbing the old gray tower, and the quiet graves in the churchyard.
Kind are the people I live with, and dear to me my religion;
Still my heart is so sad, that I wish myself back in Old England.
You will say it is wrong, but I cannot help it: I almost
Wish myself back in Old England, I feel so lonely and wretched."

Thereupon answered the youth:—" Indeed I do not condemn you;
Stouter hearts than a woman's have quailed in this terrible winter.
Yours is tender and trusting, and needs a stronger to lean on;
So I have come to you now, with an offer and proffer of marriage
Made by a good man and true, Miles Standish the Captain of
    Plymouth! "

Thus he delivered his message, the dexterous writer of letters,—
Did not embellish the theme, nor array it in beautiful phrases,
But came straight to the point, and blurted it out like a schoolboy;
Even the Captain himself could hardly have said it more bluntly.
Mute with amazement and sorrow, Priscilla the Puritan maiden
Looked into Alden's face, her eyes dilated with wonder,
Feeling his words like a blow, that stunned her and rendered her
    speechless;

Till at length she exclaimed, interrupting the ominous silence:
" If the great Captain of Plymouth is so very eager to wed me,
Why does he not come himself, and take the trouble to woo me?
If I am not worth the wooing, I surely am not worth the winning! "
Then John Alden began explaining and smoothing the matter,
Making it worse as he went, by saying the Captain was busy,—
Had no time for such things;—such things! the words grating harshly
Fell on the ear of Priscilla; and swift as a flash she made answer:
" Has he no time for such things, as you call it, before he is married,
Would he be likely to find it, or make it, after the wedding?
That is the way with you men; you don't understand us, you cannot.
When you have made up your minds, after thinking of this one and
    that one,
Choosing, selecting, rejecting, comparing one with another,
Then you make known your desire, with abrupt and sudden avowal,
And are offended and hurt, and indignant perhaps, that a woman
Does not respond at once to a love that she never suspected,
Does not attain at a bound the height to which you have been climbing.
This is not right nor just: for surely a woman's affection
Is not a thing to be asked for, and had for only the asking.
When one is truly in love, one not only says it, but shows it.
Had he but waited awhile, had he only showed that he loved me,
Even this Captain of yours—who knows?—at last might have won me,
Old and rough as he is; but now it never can happen."

    Still John Alden went on, unheeding the words of Priscilla,
Urging the suit of his friend, explaining, persuading, expanding;
Spoke of his courage and skill, and of all his battles in Flanders,
How with the people of God he had chosen to suffer affliction,
How, in return for his zeal, they had made him Captain of Plymouth;
He was a gentleman born, could trace his pedigree plainly
Back to Hugh Standish of Duxbury Hall, in Lancashire, England,
Who was the son of Ralph, and the grandson of Thurston de Standish;
Heir unto vast estates, of which he was basely defrauded.
Still bore the family arms, and had for his crest a cock argent
Combed and wattled gules, and all the rest of the blazon.
He was a man of honour, of noble and generous nature;
Though he was rough, he was kindly; she knew how during the winter
He had attended the sick, with a hand as gentle as woman's;
Somewhat hasty and hot, he could not deny it, and headstrong,
Stern as a soldier might be, but hearty, and placable always,
Not to be laughed at and scorned, because he was little of stature;
For he was great of heart, magnanimous, courtly, courageous;
Any woman in Plymouth, nay, any woman in England,
Might be happy and proud to be called the wife of Miles Standish!

    But as he warmed and glowed, in his simple and eloquent language,
Quite forgetful of self, and full of the praise of his rival,
Archly the maiden smiled, and, with eyes overrunning with laughter,
Said, in a tremulous voice, " Why don't you speak for yourself, John? "

IV.

JOHN ALDEN

Into the open air John Alden, perplexed and bewildered,
Rushed like a man insane, and wandered alone by the seaside;
Paced up and down the sands, and bared his head to the east wind,
Cooling his heated brow, and the fire and fever within him.
Slowly as out of the heavens, with apocalyptical splendours,
Sank the City of God, in the vision of John the Apostle,
So, with its cloudy walls of chrysolite, jasper, and sapphire,
Sank the broad red sun, and over its turrets uplifted
Glimmered the golden reed of the angel who measured the city.

"Welcome, O wind of the East!" he exclaimed in his wild exulta-
    tion,
"Welcome, O wind of the East, from the caves of the misty Atlantic!
Blowing o'er fields of dulse, and measureless meadows of sea-grass,
Blowing o'er rocky wastes, and the grottos and gardens of ocean!
Lay thy cold, moist hand on my burning forehead, and wrap me
Close in thy garments of mist, to allay the fever within me!"

Like an awakened conscience, the sea was moaning and tossing,
Beating remorseful and loud the mutable sands of the sea-shore.
Fierce in his soul was the struggle and tumult of passions contending;
Love triumphant and crowned, and friendship wounded and bleeding,
Passionate cries of desire, and importunate pleadings of duty!
"Is it my fault," he said, "that the maiden has chosen between us?
Is it my fault that he failed,—my fault that I am the victor?"
Then within him there thundered a voice, like the voice of the Prophet:
"It hath displeased the Lord!"—and he thought of David's trans-
    gression,
Bathsheba's beautiful face, and his friend in the front of the battle!
Shame and confusion of guilt, and abasement and self-condemnation,
Overwhelmed him at once; and he cried in the deepest contrition:
"It hath displeased the Lord!   It is the temptation of Satan!"

Then, uplifting his head, he looked at the sea, and beheld there
Dimly the shadowy form of the May Flower riding at anchor,
Rocked on the rising tide, and ready to sail on the morrow;
Heard the voices of men through the mist, the rattle of cordage
Thrown on the deck, the shouts of the mate, and the sailors' "Ay, ay,
    Sir!"
Clear and distinct, but not loud, in the dripping air of the twilight.
Still for a moment he stood, and listened, and stared at the vessel,
Then went hurriedly on, as one who, seeing a phantom,
Stops, then quickens his pace, and follows the beckoning shadow.

" Yes, it is plain to me now," he murmured; " the hand of the Lord is
Leading me out of the land of darkness, the bondage of error.
Through the sea, that shall lift the walls of its waters around me,
Hiding me, cutting me off, from the cruel thoughts that pursue me.
Back will I go o'er the ocean, this dreary land will abandon,
Her whom I may not love, and him whom my heart has offended.
Better to be in my grave in the green old churchyard in England,
Close by my mother's side, and among the dust of my kindred;
Better be dead and forgotten, than living in shame and dishonour!
Sacred and safe and unseen, in the dark of the narrow chamber
With me my secret shall lie, like a buried jewel that glimmers
Bright on the hand that is dust, in the chambers of silence and dark-
     ness,—
Yes, as the marriage ring of the great espousal hereafter! "

    Thus as he spake, he turned, in the strength of his strong resolution,
Leaving behind him the shore, and hurried along in the twilight,
Through the congenial gloom of the forest silent and sombre,
Till he beheld the lights in the seven houses of Plymouth,
Shining like seven stars in the dusk and mist of the evening.
Soon he entered his door, and found the redoubtable Captain
Sitting alone, and absorbed in the martial pages of Cæsar,
Fighting some great campaign in Hainault or Brabant or Flanders.
" Long have you been on your errand," he said with a cheery de-
     meanour,
Even as one who is waiting an answer, and fears not the issue.
" Nor far off is the house, although the woods are between us;
But you have lingered so long, that while you were going and coming
I have fought ten battles and sacked and demolished a city.
Come, sit down, and in order relate to me all that has happened."

    Then John Alden spake, and related the wondrous adventure,
From beginning to end, minutely, just as it happened;
How he had seen Priscilla, and how he had sped in his courtship,
Only smoothing a little, and softening down her refusal.
But when he came at length to the words Priscilla had spoken,
Words so tender and cruel: " Why don't you speak for yourself,
     John? "
Up leaped the Captain of Plymouth, and stamped on the floor, till his
     armour
Clanged on the wall, where it hung, with a sound of sinister omen.
All his pent-up wrath burst forth in a sudden explosion,
Even as a hand-grenade, that scatters destruction around it.
Wildly he shouted, and loud: " John Alden! you have betrayed me!
Me, Miles Standish, your friend! have supplanted, defrauded, be-
     trayed me!
One of my ancestors ran his sword through the heart of Wat Tyler;
Who shall prevent me from running my own through the heart of a
     traitor?

Yours is the greater treason, for yours is a treason to friendship!
You, who lived under my roof, whom I cherished and loved as a
    brother;
You, who have fed at my board, and drunk at my cup, to whose
    keeping
I have intrusted my honour, my thoughts the most sacred and secret,—
You, too, Brutus! ah woe to the name of friendship hereafter!
Brutus was Cæsar's friend, and you were mine, but henceforward
Let there be nothing between us save war, and implacable hatred!"

So spake the Captain of Plymouth, and strode about in the chamber,
Chafing and choking with rage; like cords were the veins on his temples.
But in the midst of his anger a man appeared at the doorway,
Bringing in uttermost haste a message of urgent importance,
Rumours of danger and war and hostile incursions of Indians!
Straightway the Captain paused, and, without further question or
    parley,
Took from the nail on the wall his sword with its scabbard of iron,
Buckled the belt round his waist, and, frowning fiercely, departed.
Alden was left alone.   He heard the clank of the scabbard
Growing fainter and fainter, and dying away in the distance.
Then he arose from his seat, and looked forth into the darkness,
Felt the cool air blow on his cheek, that was hot with the insult,
Lifted his eyes to the heavens, and, folding his hands as in childhood,
Prayed in the silence of night to the Father who seeth in secret.

Meanwhile the choleric Captain strode wrathful away to the council,
Found it already assembled, impatiently waiting his coming;
Men in the middle of life, austere and grave in deportment,
Only one of them old, the hill that was nearest to heaven,
Covered with snow, but erect, the excellent Elder of Plymouth.
God had sifted three kingdoms to find the wheat for this planting,
Then had sifted the wheat, as the living seed of a nation;
So say the chronicles old, and such is the faith of the people!
Near them was standing an Indian, in attitude stern and defiant,
Naked down to the waist, and grim and ferocious in aspect;
While on the table before them was lying unopened a Bible,
Ponderous, bound in leather, brass-studded, printed in Holland,
And beside it outstretched the skin of a rattlesnake glittered,
Filled, like a quiver, with arrows; a signal and challenge of warfare,
Brought by the Indian, and speaking with arrowy tongues of defiance.
This Miles Standish beheld, as he entered, and heard them debating
What were an answer befitting the hostile message and menace,
Talking of this and of that, contriving, suggesting, objecting;
One voice only for peace, and that the voice of the Elder,
Judging it wise and well that some at least were converted,
Rather than any were slain, for this was but Christian behaviour!
Then outspake Miles Standish, the stalwart Captain of Plymouth,
Muttering deep in his throat, for his voice was husky with anger,

"What! do you mean to make war with milk and the water of roses?
Is it to shoot red squirrels you have your howitzer planted
There on the roof of the church, or is it to shoot red devils?
Truly the only tongue that is understood by a savage
Must be the tongue of fire that speaks from the mouth of the cannon!"
Thereupon answered and said the excellent Elder of Plymouth,
Somewhat amazed and alarmed at this irreverent language:
"Not so thought Saint Paul, nor yet the other Apostles;
Not from the cannon's mouth were the tongues of fire they spake with!"
But unheeded fell this mild rebuke on the Captain,
Who had advanced to the table, and thus continued discoursing:
"Leave this matter to me, for to me by right it pertaineth.
War is a terrible trade; but in the cause that is righteous,
Sweet is the smell of powder; and thus I answer the challenge!"

Then from the rattlesnake's skin, with a sudden, contemptuous gesture,
Jerking the Indian arrows, he filled it with powder and bullets
Full to the very jaws, and handed it back to the savage,
Saying, in thundering tones: "Here, take it! this is your answer!"
Silently out of the room then glided the glistening savage,
Bearing the serpent's skin, and seeming himself like a serpent,
Winding his sinuous way in the dark to the depths of the forest.

V.

THE SAILING OF THE MAY FLOWER

Just in the gray of the dawn, as the mists up-rose from the meadows,
There was a stir and a sound in the slumbering village of Plymouth;
Clanging and clicking of arms, and the order imperative, "Forward!"
Given in tone suppressed, a tramp of feet, and then silence.
Figures ten, in the mist, marched slowly out of the village.
Standish the stalwart it was, with eight of his valorous army,
Led by their Indian guide, by Hobomok, friend of the white men,
Northward marching to quell the sudden revolt of the savage.
Giants they seemed in the mist, or the mighty men of King David;
Giants in heart they were, who believed in God and the Bible,—
Ay, who believed in the smiting of Midianites and Philistines.
Over them gleamed far off the crimson banners of morning;
Under them loud on the sands, the serried billows, advancing,
Fired along the line, and in regular order retreated.

Many a mile had they marched, when at length the village of Plymouth
Woke from its sleep, and arose, intent on its manifold labours.
Sweet was the air and soft; and slowly the smoke from the chimneys

Rose over roofs of thatch, and pointed steadily eastward;
Men came forth from the doors, and paused and talked of the weather,
Said that the wind had changed, and was blowing fair for the May
　　Flower;
Talked of their Captain's departure, and all the dangers that menaced,
He being gone, the town, and what should be done in his absence.
Merrily sang the birds, and the tender voices of women
Consecrated with hymns the common cares of the household.
Out of the sea rose the sun, and the billows rejoiced at his coming;
Beautiful were his feet on the purple tops of the mountains;
Beautiful on the sails of the May Flower riding at anchor,
Battered and blackened and worn by all the storms of the winter.
Loosely against her masts was hanging and flapping her canvas,
Rent by so many gales, and patched by the hands of the sailors.
Suddenly from her side, as the sun rose over the ocean,
Darted a puff of smoke, and floated seaward; anon rang
Loud over field and forest the cannon's roar, and the echoes
Heard and repeated the sound, the signal-gun of departure!
Ah! but with louder echoes replied the hearts of the people!
Meekly, in voices subdued, the chapter was read from the Bible,
Meekly the prayer was begun, but ended in fervent entreaty!
Then from their houses in haste came forth the Pilgrims of Plymouth,
Men and women and children, all hurrying down to the sea-shore,
Eager, with tearful eyes, to say farewell to the May Flower,
Homeward bound o'er the sea, and leaving them here in the desert.

　　Foremost among them was Alden. All night he had lain without
　　　slumber,
Turning and tossing about in the heat and unrest of his fever.
He had beheld Miles Standish, who came back late from the council,
Stalking into the room, and heard him mutter and murmur,
Sometimes it seemed a prayer, and sometimes it sounded like swearing.
Once he had come to the bed, and stood there a moment in silence;
Then he had turned away, and said: " I will not awake him;
Let him sleep on, it is best; for what is the use of more talking! "
Then he extinguished the light, and threw himself down on his pallet,
Dressed as he was, and ready to start at the break of the morning,—
Covered himself with the cloak he had worn in his campaigns in
　　Flanders,—
Slept as a soldier sleeps in his bivouac, ready for action.
But with the dawn he arose: in the twilight Alden beheld him
Put on his corselet of steel, and all the rest of his armour,
Buckle about his waist his trusty blade of Damascus,
Take from the corner his musket, and so stride out of the chamber.
Often the heart of the youth had burned and yearned to embrace him,
Often his lips had essayed to speak, imploring for pardon;
All the old friendship came back, with its tender and grateful emotions;
But his pride overmastered the nobler nature within him,—
Pride, and the sense of his wrong, and the burning fire of the insult.

So he beheld his friend departing in anger, but spake not,
Saw him go forth to danger, perhaps to death, and he spake not!
Then he arose from his bed, and heard what the people were saying,
Joined in the talk at the door, with Stephen and Richard and Gilbert,
Joined in the morning prayer, and in the reading of Scripture,
And, with the others, in haste went hurrying down to the sea-shore,
Down to the Plymouth Rock, that had been to their feet as a door-step
Into a world unknown,—the corner-stone of a nation!

There with his boat was the Master, already a little impatient
Lest he should lose the tide, or the wind might shift to the eastward,
Square-built, hearty, and strong, with an odour of ocean about him,
Speaking with this one and that, and cramming letters and parcels
Into his pockets capacious, and messages mingled together
Into his narrow brain, till at last he was wholly bewildered.
Nearer the boat stood Alden, with one foot placed on the gunwale,
One still firm on the rock, and talking at times with the sailors,
Seated erect on the thwarts, all ready and eager for starting.
He too was eager to go, and thus put an end to his anguish,
Thinking to fly from despair, that swifter than keel is or canvas,
Thinking to drown in the sea the ghost that would rise and pursue
     him.
But as he gazed on the crowd, he beheld the form of Priscilla
Standing dejected among them, unconscious of all that was passing.
Fixed were her eyes upon his, as if she divined his intention,
Fixed with a look so sad, so reproachful, imploring, and patient,
That with a sudden revulsion his heart recoiled from its purpose,
As from the verge of a crag, where one step more is destruction.
Strange is the heart of man, with its quick, mysterious instincts!
Strange is the life of man, and fatal or fated are moments,
Whereupon turn, as on hinges, the gates of the wall adamantine!
" Here I remain! " he exclaimed, as he looked at the heavens above
     him,
Thanking the Lord whose breath had scattered the mist and the mad-
     ness,
Wherein, blind and lost, to death he was staggering headlong.
" Yonder snow-white cloud, that floats in the ether above me,
Seems like a hand that is pointing and beckoning over the ocean.
There is another hand, that is not so spectral and ghost-like,
Holding me, drawing me back, and clasping mine for protection.
Float, O hand of cloud, and vanish away in the ether!
Roll thyself up like a fist, to threaten and daunt me; I heed not
Either your warning or menace, or any omen of evil!
There is no land so sacred, no air so pure and so wholesome,
As is the air she breathes, and the soil that is pressed by her footsteps.
Here for her sake will I stay, and like an invisible presence
Hover around her for ever, protecting, supporting her weakness;
Yes! as my foot was the first that stepped on this rock at the landing,
So, with the blessing of God, shall it be the last at the leaving! "

Meanwhile the Master alert, but with dignified air and important,
Scanning with watchful eye the tide and the wind and the weather,
Walked about on the sands; and the people crowded around him
Saying a few last words, and enforcing his careful remembrance.
Then, taking each by the hand, as if he were grasping a tiller,
Into the boat he sprang, and in haste shoved off to his vessel,
Glad in his heart to get rid of all this worry and flurry,
Glad to be gone from a land of sand and sickness and sorrow,
Short allowance of victual, and plenty of nothing but Gospel!
Lost in the sound of the oars was the last farewell of the Pilgrims.
O strong hearts and true! not one went back in the May Flower!
No, not one looked back, who had set his hand to this ploughing!

Soon were heard on board the shouts and songs of the sailors
Heaving the windlass round, and hoisting the ponderous anchor.
Then the yards were braced, and all sails set to the west-wind,
Blowing steady and strong; and the May Flower sailed from the
    harbour,
Rounded the point of the Gurnet, and leaving far to the southward
Island and cape of sand, and the Field of the First Encounter,
Took the wind on her quarter, and stood for the open Atlantic,
Borne on the send of the sea, and the swelling hearts of the Pilgrims.

Long in silence they watched the receding sail of the vessel,
Much endeared to them all, as something living and human;
Then, as if filled with the spirit, and wrapt in a vision prophetic,
Baring his hoary head, the excellent Elder of Plymouth,
Said, " Let us pray! " and they prayed, and thanked the Lord and
    took courage.
Mournfully sobbed the waves at the base of the rock, and above them
Bowed and whispered the wheat on the hill of death, and their kindred
Seemed to awake in their graves, and to join in the prayer that they
    uttered.
Sun-illumined and white, on the eastern verge of the ocean
Gleamed the departing sail, like a marble slab in a graveyard;
Buried beneath it lay for ever all hope of escaping.
Lo! as they turned to depart, they saw the form of an Indian,
Watching them from the hill; but while they spake with each other,
Pointing with outstretched hands, and saying, " Look! " he had
    vanished.
So they returned to their homes; but Alden lingered a little,
Musing alone on the shore, and watching the wash of the billows
Round the base of the rock, and the sparkle and flash of the sunshine,
Like the spirit of God, moving visibly over the waters.

VI.

PRISCILLA

THUS for a while he stood, and mused by the shore of the ocean
Thinking of many things, and most of all of Priscilla;
And as if thought had the power to draw to itself, like the loadstone,
Whatsoever it touches, by subtile laws of its nature,
Lo! as he turned to depart, Priscilla was standing beside him.

" Are you so much offended, you will not speak to me ? " said she.
" Am I so much to blame, that yesterday, when you were pleading
Warmly the cause of another, my heart, impulsive and wayward,
Pleaded your own, and spake out, forgetful perhaps of decorum ?
Certainly you can forgive me for speaking so frankly, for saying
What I ought not to have said, yet now I can never unsay it;
For there are moments in life, when the heart is so full of emotion,
That if by chance it be shaken, or into its depths like a pebble
Drops some careless word, it overflows, and its secret,
Spilt on the ground like water, can never be gathered together.
Yesterday I was shocked, when I heard you speak of Miles Standish
Praising his virtues, transforming his very defects into virtues,
Praising his courage and strength, and even his fighting in Flanders,
As if by fighting alone you could win the heart of a woman,
Quite overlooking yourself and the rest, in exalting your hero.
Therefore I spake as I did, by an irresistible impulse.
You will forgive me, I hope, for the sake of the friendship between us,
Which is too true and too sacred to be so easily broken! "
Thereupon answered John Alden, the scholar, the friend of Miles
          Standish:
" I was not angry with you, with myself alone I was angry,
Seeing how badly I managed the matter I had in my keeping."
" No! " interrupted the maiden, with answer prompt and decisive;
" No; you were angry with me, for speaking so frankly and freely.
It was wrong, I acknowledge; for it is the fate of a woman
Long to be patient and silent, to wait like a ghost that is speechless,
Till some questioning voice dissolves the spell of its silence.
Hence is the inner life of so many suffering women
Sunless and silent and deep, like subterranean rivers
Running through caverns of darkness, unheard, unseen, and unfruitful,
Chafing their channels of stone, with endless and profitless murmurs."
Thereupon answered John Alden, the young man, the lover of women:
" Heaven forbid it, Priscilla; and truly they seem to me always
More like the beautiful rivers that watered the garden of Eden,
More like the river Euphrates, through deserts of Havilah flowing,
Filling the land with delight, and memories sweet of the garden! "
" Ah, by these words, I can see," again interrupted the maiden,

" How very little you prize me, or care for what I am saying.
When from the depths of my heart, in pain and with secret misgiving,
Frankly I speak to you, asking for sympathy only and kindness,
Straightway you take up my words, that are plain and direct and in earnest,
Turn them away from their meaning, and answer with flattering phrases.
This is not right, is not just, is not true to the best that is in you;
For I know and esteem you, and feel that your nature is noble,
Lifting mine up to a higher, a more ethereal level.
Therefore I value your friendship, and feel it perhaps the more keenly
If you say aught that implies I am only as one among many,
If you make use of those common and complimentary phrases
Most men think so fine, in dealing and speaking with women,
But which women reject as insipid, if not as insulting."

Mute and amazed was Alden; and listened and looked at Priscilla,
Thinking he never had seen her more fair, more divine in her beauty.
He who but yesterday pleaded so glibly the cause of another,
Stood there embarrassed and silent, and seeking in vain for an answer.
So the maiden went on, and little divined or imagined
What was at work in his heart, that made him so awkward and speechless.
" Let us, then, be what we are, and speak what we think, and in all things
Keep ourselves loyal to truth, and the sacred professions of friendship.
It is no secret I tell you, nor am I ashamed to declare:
I have liked to be with you, to see you, to speak with you always.
So I was hurt at your words, and a little affronted to hear you
Urge me to marry your friend, though he were the Captain Miles Standish.
For I must tell you the truth: much more to me is your friendship
Than all the love he could give, were he twice the hero you think him."
Then she extended her hand, and Alden, who eagerly grasped it,
Felt all the wounds in his heart, that were aching and bleeding so sorely,
Healed by the touch of that hand, and he said, with a voice full of feeling:
" Yes, we must ever be friends, and of all who offer you friendship
Let me be ever the first, the truest, the nearest and dearest! "

Casting a farewell look at the glimmering sail of the May Flower,
Distant, but still in sight, and sinking below the horizon,
Homeward together they walked, with a strange, indefinite feeling,
That all the rest had departed and left them alone in the desert.
But, as they went through the fields in the blessing and smile of the sunshine,
Lighter grew their hearts, and Priscilla said very archly:
" Now that our terrible Captain has gone in pursuit of the Indians,

Where he is happier far than he would be commanding a household,
You may speak boldly, and tell me of all that happened between you,
When you returned last night, and said how ungrateful you found me."
Thereupon answered John Alden, and told her the whole of the story,—
Told her his own despair, and the direful wrath of Miles Standish.
Whereat the maiden smiled, and said between laughing and earnest,
" He is a little chimney, and heated hot in a moment! "
But as he gently rebuked her, and told her how much he had suffered,—
How he had even determined to sail that day in the May Flower,
And had remained for her sake, on hearing the dangers that threatened,—
All her manner was changed, and she said with a faltering accent,
" Truly I thank you for this: how good you have been to me always! "

Thus, as a pilgrim devout, who toward Jerusalem journeys,
Taking three steps in advance, and one reluctantly backward,
Urged by importunate zeal, and withheld by pangs of contrition;
Slowly but steadily onward, receding yet ever advancing,
Journeyed this Puritan youth to the Holy Land of his longings
Urged by the fervour of love, and withheld by remorseful misgivings.

VII.

THE MARCH OF MILES STANDISH

Meanwhile the stalwart Miles Standish was marching steadily northward
Winding through forest and swamp, and along the trend of the seashore,
All day long, with hardly a halt, the fire of his anger
Burning and crackling within, and the sulphurous odour of powder
Seeming more sweet to his nostrils than all the scents of the forest.
Silent and moody he went, and much he revolved his discomfort;
He who was used to success, and to easy victories always,
Thus to be flouted, rejected, and laughed to scorn by a maiden,
Thus to be mocked and betrayed by the friend whom most he had trusted!
Ah! 'twas too much to be borne, and he fretted and chafed in his armour!

" I alone am to blame," he muttered, " for mine was the folly.
What has a rough old soldier, grown grim and gray in the harness,
Used to the camp and its ways, to do with the wooing of maidens?
'Twas but a dream,—let it pass,—let it vanish like so many others!
What I thought was a flower, is only a weed, and is worthless;
Out of my heart will I pluck it, and throw it away, and henceforward
Be but a fighter of battles, a lover and wooer of dangers! "
Thus he revolved in his mind his sorry defeat and discomfort,

While he was marching by day or lying at night in the forest,
Looking up at the trees, and the constellations beyond them.

After a three days' march he came to an Indian encampment
Pitched on the edge of a meadow, between the sea and the forest;
Women at work by the tents, and the warriors, horrid with war-paint,
Seated about a fire, and smoking and talking together;
Who, when they saw from afar the sudden approach of the white men,
Saw the flash of the sun on breastplate and sabre and musket,
Straightway leaped to their feet, and two, from among them advancing,
Came to parley with Standish, and offer him furs as a present;
Friendship was in their looks, but in their hearts there was hatred.
Braves of the tribe were these, and brothers gigantic in stature,
Huge as Goliath of Gath, or the terrible Og, king of Bashan;
One was Pecksuot named, and the other was called Wattawamat.
Round their necks were suspended their knives in scabbards of wam-
    pum,
Two-edged, trenchant knives, with points as sharp as a needle.
Other arms had they none, for they were cunning and crafty.
"Welcome, English!" they said,—these words they had learned from
    the traders
Touching at times on the coast, to barter and chaffer for peltries.
Then in their native tongue they began to parley with Standish,
Through his guide and interpreter, Hobomok, friend of the white man,
Begging for blankets and knives, but mostly for muskets and powder,
Kept by the white man, they said, concealed, with the plague, in his
    cellars,
Ready to be let loose, and destroy his brother the red man!
But when Standish refused, and said he would give them the Bible,
Suddenly changing their tone, they began to boast and to bluster.
Then Wattawamat advanced with a stride in front of the other,
And, with a lofty demeanour, thus vauntingly spake to the Captain:
"Now Wattawamat can see, by the fiery eyes of the Captain,
Angry is he in his heart; but the heart of the brave Wattawamat
Is not afraid at the sight. He was not born of a woman,
But on a mountain, at night, from an oak-tree riven by lightning,
Forth he sprang at a bound, with all his weapons about him,
Shouting, 'Who is there here to fight with the brave Wattawamat?'"
Then he unsheathed his knife, and, whetting the blade on his left hand,
Held it aloft and displayed a woman's face on the handle,
Saying, with bitter expression and look of sinister meaning:
"I have another at home, with the face of a man on the handle;
By and by they shall marry; and there will be plenty of children!"

Then stood Pecksuot forth, self-vaunting, insulting Miles Standish:
While with his fingers he patted the knife that hung at his bosom,
Drawing it half from its sheath, and plunging it back, as he muttered,
"By and by it shall see; it shall eat; ah, ah! but shall speak not!
This is the mighty Captain the white men have sent to destroy us!
He is a little man; let him go and work with the women!"

Meanwhile Standish had noted the faces and figures of Indians
Peeping and creeping about from bush to tree in the forest,
Feigning to look for game, with arrows set on their bow-strings,
Drawing about him still closer and closer the net of their ambush.
But undaunted he stood, and dissembled and treated them smoothly;
So the old chronicles say, that were writ in the days of the fathers.
But when he heard their defiance, the boast, the taunt, and the insult,
All the hot blood of his race, of Sir Hugh and of Thurston de Standish,
Boiled and beat in his heart, and swelled in the veins of his temples.
Headlong he leaped on the boaster, and, snatching his knife from its
 scabbard,
Plunged it into his heart, and, reeling backward, the savage
Fell with his face to the sky, and a fiendlike fierceness upon it.
Straight there arose from the forest the awful sound of the war-whoop,
And, like a flurry of snow on the whistling wind of December,
Swift and sudden and keen came a flight of feathery arrows.
Then came a cloud of smoke, and out of the cloud came the lightning,
Out of the lightning thunder; and death unseen ran before it.
Frightened the savages fled for shelter in swamp and in thicket,
Hotly pursued and beset; but their sachem, the brave Wattawamat,
Fled not; he was dead. Unswerving and swift had a bullet
Passed through his brain, and he fell with both hands clutching the
 greensward,
Seeming in death to hold back from his foe the land of his fathers.

There on the flowers of the meadow the warriors lay, and above them,
Silent, with folded arms, stood Hobomok, friend of the white man.
Smiling at length he exclaimed to the stalwart Captain of Plymouth:
" Pecksuot bragged very loud, of his courage, his strength, and his
 stature,—
Mocked the great Captain, and called him a little man; but I see now
Big enough have you been to lay him speechless before you! "

Thus the first battle was fought and won by the stalwart Miles
 Standish.
When the tidings thereof were brought to the village of Plymouth,
And as a trophy of war the head of the brave Wattawamat
Scowled from the roof of the fort, which at once was a church and a
 fortress,
All who beheld it rejoiced, and praised the Lord, and took courage.
Only Priscilla averted her face from this spectre of terror,
Thanking God in her heart that she had not married Miles Standish;
Shrinking, fearing almost, lest, coming home from his battles,
He should lay claim to her hand, as the prize and reward of his valour.

VIII.

THE SPINNING-WHEEL

Month after month passed away, and in Autumn the ships of the
    merchants
Came with kindred and friends, with cattle and corn for the Pilgrims.
All in the village was peace; the men were intent on their labours,
Busy with hewing and building, with garden-plot and with merestead,
Busy with breaking the glebe, and mowing the grass in the meadows,
Searching the sea for its fish, and hunting the deer in the forest.
All in the village was peace; but at times the rumour of warfare
Filled the air with alarm, and the apprehension of danger.
Bravely the stalwart Miles Standish was scouring the land with his
    forces,
Waxing valiant in fight and defeating the alien armies,
Till his name had become a sound of fear to the nations.
Anger was still in his heart, but at times the remorse and contrition
Which in all noble natures succeed the passionate outbreak,
Came like a rising tide, that encounters the rush of a river,
Staying its current awhile, but making it bitter and brackish.

Meanwhile Alden at home had built him a new habitation,
Solid, substantial, of timber rough-hewn from the firs of the forest.
Wooden-barred was the door, and the roof was covered with rushes;
Latticed the windows were, and the window-panes were of paper,
Oiled to admit the light, while wind and rain were excluded.
There too he dug a well, and around it planted an orchard:
Still may be seen to this day some trace of the well and the orchard.
Close to the house was the stall, where, safe and secure from annoyance,
Raghorn, the snow-white steer, that had fallen to Alden's allotment
In the division of cattle, might ruminate in the night-time
Over the pastures he cropped, made fragrant by sweet pennyroyal.

Oft when his labour was finished, with eager feet would the dreamer
Follow the pathway that ran through the woods to the house of Priscilla,
Led by illusions romantic and subtile deceptions of fancy,
Pleasure disguised as duty, and love in the semblance of friendship.
Ever of her he thought, when he fashioned the walls of his dwelling;
Ever of her he thought, when he delved in the soil of his garden;
Ever of her he thought, when he read in his Bible on Sunday
Praise of the virtuous woman, as she is described in the Proverbs,—
How the heart of her husband doth safely trust in her always,
How all the days of her life she will do him good, and not evil,
How she seeketh the wool and the flax and worketh with gladness,
How she layeth her hand to the spindle and holdeth the distaff,
How she is not afraid of the snow for herself or her household,
Knowing her household are clothed with the scarlet cloth of her
    weaving!

So as she sat at her wheel one afternoon in the Autumn,
Alden, who opposite sat, and was watching her dexterous fingers,
As if the thread she was spinning were that of his life and his fortun
After a pause in their talk, thus spake to the sound of the spindle.
" Truly, Priscilla," he said, " when I see you spinning and spinning,
Never idle a moment, but thrifty and thoughtful of others,
Suddenly you are transformed, are visibly changed in a moment;
You are no longer Priscilla, but Bertha the Beautiful Spinner."
Here the light foot on the treadle grew swifter and swifter; the spindl
Uttered an angry snarl, and the thread snapped short in her fingers
While the impetuous speaker, not heeding the mischief, continued:
" You are the beautiful Bertha, the spinner, the queen of Helvetia;
She whose story I read at a stall in the streets of Southampton,
Who, as she rode on her palfrey, o'er valley and meadow and mountain.
Ever was spinning her thread from a distaff fixed to her saddle.
She was so thrifty and good, that her name passed into a proverb.
So shall it be with your own, when the spinning-wheel shall no longe
Hum in the house of the farmer, and fill its chambers with music.
Then shall the mothers, reproving, relate how it was in their childhood
Praising the good old times, and the days of Priscilla the spinner! "
Straight uprose from her wheel the beautiful Puritan maiden,
Pleased with the praise of her thrift from him whose praise was the
   sweetest,
Drew from the reel on the table a snowy skein of her spinning,
Thus making answer, meanwhile, to the flattering phrases of Alden:
" Come, you must not be idle; if I am a pattern for housewives,
Show yourself equally worthy of being the model of husbands.
Hold this skein on your hands, while I wind it, ready for knitting;
Then who knows but hereafter, when fashions have changed and the
   manners,
Fathers may talk to their sons of the good old times of John Alden! "
Thus, with a jest and a laugh, the skein on his hands she adjusted,
He sitting awkwardly there, with his arms extended before him,
She standing graceful, erect, and winding the thread from his fingers,
Sometimes chiding a little his clumsy manner of holding,
Sometimes touching his hands, as she disentangled expertly
Twist or knot in the yarn, unawares—for how could she help it ?—
Sending electrical thrills through every nerve in his body.

Lo! in the midst of this scene, a breathless messenger entered,
Bringing in hurry and heat the terrible news from the village.
Yes; Miles Standish was dead!—an Indian had brought them the
   tidings,—
Slain by a poisoned arrow, shot down in the front of the battle,
Into an ambush beguiled, cut off with the whole of his forces;
All the town would be burned, and all the people be murdered!
Such were the tidings of evil that burst on the hearts of the hearers.
Silent and statue-like stood Priscilla, her face looking backward
Still at the face of the speaker, her arms uplifted in horror;

But John Alden, upstarting, as if the barb of the arrow
Piercing the heart of his friend had struck his own, and had sundered
Once and for ever the bonds that held him bound as a captive,
Wild with excess of sensation, the awful delight of his freedom,
Mingled with pain and regret, unconscious of what he was doing,
Clasped, almost with a groan, the motionless form of Priscilla,
Pressing her close to his heart, as for ever his own, and exclaiming:
" Those whom the Lord hath united, let no man put them asunder! "

Even as rivulets twain, from distant and separate sources,
Seeing each other afar, as they leap from the rocks, and pursuing
Each one its devious path, but drawing nearer and nearer,
Rush together at last, at their trysting-place in the forest;
So these lives that had run thus far in separate channels,
Coming in sight of each other, then swerving and flowing asunder,
Parted by barriers strong, but drawing nearer and nearer,
Rushed together at last, and one was lost in the other.

IX.

THE WEDDING-DAY

Forth from the curtain of clouds, from the tent of purple and scarlet,
Issued the sun, the great High-Priest, in his garments resplendent,
Holiness unto the Lord, in letters of light, on his forehead,
Round the hem of his robe the golden bells and pomegranates.
Blessing the world he came, and the bars of vapour beneath him
Gleamed like a grate of brass, and the sea at his feet was a laver!

This was the wedding-morn of Priscilla the Puritan maiden.
Friends were assembled together; the Elder and Magistrate also
Graced the scene with their presence, and stood like the Law and the
    Gospel,
One with the sanction of earth and one with the blessing of heaven.
Simple and brief was the wedding, as that of Ruth and of Boaz.
Softly the youth and the maiden repeated the words of betrothal,
Taking each other for husband and wife in the Magistrate's presence,
After the Puritan way, and the laudable custom of Holland.
Fervently then, and devoutly, the excellent Elder of Plymouth
Prayed for the hearth and the home, that were founded that day in
    affection,
Speaking of life and of death, and imploring divine benedictions.

Lo! when the service was ended, a form appeared on the threshold,
Clad in armour of steel, a sombre and sorrowful figure!
Why does the bridegroom start and stare at the strange apparition?
Why does the bride turn pale, and hide her face on his shoulder?

Is it a phantom of air,—a bodiless, spectral illusion?
Is it a ghost from the grave, that has come to forbid the betrothal?
Long had it stood there unseen, a guest uninvited, unwelcomed;
Over its clouded eyes there had passed at times an expression
Softening the gloom and revealing the warm heart hidden beneath
  them,
As when across the sky the driving rack of the rain-cloud
Grows for a moment thin, and betrays the sun by its brightness.
Once it had lifted its hand, and moved its lips, but was silent,
As if an iron will had mastered the fleeting intention.
But when were ended the troth and the prayer and the last benediction,
Into the room it strode, and the people beheld with amazement
Bodily there in his armour Miles Standish, the Captain of Plymouth!
Grasping the bridegroom's hand, he said with emotion, " Forgive me!
I have been angry and hurt,—too long have I cherished the feeling;
I have been cruel and hard, but now, thank God! it is ended.
Mine is the same hot blood that leaped in the veins of Hugh Standish,
Sensitive, swift to resent, but as swift in atoning for error.
Never so much as now was Miles Standish the friend of John Alden."
Thereupon answered the bridegroom: " Let all be forgotten between
  us,—
All save the dear, old friendship, and that shall grow older and dearer! "
Then the Captain advanced, and, bowing, saluted Priscilla,
Gravely, and after the manner of old-fashioned gentry in England,
Something of camp and of court, of town and of country, commingled,
Wishing her joy of her wedding, and loudly lauding her husband.
Then he said with a smile: " I should have remembered the adage,—
If you would be well served, you must serve yourself; and moreover,
No man can gather cherries in Kent at the season of Christmas! "

Great was the people's amazement, and greater yet their rejoicing,
Thus to behold once more the sun-burnt face of their Captain,
Whom they had mourned as dead; and they gathered and crowded
  about him,
Eager to see him and hear him, forgetful of bride and of bridegroom,
Questioning, answering, laughing, and each interrupting the other,
Till the good Captain declared, being quite overpowered and bewildered,
He had rather by far break into an Indian encampment,
Than come again to a wedding to which he had not been invited.

Meanwhile the bridegroom went forth and stood with the bride at
  the doorway,
Breathing the perfumed air of that warm and beautiful morning.
Touched with autumnal tints, but lonely and sad in the sunshine,
Lay extended before them the land of toil and privation;
There were the graves of the dead, and the barren waste of the sea-
  shore,
There the familiar fields, the groves of pine, and the meadows;
But to their eyes transfigured, it seemed as the Garden of Eden,
Filled with the presence of God, whose voice was the sound of the ocean.

Soon was their vision disturbed by the noise and stir of departure,
Friends coming forth from the house, and impatient of longer delaying,
Each with his plan for the day, and the work that was left uncompleted.
Then from a stall near at hand, amid exclamations of wonder,
Alden the thoughtful, the careful, so happy, so proud of Priscilla,
Brought out his snow-white steer, obeying the hand of its master,
Led by a cord that was tied to an iron ring in its nostrils,
Covered with crimson cloth, and a cushion placed for a saddle.
She should not walk, he said, through the dust and heat of the noon-
day;
Nay, she should ride like a queen, not plod along like a peasant.
Somewhat alarmed at first, but reassured by the others,
Placing her hand on the cushion, her foot in the hand of her husband,
Gaily, with joyous laugh, Priscilla mounted her palfrey.
" Nothing is wanting now," he said with a smile, " but the distaff;
Then you would be in truth my queen, my beautiful Bertha! "

Onward the bridal procession now moved to their new habitation,
Happy husband and wife, and friends conversing together.
Pleasantly murmured the brook, as they crossed the ford in the forest,
Pleased with the image that passed, like a dream of love through its
bosom,
Tremulous, floating in air, o'er the depths of the azure abysses.
Down through the golden leaves the sun was pouring his splendours,
Gleaming on purple grapes, that, from branches above them suspended,
Mingled their odorous breath with the balm of the pine and the fir-tree,
Wild and sweet as the clusters that grew in the valley of Eshcol.
Like a picture it seemed of the primitive, pastoral ages,
Fresh with the youth of the world, and recalling Rebecca and Isaac,
Old and yet ever new, and simple and beautiful always,
Love immortal and young in the endless succession of lovers.
So through the Plymouth woods passed onward the bridal procession.

THE SONG OF HIAWATHA

INTRODUCTION

Should you ask me, whence these
stories?
Whence these legends and tradi-
tions,
With the odours of the forest,
With the dew and damp of
meadows,
With the curling smoke of wig-
wams,
With the rushing of great rivers,
With their frequent repetitions,
And their wild reverberations,
As of thunder in the mountains?
   I should answer, I should tell
you,
" From the forests and the prairies,
From the great lakes of the North-
land,
From the land of the Ojibways,
From the land of the Dakotahs,
From the mountains, moors, and
fen-lands,
Where the heron, and Shuh-shuh-
gah,
Feeds among the reeds and rushes.
I repeat them as I heard them
From the lips of Nawadaha,
The musician, the sweet singer."
   Should you ask where Nawadaha
Found these songs, so wild and
wayward,
Found these legends and traditions,
I should answer, I should tell you,
" In the bird's-nests of the forest,
In the lodges of the beaver,
In the hoof-prints of the bison,
In the eyrie of the eagle!
" All the wild-fowl sang them to
him,

In the moorlands and the fen-
lands,
In the melancholy marshes;
Chetowaik, the plover, sang them,
Mahng, the loon, the wild-goose,
Wawa,
The blue heron, the Shuh-shuh-gah,
And the grouse, the Mushkodasa! "
   If still further you should ask me
Saying, " Who was Nawadaha?
Tell us of this Nawadaha,"
I should answer your inquiries
Straightway in such words as
follow:
   In the Vale of Tawasentha,[1]
In the green and silent valley,
By the pleasant watercourses,
Dwelt the singer Nawadaha.
Round about the Indian village
Spread the meadows and the corn-
fields,
And beyond them stood the forest,
Stood the groves of the singing
pine-trees,
Green in Summer, white in Winter,
Ever sighing, ever singing.
   " And the pleasant watercourses,
You could trace them through the
valley,
By the rushing in the Spring-time,
By the alders in the Summer,
By the white fog in the Autumn,
By the black line in the Winter;
And beside them dwelt the singer,
In the vale of Tawasentha,
In the green and silent valley.
   " There he sang of Hiawatha,
Sang the Song of Hiawatha,
Sang his wondrous birth and being,

[1] Now called Norman's Kill; the
valley is in Albany County, New York.

How he prayed and how he fasted,
How he lived, and toiled, and
    suffered,
That the tribes of men might
    prosper,
That he might advance his people!"
    Ye who love the haunts of
        Nature,
Love the sunshine of the meadow,
Love the shadow of the forest,
Love the wind among the branches,
And the rain-shower and the snow-
    storm,
And the rushing of great rivers
Through their palisades of pine-
    trees,
And the thunder in the mountains,
Whose innumerable echoes
Flap like eagles in their eyries;—
Listen to these wild traditions,
To this Song of Hiawatha!
    Ye who love a nation's legends,
Love the ballads of a people,
That like voices from afar off
Waving like a hand that beckons,
Call to us to pause and listen,
Speak in tones so plain and child-
    like,
Scarcely can the ear distinguish
Whether they are sung or spoken;—
Listen to this Indian Legend,
To this Song of Hiawatha!
    Ye whose hearts are fresh and
        simple,
Who have faith in God and Nature,
Who believe, that in all ages
Every human heart is human,
That in even savage bosoms
There are longings, yearnings,
    strivings
For the good they comprehend not,
That the feeble hands and helpless,
Groping blindly in the darkness,
Touch God's right hand in that
    darkness
And are lifted up and strength-
    ened;—
Listen to this simple story,
To this Song of Hiawatha!

Ye, who sometimes in your
    rambles
Through the green lanes of the
    country,
Where the tangled barberry-bushes
Hang their tufts of crimson berries
Over stone walls gray with mosses,
Pause by some neglected grave-
    yard,
For a while to muse, and ponder
On a half-effaced inscription,
Written with little skill of song-
    craft,
Homely phrases, but each letter
Full of hope, and yet of heart-
    break,
Full of all the tender pathos
Of the Here and the Hereafter;—
Stay and read this rude inscription,
Read this Song of Hiawatha!

I.

THE PEACE-PIPE

On the Mountains of the Prairie,[1]
On the great Red Pipe-stone
    Quarry,

[1] Mr. Catlin, in his *Letters and Notes
on the Manners, Customs, and Con-
ditions of the North American Indians,*
Vol. ii., p. 160, gives an interesting
account of the *Côteau des Prairies,*
and the Red Pipe-stone Quarry. He
says:—
    "Here (according to their tradi-
tions) happened the mysterious birth
of the red pipe, which has blown its
fumes of peace and war to the remotest
corners of the continent; which has
visited every warrior and passed
through its reddened stem the irre-
vocable oath of war and desolation.
And here also the peace-breathing
calumet was born, and fringed with
the eagle's quills, which had shed its
thrilling fumes over the land, and
soothed the fury of the relentless
savage.
    "The Great Spirit at an ancient
period here called the Indian nations
together, and standing on the precipice

Gitche Manito, the mighty,
He the Master of Life, descending,
On the red crags of the quarry
Stood erect, and called the nations,
Called the tribes of men together.
　From his footprints flowed a river,
Leaped into the light of morning,
O'er the precipice plunging downward
Gleamed like Ishkoodah, the comet.
And the Spirit, stooping earthward,
With his finger on the meadow
Traced a winding pathway for it,
Saying to it, " Run in this way! "
　From the red stone of the quarry
With his hand he broke a fragment,
Moulded it into a pipe-head,
Shaped and fashioned it with figures;
From the margin of the river
Took a long reed for a pipe-stem,
With its dark green leaves upon it;
Filled the pipe with bark of willow,
With the bark of the red willow;
Breathed upon the neighbouring forest,

of the red pipe-stone rock, broke from its wall a piece, and made a huge pipe by turning it in his hand, which he smoked over them, and to the North, the South, the East, and the West, and told them that this stone was red,—that it was their flesh,—that they must use it for their pipes of peace,—that it belonged to them all, and that the war-club and scalping-knife must not be raised on its ground. At the last whiff of of his pipe his head went into a great cloud, and the whole surface of the rock for several miles was melted and glazed; two great ovens were opened beneath, and two women (guardian spirits of the place) entered them in a blaze of fire; and they are heard there yet (Tso-mec-cos-tee and Tso-me-cos-te-won-dee), answering to the invocations of the high-priests or medicine-men, who consult them when they are visitors to this sacred place."

Made its great boughs chafe together,
Till in flame they burst and kindled;
And erect upon the mountains,
Gitche Manito, the mighty,
Smoked the calumet, the Peace-Pipe,
As a signal to the nations.
　And the smoke rose slowly, slowly,
Through the tranquil air of morning,
First a single line of darkness,
Then a denser, bluer vapour,
Then a snow-white cloud unfolding,
Like the tree-tops of the forest,
Ever rising, rising, rising,
Till it touched the top of heaven,
Till it broke against the heaven,
And rolled outward all around it.
　From the Vale of Tawasentha,
From the Valley of Wyoming,
From the groves of Tuscaloosa,
From the far-off Rocky Mountains,
From the Northern lakes and rivers
All the tribes beheld the signal,
Saw the distant smoke ascending,
The Pukwana of the Peace-Pipe.
　And the Prophets of the nations
Said: " Behold it, the Pukwana,
By this signal from afar off,
Bending like a wand of willow,
Gitche Manito, the mighty,
Calls the tribes of men together,
Calls the warriors to his council! "
　Down the rivers o'er the prairies,
Came the warriors of the nations,
Came the Delawares and Mohawks,
Came the Choctaws and Camanches,
Came the Shoshonies and Blackfeet,
Came the Pawnees and Omawhas,
Came the Mandans and Dacotahs,
Came the Hurons and Ojibways,
All the warriors drawn together
By the signal of the Peace-Pipe,
To the Mountains of the Prairie,

To the Great Red Pipe-stone
   Quarry.
     And they stood there on the
     meadow,
With their weapons and their war-
   gear,
Painted like the leaves of Autumn,
Painted like the sky of morning,
Wildly glaring at each other;
In their faces stern defiance,
In their hearts the feuds of ages,
The hereditary hatred,
The ancestral thirst of vengeance.
  Gitche Manito, the mighty,
The creator of the nations,
Looked upon them with compas-
   sion,
With paternal love and pity;
Looked upon their wrath and
   wrangling
But as quarrels among children,
But as feuds and fights of children!
    Over them he stretched his right
   hand,
To subdue their stubborn natures,
To allay their thirst and fever,
By the shadow of his right hand;
Spake to them with voice majestic
As the sound of far-off waters,
Falling into deep abysses,
Warning, chiding, spake in this
   wise:—
   "O my children! my poor
   children!
Listen to the words of wisdom,
Listen to the words of warning,
From the lips of the Great Spirit,
From the Master of Life, who made
   you:
   "I have given you lands to hunt
   in,
I have given you streams to fish in,
I have given you bear and bison,
I have given you roe and reindeer,
I have given you brant and beaver,
Filled the marshes full of wild fowl,
Filled the rivers full of fishes;
Why then are you not contented?
Why then will you hunt each other?

   "I am weary of your quarrels,
Weary of your wars and bloodshed,
Weary of your prayers for venge-
   ance,
Of your wranglings and dissensions;
All your strength is in your union,
All your danger is in discord;
Therefore be at peace hencefor-
   ward,
And as brothers live together.
   "I will send a Prophet to you,
A Deliverer of the nations,
Who shall guide you and shall
   teach you,
Who shall toil and suffer with
   you.
If you listen to his counsels,
You will multiply and prosper;
If his warnings pass unheeded,
You will fade away and perish!
   "Bathe now in the stream be-
   fore you,
Wash the war-paint from your
   faces,
Wash the blood-stains from your
   fingers,
Bury your war-clubs and your
   weapons,
Break the red stone from this
   quarry,
Mould and make it into Peace-
   Pipes,
Take the reeds that grow beside
   you,
Deck them with your brightest
   feathers,
Smoke the calumet together,
And as brothers live hencefor-
   ward!"
   Then upon the ground the war-
   riors
Threw their cloaks and shirts of
   deerskin,
Threw their weapons and their
   war-gear,
Leaped into the rushing river,
Washed the war-paint from their
   faces,
Clear above them flowed the water,

Clear and limpid from the foot-
prints
Of the Master of Life descending;
Dark below them flowed the water,
Soiled and stained with streaks of
crimson,
As if blood were mingled with it!
From the river came the warriors,
Clean and washed from all their
war-paint;
On the banks their clubs they
buried,
Buried all their warlike weapons.
Gitche Manito, the mighty,
The Great Spirit, the creator,
Smiled upon his helpless children!
And in silence all the warriors
Broke the red stone of the quarry,
Smoothed and formed it into
Peace-Pipes,
Broke the long reeds by the river,
Decked them with their brightest
feathers,
And departed each one homeward,
While the Master of Life, ascend-
ing,
Through the opening of cloud-
curtains,
Through the doorway of the
heaven,
Vanished from before their faces,
In the smoke that rolled around
him,
The Pukwana of the Peace-Pipe!

II.

THE FOUR WINDS

" Honour be to Mudjekeewis! "
Cried the warriors, cried the old
men,
When he came in triumph home-
ward
With the sacred Belt of Wampum.
From the regions of the North-
Wind,
From the kingdom of Wabasso,
From the land of the White Rabbit.

He had stolen the Belt of Wam-
pum
From the neck of Mishe-Mokwa,
From the Great Bear of the moun-
tains,
From the terror of the nations,
As he lay asleep and cumbrous
On the summit of the mountains,
Like a rock with mosses on it.
Spotted brown and gray with
mosses.
Silently he stole upon him,
Till the red nails of the monster
Almost touched him, almost scared
him,
Till the hot breath of his nostrils
Warmed the hands of Mudjekeewis,
As he drew the Belt of Wampum
Over the round ears, that heard
not,
Over the small eyes, that saw not,
Over the long nose and nostrils,
The black muffle of the nostrils,
Out of which the heavy breathing
Warmed the hands of Mudjekeewis.
Then he swung aloft his war-
club,
Shouted loud and long his war-cry,
Smote the mighty Mishe-Mokwa
In the middle of the forehead,
Right between the eyes he smote
him.
With the heavy blow bewildered,
Rose the Great Bear of the moun-
tains;
But his knees beneath him
trembled,
And he whimpered like a woman,
As he reeled and staggered forward,
As he sat upon his haunches;
And the mighty Mudjekeewis,
Standing fearlessly before him,
Taunted him in loud derision,
Spake disdainfully in this wise:—
" Hark you, Bear! you are a
coward,[1]

[1] This anecdote is from Hecke-
welder. In his account of the *Indian
Nations*, he describes an Indian

And no Brave, as you pretended;
Else you would not cry and
  whimper
Like a miserable woman!
Bear! you know our tribes are
  hostile,
Long have been at war together;
Now you find that we are strongest,
You go sneaking in the forest,
You go hiding in the mountains!
Had you conquered me in battle
Not a groan would I have uttered;
But you, Bear! sit here and
  whimper,
And disgrace your tribe by cry-
  ing,
Like a wretched Shaugodaya,
Like a cowardly old woman!"
  Then again he raised his war-
    club,
Smote again the Mishe-Mokwa
In the middle of his forehead,
Broke his skull, as ice is broken
When one goes to fish in Winter.
Thus was slain the Mishe-Mokwa,
He the Great Bear of the moun-
  tains,
He the terror of the nations.
  " Honour be to Mudjekeewis!"
With a shout exclaimed the people,
" Honour be to Mudjekeewis!"
Henceforth he shall be the West-
  Wind,
And hereafter and forever
Shall he hold supreme dominion
Over all the winds of heaven.
Call him no more Mudjekeewis,

Call him Kabeyun, the West-
  Wind!"
  Thus was Mudjekeewis chosen
Father of the Winds of Heaven.
For himself he kept the West-Wind,
Gave the others to his children;
Unto Wabun gave East-Wind,
Gave the South to Shawondasee,
And the North-Wind, wild and
  cruel,
To the fierce Kabibonokka.
  Young and beautiful was Wabun;
He it was who brought the morn-
  ing,
He it was whose silver arrows
Chased the dark o'er hill and
  valley;
He it was whose cheeks were
  painted
With the brightest streaks of
  crimson,
And whose voice awoke the village,
Called the deer, and called the
  hunter.
  Lonely in the sky was Wabun;
Though the birds sang gaily to
  him,
Though the wild-flowers of the
  meadow
Filled the air with odours for him,
Though the forests and the rivers
Sang and shouted at his coming,
Still his heart was sad within him,
For he was alone in heaven.
  But one morning, gazing earth-
  ward,
While the village still was sleeping,
And the fog lay on the river,
Like a ghost, that goes at sunrise,
He beheld a maiden walking
All alone upon a meadow,
Gathering water-flags and rushes
By a river in the meadow.
  Every morning, gazing earth-
  ward,
Still the first thing he beheld there
Was her blue eyes looking at him,
Two blue lakes among the rushes.
And he loved the lonely maiden,

---

hunter as addressing a bear in nearly
these words. " I was present," he
says, " at the delivery of this curious
invective; when the hunter had
despatched the bear, I asked him how
he thought that poor animal could
understand what he said to it? ' O,'
said he in answer, ' the bear under-
stood me very well; did you not
observe how *ashamed* he looked
while I was upbraiding him?'"—
*Transactions of the American Philo-
sophical Society*, Vol. i., p. 240.

Who thus waited for his coming;
For they both were solitary,
She on earth and he in heaven.

And he wooed her with caresses,
Wooed her with his smile of sunshine,
With his flattering words he wooed her,
With his sighing and his singing,
Gentlest whispers in the branches,
Softest music, sweetest odours,
Till he drew her to his bosom,
Folded in his robes of crimson,
Till into a star he changed her,
Trembling still upon his bosom;
And for ever in the heavens
They are seen together walking,
Wabun and the Wabun-Annung,
Wabun and the Star of Morning.

But the fierce Kabibonokka
Had his dwelling among icebergs,
In the everlasting snowdrifts,
In the kingdom of Wabasso,
In the land of the White Rabbit.
He it was whose hand in Autumn
Painted all the trees with scarlet,
Stained the leaves with red and yellow;
He it was who sent the snowflakes,
Sifting, hissing through the forest,
Froze the ponds, the lakes, the rivers,
Drove the loon and sea-gull southward,
Drove the cormorant and curlew
To their nests of sedge and sea-tang
In the realms of Shawondasee.

Once the fierce Kabibonokka
Issued from his lodge of snowdrifts,
From his home among the icebergs,
And his hair, with snow besprinkled,
Streamed behind him like a river,
Like a black and wintry river,
As he howled and hurried southward,
Over frozen lakes and moorlands.

There among the reeds and rushes

Found he Shingebis, the diver,
Trailing strings of fish behind him,
O'er the frozen fens and moorlands,
Lingering still among the moorlands,
Though his tribe had long departed
To the land of Shawondasee.

Cried the fierce Kabibonokka,
"Who is this that dares to brave me?
Dares to stay in my dominions,
When the Wawa has departed,
When the wild-goose has gone southward,
And the heron, the Shuh-shuh-gah,
Long ago departed southward?
I will go into his wigwam,
I will put his smouldering fire out!"

And at night Kabibonokka
To the lodge came wild and wailing,
Heaped the snow in drifts about it,
Shouted down into the smoke-flue,
Shook the lodge-poles in his fury,
Flapped the curtain of the door-way.

Shingebis, the diver, feared not,
Shingebis, the diver, cared not;
Four great logs had he for fire-wood,
One for each moon of the winter,
And for food the fishes served him.
By his blazing fire he sat there,
Warm and merry, eating, laughing,
Singing "O Kabibonokka,
You are but my fellow-mortal!"

Then Kabibonokka entered,
And though Shingebis, the diver,
Felt his presence by the coldness,
Felt his icy breath upon him,
Still he did not cease his singing,
Still he did not leave his laughing,
Only turned the log a little,
Only made the fire burn brighter,
Made the sparks fly up the smoke-flue.

From Kabibonokka's forehead,
From his snow-besprinkled tresses,
Drops of sweat fell fast and heavy,

Making dints upon the ashes,
As along the eaves of lodges,
As from drooping boughs of hem-
lock,
Drips the melting snow in spring-
time,
Making hollows in the snowdrifts.
Till at last he rose defeated,
Could not bear the heat and
laughter,
Could not bear the merry singing,
But rushed headlong through the
doorway,
Stamped upon the crusted snow-
drifts,
Stamped upon the lakes and rivers,
Made the snow upon them harder,
Made the ice upon them thicker,
Challenged Shingebis, the diver,
To come forth and wrestle with
him,
To come forth and wrestle naked
On the frozen fens and moorlands.
Forth went Shingebis, the diver,
Wrestled all night with the North-
Wind,
Wrestled naked on the moor-
lands
With the fierce Kabibonokka,
Till his panting breath grew fainter,
Till his frozen grasp grew feebler,
Till he reeled and staggered back-
ward,
And retreated, baffled, beaten,
To the kingdom of Wabasso,
To the land of the White Rabbit,
Hearing still the gusty laughter,
Hearing Shingebis, the diver,
Singing, " O Kabibonokka,
You are but my fellow-mortal! "
Shawondasee, fat and lazy,
Had his dwelling far to southward,
In the drowsy, dreamy sunshine,
In the never-ending Summer.
He it was who sent the wood-birds,
Sent the Opechee, the robin,
Sent the blue-bird the Owaissa,
Sent the Shawshaw, sent the
swallow,

Sent the wild-goose, Wawa, north-
ward,
Sent the melons and tobacco,
And the grapes in purple clusters.
From his pipe the smoke ascend-
ing
Filled the sky with haze and
vapour,
Filled the air with dreamy softness,
Gave a twinkle to the water,
Touched the rugged hills with
smoothness,
Brought the tender Indian Summer
To the melancholy north-land,
In the dreary Moon of Snow-shoes.
Listless, careless, Shawondasee!
In his life he had one shadow,
In his heart one sorrow had he.
Once, as he was gazing northward,
Far away upon a prairie
He beheld a maiden standing,
Saw a tall and slender maiden
All alone upon a prairie;
Brightest green were all her gar-
ments
And her hair was like the sunshine.
Day by day he gazed upon her,
Day by day he sighed with passion,
Day by day his heart within him
Grew more hot with love and long-
ing
For the maid with yellow tresses.
But he was too fat and lazy
To bestir himself and woo her;
Yes, too indolent and easy
To pursue her and persuade her.
So he only gazed upon her,
Only sat and sighed with passion
For the maiden of the prairie.
Till one morning, looking north-
ward,
He beheld her yellow tresses
Changed and covered o'er with
whiteness,
Covered as with whitest snowflakes.
" Ah! my brother from the North-
land,
From the kingdom of Wabasso,
From the land of the White Rabbit!

You have stolen the maiden from me,
You have laid your hand upon her,
You have wooed and won my maiden,
With your stories of the Northland!"
  Thus the wretched Shawondasee
Breathed into the air his sorrow;
And the South-Wind o'er the prairie
Wandered warm with sighs of passion
With the sighs of Shawondasee,
Till the air seemed full of snowflakes,
Full of thistle-down the prairie,
And the maid with hair like sunshine
Vanished from his sight for ever;
Nevermore did Shawondasee
See the maid with yellow tresses!
  Poor, deluded Shawondasee!
'Twas no woman that you gazed at,
'Twas no maiden that you sighed for,
'Twas the prairie dandelion
That through all the dreamy Summer
You had gazed at with such longing,
You had sighed for with such passion
And had puffed away for ever,
Blown into the air with sighing.
Ah! deluded Shawondasee!
  Thus the Four Winds were divided;
Thus the sons of Mudjekeewis
Had their stations in the heavens,
At the corners of the heavens;
For himself the West-Wind only
Kept the mighty Mudjekeewis.

III.

HIAWATHA'S CHILDHOOD

Downward through the evening twilight,
In the days that are forgotten,
In the unremembered ages,
From the full moon fell Nokomis,
Fell the beautiful Nokomis,
She a wife, but not a mother.
  She was sporting with her women
Swinging in a swing of grape-vines,
When her rival, the rejected,
Full of jealousy and hatred,
Cut the leafy swing asunder,
Cut in twain the twisted grapevines,
And Nokomis fell affrighted
Downward through the evening twilight,
On the Muskoday, the meadow,
On the prairie full of blossoms.
"See! a star falls!" said the people;
"From the sky a star is falling!"
There among the ferns and mosses,
There among the prairie lilies,
On the Muskoday the meadow,
In the moonlight and the starlight,
Fair Nokomis bore a daughter.
And she called her name Wenonah,
As the first-born of her daughters.
And the daughter of Nokomis
Grew up like the prairie lilies,
Grew a tall and slender maiden,
With the beauty of the moonlight,
With the beauty of the starlight.
  And Nokomis warned her often,
Saying oft, and oft repeating,
"O, beware of Mudjekeewis,
Of the West-Wind, Mudjekeewis;
Listen not to what he tells you;
Lie not down upon the meadow,
Stoop not down among the lilies,
Lest the West-Wind come and harm you!"
  But she heeded not the warning,
Heeded not those words of wisdom,
And the West-Wind came at evening,
Walking lightly o'er the prairie,
Whispering to the leaves and blossoms,
Bending low the flowers and grasses,

Found the beautiful Wenonah,
Lying there among the lilies,
Wooed her with his words of
    sweetness,
Wooed her with his soft caresses,
Till she bore a son in sorrow,
Bore a son of love and sorrow.

Thus was born my Hiawatha,
Thus was born the child of wonder;
But the daughter of Nokomis,
Hiawatha's gentle mother,
In her anguish died deserted
By the West-Wind, false and faith-
    less,
By the heartless Mudjekeewis.

For her daughter, long and
    loudly
Wailed and wept the sad Nokomis;
"O that I were dead!" she mur-
    mured,
"O that I were dead, as thou art!
No more work, and no more weep-
    ing,
Wahonowin! Wahonowin!"

By the shores of Gitche Gumee,
By the shining Big-Sea-Water,
Stood the wigwam of Nokomis,
Daughter of the Moon, Nokomis.
Dark behind it rose the forest,
Rose the black and gloomy pine-
    trees,
Rose the firs with cones upon them;
Bright before it beat the water,
Beat the clear and sunny water,
Beat the shining Big-Sea-Water.

There the wrinkled, old Nokomis
Nursed the little Hiawatha,
Rocked him in his linden cradle,
Bedded soft in moss and rushes,
Safely bound with reindeer sinews;
Stilled his fretful wail by saying,
"Hush! the Naked Bear [1] will get
    thee!"

Lulled him into slumber, singing,
"Ewa-yea! my little owlet!
Who is this, that lights the wig-
    wam?
With his great eyes lights the wig-
    wam?
Ewa-yea! my little-owlet!"

Many things Nokomis taught
    him
Of the stars that shine in heaven;
Showed him Ishkoodah, the comet,
Ishkoodah, with fiery tresses;
Showed the Death-Dance of the
    spirits,
Warriors with their plumes and
    war-clubs,
Flaring far away to northward
In the frosty nights of Winter;
Showed the broad, white road in
    heaven,
Pathway of the ghosts, the shadows,
Running straight across the
    heavens,
Crowded with the ghosts, the
    shadows.

At the door on Summer evenings
Sat the little Hiawatha;
Heard the whispering of the pine-
    trees,
Heard the lapping of the water,
Sounds of music, words of wonder;
"Minne-wawa!" said the pine-
    trees,
"Mudway-aushka!" said the
    water.

---

[1] Heckewelder, in a letter published
in the *Transactions of the American
Philosophical Society*, Vol. iv., p. 260,
speaks of this tradition as prevalent
among the Mohicans and Delawares.
"Their reports," he says, "run

thus: that among all animals that had
been formerly in this country, this
was the most ferocious; that it was
much larger than the largest of the
common bears, and remarkably long-
bodied; all over (except a spot of
hair on its back of a white colour)
naked. . . .

"The history of this animal used
to be a subject of conversation among
the Indians, especially when in the
woods a-hunting. I have also heard
them say to their children when
crying: 'Hush! the naked bear will
hear you, be upon you, and devour
you.'"

Saw the fire-fly, Wah-wah-
taysee,
Flitting through the dusk of even-
ing,
With the twinkle of its candle
Lighting up the brakes and bushes,
And he sang the song of children,
Sang the song Nokomis taught
him:
" Wah-wah-taysee, little firefly,
Little, flitting, white-fire insect,
Little, dancing, white-fire creature,
Light me with your little cradle,
Ere upon my bed I lay me,
Ere in sleep I close my eyelids! "
Saw the moon rise from the
water
Rippling, rounding from the water,
Saw the flecks and shadows on it,
Whispered, " What is that, Noko-
mis? "
And the good Nokomis answered:
" Once a warrior, very angry,
Seized his grandmother, and threw
her
Up into the sky at midnight;
Right against the moon he threw
her;
'Tis her body that you see there."
Saw the rainbow in the heaven,
In the eastern sky, the rainbow,
Whispered, " What is that, Noko-
mis? "
And the good Nokomis answered:
" 'Tis the heaven of flowers you
see there;
All the wild-flowers of the forest,
All the lilies of the prairie,
When on earth they fade and
perish,
Blossom in that heaven above us."
When he heard the owls at mid-
night,
Hooting, laughing in the forest,
" What is that? " he cried in
terror
" What is that? " he said, " Noko-
mis? "
And the good Nokomis answered:

" That is but the owl and owlet,
Talking in their native language,
Talking, scolding at each other."
Then the little Hiawatha
Learned of every bird its language,
Learned their names and all their
secrets,
How they built their nests in
Summer,
Where they hid themselves in
Winter,
Talked with them whene'er he met
them,
Called them " Hiawatha's Chick-
ens."
Of all beasts he learned the
language,
Learned their names and all their
secrets,
How the beavers built their lodges,
Where the squirrels hid their
acorns,
How the reindeer ran so swiftly,
Why the rabbit was so timid,
Talked with them whene'er he met
them,
Called them Hiawatha's Brothers."
Then Iagoo, the great boaster,
He the marvellous story-teller,
He the traveller and the talker.
He the friend of old Nokomis,
Made a bow for Hiawatha:
From a branch of ash he made it,
From an oak-bough made the
arrows,
Tipped with flint, and winged with
feathers,
And the cord he made of deer-skin.
Then he said to Hiawatha:
" Go, my son, into the forest,
Where the red deer herd together,
Kill for us a famous roebuck,
Kill for us a deer with antlers! "
Forth into the forest straight-
way
All alone walked Hiawatha
Proudly, with his bow and arrows;
And the birds sang round him, o'er
him,

" Do not shoot us, Hiawatha! "
Sang the Opechee, the robin,
Sang the bluebird, the Owaissa,
" Do not shoot us, Hiawatha! "
  Up the oak-tree, close beside him,
Sprang the squirrel, Adjidaumo,
In and out among the branches,
Coughed and chattered from the
    oak-tree,
Laughed, and said between his
    laughing,
" Do not shoot me, Hiawatha! "
  And the rabbit from his pathway
Leaped aside, and at a distance
Sat erect upon his haunches,
Half in fear and half in frolic,
Saying to the little hunter,
" Do not shoot me, Hiawatha! "
  But he heeded not, nor heard
    them,
For his thoughts were with the red
    deer;
On their tracks his eyes were
    fastened,
Leading downward to the river,
To the ford across the river,
And as one in slumber walked he.
  Hidden in the alder bushes,
There he waited till the deer came,
Till he saw two antlers lifted,
Saw two eyes look from the thicket
Saw two nostrils point to wind-
    ward,
And a deer came down the path-
    way,
Flecked with leafy light and
    shadow.
And his heart within him fluttered,
Trembled like the leaves above
    him,
Like the birch-leaf palpitated,
As the deer came down the path-
    way.
  Then upon one knee uprising,
Hiawatha aimed an arrow;
Scarce a twig moved with his
    motion,
Scarce a leaf was stirred or rustled,
But the wary roebuck started,

Stamped with all his hoofs to-
    gether,
Listened with one foot uplifted,
Leaped as if to meet the arrow;
Ah! the singing, fatal arrow,
Like a wasp it buzzed and stung
    him!
  Dead he lay there in the forest,
By the ford across the river;
Beat his timid heart no longer,
But the heart of Hiawatha
Throbbed and shouted and exulted,
As he bore the red deer homeward
And Iagoo and Nokomis
Hailed his coming with applauses.
  From the red deer's hide Noko-
    mis
Made a cloak for Hiawatha,
From the red deer's flesh Nokomis
Made a banquet in his honour.
All the village came and feasted,
All the guests praised Hiawatha,
Called him Strong-heart, Soan-
    getaha!
Called him Loon-Heart, Mahn-go
    taysee!

IV.

HIAWATHA AND MUDJEKEEWIS

  Out of childhood into manhood
Now had grown my Hiawatha,
Skilled in all the craft of hunters,
Learned in all the lore of old men,
In all youthful sports and pastimes,
In all manly arts and labours.
  Swift of foot was Hiawatha;
He could shoot an arrow from
    him,
And run forward with such fleet-
    ness,
That the arrow fell behind him!
Strong of arm was Hiawatha;
He could shoot ten arrows up-
    ward,
Shoot them with such strength and
    swiftness,

That the tenth had left the bow-
string
Ere the first to earth had fallen!
He had mittens, Minjckahwun,
Magic mittens made of deer-skin;
When upon his hands he wore
them,
He could smite the rocks asunder,
He could grind them into powder,
He had moccasins enchanted,
Magic moccasins of deer-skin;
When he bound them round his
ankles,
When upon his feet he tied them,
At each stride a mile he measured!
Much he questioned old Nokomis
Of his father Mudjekeewis;
Learned from her the fatal secret
Of the beauty of his mother,
Of the falsehood of his father;
And his heart was hot within him,
Like a living coal his heart was.
Then he said to old Nokomis,
" I will go to Mudjekeewis,
See how fares it with my father,
At the doorways of the West-Wind,
At the portals of the Sunset!"
From his lodge went Hiawatha,
Dressed for travel, armed for hunt-
ing;
Dressed in deer-skin shirt and
leggings,
Richly wrought with quills and
wampum;
On his head his eagle feathers,
Round his waist his belt of wam-
pum,
In his hand his bow of ash-wood,
Strung with sinews of the reindeer;
In his quiver oaken arrows,
Tipped with jasper, winged with
feathers;
With his mittens, Minjekahwun,
With his moccasins enchanted.
Warning said the old Nokomis,
" Go not forth, O Hiawatha!
To the kingdom of the West-Wind.
To the realms of Mudjekeewis,
Lest he harm you with his magic,

Lest he kill you with his cunning!"
But the fearless Hiawatha
Heeded not her woman's warning;
Forth he strode into the forest,
At each stride a mile he measured;
Lurid seemed the sky above him,
Lurid seemed the earth beneath
him,
Hot and close the air around him,
Filled with smoke and fiery
vapours,
As of burning woods and prairies,
For his heart was hot within him,
Like a living coal his heart was.
So he journeyed westward, west-
ward,
Left the fleetest deer behind him,
Left the antelope and bison;
Crossed the rushing Esconawbaw,
Crossed the mighty Mississippi,
Passed the Mountains of the
Prairie,
Passed the land of Crows and
Foxes,
Passed the dwellings of the Black-
feet,
Came unto the Rocky Mountains,
To the kingdom of the West-Wind,
Where upon the gusty summits
Sat the ancient Mudjekeewis,
Ruler of the winds of heaven.
Filled with awe was Hiawatha
At the aspect of his father.
On the air about him wildly
Tossed and streamed his cloudy
tresses,
Gleamed like drifting snow his
tresses,
Glared like Ishkoodah, the comet,
Like the star with fiery tresses.
Filled with joy was Mudjekeewis
When he looked on Hiawatha,
Saw his youth rise up before him
In the face of Hiawatha,
Saw the beauty of Wenonah
From the grave rise up before him.
" Welcome!" said he, " Hia-
watha,
To the kingdom of the West-Wind!

Long have I been waiting for you!
Youth is lovely, age is lonely,
Youth is fiery, age is frosty;
You bring back the days departed,
You bring back my youth of pas-
sion,
And the beautiful Wenonah!"
    Many days they talked together,
Questioned, listened, waited, an-
swered
Much the mighty Mudjekeewis
Boasted of his ancient prowess,
Of his perilous adventures,
His indomitable courage,
His invulnerable body.
    Patiently sat Hiawatha,
Listening to his father's boasting;
With a smile he sat and listened,
Uttered neither threat nor menace,
Neither word nor look betrayed
him,
But his heart was hot within him,
Like a living coal his heart was.
    Then he said, " O Mudjekeewis,
Is there nothing that can harm
you?
Nothing that you are afraid of?"
And the mighty Mudjekeewis,
Grand and gracious in his boasting,
Answered, saying, " There is
nothing,
Nothing but the black rock yonder,
Nothing but the fatal Wawbeek?"
    And he looked at Hiawatha
With a wise look and benignant,
With a countenance paternal,
Looked with pride upon the beauty
Of his tall and graceful figure,
Saying, " O my Hiawatha!
Is there anything can harm you?
Anything you are afraid of?"
    But the wary Hiawatha
Paused awhile, as if uncertain,
Held his peace, as if resolving,
And then answered, " There is
nothing,
Nothing but the bulrush yonder,
Nothing but the great Apukwa!"
    And as Mudjekeewis, rising,

Stretched his hand to pluck the
bulrush,
Hiawatha cried in terror,
Cried in well-dissembled terror,
" Kago! kago! do not touch it!"
" Ah, kaween!" said Mudjekeewis,
" No, indeed, I will not touch it!"
Then they talked of other
matters;
First of Hiawatha's brothers,
First of Wabun, of the East-Wind,
Of the South Wind, Shawondasee,
Of the North, Kabibonokka;
Then of Hiawatha's mother,
Of the beautiful Wenonah,
Of her birth upon the meadow,
Of her death, as old Nokomis
Had remembered and related.
    And he cried, " O Mudjekeewis,
It was you who killed Wenonah,
Took her young life and her beauty,
Broke the Lily of the Prairie,
Trampled it beneath your foot-
steps;
You confess it! you confess it!"
And the mighty Mudjekeewis
Tossed his gray hairs to the west
wind
Bowed his hoary head in anguish,
With a silent nod assented.
    Then up started Hiawatha,
And with threatening look and
gesture
Laid his hand upon the black rock,
On the fatal Wawbeek laid it.
With his mittens, Minjekahwun,
Rent the jutting crag asunder,
Smote and crushed it into frag-
ments,
Hurled them madly at his father,
The remorseful Mudjekeewis,
For his heart was hot within him,
Like a living coal his heart was.
    But the ruler of the West-Wind
Blew the fragments backwards
from him,
With the breathing of his nostrils,
With the tempest of his anger,
Blew them back at his assailant;

Seized the bulrush, the Apukwa,
Dragged it with its roots and fibres
From the margin of the meadow,
From its ooze, the giant bulrush;
Long and loud laughed Hiawatha!
  Then began the deadly conflict,
Hand to hand among the mountains;
From his eyrie screamed the eagle,
The Keneu, the great war-eagle,
Sat upon the crags around them,
Wheeling flapped his wings above
    them.
  Like a tall tree in the tempest
Bent and lashed the giant bulrush;
And in masses huge and heavy
Crashing fell the fatal Wawbeek;
Till the earth shook with the
    tumult
And confusion of the battle,
And the air was full of shoutings,
And the thunder of the mountains,
Starting, answered, "Biam-wawa!"
  Back retreated Mudjekeewis,
Rushing westward o'er the mountains,
Stumbling westward down the
    mountains,
Three whole days retreated fighting,
Still pursued by Hiawatha
To the doorways of the West-Wind,
To the portals of the Sunset,
To the earth's remotest border,
Where into the empty spaces
Sinks the sun, as a flamingo
Drops into her nest at nightfall,
In the melancholy marshes.
  "Hold!" at length cried Mudjekeewis,
"Hold, my son, my Hiawatha!
'Tis impossible to kill me,
For you cannot kill the immortal.
I have put you to this trial,
But to know and prove your courage;
Now receive the prize of valour!

  "Go back to your home and
    people,
Live among them, toil among
    them,
Cleanse the earth from all that
    harms it,
Clear the fishing-grounds and
    rivers,
Slay all monsters and magicians,
All the giants, the Wendigoes,
All the serpents, the Kenabeeks,
As I slew the Mishe-Mokwa,
Slew the Great Bear of the mountains,
  "And at last when Death draws
    near you,
When the awful eyes of Pauguk
Glare upon you in the darkness,
I shall share my kingdom with you,
Ruler shall you be thenceforward
Of the Northwest-Wind, Keewaydin,
Of the home-wind, the Keewaydin."
  Thus was fought that famous
    battle
In the dreadful days of Shah-shah,
In the days long since departed,
In the kingdom of the West-Wind.
Still the hunter sees its traces
Scattered far o'er hill and valley;
Sees the giant bulrush growing
By the ponds and watercourses,
  Sees the masses of the Wawbeek
Lying still in every valley.
  Homeward now went Hiawatha;
Pleasant was the landscape round
    him,
Pleasant was the air above him,
For the bitterness of anger
Had departed wholly from him,
From his brain the thought of
    vengeance,
From his heart the burning fever.
  Only once his pace he slackened,
Only once he paused or halted,
Paused to purchase heads of arrows
Of the ancient Arrow-maker,
In the land of the Dacotahs,

Where the Falls of Minnehaha [1]
Flash and gleam among the oak
    trees,
Laugh and leap into the valley.
    There the ancient Arrow-maker
Made his arrow-heads of sandstone,
Arrow-heads of chalcedony,
Arrow-heads of flint and jasper,
Smoothed and sharpened at the
    edges,
Hard and polished, keen and costly.
    With him dwelt his dark-eyed
    daughter,
Wayward as the Minnehaha,
With her moods of shade and sun-
    shine,
Eyes that smiled and frowned
    alternate,
Feet as rapid as the river,
Tresses flowing like the water,
And as musical a laughter;
And he named her from the river,
From the waterfall he named her,
Minnehaha, Laughing Water.
    Was it then for heads of arrows,
Arrow-heads of chalcedony,
Arrow-heads of flint and jasper,
That my Hiawatha halted
In the land of the Dacotahs?
    Was it not to see the maiden,
See the face of Laughing Water,
Peeping from behind the curtain,
Hear the rustling of her garments
From behind the waving curtain,
As one sees the Minnehaha
Gleaming, glancing through the
    branches,
As one hears the Laughing Water

    [1] " The scenery about Fort Snelling
is rich in beauty. The Falls of St.
Anthony are familiar to travellers,
and to readers of Indian sketches.
Between the fort and these falls
are the ' Little Falls,' forty feet
in height, on a stream that empties
into the Mississippi. The Indians
call them Mine-hah-hah, or ' laughing
waters.' "—Mrs. Eastman's *Dacotah,
or Legends of the Sioux*, Introduction,
p. ii.

From behind its screen of branches?
    Who shall say what thoughts
    and visions
Fill the fiery brains of young men?
Who shall say that dreams of
    beauty
Filled the heart of Hiawatha?
All he told to old Nokomis,
When he reached the lodge at sun-
    set,
Was the meeting with his father,
Was his fight with Mudjekeewis;
Not a word he said of arrows,
Not a word of Laughing Water.

V.

HIAWATHA'S FASTING

    You shall hear how Hiawatha
Prayed and fasted in the forest,
Not for greater skill in hunting,
Not for greater craft in fishing,
Not for triumphs in the battle,
And renown among the warriors,
But for profit of the people,
For advantage of the nations.
    First he built a lodge for fasting,
Built a wigwam in the forest,
By the shining Big-Sea-Water,
In the blithe and pleasant Spring-
    time,
In the Moon of Leaves he built it,
And, with dreams and visions
    many,
Seven whole days and nights he
    fasted.
    On the first day of his fasting
Through the leafy woods he
    wandered;
Saw the deer start from the
    thicket,
Saw the rabbit in his burrow,
Heard the pheasant, Bena, drum-
    ming,
Heard the squirrel, Adjidaumo,
Rattling in his hoard of acorns,
Saw the pigeon, the Omeme,

Building nests among the pine-trees,
And in flocks the wild goose, Wawa,
Flying to the fen-lands northward,
Whirring, wailing far above him.
" Master of Life! " he cried, despending,
" Must our lives depend on these things ? "
  On the next day of his fasting
By the river's bank he wandered,
Through the Muskoday, the meadow,
Saw the wild rice, Mahnomonee,
Saw the blueberry, Meenahga,
And the strawberry, Odahmin,
And the gooseberry, Shahbomin,
And the grape-vine, the Bemahgut,
Trailing o'er the alder-branches,
Filling all the air with fragrance!
" Master of Life! " he cried, despending,
" Must our lives depend on these things ? "
  On the third day of his fasting
By the lake he sat and pondered,
By the still, transparent water;
Saw the sturgeon, Nahma, leaping,
Scattering drops like beads of wampum,
Saw the yellow perch, the Sahwa,
Like a sunbeam in the water,
Saw the pike, the Maskenozha,
And the herring, Okahahwis,
And the Shawgashee, the crawfish!
" Master of Life! " he cried despending,
" Must our lives depend on these things ? "
  On the fourth day of his fasting
In his lodge he lay exhausted;
From his couch of leaves and branches
Gazing with half-open eyelids,
Full of shadowy dreams and visions,
On the dizzy, swimming landscape,
On the gleaming of the water,
On the splendour of the sunset.

And he saw a youth approaching,
Dressed in garments green and yellow
Coming through the purple twilight,
Through the splendour of the sunset;
Plumes of green bent o'er his forehead,
And his hair was soft and golden.
  Standing at the open doorway,
Long he looked at Hiawatha,
Looked with pity and compassion
On his wasted form and features,
And, in accents like the sighing
Of the South-Wind in the tree-tops,
Said he, " O my Hiawatha!
All your prayers are heard in heaven,
For you pray not like the others;
Not for greater skill in hunting,
Not for greater craft in fishing,
Not for triumph in the battle,
Nor renown among the warriors,
But for profit of the people,
For advantage of the nations.
  " From the Master of Life descending,
I, the friend of man, Mondamin,
Come to warn you and instruct you,
How by struggle and by labour
You shall gain what you have prayed for.
Rise up from your bed of branches,
Rise, O youth, and wrestle with me! "
  Faint with famine, Hiawatha
Started from his bed of branches,
From the twilight of his wigwam
Forth into the flush of sunset
Came, and wrestled with Mondamin;
At his touch he felt new courage
Throbbing in his brain and bosom,
Felt new life and hope and vigour
Run through every nerve and fibre.
  So they wrestled there together

In the glory of the sunset,
And the more they strove and
    struggled,
Stronger still grew Hiawatha;
Till the darkness fell around them,
And the heron, the Shuh-shuh-gah,
From her haunts among the fen-
    lands,
Gave a cry of lamentation,
Gave a scream of pain and famine.
    " 'Tis enough! " then said Mon-
    damin,
Smiling upon Hiawatha,
" But to-morrow, when the sun
    sets,
I will come again to try you."
And he vanished, and was seen
    not;
Whether sinking as the rain sinks,
Whether rising as the mists rise,
Hiawatha saw not, knew not,
Only saw that he had vanished,
Leaving him alone and fainting,
With the misty lake below him,
And the reeling stars above him.
On the morrow and the next day,
When the sun through heaven de-
    scending,
Like a red and burning cinder
From the hearth of the Great Spirit,
Fell into the western waters,
Came Mondamin for the trial,
For the strife with Hiawatha;
Came as silent as the dew comes,
From the empty air appearing,
Into empty air returning,
Taking shape when earth it
    touches,
But invisible to all men
In its coming and its going.
    Thrice they wrestled there to-
    gether
In the glory of the sunset,
Till the darkness fell around them,
Till the heron, the Shuh-shuh-gah,
From her haunts among the fen-
    lands,
Uttered her loud cry of famine,
And Mondamin paused to listen.

Tall and beautiful he stood
    there,
In his garments green and yellow;
To and fro his plumes above him
Waved and nodded with his
    breathing,
And the sweat of the encounter
Stood like drops of dew upon him.
    And he cried, " O Hiawatha!
Bravely have you wrestled with
    me,
Thrice have wrestled stoutly with
    me,
And the Master of Life, who sees
    us,
He will give to you the triumph! "
    Then he smiled, and said: " To-
    morrow
Is the last day of your conflict,
Is the last day of your fasting.
You will conquer and o'ercome
    me:
Make a bed for me to lie in,
Where the rain may fall upon me,
Where the sun may come and
    warm me;
Strip these garments, green and
    yellow,
Strip this nodding plumage from
    me,
Lay me in the earth, and make it
Soft and loose and light above me.
    " Let no hand disturb my slum-
    ber,
Let no weed nor worm molest me,
Let not Kahgahgee, the raven,
Come to haunt me and molest me,
Only come yourself to watch me,
Till I wake, and start, and quicken,
Till I leap into the sunshine."
    And thus saying, he departed.
Peacefully slept Hiawatha,
But he heard the Wawonaissa,
Heard the whippoorwill complain-
    ing,
Perched upon his lonely wigwam;
Heard the rushing Sebowisha,
Heard the rivulet rippling near
    him,

Talking to the darksome forest;
Heard the sighing of the branches,
As they lifted and subsided
At the passing of the night-wind,
Heard them, as one hears in slumber
Far-off murmurs, dreamy whispers:
Peacefully slept Hiawatha.
    On the morrow came Nokomis,
On the seventh day of his fasting,
Came with food for Hiawatha,
Came imploring and bewailing,
Lest his hunger should o'ercome him,
Lest his fasting should be fatal.
    But he tasted not, and touched not,
Only said to her, " Nokomis,
Wait until the sun is setting,
Till the darkness falls around us,
Till the heron, the Shuh-shuh-gah,
Crying from the desolate marshes,
Tells us that the day is ended."
    Homeward weeping went Nokomis,
Sorrowing for her Hiawatha,
Fearing lest his strength should fail him,
Lest his fasting should be fatal.
He meanwhile sat weary waiting
For the coming of Mondamin,
Till the shadows, pointing eastward,
Lengthened over field and forest,
Till the sun dropped from the heaven,
Floating on the waters westward,
As a red leaf in the Autumn
Falls and floats upon the water,
Falls and sinks into its bosom.
    And behold! the young Mondamin,
With his soft and shining tresses,
With his garments green and yellow,
With his long and glossy plumage,
Stood and beckoned at the doorway.
And as one in slumber walking,

Pale and haggard, but undaunted,
From the wigwam Hiawatha
Came and wrestled with Mondamin.
    Round about him spun the landscape,
Sky and forest reeled together,
And his strong heart leaped within him,
As the sturgeon leaps and struggles
In a net to break its meshes.
Like a ring of fire around him
Blazed and flared the red horizon,
And a hundred suns seemed looking
At the combat of the wrestlers.
    Suddenly upon the greensward
All alone stood Hiawatha,
Panting with his wild exertion,
Palpitating with the struggle;
And before him, breathless, lifeless,
Lay the youth, with hair dishevelled,
Plumage torn, and garments tattered,
Dead he lay there in the sunset.
    And victorious Hiawatha
Made the grave as he commanded,
Stripped the garments from Mondamin,
Stripped his tattered plumage from him,
Laid him in the earth, and made it
Soft and loose and light above him;
And the heron, the Shuh-shuh-gah,
From the melancholy moorlands,
Gave a cry of lamentation,
Gave a cry of pain and anguish!
    Homeward then went Hiawatha
To the lodge of old Nokomis,
And the seven days of his fasting
Were accomplished and completed.
But the place was not forgotten
Where he wrestled with Mondamin;
Nor forgotten nor neglected

Was the grave where lay Mon-
   damin,
Sleeping in the rain and sunshine,
Where his scattered plumes and
   garments
Faded in the rain and sunshine.
   Day by day did Hiawatha
Go to wait and watch beside it;
Kept the dark mould soft above it,
Kept it clean from weeds and in-
   sects,
Drove away, with scoffs and shout-
   ings,
Kahgahgee, the king of ravens.
   Till at length a small green
   feather
From the earth shot slowly upward,
Then another and another,
And before the Summer ended
Stood the maize in all its beauty,
With its shining robes about it,
And its long, soft, yellow tresses;
And in rapture Hiawatha
Cried aloud, " It is Mondamin!
Yes, the friend of man, Mon-
   damin!"
   Then he called to old Nokomis
And Iagoo, the great boaster,
Showed them where the maize was
   growing,
Told them of his wondrous vision,
Of his wrestling and his triumph,
Of this new gift to the nations,
Which should be their food for-
   ever.
   And still later, when the Autumn
Changed the long, green leaves to
   yellow,
And the soft and juicy kernels
Grew like wampum hard and
   yellow,
Then the ripened ears he gathered,
Stripped the withered husks from
   off them,
As he once had stripped the
   wrestler,
Gave the first Feast of Mondamin,
And made known unto the people
This new gift of the Great Spirit.

VI.

HIAWATHA'S FRIENDS

   Two good friends had Hiawatha,
Singled out from all the others,
Bound to him in closest union,
And to whom he gave the right
   hand
Of his heart, in joy and sorrow;
Chibiabos, the musician,
And the very strong man, Kwasind.
   Straight between them ran the
   pathway,
Never grew the grass upon it;
Singing birds, that utter false-
   hoods,
Story-tellers, mischief-makers,
Found no eager ear to listen,
Could not breed ill-will between
   them,
For they kept each other's counsel,
Spake with naked hearts together,
Pondering much and much con-
   triving
How the tribes of men might
   prosper.
   Most beloved by Hiawatha
Was the gentle Chibiabos,
He the best of all musicians,
He the sweetest of all singers.
Beautiful and childlike was he,
Brave as man is, soft as woman,
Pliant as a wand of willow,
Stately as a deer with antlers.
   When he sang, the village
   listened:
All the warriors gathered round
   him,
All the women came to hear him;
Now he stirred their souls to pas-
   sion,
Now he melted them to pity.
   From the hollow reeds he
   fashioned
Flutes so musical and mellow,
That the brook, the Sebowisha,
Ceased to murmur in the wood-
   land,

That the wood-birds ceased from
singing,
And the squirrel, Adjidaumo,
Ceased his chatter in the oak-tree,
And the rabbit, the Wabasso,
Sat upright to look and listen.
  Yes, the brook, the Sebowisha,
Pausing, said, " O Chibiabos,
Teach my waves to flow in music,
Softly as your words in singing! "
  Yes, the bluebird, the Owaissa,
Envious, said, " O Chibiabos,
Teach me tones as wild and way-
ward,
Teach me songs as full of frenzy! "
  Yes, the Opechee, the robin,
Joyous, said, " O Chibiabos,
Teach me tones as sweet and
tender,
Teach me songs as full of glad-
ness! "
  And the whippoorwill, Wawo-
naissa,
Sobbing, said, " O Chibiabos,
Teach me tones as melancholy,
Teach me songs as full of sadness! "
  All the many sounds of nature
Borrowed sweetness from his sing-
ing;
All the hearts of men were softened
By the pathos of his music;
For he sang of peace and freedom,
Sang of beauty, love, and longing;
Sang of death, and life undying
In the Islands of the Blessed,
In the kingdom of Ponemah,
In the land of the Hereafter.
  Very dear to Hiawatha
Was the gentle Chibiabos,
He the best of all musicians,
He the sweetest of all singers;
For his gentleness he loved him,
And the magic of his singing.
  Dear, too, unto Hiawatha
Was the very strong man, Kwasind,
He the strongest of all mortals,
He the mightiest among many:
For his very strength he loved
him,

For his strength allied to goodness.
  Idle in his youth was Kwasind,
Very listless, dull, and dreamy,
Never played with other children,
Never fished and never hunted,
Not like other children was he;
But they saw that much he fasted,
Much his Manito entreated,
Much besought his Guardian Spirit.
  " Lazy Kwasind! " said his
mother,
" In my work you never help me!
In the Summer you are roaming
Idly in the fields and forests;
In the Winter you are cowering
O'er the firebrands in the wigwam!
In the coldest days of Winter
I must break the ice for fishing;
With my nets you never help me;
At the door my nets are hanging,
Dripping, freezing with the water;
Go and wring them, Yenadizze!
Go and dry them in the sunshine! "
  Slowly, from the ashes, Kwasind
Rose, but made no angry answer;
From the lodge went forth in
silence,
Took the nets, that hung together,
Dripping, freezing at the doorway,
Like a wisp of straw he wrung
them,
Like a wisp of straw he broke
them,
Could not wring them without
breaking,
Such the strength was in his fingers.
  " Lazy Kwasind! " said his
father,
" In the hunt you never help me;
Every bow you touch is broken,
Snapped asunder every arrow;
Yet come with me to the forest,
You shall bring the hunting home-
ward."
  Down a narrow pass they wan-
dered,
Where a brooklet led them onward,
Where the trail of deer and bison
Marked the soft mud on the margin,

Till they found all further passage
Shut against them, barred securely
By the trunks of trees uprooted,
Lying lengthwise, lying crosswise,
And forbidding further passage.
　"We must go back," said the
　　old man,
"O'er these logs we cannot
　clamber;
Not a woodchuck could get
　through them,
Not a squirrel clamber o'er them!"
And straightway his pipe he
　lighted,
And sat down to smoke and
　ponder.
But before his pipe was finished,
Lo! the path was cleared before
　him;
All the trunks had Kwasind lifted,
To the right hand, to the left hand,
Shot the pine-trees swift as arrows,
Hurled the cedars light as lances.
　"Lazy Kwasind!" said the
　　young men,
As they sported in the meadow:
"Why stand idly looking at us,
Leaning on the rock behind you?
Come and wrestle with the others,
Let us pitch the quoit together!"
　Lazy Kwasind made no answer,
To their challenge made no answer,
Only rose, and, slowly turning,
Seized the huge rock in his fingers,
Tore it from its deep foundation,
Poised it in the air a moment,
Pitched it sheer into the river,
Sheer into the swift Pauwating,
Where it still is seen in Summer.
　Once as down that foaming
　　river,
Down the rapids of Pauwating,
Kwasind sailed with his com-
　panions,
In the stream he saw a beaver,
Saw Ahmeek, the King of Beavers,
Struggling with the rushing cur-
　rents,
Rising, sinking in the water.

Without speaking, without paus-
　ing,
Kwasind leaped into the river,
Plunged beneath the bubbling sur-
　face,
Through the whirlpools chased the
　beaver,
Followed him among the islands,
Stayed so long beneath the water,
That his terrified companions
Cried, "Alas! good-by to Kwasind!
We shall never more see Kwasind!"
But he reappeared triumphant,
And upon his shining shoulders
Brought the beaver, dead and
　dripping,
Brought the King of all the
　Beavers.
　And these two, as I have told you,
Were the friends of Hiawatha,
Chibiabos, the musician,
And the very strong man, Kwasind.
Long they lived in peace together,
Spake with naked hearts together,
Pondering much and much con-
　triving
How the tribes of men might
　prosper.

VII.

HIAWATHA'S SAILING

　"Give me of your bark, O Birch-
　　Tree!
Of your yellow bark, O Birch-Tree!
Growing by the rushing river,
Tall and stately in the valley!
I a light canoe will build me,
Build a swift Cheemaun for sailing,
That shall float upon the river,
　Like a yellow leaf in Autumn,
Like a yellow water-lily!
　"Lay aside your cloak, O Birch-
　　Tree!
Lay aside your white-skin wrapper,
For the Summer-time is coming,
And the sun is warm in heaven,

And you need no white-skin
    wrapper!"
    Thus aloud cried Hiawatha
In the solitary forest,
By the rushing Taquamenaw,
When the birds were singing gaily,
In the Moon of Leaves were singing,
And the sun, from sleep awaking,
Started up and said, "Behold me!
Gheezis, the great Sun, behold me!'
    And the tree with all its branches
Rustled in the breeze of morning,
Saying, with a sigh of patience,
"Take my cloak, O Hiawatha!"
    With his knife the tree he
    girdled;
Just beneath its lowest branches,
Just above the roots he cut it,
Till the sap came oozing outward;
Down the trunk, from top to
    bottom,
Sheer he cleft the bark asunder,
With a wooden wedge he raised it,
Stripped it from the trunk un-
    broken.
    "Give me of your boughs, O
    Cedar!
Of your strong and pliant branches,
My canoe to make more steady,
Make more strong and firm beneath
    me!"
    Through the summit of the cedar
Went a sound, a cry of horror,
Went a murmur of resistance;
But it whispered, bending down-
    ward,
"Take my boughs, O Hiawatha!"
    Down he hewed the boughs of
    cedar,
Shaped them straightway to a
    framework,
Like two bows he formed and
    shaped them,
Like two bended bows together.
"Give me of your roots, O Tama-
    rack!
Of your fibrous roots, O Larch-
    Tree!
My canoe to bind together.

So to bind the ends together
That the water may not enter,
That the river may not wet me!"
    And the larch, with all its fibres,
Shivered in the air of morning,
Touched his forehead with its
    tassels,
Said, with one long sigh of sorrow,
"Take them all, O Hiawatha!"
    From the earth he tore the fibres,
Tore the tough roots of the Larch-
    Tree,
Closely sewed the bark together,
Bound it closely to the framework.
    "Give me of your balm, O Fir-
    Tree!
Of your balsam and your resin,
So to close the seams together
That the water may not enter,
That the river may not wet me!"
    And the Fir-Tree, tall and
    sombre,
Sobbed through all its robes of
    darkness,
Rattled like a shore with pebbles,
Answered wailing, answered weep-
    ing,
"Take my balm, O Hiawatha!"
    And he took the tears of balsam,
Took the resin of the Fir-Tree,
Smeared therewith each seam and
    fissure,
Made each crevice safe from water.
    "Give me of your quills, O
    Hedge-hog!
All your quills, O Kagh, the
    Hedgehog!
I will make a necklace of them,
Make a girdle for my beauty,
And two stars to deck her bosom!"
    From a hollow tree the Hedge-
    hog
With his sleepy eyes looked at him,
Shot his shining quills, like arrows,
Saying, with a drowsy murmur,
Through the tangle of his whiskers,
"Take my quills, O Hiawatha!"
    From the ground the quills he
    gathered,

All the little shining arrows,
Stained them red and blue and
  yellow,
With the juice of roots and berries;
Into his canoe he wrought them,
Round its waist a shining girdle,
Round its bows a gleaming neck-
  lace,
On its breast two stars resplendent.
  Thus the Birch Canoe was
    builded
In the valley, by the river,
In the bosom of the forest;
And the forest's life was in it,
All its mystery and its magic,
All the lightness of the birch-tree,
All the toughness of the cedar,
All the larch's supple sinews;
And it floated on the river
Like a yellow leaf in Autumn,
Like a yellow water-lily.
  Paddles none had Hiawatha,
Paddles none he had or needed,
For his thoughts as paddles served
  him,
And his wishes served to guide
  him;
Swift or slow at will he glided,
Veered to right or left at pleasure.
  Then he called aloud to Kwasind,
To his friend, the strong man,
  Kwasind,
Saying, " Help me clear this river
Of its sunken logs and sand-bars."
  Straight into the river Kwasind
Plunged as if he were an otter,
Dived as if he were a beaver,
Stood up to his waist in water,
To his armpits in the river,
Swam and shouted in the river,
Tugged at sunken logs and
  branches,
With his hands he scooped the
  sand-bars,
With his feet the ooze and tangle,
  And thus sailed my Hiawatha
Down the rushing Taquamenaw,
Sailed through all its bends and
  windings,

Sailed through all its deeps and
  shallows,
While his friend, the strong man
  Kwasind,
Swam the deeps, the shallows
  waded.
  Up and down the river went
    they,
In and out among its islands,
Cleared its bed of root and sand
  bar,
Dragged the dead trees from its
  channel,
Made its passage safe and certain,
Made a pathway for the people,
From its springs among the moun-
  tains,
To the water of Pauwating,
To the bay of Taquamenaw.

VIII.

HIAWATHA'S FISHING

  Forth upon the Gitche Gumee,
On the shining Big-Sea-Water,
With his fishing line of cedar,
Of the twisted bark of cedar,
Forth to catch the sturgeon
  Nahma,
Mishe-Nahma, King of Fishes,
In his birch canoe exulting
All alone went Hiawatha.
  Through the clear, transparent
    water
He could see the fishes swimming
Far down in the depths below him;
See the yellow perch, the Sahwa,
Like a sunbeam in the water,
See the Shawgashee, the crawfish,
Like a spider on the bottom,
On the white and sandy bottom.
  At the stern sat Hiawatha,
With his fishing-line of cedar;
In his plumes the breeze of morn-
  ing
Played as in the hemlock branches;
On the bows, with tail erected,
Sat the squirrel, Adjidaumo;

In his fur the breeze of morning
Played as in the prairie grasses.
  On the white sand of the bottom
Lay the monster Mishe-Nahma,
Lay the sturgeon, King of Fishes;
Through his gills he breathed the
  water,
With his fins he fanned and win-
  nowed,
With his tail he swept the sand-
  floor.
  There he lay in all his armour;
On each side a shield to guard him,
Plates of bone upon his forehead.
Down his sides and back and
  shoulders
Plates of bone with spines project-
  ing!
Painted was he with his war-paints,
Stripes of yellow, red, and azure,
Spots of brown and spots of sable;
And he lay there on the bottom,
Fanning with his fins of purple,
As above him Hiawatha
In his birch canoe came sailing,
With his fishing-line of cedar.
  "Take my bait," cried Hiawatha,
Down into the depths beneath him,
  "Take my bait, O Sturgeon,
  Nahma!
Come up from below the water,
Let us see which is the stronger!"
And he dropped his line of cedar
Through the clear, transparent
  water,
Waited vainly for an answer,
Long sat waiting for an answer,
And repeating loud and louder,
"Take my bait, O King of Fishes!"
  Quiet lay the sturgeon, Nahma,
Fanning slowly in the water,
Looking up at Hiawatha,
Listening to his call and clamour,
His unnecessary tumult,
Till he wearied of the shouting;
And he said to the Kenozha,
To the pike, the Maskenozha,
"Take the bait of this rude fellow,
Break the line of Hiawatha!"

In his fingers Hiawatha
Felt the loose line jerk and tighten
As he drew it in, it tugged so
That the birch canoe stood end
  wise,
Like a birch log in the water,
With the squirrel, Adjidaumo,
Perched and frisking on the sum-
  mit.
  Full of scorn was Hiawatha
When he saw the fish rise upward,
Saw the pike, the Maskenozha,
Coming nearer, nearer to him,
And he shouted through the water,
"Esa! esa! shame upon you!
You are but the pike, Kenozha,
You are not the fish I wanted,
You are not the King of Fishes!"
  Reeling downward to the bottom
Sank the pike in great confusion,
And the mighty sturgeon, Nahma,
Said to Ugudwash, the sun-fish,
"Take the bait of this great
  boaster,
Break the line of Hiawatha!"
  Slowly upward, wavering,
  gleaming,
Like a white moon in the water,
Rose the Ugudwash, the sun-fish,
Seized the line of Hiawatha,
Swung with all his weight upon it,
Made a whirlpool in the water,
Whirled the birch canoe in circles,
Round and round in gurgling
  eddies,
Till the circles in the water
Reached the far-off sandy beaches,
Till the water-flags and rushes
Nodded on the distant margins.
  But when Hiawatha saw him
Slowly rising through the water,
Lifting his great disk of whiteness,
Loud he shouted in derision,
"Esa! esa! shame upon you!
You are Ugudwash, the sunfish,
You are not the fish I wanted,
You are not the King of Fishes!"
Wavering downward, white and
  ghastly,

Sank the Ugudwash, the sun-fish,
And again the sturgeon, Nahma,
Heard the shout of Hiawatha,
Heard his challenge of defiance,
The unnecessary tumult,
Ringing far across the water.
     From the white sand of the bottom
Up he rose with angry gesture,
Quivering in each nerve and fibre,
Clashing all his plates of armour,
Gleaming bright with all his war-paint;
In his wrath he darted upward,
Flashing leaped into the sunshine,
Opened his great jaws, and swallowed
Both canoe and Hiawatha.
     Down into that darksome cavern
Plunged the headlong Hiawatha,
As a log on some black river
Shoots and plunges down the rapids,
Found himself in utter darkness,
Groped about in helpless wonder,
Till he felt a great heart beating,
Throbbing in that utter darkness.
     And he smote it in his anger,
With his fist, the heart of Nahma,
Felt the mighty King of Fishes
Shudder through each nerve and fibre,
Heard the water gurgle round him
As he leaped and staggered through it,
Sick at heart, and faint and weary.
     Crosswise then did Hiawatha
Drag his birch-canoe for safety,
Lest from out the jaws of Nahma,
In the turmoil and confusion,
Forth he might be hurled and perish.
And the squirrel, Adjidaumo,
Frisked and chattered very gaily,
Toiled and tugged with Hiawatha
Till the labour was completed.
     Then said Hiawatha to him,
" O my little friend, the squirrel,

Bravely have you toiled to help me;
Take the thanks of Hiawatha,
And the name which now he gives you;
For hereafter and for ever
Boys shall call you Adjidaumo,
Tail-in-air the boys shall call you! "
     And again the sturgeon, Nahma,
Gasped and quivered in the water,
Then was still, and drifted landward
Till he grated on the pebbles,
Till the listening Hiawatha
Heard him grate upon the margin,
Felt him strand upon the pebbles,
Knew that Nahma, King of Fishes,
Lay there dead upon the margin.
     Then he heard a clang and flapping,
As of many wings assembling,
Heard a screaming and confusion,
As of birds of prey contending,
Saw a gleam of light above him,
Shining through the ribs of Nahma,
Saw the glittering eyes of sea-gulls,
Of Kayoshk, the sea-gulls, peering,
Gazing at him through the opening,
Heard them saying to each other,
" 'Tis our brother, Hiawatha! "
     And he shouted from below them,
Cried exulting from the caverns:
" O ye sea-gulls! O my brothers!
I have slain the sturgeon, Nahma;
Make the rifts a little larger,
With your claws the openings widen,
Set me free from this dark prison,
And henceforward and for ever
Men shall speak of your achievements,
Calling you Kayoshk, the sea-gulls,
Yes, Kayoshk, the Noble Scratchers! "
     And the wild and clamorous sea-gulls
Toiled with beak and claws together,

Made the rifts and openings wider
In the mighty ribs of Nahma,
And from peril and from prison,
From the body of the sturgeon,
From the peril of the water,
Was released my Hiawatha.
 He was standing near his wig-
  wam,
On the margin of the water,
And he called to old Nokomis,
Called and beckoned to Nokomis,
Pointed to the sturgeon, Nahma,
Lying lifeless on the pebbles,
With the sea-gulls feeding on him.
 " I have slain the Mishe-Nahma,
Slain the King of Fishes! " said he;
" Look! the sea-gulls feed upon
  him,
Yes, my friends Kayoshk, the sea-
  gulls;
Drive them not away, Nokomis,
They have saved me from great
  peril
In the body of the sturgeon,
Wait until their meal is ended,
Till their craws are full with feast-
  ing,
Till they homeward fly, at sunset,
To their nests among the marshes;
Then bring all your pots and
  kettles
And make oil for us in Winter."
 And she waited till the sun set,
Till the pallid moon, the Night-sun,
Rose above the tranquil water,
Till Kayoshk, the sated sea-gulls,
From their banquet rose with
  clamour,
And across the fiery sunset
Winged their way to far-off islands,
To their nests among the rushes.
 To his sleep went Hiawatha,
And Nokomis to her labour,
Toiling patient in the moonlight,
Till the sun and moon changed
  places,
Till the sky was red with sunrise,
And Kayoshk, the hungry sea-gulls,
Came back from the reedy islands,

Clamorous for their morning ban-
  quet.
 Three whole days and nights
  alternate
Old Nokomis and the sea-gulls
Stripped the oily flesh of Nahma,
Till the waves washed through the
  rib-bones,
Till the sea-gulls came no longer,
And upon the sands lay nothing
But the skeleton of Nahma.

IX.

HIAWATHA AND THE PEARL-FEATHER

 On the shores of Gitche Gumee,
Of the shining Big-Sea-Water,
Stood Nokomis, the old woman,
Pointing with her finger westward,
O'er the water pointing westward,
To the purple clouds of sunset.
 Fiercely the red sun descending
Burned his way along the heavens,
Set the sky on fire behind him,
As war-parties, when retreating,
Burn the prairies on their war-trail;
And the moon, the Night-sun, east-
  ward,
Suddenly starting from his ambush,
Followed fast those bloody foot-
  prints,
Followed in that fiery war-trail,
With its glare upon his features.
 And Nokomis, the old woman,
Pointing with her finger westward,
Spake these words to Hiawatha:
" Yonder dwells the great Pearl-
  Feather,
Megissogwon, the Magician,
Manito of Wealth and Wampum,
Guarded by his fiery serpents,
Guarded by the black pitch-water.
You can see his fiery serpents,
The Kenabeek, the great serpents,
Coiling, playing in the water;
You can see the black pitch-water
Stretching far away beyond them,

To the purple clouds of sunset!
"He it was who slew my father,
By his wicked wiles and cunning,
When he from the moon descended,
When he came on earth to seek me.
He, the mightiest of Magicians,
Sends the fever from the marshes,
Sends the pestilential vapours,
Sends the poisonous exhalations,
Sends the white fog from the fen-lands,
Sends disease and death among us!
"Take your bow, O Hiawatha,
Take your arrows, jasper-headed,
Take your war-club, Puggawaugun,
And your mittens, Minjekahwun,
And your birch-canoe for sailing,
And the oil of Mishe-Nahma,
So to smear its sides, that swiftly
You may pass the black pitch-water;
Slay this merciless magician,
Save the people from the fever
That he breathes across the fen-lands,
And avenge my father's murder!"
  Straightway then my Hiawatha
Armed himself with all his war-gear,
Launched his birch-canoe for sail-ing;
With his palm its sides he patted,
Said with glee, "Cheemaun, my darling,
O my Birch-Canoe! leap forward,
Where you see the fiery serpents,
Where you see the black pitch-water!"
  Forward leaped Cheemaun ex-ulting,
And the noble Hiawatha
Sang his war-song wild and woeful,
And above him the war-eagle,
The Keneu, the great war-eagle,
Master of all fowls with feathers,
Screamed and hurtled through the heavens.

  Soon he reached the fiery ser-pents,
The Kenabeek, the great serpents,
Lying huge upon the water,
Sparkling, rippling in the water,
Lying coiled across the passage,
With their blazing crests uplifted,
Breathing fiery fogs and vapours,
So that none could pass beyond them.
  But the fearless Hiawatha
Cried aloud, and spake in this wise:
"Let me pass my way, Kenabek,
Let me go upon my journey!"
And they answered, hissing fiercely,
With their fiery breath made answer:
"Back, go back! O Shaugodaya!
Back to old Nokomis, Faint-heart!"
  Then the angry Hiawatha
Raised his mighty bow of ash-tree,
Seized his arrows, jasper-headed,
Shot them fast among the serpents;
Every twanging of the bowstring
Was a war-cry and a death-cry,
Every whizzing of an arrow
Was a death-song of Kenabeek.
  Weltering in the bloody water,
Dead lay all the fiery serpents,
And among them Hiawatha
Harmless sailed, and cried exult-ing:
"Onward, O Cheemaun, my dar-ling!
Onward to the black pitch-water!"
  Then he took the oil of Nahma,
And the bows and sides anointed,
Smeared them well with oil, that swiftly
He might pass the black pitch-water.
  All night long he sailed upon it,
Sailed upon that sluggish water,
Covered with its mould of ages,
Black with rotting water-rushes,
Rank with flags and leaves of lilies,
Stagnant, lifeless, dreary, dismal,

Lighted by the shimmering moon-
light,
And by will-o'-the-wisps illumined,
Fires by ghosts of dead men
kindled,
In their weary night-encampments.
All the air was white with moon-
light,
All the water black with shadow,
And around him the Suggema,
The mosquito, sang their war-song,
And the fireflies, Wah-wah-taysee,
Waved their torches to mislead
him:
And the bullfrog, the Dahinda,
Thrust his head into the moon-
light,
Fixed his yellow eyes upon him,
Sobbed and sank beneath the sur-
face;
And anon a thousand whistles,
Answered over all the fen-lands,
And the heron, the Shuh-shuh-gah,
Far off on the reedy margin,
Heralded the hero's coming.

Westward thus fared Hiawatha,
Toward the realm of Megissogwon,
Toward the land of the Pearl-
Feather,
Till the level moon stared at him,
In his face stared pale and haggard,
Till the sun was hot behind him,
Till it burned upon his shoulders,
And before him on the upland
He could see the Shining Wigwam
Of the Manito of Wampum,
Of the mightiest of Magicians.

Then once more Cheemaun he
patted,
To his birch-canoe said, " On-
ward! "
And it stirred in all its fibres,
And with one great bound of
triumph
Leaped across the water-lilies,
Leaped through tangled flags and
rushes,
And upon the beach beyond them
Dry-shod landed Hiawatha.

Straight he took his bow of ash-
tree,
One end on the sand he rested,
With his knee he pressed the
middle,
Stretched the faithful bowstring
tighter,
Took an arrow, jasper-headed,
Shot it at the Shining Wigwam,
Sent it singing as a herald,
As a bearer of his message,
Of his challenge loud and lofty:
" Come forth from your lodge,
Pearl-Feather!
Hiawatha waits your coming! "

Straightway from the Shining
Wigwam
Came the mighty Megissogwon,
Tall of stature, broad of shoulder,
Dark and terrible in aspect,
Clad from head to foot in wampum,
Armed with all his warlike
weapons,
Painted like the sky of morning,
Streaked with crimson, blue, and
yellow,
Crested with great eagle-feathers,
Streaming upward, streaming out-
ward,
" Well I know you, Hiawatha! "
Cried he in a voice of thunder,
In a tone of loud derision.
" Hasten back, O Shaugodaya!
Hasten back among the women,
Back to old Nokomis, Faint-heart,
I will slay you as you stand there,
As of old I slew her father! "

But my Hiawatha answered,
Nothing daunted, fearing nothing:
" Big words do not smite like war-
clubs,
Boastful breath is not a bowstring,
Taunts are not so sharp as arrows,
Deeds are better things than words
are,
Actions mightier than boastings! "
Then began the greatest battle
That the sun had ever looked on,
That the war-birds ever witnessed.

All a Summer's day it lasted,
From the sunrise to the sunset;
For the shafts of Hiawatha
Harmless hit the shirt of wampum,
Harmless fell the blows he dealt it
With his mittens, Minjekahwun,
Harmless fell the heavy war-club;
It could dash the rocks asunder,
But it could not break the meshes
Of that magic shirt of wampum.

Till at sunset Hiawatha,
Leaning on his bow of ash-tree,
Wounded, weary, and desponding,
With his mighty war-club broken,
With his mittens torn and tattered,
And three useless arrows only,
Paused to rest beneath a pine-tree,
From whose branches trailed the
    mosses,
And whose trunk was coated over
With the Dead-man's Moccasin-
    leather,
With the fungus white and yellow.
    Suddenly from the boughs above
        him
Sang the Mama, the woodpecker:
" Aim your arrows, Hiawatha,
At the head of Megissogwon,
Strike the tuft of hair upon it,
At their roots the long black
    tresses;
There alone can he be wounded! "
    Winged with feathers, tipped
        with jasper,
Swift flew Hiawatha's arrow,
Just as Megissogwon, stooping,
Raised a heavy stone to throw it.
Full upon the crown it struck him,
At the roots of his long tresses,
And he reeled and staggered for-
    ward,
Plunging like a wounded bison,
Yes, like Pezhekee, the bison,
When the snow is on the prairie.
    Swifter flew the second arrow.
In the pathway of the other,
Piercing deeper than the other,
Wounding sorer than the other,
And the knees of Megissogwon

Shook like windy reeds beneath
    him,
Bent and trembled like the rushes.
    But the third and latest arrow
Swiftest flew, and wounded sorest,
And the mighty Megissogwon
Saw the fiery eyes of Pauguk,
Saw the eyes of Death glare at him,
Heard his voice call in the darkness;
At the feet of Hiawatha
Lifeless lay the great Pearl-
    Feather,
Lay the mightiest of Magicians.
    Then the grateful Hiawatha
Called the Mama, the woodpecker,
From his perch among the branches
Of the melancholy pine-tree,
And in honour of his service,
Stained with blood the tuft of
    feathers
On the little head of Mama;
Even to this day he wears it,
Wears the tuft of crimson feathers,
As a symbol of his service.
    Then he stripped the shirt of
        wampum
From the back of Megissogwon,
As a trophy of the battle,
As a signal of his conquest.
On the shore he left the body,
Half on land and half in water,
In the sand his feet were buried,
And his face was in the water,
And above him, wheeled and
    clamoured
The Keneu, the great war-eagle,
Sailing round in narrower circles,
Hovering nearer, nearer, nearer.
    From the wigwam Hiawatha
Bore the wealth of Megissogwon,
All his wealth of skins and wam-
    pum,
Furs of bison and of beaver,
Furs of sable and of ermine,
Wampum belts and strings and
    pouches,
Quivers wrought with beads of
    wampum,
Filled with arrows, silver-headed.

Homeward then he sailed exulting,
Homeward through the black pitch-water,
Homeward through the weltering serpents,
With the trophies of the battle,
With a shout and song of triumph.
On the shore stood old Nokomis,
On the shore stood Chibiabos,
And the very strong man, Kwasind,
Waiting for the hero's coming,
Listening to his song of triumph.
And the people of the village
Welcomed him with songs and dances,
Made a joyous feast, and shouted!
"Honour be to Hiawatha!
He has slain the great Pearl-Feather,
Slain the mightiest of Magicians,
Him, who sent the fiery fever,
Sent the white fog from the fen-lands,
Sent disease and death among us!"
Ever dear to Hiawatha
Was the memory of Mama!
And in token of his friendship,
As a mark of his remembrance,
He adorned and decked his pipe-stem
With the crimson tuft of feathers,
With the blood-red crest of Mama.
But the wealth of Megissogwon,
All the trophies of the battle,
He divided with his people,
Shared it equally among them.

X.

HIAWATHA'S WOOING

"As unto the bow the cord is,
So unto the man is woman,
Though she bends him, she obeys him,
Though she draws him, yet she follows,
Useless each without the other!"

Thus the youthful Hiawatha
Said within himself and pondered,
Much perplexed by various feelings,
Listless, longing, hoping, fearing,
Dreaming still of Minnehaha,
Of the lovely Laughing Water,
In the land of the Dacotahs.
"Wed a maiden of your people,"
Warning said the old Nokomis;
"Go not eastward, go not westward,
For a stranger, whom we know not!
Like a fire upon the hearthstone
Is a neighbour's homely daughter,
Like the starlight or the moonlight
Is the handsomest of strangers!"
Thus dissuading spake Nokomis,
And my Hiawatha answered
Only this: "Dear old Nokomis,
Very pleasant is the firelight,
But I like the starlight better,
Better do I like the moonlight!"
Gravely then said old Nokomis:
"Bring not here an idle maiden,
Bring not here a useless woman,
Hands unskilful, feet unwilling;
Bring a wife with nimble fingers,
Heart and hand that move together,
Feet that run on willing errands!"
Smiling answered Hiawatha:
"In the land of the Dacotahs
Lives the Arrow-maker's daughter,
Minnehaha, Laughing Water,
Handsomest of all the women.
I will bring her to your wigwam,
She shall run upon your errands,
Be your starlight, moonlight, fire-light,
Be the sunlight of my people!"
Still dissuading said Nokomis:
"Bring not to my lodge a stranger
From the land of the Dacotahs!
Very fierce are the Dacotahs,
Often is there war between us,
There are feuds yet unforgotten,
Wounds that ache and still may open!"
Laughing answered Hiawatha:

" For that reason, if no other,
Would I wed the fair Dacotah,
That our tribes might be united,
That old feuds might be forgotten,
And old wounds be healed for
    ever!"
    Thus departed Hiawatha
To the land of the Dacotahs,
To the land of handsome women;
Striding over moor and meadow,
Through interminable forests,
Through uninterrupted silence.
    With his moccasins of magic,
At each stride a mile he measured;
Yet the way seemed long before
    him,
And his heart outrun his footsteps;
And he journeyed without resting,
Till he heard the cataract's thunder,
Heard the Falls of Minnehaha,
Calling to him through the silence.
" Pleasant is the sound!" he mur-
    mured,
" Pleasant is the voice that calls
    me!"
    On the outskirts of the forest,
'Twixt the shadow and the sun-
    shine,
Herds of fallow deer were feeding,
But they saw not Hiawatha;
To his bow he whispered, " Fail
    not!"
To his arrow whispered, " Swerve
    not!"
Sent it singing on its errand,
To the red heart of the roebuck;
Threw the deer across his shoulder,
And sped forward without pausing.
    At the doorway of his wigwam
Sat the ancient Arrow-maker,
In the land of the Dacotahs,
Making arrow-heads of jasper,
Arrow-heads of chalcedony.
At his side, in all her beauty,
Sat the lovely Minnehaha,
Sat his daughter, Laughing Water,
Plaiting mats of flags and rushes;
Of the past the old man's thoughts
    were,

And the maiden's of the future.
    He was thinking, as he sat there,
Of the days when with such arrows
He had struck the deer and bison,
On the Muskoday, the meadow;
Shot the wild goose, flying south-
    ward,
On the wing, the clamorous Wawa;
Thinking of the great war-parties,
How they came to buy his arrows,
Could not fight without his arrows.
Ah, no more such noble warriors
Could be found on earth as they
    were!
Now the men were all like women,
Only used their tongues for
    weapons!
    She was thinking of a hunter,
From another tribe and country,
Young and tall and very handsome,
Who one morning, in the Spring-
    time,
Came to buy her father's arrows,
Sat and rested in the wigwam,
Lingered long about the doorway,
Looking back as he departed.
She had heard her father praise
    him,
Praise his courage and his wisdom;
Would he come again for arrows
To the Falls of Minnehaha?
On the mat her hands lay idle,
And her eyes were very dreamy.
    Through their thoughts they
        heard a footstep,
Heard a rustling in the branches,
And with glowing cheek and fore-
    head,
With the deer upon his shoulders,
Suddenly from out the woodlands
Hiawatha stood before them.
    Straight the ancient Arrow-
        maker
Looked up gravely from his labour,
Laid aside the unfinished arrow,
Bade him enter at the doorway,
Saying, as he rose to meet him,
" Hiawatha, you are welcome!"
    At the feet of Laughing Water

Hiawatha laid his burden,
Threw the red deer from his shoulders;
And the maiden looked up at him,
Looked up from her mat of rushes,
Said with gentle look and accent,
" You are welcome, Hiawatha! "
    Very spacious was the wigwam,
Made of deerskin dressed and whitened,
With the Gods of the Dacotahs
Drawn and painted on its curtains,
And so tall the doorway, hardly
Hiawatha stooped to enter,
Hardly touched his eagle-feathers
As he entered at the doorway.
    Then uprose the Laughing Water,
From the ground fair Minnehaha,
Lay aside her mat unfinished,
Brought forth food and set before them,
Water brought them from the brooklet,
Gave them food in earthen vessels,
Gave them drink in bowls of basswood,
Listened while the guest was speaking,
Listened while her father answered,
But not once her lips she opened,
Not a single word she uttered.
    Yes, as in a dream she listened
To the words of Hiawatha,
As he talked of old Nokomis,
Who had nursed him in his childhood,
As he told of his companions,
Chibiabos, the musician,
And the very strong man, Kwasind,
And of happiness and plenty
In the land of the Ojibways,
In the pleasant land and peaceful.
    " After many years of warfare,
Many years of strife and bloodshed,
There is peace between the Ojibways
And the tribe of the Dacotahs."
Thus continued Hiawatha,

And then added, speaking slowly,
" That this peace may last for ever,
And our hands be clasped more closely,
And our hearts be more united,
Give me as my wife this maiden,
Minnehaha, Laughing Water,
Loveliest of Dacotah women! "
    And the ancient Arrow-maker
Paused a moment ere he answered,
Smoked a little while in silence,
Looked at Hiawatha proudly,
Fondly looked at Laughing Water,
And made answer very gravely:
" Yes. if Minnehaha wishes;
Let your heart speak, Minnehaha! "
    And the lovely Laughing Water
Seemed more lovely, as she stood there,
Neither willing nor reluctant,
As she went to Hiawatha,
Softly took the seat beside him,
While she said, and blushed to say it,
" I will follow you, my husband! "
    This was Hiawatha's wooing!
Thus it was he won the daughter
Of the ancient Arrow-maker,
In the land of the Dacotahs!
    From the wigwam he departed,
Leading with him Laughing Water;
Hand in hand they went together,
Through the woodland and the meadow,
Left the old man standing lonely
At the doorway of his wigwam,
Heard the Falls of Minnehaha
Calling to them from the distance,
Crying to them from afar off,
" Fare thee well, O Minnehaha! "
    And the ancient Arrow-maker
Turned again unto his labour,
Sat down by his sunny doorway,
Murmuring to himself, and saying:
" Thus it is our daughters leave us,
Those we love, and those who love us!
Just when they have learned to help us,

When we are old and lean upon
them,
Comes a youth with flaunting
feathers,
With his flute of reeds, a stranger
Wanders piping through the village,
Beckons to the fairest maiden,
As she follows where he leads her,
Leaving all things for the
stranger!"
　Pleasant was the journey home-
ward,
Through interminable forests,
Over meadow, over mountain,
Over river, hill, and hollow.
Short it seemed to Hiawatha,
Though they journeyed very
slowly,
Though his pace he checked and
slackened
To the steps of Laughing Water.
　Over wide and rushing rivers
In his arms he bore the maiden;
Light he thought her as a feather,
As the plume upon his headgear;
Cleared the tangled pathway for
her,
Bent aside the swaying branches,
Made at night a lodge of branches,
And a bed with boughs of hemlock,
And a fire before the doorway
With the dry cones of the pine tree.
　All the travelling winds went
with them,
O'er the meadow, through the forest;
All the stars of night looked at
them,
Watched with sleepless eyes their
slumber;
From his ambush in the oak tree
Peeped the squirrel, Adjidaumo,
Watched with eager eyes the lovers;
And the rabbit, the Wabasso,
Scampered from the path before
them,
Peering, peeping from his burrow,
Sat erect upon his haunches,
Watched with curious eyes the
lovers.

Pleasant was the journey home-
ward!
All the birds sang loud and sweetly
Songs of happiness and heart's-
ease;
Sang the bluebird, the Owaissa,
" Happy are you, Hiawatha,
Having such a wife to love you!"
Sang the Opechee, the robin,
" Happy are you, Laughing Water,
Having such a noble husband!"
　From the sky the sun benignant
Looked upon them through the
branches,
Saying to them, " O my children,
Love is sunshine, hate is shadow,
Life is checkered shade and sun-
shine,
Rule by love, O Hiawatha!"
　From the sky the moon looked
at them,
Filled the lodge with mystic splen-
dours,
Whispered to them, " O my chil-
dren,
Day is restless, night is quiet,
Man imperious, woman feeble;
Half is mine, although I follow;
Rule by patience, Laughing
Water!"
　Thus it was they journeyed
homeward;
Thus it was that Hiawatha
To the lodge of old Nokomis
Brought the moonlight, starlight,
firelight,
Brought the sunshine of his people,
Minnehaha, Laughing Water,
Handsomest of all the women
In the land of the Dacotahs,
In the land of handsome women.

XI.

HIAWATHA'S WEDDING-FEAST

You shall hear how Pau - Puk-
Kee-wis,
How the handsome Yenadizze

Danced at Hiawatha's wedding;
How the gentle Chibiabos,
He the sweetest of musicians,
Sang his songs of love and longing;
How Iagoo, the great boaster,
He the marvellous story-teller,
Told his tales of strange adventure,
That the feast might be more joyous,
That the time might pass more gaily,
And the guests be more contented.
    Sumptuous was the feast Nokomis
Made at Hiawatha's wedding;
All the bowls were made of basswood,
White and polished very smoothly,
All the spoons of horn and bison,
Black and polished very smoothly.
    She had sent through all the village
Messengers with wands of willow,
As a sign of invitation,
As a token of the feasting;
And the wedding guests assembled,
Clad in all their richest raiment,
Robes of fur and belts of wampum,
Splendid with their paint and plumage,
Beautiful with beads and tassels.
    First they ate the sturgeon, Nahma,
And the pike, the Maskenozha,
Caught and cooked by old Nokomis;
Then on pemican they feasted,
Pemican and buffalo marrow,
Haunch of deer and hump of bison,
Yellow cakes of the Mondamin,
And the wild rice of the river.
    But the gracious Hiawatha,
And the lovely Laughing Water,
And the careful old Nokomis,
Tasted not the food before them,
Only waited on the others,
Only served their guests in silence.
    And when all the guests had finished,

Old Nokomis, brisk and busy,
From an ample pouch of otter,
Filled the redstone pipes for smoking
With tobacco from the South-land,
Mixed with bark of the red willow,
And with herbs and leaves of fragrance.
    Then she said, "O Pau-Puk-Keewis,
Dance for us your merry dances,
Dance the Beggar's Dance to please us,
That the feast may be more joyous,
That the time may pass more gaily,
And our guests be more contented!"
    Then the handsome Pau-Puk-Keewis,
He the idle Yenadizze,
He the merry mischief-maker,
Whom the people called the Storm-Fool,
Rose among the guests assembled.
Skilled was he in sports and pastimes,
In the merry dance of snowshoes,
In the play of quoits and ball-play;
Skilled was he in games of hazard,
In all games of skill and hazard,
Pugasaing, the Bowl and Counters,
Kuntassoo, the Game of Plum-stones.
    Though the warriors called him Faint-Heart,
Called him coward, Shaugodaya,
Idler, gambler, Yenadizze,
Little heeded he their jesting,
Little cared he for their insults,
For the women and the maidens
Loved the handsome Pau-Puk-Keewis.
    He was dressed in shirt of doeskin,
White and soft, and fringed with ermine,
All inwrought with beads of wampum;
He was dressed in deerskin leggings,

Fringed with hedgehog quills and
    ermine,
And in moccasins of buckskin,
Thick with quills and beads em-
    broidered.
On his head were plumes of swan's
    down,
On his heels were tails of foxes,
In one hand a fan of feathers,
And a pipe was in the other.

    Barred with streaks of red and
    yellow,
Streaks of blue and bright ver-
    milion,
Shone the face of Pau-Puk-Keewis.
From his forehead fell his tresses,
Smooth, and parted like a woman's,
Shining bright with oil, and
    plaited,
Hung with braids of scented
    grasses,
As among the guests assembled.
To the sound of flutes and singing,
To the sound of drums and voices,
Rose the handsome Pau - Puk -
    Keewis,
And began his mystic dances.

    First he danced a solemn measure,
Very slow in step and gesture,
In and out among the pine trees,
Through the shadows and the sun-
    shine,
Treading softly like a panther,
Then more swiftly and still swifter,
Whirling, spinning round in circles,
Leaping o'er the guests assembled,
Eddying round and round the
    wigwam,
Till the leaves went whirling with
    him,
Till the dust and wind together
Swept in eddies round about him.

    Then along the sandy margin
Of the lake, the Big-Sea-Water,
On he sped with frenzied gestures,
Stamped upon the sand, and
    tossed it
Wildly in the air around him;
Till the wind became a whirlwind,

Till the sand was blown and sifted
Like great snowdrifts o'er the
    landscape,
Heaping all the shores with Sand
    Dunes,
Sand Hills of the Nagow Wud-
    joo! [1]

    Thus the merry Pau-Puk-Keewis
Danced his Beggar's Dance to
    please them,
And, returning, sat down laughing
There among the guests assembled,
Sat and fanned himself serenely
With his fan of turkey-feathers.

    Then they said to Chibiabos,
To the friend of Hiawatha,
To the sweetest of all singers,
To the best of all musicians,
" Sing to us, O Chibiabos!
Songs of love and songs of longing,
That the feast may be more joyous,
That the time may pass more gaily,
And our guests be more con-
    tented! "

    And the gentle Chibiabos
Sang in accents sweet and tender,
Sang in tones of deep emotion,
Songs of love and songs of longing;
Looking still at Hiawatha,
Looking at fair Laughing Water,
Sang he softly, sang in this wise.

[1] A description of the *Grand Sable*,
or great sand dunes of Lake Superior,
is given in Foster and Whitney's
*Report on the Geology of the Lake
Superior Land District*, Part II., p. 131.
" The Grand Sable possesses a
scenic interest little inferior to that
of the Pictured Rocks. The explorer
passes abruptly from a coast of con-
solidated sand to one of loose materials;
and although in the one case the cliffs
are less precipitous, yet in the other
they attain a higher altitude. He
sees before him a long reach of coast,
resembling a vast sand-bank, more
than three hundred and fifty feet in
height, without a trace of vegetation.
Ascending to the top, rounded hillocks
of blown sand are observed, with
occasional clumps of trees, standing
out like oases in the desert."

" Onaway! Awake, beloved! [1]
Thou the wild flower of the forest!
Thou the wild bird of the prairie!
Thou with eyes so soft and fawn-
    like!
  " If thou only lookest on me,
I am happy, I am happy,
As the lilies of the prairie,
When they feel the dew upon
    them!
  " Sweet thy breath is as the fra-
    grance
Of the wild flowers in the morning,
As their fragrance is at evening,
In the Moon when leaves are fall-
    ing.
  " Does not all the blood within
    me,
Leap to meet thee, leap to meet
    thee,
As the springs to meet the sun-
    shine,
In the Moon when nights are
    brightest?
  " Onaway! my heart sings to
    thee,
Sings with joy when thou art near
    me,
As the sighing, singing branches
In the pleasant Moon of Straw-
    berries!
  " When thou art not pleased,
    beloved,
Then my heart is sad and darkened,
As the shining river darkens
When the clouds drop shadows on
    it!
  " When thou smilest, my be-
    loved,
Then my troubled heart is bright-
    ened,
As in sunshine gleam the ripples
That the cold wind makes in rivers.
  " Smiles the earth, and smile the
    waters,
Smile the cloudless skies above us,

  [1] The original of this song may be
found in Littell's *Living Age*, Vol.
XXV., p. 45.

But I lose the way of smiling
When thou art no longer near me!
  " I myself, myself! behold me!
Blood of my beating heart, behold
    me!
O awake, awake, beloved!
Onaway! awake, beloved! "
    Thus the gentle Chibiabos
Sang his song of love and longing;
And Iagoo, the great boaster,
He the marvellous story-teller,
He the friend of old Nokomis,
Jealous of the sweet musician,
Jealous of the applause they gave
    him,
Saw in all the eyes around him,
Saw in all their looks and gestures,
That the wedding guests assembled
Longed to hear his pleasant stories,
His immeasurable falsehoods.
    Very boastful was Iagoo;
Never heard he an adventure
But himself had met a greater;
Never any deed of daring
But himself had done a bolder;
Never any marvellous story
But himself could tell a stranger.
    Would you listen to his boasting,
Would you only give him credence,
No one ever shot an arrow
Half so far and high as he had;
Ever caught so many fishes,
Ever killed so many reindeer,
Ever trapped so many beaver!
    None could run so fast as he
    could,
None could dive so deep as he could,
None could swim as far as he could;
None had made so many journeys,
None had seen so many wonders,
As this wonderful Iagoo,
As this marvellous story-teller!
    Thus his name became a by-word
And a jest among the people;
And whene'er a boastful hunter
Praised his own address too highly,
Or a warrior, home returning,
Talked too much of his achieve-
    ments,

All his hearers cried, " Iagoo!
Here's Iagoo come among us! "
He it was who carved the cradle
Of the little Hiawatha,
Carved its framework out of linden,
Bound it strong with reindeer
    sinews;
He it was who taught him later
How to make his bows and arrows,
How to make the bows of ash tree,
And the arrows of the oak tree,
So among the guests assembled
At my Hiawatha's wedding
Sat Iagoo, old and ugly,
Sat the marvellous story-teller.

    And they said, " O good Iagoo,
Tell us now a tale of wonder,
Tell us of some strange adventure,
That the feast may be more joyous,
That the time may pass more gaily,
And our guests be more con-
    tented! "
And Iagoo answered straightway,
" You shall hear a tale of wonder.
You shall hear the strange adven-
    tures
Of Osseo, the magician,
From the Evening Star descended."

XII.

THE SUN OF THE EVENING STAR

Can it be the sun descending
O'er the level plain of water?
Or the Red Swan floating, flying,[1]
Wounded by the magic arrow,

[1] The fanciful tradition of the Red
Swan may be found in Schoolcraft's
Algic Researches, Vol. II., p. 9.
Three brothers were hunting on a
wager to see who would bring home
the first game.
    " They were to shoot no other
animal," so the legend says, " but
such as each was in the habit of killing.
They set out different ways; Odjibwa,
the youngest, had not gone far before
he saw a bear, an animal he was not
to kill, by the agreement. He followed
him close, and drove an arrow through

Staining all the waves with crim-
    son,

him, which brought him to the ground.
Although contrary to the bet, he im-
mediately commenced skinning him,
when suddenly something red tinged
all the air around him. He rubbed his
eyes, thinking he was perhaps de-
ceived, but without effect, for the red
hue continued. At length he heard
a strange noise at a distance. It first
appeared like a human voice; but
after following the sound for some
distance, he reached the shores of a
lake, and soon saw the object he was
looking for. At a distance out in the
lake sat a most beautiful Red Swan
whose plumage glittered in the sun,
and who would now and then make
the same noise he had heard. He was
within long bow-shot, and pulling the
arrow from the bow-string up to his
ear, took deliberate aim and shot.
The arrow took no effect; and he shot
and shot again till his quiver was
empty. Still the swan remained,
moving round and round, stretching
its long neck and dipping its bill
into the water, as if heedless of the
arrows shot at it. Odjibwa ran home,
and got all his own and his brother's
arrows, and shot them all away. He
then stood and gazed at the beautiful
bird. While standing, he remembered
his brother's saying that in their
deceased father's medicine-sack were
three magic arrows. Off he started,
his anxiety to kill the swan over-
coming all scruples. At any other
time he would have deemed it sacri-
lege to open his father's medicine-
sack; but now he hastily seized the
three arrows and ran back, leaving the
other contents of the sack scattered
over the lodge. The swan was still
there. He shot the first arrow with
great precision, and came very near to
it. The second came still closer; as
he took the last arrow, he felt his arm
firmer, and drawing it up with vigour,
saw it pass through the neck of the
swan a little above the breast. Still
it did not prevent the bird from flying
off, which it did, however, at first
slowly, flapping its wings and rising
gradually into the air, and then flying
off toward the sinking of the sun."—
Pp. 10-12.

With the crimson of its life-blood,
Filling all the air with splendour,
With the splendour of its plumage?
Yes; it is the sun descending,
Sinking down into the water;
All the sky is stained with purple,
All the water flushed with crimson!
No; it is the Red Swan floating,
Diving down beneath the water,
To the sky its wings are lifted,
With its blood the waves are
    reddened!
    Over it the Star of Evening
Melts and trembles through the
    purple,
Hangs suspended in the twilight.
No; it is a bead of wampum
On the robes of the Great Spirit,
As he passes through the twilight,
Walks in silence through the
    heavens.
    This with joy beheld Iagoo
And he said in haste: " Behold it!
See the sacred Star of Evening!
You shall hear a tale of wonder,
Hear the story of Osseo,
Son of the Evening Star, Osseo!
    " Once, in days no more remem-
    bered,
Ages nearer the beginning,
When the heavens were closer to
    us,
And the Gods were more familiar,
In the North-land lived a hunter,
With ten young and comely
    daughters,
Tall and lithe as wands of willow;
Only Oweenee, the youngest,
She the wilful and the wayward,
She the silent, dreamy maiden,
Was the fairest of the sisters.
    " All these women married war-
    riors,
Married brave and haughty hus-
    bands;
Only Oweenee, the youngest,
Laughed and flouted all her lovers,
All her young and handsome
    suitors,

And then married old Osseo,
Old Osseo, poor and ugly,
Broken with age and weak from
    coughing,
Always coughing like a squirrel.
    " Ah, but beautiful within him
Was the spirit of Osseo,
From the Evening Star descended,
Star of Evening, Star of Woman,
Star of tenderness and passion!
All its fire was in his bosom,
All its beauty in his spirit,
All its mystery in his being,
All its splendour in his language!
    " And her lovers, the rejected,
Handsome men with belts of wam-
    pum,
Handsome men with paint and
    feathers,
Pointed at her in derision,
Followed her with jest and
    laughter.
But she said: ' I care not for you,
Care not for your belts of wampum,
Care not for your paint and
    feathers,
Care not for your jests and
    laughter;
I am happy with Osseo! '
    " Once to some great feast in-
    vited,
Through the damp and dusk of
    evening
Walked together the ten sisters,
Walked together with their hus-
    bands;
Slowly followed old Osseo,
With fair Oweenee beside him;
All the others chatted gaily,
These two only walked in silence.
    " At the western sky Osseo
Gazed intent, as if imploring,
Often stopped and gazed imploring
At the trembling Star of Evening,
At the tender Star of Woman;
And they heard him murmur
    softly,
' Ah, *showain nemeshin, Nosa !*
Pity, pity me, my father! '

" ' Listen! ' said the eldest sister,
' He is praying to his father!
What a pity that the old man
Does not stumble in the pathway,
Does not break his neck by fall-
ing! '
And they laughed till all the forest
Rang with their unseemly laughter.
    " On their pathway through the
        woodlands
Lay an oak, by storms uprooted,
Lay the great trunk of an oak tree,
Buried half in leaves and mosses,
Mouldering, crumbling, huge and
    hollow
And Osseo, when he saw it,
Gave a shout, a cry of anguish,
Leaped into its yawning cavern,
At one end went in an old man,
Wasted, wrinkled, old, and ugly;
From the other came a young man,
Tall and straight and strong and
    handsome.
    " Thus Osseo was transfigured,
Thus restored to youth and beauty;
But alas for good Osseo,
And for Oweenee, the faithful!
Strangely, too, was she trans-
    figured.
Changed into a weak old woman,
With a staff she tottered onward,
Wasted, wrinkled, old, and ugly!
And the sisters and their husbands
Laughed until the echoing forest
Rang with their unseemly laughter.
    " But Osseo turned not from her,
Walked with slower step beside her,
Took her hand, as brown and
    withered
As an oak-leaf is in Winter,
Called her sweetheart, Nenomoo-
    sha,
Soothed her with soft words of
    kindness,
Till they reached the lodge of
    feasting,
Till they sat down in the wigwam,
Sacred to the Star of Evening,
To the tender Star of Woman.

    " Wrapt in visions, lost in
        dreaming,
At the banquet sat Osseo;
All were merry, all were happy,
All were joyous but Osseo,
Neither food nor drink he tasted,
Neither did he speak nor listen,
But as one bewildered sat he,
Looking dreamily and sadly,
First at Oweenee, then upward
At the gleaming sky above them.
    " Then a voice was heard, a
        whisper,
Coming from the starry distance.
Coming from the empty vastness,
Low, and musical, and tender;
And the voice said: ' O Osseo!
O my son, my best beloved!
Broken are the spells that bound
    you,
All the charms of the magicians,
All the magic powers of evil;
Come to me; ascend, Osseo!
    " ' Taste the food that stands
        before you;
It is blessed and enchanted,
It has magic virtues in it,
It will change you to a spirit.
All your bowls and all your kettles
Shall be wood and clay no longer;
But the bowls be changed to wam-
    pum,
And the kettles shall be silver;
They shall shine like shells of
    scarlet,
Like the fire shall gleam and glim-
    mer.
    " ' And the women shall no
        longer
Bear the dreary doom of labour,
But be changed to birds, and
    glisten
With the beauty of the starlight,
Painted with the dusky splendours
Of the skies and clouds of even-
    ing! '
    " What Osseo heard as whispers,
What as words he comprehended,
Was but music to the others,

Music as of birds afar off,
Of the whippoorwill afar off,
Of the lonely Wawonaissa
Singing in the darksome forest.
    "Then the lodge began to tremble,
Straight began to shake and tremble,
And they felt it rising, rising,
Slowly through the air ascending,
From the darkness of the tree-tops
Forth into the dewy starlight,
Till it passed the topmost branches;
And behold! the wooden dishes
All were changed to shells of scarlet!
And behold! the earthen kettles
All were changed to bowls of silver!
And the roof-poles of the wigwam
Were as glittering rods of silver,
And the roof of bark upon them
As the shining shards of bettles.
    "Then Osseo gazed around him,
And he saw the nine fair sisters,
All the sisters and their husbands,
Changed to birds of various plumage.
Some were jays and some were magpies,
Others thrushes, others blackbirds;
And they hopped, and sang, and twittered,
Pecked and fluttered all their feathers,
Strutted in their shining plumage,
And their tails like fans unfolded.
    "Only Oweenee, the youngest,
Was not changed, but sat in silence,
Wasted, wrinkled, old, and ugly,
Looking sadly at the others;
Till Osseo, gazing upward,
Gave another cry of anguish,
Such a cry as he had uttered
By the oak tree in the forest.
    "Then returned her youth and beauty
And her soiled and tattered garments
Were transformed to robes of ermine,
And her staff became a feather,
Yes, a shining silver feather!
    "And again the wigwam trembled,
Swayed and rushed through airy currents,
Through transparent cloud and vapour,
And amid celestial splendours
On the Evening Star alighted,
As a snowflake falls on snowflake,
As a leaf drops on a river,
As the thistledown on water.
    "Forth with cheerful words of welcome
Came the father of Osseo,
He with radiant locks of silver,
He with eyes serene and tender,
And he said: 'My son, Osseo,
Hang the cage of birds you bring there,
Hang the cage with rods of silver,
And the birds with glistening feathers,
At the doorway of my wigwam.'
    "At the door he hung the birdcage,
And they entered in and gladly
Listened to Osseo's father,
Ruler of the Star of Evening,
As he said: 'O my Osseo!
I have had compassion on you,
Given you back your youth and beauty,
Into birds of various plumage
Changed your sisters and their husbands;
Changed them thus because they mocked you
In the figure of the old man,
In that aspect sad and wrinkled,
Could not see your heart of passion,
Could not see your youth immortal;
Only Oweenee, the faithful,
Saw your naked heart and loved you.

" ' In the lodge that glimmers
yonder,
In the little star that twinkles
Through the vapours, on the left
hand,
Lives the envious Evil Spirit,
The Wabeno, the magician,
Who transformed you to an old
man.
Take heed lest his beams fall on
you,
For the rays he darts around
him
Are the power of his enchantment,
Are the arrows that he uses.'
" Many years, in peace and
quiet,
On the peaceful Star of Evening
Dwelt Osseo with his father;
Many years, in song and flutter,
At the doorway of the wigwam,
Hung the cage with rods of silver,
And fair Oweenee, the faithful,
Bore a son unto Osseo,
With the beauty of his mother,
With the courage of his father.
" And the boy grew up and
prospered,
And Osseo, to delight him,
Made him little bows and arrows,
Opened the great cage of silver,
And let loose his aunts and uncles,
All those birds with glossy feathers,
For his little son to shoot at.
" Round and round they
wheeled and darted,
Filled the Evening Star with
music,
With their songs of joy and free-
dom;
Filled the Evening Star with splen-
dour,
With the fluttering of their plu-
mage;
Till the boy, the little hunter,
Bent his bow and shot an arrow,
Shot a swift and fatal arrow,
And a bird, with shining feathers,
At his feet fell wounded sorely.

" But, O wondrous transforma-
tion!
'Twas no bird he saw before
him,
'Twas a beautiful young woman,
With the arrow in her bosom!
" When her blood fell on the
planet,
On the sacred Star of Evening,
Broken was the spell of magic,
Powerless was the strange en-
chantment,
And the youth, the fearless bow-
man,
Suddenly felt himself descending,
Held by unseen hands, but sinking
Downward through the empty
spaces,
Downward through the clouds and
vapours,
Till he rested on an island,
On an island, green and grassy,
Yonder in the Big-Sea-Water.
" After him he saw descending
All the birds with shining feathers,
Fluttering, falling, wafted down-
ward,
Like the painted leaves of Autumn;
And the lodge with poles of silver,
With its roof like wings of beetles,
Like the shining shards of beetles,
By the winds of heaven uplifted,
Slowly sank upon the island,
Bringing back the good Osseo,
Bringing Oweenee, the faithful.
" Then the birds again trans-
figured,
Reassumed the shape of mortals,
Took their shape but not their
stature;
They remained as Little People,
Like the pygmies, the Puk-Wud-
jies,
And on pleasant nights of Summer
When the Evening Star was shin-
ing,
Hand in hand they danced together
On the island's craggy headlands,
On the sand-beach low and level.

" Still their glittering lodge is
    seen there,
On the tranquil Summer evenings,
And upon the shore the fisher,
Sometimes hears their happy
    voices,
Sees them dancing in the star-
    light! "
    When the story was completed,
When the wondrous tale was ended,
Looking round upon his listeners,
Solemnly Iagoo added:
" There are great men, I have
    known such,
Whom their people understand not,
Whom they even make a jest of,
Scoff and jeer at in derision.
From the story of Osseo
Let them learn the fate of jesters! "
    All the wedding guests delighted
Listened to the marvellous story,
Listened laughing and applauding,
And they whispered to each other:
" Does he mean himself, I wonder?
And are we the aunts and uncles ? "
    Then again sang Chibiabos,
Sang a song of love and longing,
In those accents sweet and tender,
In those tones of pensive sadness,
Sang a maiden's lamentation
For her lover her Algonquin.
" When I think of my beloved,[1]
Ah me! think of my beloved,
When my heart is thinking of him,
O my sweetheart, my Algonquin!
" Ah me! when I parted from
    him,
Round my neck he hung the wam-
    pum,
As a pledge, the snow-white wam-
    pum,
O my sweetheart, my Algonquin!
" I will go with you, he whis-
    pered,
Ah me! to your native country;
Let me go with you, he whispered,
O my sweetheart, my Algonquin!

[1] The original of this song may be
found in *Oneóta*, p. 15.

" Far away, away, I answered,
Very far away, I answered,
Ah me! is my native country,
O my sweetheart, my Algonquin!
" When I looked back to behold
    him,
Where we parted, to behold him,
After me he still was gazing,
O my sweetheart, my Algonquin!
" By the tree he still was stand-
    ing,
By the fallen tree was standing,
That had dropped into the water,
O my sweetheart, my Algonquin!
" When I think of my beloved,
Ah me! think of my beloved,
When my heart is thinking of him
O my sweetheart, my Algonquin! "
    Such was Hiawatha's Wedding,
Such the dance of Pau-Puk-Kee-
    wis,
Such the story of Iagoo,
Such the songs of Chibiabos;
Thus the wedding banquet ended,
And the wedding guests departed,
Leaving Hiawatha happy
With the night and Minnehaha.

XIII.

BLESSING THE CORNFIELDS

Sing, O Song of Hiawatha,
Of the happy days that followed,
In the land of the Ojibways,
In the pleasant land and peaceful
Sing the mysteries of Mondamin.[1]

[1] The Indians hold the maize, or
Indian corn, in great veneration.
" They esteem it so important and
divine a grain," says Schoolcraft,
" that their story-tellers invented
various tales, in which this idea is
symbolised under the form of a special
gift from the Great Spirit. The
Odjibwa-Algonquins, who call it
Mon-dà-min, that is, the Spirit's
grain or berry, have a pretty story
of this kind, in which the stalk in
full tassel is represented as descending
from the sky, under the guise of a

Sing the Blessing of the Cornfields!
  Buried was the bloody hatchet,
Buried was the dreadful war-club,
Buried were all warlike weapons,
And the war-cry was forgotten.
There was peace among the nations;
Unmolested roved the hunters,
Built the birch canoe for sailing,
Caught the fish in lake and river,
Shot the deer and trapped the
      beaver;
Unmolested worked the women,
Made their sugar from the maple,
Gathered wild rice in the meadows,
Dressed the skins of deer and
      beaver.
  All around the happy village,
Stood the maize fields, green and
      shining,
Waved the green plumes of Mon-
      damin,
Waved his soft and sunny tresses,
Filling all the land with plenty.
'Twas the women who in Spring-
      time
Planted the broad fields and fruit-
      ful,
Buried in the earth Mondamin;

'Twas the women who in Autumn
Stripped the yellow husks of har-
      vest,
Stripped the garments from Mon-
      damin,
Even as Hiawatha taught them.
  Once, when all the maize was
      planted,
Hiawatha, wise and thoughtful,
Spake and said to Minnehaha,
To his wife, the Laughing Water:
" You shall bless to-night the corn-
      fields,
Draw a magic circle round them,
To protect them from destruction,
Blast of mildew, blight of insect,
Wagemin, the thief of cornfields,
Paimosaid, who steals the maize-
      ear!
  " In the night, when all is
      silence,
In the night, when all is darkness,
When the Spirit of Sleep, Nepah-
      win,
Shuts the doors of all the wigwams,
So that not an ear can hear you,
So that not an eye can see you,
Rise up from your bed in silence,
Lay aside your garments wholly,
Walk around the fields you planted,
Round the borders of the corn-
      fields,
Covered by your tresses only,
Robed with darkness as a garment.
  " Thus the fields shall be more
      fruitful,[1]

---

handsome youth, in answer to the
prayers of a young man at his fast of
virility, or coming to manhood.
  " It is well known that corn-
planting and corn-gathering, at least
among all the still *uncolonised* tribes,
are left entirely to the females and
children, and a few superannuated
old men. It is not generally known,
perhaps, that this labour is not com-
pulsory, and that it is assumed by
the females as a just equivalent, in
their view, for the onerous and con-
tinuous labour of the other sex, in
providing meats and skins for clothing
by the chase, and in defending their
villages against their enemies, and
keeping intruders off their territories.
A good Indian housewife deems this
a part of her prerogative, and prides
herself to have a store of corn to
exercise her hospitality, or duly
honour her husband's hospitality,
in the entertainment of the lodge
guests."—*Oneóta*, p. 82.

[1] " A singular proof of this belief,
in both sexes, of the mysterious
influence of the steps of a woman
on the vegetable and insect creation,
is found in an ancient custom, which
was related to me, respecting corn-
planting. It was the practice of the
hunter's wife, when the field of corn
had been planted, to choose the first
dark or over-clouded evening to
perform a secret circuit, *sans habille-
ment*, around the field. For this
purpose she slipped out of the lodge
in the evening, unobserved, to some
obscure nook, where she completely

And the passing of your footsteps
Draw a magic circle round them,
So that neither blight nor mildew,
Neither burrowing word nor insect,
Shall pass o'er the magic circle;
Not the dragon fly, Kwo-ne-she,
Nor the Spider, Subbekashe,
Nor the grasshopper, Paw-Puk-keena,
Nor the mighty caterpillar,
Way-muk-kwana, with the bear-skin,
King of all the caterpillars! "
On the tree-tops near the corn-fields
Sat the hungry crows and ravens,
Kahgahgee, the King of Ravens,
With his band of black marauders.
And they laughed at Hiawatha,
Till the tree-tops shook with laughter,
With his melancholy laughter,
At the words of Hiawatha.
" Hear him! " said they; " hear the Wise Man,
Hear the plots of Hiawatha! "
When the noiseless night descended
Broad and dark o'er field and forest,
When the mournful Wawonaissa,
Sorrowing sang among the hemlocks,
And the Spirit of Sleep, Nepahwin,
Shut the doors of all the wigwams,
From her bed rose Laughing Water,
Laid aside her garments wholly,
And with darkness clothed and guarded,
Unashamed and unaffrighted,
Walked securely round the cornfields,

Drew the sacred, magic circle
Of her footprints round the cornfields.
No one but the Midnight only
Saw her beauty in the darkness,
No one but the Wawonaissa
Heard the panting of her bosom;
Guskewau, the darkness, wrapped her
Closely in his sacred mantle,
So that none might see her beauty,
So that none might boast, " I saw her! "
On the morrow, as the day dawned,
Kahgahgee, the King of Ravens,
Gathered all his black marauders,
Crows and blackbirds, jays, and ravens,
Clamorous on the dusky tree-tops,
And descended, fast and fearless,
On the fields of Hiawatha,
On the grave of the Mondamin.
" We will drag Mondamin," said they,
" From the grave where he is buried,
Spite of all the magic circles
Laughing Water draws around it,
Spite of all the sacred footprints
Minnehaha stamps upon it! "
But the wary Hiawatha,
Ever thoughtful, careful, watchful,
Had o'erheard the scornful laughter
When they mocked him from the tree-tops.
" Kaw! " he said, " my friends the ravens!
Kahgahgee, my King of Ravens!
I will teach you all a lesson
That shall not be soon forgotten! "
He had risen before the day-break,
He had spread o'er all the corn-fields
Snares to catch the black marauders,
And was lying now in ambush

disrobed. Then, taking her matche-cota, or principal garment, in one hand, she dragged it around the field. This was thought to insure a prolific crop, and to prevent the assaults of insects and worms upon the grain. It was supposed they could not creep over the charmed line."—*Oneóta*, p. 83.

In the neighbouring grove of pine
    trees,
Waiting for the crows and black-
    birds,
Waiting for the jays and ravens.
    Soon they came with caw and
    clamour,
Rush of wings and cry of voices,
To their work of devastation,
Settling down upon the cornfields,
Delving deep with beak and talon,
For the body of Mondamin.
And with all their craft and cun-
    ning,
All their skill in wiles of warfare,
They perceived no danger near
    them.
Till their claws became entangled,
Till they found themselves im-
    prisoned
In the snares of Hiawatha.
    From his place of ambush came
    he,
Striding terrible among them,
And so awful was his aspect
That the bravest quailed with
    terror.
Without mercy he destroyed them
Right and left, by tens and twen-
    ties,
And their wretched, lifeless bodies
Hung aloft on poles for scarecrows
Round the consecrated cornfields,
As a signal of his vengeance,
As a warning to marauders.
    Only Kahgahgee, the leader,
Kahgahgee, the King of Ravens,
He alone was spared among them
As a hostage for his people.
With his prisoner-string he bound
    him,[1]

Led him captive to his wigwam,
Tied him fast with cords of elm
    bark
To the ridgepole of his wigwam.
    "Kahgahgee, my raven!" said
    he.
"You the leader of the robbers,
You the plotter of this mischief,
The contriver of this outrage,
I will keep you, I will hold you,
As a hostage for your people,
As a pledge of good behaviour!"
    And he left him, grim and sulky,
Sitting in the morning sunshine
On the summit of the wigwam,
Croaking fiercely his displeasure,
Flapping his great sable pinions,
Vainly struggling for his freedom,
Vainly calling on his people!
    Summer passed, and Shawonda-
    see
Breathed his sighs o'er all the land-
    scape,
From the Southland sent his
    ardours,
Wafted kisses warm and tender;
And the maize field grew and
    ripened,
Till it stood in all the splendour,
Of its garments green and yellow,
Of its tassels and its plumage,
And the maize ears full and shin-
    ing
Gleamed from bursting sheaths of
    verdure.
    Then Nokomis, the old woman,
Spake, and said to Minnehaha:
"'Tis the Moon when leaves are
    falling;
All the wild rice has been gathered,
And the maize is ripe and ready;
Let us gather in the harvest,
Let us wrestle with Mondamin,
Strip him of his plumes and tassels,
Of his garments green and yellow!"

[1] "These cords," says Mr. Tanner,
"are made of the bark of the elm-
tree, by boiling and then immersing
it in cold water. . . . The leader of
a war party commonly carries several
fastened about his waist; and if, in
the course of the fight, any one of
his young men takes a prisoner, it is
his duty to bring him immediately
to the chief, to be tied, and the
latter is responsible for his safe-
keeping."—*Narrative of Captivity and
Adventures*, p. 412.

And the merry Laughing Water
Went rejoicing from the wigwam,
With Nokomis old and wrinkled,
And they called the women round
them,
Called the young men and the
maidens,
To the harvest of the cornfields,
To the husking of the maize ear.
On the border of the forest,
Underneath the fragrant pine
trees,
Sat the old man and the warriors
Smoking in the pleasant shadow.
In uninterrupted silence
Looked they at the gamesome
labour
Of the young men and the women;
Listened to their noisy talking,
To their laughter and their singing,
Heard them chattering like the
magpies,
Heard them laughing like the blue-
jays,
Heard them singing like the robins.
And whene'er some lucky
maiden
Found a red ear in the husking,
Found a maize ear red as blood is,
" Nushka! " cried they all together,
" Nushka! you shall have a sweet-
heart,
You shall have a handsome hus-
band! "
" Ugh! " the old men all responded
From their seats beneath the pine
trees.
And whene'er a youth or maiden
Found a crooked ear in husking,
Found a maize ear in the husk-
ing
Blighted, mildewed, or misshapen,
Then they laughed and sang to-
gether,
Crept and limped about the corn-
fields,
Mimicked in their gait and gestures
Some old man bent almost double,
Singing singly or together:

" Wagemin, the thief of corn-
fields! [1]
Paimosid, the skulking robber! "
Till the cornfields rang with
laughter,
Till from Hiawatha's wigwam
Kahgahgee, the King of Ravens,
Screamed and quivered in his
anger,
And from all the neighbouring tree-
tops
Cawed and croaked the black
marauders.

[1] " If one of the young female huskers find a *red* ear of corn, it is typical of a brave admirer, and is regarded as a fitting present to some young warrior. But if the ear be *crooked*, and tapering to a point, no matter what colour, the whole circle is set in a roar, and *wa-ge-min* is the word shouted aloud. It is the symbol of a thief in the cornfield. It is con- sidered as the image of an old man stooping as he enters the lot. Had the chisel of Praxiteles been employed to produce this image, it could not more vividly bring to the minds of the merry group the idea of a pilferer of their favourite mondámin. . . .

" The literal meaning of the term is a mass, or crooked ear of grain; but the ear of corn so called is a con- ventional type of a little old man pilfering ears of corn in a cornfield. It is in this manner that a single word or term, in these curious languages, becomes the fruitful parent of many ideas. And we can thus perceive why it is that the word *wagemin* is alone competent to excite merriment in the husking circle.

" This term is taken as the basis of the cereal chorus, or corn song, as sung by the Northern Algonquin tribes. It is coupled with the phrase *Paimosaid,*—a permutative form of the Indian substantive, made from the verb *pim-o-sa,* to walk. Its literal meaning is, *he who walks,* or *the walker ;* but the ideas conveyed by it are, he who walks by night to pilfer corn. It offers, therefore, a kind of parallelism in expression to the pre- ceding term."—*Oneóta,* p. 264.

"Ugh!" the old men all responded,
From their seats beneath the pine trees!

XIV.

PICTURE-WRITING

In those days said Hiawatha,
"Lo! how all things fade and perish!
From the memory of the old men
Fade away the great traditions,
The achievements of the warriors,
The adventures of the hunters,
All the wisdom of the Medas,
All the craft of the Wabenos,
All the marvellous dreams and visions
Of the Jossakeeds, the Prophets!
"Great men die and are forgotten,
Wise men speak; their words of wisdom
Perish in the ears that hear them,
Do not reach the generations
That, as yet unborn, are waiting
In the great, mysterious darkness
Of the speechless days that shall be!
"On the grave-posts of our fathers
Are no signs, no figures painted;
Who are in those graves we know not,
Only know they are our fathers.
Of what kith they are and kindred,
From what old, ancestral Totem,
Be it Eagle, Bear, or Beaver,
They descended, this we know not,
Only know they are our fathers.
"Face to face we speak together,
But we cannot speak when absent,
Cannot send our voices from us
To the friends that dwell afar off;
Cannot send a secret message,
But the bearer learns our secret,
May pervert it, may betray it,
May reveal it unto others."
Thus said Hiawatha, walking

In the solitary forest,
Pondering, musing in the forest,
On the welfare of his people.
From his pouch he took his colours,
Took his paints of different colours,
On the smooth bark of a birch tree
Painted many shapes and figures,
Wonderful and mystic figures,
And each figure had a meaning,
Each some word or thought suggested.
Gitche Manito the Mighty,
He, the Master of Life, was painted
As an egg, with points projecting
To the four winds of the heavens.
Everywhere is the Great Spirit,
Was the meaning of this symbol.
Mitche Manito the Mighty,
He the dreadful Spirit of Evil,
As a serpent was depicted,
As Kenabeek, the great serpent.
Very crafty, very cunning,
Is the creeping Spirit of Evil,
Was the meaning of this symbol.
Life and Death he drew as circles,
Life was white, but Death was darkness;
Sun and moon and stars he painted,
Man and beast, and fish and reptile,
Forests, mountains, lakes, and rivers.
For the earth he drew a straight line,
For the sky a bow above it;
White the space between for daytime,
Filled with little stars for nighttime;
On the left a point for sunrise,
On the right a point for sunset,
On the top a point for noontide,
And for rain and cloudy weather
Waving lines descending from it.
Footprints pointing toward a wigwam
Were a sign of invitation,
Were a sign of guests assembling;

Bloody hands with palms uplifted
Were a symbol of destruction,
Were a hostile sign and symbol.

All these things did Hiawatha
Show unto his wondering people,
And interpreted their meaning,
And he said: " Behold, your grave-
        posts
Have no mark, no sign, nor symbol.
Go and paint them all with figures;
Each one with its household sym-
        bol,
With its own ancestral Totem;
So that those who follow after
May distinguish them and know
        them."

And they painted on the grave-
        posts
Of the graves yet unforgotten,
Each his own ancestral Totem,
Each the symbol of his household;
Figures of the Bear and Reindeer,
Of the Turtle, Crane, and Beaver,
Each inverted as a token
That the owner was departed,
That the chief who bore the symbol
Lay beneath in dust and ashes.

And the Jossakeeds, the
        Prophets,
The Wabenos, the Magicians,
And the Medicine-men, the Medas,
Painted upon bark and deerskin
Figures for the songs they chaunted,
For each song a separate symbol,
Figures mystical and awful,
Figures strange and brightly
        coloured;
And each figure had its meaning,
Each some magic song suggested.

The Great Spirit, the Creator,
Flashing light through all the
        heaven;
The Great Serpent, the Kenabeek,
With his bloody crest erected,
Creeping, looking into heaven;
In the sky the sun, that listens,
And the moon eclipsed and dying;
Owl and eagle, crane and henhawk,
And the cormorant, bird of magic;

Headless men, that walk the
        heavens,
Bodies lying pierced with arrows
Bloody hands of death uplifted,
Flags on graves, and great war
        captains
Grasping both the earth and
        heaven!

Such as these the shapes they
        painted
On the birchbark and the deerskin;
Songs of war and songs of hunting,
Songs of medicine and of magic,
All were written in these figures,
For each figure had its meaning,
Each its separate song recorded.

Nor forgotten was the Love-Song,
The most subtle of all medicines,
The most potent spell of magic,
Dangerous more than war or hunt-
        ing!
Thus the Love-Song was recorded,
Symbol and interpretation.

First a human figure standing,
Painted in the brightest scarlet;
'Tis the lover, the musician,
And the meaning is, " My painting
Makes me powerful over others."

Then the figure seated, singing,
Playing on a drum of magic,
And the interpretation, " Listen!
'Tis my voice you hear, my sing-
        ing!"

Then the same red figure seated
In the shelter of a wigwam,
And the meaning of the symbol,
" I will come and sit beside you
In the mystery of my passion!"

Then two figures, man and
        woman,
Standing hand in hand together
With their hands so clasped to-
        gether
That they seem in one united,
And the words thus represented
Are, " I see your heart within you,
And your cheeks are red with
        blushes!"

Next the maiden on an island,

In the centre of an island;
And the song this shape suggested
Was, "Though you were at a distance,
Were upon some far-off island,
Such the spell I cast upon you,
Such the magic power of passion,
I could straightway draw you to me!"
Then the figure of the maiden
Sleeping, and the lover near her,
Whispering to her in her slumbers,
Saying, "Though you were far from me
In the land of Sleep and Silence,
Still the voice of love would reach you!"
And the last of all the figures
Was a heart within a circle,
Drawn within a magic circle,
And the image had this meaning:
"Naked lies your heart before me,
To your naked heart I whisper!"
Thus it was that Hiawatha,
In his wisdom, taught the people
All the mysteries of painting,
All the art of Picture-Writing,
On the smooth bark of the birch tree,
On the white skin of the reindeer,
On the grave-posts of the village.

XV.

HIAWATHA'S LAMENTATION

In those days the Evil Spirits,
All the Manitos of mischief,
Fearing Hiawatha's wisdom,
And his love for Chibiabos,
Jealous of their faithful friendship,
And their noble words and actions,
Made at length a league against them,
To molest them and destroy them.
Hiawatha, wise and wary,
Often said to Chibiabos,
"O my brother! do not leave me,
Lest the Evil Spirits harm you!"

Chibiabos, young and heedless,
Laughing shook his coal-black tresses,
Answered ever sweet and childlike.
"Do not fear for me, O brother!
Harm and evil come not near me!"
Once when Peboan, the Winter,
Roofed with ice the Big-Sea-Water,
When the snowflakes whirling downward,
Hissed among the withered oak leaves,
Changed the pine trees into wigwams,
Covered all the earth with silence,—
Armed with arrows, shod with snowshoes,
Heeding not his brother's warning,
Fearing not the Evil Spirits,
Forth to hunt the deer with antlers
All alone went Chibiabos.
Right across the Big-Sea-Water
Sprang with speed the deer before him,
With the wind and snow he followed,
O'er the treacherous ice he followed,
Wild with all the fierce commotion
And the rapture of the hunting.
But beneath, the Evil Spirits
Lay in ambush, waiting for him,
Broke the treacherous ice beneath him,
Dragged him downward to the bottom,
Buried in the sand his body,
Unktahee, the god of water,
He the god of the Dacotahs,
Drowned him in the deep abysses
Of the lake of Gitche Gumee.
From the headlands Hiawatha
Sent forth such a wail of anguish,
Such a fearful lamentation,
That the bison paused to listen,
And the wolves howled from the prairies,
And the thunder in the distance
Woke and answered "Baimwawa!"

Then his face with black he
　　painted,
With his robe his head he covered,
In his wigwam sat lamenting,
Seven long weeks he sat lamenting,
Uttering still this moan of sorrow:
　" He is dead, the sweet musician!
He the sweetest of all singers! "
He has gone from us for ever,
He has moved a little nearer
To the Master of all music,
To the Master of all singing!
O my brother, Chibiabos! "
　And the melancholy fir trees
Waved their dark-green fans above
　　him,
Waved their purple cones above
　　him,
Sighing with him to console him,
Mingling with his lamentation
Their complaining, their lamenting.
　Came the Spring, and all the
　　forest
Looked in vain for Chibiabos;
Sighed the rivulet, Sebowisha,
Sighed the rushes in the meadow.
　From the tree-tops sang the blue-
　　bird,
Sang the bluebird, the Owaissa,
" Chibiabos!　Chibiabos!
He is dead, the sweet musician! "
　From the wigwam sang the
　　robin,
Sang the Opechee, the robin,
" Chibiabos!　Chibiabos!
He is dead, the sweetest singer! "
　And at night through all the
　　forest
Went the whippoorwill complain-
　　ing,
Wailing went the Wawonaissa,
" Chibiabos!　Chibiabos!
He is dead, the sweet musician!
He the sweetest of all singers! "
　Then the Medicine-men, the
　　Medas,
The magicians, the Wabenos,
And the Jossakeeds, the prophets,
Came to visit Hiawatha;

Built a Sacred Lodge beside him,
To appease him, to console him,
Walked in silent, grave procession,
Bearing each a pouch of healing,
Skin of beaver, lynx, or otter,
Filled with magic roots and simples,
Filled with very potent medicines.
　When he heard their steps ap-
　　proaching,
Hiawatha ceased lamenting,
Called no more on Chibiabos;
Naught he questioned, naught he
　answered
But his mournful head uncovered,
From his face the mourning colours
Washed he slowly and in silence,
Slowly and in silence followed
Onward to the Sacred Wigwam.
　There a magic drink they gave
　　him,
Made of Nahma-wusk, the spear-
　　mint,
And Wabeno-wusk, the yarrow,
Roots of power, and herbs of heal-
　　ing;
Beat their drums, and shook their
　rattles;
Chaunted singly and in chorus,
Mystic songs like these, they
　chaunted.
　" I myself, myself! behold me!
'Tis the great Gray Eagle talk-
　　ing;
Come, ye white crows, come and
　hear him!
The loud-speaking thunder helps
　me;
All the unseen spirits help me;
I can hear their voices calling,
All around the sky I hear them!
I can blow you strong, my brother,
I can heal you, Hiawatha! "
　" Hi-au-ha! " replied the chorus,
" Way-ha-way! " the mystic
　chorus,
　" Friends of mine are all the
　　serpents!
Hear me shake my skin of hen-
　hawk!

Mahng, the white loon, I can kill
  him;
I can shoot your heart and kill it!
I can blow you strong, my brother,
I can heal you, Hiawatha!"
  "Hi-au-ha!" replied the chorus,
"Way-ha-way!" the mystic
  chorus.
  "I myself, myself! the prophet!
When I speak the wigwam
  trembles,
Shakes the Sacred Lodge with
  terror,
Hands unseen begin to shake it!
When I walk, the sky I tread on
Bends and makes a noise beneath
  me!
I can blow you strong, my brother!
Rise and speak, O Hiawatha!"
  "Hi-au-ha!" replied the chorus,
"Way-ha-way!" the mystic
  chorus.
Then they shook their medicine-
  pouches
O'er the head of Hiawatha,
Danced their medicine-dance
  around him;
And upstarting wild and haggard,
Like a man from dreams awakened,
He was healed of all his madness.
As the clouds are swept from
  heaven,
Straightway from his brain de-
  parted
All his moody melancholy;
As the ice is swept from rivers,
Straightway from his heart de-
  parted
All his sorrow and affliction.
  Then they summoned Chibiabos
From his grave beneath the waters,
From the sands of Gitche Gumee
Summoned Hiawatha's brother.
And so mighty was the magic
Of that cry and invocation,
That he heard it as he lay there
Underneath the Big-Sea-Water;
From the sand he rose and listened,
Heard the music and the singing,

Came, obedient to the summons,
To the doorway of the wigwam,
But to enter they forbade him.
Through a chink a coal they gave
  him,
Through the door a burning fire-
  brand;
Ruler in the Land of Spirits,
Ruler o'er the dead, they made
  him,
Telling him a fire to kindle
For all those that died thereafter,
Camp-fires for their night encamp-
  ments
On their solitary journey
To the kingdom of Ponemah,
To the land of the Hereafter.
  From the village of his child-
  hood,
From the homes of those who
  knew him,
Passing silent through the forest,
Like a smoke-wreath wafted side-
  ways,
Slowly vanished Chibiabos!
Where he passed, the branches
  moved not,
Where he trod the grasses bent not,
And the fallen leaves of last year
Made no sound beneath his foot-
  steps.
  Four whole days he journeyed
  onward
Down the pathway of the dead
  men;
On the dead man's strawberry
  feasted,
Crossed the melancholy river,
On the swinging log he crossed it,
Came unto the Lake of Silver,
In the Stone Canoe was carried
To the Islands of the Blessed,
To the land of ghosts and shadows.
  On that journey, moving slowly,
Many weary spirits saw he,
Panting under heavy burdens,
Laden with war-clubs, bows and
  arrows,
Robes of fur, and pots and kettles,

And with food that friends had
    given
For that solitary journey.
  " Ay! why do the living," said
    they,
" Lay such heavy burdens on us!
Better were it to go naked,
Better were it to go fasting,
Than to bear such heavy burdens
On our long and weary journey! "
  Forth then issued Hiawatha,
Wandered eastward, wandered
    westward,
Teaching men the use of simples
And the antidotes for poisons,
And the cure of all diseases.
Thus was first made known to
    mortals
All the mystery of Medamin,
All the sacred art of healing.

XVI.

PAU-PUK-KEEWIS

  You shall hear how Pau-Puk-
    Keewis
He, the handsome Yenadizze,
Whom the people called the Storm
    Fool,
Vexed the village with disturb-
    ance;
You shall hear of all his mischief,
And his flight from Hiawatha,
And his wondrous transmigrations,
At the end of his adventures.
  On the shores of Gitche Gumee,
On the dunes of Nagow Wudjoo,
By the shining Big-Sea-Water,
Stood the lodge of Pau-Puk-Kee-
    wis.
It was he who in his frenzy
Whirled these drifting sands to-
    gether,
On the dunes of Nagow Wudjoo,
When, among the guests assembled,
He so merrily and madly
Danced at Hiawatha's wedding,

Danced the Beggar's Dance to
    please them.
  Now, in search of new adven-
    tures,
From his lodge went Pau-Puk-
    Keewis,
Came with speed into the village,
Found the young men all assembled
In the lodge of old Iagoo,
Listening to his monstrous stories,
To his wonderful adventures.
  He was telling them the story
Of Ojeeg, the Summer-Maker,
How he made a hole in heaven,
How he climbed up into heaven,
And let out the summer weather,
The perpetual, pleasant Summer;
How the Otter first essayed it;
How the Beaver, Lynx, and
    Badger,
Tried in turn the great achieve-
    ment,
From the summit of the moun-
    tain
Smote their fists against the
    heavens,
Smote against the sky their fore-
    heads,
Cracked the sky, but could not
    break it,
How the Wolverine, uprising,
Made him ready for the encounter,
Bent his knees down, like a squirrel,
Drew his arms back, like a cricket.
  " Once he leaped," said Old
    Iagoo,
" Once he leaped, and lo! above
    him
Bent the sky, as ice in rivers
When the waters rise beneath it;
Twice he leaped, and lo! above
    him
Cracked the sky, as ice in rivers
When the freshet is at highest!
Thrice he leaped, and lo! above
    him
Broke the shattered sky asunder,
And he disappeared within it,
And Ojeeg, the Fisher Weasel,

With a bound went in behind
　　him!"
"Hark you!" shouted Pau-
　　Puk-Keewis
As he entered at the doorway:
"I am tired of all this talking,
Tired of old Iagoo's stories,
Tired of Hiawatha's wisdom.
Here is something to amuse
　　you,
Better than this endless talking."
　　Then from out his pouch of wolf-
　　　skin
Forth he drew, with solemn
　　manner,
All the game of Bowl and
　　Counters,
Pugasaing, with thirteen pieces.[1]

[1] This Game of the Bowl is the principal game of hazard among the Northern tribes of Indians. Mr. Schoolcraft gives a particular account of it in *Oneóta*, p. 85. "This game," he says, "is very fascinating to some portions of the Indians. They stake at it their ornaments, weapons, clothing, canoes, horses, everything in fact they possess; and have been known, it is said, to set up their wives and children, and even to forfeit their own liberty. Of such desperate stakes I have seen no examples, nor do I think the game itself in common use. It is rather confined to certain persons, who hold the relative rank of gamblers in Indian society,—men who are not noted as hunters or warriors, or steady providers for their families. Among these are persons who bear the term of *Ienadizzewug*, that is, wanderers about the country, braggadocios, or fops. It can hardly be classed with the popular games of amusement, by which skill and dexterity are acquired. I have generally found the chiefs and graver men of the tribes, who encouraged the young men to play ball, and are sure to be present at the customary sports, to witness and sanction and applaud them, speak lightly and disparagingly of this game of hazard. Yet it cannot be denied that some of the chiefs, distinguished in war and the chase at the West, can be referred to as

White on one side were they
　　painted,
And vermilion on the other;
Two Kenabeeks or great serpents,
Two Ininewug or wedge-men,
One great war-club, Pugamaugun,
And one slender fish, the Keego,
Four round pieces, Ozawabeeks,
And three Sheshebwug or duck-
　　lings,
All were made of bone and painted,
All except the Ozawabeeks;
These were brass, on one side bur-
　　nished,
And were black upon the other.
　　In a wooden bowl he placed
　　　them,
Shook and jostled them together,
Threw them on the ground before
　　him.
Thus exclaiming and explaining:
"Red side up are all the pieces,
And one great Kenabeek standing
On the bright side of a brass piece,
On a burnished Ozawabeek;
Thirteen tens and eight are
　　counted."
　　Then again he shook the pieces,
Shook and jostled them together,
Threw them on the ground before
　　him,
Still exclaiming and explaining:
"White are both the great Kena-
　　beeks,
White the Ininewug, the wedge-
　　men,
Red are all the other pieces;
Five tens and an eight are counted.
　　Thus he taught the game of
　　　hazard,
Thus displayed it and explained it,
Running through its various
　　chances,
Various changes, various meanings;

lending their examples to its fascinating power."
　　See also his *History, Condition, and Prospects of the Indian Tribes*, Part II., p. 72.

Twenty curious eyes stared at him,
Full of eagerness stared at him.
" Many games," said old Iagoo,
" Many games of skill and hazard
Have I seen in different nations,
Have I played in different coun-
    tries.
He who plays with old Iagoo
Must have very nimble fingers;
Though you think yourself so skil-
    ful
I can beat you, Pau-Puk-Keewis,
I can even give you lessons
In your game of Bowl and Coun-
    ters!"
    So they sat and played together,
All the old men and the young men
Played for dresses, weapons, wam-
    pum,
Played till midnight, played till
    morning,
Played until the Yenadizze,
Till the cunning Pau-Puk-Keewis
Of their treasures had despoiled
    them,
Of the best of all their dresses,
Shirts of deerskin, robes of ermine,
Belts of wampum, crests of
    feathers,
Warlike weapons, pipes and
    pouches.
Twenty eyes glared wildly at him,
Like the eyes of wolves glared at
    him.
    Said the lucky Pau-Puk-Keewis:
" In my wigwam I am lonely,
In my wanderings and adventures
I have need of a companion,
Fain would have a Meshinauwa,
An attendant and pipe-bearer.
I will venture all these winnings,
All these garments heaped about
    me,
All this wampum, all these
    feathers,
On a single throw will venture
All against the young man yon-
    der!"
'Twas a youth of sixteen summers,

'Twas a nephew of Iagoo;
Face-in-a-Mist the people called
    him.
    As the fire burns in a pipe-head
Dusky red beneath the ashes,
So beneath his shaggy eyebrows
Glowed the eyes of old Iagoo.
" Ugh!" he answered very fiercely;
" Ugh!" they answered all and
    each one.
    Seized the wooden bowl the old
    man,
Closely in his bony fingers
Clutched the fatal bowl, Onagon,
Shook it fiercely and with fury,
Made the pieces ring together
As he threw them down before him.
    Red were both the great Kena-
    beeks,
Red the Ininewug, the wedge-men,
Red the Sheshebwug, the ducklings,
Black the four brass Ozawabeeks,
White alone the fish, the Keego;
Only five the pieces counted!
    Then the smiling Pau-Puk-Kee-
    wis
Shook the bowl and threw the
    pieces;
Lightly in the air he tossed them,
And they fell about him scattered;
Dark and bright the Ozawabeeks,
Red and white the other pieces,
And upright among the others
One Ininewug was standing,
Even as crafty Pau-Puk-Keewis
Stood alone among the players,
Saying, " Five tens! mine the
    game is!"
    Twenty eyes glared at him
    fiercely,
Like the eyes of wolves glared at
    him,
As he turned and left the wigwam,
Followed by his Meshinauwa,
By the nephew of Iagoo,
By the tall and graceful stripling,
Bearing in his arms the winnings,
Shirts of deerskin, robes of er-
    mine,

Belts of wampum, pipes and
   weapons.
  "Carry them," said Pau-Puk-
   Keewis,
Pointing with his fan of feathers,
"To my wigwam far to eastward,
On the dunes of Nagow Wudjoo!"
  Hot and red with smoke and
   gambling
Were the eyes of Pau-Puk-Keewis
As he came forth to the freshness
Of the pleasant summer morning.
All the birds were singing gaily,
All the streamlets flowing swiftly,
And the heart of Pau-Puk-Keewis
Sang with pleasure as the birds
   sing,
Beat with triumph like the stream-
   lets,
As he wandered through the village,
In the early gray of morning,
With his fan of turkey-feathers,
With his plumes and tufts of
   swan's-down,
Till he reached the farthest wig-
   wam,
Reached the lodge of Hiawatha.
  Silent was it and deserted;
No one met him at the doorway,
No one came to bid him welcome;
But the birds were singing round it,
In and out and round the doorway,
Hopping, singing, fluttering, feed-
   ing,
And aloft upon the ridge-pole
Kahgahgee, the King of Ravens,
Sat with fiery eyes, and, screaming,
Flapped his wings at Pau-Puk-
   Keewis.
  "All are gone! the lodge is
   empty!"
Thus it was spake Pau-Puk-Kee-
   wis,
In his heart resolving mischief;—
"Gone is wary Hiawatha,
Gone the silly Laughing Water,
Gone Nokomis, the old woman,
And the lodge is left unguarded!"
  By the neck he seized the raven,

Whirled it round him like a rattle,
Like a medicine-pouch he shook
   it,
Strangled Kahgahgee, the raven,
From the ridge-pole of the wigwam
Left its lifeless body hanging,
As an insult to its master,
As a taunt to Hiawatha.
  With a stealthy step he entered,
Round the lodge in wild disorder
Threw the household things about
   him,
Piled together in confusion
Bowls of wood and earthen kettles,
Robes of buffalo and beaver,
Skins of otter, lynx, and ermine,
As an insult to Nokomis,
As a taunt to Minnehaha.
  Then departed Pau-Puk-Keewis,
Whistling, singing through the
   forest,
Whistling gaily to the squirrels,
Who from hollow boughs above
   him
Dropped their acorn-shells upon
   him,
Singing gaily to the wood birds,
Who from out the leafy darkness
Answered with a song as merry.
  Then he climbed the rocky head-
   lands,
Looking o'er the Gitche Gumee,
Perched himself upon the summit,
Waiting full of mirth and mischief
The return of Hiawatha.
  Stretched upon his back he lay
   there;
Far below him plashed the waters,
Plashed and washed the dreamy
   waters;
Far above him swam the heavens,
Swam the dizzy, dreamy heavens;
Round him hovered, fluttered,
   rustled,
Hiawatha's mountain chickens,
Flock-wise swept and wheeled
   about him,
Almost brushed him with their
   pinions,

And he killed them as he lay
there,
Slaughtered them by tens and
twenties,
Threw their bodies down the head-
land,
Threw them on the beach below
him,
Till at length Kayoshk, the sea-
gull,
Perched upon a crag above them,
Shouted: "It is Pau-Puk-Keewis!
He is slaying us by hundreds!
Send a message to our brother,
Tidings send to Hiawatha!"

XVII.

THE HUNTING OF PAU-PUK-KEEWIS

Full of wrath was Hiawatha,
When he came into the village,
Found the people in confusion,
Heard of all the misdemeanours,
All the malice and the mischief
Of the cunning Pau-Puk-Keewis.
Hard his breath came through
his nostrils,
Through his teeth he buzzed and
muttered
Words of anger and resentment,
Hot and humming like a hornet.
"I will slay this Pau-Puk-Keewis,
Slay this mischief-maker!" said
he.
"Not so long and wide the world is,
Not so rude and rough the way is,
That my wrath shall not attain
him,
That my vengeance shall not
reach him!"
Then in swift pursuit departed,
Hiawatha and the hunters
On the trail of Pau-Puk-Keewis,
Through the forest, where he
passed,
To the headlands where he rested;

But they found not Pau-Puk-Kee-
wis,
Only in the trampled grasses,
In the whortleberry bushes,
Found the couch where he had
rested,
Found the impress of his body.
From the lowlands far beneath
them,
From the Muskoday, the meadow,
Pau-Puk-Keewis, turning back-
ward,
Made a gesture of defiance,
Made a gesture of derision;
And aloud cried Hiawatha,
From the summit of the mountain:
"Not so long and wide the world is,
Not so rude and rough the way is,
But my wrath shall overtake you,
And my vengeance shall attain
you!"
Over rock and over river,
Through bush, and brake, and
forest,
Ran the cunning Pau-Puk-Keewis;
Like an antelope he bounded,
Till he came unto a streamlet
In the middle of the forest.
To a streamlet still and tranquil,
That had overflowed its margin,
To a dam made by the beavers,
To a pond of quiet water,
Where knee-deep the trees were
standing,
Where the water-lilies floated,
Where the rushes waved and whis-
pered.
On the dam stood Pau-Puk-Kee-
wis,
On the dam of trunks and branches,
Through whose chinks the water
spouted,
O'er whose summit flowed the
streamlet.
From the bottom rose the beaver,
Looked with two great eyes of
wonder,
Eyes that seemed to ask a question,
At the stranger, Pau-Puk-Keewis.

On the dam stood Pau-Puk-Keewis,
O'er his ankles flowed the streamlet,
Flowed the bright and silvery water,
And he spake unto the beaver,
With a smile he spake in this wise:
"O my friend Ahmeek, the beaver,
Cool and pleasant is the water;
Let me dive into the water,
Let me rest there in your lodges;
Change me, too, into a beaver!"
  Cautiously replied the beaver,
With reserve he thus made answer:
"Let me first consult the others,
Let me ask the other beavers."
  Down he sank into the water,
Heavily sank he, as a stone sinks,
Down among the leaves and branches,
Brown and matted at the bottom.
  On the dam stood Pau-Puk-Keewis,
O'er his ankles flowed the streamlet,
Spouted through the chinks below him,
Dashed upon the stones beneath him,
Spread serene and calm before him,
And the sunshine and the shadows
Fell in flecks and gleams upon him,
Fell in little shining patches,
Through the waving, rustling branches.
  From the bottom rose the beavers,
Silently above the surface
Rose one head and then another,
Till the pond seemed full of beavers,
Full of black and shining faces.
  To the beavers Pau-Puk-Keewis
Spake entreating, said in this wise:
"Very pleasant is your dwelling,
O my friends! and safe from danger;

Can you not with all your cunning,
All your wisdom and contrivance,
Change me, too, into a beaver?"
  "Yes!" replied Ahmeek, the beaver,
He the King of all the beavers,
"Let yourself slide down among us,
Down into the tranquil water."
  Down into the pond among them
Silently sank Pau-Puk-Keewis;
Black became his shirt of deerskin,
Black his moccasins and leggings,
In a broad black tail behind him
Spread his foxtails and his fringes;
He was changed into a beaver.
  "Make me large," said Pau-Puk-Keewis,
"Make me large and make me larger,
Larger than the other beavers."
  "Yes," the beaver chief responded,
"When our lodge below you enter,
In our wigwam we will make you
Ten times larger than the others."
  Thus into the clear, brown water
Silently sank Pau-Puk-Keewis;
Found the bottom covered over
With the trunks of trees and branches,
Hoards of food against the winter,
Piles and heaps against the famine;
Found the lodge with arching doorway,
Leading into spacious chambers.
  Here they made him large and larger,
Made him largest of the beavers,
Ten times larger than the others.
"You shall be our ruler," said they;
"Chief and King of all the beavers."
  But not long had Pau-Puk-Keewis
Sat in state among the beavers,
When there came a voice of warning
From the watchman at his station

In the water-flags and lilies,
Saying, " Here is Hiawatha!
Hiawatha with his hunters! "
　Then they heard a cry above
　　them,
Heard a shouting and a tramping,
Heard a crashing and a rushing,
And the water round and o'er them
Sank and sucked away in eddies,
And they knew their dam was
　broken.
　On the lodge's roof the hunters
Leaped, and broke it all asunder;
Streamed the sunshine through
　the crevice,
Sprang the beavers through the
　doorway,
Hid themselves in deeper water,
In the channel of the streamlet;
But the mighty Pau-Puk-Keewis
Could not pass beneath the door-
　way;
He was puffed with pride and feed-
　ing,
He was swollen like a bladder.
　Through the roof looked Hia-
　　watha,
Cried aloud, " O Pau-Puk-Keewis!
Vain are all your craft and cun-
　ning,
Vain your manifold disguises!
Well I know you, Pau-Puk-Kee-
　wis! "
　With their clubs they beat and
　　bruised him,
Beat to death poor Pau-Puk-Kee-
　wis,
Pounded him as maize is pounded,
Till his skull was crushed to pieces.
Six tall hunters, lithe and limber,
Bore him home on poles and
　branches,
Bore the body of the beaver;
But the ghost, the Jeebi in him,
Thought and felt as Pau-Puk-Kee-
　wis,
Still lived on as Pau-Puk-Keewis.
　And it fluttered, strove, and
　struggled,

Waving hither, waving thither,
As the curtains of a wigwam
Struggle with their thongs of deer-
　skin,
When the wintry wind is blowing;
Till it drew itself together,
Till it rose up from the body,
Till it took the form and features
Of the cunning Pau-Puk-Keewis,
Vanishing into the forest.
　But the wary Hiawatha
Saw the figure ere it vanished,
Saw the form of Pau-Puk-Keewis
Glide into the soft blue Shadow
Of the pine-trees of the forest;
Toward the squares of white
　beyond it,
Toward an opening in the forest,
Like a wind it rushed and panted,
Bending all the boughs before it,
And behind it, as the rain comes,
Came the steps of Hiawatha.
　To a lake with many islands
Came the breathless Pau-Puk-Kee-
　wis,
Where among the water-lilies
Pishnekuh, the brant, was sailing;
Through the tufts of rushes float-
　ing,
Steering through the reedy islands,
Now their broad black beaks they
　lifted,
Now they plunged beneath the
　water,
Now they darkened in the shadow,
Now they brightened in the sun-
　shine.
　" Pishnekuh! " cried Pau-Puk-
　　Keewis,
" Pishnekuh! my brothers! " said
　he,
" Change me to a brant with
　plumage,
With a shining neck and feathers,
Make me large, and make me
　larger,
Ten times larger than the others."
　Straightway to a brant they
　changed him,

With two huge and dusky pinions,
With a bosom smooth and rounded,
With a bill like two great paddles,
Made him larger than the others,
Ten times larger than the largest,
Just as, shouting from the forest,
On the shore stood Hiawatha.

Up they rose with cry and clamour,
With a whir and beat of pinions,
Rose up from the reedy islands,
From the water-flags and lilies.
And they said to Pau-Puk-Keewis:
" In your flying, look not downward,
Take good heed and look not downward,
Lest some strange mischance should happen,
Lest some great mishap befall you! "

Fast and far they fled to northward,
Fast and far through mist and sunshine,
Fed among the moors and fenlands,
Slept among the reeds and rushes.

On the morrow as they journeyed,
Buoyed and lifted by the South-wind,
Wafted onward by the South-wind,
Blowing fresh and strong behind them,
Rose a sound of human voices,
Rose a clamour from beneath them,
From the lodges of a village,
From the people miles beneath them.

For the people of the village
Saw the flock of brant with wonder,
Saw the wings of Pau-Puk-Keewis
Flapping far up in the ether,
Broader than two doorway curtains.
Pau-Puk-Keewis heard the shouting,
Knew the voice of Hiawatha,

Knew the outcry of Iagoo,
And, forgetful of the warning,
Drew his neck in, and looked downward,
And the wind that blew behind him
Caught his mighty fan of feathers,
Sent him wheeling, whirling downward!

All in vain did Pau-Puk-Keewis
Struggle to regain his balance!
Whirling round and round and downward,
He beheld in turn the village
And in turn the flock above him,
Saw the village coming nearer,
And the flock receding farther,
Heard the voices growing louder,
Heard the shouting and the laughter;
Saw no more the flock above him,
Only saw the earth beneath him;
Dead out of the empty heaven,
Dead among the shouting people,
With a heavy sound and sullen,
Fell the brant with broken pinions.

But his soul, his ghost, his shadow,
Still survived as Pau-Puk-Keewis,
Took again the form and features
Of the handsome Yenadizze,
And again went rushing onward,
Followed fast by Hiawatha,
Crying: " Not so wide the world is,
Not so long and rough the way is,
But my wrath shall overtake you,
But my vengeance shall attain you! "

And so near he came, so near him,
That his hand was stretched to seize him,
His right hand to seize and hold him,
When the cunning Pau-Puk-Keewis
Whirled and spun about in circles,
Fanned the air into a whirlwind,

Danced the dust and leaves about him,
And amid the whirling eddies
Sprang into a hollow oak-tree,
Changed himself into a serpent,
Gliding out through root and rubbish.

With his right hand Hiawatha
Smote amain the hollow oak-tree,
Rent it into shreds and splinters,
Left it lying there in fragments.
But in vain; for Pau-Puk-Keewis,
Once again in human figure,
Full in sight ran on before him,
Sped away in gust and whirlwind,
On the shores of Gitche Gumee,
Westward by the Big-Sea-Water,
Came unto the rocky headlands,
To the Pictured Rocks of sandstone,[1]

Looking over lake and landscape.
And the Old Man of the Mountain,
He the Manito of Mountains,
Opened wide his rocky doorways,
Opened wide his deep abysses,
Giving Pau-Puk-Keewis shelter
In his caverns dark and dreary,
Bidding Pau-Puk-Keewis welcome
To his gloomy lodge of sandstone.

There without stood Hiawatha,
Found the doorways closed against him,
With his mittens, Minjekahwun,
Smote great caverns in the sandstone,
Cried aloud in tones of thunder,
"Open! I am Hiawatha!"
But the Old Man of the Mountain
Opened not, and made no answer
From the silent crags of sandstone,

---

[1] The reader will find a long description of the Pictured Rocks in Foster and Whitney's *Report on the Geology of the Lake Superior Land District*, Part II., p. 124. From this I make the following extract:—

"The Pictured Rocks may be described, in general terms, as a series of sandstone bluffs extending along the shore of Lake Superior for about five miles, and rising, in most places vertically from the water, without any beach at the base, to a height varying from fifty to nearly two hundred feet. Were they simply a line of cliffs they might not, so far as relates to height or extent, be worthy of rank among great natural curiosities, although such an assemblage of rocky strata, washed by the waves of the great lake, would not, under any circumstances, be destitute of grandeur. To the voyager coasting along their base in his frail canoe they would at all times be an object of dread; the recoil of the surf, the rockbound coast affording for miles no place of refuge, the lowering sky, the rising wind, all these would excite his apprehension, and induce him to ply a vigorous oar until the dreaded wall was passed. But in the Pictured Rocks there are two features which communicate to the scenery a wonderful and almost unique character. These are first, the curious manner in which the cliffs have been excavated and worn away by the action of the lake, which for centuries has dashed an ocean-like surf against their base; and second, the equally curious manner in which large portions of the surface have been coloured by bands of brilliant hues.

"It is from the latter circumstance that the name by which these cliffs are known to the American traveller is derived; while that applied to them by the French voyagers ('Les Portals') is derived from the former, and by far the most striking peculiarity.

"The term *Pictured Rocks* has been in use for a great length of time; but when it was first applied we have been unable to discover. It would seem that the first travellers were more impressed with the novel and striking distribution of colours on the surface than with the astonishing variety of form into which the cliffs themselves have been worn. . . .

"Our voyagers had many legends to relate of the pranks of the *Mennibojou* in these caverns, and in answer to our inquiries, seemed disposed to fabricate stories without end of the achievements of this Indian deity."

From the gloomy rock abysses.
  Then he raised his hands to
    heaven,
Called imploring on the tempest,
Called Waywassimo, the lightning,
And the thunder, Annemeekee;
And they came with night and
  darkness,
Sweeping down the Big-Sea-Water
From the distant Thunder Moun-
  tains;
And the trembling Pau-Puk-Kee-
  wis
Heard the footsteps of the thunder,
Saw the red eyes of the lightning,
Was afraid, and crouched and
  trembled.
  Then Waywassimo, the light-
    ning,
Smote the doorways of the caverns,
With his war club smote the door-
  ways,
Smote the jutting crags of sand-
  stone,
And the thunder, Annemeekee,
Shouted down into the caverns,
Saying, " Where is Pau-Puk-Kee-
  wis!"
And the crags fell, and beneath
  them
Dead among the rocky ruins
Lay the cunning Pau-Puk-Keewis,
Lay the handsome Yenadizze,
Slain in his own human figure.
  Ended were his wild adventures,
Ended were his tricks and gambols,
Ended all his craft and cunning,
Ended all his mischief-making,
All his gambling and his dancing,
All his wooing of the miadens.
  Then the noble Hiawatha
Took his soul, his ghost, his
  shadow,
Spake and said: " O Pau-Puk-
  Keewis,
Never more in human figure
Shall you search for new adven-
  tures;
Never more with jest and laughter

Dance the dust and leaves in whirl-
  winds;
But above there in the heavens
You shall soar and sail in circles;
I will change you to an eagle,
To Keneu, the great war-eagle,
Chief of all the fowls with feathers,
Chief of Hiawatha's chickens."
  And the name of Pau-Puk-Kee-
  wis
Lingers still among the people,
Lingers still among the singers,
And among the story-tellers;
And in Winter, when the snow-
  flakes
Whirl in eddies round the lodges,
When the wind in gusty tumult
O'er the smoke-flue pipes and
  whistles,
" There," they cry, " comes Pau-
  Puk-Keewis;
He is dancing through the village,
He is gathering in his harvest!"

XVIII.

THE DEATH OF KWASIND

  Far and wide among the nations
Spread the name and fame of
  Kwasind;
No man dared to strive with
  Kwasind,
No man could compete with
  Kwasind.
But the mischievous Puk-Wudjies,
They the envious Little People,
They the fairies and the pygmies,
Plotted and conspired against him.
  " If this hateful Kwasind," said
  they,
" If this great, outrageous fellow
Goes on thus a little longer,
Tearing everything he touches,
Rending everything to pieces,
Filling all the world with wonder,
What becomes of the Puk-Wud
  jies!

Who will care for the Puk-Wud-
     jies?
He will tread us down like mush-
     rooms,
Drive us all into the water,
Give our bodies to be eaten
By the wicked Nee-ba-naw-baigs,
By the Spirits of the water!"
     So the angry Little People
All conspired against the Strong
     Man,
All conspired to murder Kwasind,
Yes, to rid the world of Kwasind,
The audacious, overbearing,
Heartless, haughty, dangerous
     Kwasind!
     Now this wondrous strength of
     Kwasind
In his crown alone was seated;
In his crown, too, was his weakness;
There alone could he be wounded,
Nowhere else could weapon pierce
     him,
Nowhere else could weapon harm
     him.
     Even there the only weapon
That could wound him, that could
     slay him,
Was the seed-cone of the pine-tree,
Was the blue cone of the fir-tree.
This was Kwasind's fatal secret,
Known to no man among mortals;
But the cunning Little People,
The Puk-Wudjies, knew the secret,
Knew the only way to kill him.
     So they gathered cones together,
Gathered seed-cones of the pine-
     tree,
Gathered blue cones of the fir-tree,
In the woods by Taquamenaw,
Brought them to the river's mar-
     gin,
Heaped them in great piles to-
     gether,
Where the red rocks from the mar-
     gin
Jutting overhang the river.
There they lay in wait for Kwasind,
The malicious Little People.

'Twas an afternoon in Summer;
Very hot and still the air was,
Very smooth the gliding river,
Motionless the sleeping shadows;
Insects glistened in the sunshine,
Insects skated on the water,
Filled the drowsy air with buzzing,
With a far resounding war-cry.
     Down the river came the Strong
     Man,
In his birch canoe came Kwasind,
Floating slowly down the current
Of the sluggish Taquamenaw,
Very languid with the weather,
Very sleepy with the silence.
     From the overhanging branches,
From the tassels of the birch-trees,
Soft the Spirit of Sleep descended;
By his airy hosts surrounded,
His invisible attendants,
Came the Spirit of Sleep, Nepahwin;
Like the burnished Dush-kwo-ne-
     she,
Like a dragon-fly he hovered
O'er the drowsy head of Kwasind.
     To his ear there came a murmur
As of waves upon a seashore,
As of far-off tumbling waters,
As of wind among the pine-trees;
As he felt upon his forehead
Blows of little airy war-clubs,
Wielded by the slumbrous legions
Of the Spirit of Sleep, Nepahwin,
As of some one breathing on him.
     At the first blow of their war-
     clubs,
Fell a drowsiness on Kwasind;
At the second blow they smote
     him,
Motionless his paddle rested;
At the third, before his vision
Reeled the landscape into darkness,
Very sound asleep was Kwasind.
     So he floated down the river,
Like a blind man seated upright,
Floated down the Taquamenaw,
Underneath the trembling birch-
     trees,
Underneath the wooded headlands.

Underneath the war encampment
Of the pygmies, the Puk-Wudjies.
　　There they stood, all armed and
　　　waiting,
Hurled the pine-cones down upon
　　him,
Struck him on his brawny shoul-
　　ders,
On his crown defenceless struck
　　him.
"Death to Kwasind!" was the
　　sudden
War-cry of the Little People.
　　And he sideways swayed and
　　　tumbled,
Sideways fell into the river,
Plunged beneath the sluggish
　　water
Headlong, as an otter plunges;
And the birch-canoe, abandoned,
Drifted empty down the river,
Bottom upward swerved and
　　drifted;
Nothing more was seen of Kwasind.
　　But the memory of the Strong
　　　Man
Lingered long among the people,
And whenever through the forest
Raged and roared the wintry
　　tempest,
And the branches, tossed and
　　troubled,
Creaked and groaned and split
　　asunder,
"Kwasind!" cried they; "that
　　is Kwasind!
He is gathering in his firewood!"

XIX.

THE GHOSTS

　　Never stoops the soaring vulture
On his quarry in the desert,
On the sick or wounded bison,
But another vulture, watching
From his high aerial lookout,
Sees the downward plunge, and
　　follows;

And a third pursues the second,
Coming from the invisible ether,
First a speck, and then a vulture,
Till the air is dark with pinions.
　　So disasters come not singly;
But as if they watched and waited,
Scanning one another's motions,
When the first descends, the others
Follow, follow, gathering flock-
　　wise
Round their victim, sick and
　　wounded,
First a shadow, then a sorrow,
Till the air is dark with anguish.
　　Now, o'er all the dreary North-
　　　land,
Mighty Peboan, the Winter,
Breathing on the lakes and rivers,
Into stone had changed their
　　waters.
From his hair he shook the snow-
　　flakes,
Till the plains were strewn with
　　whiteness,
One uninterrupted level,
As if, stooping, the Creator
With his hands had smoothed them
　　over.
　　Through the forest, wide and
　　　wailing,
Roamed the hunter on his snow-
　　shoes;
In the village worked the women,
Pounded maize, or dressed the
　　deer-skin;
And the young men played to-
　　gether
On the ice the noisy ball-play.
On the plain the dance of snow-
　　shoes.
　　One dark evening, after sun-
　　　down,
In her wigwam Laughing Water
Sat with old Nokomis, waiting
For the steps of Hiawatha
Homeward from the hunt return-
　　ing.
　　On their faces gleamed the fire-
　　　light,

Painting them with streaks of crimson,
In the eyes of old Nokomis
Glimmered like the watery moonlight,
In the eyes of Laughing Water
Glistened like the sun in water;
And behind them crouched their shadows
In the corners of the wigwam,
And the smoke in wreaths above them
Climbed and crowded through the smoke-flue.
　Then the curtain of the doorway
From without was slowly lifted;
Brighter glowed the fire a moment,
And a moment swerved the smoke-wreath,
As two women entered softly,
Passed the doorway uninvited,
Without word of salutation,
Without sign of recognition,
Sat down in the farthest corner,
Crouching low among the shadows.
　From their aspect and their garments,
Strangers seemed they in the village;
Very pale and haggard were they,
As they sat there sad and silent,
Trembling, cowering with the shadows.
　Was it the wind above the smoke-flue.
Muttering down into the wigwam?
Was it the owl, the Koko-koho,
Hooting from the dismal forest?
Sure a voice said in the silence:
"These are corpses clad in garments,
These are ghosts that come to haunt you,
From the kingdom of Ponemah,
From the land of the Hereafter!"
　Homeward now came Hiawatha
From his hunting in the forest,
With the snow upon his tresses,
And the red deer on his shoulders.

At the feet of Laughing Water
Down he threw his lifeless burden;
Nobler, handsomer she thought him,
Than when first he came to woo her,
First threw down the deer before her,
As a token of his wishes,
As a promise of the future.
　Then he turned and saw the strangers,
Cowering, crouching with the shadows,
Said within himself, "Who are they?
What strange guests has Minnehaha?"
But he questioned not the strangers,
Only spake to bid them welcome
To his lodge, his food, his fireside.
　When the evening meal was ready,
And the deer had been divided,
Both the pallid guests, the strangers,
Springing from among the shadows,
Seized upon the choicest portions,
Seized the white fat of the roebuck,
Set apart for Laughing Water,
For the wife of Hiawatha;
Without asking, without thanking,
Eagerly devoured the morsels,
Flitted back among the shadows
In the corner of the wigwam.
　Not a word spake Hiawatha,
Not a motion made Nokomis,
Not a gesture Laughing Water;
Not a change came o'er their features,
Only Minnehaha softly
Whispered, saying, "They are famished;
Let them do what best delights them;
Let them eat, for they are famished."
　Many a daylight dawned and darkened,

Many a night shook off the day-
light
As the pine shakes off the snow-
flakes
From the midnight of its branches;
Day by day the guests unmoving
Sat there silent in the wigwam;
But by night, in storm or starlight,
Forth they went into the forest,
Bringing firewood to the wigwam,
Bringing pine cones for the burn-
ing,
Always sad and always silent.
And whenever Hiawatha
Came from fishing or from hunting,
When the evening meal was ready,
And the food had been divided,
Gliding from their darksome corner,
Came the pallid guests, the stran-
gers,
Seized upon the choicest portions
Set aside for Laughing Water,
And without rebuke or question
Flitted back among the shadows.
    Never once had Hiawatha
By a word or look reproved them;
Never once had old Nokomis
Made a gesture of impatience;
Never once had Laughing Water
Shown resentment at the outrage.
All had they endured in silence,
That the rights of guest and stran-
ger,
That the virtue of free-giving,
By a look might not be lessened,
By a word might not be broken.
    Once at midnight Hiawatha,
Ever wakeful, ever watchful,
In the wigwam, dimly lighted
By the brands that still were burn-
ing,
By the glimmering, flickering fire-
light,
Heard a sighing, oft repeated,
Heard a sobbing, as of sorrow.
    From his couch rose Hiawatha,
From his shaggy hides of bison,
Pushed aside the deerskin curtain,
Saw the pallid guests, the shadows,

Sitting upright on their couches,
Weeping in the silent midnight.
    And he said: " O guests ! why
is it
That your hearts are so afflicted,
That you sob so in the midnight ?
Has perchance the old Nokomis,
Has my wife, my Minnehaha,
Wronged or grieved you by un-
kindness,
Failed in hospitable duties ? "
    Then the shadows ceased from
weeping,
Ceased from sobbing and lament-
ing,
And they said, with gentle voices,
" We are ghosts of the departed,
Souls of those who once were with
you,
From the realm of Chibiabos
Hither have we come to try you,
Hither have we come to warn you:
    " Cries of grief and lamentation
Reach us in the Blessed Islands;
Cries of anguish from the living,
Calling back their friends departed,
Sadden us with useless sorrow.
Therefore have we come to try
you:
No one knows us, no one heeds us.
We are but a burden to you,
And we see that the departed
Have no place among the living.
    " Think of this, O Hiawatha!
Speak of it to all the people,
That henceforward and for ever
They no more with lamentations
Sadden the souls of the departed
In the Islands of the Blessed.
    " Do not lay such heavy burdens
In the graves of those you bury,
Not such weight of furs and wam-
pum,
Not such weight of pots and kettles,
For the spirits faint beneath them.
Only give them food to carry,
Only give them fire to light them.
    " Four days is the spirit's
journey

To the land of ghosts and shadows,
Four its lonely night encamp-
ments;
Four times must their fires be
lighted.
Therefore, when the dead are
buried,
Let a fire, as night approaches,
Four times on the grave be kindled,
That the soul upon its journey
May not lack the cheerful firelight,
May not grope about in darkness.
" Farewell, noble Hiawatha!
We have put you to the trial,
To the proof have put your
patience,
By the insult of our presence,
By the outrage of our actions.
We have found you great and
noble.
Fail not in the greater trial,
Faint not in the harder struggle."
When they ceased, a sudden
darkness
Fell and filled the silent wigwam.
Hiawatha heard a rustle
As of garments trailing by him,
Heard the curtain of the doorway
Lifted by a hand he saw not,
Felt the cold breath of the night
air,
For a moment saw the starlight;
But he saw the ghosts no longer,
Saw no more the wandering spirits
From the kingdom of Ponemah,
From the land of the Hereafter.

XX.

THE FAMINE

O the long and dreary Winter!
O the cold and cruel Winter!
Ever thicker, thicker, thicker
Froze the ice on lake and river,
Ever deeper, deeper, deeper
Fell the snow o'er all the land-
scape,
Fell the covering snow, and drifted

Through the forest, round the vil
lage.
Hardly from his buried wigwam
Could the hunter force a passage;
With his mittens and his snow-
shoes
Vainly walked he through the
forest,
Sought for bird or beast and found
none,
Saw no track of deer or rabbit,
In the snow beheld no footprints,
In the ghastly, gleaming forest
Fell, and could not rise from weak-
ness,
Perished there from cold and
hunger.
O the famine and the fever!
O the wasting of the famine!
O the blasting of the fever!
O the wailing of the children!
O the anguish of the women!
All the earth was sick and fam-
ished;
Hungry was the air around them,
Hungry was the sky above them,
And the hungry stars in heaven
Like the eyes of wolves glared at
them!
Into Hiawatha's wigwam
Came two other guests, as silent
As the ghosts were, and as gloomy,
Waited not to be invited,
Did not parley at the doorway,
Sat there without word of welcome
In the seat of Laughing Water;
Looked with haggard eyes and
hollow
At the face of Laughing Water.
And the foremost said: " Be-
hold me!
I am Famine, Bukadawin! "
And the other said: " Behold me!
I am Fever, Ahkosewin! "
And the lovely Minnehaha
Shuddered as they looked upon her,
Shuddered at the words they
uttered,
Lay down on her bed in silence,

Hid her face, but made no answer;
Lay there trembling, freezing,
    burning
At the looks they cast upon her,
At the fearful words they uttered.
    Forth into the empty forest
Rushed the maddened Hiawatha;
In his heart was deadly sorrow,
In his face a stony firmness;
On his brow the sweat of anguish
Started, but it froze and fell not.
    Wrapped in furs and armed for
        hunting,
With his mighty bow of ash-tree,
With his quiver full of arrows,
With his mittens, Minjekahwun,
Into the vast and vacant forest
On his snow-shoes strode he for-
    ward.
    " Gitche Manito, the Mighty! "
Cried he with his face uplifted
In that bitter hour of anguish,
" Give your children food, O
        father!
Give us food, or we must perish!
Give me food for Minnehaha,
For my dying Minnehaha! "
    Through the far-resounding
        forest,
Through the forest vast and vacant
Rang that cry of desolation.
But there came no other answer
Than the echo of his crying,
Than the echo of the woodlands,
" Minnehaha! Minnehaha! "
    All day long roved Hiawatha
In that melancholy forest,
Through the shadow of whose
    thickets,
In the pleasant days of Summer,
Of that ne'er forgotten Summer,
He had brought his young wife
        homeward
From the land of the Dacotahs;
When the birds sang in the thickets,
And the streamlets laughed and
        glistened,
And the air was full of fragrance,
And the lovely Laughing Water

Said with voice that did not
    tremble,
" I will follow you, my husband! "
In the wigwam with Nokomis,
With those gloomy guests, that
    watched her,
With the Famine and the Fever,
She was lying, the Beloved,
She the dying Minnehaha.
    " Hark! " she said; " I hear a
        rushing,
Hear a roaring and a rushing,
Hear the Falls of Minnehaha
Calling to me from a distance! "
" No, my child! " said old Noko-
    mis
" 'Tis the night-wind in the pine-
    trees! "
" Look! " she said; " I see my
        father
Standing lonely at his doorway,
Beckoning to me from his wigwam
In the land of the Dacotahs! "
" No, my child! " said old Noko-
    mis,
" 'Tis the smoke, that waves and
    beckons! "
    " Ah! " said she, " the eyes of
        Pauguk
Glare upon me in the darkness,
I can feel his icy fingers
Clasping mine amid the darkness!
Hiawatha! Hiawatha! "
    And the desolate Hiawatha,
Far away amid the forest,
Miles away among the mountains,
Heard that sudden cry of anguish,
Heard the voice of Minnehaha
Calling to him in the darkness,
" Hiawatha! Hiawatha! "
    Over snowfields waste and path-
        less
Under snow-encumbered branches,
Homeward hurried Hiawatha,
Empty-handed, heavy-hearted,
Heard Nokomis moaning, wailing:
" Wahonowin! Wahonowin!
Would that I had perished for you,
Would that I were dead as you are!

Wahonowin! Wahonowin!"
And he rushed into the wigwam,
Saw the old Nokomis slowly
Rocking to and fro and moaning,
Saw his lovely Minnehaha
Lying dead and cold before him,
And his bursting heart within him
Uttered such a cry of anguish,
That the forest moaned and shuddered,
That the very stars in heaven
Shook and trembled with his anguish.
  Then he sat down, still and speechless,
On the bed of Minnehaha,
At the feet of Laughing Water,
At those willing feet, that never
More would lightly run to meet him,
Never more would lightly follow.
  With both hands his face he covered,
Seven long days and nights he sat there,
As if in a swoon he sat there,
Speechless, motionless, unconscious
Of the daylight or the darkness.
  Then they buried Minnehaha;
In the snow a grave they made her,
In the forest deep and darksome,
Underneath the moaning hemlocks;
Clothed in her richest garments,
Wrapped in her robes of ermine;
Covered her with snow, like ermine,
Thus they buried Minnehaha.
  And at night a fire was lighted,
On her grave four times was kindled,
For her soul upon its journey
To the Islands of the Blessed.
From his doorway Hiawatha
Saw it burning in the forest,
Lighting up the gloomy hemlocks;
From his sleepless bed uprising,
From the bed of Minnehaha,
Stood and watched it at the doorway,
That it might not be extinguished,
Might not leave her in the darkness.
  "Farewell!" said he, "Minnehaha!
Farewell, O my Laughing Water!
All my heart is buried with you,
All my thoughts go onward with you!
Come not back again to labour,
Come not back again to suffer,
Where the Famine and the Fever
Wear the heart and waste the body.
Soon my task will be completed,
Soon your footsteps I shall follow
To the Islands of the Blessed,
To the Kingdom of Ponemah,
To the Land of the Hereafter!"

XXI.

THE WHITE MAN'S FOOT

  In his lodge beside a river,
Close beside a frozen river,
Sat an old man, sad and lonely.
White his hair was as a snowdrift;
Dull and low his fire was burning,
And the old man shook and trembled,
Folded in his Waubewyon,
In his tattered white skin wrapper,
Hearing nothing but the tempest
As it roared along the forest,
Seeing nothing but the snowstorm,
As it whirled and hissed and drifted.
  All the coals were white with ashes,
And the fire was slowly dying,
As a young man, walking lightly,
At the open doorway entered.
Red with blood of youth his cheeks were,
Soft his eyes, as stars in Springtime,

Bound his forehead was with
  grasses,
Bound and plumed with scented
  grasses;
On his lips a smile of beauty,
Filling all the lodge with sunshine,
In his hand a bunch of blossoms
Filling all the lodge with sweetness.
  " Ah, my son! " exclaimed the
  old man,
" Happy are my eyes to see you.
Sit here on the mat beside me,
Sit here by the dying embers,
Let us pass the night together.
Tell me of your strange adventures,
Of the lands where you have
  travelled;
I will tell you of my prowess,
Of my many deeds of wonder."
  From his pouch he drew his
  peace-pipe,
Very old and strangely fashioned;
Made of red stone was the pipe-
  head,
And the stem a reed with feathers,
Filled the pipe with bark of willow,
Placed a burning coal upon it,
Gave it to his guest, the stranger,
And began to speak in this wise:
  " When I blow my breath about
  me,
When I breathe upon the land-
  scape,
Motionless are all the rivers,
Hard as stones become the water! "
  And the young man answered,
  smiling:
" When I blow my breath about
  me,
When I breathe upon the land-
  scape,
Flowers spring up o'er all the
  meadows,
Singing, onward rush the rivers! "
  " When I shake my hoary
  tresses,"
Said the old man darkly frowning,
" All the land with snow is covered;
All the leaves from all the branches

Fall and fade and die and wither,
For I breathe, and lo! they are
  not.
From the waters and the marshes
Rise the wild goose and the heron,
Fly away to distant regions,
For I speak, and lo! they are not.
And where'er my footsteps wander,
All the wild beasts of the forest
Hide themselves in holes and
  caverns,
And the earth becomes as flint-
  stone! "
  " When I shake my flowing
  ringlets,"
Said the young man, softly laugh-
  ing,
" Showers of rain fall warm and
  welcome,
Plants lift up their heads rejoicing,
Back unto their lakes and marshes
Come the wild goose and the heron,
Homeward shoots the arrowy
  swallows,
Sing the bluebird and the robin,
And where'er my footsteps wander,
All the meadows wave with blos-
  soms,
All the woodlands ring with music,
All the trees are dark with foliage! "
  While they spake, the night de-
  parted:
From the distant realms of Wabun,
From his shining lodge of silver,
Like a warrior robed and painted,
Came the sun, and said, " Behold
  me!
Gheezis, the great sun, behold
  me! "
  Then the old man's tongue was
  speechless.
And the air grew warm and
  pleasant,
And upon the wigwam sweetly
Sang the bluebird and the robin,
And the stream began to murmur,
And a scent of growing grasses
Through the lodge was gently
  wafted.

And Segwun, the youthful stranger,
More distinctly in the daylight
Saw the icy face before him;
It was Peboan, the Winter!
  From his eyes the tears were flowing,
As from melting lakes the streamlets,
And his body shrunk and dwindled
As the shouting sun ascended,
Till into the air it faded,
Till into the ground it vanished,
And the young man saw before him,
On the hearth-stone of the wigwam,
Where the fire had smoked and smouldered,
Saw the earliest flower of Spring-time,
Saw the beauty of the Spring-time,
Saw the Miskodeed in blossom.
  Thus it was that in the Northland
After that unheard-of coldness,
That intolerable Winter,
Came the Spring with all its splendour,
All its birds and all its blossoms,
All its flowers and leaves and grasses,
  Sailing on the wind to northward,
Flying in great flocks, like arrows,
Like huge arrows shot through heaven,
Passed the swan, the Mahnahbezee,
Speaking almost as a man speaks;
And in long lines waving, bending
Like a bow-string snapped asunder,
Came the white goose, Wawbewawa;
And the pairs or singly flying,
Mahng the loon, with clangorous pinions,
The blue heron, the Shuh-shuh-gah,
And the grouse, the Mushkodasa.
  In the thickets and the meadows
Piped the bluebird, the Owaissa,
On the summit of the lodges
Sang the Opechee, the robin,
In the covert of the pine-trees
Cooed the pigeon, the Omemee,
And the sorrowing Hiawatha,
Speechless in his infinite sorrow,
Heard their voices calling to him,
Went forth from his gloomy doorway,
Stood and gazed into the heaven,
Gazed upon the earth and waters.
  From his wanderings far to eastward,
From the regions of the morning,
From the shining land of Wabun,
Homeward now returned Iagoo,
The great traveller, the great boaster,
Full of new and strange adventures,
Marvels many and many wonders.
  And the people of the village
Listened to him as he told them
Of his marvellous adventures,
Laughing answered him in this wise:
"Ugh! it is indeed Iagoo!
No one else beholds such wonders!
  He had seen, he said, a water,
Bigger than the Big-Sea-Water,
Broader than the Gitche Gumee,
Bitter so that none could drink it!
At each other looked the warriors,
Looked the women at each other,
Smiled, and said, "It cannot be so!
Kaw!" they said, "It cannot be so!"
  O'er it, said he, o'er this water
Came a great canoe with pinions,
A canoe with wings came flying,
Bigger than a grove of pine-trees,
Taller than the tallest tree-tops!
And the old men and the women
Look and tittered at each other;
"Kaw!" they said, "we don't believe it!"

From its mouth, he said, to greet
   him,
Came Waywassimo, the lightning,
Came the thunder, Annemeekee!
And the warriors and the women
Laughed aloud at poor Iagoo;
"Kaw!" they said, "what tales
   you tell us!"
   In it, said he, came a people,
In the great canoe with pinions
Came, he said, a hundred warriors;
Painted white were all their faces
And with hair their chins were
   covered!
And the warriors and the women
Laughed and shouted in derision,
Like the ravens on the tree-tops,
Like the crows upon the hemlocks.
"Kaw!" they said, "what lies
   you tell us!
Do not think that we believe
   them!"
   Only Hiawatha laughed not,
But he gravely spake and answered
To their jeering and their jesting:
"True is all Iagoo tells us;
I have seen it in a vision,
Seen the great canoe with pinions,
Seen the people with white faces,
Seen the coming of this bearded
People of the wooden vessel
From the regions of the morning,
From the shining land of Wabun.
   "Gitche Manito, the Mighty,
The Great Spirit, the Creator,
Sends them hither on his errand,
Sends them to us with his message.
Wheresoe'er they move, before
   them
Swarms the stinging fly, the Ahmo,
Swarms the bee, the honey-maker;
Wheresoe'er they tread, beneath
   them
Springs a flower unknown among
   us,
Springs the White-man's Foot in
   blossom.
   "Let us welcome, then, the
   strangers,

Hail them as our friends and
   brothers,
And the heart's right hand of
   friendship
Give them when they come to see
   us.
Gitche Manito, the Mighty,
Said this to me in my vision.
   "I beheld, too, in that vision,
All the secrets of the future,
Of the distant days that shall be.
I beheld the westward marches
Of the unknown, crowded nations.
All the land was full of people,
Restless, struggling, toiling, striv-
   ing,
Speaking many tongues, yet feel-
   ing
But one heart-beat in their bosoms.
In the woodlands rang their axes,
Smoked their towns in all the
   valleys,
Over all the lakes and rivers
Rushed their great canoes of
   thunder.
   "Then a darker, drearier vision
Passed before me, vague and
   cloud-like
I beheld our nation scattered,
All forgetful of my counsels,
Weakened, warring with each
   other;
Saw the remnants of our people
Sweeping westward, wild and wo-
   ful,
Like the cloud-rack of a tempest,
Like the withered leaves of
   Autumn!"

XXII.

HIAWATHA'S DEPARTURE

By the shore of Gitche Gumee,
By the shining Big-Sea-Water,
At the doorway of his wigwam,
In the pleasant Summer morning,
Hiawatha stood and waited.
   All the air was full of freshness

All the earth was bright and joyous,
And before him through the sun-
    shine,
Westward toward the neighbour-
    ing forest
Passed in golden swarms the Ahmo,
Passed the bees, the honey-
    makers,
Burning, singing in the sunshine.
    Bright above him shone the
        heavens,
Level spread the lake before him;
From its bosom leaped the stur-
    geon,
Sparkling, flashing in the sunshine;
On its margin the great forest
Stood reflected in the water,
Every tree-top had its shadow,
Motionless beneath the water.
    From the brow of Hiawatha
Gone before was every trace of sorrow,
As the fog from off the water,
As the mist from off the meadow.
With a smile of joy and triumph,
With a look of exultation.
As of one who in a vision
Sees what is to be, but is not,
Stood and waited Hiawatha.
    Toward the sun his hands were
        lifted,[1]
Both the palms spread out against
    it,
And between the parted fingers
Fell the sunshine on his features,
Flecked with light his naked
    shoulders,
As it falls and flecks an oak tree
Through the rifted leaves and
    branches.
    O'er the water floating, flying,
Something in the hazy distance,
Something in the mists of morning,
Loomed and lifted from the water,
Now seemed floating, now seemed
    flying,

[1] In this manner, and with such salutations, was Father Marquette received by the Illinois. See his *Voyage et Découvertes*, Section V.

Coming nearer, nearer, nearer.
    Was it Shingebis, the diver?
Was it the pelican, the Shada?
Or the heron, the Shuh-shuh-gah?
Or the white goose, Waw-be-wawa,
With the water dripping, flashing,
From its glossy neck and feathers?
    It was neither goose nor diver,
Neither pelican nor heron,
O'er the water floating, flying,
Through the shining mist of morn-
    ing,
But a birch canoe with paddles,
Rising, sinking on the water,
Dripping, flashing in the sunshine;
And within it came a people
From the distant land of Wabun,
From the farthest realms of morn-
    ing
Came the Black-Robe chief, the
    Prophet,
He the Priest of Prayer, the Pale-
    face,
With his guides and his com-
    panions.
    And the noble Hiawatha,
With his hands aloft extended,
Held aloft in sign of welcome,
Waited, full of exultation,
Till the birch canoe with paddles
Grated on the shining pebbles,
Stranded on the sandy margin,
Till the Black-Robe chief, the Pale-
    face,
With the cross upon his bosom,
Landed on the sandy margin.
    Then the joyous Hiawatha
Cried aloud and spake in this wise:
" Beautiful is the sun, O strangers,
When you come so far to see us!
All our town in peace awaits you,
All our doors stand open for you;
You shall enter all our wigwams,
For the heart's right hand we give
    you.
    " Never bloomed the earth so
        gaily,
Never shone the sun so brightly,
As to-day they shine and blossom

When you come so far to see us!
Never was our lake so tranquil,
Nor so free from rocks and sand-
    bars;
For our birch canoe in passing
Has removed both rock and sand-
    bar.
    "Never before had our tobacco
Such a sweet and pleasant flavour,
Never the broad leaves of our corn-
    fields
Were so beautiful to look on,
As they seem to us this morning,
When you come so far to see us!"
    And the Black-Robe chief made
        answer,
Stammered in his speech a little,
Speaking words yet unfamiliar:
"Peace be with you, Hiawatha,
Peace be with you and your people,
Peace of prayer, and peace of par-
    don,
Peace of Christ, and joy of Mary!"
    Then the generous Hiawatha
Led the strangers to his wigwam,
Seated them on skins of bison,
Seated them on skins of ermine,
And the careful, old Nokomis
Brought them food in bowls of
    bass-wood,
Water brought in birchen dippers,
And the calumet, the peace-pipe,
Filled and lighted for their smok-
    ing.
    All the old men of the village,
All the warriors of the nation,
All the Jossakeeds, the prophets,
The magicians, the Wabenos,
And the medicine-men, the Medas,
Came to bid the strangers welcome;
"It is well," they said, "O
    brothers,
That you come so far to see us!"
    In a circle round the doorway,
With their pipes they sat in silence,
Waiting to behold the strangers,
Waiting to receive their message;
Till the Black-Robe chief, the Pale-
    face,

From the wigwam came to greet
    them,
Stammering in his speech a little,
Speaking words yet unfamiliar;
"It is well," they said, "O
    brother,
That you come so far to see us!"
    Then the Black-Robe chief, the
        prophet,
Told his message to the people,
Told the purport of his mission,
Told them of the Virgin Mary,
And her blessed Son, the Saviour,
How in distant lands and ages
He had lived on earth as we do;
How he fasted, prayed, and
    laboured;
How the Jews, the tribe accursed,
Mocked him, scourged him, cruci-
    fied him;
How he rose from where they laid
    him,
Walked again with his disciples,
And ascended into heaven.
    And the chiefs made answer,
        saying:
"We have listened to your mes-
    sage,
We have heard your words of wis-
    dom,
We will think on what you tell us.
It is well for us, O brothers,
That you come so far to see us!"
    Then they rose up and departed
Each one homeward to his wigwam,
To the young men and the women
Told the story of the strangers
Whom the Master of Life had sent
    them
From the shining land of Wabun.
    Heavy with the heat and silence
Grew the afternoon of Summer;
With a drowsy sound the forest
Whispered round the sultry wig-
    wam.
With a sound of sleep the water
Rippled on the beach below it;
From the cornfields shrill and
    ceaseless

Sang the grasshopper, Pah-puk-keena;
And the guests of Hiawatha,
Weary with the heat of Summer,
Slumbered in the sultry wigwam.
　　Slowly o'er the simmering landscape
Fell the evening's dusk and coolness,
And the long and level sunbeams
Shot their spears into the forest,
Breaking through its shields of shadow,
Rushed into each secret ambush,
Searched each thicket, dingle, hollow;
Still the guests of Hiawatha
Slumbered in the silent wigwam.
　　From his place rose Hiawatha,
Bade farewell to old Nokomis,
Spake in whispers, spake in this wise,
Did not wake the guests, that slumbered:
　" I am going, O Nokomis,
On a long and distant journey,
To the portals of the Sunset,
To the regions of the home-wind,
Of the Northwest wind, Keeway-din.
But these guests I leake behind me,
In your watch and ward I leave them;
See that never harm comes near them,
See that never fear molests them,
Never danger nor suspicion,
Never want of food or shelter,
In the lodge of Hiawatha!
　　Forth into the village went he,
Bade farewell to all the warriors,
Bade farewell to all the young men,
Spake persuading, spake in this wise:
　" I am going, O my people,
On a long and distant journey;
Many moons and many winters
Will have come, and will have vanished,
Ere I come again to see you.
But my guests I leave behind me;
Listen to their words of wisdom,
Listen to the truth they tell you,
For the Master of Life has sent them
From the land of light and morning! "
　　On the shore stood Hiawatha,
Turned and waved his hands at parting;
On the clear and luminous water
Launched his birch canoe for sailing,
From the pebbles of the margin
Shoved it forth into the water;
Whispered to it, " Westward! westward! "
And with speed it darted forward.
　　And the evening sun descending
Set the clouds on fire with redness,
Burned the broad sky, like a prairie,
Left upon the level water
One long track and trail of splendour,
Down whose stream, as down a river,
Westward, westward Hiawatha
Sailed into the fiery sunset,
Sailed into the purple vapours,
Sailed into the dusk of evening.
　　And the people from the margin
Watched him floating, rising, sinking,
Till the birch canoe seemed lifted
High into that sea of splendour,
Till it sank into the vapours
Like the new moon slowly, slowly
Sinking in the purple distance.
　　And they said, " Farewell for ever! "
Said, " Farewell, O Hiawatha! "
And the forests, dark and lonely,
Moved through all their depths of darkness,
Sighed, " Farewell, O Hiawatha! "

And the waves upon the margin
　Rising, rippling on the pebbles,
Sobbed, " Farewell, O Hiawatha!"
And the heron, the Shuh-shuh-gah,
　From her haunts among the fen-
　　lands
Screamed, " Farewell, O Hia-
　　watha! "
　　Thus departed Hiawatha!

Hiawatha the Beloved,
In the glory of the sunset,
In the purple mists of evening,
To the regions of the home-wind,
Of the Northwest wind, Keeway-
　din,
To the Islands of the Blessed,
To the Kingdom of Ponemah,
To the land of the Hereafter!

THE VILLAGE BLACKSMITH AND OTHER POEMS

THE VILLAGE BLACKSMITH

UNDER a spreading chestnut tree
　The village smithy stands;
The smith, a mighty man is he,
　With large and sinewy hands;
And the muscles of his brawny
　　arms
　Are strong as iron bands.

His hair is crisp, and black, and
　　long,
　His face is like the tan;
His brow is wet with honest sweat,
　He earns whate'er he can,
And looks the whole world in the
　　face,
　For he owes not any man.

Week in, week out, from morn till
　　night,
　You can hear his bellows blow;
You can hear him swing his heavy
　　sledge,
　With measured beat and slow,
Like a sexton ringing the village
　　bell,
　When the evening sun is low.

And children coming home from
　　school
　Look in at the open door;

They love to see the flaming forge,
　And hear the bellows roar,
And catch the burning sparks that
　　fly
　Like chaff from a threshing floor.

He goes on Sunday to the church,
　And sits among his boys;
He hears the parson pray and
　　preach,
　He hears his daughter's voice,
Singing in the village choir,
　And it makes his heart rejoice.

It sounds to him like her mother's
　　voice,
　Singing in Paradise!
He needs must think of her once
　　more,
　How in the grave she lies;
And with his hard, rough hand he
　　wipes
　A tear out of his eyes.

Toiling,—rejoicing,—sorrowing,
　Onward through life he goes;
Each morning sees some task begin,
　Each evening sees it close;
Something attempted, something
　　done,
　Has earned a night's repose.

Thanks. thanks to thee, my worthy
    friend,
  For the lesson thou hast taught!
Thus at the flaming forge of life
  Our fortunes must be wrought;
Thus on its sounding anvil shaped
  Each burning deed and thought!

ENDYMION

The rising moon has hid the stars;
Her level rays, like golden bars,
    Lie on the landscape green,
    With shadows brown between.

And silver white the river gleams,
As if Diana, in her dreams,
    Had dropt her silver bow
    Upon the meadows low.

On such a tranquil night as this,
She woke Endymion with a kiss,
    When, sleeping in the grove,
    He dreamed not of her love.

Like Dian's kiss, unaskt, unsought,
Love gives itself, but is not bought!
    Nor voice, nor sound betrays
    Its deep, impassioned gaze.

It comes,—the beautiful, the free,
The crown of all humanity,—
    In silence and alone
    To seek the elected one.

It lifts the boughs, whose shadows
    deep,
Are Life's oblivion, the soul's sleep,
    And kisses the closed eyes
    Of him, who slumbering lies.

O, weary hearts! O, slumbering
    eyes!
O, drooping souls, whose destinies
    Are fraught with fear and
        pain,
    Ye shall be loved again!

No one is so accurst by fate,
No one so utterly desolate,
    But some heart, though un-
        known,
    Responds unto his own.

Responds,—as if with unseen wings,
An angel touched its quivering
        strings;
    And whispers in its song,
    " Where hast thou stayed so
        long! "

THE TWO LOCKS OF HAIR

FROM THE GERMAN OF PFIZER

A youth, light-hearted and content,
  I wander through the world;
Here, Arab-like, is pitched my tent
  And straight again is furled.

Yet oft I dream, that once a wife
  Close in my heart was locked,
And in the sweet repose of life
  A blessèd child I rocked.

I wake! Away that dream,—
        away!
  Too long did it remain!
So long, that both by night and
        day
  It ever comes again.

The end lies ever in my thought;
  To a grave so cold and deep
The mother beautiful was brought;
  Then dropt the child asleep.

But now the dream is wholly o'er,
  I bathe mine eyes and see;
And wander through the world once
        more,
  A youth so light and free.

Two locks,—and they are won-
        drous fair,—
  Left me that vision mild;

The brown is from the mother's
hair,
The blond is from the child.

And when I see that lock of gold,
Pale grows the evening-red;
And when the dark lock I behold,
I wish that I were dead.

IT IS NOT ALWAYS MAY

NO HAY PÁJAROS EN LOS NIDOS DE
ANTAÑO

Spanish Proverb.

The sun is bright,—the air is clear,
The darting swallows soar and
sing,
And from the stately elms I hear
The bluebird prophesying Spring.

So blue yon winding river flows,
It seems an outlet from the sky,
Where waiting till the west wind
blows,
The freighted clouds at anchor
lie.

All things are new;—the buds, the
leaves,
That gild the elm-tree's nodding
crest,
And even the nest beneath the
eaves;—
There are no birds in last year's
nest!

All things rejoice in youth and love,
The fulness of their first delight!
And learn from the soft heavens
above
The melting tenderness of night.

Maiden, that read'st this simple
rhyme,
Enjoy thy youth, it will not stay;
Enjoy the fragrance of thy prime,
For O! it is not always May!

Enjoy the Spring of Love and
Youth,
To some good angel leave the
rest;
For Time will teach thee soon the
truth,
There are no birds in last year's
nest!

THE RAINY DAY

The day is cold, and dark, and
dreary;
It rains, and the wind is never
weary;
The vine still clings to the moulder-
ing wall,
But at every gust the dead leaves
fall,
And the day is dark and dreary.

My life is cold, and dark, and
dreary;
It rains, and the wind is never
weary;
My thoughts still cling to the
mouldering Past,
But the hopes of youth fall thick in
the blast,
And the days are dark and
dreary.

Be still, sad heart! and cease re-
pining;
Behind the clouds is the sun still
shining;
Thy fate is the common fate of all,
Into each life some rain must fall,
Some days must be dark and
dreary.

GOD'S-ACRE

I like that ancient Saxon phrase
which calls
The burial-ground God's-Acre!
It is just;

It consecrates each grave within
its walls,
And breathes a benison o'er the
sleeping dust.

God's-Acre! Yes, that blessèd
name imparts
Comfort to those, who in the
grave have sown
The seed, that they had garnered
in their hearts,
Their bread of life, alas! no
more their own.

Into its furrows shall we all be cast,
In the sure faith, that we shall
rise again
At the great harvest, when the
arch-angel's blast
Shall winnow, like a fan, the
chaff and grain.

Then shall the good stand in im-
mortal bloom,
In the fair gardens of that second
birth;
And each bright blossom, mingle
its perfume
With that of flowers, which
never bloomed on earth.

With thy rude ploughshare, Death,
turn up the sod,
And spread the furrow for the
seed we sow;
This is the field and Acre of our
God,
This is the place, where human
harvests grow!

TO THE RIVER CHARLES

River! that in silence windest
Through the meadows, bright
and free,
Till at length thy rest thou findest
In the bosom of the sea!

Four long years of mingled feeling,
Half in rest, and half in strife,
I have seen thy waters stealing
Onward, like the stream of life.

Thou has taught me, Silent River!
Many a lesson, deep and long;
Thou hast been a generous giver;
I can give thee but a song.

Oft in sadness and in illness,
I have watched thy current
glide,
Till the beauty of its stillness
Overflowed me, like a tide.

And in better hours and brighter,
When I saw thy waters gleam,
I have felt my heart beat lighter,
And leap onward with thy
stream.

Not for this alone I love thee,
Nor because, thy waves of blue
From celestial seas above thee
Take their own celestial hue.

Where yon shadowy woodlands
hide thee,
And thy waters disappear,
Friends I love have dwelt beside
thee,
And have made thy margin dear.

More than this;—thy name re-
minds me
Of three friends, all true and
tried;
And that name, like magic, binds
me
Closer, closer to thy side.

Friends my soul with joy remem-
bers!
How like quivering flames they
start,
When I fan the living embers
On the hearth-stone of my
heart!

'Tis for this, thou Silent River!
   That my spirit leans to thee;
Thou hast been a generous giver,
   Take this idle song from me.

BLIND BARTIMEUS

Blind Bartimeus at the gates
Of Jericho in darkness waits;
He hears the crowd;—he hears a
      breath
Say, " It is Christ of Nazareth! "
And calls in tones of agony,
Ἰησοῦ, ἐλέησόν με *!*

The thronging multitudes in-
      crease;
Blind Bartimeus, hold thy peace!
But still, above the noisy crowd,
The beggar's cry is shrill and loud;
Until they say, " He calleth thee! "
Θάρσει, ἔγειραι, φωνεῖ σε *!*

Then saith the Christ, as silent
      stands
The crowd, " What wilt thou at
      my hands ? "
And he replies, " O give me light!"
Rabbi, restore the blind man's
      sight!
And Jesus answers, Ὕπαγε.
Ἡ πίστις σου σέσωκέ σε *!*

Ye that have eyes, yet cannot see,
In darkness and in misery,
Recall those mighty Voices Three,
Ἰησοῦ ἐλέησόν με *!*
Θάρσει, ἔγειραι, Ὕπαγε *!*
Ἡ πίστις σου σέσωκε σε *!*

THE GOBLET OF LIFE

Filled is Life's goblet to the brim;
And though my eyes with tears are
      dim,

I see its sparkling bubbles swim,
And chaunt a melancholy hymn
   With solemn voice and slow.

No purple flowers,—no garlands
      green,
Conceal the goblet's shade or
      sheen.
Nor maddening draughts of Hippo-
      crene,
Like gleams of sunshine, flash be-
      tween
   Thick leaves of mistletoe.

This goblet, wrought with curious
      art,
Is filled with waters, that upstart,
When the deep fountains of the
      heart,
By strong convulsions rent apart,
   Are running all to waste.

And as it mantling passes round,
With fennel it is wreathed and
      crowned,
Whose seed and foliage sun-im-
      browned
Are in its waters steeped and
      drowned,
   And give a bitter taste.

Above the lowly plants it towers.
The fennel, with its yellow flowers,
And in an earlier age than ours
Was gifted with the wondrous
      powers,
   Lost vision to restore.

It gave new strength, and fearless
      mood;
And gladiators, fierce and rude,
Mingled it in their daily food;
And he who battled and subdued,
   A wreath of fennel wore.

Then in Life's goblet freely press,
The leaves that give it bitterness,
Nor prize the coloured waters less,
For in thy darkness and distress
   New light and strength they
      give!

And he who has not learned to
know
How false its sparkling bubbles
show,
How bitter are the drops of woe,
With which its brim may overflow,
He has not learned to live.

The prayer of Ajax was for light;
Through all that dark and desper-
ate fight,
The blackness of that noonday
night,
He asked but the return of sight,
To see his foeman's face.

Let our unceasing, earnest prayer
Be, too, for light,—for strength to
bear
Our portion of the weight of care,
That crushes into dumb despair
One half the human race.

O suffering, sad humanity!
O ye afflicted ones, who lie
Steeped to the lips in misery,
Longing, and yet afraid to die,
Patient, though sorely tried!

I pledge you in this cup of grief,
Where floats the fennel's bitter leaf!
The Battle of our Life is brief,
The alarm,—the struggle,—the
relief,—
Then sleep we side by side.

MAIDENHOOD

Maiden! with the meek, brown
eyes,
In whose orbs a shadow lies
Like the dusk in evening skies!

Thou whose locks outshine the sun,
Golden tresses, wreathed in one,
As the braided streamlets run!

Standing, with reluctant feet,
Where the brook and river meet,
Womanhood and childhood fleet!

Gazing, with a timid glance,
On the brooklet's swift advance,
On the river's broad expanse!

Deep and still, that gliding stream
Beautiful to thee must seem,
As the river of a dream.

Then why pause with indecision,
When bright angels in thy vision
Beckon thee to fields Elysian?

Seest thou shadows sailing by,
As the dove, with startled eye,
Sees the falcon's shadow fly?

Hearest thou voices on the shore,
That our ears perceive no more,
Deafened by the cataract's roar?

O, thou child of many prayers!
Life hath quicksands,—Life hath
snares!
Care and age come unawares!

Like the swell of some sweet
tune,
Morning rises into noon,
May glides onward into June.

Childhood is the bough, where
slumbered
Birds and blossoms many-num-
bered;—
Age, that bough with snows en-
cumbered.

Gather, then, each flower that
grows,
When the young heart overflows,
To embalm that tent of snows.

Bear a lily in thy hand;
Gates of brass cannot withstand
The touch of that magic wand.

Bear through sorrow, wrong, and
　　ruth,
In thy heart the dew of youth,
On thy lips the smile of truth.

O, that dew, like balm, shall steal
Into wounds, that cannot heal,
Even as sleep our eyes doth seal;

And that smile, like sunshine, dart
Into many a sunless heart,
For a smile of God thou art.

EXCELSIOR

The shades of night were falling
　　fast,
As through an Alpine village passed
A youth, who bore, 'mid snow and
　　ice,
A banner with the strange device,
　　　　Excelsior!

His brow was sad; his eye beneath
Flashed like a falchion from its
　　sheath,
And like a silver clarion rung
The accents of that unknown
　　tongue,
　　　　Excelsior!

In happy homes he saw the light
Of household fires gleam warm and
　　bright;
Above, the spectral glaciers shone,
And from his lips escaped a groan,
　　　　Excelsior!

" Try not the Pass! " the old man
　　said;

" Dark lowers the tempest over-
　　head,
The roaring torrent is deep and
　　wide!
And loud that clarion voice replied,
　　　　Excelsior!

" O stay," the maiden said, " and
　　rest
Thy weary head upon this breast! "
A tear stood in his bright blue eye,
But still he answered, with a sigh,
　　　　Excelsior!

" Beware the pine-tree's withered
　　branch!
Beware the awful avalanche! "
This was the peasant's last Good-
　　night,
A voice replied, far up the height,
　　　　Excelsior!

At break of day, as heavenward
The pious monks of Saint Bernard
Uttered the oft-repeated prayer,
A voice cried through the startled
　　air,
　　　　Excelsior!

A traveller, by the faithful hound,
Half-buried in the snow was found,
Still grasping in his hand of ice
That banner with the strange de-
　　vice,
　　　　Excelsior!

There in the twilight cold and gray,
Lifeless, but beautiful, he lay,
And from the sky, serene and far,
A voice fell, like a falling star,
　　　　Excelsior!

THE SPANISH STUDENT

1843

DRAMATIS PERSONÆ

VICTORIAN }
HYPOLITO } · · *Students of Alcalá.*
THE COUNT OF LARA } *Gentlemen of*
DON CARLOS } *Madrid*
THE ARCHBISHOP OF TOLEDO.
A CARDINAL.
BELTRAN CRUZADO. *Count of the Gypsies.*
BARTOLOMÉ ROMAN *A young Gypsy.*
THE PADRE CURA OF GUADARRAMA.
PEDRO CRESPO . . *Alcalde.*
PANCHO. . . . *Alguacil.*
FRANCISCO. . . . *Lara's servant.*
CHISPA. . . . . *Victorian's servant.*
BALTASAR. . . . *Innkeeper.*
PRECIOSA. . . . *A Gypsy girl.*
ANGELICA. . . . *A poor girl.*
MARTINA... . . . *The Padre Cura's niece.*
DOLORES. . . . *Preciosa's maid.*
Gypsies, Musicians, etc.

ACT I.

SCENE I.—*The* COUNT OF LARA'S *chambers. Night. The* COUNT *in his dressing-gown, smoking and conversing with* DON CARLOS.

Lara. You were not at the play to-night, Don Carlos;
How happened it?
Don Carlos. I had engagements elsewhere.
Pray who was there?
Lara. Why, all the town and court.
The house was crowded; and the busy fans
Among the gaily dressed and perfumed ladies
Fluttered like butterflies among the flowers.

There was the Countess of Medina Celi;
The Goblin Lady with her Phantom Lover,
Her Lindo Don Diego; Doña Sol,
And Doña Serafina, and her cousins.
Don Carlos. What was the play?
Lara. It was a dull affair
One of those comedies in which you see,
As Lope says,[1] the history of the world
Brought down from Genesis to the Day of Judgment.
There were three duels fought in the first act,
Three gentlemen receiving deadly wounds,
Laying their hands upon their hearts, and saying,
"O, I am dead!" a lover in a closet,
An old hidalgo, and a gay Don Juan,
A Doña Inez with a black mantilla,
Followed at twilight by an unknown lover.
Who looks intently where he knows she is not!
Don Carlos. Of course, the Preciosa danced to-night?
Lara. And never better. Every footstep fell
As lightly as a sunbeam on the water.

[1] *As Lope says.*
"La cólera
de un Español sentado no se templa,
sino le representan en dos horas
hasta el final juicio desde el Génesis."
Lope de Vega.

265

I think the girl extremely beautiful.

Don Carlos. Almost beyond the privilege of woman!
I saw her in the Prado yesterday.
Her step was royal,—queen-like,—and her face
As beautiful as a saint's in Paradise.

Lara. May not a saint fall from her Paradise,
And be no more a saint?

Don Carlos. Why do you ask?

Lara. Because I have heard it said this angel fell,
And, though she is a virgin outwardly,
Within she is a sinner; like those panels
Of doors and altar-pieces the old monks
Painted in convents, with the Virgin Mary
On the outside, and on the inside Venus!

Don Carlos. You do her wrong; indeed, you do her wrong!
She is as virtuous as she is fair.

Lara. How credulous you are!
Why, look you, friend,
There's not a virtuous woman in Madrid,
In this city whole! And would you persuade me
That a mere dancing-girl, who shows herself,
Nightly, half-naked, on the stage, for money,
And with voluptuous motions fires the blood
Of inconsiderate youth, is to be held
A model for her virtue?

Don Carlos. You forget
She is a Gypsy girl.

Lara. And therefore won
The easier.

Don Carlos. Nay, not to be won at all!

The only virtue that a Gypsy prizes
Is chastity. That is her only virtue.
Dearer than life she holds it. I remember
A Gypsy woman, a vile, shameless bawd,
Whose craft was to betray the young and fair;
And yet this woman was above all bribes.
And when a noble lord, touched by her beauty,
The wild and wizard beauty of her race,
Offered her gold to be what she made others,
She turned upon him, with a look of scorn,
And smote him in the face!

Lara. And does that prove
That Preciosa is above suspicion?

Don Carlos. It proves a nobleman may be repulsed
When he thinks conquest easy. I believe
That woman, in her deepest degradation,
Holds something sacred, something undefiled,
Some pledge and keepsake of her higher nature,
And, like the diamond in the dark, retains
Some quenchless gleam of the celestial light!

Lara. Yet Preciosa would have taken the gold.

Don Carlos (*rising*). I do not think so.

Lara. I am sure of it,
But why this haste? Stay yet a little longer,
And fight the battles of your Dulcinea.

Don Carlos. 'Tis late. I must begone, for if I stay
You will not be persuaded.

Lara.   Yes; persuade me.

Don Carlos. No one so deaf as he who will not hear!

Lara. No one so blind as he who will not see!

Don Carlos. And so good-night.
I wish you pleasant dreams,
And greater faith in woman.

[*Exit.*

Lara.   Greater faith!
I have the greatest faith; for I
    believe
Victorian is her lover.   I believe
That I shall be to-morrow; and
    thereafter
Another, and another, and another,
Chasing each other through her
    zodiac,
As Taurus chases Aries.

(*Enter* FRANCISCO *with a casket.*)

                    Well, Francisco,
What speed with Preciosa?

Francisco.   None, my lord.
She sends your jewels back, and
    bids me tell you
She is not to be purchased by your
    gold.

Lara. Then I will try some other
    way to win her.
Pray, dost thou know Victorian?

Francisco.   Yes, my lord;
I saw him at the jeweller's to-
    day.

Lara. What was he doing there?

Francisco.   I saw him buy
A golden ring, that had a ruby in
    it.

Lara. Was there another like
    it?

Francisco.   One so like it
I could not choose between
    them.

Lara.   It is well.
To-morrow morning bring that
    ring to me.
Do not forget.   Now light me to
    my bed.

[*Exeunt.*

SCENE II.—*A street in Madrid.*
Enter CHISPA, *followed by musi-
cians, with a bagpipe, guitars, and
other instruments.*

Chispa. Abernuncio Satanas![1]
and a plague on all lovers who
ramble about at night, drinking
the elements, instead of sleeping
quietly in their beds.   Every dead
man to his cemetery, say I; and
every friar to his monastery.
Now, here's my master, Victorian,
yesterday a cow-keeper, and to-
day a gentleman; yesterday a
student, and to-day a lover; and
I must be up later than the night-
ingale, for as the abbot sings so
must the sacristan respond.   God
grant he may soon be married,
for then shall all this serenad-
ing cease.   Ay, marry! marry!
marry!   Mother, what does marry
mean?   It means to spin, to bear
children, and to weep, my daugh-
ter!   And of a truth, there is
something more in matrimony
than the wedding-ring. (*To the
musicians*).   And now, gentlemen,
Pax vobiscum! as the ass said to
the cabbages.   Pray, walk this
way; and don't hang down your
heads.   It is no disgrace to have
an old father and a ragged shirt.
Now, look you, you are gentlemen
who lead the life of crickets; you
enjoy hunger by day and noise by
night.   Yet, I beseech you, for this
once be not loud, but pathetic; for
it is a serenade to a damsel in bed,
and not to the Man in the Moon.
Your object is not to arouse and
terrify, but to soothe and bring

[1] *Abernuncio Satanas.*
" Digo, Señora, respondeió Sancho,
lo que tengo dicho, que de los azotes
abernuncio.   Abernuncio habeis de
decir, Sancho, y no como decis, dijo
el Duque."—*Don Quixote*, Part II.,
ch. 35.

lulling dreams. Therefore, each shall not play upon his instrument as if it were the only one in the universe, but gently, and with a certain modesty according with the others. Pray, how may I call thy name, friend?

First Musician. Gerónimo Gil, at your service.

Chispa. Every tub smells of the wine that is in it. Pray, Gerónimo, is not Saturday an unpleasant day with thee?

First Musician. Why so?

Chispa. Because I have heard it said that Saturday is an unpleasant day with those who have but one shirt. Moreover, I have seen thee at the tavern, and if thou canst run as fast as thou canst drink, I should like to hunt hares with thee. What instrument is that?

First Musician. An Aragonese bagpipe.

Chispa. Pray, art thou related to the bagpiper of Bujalance, who asked a maravedi for playing, and ten for leaving off?

First Musician. No, your honour.

Chispa. I am glad of it. What other instruments have we?

Second and Third Musicians. We play the bandurria.

Chispa. A pleasing instrument. And thou!

Fourth Musician. The fife.

Chispa. I like it; it has a cheerful, soul-stirring sound, that soars up to my lady's window like the song of a swallow. And you others?

Other Musicians. We are the singers, please your honour.

Chispa. You are too many. Do you think we are going to sing mass in the cathedral of Córdova? Four men can make but little use of one shoe, and I see not how you can all sing in one song. But follow me along the garden wall. That is the way my master climbs to the lady's window. It is by the Vicar's skirts that the devil climbs into the belfry. Come, follow me, and make no noise.

[*Exeunt.*

SCENE III. PRECIOSA'S *chamber. She stands at the open window.*

Preciosa. How slowly through the lilac-scented air
Descends the tranquil moon!
　　Like thistle-down
The vapoury clouds float in the peaceful sky;
And sweetly from yon hollow vaults of shade
The nightingales breathe out their souls in song.
And hark! what songs of love, what soul-like sounds,
Answer them from below!

SERENADE

Stars of the summer night!
　　Far in yon azure deeps,
Hide, hide your golden light!
　　　She sleeps!
My lady sleeps!
　　　Sleeps!

Moon of the summer night!
　　Far down yon western steeps,
Sink, sink in silver light!
　　　She sleeps!
My lady sleeps!
　　　Sleeps!

Wind of the summer night!
　　Where yonder woodbine creeps,
Fold, fold thy pinions light!
　　　She sleeps!
My lady sleeps!
　　　Sleeps!

Dreams of the summer night!
　　Tell her, her lover keeps
Watch! while in slumbers light
　　　She sleeps!
My lady sleeps!
　　　Sleeps!

(Enter VICTORIAN *by the balcony.)*

Victorian. Poor, little dove!
Thou tremblest like a leaf!

Preciosa. I am so frightened!
'Tis for thee I tremble!
I hate to have thee climb that wall
by night!
Did no one see thee?

Victorian. None, my love, but
thou.

Preciosa. 'Tis very dangerous;
and when thou art gone
I chide myself for letting thee come
here
Thus stealthily by night. Where
hast thou been?
Since yesterday I have no news
from thee.

Victorian. Since yesterday I've
been in Alcala.
Ere long the time will come, sweet
Preciosa,
When that dull distance shall no
more divide us;
And I no more shall scale thy wall
by night
To steal a kiss from thee, as I do
now.

Preciosa. An honest thief, to
steal but what thou givest.

Victorian. And we shall sit to-
gether unmolested,
And words of true love pass from
tongue to tongue,
As singing birds from one bough to
another.

Preciosa. That were a life indeed
to make time envious!
I knew that thou wouldst visit me
to-night.
I saw thee at the play.

Victorian. Sweet child of air!
Never did I behold thee so attired
And garmented in beauty as to-
night!
What hast thou done to make thee
look so fair?

Preciosa. Am I not always fair?

Victorian. Ay, and so fair
That I am jealous of all eyes that
see thee,
And wish that they were blind.

Preciosa. I heed them not;
When thou art present, I see none
but thee!

Victorian. There's nothing fair
nor beautiful, but takes
Something from thee, that makes
it beautiful.

Preciosa. And yet thou leavest
me for those dusty books.

Victorian. Thou comest between
me and those books too often!
I see thy face in everything I see!
The paintings in the chapel wear
thy looks,
The canticles are changed to sara-
bands,
And with the learnèd doctors of
the schools
I see thee dance cachuchas.

Preciosa. In good sooth,
I dance with learned doctors of the
schools
To-morrow morning.

Victorian. And with whom, I
pray?

Preciosa. A grave and reverend
Cardinal, and his Grace
The Archbishop of Toledo.

Victorian. What mad jest
Is this?

Preciosa. It is no jest; indeed it
is not.

Victorian. Prithee, explain thy-
self.

Preciosa. Why, simply thus.
Thou knowest the Pope has sent
here into Spain
To put a stop to dances on the
stage.

Victorian. I have heard it whis-
pered.

Preciosa. Now the Cardinal,
Who for this purpose comes, would
fain behold
With his own eyes these dances;
and the Archbishop

Has sent for me—
   Victorian. That thou may'st
dance before them!
Now viva la cachucha! It will
  breathe
The fire of youth into these gray
  old men!
'Twill be thy proudest conquest!
   Preciosa.   Saving one;
And yet I fear these dances will be
  stopped,
And Preciosa be once more a
  beggar.
   Victorian. The sweetest beggar
that e'er asked for alms;
With such beseeching eyes, that
  when I saw thee
I gave my heart away!
   Preciosa.   Dost thou remember
When first we met?
   Victorian.   It was at Córdova,
In the cathedral garden. Thou
  wast sitting
Under the orange trees, beside a
  fountain.
   Preciosa. 'Twas Easter-Sunday.
  The full-blossomed trees
Filled all the air with fragrance and
  with joy.
The priests were singing, and the
  organ sounded,
And then anon the great cathedral
  bell.
It was the elevation of the Host.
We both of us fell down upon our
  knees,
Under the orange boughs, and
  prayed together
I never had been happy till that
  moment.
   Victorian. Thou blessed angel!
   Preciosa. And when thou wast
  gone
I felt an aching here. I did not
  speak
To any one that day. But from
  that day
Bartolomé grew hateful unto
  me.

   Victorian. Remember him no
  more. Let not his shadow
Come between thee and me.
  Sweet Preciosa.
I loved thee even then, though I
  was silent!
   Preciosa. I thought I ne'er
  should see thy face again.
Thy farewell had a sound of sorrow
  in it.
   Victorian. That was the first
  sound in the song of love!
Scarce more than silence is, and
  yet a sound.
Hands of invisible spirits touch
  the strings
Of that mysterious instrument, the
  soul,
And play the prelude of our fate.
  We hear
The voice prophetic, and are not
  alone.
   Preciosa. That is my faith.
  Dost thou believe these warn-
  ings?
   Victorian. So far as this. Our
  feelings and our thoughts
Tend ever on, and rest not in the
  Present.
As drops of rain fall into some dark
  well,
And from below comes a scarce
  audible sound,
So fall our thoughts into the dark
  Hereafter,
And their mysterious echo reaches
  us.
   Preciosa. I have felt it so, but
  found no words to say it!
I cannot reason; I can only
  feel!
But thou hast language for all
  thoughts and feelings.
Thou art a scholar; and some-
  times I think
We cannot walk together in this
  world!
The distance that divides us is too
  great!

Henceforth thy pathway lies
   among the stars;
I must not hold thee back.
   Victorian.   Thou little sceptic!
Dost thou still doubt? What I
   most prize in woman
Is her affections, not her intellect!
The intellect is finite; but the
   affections
Are infinite, and cannot be ex-
   hausted.
Compare me with the great men
   of the earth;
What am I? Why, a pygmy
   among giants!
But if thou lovest,—mark me! I
   say lovest,
The greatest of thy sex excels thee
   not!
The world of the affections is thy
   world,
Not that of man's ambition. In
   that stillness
Which most becomes a woman,
   calm and holy,
Thou sittest by the fireside of the
   heart,
Feeding its flame. The element
   of fire
Is pure. It cannot change nor
   hide its nature,
But burns as brightly in a Gypsy
   camp
As in a palace hall. Art thou
   convinced?
   Preciosa. Yes, that I love thee,
   as the good love heaven;
But not that I am worthy of that
   heaven.
How shall I more deserve it?
   Victorian.   Loving more.
   Preciosa. I cannot love thee
   more; my heart is full.
   Victorian. Then let it overflow,
   and I will drink it,
As in the summer-time the thirsty
   sands
Drink the swift waters of the Man-
   zanares,

And still do thirst for more.
   A Watchman (in the street).
               Ave Maria
Purissima!   'Tis midnight and
   serene!
   Victorian. Hear'st thou that
   cry?
   Preciosa. It is a hateful sound,
To scare thee from me!
   Victorian. As the hunter's horn
Doth scare the timid stag, or bark
   of hounds
The moor-fowl from his mate.
   Preciosa.   Pray, do not go!
   Victorian. I must away to Al-
   calá to-night.
Think of me when I am away.
   Preciosa.   Fear not!
I have no thoughts that do not
   think of thee.
   Victorian, giving her a ring.
And to remind thee of my love,
   take this;
A serpent, emblem of Eternity;
A ruby,—say, a drop of my heart's
   blood.
   Preciosa. It is an ancient say-
   ing, that the ruby
Brings gladness to the wearer, and
   preserves
The heart pure, and if laid beneath
   the pillow,
Drives away evil dreams. But
   then, alas!
It was a serpent tempted Eve to
   sin.
   Victorian. What convent of
   barefooted Carmelites
Taught thee so much theology?
   *Preciosa, laying her hand upon
   his mouth.* Hush! Hush!
Good-night! and may all holy
   angels guard thee!
   Victorian. Good-night! good-
   night! Thou art my guardian
   angel!
I have no other saint than thou to
   pray to!
   (He descends by the balcony).

Preciosa. Take care, and do not hurt thee. Art thou safe?

Victorian, from the garden.

Safe as my love for thee! But art thou safe?
Others can climb a balcony by moonlight
As well as I. Pray, shut thy window close;
I am jealous of the perfumed air of night
That from this garden climbs to kiss thy lips.

Preciosa, throwing down her handkerchief. Thou silly child!
Take this to blind thine eyes.
It is my benison!

Victorian. And brings to me
Sweet fragrance from thy lips, as the soft wind
Wafts to the out-bound mariner the breath
Of the belovèd land he leaves behind.

Preciosa. Make not thy voyage long.

Victorian. To-morrow night
Shall see me safe returned. Thou art the star
To guide me to an anchorage. Good-night!
My beauteous star! My star of love, good-night!

Preciosa. Good-night!

Watchman (at a distance).
Ave Maria Purissima!

SCENE IV.—*An inn on the road to Alcalá.* BALTASAR *asleep on a bench. Enter* CHISPA.

Chispa. And here we are, half-way to Alcala, between cocks and midnight. Body o' me! what an inn this is! The lights out, and the landlord asleep. Hola! ancient Baltasar!

Baltasar, waking. Here I am.

Chispa. Yes, there you are, like a one-eyed Alcalde in a town without inhabitants. Bring a light, and let me have supper.

Baltasar. Where is your master?

Chispa. Do not trouble yourself about him. We have stopped a moment to breathe our horses; and, if he chooses to walk up and down in the open air, looking into the sky as one who hears it rain, that does not satisfy my hunger, you know. But be quick, for I am in a hurry, and every man stretches his legs according to the length of his coverlet. What have we here?

Baltasar, setting a light on the table. Stewed rabbit.

Chispa, eating. Conscience of Portalegre! Stewed kitten, you mean!

Baltashar. And a pitcher of Pedro Ximenes, with a roasted pear in it.

Chispa, drinking. Ancient Baltasar, amigo! You know how to cry wine and sell vinegar. I tell you this is nothing but Vino Tinto of La Mancha, with a tang of the swine-skin.

Baltasar. I swear to you by Saint Simon and Judas, it is all as I say.

Chispa. And I swear to you, by Saint Peter and Saint Paul, that it is no such thing. Moreover, your supper is like the hidalgo's dinner, very little meat, and a great deal of tablecloth.

Baltasar. Ha! ha! ha!

Chispa. And more noise than nuts.

Baltasar. Ha! ha! ha! You must have your joke, Master Chispa. But shall I not ask Don Victorian in, to take a draught of the Pedro Ximenes?

Chispa. No; you might as well say, "Don't-you-want-some?" to a dead man.

Baltasar. Why does he go so often to Madrid?

Chispa. For the same reason that he eats no supper. He is in love. Were you ever in love, Baltasar?

Baltasar. I was never out of it, good Chispa. It has been the torment of my life.

Chispa. What! are you on fire, too, old hay-stack? Why, we shall never be able to put you out.

Victorian, without. Chispa!

Chispa. Go to bed, Pero Grullo, for the cocks are crowing.

Victorian. Ea! Chispa! Chispa!

Chispa. Ea! Señor. Come with me, ancient Baltasar, and bring water for the horses. I will pay for the supper to-morrow.

[*Exeunt.*

SCENE V.—VICTORIAN'S *chambers at Alcalá.* HYPOLITO *asleep in an arm-chair. He awakes slowly.*

Hypolito. I must have been asleep! ay, sound asleep!
And it was all a dream. O sleep, sweet!
Whatever form thou takest, thou art fair,
Holding unto our lips thy goblet filled
Out of Oblivion's well, a healing draught!
The candles have burned low; it must be late.
Where can Victorian be? Like Fray Carrillo [1]
The only place in which one cannot find him
Is his own cell. Here's his guitar, that seldom

[1] *Fray Carrillo.* The allusion here is to a Spanish epigram.
" Siempre Fray Carrillo estás
cansándonos acá fuera:
quién en tu celda estuviera
para no verte jamás!"
Böhl de Faber. Floresu., No. 611.

Feels the caresses of its master's hand.
Open thy silent lips, sweet instrument!
And make a dull midnight merry with a song.

(*He plays and sings*).

Padre Francisco! [1]
Padre Francisco!
What do you want of Padre Francisco?
Here is a pretty young maiden
Who wants to confess her sins!
Open the door and let her come in,
I will shrive her from every sin.

(*Enter* VICTORIAN).

Victorian. Padre Hypolito!
Padre Hypolito!

Hypolito. What do you want of Padre Hypolito!

Victorian. Come, shrive me straight; for, if love be a sin,
I am the greatest sinner that doth live.
I will confess the sweetest of all crimes,
A maiden wooed and won.

Hypolito.　　The same old tale
Of the old woman in the chimney corner,
Who, while the pot boils, says,
"Come here, my child;
I'll tell thee a story of my wedding-day."

Victorian. Nay, listen, for my heart is full; so full
That I must speak.

Hypolito. Alas! that heart of thine

[1] *Padre Francisco.* This is from an Italian popular song.
" ' Padre Francesco,
Padre Francesco! '
—Cosa volete del Padre Francesco—
' V'è una bella ragazzina
Che si vuole confessar! '
Fatte l'entrare, fatte l'entrare
Che la voglio confessare."
Kopisch. Volksthümliche. Poesien aus allen Mundarten Italiens und seiner Inseln, p. 194.

Is like a scene in the old play; the
curtain
Rises to solemn music, and lo!
enter
The eleven thousand virgins of
Cologne!
    Victorian. Nay, like the Sibyl's
volumes, thou shouldst say;
Those that remained, after the six
were burned,
Being held more precious than the
nine together.
But listen to my tale. Dost thou
remember
The Gypsy girl we saw at Córdova
Dance the Romalis in the market-
place?
    Hypolito. Thou meanest Pre-
ciosa.
    Victorian.   Ay, the same.
Thou knowest how her image
haunted me
Long after we returned to Alcalá.
She's in Madrid.
    Hypolito.   I know it.
    Victorian.   And I'm in love.
    Hypolito.   And therefore in
Madrid when thou shouldst be
In Alcalá.
    Victorian. O pardon me, my
friend,
If I so long have kept this secret
from thee;
But silence is the charm that
guards such treasures,
And, if a word be spoken ere the
time,
They sink again, they were not
meant for us.
    Hypolito. Alas! alas! I see thou
art in love.
Love keeps the cold out better than
a cloak.
It serves for food and raiment.
Give a Spaniard
His mass, his olla, and his Doña
Luisa,—
Thou knowest the proverb. But
pray tell me, lover,

How speeds thy wooing? Is the
maiden coy?
Write her a song, beginning with
an *Ave;*
Sing as the monk sang to the Vir-
gin Mary,
    Ave! cujus calcem clare,[1]
    Nec centenni commendare
      Sciret Seraph studio!
    Victorian. Pray, do not jest!
This is no time for it!
I am in earnest!
    Hypolito. Seriously enamoured?
What, ho! The Primus of great
Alcalá
Enamoured of a Gypsy? Tell me
frankly,
How meanest thou?
    Victorian. I mean it honestly.
    Hypolito. Surely thou wilt not
marry her!
    Victorian.   Why not?
    Hypolito. She was betrothed to
one Bartolomé
If I remember rightly, a young
Gypsy
Who danced with her at Córdova.
    Victorian.   They quarrelled,
And so the matter ended.
    Hypolito.   But in truth
Thou wilt not marry her.
    Victorian.   In truth I will.
The angels sang in heaven when
she was born!
She is a precious jewel I have found
Among the filth and rubbish of the
world.
I'll stoop for it; but when I wear it
here,
Set on my forehead like the morn-
ing star,
The world may wonder, but it will
not laugh.

---

[1] *Ave! cujus calcem clare.*
From a monkish hymn of the
twelfth century, in Sir Alexander
Croke's *Essay on the Origin, Progress
and Decline of Rhyming Latin Verse,*
p. 109.

Hypolito. If thou wear'st nothing else upon thy forehead,
'Twill be indeed a wonder.
　　Victorian.　　　Out upon thee,
With thy unseasonable jests!
Pray, tell me,
Is there no virtue in the world?
　　Hypolito.　　　Not much.
What, think'st thou, is she doing at this moment;
Now, while we speak of her?
　　Victorian.　　　She lies asleep,
And, from her parted lips, her gentle breath
Comes like the fragrance from the lips of flowers.
Her tender limbs are still, and, on her breast,
The cross she prayed to, ere she fell asleep,
Rises and falls with the soft tide of dreams,
Like a light barge safe moored.
　　Hypolito. Which means, in prose,
She's sleeping with her mouth a little open!
　　Victorian. O, would I had the old magician's glass
To see her as she lies in child-like sleep!
　　Hypolito. And wouldst thou venture?
　　Victorian. Ay, indeed I would!
　　Hypolito. Thou art courageous.
Hast thou e'er reflected
How much lies hidden in that one word, *now?*
　　Victorian. Yes; all the awful mystery of Life!
I oft have thought, my dear Hypolito,
That could we, by some spell of magic, change
The world and its inhabitants to stone,
In the same attitudes they now are in,
What fearful glances downward might we cast

Into the hollow chasms of human life!
What groups should we behold about the deathbed,
Putting to shame the group of Niobe!
What joyful welcomes, and what sad farewells!
What stony tears in those congealèd eyes!
What visible joy or anguish in those cheeks!
What bridal pomps, and what funereal shows!
What foes, like gladiators, fierce and struggling!
What lovers with their marble lips together!
　　Hypolito. Ay, there it is! and, if I were in love,
That is the very point I most should dread.
This magic glass, these magic spells of thine,
Might tell a tale were better left untold.
For instance, they might show us thy fair cousin,
The Lady Violante, bathed in tears
Of love and anger, like the maid of Colchis,
Whom thou, another faithless Argonaut,
Having won that golden fleece, a woman's love,
Desertest for this Glaucè.
　　Victorian.　　　Hold thy peace:
She cares not for me. She may wed another,
Or go into a convent, and, thus dying,
Marry Achilles in the Elysian Fields.
　　Hypolito, rising. And so, good-night! Good - morning, I should say.
　　　　　(*Clock strikes three.*)
Hark! how the loud and ponderous mace of Time

Knocks at the golden portals of the
    day!
And so, once more, good-night!
We'll speak more largely
Of Preciosa when we meet again.
Get thee to bed, and the magician,
    Sleep,
Shall show her to thee, in his magic
    glass,
In all her loveliness.   Good-night!
                             [*Exit.*
    Victorian.   Good-night!
But not to bed; for I must read
    awhile.
    (*Throws himself into the arm-*
    chair which HYPOLITO *has*
    left, and lays a large book
    open upon his knees.)
Must read, or sit in reverie and
    watch
The changing colour of the waves
    that break
Upon the idle seashore of the mind!
Visions of Fame! that once did
    visit me,
Making night glorious with your
    smile, where are ye?
O, who shall give me, now that ye
    are gone,
Juices of those immortal plants
    that bloom
Upon Olympus, making us im-
    mortal?
Or teach me where that wondrous
    mandrake grows
Whose magic root, torn from the
    earth with groans,
At midnight hour, can scare the
    fiends away,
And make the mind prolific in its
    fancies?
I have the wish, but want the will
    to act!
Souls of great men departed!   Ye
    whose words
Have come to light from the swift
    river of Time,
Like Roman swords found in the
    Tagus' bed,

Where is the strength to wield the
    arms ye bore?
From the barred visor of Antiquity
Reflected shines the eternal light of
    Truth,
As from a mirror!   All the means
    of action—
The shapeless masses—the materi-
    als—
Lie everywhere about us.   What
    we need
Is the celestial fire to change the
    flint
Into transparent crystal, bright
    and clear.
That fire is genius!   The rude
    peasant sits
At evening in his smoky cot, and
    draws
With charcoal uncouth figures on
    the wall.
The son of genius comes, foot-sore
    with travel,
And begs a shelter from the incle-
    ment night.
He takes the charcoal from the
    peasant's hand,
And, by the magic of his touch at
    once
Transfigured, all its hidden virtues
    shine,
And, in the eyes of the astonished
    clown,
It gleams a diamond!   Even thus
    transformed,
Rude popular traditions and old
    tales
Shine as immortal poems, at the
    touch
Of some poor, houseless, homeless,
    wandering bard,
Who had but a night's lodging for
    his pains.
But there are brighter dreams than
    those of Fame,
Which are the dreams of Love!
    Out of the heart
Rises the bright ideal of these
    dreams,

And from some woodland fount a
  spirit rises
And sinks again into its silent
  deeps,
Ere the enamoured knight can
  touch her robe!
'Tis this ideal that the soul of man,
Like the enamoured knight beside
  the fountain,
Waits for upon the margin of Life's
  stream;
Waits to behold her rise from the
  dark waters,
Clad in a mortal shape! Alas!
  how many
Must wait in vain! The stream
  flows evermore,
But from its silent deeps no spirit
  rises!
Yet I, born under a propitious star,
Have found the bright ideal of my
  dreams.
Yes! she is ever with me. I can
  feel,
Here, as I sit at midnight and alone,
Her gentle breathing! on my breast
  can feel
The pressure of her head! God's
  benison
Rest ever on it! Close those
  beauteous eyes,
Sweet Sleep! and all the flowers
  that bloom at night
With balmy lips breathe in her
  ears my name!
    (Gradually sinks asleep).

ACT II

SCENE I.—PRECIOSA's *chamber.*
Morning. PRECIOSA *and* AN-
GELICA.

Preciosa. Why will you go so
  soon? Stay yet awhile.
The poor too often turn away un-
  heard
From hearts that shut against
  them with a sound

That will be heard in heaven.
  Pray, tell me more
Of your adversities. Keep noth-
  ing from me.
What is your landlord's name?
  Angelica. The Count of Lara.
  Preciosa. The Count of Lara?
  O, beware that man
Mistrust his pity,—hold no parley
  with him!
And rather die an outcast in the
  streets
Than touch his gold.
  Angelica. You know him, then!
  Preciosa.   As much
As any woman may, and yet be
  pure.
As you would keep your name
  without a blemish,
Beware of him!
  Angelica. Alas! what can I
  do?
I cannot choose my friends. Each
  word of kindness,
Come whence it may, is welcome
  to the poor.
  Preciosa. Make me your friend.
  A girl so young and fair
Should have no friends but those
  of her own sex.
What is your name?
  Angelica.   Angelica.
  Preciosa.   That name
Was given you, that you might be
  an angel
To her who bore you! When your
  infant smile
Made her home Paradise, you were
  her angel.
O, be an angel still! She needs
  that smile.
So long as you are innocent, fear
  nothing.
No one can harm you! I am a
  poor girl,
Whom chance has taken from the
  public streets.
I have no other shield than mine
  own virtue:

That is the charm which has protected me!

Amid a thousand perils, I have worn it

Here on my heart! It is my guardian angel.

Angelica, rising. I thank you for this counsel, dearest lady.

Preciosa. Thank me by following it.

Angelica.   Indeed I will.

Preciosa. Pray, do not go. I have much more to say.

Angelica. My mother is alone. I dare not leave her.

Preciosa. Some other time, then, when we meet again.

You must not go away with words alone.

(Gives her a purse).

Take this. Would it were more.

Angelica. I thank you, lady.

Preciosa.   No thanks. To-morrow come to me again.

I dance to-night,—perhaps for the last time.

But what I gain, I promise shall be yours,

If that can save you from the Count of Lara.

Angelica. O, my dear lady! how shall I be grateful

For so much kindness?

Preciosa.   I deserve no thanks.

Thank Heaven, not me.

Angelica. Both Heaven and you

Preciosa.   Farewell!

Remember that you come again to-morrow.

Angelica. I will. And may the blessed Virgin guard you,

And all good angels.   [*Exit.*

Preciosa. May they guard thee too,

And all the poor; for they have need of angels.

Now bring me, dear Dolores, my basquiña,

My richest maja dress,—my dancing dress,

And my most precious jewels! Make me look

Fairer than night e'er saw me! I've a prize

To win this day, worthy of Preciosa!

(Enter BELTRAN CRUZADO).

Cruzado. Ave Maria!

Preciosa. O God! my evil genius! What seekest thou here to-day?

Cruzado.   Thyself,—my child.

Preciosa. What is thy will with me?

Cruzado.   Gold! gold!

Preciosa. I gave thee yesterday; I have no more.

Cruzado. The gold of the Busné, —give me his gold!

Preciosa. I gave the last in charity to-day.

Cruzado. That is a foolish lie.

Preciosa. It is the truth.

Cruzado.   Curses upon thee! Thou art not my child!

Hast thou given gold away, and not to me?

Not to thy father? To whom, then?

Preciosa.   To one

Who needs it more.

Cruzado. No one can need it more.

Preciosa. Thou art not poor.

Cruzado. What, I, who lurk about

In dismal suburbs and unwholesome lanes;

I, who am housed worse than the galley slave;

I, who am fed worse than the kennelled hound;

I, who am clothed in rags,—Beltran Cruzado,—

Not poor!

Preciosa. Thou hast a stout heart and strong hands.

Thou canst supply thy wants;
what wouldst thou more?
  Cruzado. The gold of the
  Busné![1] give me his gold!
  Preciosa. Beltran Cruzado! hear
  me once for all.
I speak the truth. So long as I
  had gold,
I gave it to thee freely, at all times,
Never denied thee; never had a wish
But to fulfil thine own. Now go in
  peace!
Be merciful, be patient, and, ere
  long,
Thou shalt have more.
  Cruzado. And if I have it not.
Thou shalt no longer dwell here in
  rich chambers,
Wear silken dresses, feed on
  dainty food,
And live in idleness; but go with
  me,
Dance the Romalis in the public
  streets,
And wander wild again o'er field
  and fell;
For here we stay not long.
  Preciosa. What! march again?
  Cruzado. Ay, with all speed. I
  hate the crowded town!
I cannot breathe shut up within its
  gates!
Air,—I want air, and sunshine, and
  blue sky,
The feeling of the breeze upon my
  face,
The feeling of the turf beneath my
  feet,
And no walls but the far-off moun-
  tain tops.
Then I am free and strong,—once
  more myself,
Beltran Cruzado, Count of the
  Calés![2]

[1] *The gold of Busné.*
Busné is the name given by the
Gypsies to all who are not of their
race.
[2] *Count of the Calés.*
The Gypsies call themselves Calés.

  Preciosa. God speed thee on thy
  march!—I cannot go.
  Cruzado. Remember who I am,
  and who thou art!
Be silent and obey! Yet one thing
  more.
Bartolomé Román—
  Preciosa, with emotion. O I be-
  seech thee!
If my obedience and blameless life,
If my humility and meek submis-
  sion
In all things hitherto, can move in
  thee
One feeling of compassion; if thou
  art
Indeed my father, and canst trace
  in me
One look of her who bore me, or
  one tone
That doth remind thee of her, let
  it plead
In my behalf, who am a feeble
  girl,
Too feeble to resist, and do not
  force me
To wed that man! I am afraid of
  him!
I do not love him! On my knees I
  beg thee
To use no violence, nor do in haste
What cannot be undone!
  Cruzado. O child, child, child!
Thou hast betrayed thy secret, as
  a bird
Betrays her nest, by striving to
  conceal it.
I will not leave thee here in the
  great city
To be grandee's mistress. Make
  thee ready
To go with us; and until then re-
  member
A watchful eye is on thee. [*Exit.*
  Preciosa. Woe is me!

See Borrow's valuable and extremely
interesting work, *The Zincali; or an
Account of the Gypsies in Spain.*
London, 1841.

I have a strange misgiving in my heart!
But that one deed of charity I'll do,
Befall what may; they cannot take that from me.   [*Exit.*

SCENE II.—*A room in the* ARCH-
BISHOP'S *Palace, the* ARCH-
BISHOP *and a* CARDINAL *seated.*

   Archbishop. Knowing how near
it touched the public morals,
And that our age is grown corrupt and rotten
By such excesses, we have sent to Rome,
Beseeching that his Holiness would aid
In curing the gross surfeit of the time,
By seasonable stop put here in Spain
To bull-fights and lewd dances on the stage.
All this you know.
   Cardinal.   Know and approve.
   Archbishop.   And farther,
That, by a mandate from his Holiness,
The first have been suppressed.
   Cardinal.   I trust for ever.
It was a cruel sport.
   Archbishop.   A barbarous pastime,
Disgraceful to the land that calls itself
Most Catholic and Christian.
   Cardinal.   Yet the people
Murmur at this; and, if the public dances
Should be condemned upon too slight occasion,
Worse ills might follow than the ills we cure.
As *Panem et Circenses* was the cry,
Among the Roman populace of old,
So *Pan y Toros* is the cry in Spain.
Hence I would act advisedly herein;

And therefore have induced your grace to see
These national dances, ere we interdict them.
    (*Enter a Servant*).
   Servant. The dancing-girl, and with her the musicians
Your grace was pleased to order, wait without.
   Archbishop. Bid them come in.
Now shall your eyes behold
In what angelic yet voluptuous shape
The Devil came to tempt Saint Anthony.
    (*Enter* PRECIOSA, *with a mantle
thrown over her head. She
advances slowly, in a modest,
half-timid attitude.*)
   Cardinal, aside. O, what a fair and ministering angel
Was lost to heaven when this sweet woman fell!
   Preciosa, kneeling before the
ARCHBISHOP. I have obeyed the order of your grace.
If I intrude upon your better hours,
I proffer this excuse, and here beseech
Your holy benediction.
   Archbishop. May God bless thee,
And lead thee to a better life. Arise.
   Cardinal, aside. Her acts are modest, and her words discreet!
I did not look for this. Come hither, child.
Is thy name Preciosa?
   Preciosa.   Thus I am called.
   Cardinal. That is a Gypsy name. Who is thy father?
   Preciosa. Beltran Cruzado, Count of the Calés.
   Archbishop. I have a dim remembrance of that man;
He was a bold and reckless character,
A sun-burnt Ishmael!

Cardinal. Dost thou remember
Thy earlier days?

Preciosa. Yes; by the Darro's
side
My childhood passed. I can re-
member still
The river, and the mountains
capped with snow;
The villages, where, yet a little
child,
I told the traveller's fortune in the
street;
The smuggler's horse, the brigand
and the shepherd;
The march across the moor; the
halt at noon;
The red fire of the evening camp,
that lighted
The forest where we slept; and,
farther back,
As in a dream or in some former
life,
Gardens and palace walls.

Archbishop. 'Tis the Alhambra,
Under whose towers the Gypsy
camp was pitched.
But the time wears; and we
would see thee dance.

Preciosa. Your grace shall be
obeyed.

(*She lays aside her mantilla. The
music of the cachucha is
played, and the dance begins.
The* ARCHBISHOP *and the*
CARDINAL *look on with
gravity and an occasional
frown : then make signs to
each other ; and, as the dance
continues, become more and
more pleased and excited ;
and at length rise from their
seats, throw their caps in the
air, and applaud vehemently
as the scene closes.*)

SCENE III.—*The Prado. A long
avenue of trees leading to the gate
of Atocha. On the right the dome
and spires of a convent. A foun-*
tain. Evening. DON CARLOS *and*
HYPOLITO *meeting.*

Don Carlos. Hola! good-even-
ing, Don Hypolito.

Hypolito. And a good-evening
to my friend, Don Carlos,
Some lucky star has led my steps
this way.
I was in search of you.

Don Carlos. Command me al-
ways.

Hypolito. Do you remember, in
Quevedo's Dreams,
The miser, who, upon the Day of
Judgment,
Asks if his money-bags would
rise?[1]

Don Carlos. I do;
But what of that?

Hypolito. I am that wretched
man.

Don Carlos. You mean to tell
me yours have risen empty?

Hypolito. And amen! said my
Cid Campeador.[2]

Don Carlos. Pray, how much
need you?

Hypolito. Some half dozen ounces
Which, with due interest—

Don Carlos, giving his purse.
What, am I a Jew
To put my moneys out at usury?
Here is my purse.

Hypolito. Thank you. A pretty
purse,
Made by the hand of some fair
Madrileña;

[1] *Asks if his money-bags would rise.*
" Y volviéndome á un lado, vi á
un Avariento, que estaba preguntando
á otro, (que por haber sido embalsa-
mado, y estar léjos sus tripas, no
hablaba proque no habian llegado
si habian de resucitar aquel dia todos
los enterrados,) ¿si resucitarian unos
bolsones suyos? "—*El Sueño de las
Calaveras.*

[2] *And amen! said my Cid Campeador.*
A line from the ancient *Poema del Cid.*
" Amen, dixo Mio Cid el Campeador."
Line 3044.

Perhaps a keepsake.

Don Carlos.　　No, 'tis at your service.

Hypolito. Thank you again. Lie there, good Chrysostom,
And with thy golden mouth re-mind me often,
I am the debtor of my friend.

Don Carlos.　　But tell me,
Come you to-day from Alcalá?

Hypolito.　　This moment.

Don Carlos. And pray, how fares the brave Victorian?

Hypolito. Indifferent well; that is to say, not well.
A damsel has ensnared him with the glances
Of her dark, roving eyes, as herds-men catch
A steer of Andalusia with a lazo.
He is in love.

Don Carlos.　　And is it faring ill
To be in love?

Hypolito. In his case very ill.

Don Carlos. Why so?

Hypolito. For many reasons.
First and foremost,
Because he is in love with an ideal,
A creature of his own imagination;
A child of air; an echo of his heart;
And, like a lily on a river floating,
She floats upon the river of his thoughts! [1]

Don Carlos. A common thing with poets. But who is
This floating lily? For, in fine, some woman,
Some living woman,—not a mere ideal,—
Must wear the outward semblance of his thought.
Who is it? Tell me.

Hypolito. Well, it is a woman!

[1] *The river of his thoughts.* This expression is from Dante;
　　" Si she chiaro
Per essa scenda della mente il fiume."
Byron has likewise used the ex-pression; though I do not recollect in which of his poems.

But, look you, from the coffer of his heart
He brings forth precious jewels to adorn her,
As pious priests adorn some favourite saint
With gems and gold, until at length she gleams
One blaze of glory. Without these, you know,
And the priest's benediction, 'tis a doll.

Don Carlos. Well, well! who is this doll?

Hypolito.　　Why, who do you think?

Don Carlos. His cousin Violante.

Hypolito.　　Guess again.
To ease his labouring heart, in the last storm
He threw her overboard, with all her ingots.

Don Carlos. I cannot guess; so tell me who it is.

Hypolito. Not I.

Don Carlos.　　Why not?

Hypolito, mysteriously.　　Why?
Because Mari Franca[1]
Was married four leagues out of Salamanca!

Don Carlos. Jesting aside, who is it?

Hypolito.　　Preciosa.

Don Carlos. Impossible! The Count of Lara tells me
She is not virtuous.

Hypolito. Did I say she was?
The Roman Emperor Claudius had a wife
Whose name was Messalina, as I think;
Valeria Messalina was her name.
But hist! I see him yonder through the trees,

[1] *Mari Franca.* A common Spanish proverb, used to turn aside a question one does not wish to answer;
　　" Porque casó Mari Franca
　　Cuatro leguas de Salamanca."

Walking as in a dream.

Don Carlos. He comes this way.

Hypolito. It has been truly said
by some wise man,
That money, grief, and love cannot
be hidden.

(*Enter* VICTORIAN *in front*).

Victorian. Where'er thy step
has passed is holy ground:
These groves are sacred! I behold
thee walking   ..
Under these shadowy trees, where
we have walked
At evening, and I feel thy presence
now;
Feel that the place has taken a
charm from thee,
And is for ever hallowed.

Hypolito.   Mark him well!
See how he strides away with
lordly air,
Like that odd guest of stone, that
grim Commander
Who comes to sup with Juan in
the play.

Don Carlos. What ho! Vic-
torian!

Hypolito. Wilt thou sup with us?

Victorian. Hola! amigos! Faith,
I did not see you.
How fares Don Carlos?

Don Carlos. At your service ever.

Victorian. How is that young
and green-eyed Gaditana
That you both wot of?

Don Carlos. Ay, soft, emerald
eyes. [1]

---

[1] *Ay, soft, emerald eyes.* The
Spaniards, with good reason, consider
this colour of the eye as beautiful,
and celebrate it in song; as, for ex-
ample in the well known *Villancico*—
"¡Ay ojuelos verdes,
ay los mis ojuelos,
ay hagan los cielos
que de mi te acuerdes!

.   .   .   .   .

Tengo confianza
de mis verdes ojos."
Böhl de Faber. Floresta, No. 255.
Dante speaks of Beatrice's eyes

She has gone back to Cadiz.

Hypolito.   *Ay de mi!*

Victorian. You are much to
blame for letting her go back.
A pretty girl; and in her tender
eyes
Just that soft shade of green we
sometimes see
In evening skies.

Hypolito. But, speaking of green
eyes
Are thine green?

Victorian. Not a whit. Why so?

Hypolito.   I think
The slightest shade of green would
be becoming,
For thou art jealous.

Victorian. No, I am not jealous.

Hypolito. Thou shouldst be.

Victorian.   Why?

Hypolito. Because thou art in
love.
And they who are in love are al-
ways jealous.
Therefore thou shouldst be.

Victorian.   Marry, is that all?
Farewell; I am in haste. Fare-
well, Don Carlos.
Thou sayest I should be jealous?

Hypolito.   Ay, in truth
I fear there is reason. Be upon
thy guard.
I hear it whispered that the Count
of Lara
Lays siege to the same citadel.

Victorian.   Indeed!
Then he will have his labour for his
pains.

Hypolito. He does not think so,
and Don Carlos tells me
He boasts of his success.

Victorian.   How's this, Don
Carlos?

Don Carlos. Some hints of it I
heard from his own lips.

---

as emeralds. *Purgatorio,* xxxi. 116.
Lami says, in his *Annotazioni,* "Erano
i suoi occhi d' un turchino verdiccio,
simile e quel del mare."

He spoke but lightly of the lady's
virtue,
As a gay man might speak.
   Victorian.   Death and damna-
tion!
I'll cut his lying tongue out of his
mouth,
And throw it to my dog! But no,
no, no!
This cannot be. You jest, indeed
you jest.
Trifle with me no more. For
otherwise
We are no longer friends. And so,
farewell!   [*Exit.*
   Hypolito. Now what a coil is
here! The Avenging Child [1]
Hunting the traitor Quadros to his
death,
And the great Moor Calaynos,
when he rode
To Paris for the ears of Oliver,
Were nothing to him! O hot-
headed youth!
But come; we will not follow.
Let us join
The crowd that pours into the
Prado. There
We shall find merrier company; I
see
The Marialonzos and the Alma-
vivas,
And fifty fans, that beckon me
already.   [*Exeunt.*

SCENE IV.—PRECIOSA'S *chamber.*
*She is sitting, with a book in her
hand, near a table on which are
flowers. A bird singing in its
cage. The* COUNT OF LARA
enters behind unperceived.

   Preciosa, reads.

   All are sleeping, weary heart! [2]
   Thou, thou only sleepless art!

[1] *The Avenging Child.* See the
ancient Ballads of *El Infante Vengador*
and *Calaynos.*
[2] *All are sleeping.* From the
Spanish. *Böhl's Floresta,* No. 282.

Heigho! I wish Victorian were here.
I know not what it is makes me so
restless!
      (*The bird sings.*)
Thou little prisoner with thy mot-
ley coat,
That from thy vaulted, wiry dun-
geon singest,
Like thee I am a captive, and,
like thee,
I have a gentle gaoler. Lack-a-
day!

   All are sleeping, weary heart!
   Thou, thou only sleepless art!
   All this throbbing, all this aching,
   Evermore shall keep thee waking,
   For a heart in sorrow breaking
   Thinketh ever of its smart!

Thou speakest truly, poet! and
methinks
More hearts are breaking in this
world of ours
Than one would say. In distant
villages
And solitudes remote, where winds
have wafted
The barbèd seeds of love, or birds
of passage
Scattered them in their flight, do
they take root,
And grow in silence, and in silence
perish.
Who hears the falling of the forest
leaf?
Or who takes note of every flower
that dies?
Heigho! I wish Victorian would
come.
Dolores!
(*Turns to lay down her book and
perceives the* COUNT.)
      Ha!
   Lara.   Señora, pardon me!
   Preciosa. How's this? Dolores!
   Lara.   Pardon me—
   Preciosa.   Dolores!
   Lara. Be not alarmed; I found
no one in waiting.
If I have been too bold—

Preciosa, turning her back upon him. You are too bold!
Retire! retire, and leave me!

Lara. My dear lady,
First hear me! I beseech you, let me speak!
'Tis for your good I come.

Preciosa, turning toward him with indignation. Begone! Begone!
You are the Count of Lara, but your deeds
Would make the statues of your ancestors
Blush on their tombs! Is it Castilian honour,
Is it Castilian pride, to steal in here
Upon a friendless girl, to do her wrong?
O shame! shame! shame that you, a nobleman,
Should be so little noble in your thoughts
As to send jewels here to win my love,
And think to buy my honour with your gold!
I have no words to tell you how I scorn you!
Begone! The sight of you is hateful to me!
Begone, I say!

Lara. Be calm; I will not harm you.

Preciosa. Because you dare not.

Lara. I dare anything!
Therefore beware! You are deceived in me.
In this false world, we do not always know
Who are our friends and who our enemies.
We all have enemies, and all need friends.
Even you, fair Preciosa, here at court
Have foes, who seek to wrong you.

Preciosa. If to this
I owe the honour of the present visit,
You might have spared the coming. Having spoken,
Once more I beg you, leave me to myself.

Lara. I thought it but a friendly part to tell you
What strange reports are current here in town.
For my own self, I do not credit them;
But there are many who, not knowing you,
Will lend a readier ear.

Preciosa. There was no need
That you should take upon yourself the duty
Of telling me these tales.

Lara. Malicious tongues
Are ever busy with your name.

Preciosa. Alas!
I have no protectors. I am a poor girl,
Exposed to insults and unfeeling jests.
They wound me, yet I cannot shield myself.
I give no cause for these reports. I live
Retired; am visited by none.

Lara. By none?
O, then, indeed, you are much wronged!

Preciosa. How mean you?

Lara. Nay, nay; I will not wound your gentle soul
By the report of idle tales.

Preciosa. Speak out!
What are these idle tales? You need not spare me.

Lara. I will deal frankly with you. Pardon me;
This window, as I think, looks toward the street,
And this into the Prado, does it not?
In yon high house, beyond the garden wall,—

You see the roof there just above the trees,—
There lives a friend, who told me yesterday,
That on a certain night,—be not offended
If I too plainly speak,—he saw a man
Climb to your chamber window. You are silent!
I would not blame you, being young and fair—

(*He tries to embrace her. She starts back and draws a dagger from her bosom.*)

   Preciosa. Beware! beware! I am a Gypsy girl!
Lay not your hand upon me. One step nearer
And I will strike!
   Lara. Pray you, put up that dagger.
Fear not.
   Preciosa. I do not fear. I have a heart
In whose strength I can trust.
   Lara. Listen to me.
I come here as your friend,—I am your friend,—
And by a single word can put a stop
To all those idle tales, and make your name
Spotless as lilies are. Here on my knees,
Fair Preciosa! on my knees I swear,
I love you even to madness, and that love
Has driven me to break the rules of custom,
And force myself unasked into your presence.

(VICTORIAN *enters behind.*)

   Preciosa. Rise, Count of Lara! That is not the place
For such as you are. It becomes you not
To kneel before me. I am strangely moved

To see one of your rank thus low and humbled;
For your sake I will put aside all anger,
All unkind feeling, all dislike, and speak
In gentleness, as most becomes a woman,
And as my heart now prompts me. I no more
Will hate you, for all hate is painful to me.
But if, without offending modesty
And that reserve which is a woman's glory,
I may speak freely, I will teach my heart
To love you.
   Lara. O sweet angel!
   Preciosa. Ay, in truth,
Far better than you love yourself or me.
   Lara. Give me some sign of this,
—the slightest token.
Let me but kiss your hand.
   Preciosa. Nay, come no nearer.
The words I utter are its sign and token.
Misunderstand me not! Be not deceived!
The love wherewith I love you is not such
As you would offer me. For you come here
To take from me the only thing I have,
My honour. You are wealthy, you have friends
And kindred, and a thousand pleasant hopes
That fill your heart with happiness; but I
Am poor, and friendless, having but one treasure,
And you would take that from me, and for what?
To flatter your own vanity, and make me

What you would most despise. O
Sir, such love,
That seeks to harm me, cannot be
true love.
Indeed it cannot. But my love for
you
Is of a different kind. It seeks your
good.
It is a holier feeling. It rebukes
Your earthly passion, your un-
chaste desires,
And bids you look into your heart,
and see
How you do wrong that better
nature in you,
And grieve your soul with sin.

Lara. I swear to you,
I would not harm you; I would
only love you.
I would not take your honour, but
restore it,
And in return I ask but some
slight mark
Of your affection. If indeed you
love me,
As you confess you do, O let me
thus
With this embrace—

Victorian, rushing forward.
Hold! hold! This is too much.
What means this outrage?

Lara. First, what right have you
To question thus a nobleman of
Spain?

Victorian. I too am noble, and
you are no more!
Out of my sight!

Lara. Are you the master here?

Victorian. Ay, here and else-
where, when the wrong of
others
Gives me the right!

Preciosa, to Lara. Go! I be-
seech you, go!

Victorian. I shall have business
with you, Count, anon!

Lara. You cannot come too
soon!   [*Exit.*

Preciosa.   Victorian!

O we have been betrayed!

Victorian. Ha! ha! betrayed!
'Tis I have been betrayed, not we!
—not we!

Preciosa. Dost thou imagine—

Victorian. I imagine nothing;
I see how 'tis thou whilest the
time away
When I am gone!

Preciosa. O speak not in that
tone!
It wounds me deeply.

Victorian. 'Twas not meant to
flatter.

Preciosa. Too well thou knowest
the presence of that man
Is hateful to me!

Victorian. Yet I saw thee stand
And listen to him, when he told
his love.

Preciosa. I did not heed his
words.

Victorian. Indeed thou didst,
And answeredst them with love.

Preciosa. Hadst thou heard all—

Victorian. I heard enough.

Preciosa. Be not so angry with
me.

Victorian. I am not angry; I am
very calm.

Preciosa. If thou wilt let me
speak—

Victorian. Nay, say no more.
I know too much already. Thou
art false!
I do not like these Gypsy mar-
riages!
Where is the ring I gave thee?

Preciosa. In my casket.

Victorian. There let it rest! I
would not have thee wear it;
I thought thee spotless, and thou
art polluted!

Preciosa. I call the Heavens to
witness—

Victorian. Nay, nay, nay!
Take not the name of Heaven upon
thy lips!
They are forsworn!

Preciosa. Victorian! dear Victorian!

Victorian. I gave up all for thee; myself, my fame,
My hopes of fortune, ay, my very soul!
And thou hast been my ruin! Now, go on!
Laugh at my folly with thy paramour,
And, sitting on the Count of Lara's knee,
Say what a poor, fond fool Victorian was!
(*He casts her from him and rushes out.*)
    Preciosa. And this from thee!
    (*Scene closes.*)

SCENE V.—*The* COUNT OF LARA'S *rooms. Enter the* COUNT.

    Lara. There's nothing in this world so sweet as love,
And next to love the sweetest thing is hate!
I've learned to hate, and therefore am revenged.
A silly girl to play the prude with me!
The fire that I have kindled—
    (*Enter* FRANCISCO).
               Well, Francisco.
What tidings from Don Juan?
    Francisco. Good, my lord;
He will be present.
    Lara. And the Duke of Lermos?
    Francisco. Was not at home.
    Lara. How with the rest?
    Francisco.   I've found
The men you wanted. They will all be there,
And at the given signal raise a whirlwind
Of such discordant noises, that the dance
Must cease for lack of music.
    Lara.   Bravely done.
Ah! little dost thou dream, sweet Preciosa,

What lies in wait for thee. Sleep shall not close
Thine eyes this night! Give me my cloak and sword.
               [*Exeunt.*

SCENE VI.—*A retired spot beyond the city gates. Enter* VICTORIAN *and* HYPOLITO.

    Victorian. O shame! O shame! Why do I walk abroad
By daylight, when the very sunshine mocks me,
And voices, and familiar sights and sounds
Cry, "Hide thyself!" O what a thin partition
Doth shut out from the curious world the knowledge
Of evil deeds that have been done in darkness!
Disgrace has many tongues. My fears are windows,
Through which all eyes seem gazing. Every face
Expresses some suspicion of my shame,
And in derision seems to smile at me!
    Hypolito. Did I not caution thee? Did I not tell thee
I was but half persuaded of her virtue?
    Victorian. And yet, Hypolito, we may be wrong,
We may be over-hasty in condemning!
The Count of Lara is a cursed villain.
    Hypolito. And therefore is she cursed, loving him.
    Victorian. She does not love him! 'Tis for gold! for gold!
    Hypolito. Ay, but remember, in the public streets
He shows a golden ring the Gypsy gave him,
A serpent with a ruby in its mouth.

Victorian. She had that ring from me! God! she is false!
But I will be revenged! The hour is passed.
Where stays the coward?
Hypolito. Nay, he is no coward;
A villain, if thou wilt, but not a coward.
I've seen him play with swords; it is his pastime,
And therefore be not over-confident,
He'll task thy skill anon. Look, here he comes.

(*Enter* LARA *followed by* FRANCISCO.)

Lara. Good-evening, gentlemen.
Hypolito. Good-evening, Count.
Lara. I trust I have not kept you long in waiting.
Victorian. Not long and yet too long. Are you prepared?
Lara. I am.
Hypolito. It grieves me much to see this quarrel
Between you, gentlemen. Is there no way
Left open to accord this difference,
But you must make one with your swords?
Victorian.   No! none!
I do entreat thee, dear Hypolito,
Stand not between me and my foe. Too long
Our tongues have spoken. Let these tongues of steel
End our debate. Upon your guard, Sir Count!

(*They fight.* VICTORIAN *disarms the* COUNT.)

Your life is mine; and what shall now withhold me
From sending your vile soul to its account?
Lara. Strike! strike!
Victorian. You are disarmed.
I will not kill you.
I will not murder you. Take up your sword.

(FRANCISCO *hands the* COUNT *his sword, and* HYPOLITO *interposes.*)

Hypolito. Enough! Let it end here! The Count of Lara
Has shown himself a brave man, and Victorian
A generous one, as ever. Now be friends.
Put up your swords; for, to speak frankly to you,
Your cause of quarrel is too slight a thing
To move you to extremes.
Lara.   I am content.
I sought no quarrel. A few hasty words,
Spoken in the heat of blood, have led to this.
Victorian. Nay, something more than that.
Lara.   I understand you.
Therein I did not mean to cross your path.
To me the door stood open, as to others.
But, had I known the girl belonged to you,
Never would I have sought to win her from you.
The truth stands now revealed; she has been false
To both of us.
Victorian. Ay, false as hell itself!
Lara. In truth I did not seek her; she sought me;
And told me how to win her, telling me
The hours when she was oftenest left alone.
Victorian. Say, can you prove this to me? O, pluck out
These awful doubts, that goad me into madness!
Let me know all! all! all!
Lara.   You shall know all.
Here is my page, who was the messenger

Between us. Question him. Was
it not so,
Francisco?
   Francisco.   Ay, my lord.
   Lara.   If farther proof
Is needful, I have here a ring she
gave me.
   Victorian. Pray let me see that
ring! It is the same!
(*Throws it upon the ground, and
   tramples upon it.*)
Thus may she perish who once
wore that ring!
Thus do I spurn her from me; do
thus trample
Her memory in the dust! O
Count of Lara,
We both have been abused, been
much abused!
I thank you for your courtesy and
frankness.
Though, like the surgeon's hand,
yours gave me pain,
Yet it has cured my blindness, and
I thank you.
I now can see the folly I have done,
Though 'tis, alas! too late. So
fare you well!
To-night I leave this hateful town
for ever.
Regard me as your friend. Once
more, farewell!
   Hypolito. Farewell, Sir Count.
[*Exeunt* VICTORIAN *and* HYPOLITO.
   Lara.   Farewell! farewell!
Thus have I cleared the field of my
worst foe!
I have none else to fear; the fight
is done,
The citadel is stormed, the victory
won!
              [*Exit with* FRANCISCO.

SCENE VII.—*A lane in the sub-
   urbs. Night. Enter* CRUZADO
   and BARTOLOMÉ.

   Cruzado. And so, Bartolomé,
the expedition failed. But where
wast thou for the most part?

   Bartolomé. In the Guadarrama
mountains, near San Ildefonso.
   Cruzado.   And thou bringest
nothing back with thee? Didst
thou rob no one?
   Bartolomé. There was no one to
rob, save a party of students from
Segovia, who looked as if they
would rob us; and a jolly little
friar, who had nothing in his
pockets but a missal and a loaf of
bread.
   Cruzado. Pray, then, what brings
thee back to Madrid?
   Bartolomé. First tell me what
keeps thee here?
   Cruzado. Preciosa.
   Bartolomé. And she brings me
back. Hast thou forgotten thy
promise?
   Cruzado. The two years are not
passed yet. Wait patiently. The
girl shall be thine.
   Bartolomé. I hear she has a
Busné lover.
   Cruzado. That is nothing.
   Bartolomé. I do not like it. I
hate him—the son of a Busné har-
lot. He goes in and out, and
speaks with her alone, and I must
stand aside, and wait his pleasure.
   Cruzado. Be patient, I say.
Thou shalt have thy revenge.
When the time comes, thou shalt
waylay him.
   Bartolomé. Meanwhile, show me
her house.
   Cruzado. Come this way. But
thou wilt not find her. She dances
at the play to-night.
   Bartolomé. No matter. Show
me the house.   [*Exeunt.*

SCENE VIII.—*The theatre. The
   orchestra plays the cachucha.
   Sounds of castanets behind the
   scenes. The curtain rises and
   discovers* PRECIOSA *in the atti-
   tude of commencing the dance.*

The cachucha. Tumult ; hisses ; cries of " Brava ! " and " Afuera ! " She falters and pauses. The music stops. General confusion. PRECIOSA *faints.*

SCENE IX. — *The* COUNT OF LARA'S *chambers.* LARA *and his friends at supper.*

Lara. So, Caballeros, once more many thanks!
You have stood by me bravely in this matter.
Pray fill your glasses.
Don Juan. Did you mark, Don Luis,
How pale she looked, when first the noise began,
And then stood still, with her large eyes dilated!
Her nostrils spread! her lips apart! her bosom
Tumultuous as the sea!
Don Luis.   I pitied her.
Lara. Her pride is humbled; and this very night
I mean to visit her.
Don Juan. Will you serenade her ?
Lara.   No music! no more music!
Don Luis.   Why not music ?
It softens many hearts.
Lara.   Not in the humour
She now is in. Music would madden her.
Don Juan. Try golden cymbals.
Don Luis. Yes, try Don Dinero;
A mighty wooer is your Don Dinero.
Lara. To tell the truth, then, I have bribed her maid.
But, Caballeros, you dislike this wine.
A bumper and away; for the night wears.
A health to Preciosa!
        (*They rise and drink.*)
All.   Preciosa.

Lara, holding up his glass.
Thou bright and flaming minister of Love!
Thou wonderful magician! who hast stolen
My secret from me, and mid sighs of passion
Caught from my lips, with red and fiery tongue,
Her precious name! O never more henceforth
Shall mortal lips press thine; and never more
A mortal name be whispered in thine ear.
Go! keep my secret!
(*Drinks and dashes the goblet down*).
Don Juan.   Ite ! missa est !
        (*Scene closes.*)

SCENE X.—*Street and garden wall. Night.   Enter* CRUZADO *and* BARTOLOMÉ.

Cruzado. This is the garden wall, and above it yonder is her house. The window in which thou seest the light is her window. But we will not go in now.
Bartolomé. Why not ?
Cruzado. Because she is not at home.
Bartolomé. No matter; we can wait. But how is this ? The gate is bolted. (*Sound of guitars and voices in a neighbouring street*). Hark! There comes her lover with his infernal serenade! Hark!

SONG

Good-night! [1] Good-night, beloved!
    I come to watch o'er thee!
To be near thee,—to be near thee,
    Alone is peace for me.

Thine eyes are stars of morning,
    Thy lips are crimson flowers,
Good-night! Good-night, beloved,
    While I count the weary hours.

---

[1] *Good-night.* From the Spanish; as are likewise the songs immediately following, and that which commences the first scene of Act III.

Cruzado. They are not coming this way.

Bartolomé.   Wait, they begin again.

SONG (*coming nearer*).

Ah! thou moon that shinest
    Argent-clear above!
All night long enlighten
    My sweet lady-love!
Moon that shinest,
All night long enlighten us!

Bartolomé. Woe be to him, if he comes this way!

Cruzado. Be quiet, they are passing down the street.

SONG (*dying away*).

The nuns in the cloister
    Sang to each other;
For so many sisters
    Is there not one brother!
Ay, for the partridge, mother!
    The cat has run away with the partridge!
Puss! puss! puss!

Bartolomé. Follow that! follow that! Come with me. Puss! puss!
        (*Exeunt. On the opposite side enter the* COUNT OF LARA *and gentlemen with* FRANCISCO.)

Lara. The gate is fast. Over the wall, Francisco,
And draw the bolt. There, so, and so, and over.
Now, gentlemen, come in, and help me scale
Yon balcony. How now? Her light still burns.
Move warily. Make fast the gate, Francisco.
        (*Exeunt. Re-enter* CRUZADO *and* BARTOLOMÉ).

Bartolomé. They went in at the gate. Hark! I hear them in the garden. (*Tries the gate*). Bolted again! Vive Cristo! Follow me over the wall.
        (*They climb the wall.*)

SCENE XI. — PRECIOSA'S *bedchamber. Midnight. She is sleeping in an arm-chair, in an undress.* DOLORES *watching her.*

Dolores. She sleeps at last!
        (*Opens the window and listens.*)
                    All silent in the street,
And in the garden. Hark!
Preciosa, in her sleep. I must go hence!
Give me my cloak!
Dolores. He comes! I hear his footsteps!
Preciosa. Go tell them that I cannot dance to-night;
I am too ill! Look at me! See the fever
That burns upon my cheek! I must go hence.
I am too weak to dance.
        (*Signal from the garden.*)
Dolores, from the window.
                    Who's there?
Voice, from below.   A friend.
Dolores. I will undo the door.
Wait till I come.
Preciosa. I must go hence. I pray you do not harm me!
Shame! shame! to treat a feeble woman thus!
Be you but kind, I will do all things for you.
I'm ready now,—give me my castanets.
Where is Victorian? Oh, those hateful lamps!
They glare upon me like an evil eye.
I cannot stay. Hark! how they mock at me!
They hiss at me like serpents! Save me! save me!
        (*She wakes.*)
How late is it, Dolores?
Dolores.   It is midnight.
Preciosa. We must be patient. Smooth this pillow for me.
        (*She sleeps again. Noise from the garden, and voices.*)

Voice. Muera!
Another Voice.   O villains!
villains!
Lara.   So! have at you!
Voice. Take that!
Lara.   O, I am wounded!
Dolores, shutting the window.
                    Jesu Maria!

ACT III

SCENE I.—*A cross-road through a wood. In the background a distant village spire.* VICTORIAN *and* HYPOLITO, *as travelling students, with guitars, sitting under the trees.* HYPOLITO *plays and sings.*

SONG

Ah, Love!
Perjured, false, treacherous Love!
        Enemy
Of all that mankind may not rue!
        Most untrue
To him who keeps most faith with thee,
        Woe is me!
The falcon has the eyes of the dove,
        Ah, Love!
Perjured, false, treacherous Love!

Victorian. Yes, love is ever busy
        with his shuttle,
Is ever weaving into life's dull warp
Bright, gorgeous flowers and scenes
        Arcadian;
Hanging our gloomy prison-house
        about
With tapestries, that make its
        walls dilate
In never-ending vistas of delight.
Hypolito. Thinking to walk in
        those Arcadian pastures,
Thou hast run thy noble head
        against the wall.

SONG (*continued*).

        Thy deceits
Give us clearly to comprehend,
        Whither tend
All thy pleasures, all the sweets!
        They are cheats,
Thorns below and flowers above,
        Ah, Love!
Perjured, false, treacherous Love!

Victorian. A very pretty song.
        I thank thee for it.
Hypolito. It suits thy case.
Victorian. Indeed, I think it
        does.
What wise man wrote it?
Hypolito.   Lopez Maldonado.
Victorian. In truth, a pretty
        song.
Hypolito. With much truth in it.
I hope thou wilt profit by it; and
        in earnest
Try to forget this lady of thy love.
Victorian. I will forget her! All
        dear recollections
Pressed in my heart, like flowers
        within a book,
Shall be torn out, and scattered to
        the winds!
I will forget her! But perhaps
        hereafter,
When she shall learn how heartless
        is the world,
A voice within her will repeat my
        name,
And she will say, "He was indeed
        my friend!"
O, would I were a soldier, not a
        scholar,
That the loud march, the deafening beat of drums,
The shattering blast of the brass-throated trumpet,
The din of arms, the onslaught and
        the storm,
And a swift death, might make me
        deaf for ever
To the upraidings of this foolish
        heart!
Hypolito. Then let that foolish
        heart upbraid no more!
To conquer love, one need but will
        to conquer.
Victorian. Yet, good Hypolito,
        it is in vain
I throw into Oblivion's sea the
        sword
That pierces me; for, like Excalibar,

With gemmed and flashing hilt, it
will not sink.
There rises from below a hand
that grasps it,
And waves it in the air; and wail-
ing voices
Are heard along the shore.
Hypolito. And yet at last
Down sank Excalibar to rise no
more.
This is not well. In truth, it
vexes me.
Instead of whistling to the steeds
of Time,
To make them jog on merrily with
life's burden,
Like a dead weight thou hangest
on the wheels.
Thou art too young, too full of
lusty health
To talk of dying.
Victorian. Yet I fain would
die!
To go through life, unloving and
unloved;
To feel that thirst and hunger of
the soul
We cannot still; that longing, that
wild impulse,
And struggle after something we
have not
And cannot have; the effort to be
strong;
And, like the Spartan boy, to
smile, and smile,
While secret wounds do bleed be-
neath our cloaks;
All this the dead feel not,—the
dead alone!
Would I were with them!
Hypolito. We shall all be soon.
Victorian. It cannot be too soon;
for I am weary
Of the bewildering masquerade of
Life,
Where strangers walk as friends,
and friends as strangers;
Where whispers overheard betray
false hearts;

And through the mazes of the
crowd we chase
Some form of loveliness, that
smiles, and beckons,
And cheats us with fair words, only
to leave us
A mockery and a jest; maddened,
—confused,—
Not knowing friend from foe.
Hypolito. Why seek to know?
Enjoy the merry shrove-tide of thy
youth!
Take each fair mask for what it
gives itself,
Nor strive to look beneath it.
Victorian. I confess,
That were the wiser part. But
Hope no longer
Comforts my soul. I am a
wretched man,
Much like a poor and shipwrecked
mariner,
Who, struggling to climb up into
the boat,
Has both his bruised and bleeding
hands cut off,
And sinks again into the weltering
sea,
Helpless and hopeless!
Hypolito. Yet thou shalt not
perish.
The strength of thine own arm is
thy salvation.
Above thy head, through rifted
clouds, there shines
A glorious star. Be patient. Trust
thy star!

(*Sound of a village bell in the dis-
tance.*)

Victorian. Ave Maria! I hear the
sacristan
Ringing the chimes from yonder
village belfry!
A solemn sound, that echoes far
and wide
Over the red roofs of the cottages,
And bids the labouring hind a-
field, the shepherd,

Guarding his flock, the lonely
  muleteer,
And all the crowd in village
  streets, stand still,
And breathe a prayer unto the
  blessed Virgin!
  Hypolito. Amen! amen! Not
half a league from hence
The village lies.
  Victorian. This path will lead
us to it,
Over the wheat fields, where the
  shadows sail
Across the running sea, now green,
  now blue,
And, like an idle mariner on the
  main,
Whistles the quail. Come, let us
  hasten on.   [*Exeunt.*

SCENE II.—*Public square in the
  village of Guadarrama.   The Ave
  Maria still tolling.   A crowd of
  villagers, with their hats in their
  hands, as if in prayer.   In front,
  a group of Gypsies.   The bell
  rings a merrier peal.   A Gypsy
  dance.   Enter* PANCHO, *followed
  by* PEDRO CRESPO.

  Pancho. Make room, ye vaga-
bonds and Gypsy thieves!
Make room for the Alcalde and for
  me!
  Pedro Crespo. Keep silence all!
I have an edict here
From our most gracious lord, the
  King of Spain,
Jerusalem, and the Canary Islands,
Which I shall publish in the
  market-place.
Open your ears and listen!
(*Enter the* PADRE CURA *at the door
  of his cottage.*)
                Padre Cura,
Good-day! and, pray you, hear
  this edict read.
  Padre Cura. Good-day, and God
be with you! Pray, what is it?

  Pedro Crespo. An act of banish-
ment against the Gypsies!
(*Agitation and murmurs in the
  crowd.*)
  Pancho. Silence!
  Pedro Crespo, reads. " I hereby
order and command,
That the Egyptian and Chaldean
  strangers,
Known by the name of Gypsies,
  shall henceforth
Be banished from the realm, as
  vagabonds
And beggars; and if, after seventy
  days,
Any be found within our kingdom's
  bounds,
They shall receive a hundred lashes
  each;
The second time, shall have their
  ears cut off;
The third, be slaves for life to him
  who takes them,
Or burnt as heretics. Signed, I,
  the King."
Vile miscreants and creatures un-
  baptised!
You hear the law! Obey and dis-
  appear!
  Pancho. And if in seventy days
  you are not gone,
Dead or alive I make you all my
  slaves.
(*The Gypsies go out in confusion,
  showing signs of fear and dis-
  content.   Pancho follows.*)
  Padre Cura. A righteous law!
  A very righteous law!
Pray you, sit down.
  Pedro Crespo.   I thank you
  heartily.
(*They seat themselves on a bench
  at the* PADRE CURA'S *door.
  Sound of guitars heard at a
  distance, approaching during
  the dialogue which follows.*)
A very righteous judgment, as you
  say.

Now tell me, Padre Cura,—you
  know all things,—
How came these Gypsies into
  Spain?
    Padre Cura.   Why, look you;
They came with Hercules from
  Palestine,
And hence are thieves and vagrants,
  Sir Alcalde,
As the Simoniacs from Simon
  Magus.
And, look you, as Fray Jayme
  Bleda says,
There are a hundred marks to
  prove a Moor
Is not a Christian, so 'tis with the
  Gypsies.
They never marry, never go to
  mass,
Never baptise their children, nor
  keep Lent,
Nor see the inside of a church,—
  nor—nor—
    Pedro Crespo.   Good reasons,
  good, substantial reasons all!
No matter for the other ninety-
  five.
They should be burnt, I see it plain
  enough,
They should be burnt.

(*Enter* VICTORIAN *and* HYPOLITO
playing.)

    Padre Cura. And pray, whom
  have we here?
    Pedro Crespo. More vagrants!
  By Saint Lazarus, more vag-
  rants!
    Hypolito. Good-evening, gentle-
  men! Is this Guadarrama?
    Padre Cura. Yes, Guadarrama,
  and good-evening to you.
    Hypolito. We seek the Padre
  Cura of the village;
And, judging from your dress and
  reverend mien,
You must be he.
    Padre Cura. I am. Pray, what's
  your pleasure?

    Hypolito. We are poor students,
  travelling in vacation.
You know this mark?

(*Touching the wooden spoon in his
hat-band.*)

    Padre Cura, joyfully. Ay, know
  it, and have worn it.
    Pedro Crespo, aside. Soup-eaters!
  by the mass! The worst of
  vagrants!
And there is no law against them.
  Sir, your servant.   [*Exit.*
    Padre Cura.   Your servant,
  Pedro Crespo.
    Hypolito.   Padre Cura,
From the first moment I beheld
  your face,
I said within myself, " This is the
  man! "
There is a certain something in
  your looks,
A certain scholar-like and studious
  something,—
You understand,—which cannot
  be mistaken;
Which marks you as a very learned
  man,
In fine, as one of us.
    Victorian, aside. What impu-
  dence!
    Hypolito. As we approached, I
  said to my companion,
" That is the Padre Cura; mark
  my words! "
Meaning your Grace. " The other
  man," said I,
" Who sits so awkwardly upon the
  bench,
Must be the sacristan."
    Padre Cura. Ah! said you so?
Why, that was Pedro Crespo, the
  alcalde!
    Hypolito. Indeed! you much
  astonish me! His air
Was not so full of dignity and
  grace
As an alcade's should be.
    Padre Cura.   That is true.

He is out of humour with some
vagrant Gypsies,
Who have their camp here in the
neighbourhood.
There is nothing so undignified as
anger.

Hypolito. The Padre Cura will
excuse our boldness,
If, from his well-known hospitality,
We crave a lodging for the night.

Padre Cura.   I pray you!
You do me honour! I am but too
happy
To have such guests beneath my
humble roof.
It is not often that I have occasion
To speak with scholars;   and
Emollit mores,
Nec sinit esse feros, Cicero says.

Hypolito. 'Tis Ovid, is it not?

Padre Cura.   No, Cicero.

Hypolito. Your Grace is right.
You are the better scholar.
Now what a dunce was I to think it
Ovid!
But hang me if it is not!   (*Aside.*)

Padre Cura.   Pass this way.
He was a very great man, was
Cicero!
Pray you, go in, go in! no cere-
mony.   [*Exeunt.*

SCENE III.—*A room in the* PADRE
CURA'S *house.   Enter the* PADRE
and HYPOLITO.

Padre Cura. So then, Señor, you
come from Alcalá.
I am glad to hear it.   It was there
I studied.

Hypolito. And left behind an
honoured name, no doubt.
How may I call your Grace?

Padre Cura.   Gerónimo
De Santillana, at your Honour's
service.

Hypolito. Descended from the
Marquis Santillana?
From the distinguished poet?

Padre Cura. From the Marquis,
Not from the poet.

Hypolito. Why, they were the
same.
Let me embrace you?   O some
lucky star
Has brought me hither!   Yet once
more!—once more!
Your name is ever green in Alcalá,
And our professor, when we are
unruly,
Will shake his hoary head, and
say, " Alas!
It was not so in Santillana's time! "

Padre Cura. I did not think my
name remembered there.

Hypolito. More than remem-
bered; it is idolised.

Padre Cura. Of what professor
speak you?

Hypolito.   Timoneda.

Padre Cura. I don't remember
any Timoneda.

Hypolito. A grave and sombre
man, whose beetling brow
O'erhangs the rushing current of
his speech
As rocks o'er rivers hang.   Have
you forgotten?

Padre Cura. Indeed, I have.   O,
those were pleasant days,
Those college days!   I ne'er shall
see the like!
I had not buried then so many
hopes!
I had not buried then so many
friends!
I've turned my back on what was
then before me;
And the bright faces of my young
companions
Are wrinkled like my own, or are
no more.
Do you remember Cueva?

Hypolito.   Cueva? Cueva?

Padre Cura. Fool that I am!
He was before your time.
You're a mere boy, and I am an old
man.

Hypolito. I should not like to try my strength with you.

Padre Cura. Well, well. But I forget; you must be hungry. Martina! ho! Martina! 'Tis my niece.

(*Enter* MARTINA).

Hypolito. You may be proud o' such a niece as that. I wish I had a niece. *Emollit mores* (*Aside.*) He was a very great man, was Cicero!

Your servant, fair Martina.

Martina. Servant, sir.

Padre Cura. This gentleman is hungry. See thou to it. Let us have supper.

Martina. 'Twill be ready soon.

Padre Cura. And bring a bottle of my Val-de-Peñas Out of the cellar. Stay; I'll go myself, Pray you, Señor, excuse me. [*Exit.*

Hypolito. Hist! Martina! One word with you. Bless me! what handsome eyes! To-day there have been Gypsies in the village, Is it not so?

Martina. There have been Gypsies here.

Hypolito. Yes, and they told your fortune.

Martina, embarrassed. Told my fortune?

Hypolito. Yes, yes; I know they did. Give me your hand. I'll tell you what they said. They said,—they said, The shepherd boy that loved you was a clown, And him you should not marry. Was it not?

Martina, surprised. How know you that?

Hypolito. O, I know more than that.

What a soft, little hand! And then they said, A cavalier from court, handsome, and tall And rich, should come one day to marry you, And you should be a lady. Was it not? He has arrived, the handsome cavalier.

(*Tries to kiss her. She runs off. Enter* VICTORIAN, *with a letter.*)

Victorian. The muleteer has come.

Hypolito. So soon?

Victorian. I found him Sitting at supper by the tavern door, And, from a pitcher that he held aloft His whole arm's length, drinking the blood-red wine.

Hypolito. What news from Court?

Victorian. He brought this letter only. (*Reads.*) O cursed perfidy! Why did I let That lying tongue deceive me? Preciosa, Sweet Preciosa! how art thou avenged!

Hypolito. What news is this, that makes thy cheek turn pale, And thy hand tremble?

Victorian. O, most infamous! The Count of Lara is a damned villain!

Hypolito. That is no news, forsooth.

Victorian. He strove in vain To steal from me the jewel of my soul, The love of Preciosa. Not succeeding, He swore to be revenged; and set on foot A plot to ruin her, which has succeeded,

She has been hissed and hooted
from the stage,
Her reputation stained by slander-
ous lies
Too foul to speak of; and, once
more a beggar,
She roams a wanderer over God's
green earth,
Housing with Gypsies!
Hypolito.   To renew again
The Age of Gold, and make the
shepherd swains
Desperate with love, like Gasper
Gil's Diana.
Redit et Virgo !
Victorian.   Dear Hypolito,
How have I wronged that meek,
confiding heart!
I will go seek for her; and with my
tears
Wash out the wrong I've done her!
Hypolito.   O beware!
Act not that folly o'er again.
Victorian.   Ay, folly,
Delusion, madness, call it what
thou wilt,
I will confess my weakness,—I still
love her!
Still fondly love her!

(*Enter* DON CARLOS.)

Don Carlos. Are not the horses
ready yet?
Chispa. I should think not, for
the hostler seems to be asleep.
Ho! within there! Horses!
horses! horses!

(*He knocks at the gate with his
whip, and enter* MOSQUITO,
putting on his jacket.)

Mosquito. Pray, have a little
patience. I'm not a musket.
Chispa. Health and pistareens!
I'm glad to see you come on
dancing, padre! Pray, what's
the news?
Mosquito.   You cannot have
fresh horses; because there are
none.
Chispa.   Cachiporra! Throw

that bone to another dog. Do I
look like your aunt?
Mosquito. No; she has a beard.
Chispa. Go to! go to!
Mosquito. Are you from Madrid?
Chispa. Yes; and going to Estra-
madura. Get us horses.
Mosquito. What's the news at
Court?
Why, the latest news is, that I
am going to set up a coach, and I
have already bought the whip.

(*Strikes him round the legs.*)

Mosquito. Oh! oh! you hurt
me!
Don Carlos. Enough of this folly.
Let us have horses. (*Gives money
to* MOSQUITO.) It is almost dark;
and we are in haste. But tell me,
has a band of Gypsies passed this
way of late?
Mosquito. Yes; and they are
still in the neighbourhood.
Don Carlos. And where?
Mosquito.   Across the fields
yonder, in the woods near
Guadarrama.   [*Exit.*
Don Carlos. Now this is lucky.
We will visit the Gypsy camp.
Chispa. Are you not afraid of
the evil eye? [1] Have you a stag's
horn with you?

[1] *The evil eye.* "In the Gitano
language, casting the evil eye is called
Querelar nasula, which simply means
making sick, and which, according
to the common superstition, is
accomplished by casting an evil look
at people, especially children, who,
from the tenderness of their constitu-
tion, are supposed to be more easily
blighted than those of a mature age.
After receiving the evil glance, they
fall sick, and die in a few hours.
"The Spaniards have very little
to say respecting the evil eye, though
the belief in it is very prevalent,
especially in Andalusia, amongst the
lower orders. A stag's horn is con-
sidered a good safeguard, and on that
account a small horn, tipped with
silver, is frequently attached to the

Don Carlos. Fear not. We will pass the night at the village.

Chispa.   And sleep like the Squires of Herman Daza, nine under one blanket.

Don Carlos. I hope we may find the Preciosa among them.

Chispa. Among the Squires?

Don Carlos. No; among the Gypsies, blockhead!

Chispa. I hope we may; for we are giving ourselves trouble enough on her account. Don't you think so? However, there is no catching trout without wetting one's trousers. Yonder come the horses.

[*Exeunt.*

SCENE V.—*The Gypsy camp in the forest. Night. Gypsies working at a forge. Others playing cards by the firelight.*

Gypsies, at the forge sing.

On the top of the mountain I stand,[1]
With a crown of red gold in my hand,
Wild Moors come trooping over the lea,
O how from their fury shall I flee, flee, flee?
O how from their fury shall I flee?

children's necks by means of a cord braided from the hair of a black mare's tail. Should the evil glance be cast, it is imagined that the horn receives it, and instantly snaps asunder. Such horns may be purchased in some of the silversmith's shops at Seville. BORROW's *Zincali.* Vol. i. ch. ix.

[1] *On the top of a mountain I stand.*
This and the following scraps of song are from Borrow's *Zincali; or, an Account of the Gypsies in Spain.*
The Gypsy words in the same scene may be thus interpreted.

John-Dorados, pieces of gold.
Pigeon, a simpleton.
In your morocco, stripped.
Doves, sheets.
Moon, a shirt.
Chirelin, a thief.
Murcigalleros, those who steal at night-fall.
Rastilleros, foot-pads.

First Gypsy, playing. Down with your John - Dorados, my pigeon. Down with your John - Dorados, and let us make an end.

Gypsies, at the forge sing.

Loud sang the Spanish cavalier,
    And thus the ditty ran;
God send the Gypsy lassie here,
    And not the Gypsy man.

First Gypsy, playing. There you are in your morocco!

Second Gypsy. One more game. The Alcade's doves against the Padre Cura's new moon.

First Gypsy. Have at you, Chirelin.

Gypsies, at the forge sing.

At midnight, when the moon began
    To show her silver flame,
There came to him no Gypsy man,
    The Gypsy lassie came.

(*Enter* BELTRAN CRUZADO.)

Cruzado. Come hither, Murcigalleros and Rastilleros; leave work, leave play; listen to your orders for the night. (*Speaking to the right.*) You will get you to the village, mark you, by the stone cross.

Gypsies. Ay!

Cruzado, to the left. And you, by the pole with the hermit's head upon it.

Gypsies. Ay!

Cruzado. As soon as you see the planets are out, in with you, and be busy with the ten commandments, under the sly, and Saint Martin asleep. D'ye hear?

Gypsies. Ay!

Hermit, highway-robber.
Planets, candles.
Commandments, the fingers.
Saint Martin asleep, to rob a person asleep.
Lanterns, eyes.
Gablin, police officer.
Papagayo, a spy.
Vineyards and Dancing John, to take flight.

Cruzado. Keep your lanterns open, and, if you see a goblin or a papagayo, take to your trampers. "Vineyards and Dancing John" is the word. Am I comprehended?

Gypsies. Ay! ay!

Cruzado. Away, then!

(*Exeunt severally.* CRUZADO *walks up the stage, and disappears among the trees. Enter* PRECIOSA.)

Preciosa. How strangely gleams
through the gigantic trees
The red light of the forge! Wild,
beckoning shadows
Stalk through the forest ever and
anon
Rising and bending with the
flickering flame,
Then flitting into darkness! So
within me
Strange hopes and fears do beckon
to each other,
My brightest hopes giving dark
fears a being,
As the light does the shadow.
Woe is me!
How still it is about me, and how
lonely!

(BARTOLOMÉ *rushes in.*)

Bartolomé. Ho! Preciosa!

Preciosa. O, Bartolomé!
Thou here?

Bartolomé. Lo! I am here.

Preciosa. Whence comest thou?

Bartolomé. From the rough
ridges of the wild Sierra,
From caverns in the rocks, from
hunger, thirst,
And fever! Like a wild wolf to
the sheepfold
Come I for thee, my lamb.

Preciosa. O touch me not!
The Count of Lara's blood is on thy
hands!
The Count of Lara's curse is on thy
soul!

Do not come near me! Pray, begone from here!
Thou art in danger! They have
set a price
Upon thy head!

Bartolomé. Ay, and I've wandered long
Among the mountains; and for
many days
Have seen no human face, save the
rough swineherd's,
The wind and rain have been my
sole companions.
I shouted to them from the rocks
thy name,
And the loud echo sent it back to
me,
Till I grew mad. I could not stay
from thee,
And I am here! Betray me, if
thou wilt.

Preciosa. Betray thee? I betray thee?

Bartolomé. Preciosa!
I come for thee! for thee I thus
brave death!
Fly with me o'er the borders of
this realm!
Fly with me!

Preciosa. Speak of that no
more.
I cannot. I am thine no longer.

Bartolomé. O, recall the time
When we were children! how we
played together,
How we grew up together; how
we plighted
Our hearts unto each other, even
in childhood!
Fulfil thy promise, for the hour
has come.
I am hunted from the kingdom,
like a wolf!
Fulfil thy promise.

Preciosa. 'Twas my father's
promise,
Not mine. I never gave my
heart to thee,
Nor promised thee my hand!

Bartolomé. False tongue of woman!
And heart more false!
Preciosa. Nay, listen unto me.
I will speak frankly. I have never loved thee;
I cannot love thee. This is not my fault,
It is my destiny. Thou art a man
Restless and violent. What wouldst thou with me,
A feeble girl, who have not long to live,
Whose heart is broken? Seek another wife,
Better than I, and fairer; and let not
Thy rash and headlong moods estrange her from thee.
Thou art unhappy in this hopeless passion.
I never sought thy love; never did aught
To make thee love me. Yet I pity thee,
And most of all I pity thy wild heart,
That hurries thee to crimes and deeds of blood.
Beware, beware of that.
Bartolomé. For thy dear sake,
I will be gentle. Thou shalt teach me patience.
Preciosa. Then take this farewell, and depart in peace;
Thou must not linger here.
Bartolomé. Come, come with me!
Preciosa. Hark! I hear footsteps.
Bartolomé. I entreat thee, come!
Preciosa. Away! It is in vain.
Bartolomé. Wilt thou not come?
Preciosa. Never!
Bartolomé. Then woe, eternal woe, upon thee!
Thou shalt not be another's.
Thou shalt die.　　　　[*Exit.*
Preciosa. All holy angels keep me in this hour!

Spirit of her who bore me, look upon me!
Mother of God, the glorified, protect me!
Christ and the saints, be merciful unto me!
Yet why should I fear death? What is it to die?
To leave all disappointment, care, and sorrow,
To leave all falsehood, treachery, and unkindness,
All ignominy, suffering, and despair,
And be at rest for ever! O, dull heart,
Be of good cheer! When thou shalt cease to beat,
Then shalt thou cease to suffer and complain!
(*Enter* Victorian *and* Hypolito *behind.*)
　Victorian. 'Tis she! Behold, how beautiful she stands
Under the tent-like trees!
　Hypolito. A woodland nymph!
　Victorian. I pray thee, stand aside. Leave me.
　Hypolito.　　　　　　Be wary,
Do not betray thyself too soon.
　Victorian, disguising his voice.
　　　　　　　　Hist! Gypsy!
　Preciosa, aside, with emotion.
That voice! that voice from heaven! O speak again!
Who is it calls?
　Victorian.　　　　A friend.
　Preciosa, aside. 'Tis he! 'Tis he!
I thank thee, Heaven, that thou hast heard my prayer,
And sent me this protector! Now be strong,
Be strong, my heart! I must dissemble here.
False friend or true?
　Victorian. A true friend to the true;
Fear not; come hither. So; can you tell fortunes?

Preciosa. Not in the dark.
Come nearer to the fire.
Give me your hand. It is not
crossed, I see.
  *Victorian, putting a piece of gold
into her hand.* There is the
cross.
Preciosa.   Is't silver?
Victorian.   No, 'tis gold.
Preciosa. There's a fair lady at
the Court, who loves you,
And for yourself alone.
  Victorian. Fie! the old story!
Tell me a better fortune for my
money;
Not this old woman's tale!
  Preciosa. You are passionate;
And this same passionate humour
in your blood
Has marred your fortune. Yes;
I see it now;
The line of life is crossed by many
marks.
Shame! shame! O you have
wronged the maid who loved
you!
How could you do it?
  Victorian. I never loved a maid;
For she I loved was then a maid no
more.
  Preciosa. How know you that?
  Victorian. A little bird in the air
Whispered the secret.
  Preciosa. There, take back your
gold!
Your hand is cold, like a deceiver's
hand!
There is no blessing in its charity!
Make her your wife, for you have
been abused;
And you shall mend your fortunes,
mending hers.
  Victorian, aside. How like an
angel's speaks the tongue of
woman,
When pleading in another's cause
her own!—
That is a pretty ring upon your
finger.

Pray give it me. (*Tries to take
the ring*).
  Preciosa. No; never from my
hand
Shall that be taken!
  Victorian. Why, 'tis but a ring.
I'll give it back to you; or, if I
keep it,
Will give you gold to buy you
twenty such.
  Preciosa. Why would you have
this ring?
  Victorian. A traveller's fancy,
A whim, and nothing more. I
would fain keep it
As a memento of the Gypsy camp
In Guadarrama, and the fortune-
teller
Who sent me back to wed a
widowed maid.
Pray, let me have the ring.
  Preciosa. No, never! never!
I will not part with it, even when I
die;
But bid my nurse fold my pale
fingers thus,
That it may not fall from them.
'Tis a token
Of a beloved friend, who is no
more.
  Victorian.   How? dead?
  Preciosa. Yes; dead to me; and
worse than dead.
He is estranged! And yet I keep
this ring.
I will rise with it from my grave
hereafter,
To prove to him that I was never
false.
  Victorian, aside. Be still, my
swelling heart! one moment,
still!
Why, 'tis the folly of a love-sick
girl.
Come, give it me, or I will say 'tis
mine,
And that you stole it.
  Preciosa. O, you will not dare
To utter such a fiendish lie!

Victorian. Not dare?
Look in my face, and say if there is
  aught
I have not dared, I would not dare
  for thee!
  (*She rushes into his arms.*)
  Preciosa. 'Tis thou! 'tis thou!
Yes; yes; my heart's elected!
My dearest-dear Victorian! my
  soul's heaven!
Where hast thou been so long?
  Why didst thou leave me?
  Victorian. Ask me not now, my
  dearest Preciosa.
Let me forget we ever have been
  parted!
  Preciosa. Hadst thou not come—
  Victorian. I pray thee, do not
  chide me!
  Preciosa. I should have perished
  here among these Gypsies.
  Victorian. Forgive me, sweet!
  for what I made thee suffer.
Think'st thou this heart could feel
  a moment's joy,
Thou being absent? O, believe it
  not!
Indeed, since that sad hour I have
  not slept,
For thinking of the wrong I did to
  thee!
Dost thou forgive me? Say, wilt
  thou forgive me?
  Preciosa. I have forgiven thee.
  Ere those words of anger
Were in the book of Heaven writ
  down against thee,
I had forgiven thee.
  Victorian. I'm the veriest fool
That walks the earth, to have be-
  lieved thee false.
It was the Count of Lara—
  Preciosa. That bad man
Has worked me harm enough.
  Hast thou not heard—
  Victorian. I have heard all.
  And yet speak on, speak on!
Let me but hear thy voice, and I
  am happy;

For every tone, like some sweet
  incantation,
Calls up the buried past to plead
  for me.
Speak, my beloved, speak into my
  heart,
Whatever fills and agitates thine
  own.
  (*They walk aside.*)
  Hypolito. All gentle quarrels in
  the pastoral poets,
All passionate love seems in the
  best romances,
All chaste embraces on the public
  stage,
All soft adventures, which the
  liberal stars
Have winked at, as the natural
  course of things,
Have been surpassed here by my
  friend, the student,
And this sweet Gypsy lass, fair
  Preciosa!
  Preciosa. Señor Hypolito! I kiss
  your hand.
Pray, shall I tell your fortune?
  Hypolito. Not to-night;
For, should you treat me as you
  did Victorian,
And send me back to marry maids
  forlorn,
My wedding day would last from
  now till Christmas.
  Chispa, within. What ho! the
  Gypsies, ho! Beltran Cruzado!
Halloo! halloo! halloo! halloo!
  (*Enters booted, with a whip and
  lantern.*)
  Victorian. What now?
Why such a fearful din? Hast
  thou been robbed?
  Chispa. Ay, robbed and mur-
  dered; and good-evening to
  you,
My worthy masters.
  Victorian. Speak; what brings
  thee here?
  Chispa, to Preciosa. Good news

from Court; good news!
Beltran Cruzado,
The Count of the Calés, is not your
father,
But your true father has returned
to Spain
Laden with wealth. You are no
more a Gypsy.
 Victorian. Strange as a Moorish
tale!
 Chispa, aside. And I have two
to take.
I've heard my grandmother say,
that Heaven gives almonds
To those who have no teeth.
That's nuts to crack.
I've teeth to spare, but where shall
I find almonds?
 Victorian. What more of this
strange story?
 Chispa.   Nothing more.
Your friend, Don Carlos, is now at
the village,
Showing to Pedro Crespo, the Al-
calde,
The proofs of what I tell you.
The old hag,
Who stole you in your childhood,
has confessed;
And probably they'll hang her for
the crime,
To make the celebration more
complete.
 Victorian. No; let it be a day of
general joy;
Fortune comes well to all, that
comes not late.
Now let us join Don Carlos.
 Hypolito. So farewell,
The student's wandering life!
Sweet serenades,
Sung under ladies' windows in the
night,
And all that makes vacation beau-
tiful!
To you, ye cloistered shades of Al-
calá,
To you, ye radiant visions of ro-
mance,

Written in books, but here sur-
passed by truth,
The Bachelor Hypolito returns,
And leaves the Gypsy with the
Spanish Student.

SCENE VI. — *A pass in the
Guadarrama mountains. Early
morning. A muleteer crosses the
stage, sitting sideways on his mule,
and lighting a paper cigar with
flint and steel.*

SONG

If thou art sleeping, maiden,[1]
 Awake and open thy door,
'Tis the break of day, and we must
  away,
 O'er meadow, and mount, and moor.

Wait not to find thy slippers,
 But come with thy naked feet;
We shall have to pass through the
  dewy grass,
 And waters wide and fleet.

(*Disappears down the pass.
Enter a Monk. A Shep-
herd appears on the rocks
above.*)

Monk. Ave Maria, gratia plena.
Olá! good man!
Shepherd. Olá.
Monk. Is this the road to
Segovia?
Shepherd. It is, your reverence.
Monk. How far is it?
Shepherd. I do not know.
Monk. What is that yonder in
the valley?
Shepherd. San Ildefonso.
Monk. A long way to breakfast.
Shepherd. Ay, marry.
Monk. Are there robbers in
these mountains?
Shepherd. Yes, and worse than
that.
Monk. What?

[1] *If thou art sleeping, maiden.*
From the Spanish; as is likewise
the song of the Contrabandista on
next page.

Shepherd. Wolves.

Monk. Santa Maria! Come with me to San Ildefonso, and thou shalt be well rewarded.

    Shepherd. What wilt thou give me?

    Monk. An Agnus Dei and my benediction.

    (*They disappear. A mounted Contrabandista passes, wrapped in his cloak, and a gun at his saddle-bow. He goes down the pass singing.*)

SONG

Worn with speed is my good steed,
And I march me hurried, worried;
Onward caballito mio,
With the white star in thy forehead!
Onward, for here comes the Ronda,
And I hear their rifles crack!
Ay, jaléo! Ay, ay, jaléo!
Ay, jaléo! They cross our track!

    (*Song dies away. Enter* PRE-CIOSA, *on horseback, attended by* VICTORIAN, HY-POLITO, DON CARLOS, *and* CHISPA, *on foot, and armed.*)

    Victorian. This is the highest point. Here let us rest.
See, Preciosa, see how all about us
Kneeling, like hooded friars, the misty mountains
Receive the benediction of the sun!
O glorious sight!

    Preciosa. Most beautiful indeed!

    Hypolito. Most wonderful!

    Victorian. And in the vale below,
Where yonder steeples flash like lifted halberds,
San Ildefonso, from its noisy belfries,
Sends up a salutation to the morn,
As if an army smote their brazen shields,
And shouted victory!

    Preciosa. And which way lies Segovia?

    Victorian. At a great distance yonder.

Dost thou not see it?

    Preciosa. No. I do not see it.

    Victorian. The merest flaw that dents the horizon's edge.
There, yonder!

    Hypolito. 'Tis a notable old town,
Boasting an ancient Roman aqueduct,
And an Alcázar, builded by the Moors,
Wherein, you may remember, poor Gil Blas
Was fed on *Pan del Rey.* O, many a time
Out of its grated windows have I looked
Hundreds of feet plumb down to the Eresma,
That, like a serpent through the valley creeping,
Glides at its foot.

    Preciosa. O, yes! I see it now,
Yet rather with my heart, than with mine eyes,
So faint it is. And, all my thoughts sail thither,
Freighted with prayers and hopes, and forward urged
Against all stress of accident, as, in
The Eastern Tale, against the wind and tide,
Great ships were drawn to the Magnetic Mountains,
And there were wrecked, and perished in the sea!
    (*She weeps.*)

    Victorian. O gentle spirit!
Thou didst bear unmoved
Blasts of adversity and frosts of fate!
But the first ray of sunshine that falls on thee
Melts thee to tears! O, let thy weary heart
Lean upon mine! and it shall faint no more,
Nor thirst, nor hunger; but be comforted

And filled with my affection.

Preciosa.   Stay no longer!
My father waits.   Methinks I see
    him there,
Now looking from the window, and
    now watching
Each sound of wheels or foot-fall
    in the street,
And saying, "Hark! she comes!"
    O father! father!

(They descend the pass. CHISPA
    remains behind.)

Chispa. I have a father, too, but
he is a dead one. Alas and alack-
a-day! Poor was I born, and poor
do I remain. I neither win nor
lose. Thus I wag through the
world, half the time on foot, and
the other half walking; and al-
ways as merry as a thunder-storm
in the night. And so we plough
along, as the fly said to the ox.
Who knows what may happen?

Patience, and shuffle the cards!
I am not yet so bald, that you can
see my brains; and perhaps, after
all, I shall some day go to Rome,
and come back Saint Peter.
Benedicite!   *[Exit.*

(A pause. Then enter BARTO-
    LOMÉ *wildly, as if in pursuit,*
    with a carbine in his hand.)

Bartolom. They passed this way!
    I hear their horses' hoofs!
Yonder I see them! Come, sweet
    caramillo,
This serenade shall be the Gypsy's
    last!

(Fires down the pass.)

Ha! ha! Well whistled, my sweet
    caramillo!
Well whistled!—I have missed her!
    —O, my God!

(The shot is returned. BARTOLOMÉ
    falls.)

THE BELFRY OF BRUGES AND OTHER POEMS

1846

CARILLON

In the ancient town of Bruges,
In the quaint old Flemish city,
As the evening shades descended,
Low and loud and sweetly blended,
Low at times, and loud at times,
And changing like a poet's rhymes,
Rang the beautiful wild chimes
From the Belfry in the market
Of the ancient town of Bruges.

Then, with deep sonorous clangour
Calmly answering their sweet anger,
When the wrangling bells had
  ended,
Slowly struck the clock eleven,
And, from out the silent heaven,
Silence on the town descended.
Silence, silence everywhere,
On the earth and in the air,
Save that footsteps here and there
Of some burgher home returning,
By the street lamps faintly burn-
  ing,
For a moment woke the echoes
Of the ancient town of Bruges.

But amid my broken slumbers
Still I heard those magic numbers,
As they loud proclaimed the flight
And stolen marches of the night;
Till their chimes in sweet collision
Mingled with each wandering
  vision,
Mingled with the fortune-telling
Gypsy-bands of dreams and fan-
  cies,
Which amid the waste expanses

Of the silent land of trances
Have their solitary dwelling.
All else seemed asleep in Bruges,
In the quaint old Flemish city.
And I thought how like these
  chimes
Are the poet's airy rhymes,
All his rhymes and roundelays,
His conceits, and songs, and ditties,
From the belfry of his brain,
Scattered downward, though in
  vain,
On the roofs and stones of cities!
For by night the drowsy ear
Under its curtains cannot hear,
And by day men go their ways,
Hearing the music as they pass,
But deeming it no more, alas!
Than the hollow sound of brass.

Yet, perchance a sleepless wight,
Lodging at some humble inn
In the narrow lanes of life,
When the dusk and hush of night
Shut out the incessant din
Of daylight and its toil and strife,
May listen with a calm delight
To the poet's melodies,
Till he hears, or dreams he hears,
Intermingled with the song,
Thoughts that he has cherished
  long;
Hears amid the chime and singing
The bells of his own village ringing,
And wakes, and finds his slumber-
  ous eyes
Wet with most delicious tears.

Thus dreamed I, as by night I lay

In Bruges, at the Fleur-de-Blé.
Listening with a wild delight
To the chimes that, through the
   night
Rang their changes from the Belfry
Of that quaint old Flemish city.

THE BELFRY OF BRUGES

In the market-place of Bruges
   stands the belfry old and brown;
Thrice consumed and thrice re-
   builded, still it watches o'er the
   town.

As the summer morn was breaking,
   on that lofty tower I stood,
And the world threw off the dark-
   ness, like the weeds of widow-
   hood.

Thick with towns and hamlets
   studded, and with streams and
   vapours gray,
Like a shield embossed with silver,
   round and vast the landscape lay.

At my feet the city slumbered.
   From its chimneys, here and
   there,
Wreaths of snow-white smoke, as-
   cending, vanished, ghost-like,
   into air.

Not a sound rose from the city at
   that early morning hour,
But I heard a heart of iron beating
   in the ancient tower.

From their nests beneath the
   rafters sang the swallows wild
   and high;
And the world, beneath me sleep-
   ing, seemed more distant than
   the sky.

Then most musical and solemn,
   bringing back the olden times,

With their strange, unearthly
   changes rang the melancholy
   chimes,

Like the psalms from some old
   cloister, when the nuns sing in
   the choir;
And the great bell tolled among
   them, like the chanting of a
   friar.

Visions of the days departed,
   shadowy phantoms filled my
   brain;
They who live in history only
   seemed to walk the earth again;

All the Foresters of Flanders,[1]—
   mighty Baldwin Bras de Fer,
Lyderick du Bucq and Cressy,
   Philip, Guy de Dampierre.

I beheld the pageants splendid,
   that adorned those days of old;

[1] *All the Foresters of Flanders.* The title of Foresters was given to the early governors of Flanders, appointed by the kings of France. Lyderick du Bucq, in the days of Clotaire the Second, was the first of them; and Beaudoin Bras-de-Fer, who stole away the fair Judith, daughter of Charles the Bald, from the French court, and married her in Bruges, was the last. After him, the title of Forester was changed to that of Count. Philippe d'Alsace, Guy de Dampierre, and Louis de Crécy, coming later in the order of time, were therefore rather Counts than Foresters. Philippe went twice to the Holy Land as a Crusader, and died of the plague at St. Jean-d'Acre shortly after the capture of the city by the Christians. Guy de Dampierre died in the prison of Compiègne. Louis de Crécy was son and successor of Robert de Béthune, who strangled his wife, Yolande de Bourgogne, with the bridle of his horse, for having poisoned, at the age of eleven years, Charles, his son by his first wife, Blanche d'Anjou.

Stately dames, like queens at-
tended,[1] knights who bore the
Fleece of Gold; [2]

Lombard and Venetian merchants
with deep-laden argosies;
Ministers from twenty nations;
more than royal pomp and ease.

I beheld proud Maximilian, kneel-
ing humbly on the ground;
I beheld the gentle Mary,[3] hunting
with her hawk and hound;

And her lighted bridal-chamber,
where a duke slept with the
queen,
And the armed guard around them,
and the sword unsheathed be-
tween.

I beheld the Flemish weavers, with
Namur and Juliers bold,
Marching homeward from the
bloody battle of the Spurs of
Gold; [4]

[1] *Stately dames likes queens attended.*
When Phillippe-le-Bel, king of France,
visited Flanders with his queen, she
was so astonished at the magnificence
of the dames of Bruges, that she
exclaimed, " Je croyais être seule
reine ici, mais il paraît que ceux de
Flandre qui se trouvent dans nos
prisons sont tous des princes, car leur
femmes sont habillées comme des
princesses et des reines."

When the burgomasters of Ghent,
Bruges, and Ypres went to Paris to
pay homage to King John, in 1351,
they were received with great pomp
and distinction; but, being invited
to a festival, they observed that their
seats at table were not furnished with
cushions; whereupon, to make known
their displeasure at this want of regard
to their dignity, they folded their
richly embroidered cloaks and seated
themselves upon them. On rising
from table, they left their cloaks
behind them, and, being informed
of their apparent forgetfulness, Simon
van Eertrycke, burgomaster of Bruges,
replied, " We Flemings are not in the
habit of carrying away our cushions
after dinner."

[2] *Knights who bore the Fleece of Gold.*
Philippe de Bourgogne, surnamed Le
Bon, espoused Isabella of Portugal on
the 10th of January, 1430, and on the
same day instituted the famous order
of the Fleece of Gold.

[3] *I beheld the gentle Mary.* Marie de
Valois, Duchess of Burgundy, was left
by the death of her father, Charles-le-
Téméraire, at the age of twenty, the
richest heiress of Europe. She came
to Bruges, as Countess of Flanders,
in 1477, and in the same year was
married by proxy to the Archduke
Maximilian. According to the custom
of the time, the Duke of Bavaria,
Maximilian's substitute, slept with
the princess. They were both in
complete dress, separated by a naked
sword, and attended by four armed
guards. Marie was adored by her
subjects for her gentleness and her
many other virtues.

Maximilian was son of the Emperor
Frederick the Third, and is the same
person mentioned afterwards in the
poem of *Nuremberg* as the Kaiser
Maximilian, and the hero of Pfinzing's
poem of *Teuerdank.* Having been
imprisoned by the revolted burghers
of Bruges, they refused to release him
till he consented to kneel in the public
square, and to swear on the Holy
Evangelists and the body of Saint
Donatus that he would not take
vengeance upon them for their re-
bellion.

[4] *The bloody battle of the Spurs of
Gold.* This battle, the most memor-
able in Flemish history, was fought
under the walls of Courtray, on the
11th of July, 1302, between the French
and the Flemings, the former com-
manded by Robert, Comte d'Artois,
and the latter by Guillaume de Juliers,
and Jean, Comte de Namur. The
French army was completely routed,
with a loss of twenty thousand in-
fantry and seven thousand cavalry;
among whom were sixty-three princes,
dukes, and counts, seven hundred
lords-banneret, and eleven hundred
noblemen. The flower of the French
nobility perished on that day, to
which history has given the name
of the *Journée des Éperons d'Or,* from
the great number of golden spurs

Saw the fight at Minnewater,[1] saw
   the White Hoods moving west,
Saw great Artevelde victorious
   scale the Golden Dragon's nest.[2]

found on the field of battle. Seven
hundred of them were hung up as a
trophy in the church of Notre Dame
de Courtray; and, as the cavaliers
of that day wore but a single spur
each, these vouched to God for the
violent and bloody death of seven
hundred of his creatures.

[1] *Saw the fight at Minnewater.*
When the inhabitants of Bruges were
digging a canal at Minnewater, to
bring the waters of the Lys from
Deynze to their city, they were
attacked and routed by the citizens
of Ghent, whose commerce would
have been much injured by the canal.
They were led by Jean Lyons, captain
of a military company at Ghent,
called the *Chapperons Blancs.* He
had great sway over the turbulent
populace, who, in those prosperous
times of the city, gained an easy
livelihood by labouring two or three
days in the week, and had the remain-
ing four or five to devote to public
affairs. The fight at Minnewater was
followed by open rebellion against
Louis de Maele, the Count of Flanders
and Protector of Bruges. His superb
château of Wondelghem was pillaged
and burnt; and the insurgents forced
the gates of Bruges, and entered in
triumph, with Lyons mounted at
their head. A few days afterwards
he died suddenly, perhaps by poison.
Meanwhile the insurgents received
a check at the village of Nevèle;
and two hundred of them perished
in the church, which was burned by
the Count's orders. One of the chiefs,
Jean de Lannoy, took refuge in the
belfry. From the summit of the
tower he held forth his purse filled
with gold, and begged for deliverance.
It was in vain. His enemies cried to
him from below to save himself as best
he might; and, half suffocated with
smoke and flame, he threw himself
from the tower and perished at their
feet. Peace was soon afterwards
established, and the Count retired
to faithful Bruges.

[2] *The Golden Dragon's nest.* The
golden Dragon, taken from the church

And again the whiskered Spaniard
   all the land with terror smote;
And again the wild alarum sounded
   from the tocsin's throat;

Till the bell of Ghent responded
   o'er lagoon and dike of sand,
"I am Roland! I am Roland!
   there is victory in the land!"

Then the sound of drums aroused
   me. The awakened city's roar
Chased the phantoms I had sum-
   moned back into their graves
   once more.

Hours had passed away like min-
   utes; and, before I was aware,
Lo! the shadow of the belfry
   crossed the sun-illumined square.

A GLEAM OF SUNSHINE

This is the place. Stand still, my
   steed,
   Let me review the scene,
And summon from the shadowy
   Past
   The forms that once have been.

The Past and Present here unite
   Beneath Time's flowing tide
Like footprints hidden by a brook,
   But seen on either side.

Here runs the highway to the town;
   There the green lane descends,

of St. Sophia, at Constantinople, in
one of the Crusades, and placed
on the belfry of Bruges, was after-
wards transported to Ghent by Philip
van Artevelde, and still adorns the
belfry of that city.

The inscription on the alarm-bell at
Ghent is, "*Mynen naem is Roland;
als ik klep is er brand, and als ik luy
is er victorie in het land.*" My name
is Roland; when I toll there is fire,
and when I ring there is victory in
the land.

Through which I walked to church
with thee,
O gentlest of my friends!

The shadow of the linden-trees
Lay moving on the grass;
Between them and the moving
boughs,
A shadow, thou didst pass.

Thy dress was like the lilies,
And thy heart as pure as they;
One of God's holy messengers
Did walk with me that day.

I saw the branches of the trees
Bend down thy touch to meet,
The clover-blossoms in the grass
Rise up to kiss thy feet.

" Sleep, sleep to-day, tormenting
cares,
Of earth and folly born! "
Solemnly sang the village choir
On that sweet Sabbath morn,

Through the closed blinds the
golden sun
Poured in a dusty beam,
Like the celestial ladder seen,
By Jacob in his dream.

And ever and anon, the wind,
Sweet-scented with the hay,
Turned o'er the hymn-book's
fluttering leaves
That on the window lay.

Long was the good man's sermon,
Yet it seemed not so to me;
For he spake of Ruth the beautiful,
And still I thought of thee.

Long was the prayer he uttered,
Yet it seemed not so to me;
For in my heart I prayed with him,
And still I thought of thee.

But now, alas! the place seems
changed;
Thou art no longer here;

Part of the sunshine of the scene
With thee did disappear.

Though thoughts, deep-rooted in
my heart,
Like pine-trees dark and high,
Subdue the light of noon, and
breathe
A low and ceaseless sigh;

This memory brightens o'er the
past,
As when the sun, concealed
Behind some cloud that near us
hangs,
Shines on a distant field.

THE ARSENAL AT SPRING-FIELD

This is the Arsenal.   From floor to
ceiling,
Like a huge organ, rise the bur-
nished arms;
But from their silent pipes no
anthem pealing
Startles the villages with strange
alarms.

Ah! what a sound will rise, how
wild and dreary,
When the death-angel touches
those swift keys!
What loud lament and dismal Mis-
erere
Will mingle with their awful
symphonies!

I hear even now the infinite fierce
chorus,
The cries of agony, the endless
groan,
Which, through the ages that have
gone before us,
In long reverberations reach our
own.

On helm and harness rings the
Saxon hammer,
Through Cimbric forest roars the
Norseman's song,
And loud, amid the universal
clamour,
O'er distant deserts sounds the
Tartar gong.

I hear the Florentine, who from his
palace
Wheels out his battle-bell with
dreadful din,
And Aztec priests upon their teo-
callis
Beat the wild war-drums made
of serpent's skin;

The tumult of each sacked and
burning village;
The shout that every prayer for
mercy drowns;
The soldiers' revels in the midst of
pillage;
The wail of famine in be-
leaguered towns;

The bursting shell, the gateway
wrenched asunder,
The rattling musketry, the clash-
ing blade;
And ever and anon, in tones of
thunder,
The diapason of the cannonade.

Is it, O man, with such discordant
noises,
With such accursed instruments
as these,
Thou drownest Nature's sweet and
kindly voices,
And jarrest the celestial har-
monies?

Were half the power, that fills the
world with terror,
Were half the wealth, bestowed
on camps and courts,

Given to redeem the human mind
from error,
There were no need of arsenals
nor forts:

The warrior's name would be a
name abhorred!
And every nation, that should
lift again
Its hand against a brother, on its
forehead
Would wear for evermore the
curse of Cain!

Down the dark future, through
long generations,
The echoing sounds grow fainter
and then cease;
And like a bell, with solemn,
sweet vibrations,
I hear once more the voice of
Christ say, " Peace! "

Peace! and no longer from its
brazen portals
The blast of War's great organ
shakes the skies!
But beautiful as songs of the im-
mortals,
The holy melodies of love arise.

THE NORMAN BARON

Dans les moments de la vie où la
réflexion devient plus calme et
plus profonde, où l'intérêt et
l'avarice parlent moins haut que
la raison, dans les instants de
chagrin domestique, de maladie, et
de péril de mort, les nobles se re-
pentirent de posséder des serfs,
comme d'une chose peu agréable
à Dieu, qui avait créé tous les
hommes à son image.—THIERRY:
CONQUETE DE L'ANGLETERRE.

In his chamber, weak and dying,
Was the Norman baron lying;
Loud, without, the tempest thun-
dered,
And the castle turret shook.

In this fight was Death the gainer,
Spite of vassal and retainer,
And the lands his sires had plun-
    dered,
        Written in the Doomsday
        Book.

By his bed a monk was seated,
Who in humble voice repeated
Many a prayer and pater-noster,
        From the missal on his knee;

And, amid the tempest pealing,
Sounds of bells came faintly steal-
    ing,
Bells, that, from the neighbouring
    kloster,
        Rang for the Nativity.

In the hall, the serf and vassal
Held, that night, their Christmas
    wassail;
Many a carol, old and saintly,
        Sang the minstrels and the
        waifs.

And so loud these Saxon gleemen
Sang to slaves the songs of free-
    men,
That the storm was heard but
    faintly,
        Knocking at the castle gates.

Till at length the lays they chaunted
Reached the chamber terror-
    haunted,
Where the monk, with accents holy,
        Whispered at the baron's ear.

Tears upon his eyelids glistened,
As he paused awhile and listened,
And the dying baron slowly
        Turned his weary head to hear.

" Wassail for the kingly stranger
Born and cradled in a manger!
King, like David, priest, like
    Aaron,
        Christ is born to set us free! "

And the lightning showed the
    sainted
Figures on the casement painted,
And exclaimed the shuddering
    baron,
        " Miserere, Domine! "

In that hour of deep contrition,
He beheld, with clearer vision,
Through all outward show and
    fashion,
        Justice, the Avenger, rise.

All the pomp of earth had
    vanished,
Falsehood and deceit were ban-
    ished,
Reason spake more loud than pas-
    sion,
        And the truth wore no dis-
        guise.

Every vassal of his banner,
Every serf born to their manor,
All those wronged and wretched
    creatures,
        By his hand were freed again.

And, as on the sacred missal
He recorded their dismissal,
Death relaxed his iron features,
        And the monk replied,
        " Amen! "

Many centuries have been num-
    bered
Since in death the baron slumbered
By the convent's sculptured
    portal,
        Mingling with the common
        dust:

But the good deed, through the
    ages
Living in historic pages,
Brighter grows and gleams im-
    mortal,
        Unconsumed by moth or
        rust.

RAIN IN SUMMER

How beautiful is the rain!
After the dust and heat,
In the broad and fiery street,
In the narrow lane,
How beautiful is the rain!

How it clatters along the roofs,
Like the tramp of hoofs!
How it gushes and struggles out
From the throat of the overflowing
spout!
Across the window pane
It pours and pours;
And swift and wide,
With a muddy tide,
Like a river down the gutter roars
The rain, the welcome rain!

The sick man from his chamber
looks
At the twisted brooks;
He can feel the cool
Breath of each little pool;
His fevered brain
Grows calm again,
And he breathes a blessing on the
rain.

From the neighbouring school
Come the boys,
With more than their wonted noise
And commotion;
And down the wet streets
Sail their mimic fleets,
Till the treacherous pool
Engulfs them in its whirling
And turbulent ocean.

In the country, on every side,
Where far and wide,
Like a leopard's tawny and
spotted hide,
Stretches the plain,
To the dry grass and the drier
grain
How welcome is the rain!

In the furrowed land
The toilsome and patient oxen
stand;
Lifting the yoke-encumbered head,
With their dilated nostrils spread,
They silently inhale
The clover-scented gale,
And the vapours that arise
From the well-watered and smok-
ing soil;
For this rest in the furrow after
toil
Their large and lustrous eyes
Seem to thank the Lord,
More than man's spoken word.

Near at hand,
From under the sheltering trees,
The farmer sees
His pastures, and his fields of grain,
As they bend their tops
To the numberless beating drops
Of the incessant rain.
He counts it as no sin
That he sees therein
Only his own thrift and gain.

These, and far more than these,
The Poet sees!
He can behold
Aquarius old
Walking the fenceless fields of air;
And from each ample fold
Of the clouds about him rolled
Scattering everywhere
The showery rain,
As the farmer scatters his grain.

He can behold
Things manifold
That have not yet been wholly told,
Have not been wholly sung nor
said.
For his thought, that never stops,
Follows the water-drops
Down to the graves of the dead,
Down through chasms and gulfs
profound,
To the dreary fountain-head

Of lakes and rivers under ground;
And sees them, when the rain is
done,
On the bridge of colours seven
Climbing up once more to heaven,
Opposite the setting sun.

Thus the Seer,
With vision clear,
Sees forms appear and disappear,
In the perpetual round of strange,
Mysterious change
From birth to death, from death to
birth,
From earth to heaven, from heaven
to earth;
Till glimpses more sublime
Of things, unseen before,
Unto his wondering eyes reveal
The Universe, as an immeasurable
wheel
Turning for evermore
In the rapid and rushing river of
Time.

TO A CHILD

Dear child! how radiant on thy
mother's knee,
With merry-making eyes and
jocund smiles,
Thou gazest at the painted tiles,
Whose figures grace,
With many a grotesque form and
face,
The ancient chimney of thy
nursery!
The lady, with the gay macaw,
The dancing girl, the grave bashaw
With bearded lip and chin;
And, leaning idly o'er his gate,
Beneath the imperial fan of state,
The Chinese mandarin.

With what a look of proud com-
mand
Thou shakest in thy little hand

The coral rattle with its silver bells,
Making a merry tune!
Thousands of years in Indian seas
That coral grew, by slow degrees,
Until some deadly and wild mon-
soon
Dashed it on Coromandel's sand!
Those silver bells
Reposed of yore,
As shapeless ore,
Far down in the deep sunken wells
Of darksome mines,
In some obscure and sunless place,
Beneath huge Chimborazo's base,
Or Potosi's o'erhanging pines!

And thus for thee, O little child,
Through many a danger and
escape,
The tall ships passed the stormy
cape;
For thee in foreign lands remote,
Beneath the burning, tropic clime,
The Indian peasant, chasing the
wild goat,
Himself as swift and wild,
In falling, clutched the frail arbute,
The fibres of whose shallow root,
Uplifted from the soil, betrayed
The silver veins beneath it laid,
The buried treasures of the pirate,
Time.

But, lo, thy door is left ajar!
Thou hearest footsteps from afar!
And, at the sound,
Thou turnest round
With quick and questioning eyes,
Like one, who, in a foreign land,
Beholds on every hand
Some source of wonder and sur-
prise!
And, restlessly, impatiently,
Thou strivest, strugglest, to be
free.
The four walls of thy nursery
Are now like prison walls to thee.
No more thy mother's smiles,
No more the painted tiles,

Delight thee, nor the playthings on
the floor,
That won thy little, beating heart
before;
Thou strugglest for the open door.

Through these once solitary halls
Thy pattering footstep falls.
The sound of thy merry voice
Makes the old walls
Jubilant, and they rejoice
With the joy of thy young heart,
O'er the light of whose gladness
No shadows of sadness
From the sombre background of
memory start.

Once, ah, once, within these walls,
One whom memory oft recalls,
The Father of his Country, dwelt.
And yonder meadows broad and
damp
The fires of the besieging camp
Encircled with a burning belt.
Up and down these echoing stairs,
Heavy with the weight of cares,
Sounded his majestic tread;
Yes, within this very room
Sat he in those hours of gloom,
Weary both in heart and head.

But what are these grave thoughts
to thee?
Out, out! into the open air!
Thy only dream is liberty,
Thou carest little how or where.
I see thee eager at thy play,
Now shouting to the apples on the
tree
With cheeks as round and red as
they;
And now among the yellow stalks,
Among the flowering shrubs and
plants,
As restless as the bee,
Along the garden walks,
The tracks of thy small carriage-
wheels I trace;
And see at every turn how they
efface
Whole villages of sand-roofed tents,

That rise like golden domes
Above the cavernous and secret
homes
Of wandering and nomadic tribes
of ants.
Ah, cruel little Tamerlane,
Who, with thy dreadful reign,
Dost persecute and overwhelm
These hapless Troglodytes of thy
realm!

What! tired already! with those
suppliant looks,
And voice more beautiful than a
poet's books,
Or murmuring sound of water as it
flows,
Thou comest back to parley with
repose!
This rustic seat in the old apple-
tree,
With its o'erhanging golden canopy
Of leaves illuminate with autumnal
hues,
And shining with the argent light
of dews,
Shall for a season be our place of
rest.
Beneath us, like an oriole's pendent
nest,
From which the laughing birds
have taken wing,
By thee abandoned, hangs thy
vacant swing.
Dream-like the waters of the river
gleam;
A sailless vessel drops adown the
stream,
And like it, to a sea as wide and
deep,
Thou driftest gently down the
tides of sleep.

O child! O new-born denizen
Of life's great city! on thy head
The glory of the morn is shed,
Like a celestial benison!
Here at the portal thou dost stand,
And with thy little hand
Thou openest the mysterious gate

Into the future's undiscovered land.
I see its valves expand,
As at the touch of Fate!
Into those realms of love and hate,
Into that darkness blank and drear,
By some prophetic feeling taught,
I launch the bold, adventurous
    thought,
Freighted with hope and fear;
As upon subterranean streams,
In caverns unexplored and dark,
Men sometimes launch a fragile
    bark,
Laden with flickering fire,
And watch its swift-receding beams,
Until at length they disappear,
And in the distant dark expire.

By what astrology of fear or hope
Dare I to cast thy horoscope;
Like the new moon thy life ap-
    pears;
A little strip of silver light,
And widening outward into night
The shadowy disk of future years;
And yet upon its outer rim,
A luminous circle, faint and dim,
And scarcely visible to us here,
Rounds and completes the perfect
    sphere;
A prophecy and intimation,
A pale and feeble adumbration,
Of the great world of light that
    lies
Behind all human destinies.

Ah! if thy fate, with anguish
    fraught,
Should be to wet the dusty soil
With the hot tears and sweat of
    toil,—
To struggle with imperious thought,
Until the overburdened brain,
Weary with labour, faint with pain,
Like a jarred pendulum, retain
Only its motion, not its power,—
Remember, in that perilous hour,
When most afflicted and opprest,
From labour there shall come
    forth rest.

And if a more auspicious fate
On thy advancing steps await,
Still let it ever be thy pride
To linger by the labourer's side;
With words of sympathy or song
To cheer the dreary march along
Of the great army of the poor,
O'er desert sand, o'er dangerous
    moor.
Nor to thyself the task shall be
Without reward; for thou shalt
    learn
The wisdom early to discern,
True beauty in utility;
As great Pythagoras of yore,
Standing beside the blacksmith's
    door,
And hearing the hammers, as they
    smote
The anvils with a different note,
Stole from the varying tones, that
    hung
Vibrant on every iron tongue,
The secret of the sounding wire,
And formed the seven-chorded lyre.

Enough! I will not play the Seer;
I will no longer strive to ope
The mystic volume, where appear
The herald Hope, forerunning
    Fear,
And Fear, the pursuivant of Hope,
Thy destiny remains untold;
For, like Acestes' shaft of old,
The swift thought kindles as it flies,
And burns to ashes in the skies.

THE OCCULTATION OF ORION [1]

I saw, as in a dream sublime,
The balance in the hand of Time.

[1] *The Occultation of Orion.* Astro-
nomically speaking, this title is in-
correct: as I apply to a constellation
what can properly be applied to some
of its stars only. But my observa-
tion is made from the hill of song, and
not from that of science; and will, I
trust, be found sufficiently accurate
for the present purpose.

O'er East and West its beam im-
pended;
And day, with all its hours of light,
Was slowly sinking out of sight,
While, opposite, the scale of night
Silently with the stars ascended.

Like the astrologers of eld,
In that bright vision I beheld
Greater and deeper mysteries.
I saw, with its celestial keys,
Its chords of air, its frets of fire,
The Samian's great Æolian lyre,
Rising through all its sevenfold
bars,
From earth unto the fixed stars.
And through the dewy atmos[here,
Not only could I see, but hear,
Its wondrous and harmonious
strings,
In sweet vibration, sphere by
sphere,
From Dian's circle light and near,
Onward to vaster and wider rings,
Where, chanting through his beard
of snows,
Majestic, mournful, Saturn goes,
And down the sunless realms of
space
Reverberates the thunder of his
bass.

Beneath the sky's triumphal arch
This music sounded like a march,
And with its chorus seemed to be
Preluding some great tragedy.
Sirius was rising in the east;
And, slow ascending one by one,
The kindling constellation shone.
Begirt with many a blazing star,
Stood the great giant Algebar.
Orion, hunter of the beast!
His sword hung gleaming by his
side,
And, on his arm, the lion's hide
Scattered across the midnight air
The golden radiance of its hair.

The moon was pallid, but not faint,
And beautiful as some fair saint,

Serenely moving on her way
In hours of trial and dismay.
As if she heard the voice of God,
Unharmed with naked feet she trod
Upon the hot and burning stars,
As on the glowing coals and bars
That were to prove her strength,
and try
Her holiness and her purity.

Thus moving on, with silent pace,
And triumph in her sweet, pale
face,
She reached the station of Orion.
Aghast he stood in strange alarm!
And suddenly from his out-
stretched arm
Down fell the red skin of the lion
Into the river at his feet.
His mighty club no longer beat
The forehead of the bull; but he
Reeled as of yore beside the sea,
When, blinded by Œnopion,
He sought the blacksmith at his
forge,
And, climbing up the mountain
gorge,
Fixed his black eyes upon the sun.
Then, through the silence over-
head,
An angel with a trumpet said,
" For evermore, for evermore,
The reign of violence is o'er! "
And, like an instrument that flings
Its music on another's strings,
The trumpet of the angel cast
Upon the heavenly lyre its blast,
And on from sphere to sphere the
words
Re - echoed down the burning
chords,—
" For evermore, for evermore,
The reign of violence is o'er! "

THE BRIDGE

I stood on the bridge at midnight,
   As the clocks were striking the
   hour,

And the moon rose o'er the city,
   Behind the dark church-tower.

I saw her bright reflection
   In the waters under me,
Like a golden goblet falling
   And sinking into the sea.

And far in the hazy distance
   Of that lovely night in June,
The blaze of the flaming furnace
   Gleamed redder than the moon.

Among the long, black rafters
   The waving shadows lay,
And the current that came from
   the ocean
Seemed to lift and bear them
   away;

As, sweeping and eddying through
   them,
Rose the belated tide,
And, streaming into the moon-
   light,
The seaweed floated wide.

And like those waters rushing
   Among the wooden piers,
A flood of thoughts came o'er me
   That filled my eyes with tears.

How often, O, how often,
   In the days that had gone by,
I had stood on that bridge at mid-
   night,
   And gazed on that wave and sky!

How often, O, how often,
   I had wished that the ebbing tide
Would bear me away on its bosom
   O'er the ocean wild and wide!

For my heart was hot and restless,
   And my life was full of care,
And the burden laid upon me
   Seemed greater than I could bear.

But now it has fallen from me,
   It is buried in the sea;
And only the sorrow of others
   Throws its shadow over me.

Yet whenever I cross the river
   On its bridge with wooden piers,
Like the odour of brine from the
   ocean
   Comes the thought of other years.

And I think how many thousands
   Of care-encumbered men,
Each bearing his burden of sorrow,
   Have crossed the bridge since
   then.

I see the long procession
   Still passing to and fro,
The young heart hot and restless,
   And the old subdued and slow!

And for ever and for ever,
   As long as the river flows,
As long as the heart has passions,
   As long as life has woes;

The moon and its broken reflection
   And its shadows shall appear,
As the symbol of love in heaven,
   And its waving image here.

TO THE DRIVING CLOUD

Gloomy and dark art thou, O chief
   of the mighty Omawhaws;
Gloomy and dark, as the driving
   cloud, whose name thou hast
   taken!
Wrapt in thy scarlet blanket, I see
   thee stalk through the city's
Narrow and populous streets, as
   once by the margin of rivers
Stalked those birds unknown, that
   have left us only their footprints.
What, in a few short years, will re-
   main of thy race but the foot-
   prints?

How canst thou walk in these
   streets, who hast trod in the
   green turf of the prairies?

How canst thou breathe in this air,
who hast breathed the sweet air
of the mountains?
Ah! 'tis in vain that with lordly
looks of disdain thou dost chal-
lenge
Looks of dislike in return, and
question these walls and these
pavements,
Claiming the soil for thy hunting-
grounds, while down-trodden
millions
Starve in the garrets of Europe, and
cry from its caverns that they,
too,
Have been created heirs of the
earth, and claim its division!

Back, then, back to thy woods in
the regions west of the Wabash!
There as a monarch thou reignest.
In autumn the leaves of the
maple
Pave the floors of thy palace-halls
with gold, and in summer
Pine-trees waft through its cham-
bers the odorous breath of their
branches.
There thou art strong and great, a
hero, a tamer of horses!
There thou chasest the stately stag
on the banks of the Elk-horn,
Or by the roar of the Running-
Water, or where the Omawhaw
Calls thee, and leaps through the
wild ravine like a brave of the
Blackfeet!

Hark! what murmurs arise from
the heart of those mountainous
deserts!
Is it the cry of the Foxes and
Crows, or the mighty Behemoth,
Who, unharmed, on his tusks once
caught the bolts of the thunder,
And now lurks in his lair to destroy
the race of the red man?
Far more fatal to thee and thy
race than the Crows and the
Foxes,
Far more fatal to thee and thy race
than the tread of Behemoth,
Lo! the big thunder-canoe, that
steadily breasts the Missouri's
Merciless current! and yonder, afar
on the prairies, the camp-fires
Gleam through the night, and the
cloud of dust in the gray of the
daybreak
Marks not the buffalo's track, nor
the Mandan's dexterous horse-
race;
It is a caravan, whitening the
desert where dwell the Caman-
ches!
Ha! how the breath of these
Saxons and Celts, like the blast
of the east-wind,
Drifts evermore to the west the
scanty smokes of thy wigwams!

SONGS

SEAWEED

When descends on the Atlantic
　　The gigantic
Storm-wind of the equinox,
Landward in his wrath he scourges
　　The toiling surges,
Laden with seaweed from the
　　rocks:

From Bermuda's reefs; from edges
　　Of sunken ledges,
In some far-off, bright Azore;
From Bahama, and the dashing,
　　Silver-flashing
Surges of San Salvador;

From the tumbling surf, that
　　buries
　　The Orkneyan skerries,
Answering the hoarse Hebrides;
And from wrecks of ships, and
　　drifting
　　Spars, uplifting
On the desolate, rainy seas;—

Ever drifting, drifting, drifting
　　On the shifting
Currents of the restless main;
Till in sheltered coves, and reaches
　　Of sandy beaches,
All have found repose again.

So when storms of wild emotion
　　Strike the ocean
Of the poet's soul, ere long
From each cave and rocky fastness
　　In its vastness,
Floats some fragment of a song:

From the far-off isles enchanted,
　　Heaven has planted

With the golden fruit of Truth;
From the flashing surf, whose
　　vision
　　Gleams Elysian
In the tropic clime of Youth;

From the strong Will, and the En-
　　deavour
　　That for ever
Wrestles with the tides of Fate;
From the wreck of Hopes far-
　　scattered,
　　Tempest-shattered,
Floating waste and desolate;—

Ever drifting, drifting, drifting
　　On the shifting
Currents of the restless heart;
Till at length in books recorded,
　　They, like hoarded
Household words, no more depart.

THE DAY IS DONE

The day is done, and the darkness
　　Falls from the wings of Night,
As a feather is wafted downward
　　From an eagle in his flight.

I see the lights of the village
　　Gleam through the rain and the
　　　mist,
And a feeling of sadness comes o'er
　　me,
　　That my soul cannot resist:

A feeling of sadness and longing,
　　That is not akin to pain,
And resembles sorrow only
　　As the mist resembles the rain.

Come, read to me some poem,
  Some simple and heartfelt lay,
That shall soothe this restless feel-
    ing,
  And banish the thoughts of day.

Not from the grand old masters,
  Not from the bards sublime,
Whose distant footsteps echo
  Through the corridors of Time.

For, like strains of martial music,
  Their mighty thoughts suggest
Life's endless toil and endeavour;
  And to-night I long for rest.

Read from some humbler poet,
  Whose songs gushed from his
    heart,
As showers from the clouds of
    summer,
  Or tears from the eyelids start;

Who, through long days of labour,
  And nights devoid of ease,
Still heard in his soul the music
  Of wonderful melodies.

Such songs have power to quiet
  The restless pulse of care,
And come like the benediction
  That follows after prayer.

Then read from the treasured
    volume
  The poem of thy choice,
And lend to the rhyme of the poet
  The beauty of thy voice.

And the night shall be filled with
    music,
  And the cares that infest the day,
Shall fold their tents, like the
    Arabs,
  And as silently, steal away.

AFTERNOON IN FEBRUARY

The day is ending,
  The night is descending;
The marsh is frozen,
    The river dead.

Through clouds like ashes
The red sun flashes
On village windows
    That glimmer red.

The snow recommences;
The buried fences
Mark no longer
    The road o'er the plain;

While through the meadows,
Like fearful shadows,
Slowly passes
    A funeral train.

The bell is pealing,
And every feeling
Within me responds
    To the dismal knell;

Shadows are trailing,
My heart is bewailing
And toiling within
    Like a funeral bell.

TO AN OLD DANISH SONG-BOOK

Welcome, my old friend,
Welcome to a foreign fireside,
While the sullen gales of autumn
Shake the windows.

The ungrateful world
Has, it seems, dealt harshly with
    thee,
Since, beneath the skies of Den-
    mark,
First I met thee.

There are marks of age,
There are thumb-marks on thy
    margin,
Made by hands that clasped thee
    rudely,
At the alehouse.

Soiled and dull thou art;
Yellow are thy time-worn pages,
As the russet, rain-molested
Leaves of autumn.

Thou art stained with wine
Scattered from hilarious goblets,
As these leaves with the libations
Of Olympus.

Yet dost thou recall
Days departed, half-forgotten,
When in dreamy youth I wandered
By the Baltic,—

When I paused to hear
The old ballad of King Christian
Shouted from suburban taverns
In the twilight.

Thou recallest bards,
Who, in solitary chambers,
And with hearts by passion wasted,
Wrote thy pages.

Thou recallest homes
Where thy songs of love and friend-
ship
Made the gloomy Northern winter
Bright as summer.

Once some ancient Scald,
In his bleak, ancestral Iceland,
Chanted staves of these old ballads
To the Vikings.

Once in Elsinore,
At the court of old King Hamlet,
Yorick and his boon companions
Sang these ditties.

Once Prince Frederick's Guard
Sang them in their smoky bar-
racks;
Suddenly the English cannon
Joined the chorus!

Peasants in the field,
Sailors on the roaring ocean,
Students, tradesmen, pale me-
chanics,
All have sung them.

Thou hast been their friend;
They, alas! have left thee friend-
less!
Yet at least by one warm fireside
Art thou welcome.

And, as swallows build
In these wide, old-fashioned
chimneys,
So thy twittering songs shall nestle
In my bosom,—

Quiet, close, and warm,
Sheltered from all molestation,
And recalling by their voices
Youth and travel.

WALTER VON DER VOGEL-
WEID [1]

Vogelweid the Minnesinger,
  When he left this world of ours,
Laid his body in the cloister,
  Under Würtzburg's minster
    towers.

And he gave the monks his trea-
sures,
  Gave them all with this behest:
They should feed the birds at noon-
tide
  Daily on his place of rest;

Saying, " From these wandering
  minstrels
I have learned the art of song;
Let me now repay the lessons
  They have taught so well and
    long."

Thus the bard of love departed;
  And, fulfilling his desire,
On his tomb the birds were feasted
  By the children of the choir.

Day by day, o'er tower and turret,
  In foul weather and in fair,
Day by day, in vaster numbers,
  Flocked the poets of the air.

[1] *Walter von der Vogelweid.* Walter
von der Vogelweid, or Bird-Meadow,
was one of the principal Minnesingers
of the thirteenth century. He
triumphed over Heinrich van Ofter-
dingen in that poetic contest at Wart-
burg Castle, known in literary history
as the War of Wartburg.

On the tree whose heavy branches
 Overshadowed all the place,
On the pavement, on the tomb-
  stone,
 On the poet's sculptured face.

On the cross-bars of each window,
 On the lintel of each door,
They renewed the War of Wart-
  burg,
 Which the bard had fought be-
  fore.

There they sang their merry carols,
 Sang their lauds on every side;
And the name their voices uttered
 Was the name of Vogelweid.

Till at length the portly abbot
 Murmured, " Why this waste of
  food ?
Be it changed to loaves hencefor-
  ward
 For our fasting brotherhood."

Then in vain o'er tower and turret,
 From the walls and woodland
  nests,
When the minster bells rang noon-
  tide,
 Gathered the unwelcome guests.

Then in vain, with cries discordant,
 Clamorous round the Gothic
  spire,
Screamed the feathered Minne-
  singers
 For the children of the choir.

Time has long effaced the inscrip-
  tions
 On the cloister's funeral stones,
And tradition only tells us
 Where repose the poet's bones.

But around the vast cathedral,
 By sweet echoes multiplied,
Still the birds repeat the legend,
 And the name of Vogelweid.

DRINKING SONG

INSCRIPTION FOR AN ANTIQUE PITCHER

Come, old friend! sit down and
  listen!
 From the pitcher, placed be-
  tween us,
How the waters laugh and glisten
 In the head of old Silenus!

Old Silenus, bloated, drunken,
 Led by his inebriate Satyrs;
On his breast his head is sunken,
 Vacantly he leers and chatters,

Fauns with youthful Bacchus fol-
  low;
 Ivy crowns that brow supernal
As the forehead of Apollo,
 And possessing youth eternal.

Round about him, fair Bacchantes,
 Bearing cymbals, flutes, and
  thyrses,
Wild from Naxian groves, or
  Zante's
 Vineyards, sing delirious verses.

Thus he won, through all the
  nations,
 Bloodless victories, and the
  farmer
Bore, as trophies and oblations,
 Vines for banners, ploughs for
  armour.

Judged by no o'erzealous rigour,
 Much this mystic throng ex-
  presses:
Bacchus was the type of vigour,
 And Silenus of excesses.

These are ancient ethnic revels,
 Of a faith long since forsaken;
Now the Satyrs, changed to devils,
 Frighten mortals wine-o'er-
  taken.

Now to rivulets from the moun-
      tains
   Point the rods of fortune-tellers;
Youth perpetual dwells in foun-
      tains,—
      Not in flasks, and casks, and
         cellars.

Claudius, though he sang of flagons
   And huge tankards filled with
      Rhenish,
From that fiery blood of dragons
   Never would his own replenish.

Even Redi, though he chaunted
   Bacchus in the Tuscan valleys,
Never drank the wine he vaunted
   In his dithyrambic sallies.

Then with water fill the pitcher
   Wreathed about with classic
      fables;
Ne'er Falernian threw a richer
   Light upon Lucullus' tables.

Come, old friend, sit down and
      listen!
   As it passes thus between us,
How its wavelets laugh and glis-
      ten
   In the head of old Silenus!

THE OLD CLOCK ON THE STAIRS

L'éternité est une pendule, dont le
   balancier dit et redit sans cesse
   ces deux mots seulement, dans le
   silence des tombeaux; "Toujours!
   jamais! Jamais! toujours!"
                JACQUES BRIDAINE.

Somewhat back from the village
   street
Stands the old-fashioned country-
   seat.
Across its antique portico
Tall poplar-trees their shadows
   throw.
And from its station in the hall

An ancient timepiece says to all,—
      "Forever—never!
      Never—forever!"

Halfway up the stairs it stands,
And points and beckons with its
   hands
From its case of massive oak,
Like a monk, who, under his cloak,
Crosses himself, and sighs, alas!
With sorrowful voice to all who
   pass,—
      "Forever—never!
      Never—forever!"

By day its voice is low and light;
But in the silent dead of night,
Distinct as a passing footstep's fall,
It echoes along the vacant hall,
Along the ceiling, along the floor,
And seems to say, at each chamber
   door,—
      "Forever—never!
      Never—forever!"

Through days of sorrow and of
   mirth,
Through days of death and days of
   birth,
Through every swift vicissitude
Of changeful time, unchanged it
   has stood,
And as if, like God, it all things
   saw,
It calmly repeats those words of
   awe,—
      "Forever—never!
      Never—forever!"

In that mansion used to be
Free-hearted Hospitality;
His great fires up the chimney
   roared;
The stranger feasted at his board;
But, like the skeleton at the feast,
That warning timepiece never
   ceased,—
      "Forever—never!
      Never—forever!"

There groups of merry children
    played,
There youth and maidens dream-
    ing strayed;
O precious hours! O golden prime,
And affluence of love and time!
Even as a miser counts his gold,
Those hours the ancient timepiece
    told,—
        " Forever—never!
            Never—forever! "

From that chamber, clothed in
    white,
The bride came forth on her wed-
    ding night;
There, in that silent room below,
The dead lay in his shroud of
    snow;
And in the hush that followed the
    prayer,
Was heard the old clock on the
    stair,—
        " Forever—never!
            Never—forever! "

All are scattered now and fled,
Some are married, some are dead;
And when I ask, with throbs of
    pain,
" Ah! when shall they all meet
    again ? "
As in the days long since gone
    by,

The ancient timepiece makes re-
    ply,—
        " Forever—never!
            Never—forever! "

Never here, forever there,
Where all parting, pain, and
    care,
And death, and time shall dis-
    appear,—
Forever there, but never here!
The horologe of Eternity
Sayeth this incessantly,—
        " Forever—never!
            Never—forever! "

THE ARROW AND THE SONG

I shot an arrow into the air,
It fell to earth, I knew not where;
For, so swiftly it flew, the sight
Could not follow it in its flight.

I breathed a song into the air,
It fell to earth, I knew not where;
For who has sight so keen and
    strong,
That it can follow the flight of song?

Long, long afterward, in an oak
I found the arrow, still unbroke;
And the song, from beginning to
    end,
I found again in the heart of a
    friend.

SONNETS

THE EVENING STAR

Lo! in the painted oriel of the
    West,
    Whose panes the sunken sun in-
        carnadines,
    Like a fair lady at her casement,
        shines
The evening star, the star of love
    and rest!

And then anon she doth herself
    divest
    Of all her radiant garments, and
        reclines
    Behind the sombre screen of
        yonder pines,
With slumber and soft dreams of
    love opprest.

O my beloved, my sweet Hes-
    perus!

My morning and my evening star
of love!
My best and gentlest lady! even
thus,
As that fair planet in the sky
above,
Dost thou retire unto thy rest at
night,
And from thy darkened window
fades the light.

AUTUMN

Thou comest, Autumn, heralded
by the rain,
With banners, by great gales
incessant fanned,
Brighter than brightest silks of
Samarcand,
And stately oxen harnessed to thy
wain!
Thou standest, like imperial Char-
lemagne,[1]
Upon thy bridge of gold; thy
royal hand
Outstretched with benedictions
o'er the land,
Blessing the farms through all thy
vast domain.

[1] *Like imperial Charlemagne.* Char-
lemagne may be called by pre-
eminence the monarch of farmers.
According to the German tradition,
in seasons of great abundance, his
spirit crosses the Rhine on a golden
bridge at Bingen, and blesses the
cornfields and the vineyards. During
his lifetime he did not disdain, says
Montesquieu, " to sell the eggs from
the farmyards of his domains and the
superfluous vegetables of his gardens;
while he distributed among his people
the wealth of the Lombards and the
immense treasures of the Huns."

Thy shield is the red harvest moon,
suspended
So long beneath the heaven's
o'erhanging eaves;
Thy steps are by the farmer's
prayers attended;
Like flames upon an altar shine
the sheaves;
And, following thee, in thy ovation
splendid,
Thine almoner, the wind, scatters
the golden leaves!

DANTE

Tuscan, that wanderest through
the realms of gloom,
With thoughtful pace, and sad,
majestic eyes,
Stern thoughts and awful from
thy soul arise,
Like Farinata from his fiery tomb.
Thy sacred song is like the trump
of doom;
Yet in thy heart what human
sympathies,
What soft compassion glows, as
in the skies
The tender stars their clouded
lamps relume!
Methinks I see thee stand, with
pallid cheeks,
By Fra Hilario in his diocese,
As up the convent-walls, in golden
streaks,
The ascending sunbeams mark
the day's decrease;
And, as he asks what there the
stranger seeks,
Thy voice along the cloister
whispers, " Peace! "

TRANSLATIONS

THE HEMLOCK TREE

FROM THE GERMAN

O HEMLOCK tree! O hemlock
   tree! how faithful are thy
   branches!
    Green not alone in summer
    time,
    But in the winter's frost and
    rime!
O hemlock tree! O hemlock tree!
   how   faithful   are   thy
   branches!

O maiden fair! O maiden fair!
   how faithless is thy bosom!
    To love me in prosperity,
    And leave me in adversity!
O maiden fair! O maiden fair!
   how faithless is thy bosom!

The nightingale, the nightingale,
   thou tak'st for thine ex-
   ample!
    So long as summer laughs she
    sings,
    But in the autumn spreads her
    wings.
The nightingale, the nightingale,
   thou tak'st for thine ex-
   ample!

The meadow brook, the meadow
   brook, is mirror of thy
   falsehood!
    It flows so long as falls the
    rain,
    In drought its springs soon
    dry again,
The meadow brook, the meadow
   brook, is mirror of thy
   falsehood!

ANNIE OF THARAW

FROM THE LOW GERMAN OF SIMON
DACH

Annie of Tharaw, my true love of
   old,
She is my life, and my goods, and
   my gold.

Annie of Tharaw, her heart once
   again
To me has surrendered in joy and
   in pain.

Annie of Tharaw, my riches, my
   good,
Thou, O my soul, my flesh and my
   blood!

Then come the wild weather, come
   sleet or come snow,
We will stand by each other, how-
   ever it blow.

Oppression, and sickness, and sor-
   row, and pain,
Shall be to our true love as links to
   the chain.

As the palm-tree standeth so
   straight and so tall,
The more the hail beats, and the
   more the rains fall,—

So love in our hearts shall grow
   mighty and strong,
Through crosses, through sorrows,
   through manifold wrong.

Shouldst thou be torn from me to
   wander alone
In a desolate land where the sun is
   scarce known,—

Through forests I'll follow, and
where the sea flows,
Through ice, and through iron,
through armies of foes.

Annie of Tharaw, my light and my
sun,
The threads of our two lives are
woven in one.

Whate'er I have bidden thee thou
hast obeyed,
Whatever forbidden thou hast not
gainsaid.

How in the turmoil of life can love
stand,
Where there is not one heart, and
one mouth, and one hand?

Some seek for dissension, and
trouble and strife;
Like a dog and a cat live such man
and wife.

Annie of Tharaw, such is not our
love;
Thou art my lambkin, my chick,
and my dove.

Whate'er my desire is, in thine may
be seen;
I am king of the household, and
thou art its queen.

It is this, O my Annie, my heart's
sweetest rest,
That makes of us twain but one
soul in one breast.

This turns to a heaven the hut
where we dwell;
While wrangling soon changes a
home to a hell.

THE STATUE OVER THE CATHEDRAL DOOR

FROM THE GERMAN OF JULIUS MOSEN

Forms of saints and kings are
standing
The cathedral door above;

Yet I saw but one among them
Who had soothed my soul with
love.

In his mantle,—wound about him,
As their robes the sowers wind,—
Bore he swallows and their fledg-
lings,
Flowers and weeds of every kind.

And so stands he calm and child-
like,
High in wind and tempest wild;
O, were I like him exalted,
I would be like him, a child!

And my songs,—green leaves and
blossoms,—
To the doors of heaven would
bear,
Calling, even in storm and tempest,
Round me still these birds of air.

THE LEGEND OF THE CROSS-BILL

FROM THE GERMAN OF JULIUS MOSEN

On the cross the dying Saviour
Heavenward lifts his eyelids
calm,
Feels, but scarcely feels, a trem-
bling
In his pierced and bleeding palm.

And by all the world forsaken,
Sees he how with zealous care
At the ruthless nail of iron
A little bird is striving there.

Stained with blood and never tiring,
With its beak it doth not cease,
From the cross 'twould free the
Saviour,
Its Creator's Son release.

And the Saviour speaks in mild-
ness:
" Blest be thou of all the good!
Bear, as token of this moment,
Marks of blood and holy rood! "

And that bird is called the cross-
    bill;
Covered all with blood so clear,
In the groves of pine it singeth
Songs, like legends, strange to
    hear.

THE SEA HATH ITS PEARLS

FROM THE GERMAN OF HEINRICH HEINE

The sea hath its pearls,
    The heaven hath its stars;
But my heart, my heart,
    My heart hath its love.

Great are the sea and the heaven;
    Yet greater is my heart,
And fairer than pearls and stars
    Flashes and beams my love.

Thou little, youthful maiden,
    Come unto my great heart;
My heart, and the sea, and the
    heaven
Are melting away with love!

POETIC APHORISMS

FROM THE SINNGEDICHTE OF FRIEDRICH VON LOGAU. SEVENTEENTH CENTURY

MONEY

Whereunto is money good?
Who has it not wants hardihood,
Who has it has much trouble and
    care,
Who once has had it has despair.

THE BEST MEDICINE

Joy and Temperance and Repose
Slam the door in the doctor's nose.

Man-like is it to fall into sin,
Fiend-like is it to dwell therein,
Christ-like is it for sin to grieve,
God-like is it all sin to leave.

POVERTY AND BLINDNESS

A blind man is a poor man, and
    blind a poor man is;
For the former seeth no man, and
    the latter no man sees.

LAW OF LIFE

Live I, so live I,
To my Lord heartily,
To my Prince faithfully,
To my neighbour honestly,
Die I, so die I.

CREEDS

Lutheran, Popish, Calvinistic, all
    these creeds and doctrines three
Extant are; but still the doubt is,
    where Christianity may be.

THE RESTLESS HEART

A millstone and the human heart
    are driven ever round;
If they have nothing else to grind,
    they must themselves be ground.

CHRISTIAN LOVE

Whilom Love was like a fire, and
    warmth and comfort it be-
    spoke;
But, alas! it now is quenched, and
    only bites us, like the smoke.

ART AND TACT

Intelligence and courtesy not al-
    ways are combined;
Often in a wooden house a golden
    room we find.

RETRIBUTION

Though the mills of God grind
    slowly, yet they grind exceeding
    small;
Though with patience he stands
    waiting, with exactness grinds
    he all.

TRUTH

When by night the frogs are croak-
   ing, kindle but a torch's fire,
Ha! how soon they all are silent!
   Thus Truth silences the liar.

RHYMES

If perhaps these rhymes of mine
should sound not well in stran-
   gers' ears,
They have only to bethink them
   that it happens so with theirs;
For so long as words, like mortals,
   call a fatherland their own,
They will be most highly valued
   where they are best and longest
   known.

CURFEW

I.

Solemnly, mournfully,
   Dealing its dole,
The Curfew Bell
   Is beginning to toll.

Cover the embers,
   And put out the light;
Toil comes with the morning
   And rest with the night.

Dark grow the windows,
   And quenched is the fire;
Sound fades into silence,—
   All footsteps retire.

No voice in the chambers,
   No sound in the hall!
Sleep and oblivion
   Reign over all!

II.

The book is completed,
   And closed, like the day;
And the hand that has written it
   Lays it away.

Dim grow its fancies;
   Forgotten they lie;
Like coals in the ashes,
   They darken and die.

Song sinks into silence,
   The story is told,
The windows are darkened,
   The hearth-stone is cold.

Dark and darker
   The black shadows fall;
Sleep and oblivion
   Reign over all.

THE SEASIDE AND THE FIRESIDE

1850

DEDICATION

As one who walking in the twilight
    gloom,
  Hears round about him voices as
    it darkens,
And seeing not the forms from
    which they come,
  Pauses from time to time, and
    turns and hearkens;

So walking here in twilight, O my
    friends!
  I hear your voices, softened by
    the distance,
And pause, and turn to listen, as
    each sends
  His words of friendship, com-
    fort, and assistance.

If any thought of mine, or sung or
    told,
  Has ever given delight or conso-
    lation,
Ye have repaid me back a thou-
    sand fold,
  By every friendly sign and salu-
    tation.

Thanks for the sympathies that ye
    have shown!
  Thanks for each kindly word,
    each silent token,
That teaches me, when seeming
    most alone,
  Friends are around us, though
    no word be spoken.

Kind messages, that pass from
    land to land;

Kind letters, that betray the
    heart's deep history,
  In which we feel the pressure of a
    hand,—
    One touch of fire,—and all the
      rest is mystery!

The pleasant books, that silently
    among
  Our household treasures take
    familiar places,
And are to us as if a living tongue
  Spake from the printed leaves or
    pictured faces;

Perhaps on earth I never shall
    behold,
  With eye of sense, your outward
    form and semblance;
Therefore to me ye never will grow
    old,
  But live for ever young in my
    remembrance.

Never grow old, nor change, nor
    pass away!
  Your gentle voices will flow on
    for ever,
When life grows bare and tarnished
    with decay,
  As through a leafless landscape
    flows a river.

Not chance of birth or place has
    made us friends,
  Being oftentimes of different
    tongues and nations,
But the endeavour for the self-
    same ends,
  With the same hopes, and fears,
    and aspirations.

333

Therefore I hope to join your sea-
      side walk,
      Saddened, and mostly silent,
            with emotion;
Not interrupting with intrusive
      talk
      The grand, majestic symphonies
            of ocean.

Therefore I hope, as no unwelcome
      guest,
      At your warm fireside, when the
            lamps are lighted,
To have my place reserved among
            the rest,
      Nor stand as one unsought and
            uninvited!

BY THE SEASIDE

THE BUILDING OF THE SHIP

" Build me straight, O worthy
      Master!
      Staunch and strong, a goodly
            vessel,
That shall laugh at all disaster,
      And with wave and whirlwind
            wrestle! "

The merchant's word
Delighted the Master heard;
For his heart was in his work, and
      the heart
Giveth grace unto every Art.
A quiet smile played round his lips,
As the eddies and dimples of the
      tide
Play round the bows of ships,
That steadily at anchor ride.
And with a voice that was full of
      glee,
He answered, " Ere long we will
      launch
A vessel as goodly, and strong, and
      staunch,
As ever weathered a wintry sea! "

And first with nicest skill and art,
Perfect and finished in every part,
A little model the Master wrought,
Which should be to the larger plan
What the child is to the man,
Its counterpart in miniature;
That with a hand more swift and
      sure
The greater labour might be
      brought

To answer to his inward thought.
And as he laboured, his mind ran
      o'er
The various ships that were built
      of yore,
And above them all, and strangest
      of all
Towered the Great Harry, crank
      and tall,
Whose picture was hanging on the
      wall,
With bows and stern raised high in
      air,
And balconies hanging here and
      there,
And signal lanterns and flags afloat,
And eight round towers, like those
      that frown
From some old castle, looking down
Upon the drawbridge and the moat.
And he said with a smile, " Our
      ship, I wis,
Shall be of another form than
      this! "

It was of another form, indeed;
Built for freight, and yet for speed,
A beautiful and gallant craft;
Broad in the beam, that the stress
      of the blast
Pressing down upon sail and mast,
Might not the sharp bows over-
      whelm;
Broad in the beam, but sloping aft
With graceful curve and slow de-
      grees,
That she might be docile to the
      helm

And that the currents of parted seas,
Closing behind, with mighty force,
Might aid and not impede her course.

In the shipyard stood the Master,
With the model of the vessel,
That should laugh at all disaster,
And with wave and whirlwind wrestle!

Covering many a rood of ground,
Lay the timber piled around;
Timber of chestnut and elm and oak,
And scattered here and there, with these,
The knarred and crooked cedar knees;
Brought from regions far away,
From Pascagoula's sunny bay,
And the banks of the roaring Roanoke!
Oh! what a wondrous thing it is
To note how many wheels of toil
One thought, one word, can set in motion!
There's not a ship that sails the ocean,
But every climate, every soil,
Must bring its tribute, great or small,
And help to build the wooden wall!

The sun was rising o'er the sea,
And long the level shadows lay,
As if they, too, the beams would be
Of some great, airy argosy,
Framed and launched in a single day.
That silent architect, the sun,
Had hewn and laid them every one,
Ere the work of man was yet begun.
Beside the Master, when he spoke,
A youth, against an anchor leaning
Listened, to catch his slightest meansng.

Only the long waves, as they broke
In ripples on the pebbly beach,
Interrupted the old man's speech.
Beautiful they were, in sooth,
The old man and the fiery youth!
The old man, in whose busy brain
Many a ship that sailed the main
Was modelled o'er and o'er again;—
The fiery youth, who was to be
The heir of his dexterity,
The heir of his house, and his daughter's hand,
When he had built and launched from land
What the elder head had planned.

"Thus," said he, "will we build this ship!
Lay square the blocks upon the slip,
And follow well this plan of mine.
Choose the timbers with greatest care;
Of all that is unsound beware;
For only what is sound and strong
To this vessel shall belong.
Cedar of Maine and Georgia pine
Here together shall combine.
A goodly frame, and a goodly fame,
And the UNION be her name!
For the day that gives her to the sea
Shall give my daughter unto thee!"
The Master's word
Enraptured the young man heard;
And as he turned his face aside,
With a look of joy and a thrill of pride
Standing before
Her father's door,
He saw the form of his promised bride.
The sun shone on her golden hair,
And her cheek was glowing fresh and fair,
With the breath of morn and the soft sea air.
Like a beauteous barge was she,

Still at rest on the sandy beach,
Just beyond the billow's reach;
But he
Was the restless, seething, stormy
sea!

Ah, how skilful grows the hand
That obeyeth Love's command!
It is the heart and not the brain,
That to the highest doth attain,
And he who followeth Love's be-
hest
Far exceedeth all the rest!
Thus with the rising of the sun
Was the noble task begun,
And soon throughout the ship-
yard's bounds
Were heard the intermingled
sounds
Of axes and of mallets, plied
With vigorous arms on every side;
Plied so deftly and so well,
That, ere the shadows of evening
fell,
The keel of oak for a noble ship,
Scarfed and bolted, straight and
strong,
Was lying ready, and stretched
along
The blocks, well placed upon the
slip.
Happy, thrice happy, every one
Who sees his labour well begun,
And not perplexed and multiplied,
By idly waiting for time and tide!

And when the hot, long day was
o'er,
The young man at the Master's
door
Sat with the maiden calm and still.
And within the porch, a little more
Removed beyond the evening chill,
The father sat, and told them tales
Of wrecks in the great September
gales,
Of pirates upon the Spanish Main,
And ships that never came back
again,

The chance and change of a sailor's
life,
Want and plenty, rest and strife,
His roving fancy, like the wind,
That nothing can stay and nothing
can bind,
And the magic charm of foreign
lands,
With shadows of palms, and shin-
ing sands,
Where the tumbling surf,
O'er the coral reefs of Madagascar,
Washes the feet of the swarthy
Lascar,
As he lies alone and asleep on the
turf.
And the trembling maiden held her
breath
At the tales of that awful, pitiless
sea,
With all its terror and mystery,
The dim, dark sea, so like unto
Death,
That divides and yet unites man-
kind!
And whenever the old man paused,
a gleam
From the bowl of his pipe would
awhile illume
The silent group in the twilight
gloom,
And thoughtful faces, as in a
dream;
And for a moment one might
mark
What had been hidden by the dark,
That the head of the maiden lay
at rest,
Tenderly, on the young man's
breast!

Day by day the vessel grew,
With timbers fashioned strong and
true,
Stemson and keelson and sternson-
knee,
Till, framed with perfect symme-
try,
A skeleton ship rose up to view!

All around the bows and along the side
The heavy hammers and mallets plied,
Till, after many a week, at length,
Wonderful for form and strength,
Sublime in its enormous bulk,
Loomed aloft the shadowy hulk!
And around it columns of smoke, upwreathing,
Rose from the boiling, bubbling, seething
Caldron, that glowed,
And overflowed
With the black tar, heated for the sheathing.
And amid the clamours
Of clattering hammers,
He who listened heard now and then
The song of the Master and his men:—

"Build me straight, O worthy Master,
    Staunch and strong, a goodly vessel,
That shall laugh at all disaster,
    And with wave and whirlwind wrestle!"

With oaken brace and copper band,
Lay the rudder on the sand,
That, like a thought, should have control
Over the movement of the whole;
And near it the anchor, whose giant hand
Would reach down and grapple with the land,
And immovable and fast
Hold the great ship against the bellowing blast!
And at the bows an image stood,
By a cunning artist carved in wood,
With robes of white, that far behind
Seemed to be fluttering in the wind.

It was not shaped in a classic mould,
Not like a Nymph or Goddess of old,
Or Naiad rising from the water,
But modelled from the Master's daughter!
On many a dreary and misty night,
'Twill be seen by the rays of the signal light,
Speeding along through the rain and the dark,
Like a ghost in its snow-white sark,
The pilot of some phantom bark,
Guiding the vessel, in its flight,
By a path none other knows aright!
Behold, at last.[1]
Each tall and tapering mast
Is swung into its place;
Shrouds and stays
Holding it firm and fast!

Long ago,
In the deer-haunted forests of Maine,
When upon mountain and plain

[1] *Behold, at last,*
Each tall and tapering mast
Is swung into its place.

I wish to anticipate a criticism on this passage by stating, that sometimes, though not usually, vessels are launched fully rigged and sparred. I have availed myself of the exception, as better suited to my purposes than the general rule; but the reader will see that it is neither a blunder nor a poetic licence. On this subject a friend in Portland, Maine, writes me thus:—

"In this State, and also, I am told, in New York, ships are sometimes rigged upon the stocks, in order to save time, or to make a show. There was a fine, large ship launched last summer at Ellsworth, fully rigged and sparred. Some years ago a ship was launched here, with her rigging, spars, sails, and cargo aboard. She sailed the next day and—was never heard of again! I hope this will not be the fate of your poem!"

Lay the snow,
They fell,—those lordly pines!
Those grand, majestic pines!
Mid shouts and cheers
The jaded steers,
Panting beneath the goad,
Dragged down the weary, winding
    road
Those captive kings so straight and
    tall.
To be shorn of their streaming hair,
And, naked and bare,
To feel the stress and the strain
Of the wind and the reeling main,
Whose roar
Would remind them for evermore
Of their native forests they should
    not see again.

And everywhere
The slender, graceful spars
Poise aloft in the air,
And at the mast-head,
White, blue, and red,
A flag unrolls the stripes and stars.
Ah! when the wanderer, lonely,
    friendless,
In foreign harbours shall behold
That flag unrolled,
'Twill be as a friendly hand
Stretched out from his native land,
Filling his heart with memories
    sweet and endless!

All is finished! and at length
Has come the bridal day
Of beauty and of strength.
To-day the vessel shall be launched!
With fleecy clouds the sky is
    blanched,
And o'er the bay,
Slowly, in all his splendours dight,
The great sun rises to behold the
    sight.

The ocean old,
Centuries old,
Strong as youth, and as uncon-
    trolled,

Paces restless to and fro,
Up and down the sands of gold.
His beating heart is not at rest;
And far and wide,
With ceaseless flow,
His beard of snow
Heaves with the heaving of his
    breast.
He waits impatient for his bride.
There she stands,
With her foot upon the sands,
Decked with flags and streamers
    gay,
In honour of her marriage day,
Her snow-white signals fluttering,
    blending,
Round her like a veil descending,
Ready to be
The bride of the gray, old sea.

On the deck another bride
Is standing by her lover's side.
Shadows from the flags and
    shrouds,
Like the shadows cast by clouds,
Broken by many a sunny fleck,
Fall around them on the deck.

The prayer is said,
The service read,
The joyous bridegroom bows his
    head.
And in tears the good old Master
Shakes the brown hand of his son,
Kisses his daughter's glowing cheek
In silence, for he cannot speak,
And ever faster
Down his own the tears begin to
    run.
The worthy pastor—
The shepherd of that wandering
    flock,
That has the ocean for its wold,
That has the vessel for its fold,
Leaping ever from rock to rock—
Spake, with accents mild and clear,
Words of warning, words of cheer,
But tedious to the bridegroom's
    ear.

He knew the chart
Of the sailor's heart,
All its pleasures and its griefs,
All its shallows and rocky reefs,
All those secret currents, that flow
With such resistless undertow,
And lift and drift, with terrible force,
The will from its moorings and its course,
Therefore he spake, and thus said he:—
"Like unto ships far off at sea,
Outward or homeward bound, are we.
Before, behind, and all around,
Floats and swings the horizon's bound,
Seems at its distant rim to rise
And climb the crystal wall of the skies,
And then again to turn and sink,
As if we could slide from its outer brink.
Ah! it is not the sea,
It is not the sea that sinks and shelves,
But ourselves
That rock and rise
With endless and uneasy motion,
Now touching the very skies,
Now sinking into the depths of ocean.
Ah! if our souls but poise and swing
Like the compass in its brazen ring,
Ever level and ever true
To the toil and the task we have to do,
We shall sail securely, and safely reach
The Fortunate Isles, on whose shining beach
The sights we see, and the sounds we hear,
Will be those of joy and not of fear!"

Then the Master,

With a gesture of command,
Waved his hand;
And at the word,
Loud and sudden there was heard,
All around them and below,
The sound of hammers, blow on blow,
Knocking away the shores and spurs.
And see! she stirs!
She starts, — she moves, — she seems to feel
The thrill of life along her keel,
And, spurning with her foot the ground,
With one exulting, joyous, bound,
She leaps into the ocean's arms!
And lo! from the assembled crowd
There rose a shout, prolonged and loud,
That to the ocean seemed to say,—
"Take her, O bridegroom, old and gray,
Take her to thy protecting arms,
With all her youth and all her charms!"
How beautiful she is! How fair
She lies within those arms, that press
Her form with many a soft caress
Of tenderness and watchful care!
Sail forth into the sea, O ship!
Through wind and wave, right onward steer!
The moistened eye, the trembling lip,
Are not the signs of doubt or fear.
Sail forth into the sea of life,
O gentle, loving, trusting wife,
And safe from all adversity
Upon the bosom of that sea
Thy comings and thy goings be!
For gentleness and love and trust
Prevail o'er angry wave and gust;
And in the wreck of noble lives
Something immortal still survives!

Thou, too, sail on, O Ship of State!
Sail on, O UNION, strong and great!

Humanity with all its fears,
With all the hopes of future years,
Is hanging breathless on thy fate!
We know what Master laid thy
    keel,
What Workmen wrought thy ribs
    of steel,
Who made each mast, and sail, and
    rope,
What anvils rang, what hammers
    beat,
In what a forge and what a heat
Were shaped the anchors of thy
    hope!
Fear not each sudden sound and
    shock,
'Tis of the wave and not the rock;
'Tis but the flapping of the sail,
And not a rent made by the gale!
In spite of rock and tempest's roar,
In spite of false lights on the shore,
Sail on, nor fear to breast the sea!
Our hearts, our hopes, are all with
    thee,
Our hearts, our hopes, our prayers,
    our tears,
Our faith triumphant o'er our fears,
Are all with thee,—are all with
    thee!

THE EVENING STAR

Just above yon sandy bar,
    As the day grows fainter and
    dimmer,
Lonely and lovely, a single star
    Lights the air with a dusky
    glimmer.

Into the ocean faint and far
    Falls the trail of its golden splen-
    dour,
And the gleam of that single star
    Is ever refulgent, soft, and
    tender.

Chrysaor rising out of the sea,
    Showed thus glorious and thus
    emulous,

Leaving the arms of Callirrhoë,
    For ever tender, soft, and tremu-
    lous.

Thus o'er the ocean faint and far
    Trailed the gleam of his falchion
    brightly;
Is it a God, or is it a star
    That, entranced, I gaze on
    nightly!

THE SECRET OF THE SEA

Ah! what pleasant visions haunt
    me
    As I gaze upon the sea!
All the old romantic legends,
    All my dreams, come back to me.

Sails of silk and ropes of sendal,
    Such as gleam in ancient lore;
And the singing of the sailors,
    And the answer from the shore!

Most of all, the Spanish ballad
    Haunts me oft, and tarries long,
Of the noble Count Arnaldos
    And the sailor's mystic song.

Like the long waves on a sea-
    beach,
    Where the sand and silver
    shines,
With a soft, monotonous cadence,
    Flow its unrhymed lyric lines;—

Telling how the Count Arnaldos,
    With his hawk upon his hand,
Saw a fair and stately galley,
    Steering onward to the land;—

How he heard the ancient helms-
    man
    Chant a song so wild and clear,
That the sailing sea-bird slowly
    Poised upon the mast to hear,

Till his soul was full of longing,
  And he cried, with impulse
    strong,—
"Helmsman! for the love of
    heaven,
  Teach me, too, that wondrous
    song!"

"Wouldst thou,"—so the helms-
    man answered,
  "Learn the secret of the sea?
Only those who brave its dangers
  Comprehend its mystery!"

In each sail that skims the horizon,
  In each landward-blowing
    breeze,
I behold that stately galley,
  Hear those mournful melodies;

Till my soul is full of longing
  For the secret of the sea,
And the heart of the great ocean
  Sends a thrilling pulse through
    me.

TWILIGHT

The twilight is sad and cloudy,
  The wind blows wild and free,
And like the wings of sea-birds
  Flash the white caps of the sea.

But in the fisherman's cottage
  There shines a ruddier light
And a little face at the window
  Peers out into the night.

Close, close it is pressed to the win-
    dow,
  As if those childish eyes
Were looking into the darkness,
  To see some form arise.

And a woman's waving shadow
  Is passing to and fro,
Now rising to the ceiling,
  Now bowing and bending low.

What tale do the roaring ocean,
  And the night-wind, bleak and
    wild,
As they beat at the crazy casement,
  Tell to that little child?

And why do the roaring ocean,
  And the night-wind, wild and
    bleak,
As they beat at the heart of the
    mother,
  Drive the colour from her cheek?

SIR HUMPHREY GILBERT [1]

Southward with fleet of ice
  Sailed the corsair Death;
Wild and fast blew the blast,
  And the east-wind was his breath.

His lordly ships of ice
  Glistened in the sun;
On each side, like pennons wide,
  Flashing crystal streamlets run.

His sails of white sea-mist
  Dripped with silver rain;
But where he passed there were cast
  Leaden shadows o'er the main.

Eastward from Campobello
  Sir Humphrey Gilbert sailed;

[1] *Sir Humphrey Gilbert.* "When
the wind abated and the vessels were
near enough, the Admiral was seen
constantly sitting in the stern, with
a book in his hand. On the 9th of
September he was seen for the last
time, and was heard by the people of
the *Hind* to say, 'We are as near
heaven by sea as by land.' In the
following night, the lights of the ship
suddenly disappeared. The people in
the other vessel kept a good look-out
for him during the remainder of the
voyage. On the 22nd of September
they arrived, through much tempest
and peril, at Falmouth. But nothing
more was seen or heard of the Admiral.
—*Belknap's American Biography*, I.
203.

Three days or more seaward he
  bore,
    Then, alas! the land-wind
    failed.

Alas! the land-wind failed,
  And ice-cold grew the night;
And never more, on sea or shore,
  Should Sir Humphrey see the
  light.

He sat upon the deck,
  The Book was in his hand;
" Do not fear! Heaven is as near,"
  He said, " by water as by land! "

In the first watch of the night,
  Without a signal's sound,
Out of the sea, mysteriously,
  The fleet of Death rose all
  around.

The moon and the evening star
  Were hanging in the shrouds;
Every mast, as it passed,
  Seemed to rake the passing
  clouds.

They grappled with their prize,
  At midnight black and cold!
As of a rock was the shock;
  Heavily the ground-swell rolled.

Southward through day and dark,
  They drift in close embrace,
With mist and rain, to the Spanish
  Main;
    Yet there seems no change of
    place.

Southward, for ever southward,
  They drift through dark and day;
And like a dream, in the Gulf-
  Stream
    Sinking, vanish all away.

THE LIGHTHOUSE

The rocky ledge runs far into the
  sea,
    And on its outer point, some
    miles away,

The Lighthouse lifts its massive
  masonry,
    A pillar of fire by night, of cloud
    by day.

Even at this distance I can see the
  tides,
    Upheaving, break unheard along
    its base,
A speechless wrath, that rises and
  subsides
    In the white lip and tremor of
    the face.

And as the evening darkens, lo!
  how bright,
    Through the deep purple of the
    twilight air,
Beams forth the sudden radiance
  of its light
    With strange, unearthly splen-
    dour in its glare!

Not one alone; from each project-
  ing cape
    And perilous reef, along the
    ocean's verge,
Starts into life a dim, gigantic
  shape,
    Holding its lantern o'er the
    restless surge.

Like the great giant Christopher it
  stands
    Upon the brink of the tempestu-
    ous wave,
Wading far out among the rocks
  and sands,
    The night-o'ertaken mariner to
    save.

And the great ships sail outward
  and return,
    Bending and bowing o'er the
    billowy swells,
And ever joyful, as they see it burn,
    They wave their silent welcomes
    and farewells.

They come forth from the dark-
  ness, and their sails
    Gleam for a moment only in the
    blaze,

And eager faces, as the light un-
veils,
  Gaze at the tower, and vanish
while they gaze.

The mariner remembers when a
child,
  On his first voyage, he saw it
fade and sink;
And when, returning from adven-
tures wild,
  He saw it rise again o'er ocean's
brink.

Steadfast, serene, immovable, the
same
  Year after year, through all the
silent night
Burns on for evermore that
quenchless flame,
  Shines on that inextinguishable
light!

It sees the ocean to its bosom clasp
  The rocks and sea-sand with the
kiss of peace;
It sees the wild winds lift it in
their grasp,
  And hold it up, and shake it like a
fleece.

The startled waves leap over it;
the storm
  Smites it with all the scourges of
the rain,
And steadily against its solid form
  Press the great shoulders of the
hurricane.

The sea-bird wheeling round it,
with the din
  Of wings and winds and solitary
cries,
Blinded and maddened by the light
within,
  Dashes himself against the glare,
and dies.

A new Prometheus, chained upon
the rock,
  Still grasping in his hand the fire
of Jove,

It does not hear the cry, nor heed
the shock,
  But hails the mariner with words
of love.

"Sail on!" it says, "sail on, ye
stately ships!
  And with your floating bridge
the ocean span;
Be mine to guard this light from
all eclipse,
  Be yours to bring man nearer
unto man!"

THE FIRE OF DRIFT-WOOD

We sat within the farmhouse old,
  Whose windows, looking o'er
the bay,
Gave to the sea-breeze, damp and
cold,
  An easy entrance, night and day.

Not far away we saw the port,—
  The strange, old-fashioned,
silent town,—
The lighthouse,—the dismantled
fort,—
  The wooden houses, quaint and
brown.

We sat and talked until the night,
  Descending, filled the little room;
Our faces faded from the sight,
  Our voices only broke the
gloom.

We spake of many a vanished scene,
  Of what we once had thought
and said,
Of what had been, and might have
been,
  And who was changed, and who
was dead.

And all that fills the hearts of
friends,

When first they feel, with secret
  pain,
Their lives thenceforth have separ-
  ate ends,
  And never can be one again;

The first slight swerving of the
  heart,
  That words are powerless to ex-
  press,
And leave it still unsaid in part,
  Or say it in too great excess.

The very tones in which we spake
  Had something strange, I could
  but mark;
The leaves of memory seemed to
  make
  A mournful rustling in the dark.

Oft died the words upon our lips,
  As suddenly, from out the fire
Built of the wreck of stranded
  ships,
  The flames would leap and then
  expire.

And, as their splendour flashed and
  failed,

We thought of wrecks upon the
  main,—
Of ships dismasted, that were
  hailed
  And sent no answer back again.

The windows, rattling in their
  frames,—
  The ocean, roaring up the
  beach,—
The gusty blast,—the bickering
  flames,
  All mingled vaguely in our
  speech;

Until they made themselves a part
  Of fancies floating through the
  brain,
The long-lost ventures of the heart,
  That send no answers back again.

O flames that glowed! O hearts
  that yearned!
  They were indeed too much akin,
The drift-wood fire without that
  burned,
  The thoughts that burned and
  glowed within.

BY THE FIRESIDE

RESIGNATION

There is no flock, however watched
  and tended,
  But one dead lamb is there!
There is no fireside, howsoe'er de-
  fended
  But has one vacant chair!

The air is full of farewells to the
  dying,
  And mournings for the dead;
The heart of Rachel, for her chil-
  dren crying,
  Will not be comforted!

Let us be patient! These severe
  afflictions

Not from the ground arise,
But oftentimes celestial benedic-
  tions
  Assume this dark disguise.

We see but dimly through the
  mists and vapours
  Amid these earthly damps;
What seems to us but sad, funereal
  tapers
  May be heaven's distant lamps.

There is no Death! What seems
  so is transition.
  This life of mortal breath
Is but a suburb of the life elysian,
  Whose portal we call Death.

She is not dead,—the child of our
affection,—
But gone unto that school
Where she no longer needs our
poor protection,
And Christ himself doth rule.

In that great cloister's stillness and
seclusion,
By guardian angels led,
Safe from temptation, safe from
sin's pollution,
She lives, whom we call dead.

Day after day we think what she is
doing
In those bright realms of air;
Year after year, her tender steps
pursuing,
Behold her grown more fair.

Thus do we walk with her, and keep
unbroken
The bond which nature gives,
Thinking that our remembrance,
though unspoken,
May reach her where she lives.

Not as a child shall we again be-
hold her;
For when with raptures wild
In our embraces we again enfold
her,
She will not be a child;

But a fair maiden, in her Father's
mansion,
Clothed with celestial grace;
And beautiful with all the soul's
expansion
Shall we behold her face.

And though at times impetuous
with emotion
And anguish long suppressed,
The swelling heart heaves moaning
like the ocean,
That cannot be at rest,—

We will be patient, and assuage the
feeling
We may not wholly stay;
By silence sanctifying, not con-
cealing,
The grief that must have way.

THE BUILDERS

All are architects of Fate,
Working in these walls of Time;
Some with massive deeds and
great,
Some with ornaments of rhyme.

Nothing useless is, or low;
Each thing in its place is best;
And what seems but idle show
Strengthens and supports the
rest.

For the structure that we raise,
Time is with materials filled;
Our to-days and yesterdays
Are the blocks with which we
build.

Truly shape and fashion these;
Leave no yawning gaps between;
Think not, because no man sees,
Such things will remain unseen.

In the elder days of Art,
Builders wrought with greatest
care
Each minute an unseen part;
For the Gods see everywhere.

Let us do our work as well,
Both the unseen and the seen!
Make the house, where Gods may
dwell,
Beautiful, entire, and clean.

Else our lives are incomplete,
Standing in these walls of Time,
Broken stairways, where the feet
Stumble as they seek to climb.

Build to-day, then, strong and sure,
  With a firm and ample base;
And ascending and secure
  Shall to-morrow find its place.

Thus alone can we attain
  To those turrets, where the eye
Sees the world as one vast plain,
  And one boundless reach of sky.

SAND OF THE DESERT IN AN HOUR-GLASS

A handful of red sand, from the hot clime
  Of Arab deserts brought,
Within this glass becomes the spy of Time,
  The minister of Thought.

How many weary centuries has it been
  About those deserts blown!
How many strange vicissitudes has seen,
  How many histories known!

Perhaps the camels of the Ishmaelite
  Trampled and passed it o'er,
When into Egypt from the patriarch's sight
  His favourite son they bore.

Perhaps the feet of Moses, burnt and bare,
  Crushed it beneath their tread;
Or Pharaoh's flashing wheels into the air
  Scattered it as they sped;

Or Mary, with the Christ of Nazareth
  Held close in her caress,
Whose pilgrimage of hope and love and faith
  Illumed the wilderness;

Or anchorites beneath Engaddi's palms
  Pacing the Dead Sea beach,
And singing slow their old Armenian psalms
  In half-articulate speech;

Or caravans, that from Bassora's gate
  With westward steps depart;
Or Mecca's pilgrims, confident of Fate,
  And resolute in heart!

These have passed over it, or may have passed!
  Now in this crystal tower
Imprisoned by some curious hand at last,
  It counts the passing hour.

And as I gaze, these narrow walls expand:—
  Before my dreamy eye
Stretches the desert with its shifting sand,
  Its unimpeded sky.

And borne aloft by the sustaining blast,
  This little golden thread
Dilates into a column high and vast,
  A form of fear and dread.

And onward, and across the setting sun,
  Across the boundless plain,
The column and its broader shadow run,
  Till thought pursues in vain.

The vision vanishes! These walls again
  Shut out the lurid sun,
Shut out the hot, immeasurable plain;
  The half-hour's sand is run!

BIRDS OF PASSAGE

Black shadows fall
From the lindens tall,
That lift aloft their massive wall
  Against the southern sky;

And from the realms
Of the shadowy elms
A tide-like darkness overwhelms
  The fields that round us lie.

But the night is fair,
And everywhere
A warm, soft vapour fills the air,
  And distant sounds seem near;

And above, in the light
Of the star-lit night,
Swift birds of passage wing their
    flight
  Through the dewy atmosphere.

I hear the beat
Of their pinions fleet,
As from the land of snow and sleet
  They seek a southern lea.

I hear the cry
Of their voices high
Falling dreamily through the sky
  But their forms I cannot see.

O, say not so!
Those sounds that flow
In murmurs of delight and woe
  Come not from wings of birds.

They are the throngs
Of the poet's songs.
Murmurs of pleasures, and pains,
  and wrongs,
  The sound of wingèd words.

This is the cry
Of souls, that high
On toiling, beating pinions, fly,
  Seeking a warmer clime.

From their distant flight
Through realms of light
It falls into our world of night,
  With the murmuring sound of
    rhyme.

THE OPEN WINDOW

The old house by the lindens
  Stood silent in the shade,
And on the gravelled pathway
  The light and shadow played.

I saw the nursery windows
  Wide open to the air;
But the faces of the children,
  They were no longer there.

The large Newfoundland house-dog
  Was standing by the door;
He looked for his little playmates,
  Who would return no more.

They walked not under the lindens,
  They played not in the hall;
But shadow, and silence, and sad-
    ness
  Were hanging over all.

The birds sang in the branches,
  With sweet, familiar tone;
But the voices of the children
  Will be heard in dreams alone!

And the boy that walked beside me
  He could not understand
Why closer in mine, ah! closer,
  I pressed his warm, soft hand!

KING WITLAF'S DRINKING-HORN

Witlaf, a king of the Saxons,
  Ere yet his last he breathed,
To the merry monks of Croyland
  His drinking-horn bequeathed,—

That, whenever they sat at their
revels,
　And drank from the golden bowl,
They might remember the donor,
　And breathe a prayer for his soul.

So sat they once at Christmas,
　And bade the goblet pass;
In their beards the red wine glistened
　Like dewdrops in the grass.

They drank to the soul of Witlaf,
　They drank to Christ the Lord,
And to each of the Twelve Apostles,
　Who had preached his holy word.

They drank to the Saints and Martyrs
　Of the dismal days of yore,
And as soon as the horn was empty
　They remembered one Saint
more.

And the reader droned from the
pulpit,
　Like the murmur of many bees,
The legend of good Saint Guthlac,
　And Saint Basil's homilies;

Till the great bells of the convent,
　From their prison in the tower,
Guthlac and Bartholomæus,
　Proclaimed the midnight hour.

And the Yule-log cracked in the
chimney,
　And the Abbot bowed his head,
And the flamelets flapped and
flickered,
　But the Abbot was stark and
dead.

Yet still in his pallid fingers
　He clutched the golden bowl,
In which, like a pearl dissolving,
　Had sunk and dissolved his soul.

But not for this their revels
　The jovial monks forbore,

For they cried, "Fill high the goblet!
　We must drink to one Saint
more!"

GASPAR BECERRA

By his evening fire the artist
　Pondered o'er his secret shame;
Baffled, weary, and disheartened,
　Still he mused, and dreamed of
fame.

'Twas an image of the Virgin
　That had tasked his utmost
skill;
But alas! his fair ideal
　Vanished and escaped him still.

From a distant Eastern island
　Had the precious wood been
brought;
Day and night the anxious master
　At his toil untiring wrought;

Till, discouraged and desponding,
　Sat he now in shadows deep,
And the day's humiliation
　Found oblivion in sleep.

Then a voice cried, "Rise, O
master!
　From the burning brand of oak
Shape the thought that stirs within
thee!"
　And the startled artist woke,—

Woke, and from the smoking embers
　Seized and quenched the glowing wood;
And therefrom he carved an image,
　And he saw that it was good.

O thou sculptor, painter, poet!
　Take this lesson to thy heart;
That is best which lieth nearest;
　Shape from that thy work of art.

PEGASUS IN POUND

Once into a quiet village,
  Without haste and without heed,
In the golden prime of morning,
  Strayed the poet's wingèd steed.

It was Autumn, and incessant
  Piped the quails from shocks and
    sheaves,
And, like living coals, the apples
  Burned among the withering
    leaves.

Loud the clamorous bell was ring-
    ing
  From its belfry gaunt and grim;
'Twas the daily call to labour,
  Not a triumph meant for him.

Not the less he saw the landscape,
  In its gleaming vapour veiled;
Not the less he breathed the odours
  That the dying leaves exhaled.

Thus, upon the village common,
  By the school-boys he was found;
And the wise men, in their wisdom,
  Put him straightway into pound.

Then the sombre village crier,
  Ringing loud his brazen bell,
Wandered down the street pro-
    claiming
  There was an estray to sell.

And the curious country people,
  Rich and poor, and young and
    old,
Came in haste to see this wondrous
  Wingèd steed, with mane of gold.

Thus the day passed, and the
    evening
  Fell, with vapours cold and dim;
But it brought no food nor shelter,
  Brought no straw nor stall for
    him.

Patiently, and still expectant,
  Looked he through the wooden
    bars,
Saw the moon rise o'er the land-
    scape,
  Saw the tranquil, patient stars;

Till at length the bell at midnight
  Sounded from its dark abode,
And, from out a neighbouring
    farmyard,
  Loud the cock Alectryon crowed.

Then, with nostrils wide distended,
  Breaking from his iron chain,
And unfolding far his pinions,
  To those stars he soared again.

On the morrow, when the village
  Woke to all its toil and care,
Lo! the strange steed had de-
    parted,
And they knew not when nor
    where.

But they found, upon the green-
    sward
  Where his struggling hoofs had
    trod,
Pure and bright, a fountain flow-
    ing
  From the hoof-marks in the sod.

From that hour, the fount unfail-
    ing
  Gladdens the whole region round,
Strengthening all who drink its
    waters,
While it soothes them with its
    sound.

TEGNER'S DRAPA

I heard a voice, that cried,
  " Balder the Beautiful
Is dead, is dead! "
And through the misty air

Passed like the mournful cry
Of sunward sailing cranes.

I saw the pallid corpse
Of the dead sun
Borne through the Northern sky.
Blasts from Niffelheim
Lifted the sheeted mists
Around him as he passed.

And the voice for ever cried,
" Balder the Beautiful
Is dead, is dead! "
And died away
Through the dreary night,
In accents of despair.

Balder the Beautiful,
God of the summer sun,
Fairest of all the Gods!
Light from his forehead beamed,
Runes were upon his tongue,
As on the warrior's sword.

All things in earth and air
Bound were by magic spell
Never to do him harm;
Even the plants and stones;
All save the mistletoe,
The sacred mistletoe!

Hœder, the blind old God,
Whose feet are shod with silence,
Pierced through that gentle breast
With his sharp spear, by fraud
Made of the mistletoe,
The accursed mistletoe!

They laid him in his ship,
With horse and harness,
As on a funeral pyre.
Odin placed
A ring upon his finger,
And whispered in his ear.

They launched the burning ship!
It floated far away
Over the misty sea,
Till like the sun it seemed,

Sinking beneath the waves.
Balder returned no more!

So perish the old Gods!
But out of the sea of Time
Rises a new land of song,
Fairer than the old.
Over its meadows green
Walk the young bards and sing.

Build it again,
O ye bards,
Fairer than before.
Ye fathers of the new race,
Feed upon morning dew,
Sing the new Song of Love!

The law of force is dead!
The law of love prevails!
Thor, the thunderer,
Shall rule the earth no more,
No more, with threats,
Challenge the meek Christ.

Sing no more,
O ye bards of the North,
Of Vikings and of Jarls!
Of the days of Eld
Preserve the freedom only,
Not the deeds of blood!

SONNET

ON MRS. KEMBLE'S READINGS FROM
SHAKESPEARE

O precious evenings! all too
    swiftly sped!
Leaving us heirs to amplest heri-
    tages
Of all the best thoughts of the
    greatest sages,
And giving tongues unto the silent
    dead!
How our hearts glowed and
    trembled as she read,
Interpreting by tones the wondrous
    pages

Of the great poet who foreruns the
ages,
Anticipating all that shall be said!
O happy Reader! having for thy
text
The magic book, whose Sibylline
leaves have caught
The rarest essence of all human
thought!
O happy Poet! by no critic vext!
How must thy listening spirit now
rejoice
To be interpreted by such a voice!

THE SINGERS

God sent his singers upon earth
With songs of sadness and of mirth,
That they might touch the hearts
of men,
And bring them back to heaven
again.

The first a youth, with soul of fire,
Held in his hand a golden lyre;
Through groves he wandered, and
by streams,
Playing the music of our dreams.

The second, with a bearded face,
Stood singing in the market-place,
And stirred with accents deep and
loud
The hearts of all the listening
crowd.

A gray, old man, the third and last,
Sang in cathedrals dim and vast,
While the majestic organ rolled
Contrition from its mouths of gold.

And those who heard the Singers
three
Disputed which the best might be;
For still their music seemed to
start
Discordant echoes in each heart.

But the great Master said, " I see
No best in kind, but in degree;
I gave a various gift to each,
To charm, to strengthen, and to
teach.

" These are the three great chords
of might,
And he whose ear is tuned aright
Will hear no discord in the three,
But the most perfect harmony."

SUSPIRIA

Take them, O Death! and bear
away
Whatever thou canst call thine
own!
Thine image, stamped upon this
clay,
Dost give thee that, but that
alone!

Take them, O Grave! and let
them lie
Folded upon thy narrow shelves,
As garments by the soul laid by,
And precious only to ourselves!

Take them, O great Eternity!
Our little life is but a gust,
That bends the branches of thy
tree,
And trails its blossoms in the
dust.

HYMN

FOR MY BROTHER'S ORDINATION

Christ to the young man said:
" Yet one thing more;
If thou wouldst perfect be,
Sell all thou hast and give it to the
poor,
And come and follow me! "

Within this temple Christ again,
   unseen,
  Those sacred words hath said,
And his invisible hands to-day
   have been
  Laid on a young man's head.

And evermore beside him on his
   way
  The unseen Christ shall move,
That he may lean upon his arm and
   say,
   "Dost thou, dear Lord, ap-
   prove?"

Beside him at the marriage feast
   shall be,
  To make the scene more fair;
Beside him in the dark Gethsemane
  Of pain and midnight prayer.

O holy trust! O endless sense of
   rest!
  Like the beloved John
To lay his head upon the Saviour's
   breast,
  And thus to journey on!

THE BLIND GIRL OF CASTÈL-
CUILLÈ [1]

FROM THE GASCON OF JASMIN

Only the Lowland tongue of Scotland
   might
Rehearse this little tragedy aright;
Let me attempt it with an English
   quill;
And take, O Reader, for the deed the
   will.

I.

  At the foot of the mountain
    height
  Where is perched Castèl-
    Cuillè.

When the apple, the plum, and
   the almond tree
   In the plain below were grow-
    ing white,
   This is the song one might
    perceive
On a Wednesday morn of Saint
   Joseph's Eve:

"The roads should blossom, the
   roads should bloom,
So fair a bride shall leave her home!
Should blossom and bloom with
   garlands gay,
So fair a bride shall pass to-day!"

This old Te Deum, rustic rites at-
   tending,
   Seemed from the clouds de-
    scending;
When lo! a merry company
Of rosy village girls, clean as the
   eye,
   Each one with her attendant
    swain,
Came to the cliff, all singing the
   same strain;
Resembling there, so near unto the
   sky,
Rejoicing angels, that kind Heaven
   has sent
For their delight and our encour-
   agement.
   Together blending,
   And soon descending
   The narrow sweep
   Of the hillside steep,
   They wind aslant
   Towards Saint Amant,
   Through leafy alleys

[1] Jasmin, the author of this beauti-
ful poem, is to the South of France
what Burns is to the South of Scotland
—the representative of the heart of
the people—one of those happy bards
who are born with their mouths full
of birds (*la bouco pleno d'aouzelous*).
He has written his own biography in
a poetic form, and the simple narrative
of his poverty, his struggles, and his
triumphs is very touching. He still
lives at Agen on the Garonne; and
long may he live there to delight his
native land with native songs!

Of verdurous valleys
With merry sallies
Singing their chant:
" The roads should blossom, the
roads should bloom,
So fair a bride shall leave her home!
Should blossom and bloom with
garlands gay,
So fair a bride shall pass to-day! "

It is Baptiste, and his affianced
maiden,
With garlands for the bridal laden!

The sky was blue; without one
cloud of gloom,
The sun of March was shining
brightly,
And to the air the freshening wind
gave lightly
Its breathings of perfume.

When one beholds the dusky
hedges blossom,
A rustic bridal, ah! how sweet it
is!
To sounds of joyous melodies,
That touch with tenderness the
trembling bosom,
A band of maidens
Gaily frolicking,
A band of youngsters
Wildly rollicking!
Kissing,
Caressing,
With fingers pressing,
Till in the veriest
Madness of mirth, as they
dance,
They retreat and advance,
Trying whose laugh shall
be loudest and merriest;
While the bride, with roguish
eyes,
Sporting with them, now escapes
and cries:
" Those who catch me
Married verily
This year shall be! "

And all pursue with eager
haste,
And all attain what they pur-
sue,
And touch her pretty apron fresh
and new.
And the linen kirtle round her
waist.

Meanwhile, whence comes it
that among
These youthful maidens fresh
and fair,
So joyous, with such laughing
air,
Baptiste stands sighing, with
silent tongue?
And yet the bride is fair and
young!
Is it Saint Joseph would say to us
all,
That love, o'er-hasty, precedeth a
fall?
O, no! for a maiden frail, I
trow,
Never bore so lofty a brow!
What lovers! they give not a
single caress!
To see them so careless and cold
to-day,
These are grand people, one
would say,
What ails Baptiste? what grief
doth him oppress?
It is, that, half way up the hill,
In yon cottage, by whose
walls
Stand the cart-house and the
stalls,
Dwelleth the blind orphan
still.
Daughter of a veteran old;
And you must know, one year
ago,
That Margaret, the young and
tender,
Was the village pride and
splendour,
And Baptiste her lover bold.

Love, the deceiver, them en-
snared;
For them the altar was pre-
pared;
But alas! the summer's blight,
The dread disease that none
can stay,
The pestilence that walks by
night,
Took the young bride's sight
away.
All at the father's stern command
was changed;
Their peace was gone, but not
their love estranged.
Wearied at home, ere long the
lover fled;
Returned but three short days
ago,
The golden chain they round
him throw,
He is enticed, and onward
led
To marry Angela, and yet
Is thinking ever of Margaret.

Then suddenly a maiden cried,
"Anna, Theresa, Mary, Kate!
Here comes the cripple Jane!"
And by a fountain's side
A woman, bent and gray with
years,
Under the mulberry-trees ap-
pears,
And all towards her run, as
fleet,
As had they wings upon their
feet.
It is that Jane, the cripple
Jane,
Is a soothsayer, wary and
kind.
She telleth fortunes, and none com-
plain.
She promises one a village
swain,
Another a happy wedding-day,
And the bride a lovely boy
straightway.

All comes to pass as she
avers;
She never deceives, she never
errs.

But for this once the village
seer
Wears a countenance severe,
And from beneath her eyebrows
thin and white
Her two eyes flash like cannons
bright
Aimed at the bridegroom in
waistcoat blue,
Who, like a statue, stands in
view;
Changing colour, as well he
might,
When the beldame wrinkled
and gray
Takes the young bride by the
hand,
And, with the tip of her reedy
wand
Making the sign of the cross,
doth say:—
"Thoughtless Angela, beware!
Lest, when thou weddest this
false bridegroom,
Thou diggest for thyself a
tomb!"
And she was silent; and the
maidens fair
Saw from each eye escape a swollen
tear;
But on a little streamlet silver-
clear,
What are two drops of turbid
rain?
Saddened a moment, the bridal
train
Resumed the dance and song
again;
The bridegroom only was pale with
fear;—
And down green alleys
Of verdurous valleys,
With merry sallies,
They sang the refrain:—

" The roads should blossom, the
    roads should blow,
So fair a bride shall leave her home!
Should blossom and bloom with
    garlands gay,
So fair a bride shall pass to-day! "

II.

And by suffering worn and
    weary,
But beautiful as some fair angel
    yet,
    Thus lamented Margaret,
    In her cottage lone and
    dreary:—
" He has arrived! arrived at
    last!
Yet Jane has named him not these
    three days past;
    Arrived! yet keeps aloof so far!
And knows that of my night he is
    the star!
Knows that long months I waited
    alone, benighted,
And count the moments since he
    went away!
Come! keep the promise of that
    happier day,
That I may keep the faith to thee
    I plighted!
What joy have I without thee?
    what delight?
Grief wastes my life, and makes it
    misery!
Day for the others ever, but for me
    For ever night! for ever night!
When he is gone 'tis dark! my
    soul is sad!
I suffer! O my God! come, make
    me glad.
When he is near, no thoughts of
    day intrude;
Day has blue heavens, but Bap-
    tiste has blue eyes!
Within them shines for me a
    heaven of love,
A heaven all happiness, like that
    above,

No more of grief! no more of
    lassitude!
Earth I forget,—and heaven, and
    all distresses,
When seated by my side my hand
    he presses;
    But when alone, remember all!
Where is Baptiste? he hears not
    when I call!
A branch of ivy, dying on the
    ground,
    I need some bough to twine
    around!
In pity come! be to my suffering
    kind!
True love, they say, in grief doth
    more abound!
    What then—when one is
    blind?

" Who knows? perhaps I am
    forsaken!
Ah! woe is me! then bear me to
    my grave!
    O God! what thoughts
    within me waken!
Away! he will return! I do but
    rave!
    He will return! I need not fear!
    He swore it by our Saviour
    dear;
    He could not come at his own
    will;
    Is weary, or perhaps is ill!
    Perhaps his heart, in this dis-
    guise,
    Prepares for me some sweet
    surprise!
But some one comes! Though
    blind, my heart can see!
And that deceives me not! 'tis he!
    'tis he! "

And the door ajar is set,
    And poor, confiding Margaret
Rises, with outstretched arms, but
    sightless eyes;
'Tis only Paul, her brother, who
    thus cries:—

" Angela the bride has passed!
I saw the wedding guests go
by;
Tell me, my sister, why were we
not asked?
For all are there but you
and I "
" Angela married! and not
send
To tell her secret unto me!
O speak! who may the bride-
groom be? "
" My sister, 'tis Baptiste, thy
friend! "

A cry the blind girl gave, but
nothing said;
A milky whiteness spreads upon
her cheeks;
An icy hand, as heavy as lead,
Descending, as her brother
speaks,
Upon her heart, that has
ceased to beat,
Suspends awhile its life and
heat.
She stands beside the boy, now
sore distressed,
A wax Madonna as a peasant
dressed.

At length, the bridal song
again
Brings her back to her sorrow
and pain.
" Hark! the joyous airs are
ringing!
Sister, dost thou hear them
singing?
How merrily they laugh and
jest!
Would we were bidden with
the rest!
I would don my hose of home-
spun gray,
And my doublet of linen
striped and gay;
Perhaps they will come; for
they do not wed

Till to-morrow at seven
o'clock, it is said! "
" I know it! " answered Mar-
garet;
Whom the vision, with aspect black
as jet,
Mastered again; and its hand
of ice
Held her heart crushed, as in a
vice!
" Paul, be not sad! 'Tis a
holiday;
To-morrow put on thy doublet
gay!
But leave me now for a while
alone."
Away, with a hop and a jump,
went Paul,
And, as he whistled along the
hall,
Entered Jane, the crippled
crone.

" Holy Virgin! what dread-
ful heat!
I am faint, and weary, and out
of breath;
But thou art cold,—art chill as
death;
My little friend! what ails thee,
sweet? "

" Nothing! I heard them singing
home the bride;
And, as I listened to the song,
I thought my turn would come
ere long,
Thou knowest it is at Whit-
suntide.
Thy cards forsooth can never
lie,
To me such joy they prophesy,
Thy skill shall be vaunted far
and wide
When they behold him at my
side.
And poor Baptiste, what
sayest thou?
It must seem long to him;—me-
thinks I see him now! "

Jane, shuddering, her hand doth press:
"Thy love I cannot all approve;
We must not trust too much to happiness;—
Go, pray to God, that thou mayst love him less!"
    "The more I pray, the more I love!
It is no sin, for God is on my side!"
It was enough; and Jane no more replied.

Now to all hope her heart is barred and cold;
    But to deceive the beldame old
    She takes a sweet, contented air,
    Speak of foul weather or of fair,
    At every word the maiden smiles!
    Thus the beguiler she beguiles;
So that, departing at the evening's close,
    She says, "She may be saved! she nothing knows!"

Poor Jane, the cunning sorceress!
Now that thou wouldst, thou art no prophetess!
This morning, in the fulness of thy heart,
    Thou wast so, far beyond thine art!

III.

Now rings the bell, nine times reverberating,
And the white daybreak, stealing up the sky,
Sees in two cottages two maidens waiting,
    How differently!

Queen of a day, by flatterers caressed,
    The one puts on her cross and crown,
    Decks with a huge bouquet her breast,
    And flaunting, fluttering up and down,
    Looks at herself, and cannot rest.

The other, blind, within her little room,
    Has neither crown nor flower's perfume;
But in their stead for something gropes apart,
    That in a drawer's recess doth lie,
And, 'neath her bodice of bright scarlet dye,
    Convulsive clasps it to her heart.
The one, fantastic, light as air,
    'Mid kisses ringing,
    And joyous singing,
    Forgets to say her morning prayer!
The other, with cold drops upon her brow,
    Joins her two hands, and kneels upon the floor,
And whispers, as her brother opes the door,
    "O God! forgive me now!"

And then the orphan, young and blind,
    Conducted by her brother's hand,
    Towards the church, through paths unscanned,
    With tranquil air, her way doth wind.
Odours of laurel, making her faint and pale,
    Round her at times exhale,
And in the sky as yet no sunny ray,
    But brumal vapours gray.

Of verdurous valleys
With merry sallies
Singing their chant:

"The roads should blossom, the
    roads should bloom,
So fair a bride shall leave her home!
Should blossom and bloom with
    garlands gay,
So fair a bride shall pass to-day!"

It is Baptiste, and his affianced
    maiden,
With garlands for the bridal laden!

The sky was blue; without one
    cloud of gloom,
    The sun of March was shining
      brightly,
And to the air the freshening wind
    gave lightly
    Its breathings of perfume.

When one beholds the dusky
    hedges blossom,
A rustic bridal, ah! how sweet it
    is!
To sounds of joyous melodies,
That touch with tenderness the
    trembling bosom,
      A band of maidens
      Gaily frolicking,
      A band of youngsters
      Wildly rollicking!
        Kissing,
        Caressing,
      With fingers pressing,
      Till in the veriest
    Madness of mirth, as they
      dance,
      They retreat and advance,
        Trying whose laugh shall
        be loudest and merriest;
    While the bride, with roguish
      eyes,
Sporting with them, now escapes
    and cries:
      "Those who catch me
      Married verily
      This year shall be!"

And all pursue with eager
    haste,
And all attain what they pur-
    sue,
And touch her pretty apron fresh
    and new.
And the linen kirtle round her
    waist.

Meanwhile, whence comes it
    that among
These youthful maidens fresh
    and fair,
So joyous, with such laughing
    air,
Baptiste stands sighing, with
    silent tongue?
And yet the bride is fair and
    young!
Is it Saint Joseph would say to us
    all,
That love, o'er-hasty, precedeth a
    fall?
O, no! for a maiden frail, I
    trow,
Never bore so lofty a brow!
What lovers! they give not a
    single caress!
To see them so careless and cold
    to-day,
    These are grand people, one
      would say,
What ails Baptiste? what grief
    doth him oppress?
    It is, that, half way up the hill,
    In yon cottage, by whose
      walls
    Stand the cart-house and the
      stalls,
    Dwelleth the blind orphan
      still.
    Daughter of a veteran old;
    And you must know, one year
      ago,
    That Margaret, the young and
      tender,
    Was the village pride and
      splendour,
    And Baptiste her lover bold.

Mute as an idiot, sad as yester-
morning,
Thinks only of the beldame's
words of warning.

And Angela thinks of her cross, I
wis,
To be a bride is all! The pretty
lisper
Feels her heart swell to hear all
round her whisper
"How beautiful! how beautiful
she is!"
But she must calm that giddy
head,
For already the Mass is said;
At the holy table stands the
priest;
The wedding ring is blessed; Bap-
tiste receives it;
Ere on the finger of the bride he
leaves it,
He must pronounce one word
at least!
'Tis spoken; and sudden at the
groomsman's side
"'Tis he!" a well-known voice has
cried.
And while the wedding guests all
hold their breath,
Opes the confessional, and the blind
girl, see!
"Baptiste," she said, "since thou
hast wished my death,
As holy water be my blood for
thee!"
And calmly in the air a knife sus-
pended!
Doubtless her guardian angel near
attended,
For anguish did its work so
well,
That, ere the fatal stroke de-
scended,
Lifeless she fell!

At eve, instead of bridal verse,
The De Profundis filled the
air;

Decked with flowers a simple
hearse
To the churchyard forth they
bear;
Village girls in robes of snow
Follow, weeping as they go;
Nowhere was a smile that day,
No, ah no! for each one seemed to
say:—

"The roads should mourn and be
veiled in gloom,
So fair a corpse shall leave its
home!
Should mourn and should weep,
ah, well-away!
So fair a corpse shall pass to-day!"

A CHRISTMAS CAROL

FROM THE NOEL BOURGUIGNON DE
GUI BAROZAI

I hear along our street
Pass the minstrel throngs;
Hark! they play so sweet,
On their hautboys, Christmas
songs!
Let us by the fire
Ever higher
Sing them till the night expire!

In December ring
Every day the chimes;
Loud the gleemen sing

[1] "The *Suche*, or Yule-log, is thus
defined:—
"This is a huge log, which is placed
on the fire on Christmas Eve, and
which in Burgundy is called, on this
account, *lai Suche de Noel*. Then the
father of the family, particularly
among the middle classes, sings
solemnly Christmas carols with his
wife and children, the smallest of
whom he sends into the corner to
pray that the Yule-log may bear him
some sugar-plums. Meanwhile, little
parcels of them are placed under each
end of the log, and the children come
and pick them up, believing, in good
faith, that the great log has borne
them."

In the streets their merry rhymes.
   Let us by the fire
   Ever higher
Sing them till the night expire.

   Shepherds at the grange,
   Where the Babe was born,
   Sang, with many a change,
Christmas carols until morn.
   Let us by the fire
   Ever higher
Sing them till the night expire!

   These good people sang
   Songs devout and sweet;
   while the rafters rang,
There they stood with freezing
    feet.
   Let us by the fire
   Ever higher
Sing them till the night expire.

   Nuns in frigid cells
   At this holy tide,

   For want of something else,
Christmas songs at times have
   tried.
   Let us by the fire
   Ever higher
Sing them till the night expire.

   Washerwomen old,
   To the sound they beat,
   Sing by rivers cold,
With uncovered heads and feet.
   Let us by the fire
   Ever higher
Sing them till the night expire.

   Who by the fireside stands
   Stamps his feet and sings;
   But he who blows his hands
Not so gay a carol brings.
   Let us by the fire
   Ever higher
Sing them till the night expire.

BIRDS OF PASSAGE

FLIGHT THE FIRST

PROMETHEUS

OR THE POET'S FORETHOUGHT

OF Prometheus, how undaunted
   On Olympus' shining bastions
His audacious foot he planted,
Myths are told and songs are
   chaunted,
   Full of promptings and sugges-
    tions.

Beautiful is the tradition
   Of that flight through heavenly
    portals,
The old classic superstition
Of the theft and the transmission
   Of the fire of the Immortals!

First the deed of noble daring,
   Born of heavenward aspiration,
Then the fire with mortals sharing,
Then the vulture,—the despairing
   Cry of pain on crags Caucasian.

All is but a symbol painted
   Of the Poet, Prophet, Seer;
Only those are crowned and
    sainted
Who with grief have been ac-
    quainted,
   Making nations nobler, freer.

In their feverish exultations,
   In their triumph and their
    yearning,
In their passionate pulsations,

In their words among the nations,
  The Promethean fire is burning.

Shall it, then, be unavailing,
  All this toil for human culture?
Through the cloud-rack, dark and
    trailing,
Must they see above them sailing
  O'er life's barren crags the
    vulture?

Such a fate as this was Dante's,
  By defeat and exile maddened;
Thus were Milton and Cervantes,
Nature's priests and Corybantes,
  By affliction touched and
    saddened.

But the glories so transcendent
  That around their memories
    cluster,
And, on all their steps attendant,
Make their darkened lives re-
    splendent
  With such gleams of inward
    lustre!

All the melodies mysterious,
  Through the dreary darkness
    chaunted;
Thoughts in attitudes imperious,
Voices soft, and deep, and serious,
  Words that whispered, songs
    that haunted.

All the soul in rapt suspension,
  All the quivering, palpitating
Chords of life in utmost tension,
With the fervour of invention,
  With the rapture of creating!

Ah, Prometheus! heaven-scaling!
  In such hours of exultation
Even the faintest heart, unquailing
Might behold the vulture sailing
  Round the cloudy crags Cau-
    casian!

Though to all there is not given
  Strength for such sublime en-
    deavour,

Thus to scale the walls of heaven,
And to leaven with fiery leaven
  All the hearts of men for ever;

Yet all bards, whose hearts un-
    blighted
  Honour and believe the presage,
Hold aloft their torches lighted,
Gleaming through the realms be-
    nighted,
  As they onward bear the mes-
    sage!

THE LADDER OF ST.
AUGUSTINE

Saint Augustine! well hast thou
    said,
  That of our vices we can frame
A ladder,[1] if we will but tread
  Beneath our feet each deed of
    shame!

All common things, each day's
    events,
  That with the hour begin and
    end,
Our pleasures and our discontents,
  Are rounds by which we may
    ascend.

The low desire, the base design,
  That makes another's virtues
    less;
The revel of the ruddy wine,
  And all occasions of excess;

The longing for ignoble things;
  The strife for triumph more
    than truth;
The hardening of the heart, that
    brings
  Irreverence for the dreams of
    youth;

[1] The words of St. Augustine are,
"De vitiis nostris scalam nobis
facimus, si vitia ipsa calcamus."
    Sermon III. *De Ascensione.*

All thoughts of ill; all evil deeds,
That have their root in thoughts of ill;
Whatever hinders or impedes
The action of the nobler will;—

All these must first be trampled down
Beneath our feet, if we would gain
In the bright fields of fair renown
The right of eminent domain.

We have not wings, we cannot soar;
But we have feet to scale and climb
By slow degrees, by more and more,
The cloudy summits of our time.

The mighty pyramids of stone
That wedge-like cleave the desert airs,
When nearer seen, and better known,
Are but gigantic flights of stairs.

The distant mountains, that up-rear
Their solid bastions to the skies,
Are crossed by pathways, that appear
As we to higher levels rise.

The heights by great men reached and kept
Were not attained by sudden flight,
But they, while their companions slept,
Were toiling upward in the night.

Standing on what too long we bore
With shoulders bent and down-cast eyes,
We may discern—unseen before—
A path to higher destinies.

Nor deem the irrevocable Past,
As wholly wasted, wholly vain,
If, rising on its wrecks, at last
To something nobler we attain.

THE PHANTOM SHIP [1]

In Mather's Magnalia Christi,
Of the old colonial time,
May be found in prose the legend
That is here set down in rhyme.

A ship sailed from New Haven,
And the keen and frosty airs,
That filled her sails at parting,
Were heavy with good men's prayers.

"O Lord! if it be thy pleasure"
Thus prayed the old divine—
"To bury our friends in the ocean,
Take them, for they are thine!"

But Master Lamberton muttered,
And under his breath said he,
"This ship is so crank and walty
I fear our grave she will be!"

And the ships that came from England,
When the winter months were gone,
Brought no tidings of this vessel
Nor of Master Lamberton.

This put the people to praying
That the Lord would let them hear
What in his greater wisdom
He had done with friends so dear.

And at last their prayers were answered:—
It was in the month of June,

[1] A detailed account of this "apparition of a Ship in the Air" is given by Cotton Mather in his *Magnalia Christi*, Book I. Ch. VI. It is contained in a letter from the Rev. James Pierpont, Pastor of New Haven. To this account Mather adds these words:—
"Reader, there being yet living so many credible gentlemen, that were eye-witnesses of this wonderful thing, I venture to publish it for a thing as undoubted as it is wonderful."

An hour before the sunset
  Of a windy afternoon,

When, steadily steering landward,
  A ship was seen below,
And they knew it was Lamberton,
  Master,
    Who sailed so long ago.

On she came, with a cloud of can-
  vas,
Right against the wind that blew,
Until the eye could distinguish
  The faces of the crew.

Then fell her straining topmasts,
  Hanging tangled in the shrouds,
And her sails were loosened and
  lifted,
And blown away like clouds.

And the masts, with all their rig-
  ging,
  Fell slowly, one by one,
And the hulk dilated and vanished,
  As a sea-mist in the sun!

And the people who saw this
  marvel
  Each said unto his friend,
That this was the mould of their
  vessel,
  And thus her tragic end.

And the pastor of the village
  Gave thanks to God in prayer,
That, to quiet their troubled
  spirits,
  He had sent this Ship of Air.

THE WARDEN OF THE
CINQUE PORTS

A mist was driving down the
  British Channel,
  The day was just begun,
And through the window-panes, on
  floor and panel,
  Streamed the red autumn sun.

It glanced on flowing flag and rip-
  pling pennon,
  And the white sails of ships;
And, from the frowning rampart,
  the black cannon
  Hailed it with feverish lips.

Sandwich and Romney, Hastings,
  Hythe, and Dover,
  Were all alert that day,
To see the French war-steamers
  speeding over,
  When the fog cleared away.

Sullen and silent, and like cou-
  chant lions,
  Their cannon, through the
  night,
Holding their breath, had watched,
  in grim defiance,
  The sea-coast opposite.

And now they roared at drum-beat
  from their stations
  On every citadel,
Each answering each, with morn-
  ing salutations,
  That all was well.

And down the coast, all taking up
  the burden,
  Replied the distant forts,
As if to summon from his sleep the
  Warden
  And Lord of the Cinque Ports.

Him shall no sunshine from the
  fields of azure,
  No drum-beat from the wall,
No morning gun from the black
  fort's embrasure,
  Awaken with its call!

No more, surveying with an eye
  impartial
  The long line of the coast,
Shall the gaunt figure of the old
  Field-Marshal
  Be seen upon his post!

For in the night, unseen, a single
    warrior,
    In sombre harness mailed,
Dreaded of man, and surnamed the
    Destroyer,
    The rampart wall has scaled.

He passed into the chamber of the
    sleeper,
    The dark and silent room,
And as he entered, darker grew
    and deeper,
    The silence and the gloom.

He did not pause to parley or dis-
    semble,
    But smote the Warden hoar;
Ah! what a blow! that made all
    England tremble
    And groan from shore to shore.

Meanwhile without, the surly can-
    non waited,
    The sun rose bright o'erhead;
Nothing in Nature's aspect inti-
    mated
    That a great man was dead.

HAUNTED HOUSES

All houses wherein men have lived
    and died
    Are haunted houses. Through
    the open doors
The harmless phantoms on their
    errands glide,
    With feet that make no sound
    upon the floors.

We meet them at the door-way, on
    the stair,
    Along the passages they come
    and go,
Impalpable impressions on the air,
    A sense of something moving to
    and fro.

There are more guests at table,
    than the hosts
    Invited; the illuminated hall
Is thronged with quiet, inoffensive
    ghosts,
    As silent as the pictures on the
    wall.

The stranger at my fireside cannot
    see
    The forms I see, nor hear the
    sounds I hear;
He but perceives what is; while
    unto me
    All that has been is visible and
    clear.

We have no title-deeds to house or
    lands;
    Owners and occupants of earlier
    dates
From graves forgotten stretch their
    dusty hands,
    And hold in mortmain still their
    old estates.

The spirit-world around this world
    of sense
    Floats like an atmosphere, and
    everywhere
Wafts through these earthly mists
    and vapours dense
    A vital breath of more ethereal
    air.

Our little lives are kept in equipoise
    By opposite attractions and
    desires;
The struggle of the instinct that
    enjoys,
    And the more noble instinct
    that aspires.

These perturbations, this per-
    petual jar
    Of earthly wants and aspirations
    high,
Come from the influence of an
    unseen star,
    An undiscovered planet in our
    sky.

And as the moon from some dark
    gate of cloud
  Throws o'er the sea a floating
    bridge of light,
Across whose trembling planks our
    fancies crowd,
  Into the realm of mystery and
    night,—

So from the world of spirits there
    descends
  A bridge of light, connecting it
    with this,
O'er whose unsteady floor, that
    sways and bends,
  Wander our thoughts above the
    dark abyss.

IN THE CHURCHYARD AT CAMBRIDGE

In the village churchyard she lies,
Dust is in her beautiful eyes,
  No more she breathes, nor feels,
    nor stirs;
At her feet and at her head
Lies a slave to attend the dead,
  But their dust is white as hers.

Was she a lady of high degree,
So much in love with the vanity
  And foolish pomp of this world
    of ours?
Or was it Christian charity,
And lowliness and humility,
  The richest and rarest of all
    dowers?

Who shall tell us? No one speaks;
No colour shoots into those cheeks,
  Either of anger or of pride,
At the rude question we have
    asked;
Nor will the mystery be unmasked
  By those who are sleeping at her
    side.

Hereafter?—And do you think to
    look
On the terrible pages of that Book
  To find her failings, faults, and
    errors?
Ah, you will then have other cares,
In your own shortcomings and
    despairs,
  In your own secret sins and
    terrors!

THE EMPEROR'S BIRD'S-NEST

Once the Emperor Charles of
    Spain,
  With his swarthy, grave com-
    manders,
I forget in what campaign,
Long besieged, in mud and rain,
  Some old frontier town of
    Flanders.

Up and down the dreary camp,
  In great boots of Spanish leather,
Striding with a measured tramp,
These Hidalgos, dull and damp,
  Cursed the Frenchmen, cursed
    the weather.

Thus as to and fro they went,
  Over upland and through hol-
    low,
Giving their impatience vent,
Perched upon the Emperor's tent,
  In her nest, they spied a
    swallow.

Yes, it was a swallow's nest,
  Built of clay and hair of horses,
Mane, or tail, or dragoon's crest,
Found on hedgerows east and west,
  After skirmish of the forces.

Then an old Hidalgo said,
  As he twirled his gray mustachio,
"Sure this swallow overhead

Thinks the Emperor's tent a shed,
And the Emperor but a Macho!"[1]

Hearing his imperial name
Coupled with those words of
malice,
Half in anger, half in shame,
Forth in the great campaigner came
Slowly from his canvas palace.

"Let no hand the bird molest,"
Said he solemnly, "nor hurt
her!"
Adding then, by way of jest,
"Golondrina is my guest,
'Tis the wife of some deserter!"

Swift as bowstring speeds a shaft,
Through the camp was spread
the rumour,
And the soldiers, as they quaffed
Flemish beer at dinner, laughed
At the Emperor's pleasant
humour.

So unharmed and unafraid
Sat the swallow still and brooded,
Till the constant cannonade
Through the walls a breach had
made,
And the siege was thus con-
cluded.

Then the army, elsewhere bent,
Struck its tents as if disbanding,
Only not the emperor's tent,
For he ordered, ere he went,
Very curtly, "Leave it stand-
ing!"

So it stood there all alone,
Loosely flapping, torn and tat-
tered,
Till the brood was fledged and
flown,

[1] *Macho*, in Spanish, signifies a
mule. *Golondrina* is the feminine
form of *Golondrino*, a swallow, and
also a cant name for a deserter.

Singing o'er those walls of stone
Which the cannon-shot had
shattered.

THE TWO ANGELS

Two angels, one of Life and one of
Death,
Passed o'er our village as the
morning broke;
The dawn was on their faces, and
beneath,
The sombre houses hearsed with
plumes of smoke.

Their attitude and aspect were the
same,
Alike their features and their
robes of white;
But one was crowned with ama-
ranth, as with flame,
And one with asphodels, like
flakes of light.

I saw them pause on their celestial
way;
Then said I, with deep fear and
doubt oppressed,
"Beat not so loud, my heart, lest
thou betray
The place where thy beloved are
at rest!"

And he who wore the crown of
asphodels,
Descending, at my door began
to knock,
And my soul sank within me, as in
wells
The waters sink before an earth-
quake's shock.

I recognised the nameless agony,
The terror and the tremor and
the pain,
That oft before had filled or
haunted me,
And now returned with three-
fold strength again.

The door I opened to my heavenly
guest,
  And listened, for I thought I
heard God's voice;
And, knowing whatsoe'er he sent
was best,
  Dared neither to lament nor to
rejoice.

Then with a smile, that filled the
house with light,
  "My errand is not Death, but
Life," he said;
And ere I answered, passing out of
sight,
  On his celestial embassy he sped.

'Twas at thy door, O friend! and
not at mine,
  The angel with the amaranthine
wreath,
Pausing, descended, and with voice
divine,
  Whispered a word that had a
sound like Death.

Then fell upon the house a sudden
gloom,
  A shadow on those features fair
and thin;
And softly, from that hushed and
darkened room,
  Two angels issued, where but
one went in.

All is of God! If he but wave his
hand,
  The mists collect, the rain falls
thick and loud,
Till, with a smile of light on sea
and land,
  Lo! he looks back from the de-
parting cloud.

Angels of Life and Death alike are
his;
  Without his leave they pass no
threshold o'er;

Who, then, would wish or dare, be-
lieving this,
  Against his messengers to shut
the door?

DAYLIGHT AND MOONLIGHT

In broad daylight, and at noon,
Yesterday I saw the moon
Sailing high, but faint and white,
As a schoolboy's paper kite.

In broad daylight, yesterday,
I read a Poet's mystic lay;
And it seemed to me at most
As a phantom, or a ghost.

But at length the feverish day
Like a passion died away,
And the night, serene and still,
Fell on village, vale and hill,

Then the moon, in all her pride,
Like a spirit glorified,
Filled and overflowed the night
With revelations of her light.

And the Poet's song again
Passed like music through my
brain;
Night interpreted to me
All its grace and mystery.

THE JEWISH CEMETERY AT NEWPORT

How strange it seems! These
Hebrews in their graves,
  Close by the street of this fair
seaport town.
Silent beside the never-silent
waves,
  At rest in all this moving up and
down!

The trees are white with dust, that
    o'er their sleep
    Wave their broad curtains in
      the south-wind's breath,
While underneath such leafy tents
    they keep
    The long, mysterious Exodus of
      Death.

And these sepulchral stones, so old
    and brown,
    That pave with level flags their
      burial-place,
Seem like the tablets of the Law,
    thrown down
    And broken by Moses at the
      mountain's base.

The very names recorded here are
    strange,
    Of foreign accent, and of different
      climes:
Alvares and Rivera interchange
    With Abraham and Jacob of old
      times.

"Blessed be God! for he created
    Death!"
    The mourners said, "and Death
      is rest and peace";
Then added, in the certainty of
    faith,
    "And giveth Life that never
      more shall cease."

Closed are the portals of their
    Synagogue,
    No Psalms of David now the
      silence break,
No Rabbi reads the ancient Deca-
    logue
    In the grand dialect the Pro-
      phets spake.

Gone are the living, but the dead
    remain,
    And not neglected; for a hand
    unseen,

Scattering its bounty, like a
    summer rain,
    Still keeps their graves and
      their remembrance green.

How came they here? What
    burst of Christian hate,
    What persecution, merciless and
      blind,
Drove o'er the sea—that desert
    desolate—
    These Ishmaels and Hagars of
      mankind?

They lived in narrow streets and
    lanes obscure,
    Ghetto and Judenstrass, in
      mirk and mire;
Taught in the school of patience
    to endure
    The life of anguish and the
      death of fire.

All their lives long, with the un-
    leavened bread
    And bitter herbs of exile and its
      fears,
The wasting famine of the heart
    they fed,
    And slaked its thirst with marah
      of their tears.

Anathema marantha! was the cry
    That rang from town to town,
      from street to street;
At every gate the accursed Morde-
    cai
    Was mocked and jeered, and
      spurned by Christian feet.

Pride and humiliation hand in
    hand
    Walked with them through the
      world where'er they went;
Trampled and beaten were they
    as the sand,
    And yet unshaken as the con-
      tinent.

For in the background figures
vague and vast
  Of patriarchs and of prophets
  rose sublime,
And all the great traditions of the
Past
  They saw reflected in the com-
  ing time.

And thus for ever with reverted
look
  The mystic volume of the world
  they read,
Spelling it backward, like a He-
brew book.
  Till life became a Legend of the
  Dead.

But ah! what once has been shall
be no more!
  The groaning earth in travail
  and in pain
Brings forth its races, but does not
restore,
  And the dead nations never rise
  again.

OLIVER BASSELIN [1]

In the Valley of the Vire
  Still is seen an ancient mill,
With its gables quaint and queer,
  And beneath the window-sill,
    On the stone,
    These words alone:
"Oliver Basselin lived here."

Far above it, on the steep,
  Ruined stands the old Château;
Nothing but the donjon-keep
  Left for shelter or for show.

[1] Oliver Basselin, the "*Père joyeux
du Vaudeville*," flourished in the fif-
teenth century, and gave to his con-
vivial songs the name of his native
valleys, in which he sang them,
Vaux-de-Vire. This name was after-
wards corrupted into the modern
Vaudeville.

    Its vacant eyes
    Stare at the skies,
Stare at the valley green and deep.

Once a convent, old and brown,
  Looked, but ah! it looks no
  more,
From the neighbouring hillside
down
  On the rushing and the roar
    On the stream
    Whose sunny gleam
Cheers the little Norman town.

In that darksome mill of stone,
  To the water's dash and din,
Careless, humble, and unknown,
  Sang the poet Basselin
    Songs that fill
    That ancient mill
With a splendour of its own.

Never feeling of unrest
  Broke the pleasant dream he
  dreamed;
Only made to be his nest,
  All the lovely valley seemed;
    No desire
    Of soaring higher
Stirred or fluttered in his breast.

True, his songs were not divine;
  Were not songs of that high art,
Which, as winds do in the pine,
  Find an answer in each heart;
    But the mirth
    Of this green earth
Laughed and revelled in his line.

From the alehouse and the inn,
  Opening on the narrow street,
Came the loud, convivial din,
  Singing and applause of feet,
    The laughing lays
    That in those days
Sang the poet Basselin.

In the castle, cased in steel,
  Knights, who fought at Agin-
  court,

Watched and waited, spur on heel;
But the poet sang for sport
Songs that rang
Another clang,
Songs that lowlier hearts could feel.

In the convent, clad in gray,
Sat the monks in lonely cells,
Paced the cloisters, knelt to pray,
And the poet heard their bells;
But his rhymes
Found other chimes,
Nearer to the earth than they.

Gone are all the barons bold,
Gone are all the knights and squires,
Gone the abbot stern and cold,
And the brotherhood of friars;
Not a name
Remains to fame,
From those mouldering days of old!

But the poet's memory here
Of the landscape makes a part;
Like the river, swift and clear,
Flows his song through many a heart;
Haunting still
That ancient mill,
In the Valley of the Vire.

VICTOR GALBRAITH [1]

Under the walls of Monterey
At daybreak the bugles began to play,
Victor Galbraith!
In the mist of the morning damp and gray,

[1] This poem is founded on fact. Victor Galbraith was a bugler in a company of volunteer cavalry; and was shot in Mexico for some breach of discipline. It is a common superstition among soldiers, that no balls will kill them unless their names are written on them. The old proverb says, "Every bullet has its billet."

These were the words they seemed to say:
"Come forth to thy death,
Victor Galbraith!"

Forth he came, with a martial tread;
Firm was his step, erect his head;
Victor Galbraith!
He who so well the bugle played,
Could not mistake the words it said;
"Come forth to thy death,
Victor Galbraith!"

He looked at the earth, he looked at the sky,
He looked at the files of musketry,
Victor Galbraith!
And he said, with a steady voice and eye,
"Take good aim; I am ready to die!"
Thus challenges death
Victor Galbraith.

Twelve fiery tongues flashed straight and red,
Six leaden balls on their errand sped;
Victor Galbraith
Falls to the ground, but he is not dead;
His name was not stamped on those balls of lead,
And they only scath
Victor Galbraith.

Three balls are in his breast and brain,
But he rises out of the dust again,
Victor Galbraith!
The water he drinks has a bloody stain;
"O kill me, and put me out of my pain!"
In his agony prayeth
Victor Galbraith.

Forth dart once more those
tongues of flame,
And the bugler has died a death
of shame,
Victor Galbraith!
His soul has gone back to whence
it came,
And no one answers to the name,
When the Sergeant saith,
"Victor Galbraith!"

Under the walls of Monterey
By night a bugle is heard to play,
Victor Galbraith!
Through the mist of the valley
damp and gray
The sentinels hear the sound, and
say,
"That is the wraith
Of Victor Galbraith!"

MY LOST YOUTH

Often I think of the beautiful town
That is seated by the sea;
Often in thought go up and down
The pleasant streets of that dear
old town.
And my youth comes back to me,
And a verse of a Lapland song
Is haunting my memory still:
"A boy's will is the wind's will,
And the thoughts of youth are
long, long thoughts."

I can see the shadowy lines of its
trees,
And catch, in sudden gleams,
The sheen of the far-surrounding
seas,
And islands that were the Hes-
perides
Of all my boyish dreams.
And the burden of that old
song,
It murmurs and whispers still:
"A boy's will is the wind's will,
And the thoughts of youth are
long, long thoughts."

I remember the black wharves and
the slips,
And the sea-tides tossing free;
And Spanish sailors with bearded
lips,
And the beauty and mystery of
the ships,
And the magic of the sea.
And the voice of that way-
ward song,
Is singing and saying still:
"A boy's will is the wind's will,
And the thoughts of youth are
long, long thoughts."

I remember the bulwarks by the
shore,
And the fort upon the hill;
The sunrise gun, with its hollow
roar,
The drum-beat repeated o'er and
o'er,
And the bugle wild and shrill.
And the music of that old song
Throbs in my memory still:
"A boy's will is the wind's will,
And the thoughts of youth are
long, long thoughts."

I remember the sea-fight far away,[1]
How it thundered o'er the tide!
And the dead captains, as they lay
In their graves, o'erlooking the
tranquil bay,
Where they in battle died.
And the sound of that
mournful song
Goes through me with a thrill:
"A boy's will is the wind's will,
And the thoughts of youth are
long, long thoughts."

I can see the breezy dome of groves,
The shadows of Deering's Woods;

[1] This was the engagement between
the *Enterprise* and *Boxer*, off the
harbour of Portland, in which both
captains were slain. They were
buried side by side, in the cemetery
on Mountjoy.

And the friendships old and the
    early loves
Come back with a Sabbath sound,
    as of doves
    In quiet neighbourhoods.
        And the verse of that sweet
        old song,
        It flutters and murmurs still:
"A boy's will is the wind's will,
And the thoughts of youth are
    long, long thoughts."

I remember the gleams and glooms
    that dart
    Across the schoolboy's brain;
The song and the silence in the
    heart,
That in part are prophecies, and
    in part
    Are longings wild and vain.
        And the voice of that fitful
        song
        Sings on, and is never still:
"A boy's will is the wind's will,
And the thoughts of youth are
    long, long thoughts."

There are things of which I may
    not speak;
    There are dreams that cannot
    die;
There are thoughts that make the
    strong heart weak,
And bring a pallor into the cheek,
    And a mist before the eye.
        And the words to that fatal
        song
        Come over me like a chill:
"A boy's will is the wind's will,
And the thoughts of youth are
    long, long thoughts."

Strange to me now are the forms I
    meet
    When I visit the dear old town;
But the native air is pure and
    sweet,
And the trees that o'ershadow
    each well-known street,

As they balance up and down,
    Are singing the beautiful song,
    Are sighing and whispering
    still:
"A boy's will is the wind's will,
And the thoughts of youth are
    long, long thoughts."

And Deering's Woods are fresh
    and fair,
    And with joy that is almost pain
My heart goes back to wander
    there,
And among the dreams of the days
    that were,
    I find my lost youth again.
        And the strange and beautiful
        song,
        The groves are repeating it
        still:
"A boy's will is the wind's will,
And the thoughts of youth are
    long, long thoughts."

THE ROPEWALK

In that building, long and low,
With its windows all a-row,
    Like the port-holes of a hulk,
Human spiders spin and spin,
Backward down their threads so
    thin
    Dropping, each a hempen bulk.

At the end, an open door;
Squares of sunshine on the floor
    Light the long and dusky lane;
And the whirring of a wheel,
Dull and drowsy, makes me feel
    All its spokes are in my brain.

As the spinners to the end
Downward go and reascend,
    Gleam the long threads in the
    sun;
While within this brain of mine
Cobwebs brighter and more fine
    By the busy wheel are spun.

Two fair maidens in a swing,
Like white doves upon the wing,
  First before my vision pass;
Laughing, as their gentle hands
Closely clasp the twisted strands,
  At their shadow on the grass.

Then a booth of mountebanks,
With its smell of tan and planks,
  And a girl poised high in air
On a cord, in spangled dress,
With a faded loveliness,
  And a weary look of care.

Then a homestead among farms,
And a woman with bare arms
  Drawing water from a well;
As the bucket mounts apace,
With it mounts her own fair face,
  As at some magician's spell.

Then an old man in a tower,
Ringing loud the noontide hour,
  While the rope coils round and
    round
Like a serpent at his feet,
And again, in swift retreat,
  Nearly lifts him from the ground.

Then within a prison-yard,
Faces fixed, and stern, and hard,
  Laughter and indecent mirth;
Ah! it is the gallows-tree!
Breath of Christian charity,
  Blow, and sweep it from the
    earth!

Then a schoolboy, with his kite
Gleaming in a sky of light,
  And an eager, upward look;
Steeds pursued through lane and
    field;
Fowlers with their snares con-
    cealed;
  And an angler by a brook.

Ships rejoicing in the breeze,
Wrecks that float o'er unknown
    seas,

Anchors dragged through faith-
    less sand;
Sea-fog drifting overhead,
And, with lessening line and lead,
  Sailors feeling for the land.

All these scenes do I behold,
These, and many left untold,
  In that building long and low;
While the wheel goes round and
    round,
With a drowsy, dreamy sound,
  And the spinners backward go.

THE GOLDEN MILE-STONE

Leafless are the trees; their purple
    branches
Spread themselves abroad, like
    reefs of coral,
      Rising silent
In the Red Sea of the winter
    sunset.

From the hundred chimneys of the
    village,
Like the Afreet in the Arabian
    story,
      Smoky columns
Tower aloft into the air of amber.

At the window winks the flickering
    fire-light;
Here and there the lamps of even-
    ing glimmer.
      Social watch-fires
Answering one another through
    the darkness.

On the hearth the lighted logs are
    glowing,
And like Ariel in the cloven pine-
    tree
      For its freedom
Groans and sighs the air im-
    prisoned in them.

By the fireside there are old men
    seated,
Seeing ruined cities in the ashes,
        Asking sadly
Of the Past what it can ne'er
    restore them.

By the fireside there are youthful
    dreamers,
Building castles fair, with stately
    stairways,
        Asking blindly
Of the future what it cannot give
    them.

By the fireside tragedies are acted
In whose scenes appear two actors
    only,
        Wife and husband,
And above them God the sole
    spectator.

By the fireside there are peace and
    comfort,
Wives and children, with fair,
    thoughtful faces,
        Waiting, watching
For a well-known footstep in the
    passage.

Each man's chimney is his Golden
    Mile-stone;
Is the central point, from which he
    measures
        Every distance
Through the gateways of the world
    around him.

In his farthest wanderings still he
    sees it;
Hears the talking flame, the
    answering night-wind,
        As he heard them
When he sat with those who were,
    but are not.

Happy he whom neither wealth
    nor fashion,
Nor the march of the encroaching
    city,

Drives an exile
From the hearth of his ancestral
    homestead.

We may build more splendid
    habitations,
Fill our rooms with paintings and
    with sculptures,
        But we cannot
Buy with gold the old associations!

CATAWBA WINE

    This song of mine
    Is a Song of the Vine,
To be sung by the glowing embers
    Of wayside inns,
    When the rain begins
To darken the drear Novembers.

    It is not a song
    Of the Scuppernong,
From warm Carolinian valleys,
    Nor the Isabel
    And the Muscadel
That bask in our garden alleys.

    Nor the red Mustang,
    Whose clusters hang
O'er the waves of the Colorado,
    And the fiery flood
    Of whose purple blood
Has a dash of Spanish bravado.

    For richest and best
    Is the wine of the West,
That grows by the Beautiful River;
    Whose sweet perfume
    Fills all the room
With a benison on the giver.

    And as hollow trees
    Are the haunts of bees,
For ever going and coming;
    So this crystal hive
    Is all alive
With a swarming and buzzing and
    humming.

Very good in its way
Is the Verzenay,
Or the Sillery soft and creamy;
But Catawba wine
Has a taste more divine,
More dulcet, delicious, and dreamy.

There grows no vine
By the haunted Rhine,
By Danube or Guadalquivir,
Nor an island or cape,
That bears such a grape
As grows by the Beautiful River.

Drugged is their juice
For foreign use,
When shipped o'er the reeling Atlantic,
To rack our brains
With the fever pains,
That have driven the Old World frantic.

To the sewers and sinks
With all such drinks,
And after them tumble the mixer;
For a poison malign
Is such Borgia wine,
Or at best but a Devil's Elixir.

While pure as a spring
Is the wine I sing,
And to praise it, one needs but name it;
For Catawba wine
Has need of no sign,
No tavern-bush to proclaim it.

And this Song of the Vine,
This greeting of mine,
The winds and the birds shall deliver
To the Queen of the West,
In her garlands dressed,
On the banks of the Beautiful River.

SANTA FILOMENA [1]

Whene'er a noble deed is wrought,
Whene'er is spoken a noble thought,
    Our hearts, in glad surprise,
    To higher levels rise.

The tidal wave of deeper souls
Into our inmost being rolls,
    And lifts us unawares
    Out of all meaner cares.

Honour to those whose words or deeds
Thus help us in our daily needs,
    And by their overflow
    Raise us from what is low!

Thus thought I, as by night I read
Of the great army of the dead,
    The trenches cold and damp,
    The starved and frozen camp,—

The wounded from the battle-plain
In dreary hospitals of pain,
    The cheerless corridors,
    The cold and stony floors.

Lo! in that house of misery
A lady with a lamp I see
    Pass through the glimmering gloom,
    And flit from room to room.

And slow, as in a dream of bliss,
The speechless sufferer turns to kiss
    Her shadow, as it falls
    Upon the darkening walls.

[1] "At Pisa the church of San Francisco contains a chapel dedicated lately to Santa Filomena; over the altar is a picture, by Sabatelli, representing the Saint as a beautiful, nymph-like figure, floating down from heaven, attended by two angels bearing the lily, palm, and javelin, and beneath, in the foreground, the sick and maimed, who are healed by her intercession."—Mrs. Jameson, *Sacred and Legendary Art*, II. 298.

As if a door in heaven should be
Opened and then closed suddenly,
    The vision came and went,
    The light shone and was spent.

On England's annals, through the
    long
Hereafter of her speech and song,
    That light its rays shall cast
    From portals of the past.

A Lady with a Lamp shall stand
In the great history of the land,
    A noble type of good,
    Heroic womanhood.

Nor even shall be wanting here
The palm, the lily, and the spear,
    The symbols that of yore
    Saint Filomena bore.

THE DISCOVERER OF THE NORTH CAPE

A LEAF FROM KING ALFRED'S OROSIUS

Othere, the old sea-captain,
    Who dwelt in Helgoland,
To King Alfred, the Lover of
    Truth,
Brought a snow-white walrus-
    tooth,
    Which he held in his brown
    right hand.

His figure was tall and stately,
    Like a boy's his eye appeared;
His hair was yellow as hay,
But threads of a silvery gray
    Gleamed in his tawny beard.

Hearty and hale was Othere,
    His cheek had the colour of oak;
With a kind of laugh in his speech,
Like the sea-tide on a beach,
    As unto the King he spoke.

And Alfred, King of the Saxons,
    Had a book upon his knees,

And wrote down the wondrous tale
Of him who was first to sail
    Into the Arctic seas.

"So far I live to the northward,
    No man lives north of me:
To the east are wild mountain-
    chains,
And beyond them meres and
    plains;
    To the westward all is sea.

"So far I live to the northward,
    From the harbour of Skeringes-
    hale,
If you only sailed by day,
With a fair wind all the way,
    More than a month would you
    sail.

"I own six hundred reindeer,
    With sheep and swine beside;
I have tribute from the Finns,
Whalebone and reindeer-skins,
    And ropes of walrus-hide.

"I ploughed the land with horses,
    But my heart was ill at ease,
For the old seafaring men
Came to me now and then,
    With their sagas of the seas;—

"Of Iceland and of Greenland,
    And the stormy Hebrides,
And the undiscovered deep;—
Oh, I could not eat nor sleep
    For thinking of those seas.

"To the northward stretched the
    desert,
    How far I fain would know;
So at last I sallied forth,
And three days sailed due north,
    As far as the whale-ships go.

"To the west of me was the ocean,
    To the right the desolate shore,
But I did not slacken sail
For the walrus or the whale,
    Till after three days more.

"The days grew longer and longer,
    Till they became as one,
And southward through the haze
    I saw the sullen blaze
        Of the red midnight sun.

"And then uprose before me,
    Upon the water's edge,
The huge and haggard shape
Of that unknown North Cape,
    Whose form is like a wedge.

"The sea was rough and stormy,
    The tempest howled and wailed,
And the sea-fog, like a ghost,
Haunted that dreary coast,
    But onward still I sailed.

"Four days I steered to eastward,
    Four days without a night:
Round in a fiery ring
Went the great sun, O King,
    With red and lurid light."

Here Alfred, King of the Saxons,
    Ceased writing for a while;
And raised his eyes from his book,
With a strange and puzzled look,
    And an incredulous smile.

But Othere, the old sea-captain,
    He neither paused nor stirred,
Till the King listened, and then
Once more took up his pen,
    And wrote down every word.

"And now the land," said Othere,
    "Bent southward suddenly,
And I followed the curving shore
And ever southward bore
    Into a nameless sea.

"And there we hunted the walrus,
    The narwhale, and the seal;
Ha! 'twas a noble game!
And like the lightning's flame
    Flew our harpoons of steel.

"There were six of us all together,
    Norsemen of Helgoland;
In two days and no more

We killed of them threescore,
    And dragged them to the
        strand!"

Here Alfred the Truth-Teller
    Suddenly closed his book,
And lifted his blue eyes,
With doubt and strange surmise
    Depicted in their look.

And Othere the old sea-captain
    Stared at him wild and weird,
Then smiled, till his shining teeth
Gleamed white from underneath
    His tawny, quivering beard.

And to the King of the Saxons,
    In witness of the truth,
Raising his noble head,
He stretched his brown hand, and
    said,
        "Behold this walrus-tooth!"

DAYBREAK

A wind came up out of the sea,
And said, "O mists, make room
    for me."

It hailed the ships, and cried,
    "Sail on,
Ye mariners, the night is gone."

And hurried landward far away,
Crying, "Awake! it is the day."

It said unto the forest, "Shout!
Hang all your leafy banners out!"

It touched the wood-bird's folded
    wing,
And said, "O bird, awake and
    sing."

And o'er the farms, "O chanticleer
Your clarion blow; the day is
    near."

It whispered to the fields of corn,
"Bow down, and hail the coming
    morn."

It shouted through the belfry-
    tower,
"Awake, O bell! proclaim the
    hour."

It crossed the churchyard with a
    sigh,
And said, "Not yet! in quiet lie."

THE FIFTIETH BIRTHDAY
OF AGASSIZ

MAY 28, 1857

It was fifty years ago
    In the pleasant month of May,
In the beautiful Pays de Vaud,
    A child in its cradle lay.

And Nature, the old nurse, took
    The child upon her knee,
Saying: "Here is a story-book
    Thy Father has written for
        thee."

"Come, wander with me," she said,
    "Into regions yet untrod;
And read what is still unread
    In the manuscripts of God."

And he wandered away and away
    With Nature, the dear old nurse,
Who sang to him night and day
    The rhymes of the universe.

And whenever the way seemed
    long,
    Or his heart began to fail,
She would sing a more wonderful
    song,
    Or tell a more marvellous tale.

So she keeps him still a child,
    And will not let him go,

Though at times his heart beats
    wild
    For the beautiful Pays de Vaud;

Though at times he hears in his
    dreams
    The Ranz des Vaches of old,
And the rush of mountain streams
    From glaciers clear and cold;

And the mother at home says,
    "Hark!
    For his voice I listen and yearn;
It is growing late and dark,
    And my boy does not return!"

CHILDREN

Come to me, O ye children!
    For I hear you at your play,
And the questions that perplexed
    me
    Have vanished quite away.

Ye open the eastern windows,
    That look towards the sun,
Where thoughts are singing swal-
    lows
    And the brooks of morning run.

In your hearts are the birds and
    the sunshine,
    In your thoughts the brooklet's
        flow,
But in mine is the wind of Autumn
    And the first fall of the snow.

Ah! what would the world be to us
    If the children were no more?
We should dread the desert behind
    us
    Worse than the dark before.

What the leaves are to the forest,
    With light and air for food,
Ere their sweet and tender juices
    Have been hardened into
        wood,—

That to the world are children;
Through them it feels the glow
Of a brighter and sunnier climate
Than reaches the trunks below.

Come to me, O ye children!
And whisper in my ear
What the birds and the winds are
singing
In your sunny atmosphere.

For what are all our contrivings,
And the wisdom of our books,
When compared with your caresses
And the gladness of your looks?

Ye are better than all the ballads
That ever were sung or said;
For ye are living poems,
And all the rest are dead.

SANDALPHON

Have you read in the Talmud of
old,
In the Legends the Rabbins have
told
Of the limitless realms of the
air,—
Have you read it,—the marvellous
story
Of Sandalphon, the Angel of Glory,
Sandalphon, the Angel of
Prayer?

How, erect, at the outermost gates
Of the City Celestial he waits,
With his feet on the ladder of
light,
That, crowded with angels un-
numbered,
By Jacob was seen, as he slum-
bered
Alone in the desert at night?

The Angels of Wind and of Fire
Chaunt only one hymn, and expire

With the song's irresistible
stress;
Expire in their rapture and wonder
As harp-strings are broken asunder
By music they throb to express.

But serene in the rapturous throng,
Unmoved by the rush of the song,
With eyes unimpassioned and
slow,
Among the dead angels, the
deathless
Sandalphon stands listening
breathless
To sounds that ascend from be-
low;—

From the spirits on earth that
adore,
From the souls that entreat and
implore
In the fervour and passion of
prayer;
From the hearts that are broken
with losses,
And weary with dragging the
crosses
Too heavy for mortals to bear.

And he gathers the prayers as he
stands,
And they change into flowers in his
hands,
Into garlands of purple and
red;
And beneath the great arch of the
portal,
Through the streets of the City
Immortal
Is wafted the fragrance they
shed.

It is but a legend, I know,—
A fable, a phantom, a show,
Of the ancient Rabbinical lore;
Yet the old medieval tradition,
The beautiful, strange superstition
But haunts me and holds me
the more.

When I look from my window at
    night,
And the welkin above is all white,
    All throbbing and panting with
      stars,
Among them majestic is standing
Sandalphon the angel, expanding
    His pinions in nebulous bars.

And the legend, I feel, is a part
    Of the hunger and thirst of the
      heart,
    The frenzy and fire of the brain,
That grasps at the fruitage for-
      bidden,
The golden pomegranates of Eden,
    To quiet its fever and pain.

FLIGHT THE SECOND

THE CHILDREN'S HOUR

Between the dark and the daylight
    When the night is beginning to
      lower,
Comes a pause in the day's occu-
      pations,
    That is known as the Children's
      Hour.

I hear in the chamber above me
    The patter of little feet,
The sound of a door that is opened,
    And voices soft and sweet.

From my study I see in the lamp-
    light,
    Descending the broad hall stair,
Grave Alice, and laughing Allegra,
    And Edith with golden hair.

A whisper, and then a silence:
    Yet I know by their merry eyes
They are plotting and planning
    together
    To take me by surprise.

A sudden rush from the stairway,
    A sudden raid from the hall!
By three doors left unguarded
    They enter my castle wall!

They climb up into my turret
    O'er the arms and back of my
      chair;

If I try to escape, they surround
    me;
    They seem to be everywhere.

They almost devour me with kisses,
    Their arms about me entwine,
Till I think of the Bishop of Bingen
    In his Mouse-Tower on the
      Rhine!

Do you think, O blue-eyed banditti,
    Because you have scaled the wall
Such an old moustache as I am
    Is not a match for you all!

I have you fast in my fortress,
    And will not let you depart,
But put you down into the dun-
    geon
    In the round-tower of my heart.

And there will I keep you for ever,
    Yes, for ever and a day,
Till the walls shall crumble to ruin,
    And moulder in dust away!

ENCELADUS

Under Mount Etna he lies,
    It is slumber, it is not death
For he struggles at times to arise,
And above him the lurid skies
    Are hot with his fiery breath.

The crags are piled on his breast,
The earth is heaped on his head;
But the groans of his wild unrest,
Though smothered and half suppressed,
Are heard, and he is not dead.

And the nations far away
Are watching with eager eyes;
They talk together, and say,
"To-morrow, perhaps to-day,
Enceladus will arise!"

And the old gods, the austere
Oppressors in their strength,
Stand aghast and white with fear
At the ominous sounds they hear,
And tremble, and mutter, "At
length!"

Ah me! for the land that is sown
With the harvest of despair!
Where the burning cinders, blown
From the lips of the overthrown
Enceladus, fill the air.

Where ashes are heaped in drifts
Over vineyard and field and
town,
Whenever he starts and lifts
His head through the blackened
rifts
Of the crags that keep him down.

See, see! the red light shines!
'Tis the glare of his awful eyes!
And the storm - wind shouts
through the pines
Of Alps and of Apennines,
"Enceladus, arise!"

THE CUMBERLAND

At anchor in Hampton Roads we
lay,
On board of the Cumberland,
sloop-of-war;
And at times from the fortress
across the bay

The alarum of drums swept
past,
Or a bugle blast
From the camp on the shore.

Then far away to the south uprose
A little feather of snow-white
smoke,
And we knew that the iron ship of
our foes
Was steadily steering its
course
To try the force
Of our ribs of oak.

Down upon us heavily runs,
Silent and sullen, the floating
fort;
Then comes a puff of smoke from
her guns,
And leaps the terrible death,
With fiery breath,
From each open port.

We are not idle, but send her
straight,
Defiance back in a full broad-
side!
As hail rebounds from a roof of
slate,
Rebounds our heavier hail
From each iron scale
Of the monster's hide.

"Strike your flag!" the rebel cries,
In his arrogant old plantation
strain.
"Never!" our gallant Morris re-
plies;
"It is better to sink than to
yield!"
And the whole air pealed
With cheers of our men.

Then, like a kraken huge and
black,
She crushed our ribs in her iron
grasp!

Down went the Cumberland all a
　　wrack,
　　With a sudden shudder of
　　　death,
　　And the cannon's breath
For her dying gasp.

Next morn, as the sun rose over
　　the bay,
　　Still floated our flag at the main-
　　　mast-head.
Lord, how beautiful was thy day!
　　Every waft of the air
　　Was a whisper of prayer,
　　Or a dirge for the dead.

Ho! brave hearts that went down
　　in the seas!
　　Ye are at peace in the troubled
　　　stream,
Ho! brave land! with hearts like
　　these,
　　Thy flag, that is rent in twain,
　　Shall be one again,
And without a seam!

SNOWFLAKES

Out of the bosom of the Air,
　　Out of the cloud-folds of her
　　　garments shaken,
Over the woodlands brown and
　　bare
　　Over the harvest-fields forsaken,
　　Silent, and soft, and slow
　　Descends the snow.

Even as our cloudy fancies take
　　Suddenly shape in some divine
　　　expression,
Even as the troubled heart doth
　　make
　　In the white countenance con-
　　　fession,
　　The troubled sky reveals
　　The grief it feels.

This is the poem of the air,
　　Slowly in silent syllables re-
　　　corded;
This is the secret of despair,
　　Long in its cloudy bosom
　　　hoarded,
　　　Now whispered and revealed
　　To wood and field.

A DAY OF SUNSHINE

O gift of God! O perfect day:
Whereon shall no man work, but
　　play;
Whereon it is enough for me,
Not to be doing, but to be!

Through every fibre of my brain,
Through every nerve, through
　　every vein,
I feel the electric thrill, the touch
Of life, that seems almost too
　　much.

I hear the wind among the trees
Playing celestial symphonies;
I see the branches downward bent,
Like keys of some great instru-
　　ment.

And over me unrolls on high
The splendid scenery of the sky,
Where through the sapphire sea
　　the sun
Sails like a golden galleon,

Towards yonder cloud-land in the
　　West,
Towards yonder Islands of the
　　Blest,
Whose steep sierra far uplifts
Its craggy summits white with
　　drifts.

Blow, winds! and waft through all
　　the rooms
The snow-flakes of the cherry-
　　blooms!

Blow, winds! and bend within my reach
The fiery blossoms of the peach!

O Life and Love! O happy throng
Of thoughts, whose only speech is song!
O heart of man! canst thou not be
Blithe as the air is, and as free?

SOMETHING LEFT UNDONE

Labour with what zeal we will,
  Something still remains undone,
Something uncompleted still
  Waits the rising of the sun.

By the bedside, on the stair,
  At the threshold, near the gates,
With its menace or its prayer,
  Like a mendicant it waits;

Waits, and will not go away;
  Waits, and will not be gainsaid;
By the cares of yesterday
  Each to-day is heavier made;

Till at length the burden seems
  Greater than our strength can bear,
Heavy as the weight of dreams,
  Pressing on us everywhere.

And we stand from day to day,
  Like the dwarfs of times gone by,
Who, as Northern legends say,
  On their shoulders held the sky.

WEARINESS

O little feet! that such long years
Must wander on through hopes and fears,
  Must ache and bleed beneath your load;
I, nearer to the wayside inn
Where toil shall cease and rest begin,
  Am weary, thinking of your road!

O little hands! that, weak or strong,
Have still to serve or rule so long,
  Have still so long to give or ask;
I, who so much with book and pen
Have toiled among my fellow-men,
  Am weary, thinking of your task.

O little hearts! that throb and beat
With such impatient, feverish heat,
  Such limitless and strong desires;
Mine that so long has glowed and burned,
With passions into ashes turned
  Now covers and conceals its fires.

O little souls! as pure and white
And crystalline as rays of light
  Direct from heaven, their source divine;
Refracted through the mist of years,
How red my setting sun appears,
  How lurid looks this soul of mine!

FLIGHT THE THIRD

FATA MORGANA

O sweet illusions of Song,
  That tempt me everywhere,
In the lonely fields, and the throng
  Of the crowded thoroughfare!

I approach, and ye vanish away,
  I grasp you, and ye are gone;

But ever by night and by day
  The melody soundeth on.

As the weary traveller sees
  In desert or prairie vast,
Blue lakes, overhung with trees,
  That a pleasant shadow cast;

Fair towns with turrets high,
  And shining roofs of gold,
That vanish as he draws nigh,
  Like mists together rolled,—

So I wander and wander along,
  And for ever before me gleams
The shining city of song,
  In the beautiful land of dreams.

But when I would enter the gate
  Of that golden atmosphere,
It is gone, and I wander and wait
  For the vision to reappear.

THE HAUNTED CHAMBER

Each heart has its haunted
    chamber,
  Where the silent moonlight
    falls!
On the floor are mysterious foot-
    steps,
  There are whispers along the
    walls!

And mine at times is haunted
  By phantoms of the Past,
As motionless as shadows
  By the silent moonlight cast.

A form sits by the window,
  That is not seen by day,
For as soon as the dawn ap-
    proaches
  It vanishes away.

It sits there in the moonlight,
  Itself as pale and still,
And points with its airy finger
  Across the window-sill.

Without, before the window,
  There stands a gloomy pine,
Whose boughs wave upward and
    downward
  As wave these thoughts of mine.

And underneath its branches
  Is the grave of a little child,
Who died upon life's threshold,
  And never wept nor smiled.

What are ye, O pallid phantoms!
  That haunt my troubled brain?
That vanish when day approaches,
  And at night return again?

What are ye, O pallid phantoms!
  But the statues without breath,
That stand on the bridge over-
    arching
  The silent river of death?

THE MEETING

After so long an absence
  At last we meet again:
Does the meeting give us pleasure,
  Or does it give us pain?

The tree of life has been shaken,
  And but few of us linger now,
Like the Prophet's two or three
    berries
  In the top of the uppermost
    bough.

We cordially greet each other
  In the old, familiar tone;
And we think, though we do not
    say it,
  How old and gray he is grown!

We speak of a Merry Christmas
  And many a Happy New Year;
But each in his heart is thinking
  Of those that are not here.

We speak of friends and their
    fortunes,
  And of what they did and said,
Till the dead alone seem living,
  And the living alone seem dead.

And at last we hardly distinguish
　　Between the ghosts and the
　　guests;
And a mist and shadow of sadness
　　Steals over our merriest jests.

VOX POPULI

When Mazárvan the magician
　　Journeyed westward through
　　Cathay,
Nothing heard he but the praises
　　Of Badoura on his way.

But the lessening rumour ended
　　When he came to Khaledan,
There the folk were talking only
　　Of Prince Camaralzaman.

So it happens with the poets:
　　Every province hath its own;
Camaralzaman is famous
　　Where Badoura is unknown.

THE CASTLE-BUILDER

A gentle boy, with soft and
　　silken locks,
　　A dreamy boy, with brown and
　　tender eyes,
A castle-builder, with his wooden
　　blocks,
　　And towers that touch imagin-
　　ary skies.

A fearless rider on his father's
　　knee,
　　An eager listener unto stories
　　told
At the Round Table of the
　　nursery,
　　Of heroes and adventures mani-
　　fold.

There will be other towers for thee
　　to build;
　　There will be other steeds for
　　thee to ride;

There will be other legends, and
　　all filled
　　With greater marvels and more
　　glorified.

Build on, and make thy castles
　　high and fair,
　　Rising and reaching upward to
　　the skies;
Listen to voices in the upper air,
　　Nor lose thy simple faith in
　　mysteries.

CHANGED

From the outskirts of the town,
　　Where of old the mile-stone
　　stood,
Now a stranger, looking down
I behold the shadowy crown
　　Of the dark and haunted wood.

Is it changed, or am I changed?
　　Ah! the oaks are fresh and
　　green,
But the friends with whom I
　　ranged
Through their thickets are es-
　　tranged
　　By the years that intervene.

Bright as ever flows the sea,
　　Bright as ever shines the sun,
But, alas! they seem to me
Not the sun that used to be,
　　Not the tides that used to run.

THE CHALLENGE

I have vague remembrance
　　Of a story that is told
In some ancient Spanish legend
　　Or chronicle of old.

It was when brave King Sanchez
　　Was before Zamora slain,
And his great besieging army
　　Lay encamped upon the plain.

Don Diego de Ordoñez
  Sallied forth in front of all,
And shouted loud his challenge
  To the warders on the wall.

All the people of Zamora,
  Both the born and the unborn,
As traitors did he challenge
  With taunting words of scorn.

The living, in their houses,
  And in their graves, the dead!
And the waters of their rivers,
  And their wine, and oil, and
      bread!

There is a greater army
  That besets us round with strife,
A starving, numberless army,
  At all the gates of life.

The poverty-stricken millions
  Who challenge our wine and
      bread,
And impeach us all as traitors,
  Both the living and the dead.

And whenever I sit at the banquet,
  Where the feast and song are
      high,
Amid the mirth and the music
  I can hear that fearful cry.

And hollow and haggard faces
  Look into the lighted hall,
And wasted hands are extended
  To catch the crumbs that fall.

For within there is light and
      plenty,
  And odours fill the air;
But without there is cold and
      darkness,
  And hunger and despair.

And there in the camp of famine
  In wind and cold and rain,
Christ, the great Lord of the army,
  Lies dead upon the plain!

THE BROOK AND THE WAVE

The brooklet came from the
      mountain,
  As sang the bard of old,
Running with feet of silver
  Over the sands of gold!

Far away in the briny ocean
  There rolled a turbulent wave,
Now singing along the sea-beach,
  Now howling along the cave.

And the brooklet has found the
      billow,
  Though they flowed so far apart,
And has filled with its freshness
      and sweetness
  That turbulent, bitter heart!

FROM THE SPANISH CANCIONEROS

I

Eyes so tristful, eyes so tristful,
Heart so full of care and cumber,
I was lapped in rest and slumber,
Ye have made me wakeful, wistful!

In this life of labour endless
Who shall comfort my distresses?
Querulous my soul and friendless
In its sorrow shuns caresses.
Ye have made me, ye have made
      me
Querulous of you, that care not,
Eyes so tristful, yet I dare not
Say to what ye have betrayed me.

II

Some day, some day,
  O troubled breast,
  Shalt thou find rest.

If Love in thee
  To grief give birth,
  Six feet of earth

Can more than he;
There calm and free
And unoppressed
Shalt thou find rest.

The unattained
In life at last,
When life is passed
Shall all be gained;
And no more pained,
No more distressed,
Shalt thou find rest.

III

Come, O Death, so silent flying
That unheard thy coming be,
Lest the sweet delight of dying
Bring life back again to me.
For thy sure approach perceiving,
In my constancy and pain
I new life should win again,
Thinking that I am not living.
So to me, unconscious lying,
All unknown thy coming be,
Lest the sweet delight of dying
Bring life back again to me.

Unto him who finds thee hateful,
Death, thou art inhuman pain;
But to me, who dying gain,
Life is but a task ungrateful.
Come, then, with my wish comply-
      ing,
All unheard thy coming be,
Lest the sweet delight of dying
Bring life back again to me.

IV

Glove of black in white hand
      bare,
And about her forehead pale
Wound a thin, transparent veil,
That doth not conceal her hair;
Sovereign attitude and air,
Cheek and neck alike displayed,
With   coquettish   charms
    arrayed,

Laughing eyes and fugitive;—
This is killing men that live,
'Tis not mourning for the dead.

AFTERMATH

When the Summer fields are
      mown,
When the birds are fledged and
      flown,
      And the dry leaves strew the
      path;
With the falling of the snow,
With the cawing of the crow,
Once again the fields we mow
      And gather in the aftermath.

Not the sweet, new grass with
      flowers
Is this harvesting of ours;
    Not the upland clover bloom;
But the rowen mixed with weeds,
Tangled tufts from marsh and
      meads,
Where the poppy drops its seeds
    In the silence and the gloom.

EPIMETHEUS

OR THE POET'S AFTERTHOUGHT

Have I dreamed? or was it real,
    What I saw as in a vision,
When to marches hymeneal
In the land of the Ideal
    Moved my thought o'er Fields
    Elysian?

What! are these the guests whose
      glances
    Seemed like sunshine gleaming
    round me?
These the wild, bewildering fancies,
That with dithyrambic dances
    As with magic circles bound me?

Ah! how cold are their caresses!
    Pallid cheeks, and haggard
        bosoms!
Spectral gleam their snow-white
        dresses,
And from loose, dishevelled tresses
    Fall the hyacinthine blossoms!

O my songs! whose winsome
        measures
    Filled my heart with secret
        rapture!
Children of my golden leisures!
Must even your delights and
        pleasures
    Fade and perish with the cap-
        ture?

Fair they seemed, those songs
        sonorous,
    When they came to me un-
        bidden;
Voices single, and in chorus,
Like the wild birds singing o'er us
    In the dark of branches hidden.

Disenchantment! Disillusion!
    Must each noble aspiration
Come at last to this conclusion,
Jarring discord, wild confusion,
    Lassitude, renunciation?

Not with steeper fall nor faster,
    From the sun's serene domin-
        ions,
Not through brighter realms nor
        vaster,
In swift ruin and disaster,
    Icarus fell with shattered pin-
        ions!

Sweet Pandora! dear Pandora!
    Why did mighty Jove create
        thee

Coy as Thetis, fair as Flora,
Beautiful as young Aurora,
    If to win thee is to hate thee?

No, not hate thee! for this feeling
    Of unrest and long resistance
Is but passionate appealing,
A prophetic whisper stealing
    O'er the chords of our existence.

Him whom thou dost once enamour
    Thou, beloved, never leavest;
In life's discord, strife, and clamour
Still he feels thy spell of glamour;
    Him of Hope thou ne'er bereav-
        est.

Weary hearts by thee are lifted,
    Struggling souls by thee are
        strengthened,
Clouds of fear asunder rifted,
Truth from falsehood cleansed and
        sifted,
    Lives, like days in summer,
        lengthened!

Therefore art thou ever dearer,
    O my Sibyl, my deceiver!
For thou makest each mystery
        clearer,
And the unattained seems nearer,
    When thou fillest my heart with
        fever!

Muse of all the gifts and Graces!
    Though the fields around us
        wither,
There are ampler realms and
        spaces,
Where no foot has left its traces:
    Let us turn and wander thither!

TALES OF A WAYSIDE INN

PRELUDE

THE WAYSIDE INN

One Autumn night, in Sudbury
  town,
Across the meadows bare and
  brown,
The windows of the wayside inn
Gleamed red with fire-light
  through the leaves
Of woodbine, hanging from the
  eaves
Their crimson curtains rent and
  thin.

As ancient is this hostelry
As any in the land may be,
Built in the old Colonial day,
When men lived in a grander way,
With ampler hospitality;
A kind of old Hobgoblin Hall,
Now somewhat fallen to decay,
With weather-stains upon the wall,
And stairways worn, and crazy
  doors,
And creaking and uneven floors,
And chimneys huge, and tiled and
  tall.

A region of repose it seems,
A place of slumber and of dreams,
Remote among the wooded hills!
For there no noisy railway speeds,
Its torch-race scattering smoke and
  gleeds;
But noon and night, the panting
  teams
Stop under the great oaks, that
  throw
Tangles of light and shade below,
On roofs and doors and window-
  sills.

Across the road the barns display
Their lines of stalls, their mows of
  hay,
Through the wide doors the breezes
  blow,
The wattled cocks strut to and fro,
And, half effaced by rain and shine,
The Red Horse prances on the sign.
Round this old-fashioned, quaint
  abode
Deep silence reigned, save when a
  gust
Went rushing down the county
  road,
And skeletons of leaves, and dust,
A moment quickened by its breath,
Shuddered and danced their dance
  of death,
And through the ancient oaks o'er-
  head
Mysterious voices moaned and fled.

But from the parlour of the inn
A pleasant murmur smote the
  ear,
Like water rushing through a weir;
Oft interrupted by the din
Of laughter and of loud applause,
And, in each intervening pause,
The music of a violin.
The fire-light, shedding over all
The splendour of its ruddy glow,
Filled the whole parlour large and
  low;
It gleamed on wainscot and on
  wall,
It touched with more than wonted
  grace
Fair Princess Mary's pictured face;
It bronzed the rafters overhead,
On the old spinet's ivory keys
It played inaudible melodies,

It crowned the sombre clock with flame,
The hands, the hours, the maker's name,
And painted with a livelier red
The Landlord's coat-of-arms again;
And, flashing on the window-pane,
Emblazoned with its light and shade
The jovial rhymes, that still remain,
Writ near a century ago,
By the great Major Molineaux,
Whom Hawthorne has immortal made.

Before the blazing fire of wood
Erect the rapt musician stood;
And ever and anon he bent
His head upon his instrument,
And seemed to listen, till he caught
Confessions of its secret thought,—
The joy, the triumph, the lament,
The exultation and the pain;
Then, by the magic of his art,
He soothed the throbbings of its heart,
And lulled it into peace again.

Around the fireside at their ease
There sat a group of friends, entranced
With the delicious melodies;
Who from the far-off noisy town
Had to the wayside inn come down,
To rest beneath its old oak-trees.
The fire-light on their faces glanced,
Their shadows on the wainscot danced,
And, though of different lands and speech,
Each had his tale to tell, and each
Was anxious to be pleased and please.
And while the sweet musician plays,
Let me in outline sketch them all,
Perchance uncouthly as the blaze
With its uncertain touch portrays
Their shadowy semblance on the wall.

But first the Landlord will I trace;
Grave in his aspect and attire;
A man of ancient pedigree,
A Justice of the Peace was he,
Known in all Sudbury as " The Squire."
Proud was he of his name and race,
Of old Sir William and Sir Hugh,
And in the parlour, full in view,
His coat-of-arms, well framed and glazed,
Upon the wall in colours blazed;
He beareth gules upon his shield,
A chevron argent in the field,
With three wolf's heads, and for the crest
A Wyvern part-per-pale addressed
Upon a helmet barred; below
The scroll reads, " By the name of Howe."
And over this, no longer bright,
Though glimmering with a latent light,
Was hung the sword his grandsire bore,
In the rebellious days of yore,
Down there at Concord in the fight.

A youth was there, of quiet ways,
A Student of old books and days,
To whom all tongues and lands were known,
And yet a lover of his own;
With many a social virtue graced,
And yet a friend of solitude;
A man of such a genial mood
The heart of all things he embraced,
And yet of such fastidious taste,
He never found the best too good.
Books were his passion and delight,
And in his upper room at home
Stood many a rare and sumptuous tome,
In vellum bound, with gold bedight,
Great volumes garmented in white,
Recalling Florence, Pisa, Rome.
He loved the twilight that surrounds

The border-land of old romance;
Where glitter hauberk, helm, and lance,
And banner waves, and trumpet sounds,
And ladies ride with hawk on wrist,
And mighty warriors sweep along,
Magnified by the purple mist,
The dusk of centuries and of song.
The chronicles of Charlemagne,
Of Merlin and the Mort d'Arthure,
Mingled together in his brain
With tales of Flores and Blanche-
fleur,
Sir Ferumbras, Sir Eglamour,
Sir Launcelot, Sir Morgadour,
Sir Guy, Sir Bevis, Sir Gawain.

A young Sicilian, too, was there:—
In sight of Etna born and bred,
Some breath of its volcanic air
Was glowing in his heart and brain,
And, being rebellious to his liege,
After Palermo's fatal siege,
Across the western seas he fled,
In good King Bombas' happy reign.
His face was like a summer night,
All flooded with a dusky light;
His hands were small; his teeth shone white
As sea-shells, when he smiled or spoke;
His sinews supple and strong as oak;
Clean shaven was he as a priest,
Who at the mass on Sunday sings,
Save that upon his upper lip
His beard, a good palm's length at least,
Level and pointed at the tip,
Shot sideways, like a swallow's wings.
The poets read he o'er and o'er,
And most of all the Immortal Four
Of Italy; and next to those,
The story-telling bard of prose,
Who wrote the joyous Tuscan tales
Of the Decameron, that make

Fiesole's green hills and vales
Remembered for Boccaccio's sake.
Much too of music was his thought;
The melodies and measures fraught
With sunshine and the open air,
Of vineyards and the singing sea
Of his beloved Sicily;
And much it pleased him to peruse
The songs of the Sicilian muse,—
Bucolic songs by Meli sung
In the familiar peasant tongue,
That made men say, "Behold! once more
The pitying gods to earth restore
Theocritus of Syracuse!"

A Spanish Jew from Alicant
With aspect grand and grave was there;
Vender of silks and fabrics rare,
And attar of rose from the Levant.
Like an old Patriarch he appeared,
Abraham or Isaac, or at least
Some later Prophet or High-Priest;
With lustrous eyes, and olive skin,
And, wildly tossed from cheeks and chin,
The tumbling cataract of his beard.
His garments breathed a spicy scent
Of cinnamon and sandal blent,
Like the soft aromatic gales
That meet the mariner, who sails
Through the Moluccas, and the seas
That wash the shores of Celebes.
All stories that recorded are
By Pierre Alphonse he knew by heart,
And it was rumoured he could say
The Parables of Sandabar,
And all the Fables of Pilpay,
Or if not all, the greater part!
Well versed was he in Hebrew books,
Talmud and Targum, and the lore
Of Kabala; and evermore
There was a mystery in his looks;
His eyes seemed gazing far away,
As if in vision or in trance

He heard the solemn sackbut play,
And saw the Jewish maidens dance.

A Theologian, from the school
Of Cambridge on the Charles, was
   there;
Skilful alike with tongue and pen.
He preached to all men every-
   where
The Gospel of the Golden Rule,
The New Commandment given to
   men,
Thinking the deed, and not the
   creed,
Would help us in our utmost need.
With reverent feet the earth he trod,
Nor banished nature from his plan,
But studied still with deep research
To build the Universal Church,
Lofty as is the love of God,
And ample as the wants of man.

A Poet, too, was there, whose verse
Was tender, musical, and terse;
The inspiration, the delight,
The gleam, the glory, the swift
   flight,
Of thoughts so sudden, that they
   seem
The revelations of a dream,
All these were his; but with them
   came
No envy of another's fame;
He did not find his sleep less sweet
For music in some neighbouring
   street,
Nor rustling here in every breeze
The laurels of Miltiades.
Honour and blessings on his head
While living, good report when
   dead,
Who, not too eager for renown,
Accepts, but does not clutch the
   crown!
Last the Musician, as he stood
Illumined by that fire of wood;
Fair-haired, blue-eyed, his aspect
   blithe,
His figure tall and straight and
   lithe,

And every feature of his face
Revealing his Norwegian race;
A radiance, streaming from within,
Around his eyes and forehead
   beamed,
The Angel with the violin,
Painted by Raphael, he seemed.
He lived in that ideal world
Whose language is not speech, but
   song;
Around him evermore the throng
Of elves and sprites their dances
   whirled;
The Strömkarl sang, the cataract
   hurled
Its headlong waters from the
   height;
And mingled in the wild delight
The scream of sea-birds in their
   flight,
The rumour of the forest trees,
The plunge of the implacable seas,
The tumult of the wind at night,
Voices of eld, like trumpets blow-
   ing,
Of ballads, and wild melodies
Through mist and darkness pour-
   ing forth,
Like Elivagar's river flowing
Out of the glaciers of the North.

The instrument on which he played
Was in Cremona's workshops made,
By a great master of the past,
Ere yet was lost the art divine;
Fashioned of maple and of pine,
That in Tyrolian forests vast
Had rocked and wrestled with the
   blast:
Exquisite was it in design,
Perfect in each minutest part,
A marvel of the lutist's art;
And in its hollow chamber, thus,
The maker from whose hands it
   came
Had written his unrivalled name,
" Antonius Stradivarius."
And when he played, the atmo-
   sphere

Was filled with magic, and the ear
Caught echoes of that Harp of Gold,
Whose music had so weird a sound,
The hunted stag forgot to bound,
The leaping rivulet backward
  rolled,
The birds came down from bush
  and tree,
The dead came from beneath the
  sea,
The maiden to the harper's knee!

The music ceased; the applause
  was loud,
The pleased musician smiled and
  bowed;
The wood-fire clapped its hands of
  flame,
The shadows on the wainscot
  stirred,
And from the harpsichord there
  came
A ghostly murmur of acclaim,
A sound like that sent down at
  night
By birds of passage in their flight,
From the remotest distance heard.

Then silence followed; then began
A clamour for the Landlord's tale,—
The story promised them of old,
They said, but always left untold;
And he, although a bashful man,
And all his courage seemed to fail,
Finding excuse of no avail,
Yielded; and thus the story ran.

THE LANDLORD'S TALE

PAUL REVERE'S RIDE

Listen, my children, and you shall
  hear
Of the midnight ride of Paul Re-
  vere,
On the eighteenth of April, in
  Seventy-five;
Hardly a man is now alive
Who remembers that famous day
  and year.

He said to his friend, "If the
  British march
By land or sea from the town to-
  night,
Hang a lantern aloft in the belfry
  arch
Of the North Church tower as a
  signal light,—
One, if by land, and two, if by sea;
And I on the opposite shore will be,
Ready to ride and spread the alarm
Through every Middlesex village
  and farm,
For the country-folk to be up and
  to arm."

Thee he said, "Good night!" and
  with muffled oar
Silently rowed to the Charlestown
  shore,
Just as the moon rose over the bay,
Where swinging wide at her moor-
  ings lay
The Somerset, British man-of-war;
A phantom ship, with each mast
  and spar
Across the moon like a prison bar,
And a huge black hulk, that was
  magnified
By its own reflection in the tide.

Meanwhile, his friend, through
  alley and street,
Wanders and watches with eager
  ears,
Till in silence around him he hears
The muster of men at the barrack
  door,
The sound of arms, and the tramp
  of feet,
And the measured tread of the
  grenadiers,
Marching down to their boats on
  the shore.

Then he climbed to the tower of
  the church,
Up the wooden stairs, with
  stealthy tread,

To the belfry-chamber overhead,
And startled the pigeons from
   their perch
On the sombre rafters, that round
   him made
Masses and moving shapes of
   shade—
Up the trembling ladder, steep and
   tall,
To the highest window in the wall,
Where he paused to listen and look
   down
A moment on the roofs of the town,
And the moonlight flowing over all.

Beneath, in the churchyard, lay
   the dead,
In their night-encampment on the
   hill,
Wrapped in silence so deep and
   still
That he could hear, like a sentinel's
   tread,
The watchful night-wind, as it went
Creeping along from tent to tent,
And seeming to whisper, "All is
   well!"
A moment only he feels the spell
Of the place and the hour, and the
   secret dread
Of the lonely belfry and the dead;
For suddenly all his thoughts are
   bent
On a shadowy something far away,
Where the river widens to meet the
   bay,—
A line of black that bends and
   floats
On the rising tide, like a bridge of
   boats.

Meanwhile, impatient to mount
   and ride,
Booted and spurred, with a heavy
   stride
On the opposite shore walked Paul
   Revere.
Now he patted his horse's side,
Now gazed at the landscape far
   and near,

Then, impetuous, stamped the
   earth,
And turned and tightened his
   saddle-girth;
But mostly he watched with eager
   search
The belfry-tower of the Old North
   Church.

As it rose above the graves on the
   hill,
Lonely and spectral and sombre
   and still.
And lo! as he looks, on the belfry's
   height
A glimmer, and then a gleam of
   light!
He springs to the saddle, the bridle
   he turns,
But lingers and gazes, till full on
   his sight
A second lamp in the belfry burns!

A hurry of hoofs in a village street,
A shape in the moonlight, a bulk in
   the dark,
And beneath, from the pebbles, in
   passing, a spark
Struck out by a steed flying fear-
   less and fleet;
That was all! And yet, through
   the gloom and the light,
The fate of a nation was riding that
   night;
And the spark struck out by that
   steed, in his flight,
Kindled the land into flame with
   its heat.

He has left the village and
   mounted the steep,
And beneath him, tranquil and
   broad and deep,
Is the Mystic, meeting the ocean
   tides;
And under the alders, that skirt its
   edge,
Now soft on the sand, now loud on
   the ledge,

Is heard the tramp of his steed as
he rides.

It was the twelve by the village
clock
When he crossed the bridge into
Medford town.
He heard the crowing of the cock,
And the barking of the farmer's
dog,
And felt the damp of the river fog,
That rises after the sun goes down.

It was one by the village clock,
When he galloped into Lexington.
He saw the gilded weathercock
Swim in the moonlight as he passed,
And the meeting-house windows,
blank and bare,
Gaze at him with a spectral glare,
As if they already stood aghast
At the bloody work they would
look upon.

It was two by the village clock,
When he came to the bridge in
Concord town.
He heard the bleating of the flock,
And the twitter of birds among
the trees,
And felt the breath of the morning
breeze
Blowing over the meadows brown.
And one was safe and asleep in his
bed
Who at the bridge would be first to
fall,
Who that day would be lying dead,
Pierced by a British musket-ball.

You know the rest. In the books
you have read,
How the British Regulars fired
and fled,—
How the farmers gave them ball
for ball,
From behind each fence and farm-
yard wall,
Chasing the red-coats down the
lane,

Then crossing the fields to emerge
again
Under the trees at the turn of the
road,
And only pausing to fire and load.

So through the night rode Paul
Revere;
And so through the night went his
cry of alarm
To every Middlesex village and
farm,—
A cry of defiance and not of fear,
A voice in the darkness, a knock at
the door,
And a word that shall echo for
evermore!
For, borne on the night-wind of the
Past,
Through all our history, to the last,
In the hour of darkness and peril
and need,
The people will waken and listen to
hear
The hurrying hoof-beats of that
steed,
And the midnight message of Paul
Revere.

INTERLUDE

The Landlord ended thus his tale,
Then rising took down from its nail
The sword that hung there, dim
with dust,
And cleaving to its sheath with
rust,
And said, " This sword was in the
fight."
The Poet seized it, and exclaimed,
" It is the sword of a good knight,
Though homespun was his coat-of-
mail;
What matter if it be not named
Joyeuse, Colada, Durindale,
Excalibar, or Aroundight,
Or other name the books record ?
Your ancestor, who bore this sword

As Colonel of the Volunteers,
Mounted upon his old gray mare,
Seen here and there and every-
   where,
To me a grander shape appears
Than old Sir William, or what not,
Clinking about in foreign lands
With iron gauntlets on his hands,
And on his head an iron pot! "

All laughed; the Landlord's face
   grew red
As his escutcheon on the wall;
He could not comprehend at all
The drift of what the Poet said;
For those who had been longest
   dead
Were always greatest in his eyes;
And he was speechless with sur-
   prise
To see Sir William's plumed head
Brought to a level with the rest,
And made the subject of a jest.

And this perceiving, to appease
The Landlord's wrath, the others'
   fears,
The Student said, with careless
   ease,
" The ladies and the cavaliers,
The arms, the loves, the courtesies,
The deeds of high emprise, I sing!
Thus Ariosto says, in words
That have the stately stride and
   ring
Of armed knights and clashing
   swords.
Now listen to the tale I bring;
Listen! though not to me belong
The flowing draperies of his song,
The words that rouse, the voice
   that charms.
The Landlord's tale was one of
   arms,
Only a tale of love is mine,
Blending the human and divine,
A tale of the Decameron, told
In Palmieri's garden old,
By Fiametta, laurel-crowned,

While her companions lay around,
And heard the intermingled sound
Of airs that on their errands sped,
And wild birds gossiping overhead,
And lisp of leaves, and fountain's
   fall,
And her own voice more sweet than
   all,
Telling the tale, which, wanting
   these,
Perchance may lose its power to
   please."

THE STUDENT'S TALE

THE FALCON OF SER FEDERIGO

One summer morning, when the
   sun was hot,
Weary with labour in his garden-
   plot,
On a rude bench beneath his
   cottage eaves,
Ser Federigo sat among the leaves
Of a huge vine, that, with its arms
   outspread,
Hung its delicious clusters over-
   head.
Below him, through the lovely
   valley, flowed
The river Arno, like a winding road,
And from its banks were lifted
   high in air
The spires and roofs of Florence
   called the Fair;
To him a marble tomb, that rose
   above
His wasted fortunes and his buried
   love.
For there, in banquet and in tour-
   nament,
His wealth had lavished been, his
   substance spent,
To woo and lose, since ill his woo-
   ing sped,
Monna Giovanna, who his rival
   wed,

Yet ever in his fancy reigned supreme,
The ideal woman of a young man's dream.

Then he withdrew, in poverty and pain,
To this small farm, the last of his domain,
His only comfort and his only care
To prune his vines, and plant the fig and pear;
His only forester and only guest
His falcon, faithful to him, when the rest,
Whose willing hands had found so light of yore
The brazen knocker of his palace door,
Had now no strength to lift the wooden latch,
That entrance gave beneath a roof of thatch.
Companion of his solitary ways,
Purveyor of his feasts on holidays,
On him this melancholy man bestowed
The love with which his nature overflowed.
And so the empty handed years went round,
Vacant, though voiceful with prophetic sound,
And so, that summer morn, he sat and mused
With folded, patient hands, as he was used,
And dreamily before his half-closed sight
Floated the vision of his lost delight.
Beside him, motionless, the drowsy bird
Dreamed of the chase, and in his slumber heard
The sudden, scythe-like sweep of wings, that dare
The headlong plunge thro' eddying gulfs of air,

Then, starting broad awake upon his perch,
Tinkled his bells, like mass-bells in a church,
And, looking at his master, seemed to say,
" Ser Federigo, shall we hunt to-day ? "

Ser Federigo thought not of the chase;
The tender vision of her lovely face,
I will not say he seems to see, he sees
In the leaf-shadows of the trellises,
Herself, yet not herself; a lovely child
With flowing tresses, and eyes wide and wild,
Coming undaunted up the garden walk,
And looking not at him, but at the hawk.
" Beautiful falcon ! " said he, " would that I
Might hold thee on my wrist, or see thee fly ! "
The voice was hers, and made strange echoes start
Through all the haunted chambers of his heart,
As an æolian harp through gusty doors
Of some old ruin its wild music pours.

" Who is thy mother, my fair boy ? " he said,
His hand laid softly on that shining head.
" Monna Giovanna.—Will you let me stay
A little while, and with your falcon play ?
We live there, just beyond your garden wall,
In the great house behind the poplars tall."

So he spake on; and Federigo heard
As from afar each softly uttered word,
And drifted onward through the golden gleams
And shadows of the misty sea of dreams,
As mariners becalmed through vapours drift,
And feel the sea beneath them sink and lift,
And hear far off, the mournful breakers roar,
And voices calling faintly from the shore!
Then, waking from his pleasant reveries,
He took the little boy upon his knees,
And told him stories of his gallant bird,
Till in their friendship he became a third.

Monna Giovanna, widowed in her prime,
Had come with friends to pass the summer time
In her grand villa, half-way up the hill,
O'erlooking Florence, but retired and still;
With iron gates, that opened through long lines
Of sacred ilex aud centennial pines,
And terraced gardens, and broad steps of stone,
And sylvan deities, with moss o'ergrown,
And fountains palpitating in the heat,
And all Val d'Arno stretched beneath its feet.
Here in seclusion, as a widow may,
The lovely lady whiled the hours away,
Pacing in sable robes the statued hall,
Herself the stateliest statue among all,
And seeing more and more, with secret joy,
Her husband risen and living in her boy,
Till the lost sense of life returned again,
Not as delight, but as relief from pain.
Meanwhile the boy, rejoicing in his strength,
Stormed down the terraces from length to length;
The screaming peacock chased in hot pursuit,
And climbed the garden trellises for fruit.
But his chief pastime was to watch the flight
Of a gerfalcon, soaring into sight,
Beyond the trees that fringed the garden wall,
Then downward stooping at some distant call;
And as he gazed full often wondered he
Who might the master of the falcon be,
Until that happy morning, when he found
Master and falcon in the cottage ground.
And now a shadow and a terror fell
On the great house, as if a passing-bell
Tolled from the tower, and filled each spacious room
With secret awe, and preternatural gloom;
The petted boy grew ill, and day by day
Pined with mysterious malady away.
The mother's heart would not be comforted;
Her darling seemed to her already dead,

And often, sitting by the sufferer's
  side,
" What can I do to comfort thee ? "
  she cried,
At first the silent lips made no
  reply,
But, moved at length by her im-
  portunate cry,
" Give me," he answered, with im-
  ploring tone,
" Ser Federigo's falcon for my
  own ! "

No answer could the astonished
  mother make;
How could she ask, e'en for her
  darling's sake,
Such favour at a luckless lover's
  hand,
Well knowing that to ask was to
  command ?
Well knowing, what all falconers
  confessed,
In all the land that falcon was the
  best,
The master's pride and passion and
  delight,
And the sole pursuivant of this
  poor knight.
But yet, for her child's sake, she
  could no less
Than give assent, to soothe his
  restlessness,
So promised, and then promising to
  keep
Her promise sacred, saw him fall
  asleep.

The morrow was a bright Septem-
  ber morn;
The earth was beautiful as if new-
  born;
There was that nameless splendour
  everywhere,
That wild exhilaration in the air,
Which makes the passers in the
  city street
Congratulate each other as they
  meet.

Two lovely ladies, clothed in cloak
  and hood,
Passed through the garden gate
  into the wood,
Under the lustrous leaves, and
  through the sheen
Of dewy sunshine showering down
  between.
The one, close-hooded, had the
  attractive grace
Which sorrow sometimes lends a
  woman's face;
Her dark eyes moistened with the
  mists that roll
From the gulf-stream of passion in
  the soul;
The other with her hood thrown
  back, her hair
Making a golden glory in the air,
Her cheeks suffused with an aurora
  blush,
Her young heart singing louder
  than the thrush.
So walked, that morn, through
  mingled light and shade,
Each by the other's presence love-
  lier made,
Monna Giovanna and her bosom
  friend,
Intent upon their errand and its
  end.

They found Ser Federigo at his toil,
Like banished Adam, delving in
  the soil;
And when he looked and these fair
  women spied,
The garden suddenly was glorified;
His long-lost Eden was restored
  again,
And the strange river winding
  through the plain
No longer was the Arno to his eyes,
But the Euphrates watering Para-
  dise!

Monna Giovanna raised her stately
  head,
And with fair words of salutation
  said:

" Ser Federigo, we come here as
friends,
Hoping in this to make some poor
amends
For past unkindness. I who ne'er
before
Would even cross the threshold of
your door,
I who in happier days such pride
maintained,
Refused your banquets, and your
gifts disdained,
This morning come, a self-invited
guest,
To put your generous nature to the
test,
And breakfast with you under your
own vine."
To which he answered: " Poor
desert of mine,
Not your unkindness call it, for if
aught
Is good in me of feeling or of
thought,
From you it comes, and this last
grace outweighs
All sorrows, all regrets of other
days."

And after further compliment and
talk,
Among the dahlias in the garden
walk
He left his guests; and to his
cottage turned,
And as he entered for a moment
yearned
For the lost splendours of the days
of old,
The ruby glass, the silver and the
gold,
And felt how piercing is the sting
of pride,
By want embittered and intensi-
fied.
He looked about him for some
means or way
To keep this unexpected holi-
day;

Searched every cupboard, and then
searched again,
Summoned the maid, who came
but came in vain;
" The Signor did not hunt to-day,"
she said,
" There's nothing in the house but
wine and bread."
Then suddenly the drowsy falcon
shook
His little bells, with that sagacious
look,
Which said, as plain as language to
the ear,
" If anything is wanting, I am
here! "
Yes, everything is wanting, gallant
bird!
The master seized thee without
further word,
Like thine own lure, he whirled
thee round; ah me!
The pomp and flutter of brave fal-
conry,
The bells, the jesses, the bright
scarlet hood,
The flight and the pursuit o'er field
and wood,
All these for evermore are ended
now;
No longer victor, but the victim
thou!

Then on the board a snow-white
cloth he spread,
Laid on its wooden dish the loaf of
bread,
Brought purple grapes with
autumn sunshine hot,
The fragrant peach, the juicy ber-
gamot;
Then in the midst a flask of wine
he placed,
And with autumnal flowers the
banquet graced.
Ser Federigo, would not these suf-
fice
Without thy falcon stuffed with
cloves and spice?

When all was ready, and the courtly dame
With her companion to the cottage came,
Upon Ser Federigo's brain there fell
The wild enchantment of a magic spell;
The room they entered, mean and low and small,
Was changed into a sumptuous banquet-hall,
With fanfares by aerial trumpets blown;
The rustic chair she sat on was a throne;
He ate celestial food, and a divine
Flavour was given to his country wine,
And the poor falcon, fragrant with his spice,
A peacock was, or bird of paradise!

When the repast was ended, they arose
And passed again into the garden-close.
Then said the lady, " Far too well I know,
Remembering still the days of long ago,
Though you betray it not, with what surprise
You see me here in this familiar wise.
You have no children, and you cannot guess
What anguish, what unspeakable distress
A mother feels, whose child is lying ill,
Nor how her heart anticipates his will.
And yet for this, you see me lay aside
All womanly reserve and check of pride,
And ask the thing most precious in your sight,

Your falcon, your sole comfort and delight,
Which if you find it in your heart to give,
My poor, unhappy boy perchance may live."

Ser Federigo listens, and replies,
With tears of love and pity in his eyes:
" Alas, dear lady! there can be no task
So sweet to me, as giving when you ask.
One little hour ago, if I had known
This wish of yours, it would have been my own.
But thinking in what manner I could best
Do honour to the presence of my guest,
I deemed that nothing worthier could be
Than what most dear and precious was to me,
And so my gallant falcon breathed his last
To furnish forth this morning our repast."

In mute contrition, mingled with dismay,
The gentle lady turned her eyes away,
Grieving that he such sacrifice should make,
And kill his falcon for a woman's sake,
Yet feeling in her heart a woman's pride,
That nothing she could ask for was denied;
Then took her leave, and passed out at the gate
With footsteps slow and soul disconsolate.

Three days went by, and lo! a passing-bell
Tolled from the little chapel in the dell;

Ten strokes Ser Federigo heard, and said,
Breathing a prayer, " Alas! her child is dead! "
Three months went by, and lo! a merrier chime
Rang from the chapel bells at Christmas time;
The cottage was deserted, and no more
Ser Federigo sat beside its door,
But now, with servitors to do his will,
In the grand villa, half-way up the hill,
Sat at the Christmas feast, and at his side
Monna Giovanna, his beloved bride,
Never so beautiful, so kind, so fair,
Enthroned once more in the old rustic chair,
High-perched upon the back of which there stood
The image of a falcon carved in wood,
And underneath the inscription, with a date,
" All things come round to him who will but wait."

INTERLUDE

Soon as the story reached its end,
One, over eager to commend,
Crowned it with injudicious praise;
And then the voice of blame found vent,
And fanned the embers of dissent
Into a somewhat lively blaze.

The Theologian shook his head;
" These old Italian tales," he said,
" From the much-praised Decameron down
Through all the rabble of the rest,
Are either trifling, dull, or lewd;
The gossip of a neighbourhood
In some remote provincial town,
A scandalous chronicle at best!

They seem to me a stagnant fen,
Grown rank with rushes and with reeds,
Where a white lily, now and then,
Blooms in the midst of noxious weeds
And deadly nightshade on its banks."

To this the Student straight replied,
" For the white lily, many thanks!
One should not say, with too much pride,
Fountain, I will not drink of thee!
Nor were it grateful to forget,
That from these reservoirs and tanks
Even imperial Shakspeare drew
His Moor of Venice and the Jew,
And Romeo and Juliet,
And many a famous comedy."

Then a long pause; till some one said,
" An Angel is flying overhead! "
At these words spake the Spanish Jew,
And murmured with an inward breath:
" God grant, if what you say is true
It may not be the Angel of Death! "
And then another pause; and then
Stroking his beard, he said again:
" This brings back to my memory
A story in the Talmud told,
That book of gems, that book of gold,
Of wonders many and manifold,
A tale that often comes to me,
And fills my heart, and haunts my brain,
And never wearies nor grows old."

THE SPANISH JEW'S TALE

THE LEGEND OF RABBI BEN LEVI

Rabbi Ben Levi, on the Sabbath, read
A volume of the Law, in which it said,

" No man shall look upon my face
and live."
And as he read, he prayed that God
would give
His faithful servant grace with
mortal eye
To look upon His face and yet not
die.

Then fell a sudden shadow on the
page
And, lifting up his eyes, grown dim
with age,
He saw the Angel of Death before
him stand,
Holding a naked sword in his right
hand.
Rabbi Ben Levi was a righteous
man,
Yet through his veins a chill of
terror ran.

With trembling voice he said,
" What wilt thou here ? "
The angel answered, " Lo! the
time draws near
When thou must die; yet first, by
God's decree,
Whate'er thou askest shall be
granted thee."
Replied the Rabbi, " Let these
living eyes
First look upon my place in Para-
dise."

Then said the Angel, " Come with
me and look."
Rabbi Ben Levi closed the sacred
book,
And rising, and uplifting his gray
head,
" Give me thy sword," he to the
Angel said,
" Lest thou shouldst fall upon me
by the way."
The angel smiled and hastened to
obey,
Then led him forth to the Celestial
Town,

And set him on the wall, whence,
gazing down,
Rabbi Ben Levi, with his living
eyes,
Might look upon his place in Para-
dise.

Then straight into the city of the
Lord
The Rabbi leaped with the Death-
Angel's sword,
And through the streets there
swept a sudden breath
Of something there unknown,
which men call death.
Meanwhile the Angel stayed with-
out, and cried,
" Come back! "   To which the
Rabbi's voice replied,
" No! in the name of God, whom I
adore,
I swear that hence I will depart no
more! "
Then all the Angels cried, " O Holy
One,
See what the son of Levi here has
done!
The kingdom of Heaven he takes
by violence,
And in Thy name refuses to go
hence! "
The Lord replied, " My Angels, be
not wroth;
Did e'er the son of Levi break his
oath ?
Let him remain; for he with
mortal eye
Shall look upon my face and yet
not die."

Beyond the outer wall the Angel of
Death
Heard the great voice, and said,
with panting breath,
" Give back the sword, and let me
go my way."
Whereat the Rabbi paused, and
answered, " Nay!
Anguish enough already has it
caused

Among the sons of men." And
while he paused
He heard the awful mandate of the
Lord
Resounding through the air, " Give
back the sword! "

The Rabbi bowed his head in silent
prayer;
Then said he to the dreadful Angel,
" Swear,
No human eye shall look on it
again;
But when thou takest away the
souls of men,
Thyself unseen, and with an unseen
sword,
Thou wilt perform the bidding of
the Lord."

The Angel took the sword again,
and swore,
And walks on earth unseen for ever-
more.

INTERLUDE

He ended: and a kind of spell
Upon the silent listeners fell.
His solemn manner and his words
Had touched the deep, mysterious
chords,
That vibrate in each human breast
Alike, but not alike confessed.
The spiritual world seemed near;
And close above them, full of fear,
Its awful adumbration passed,
A luminous shadow, vague and
vast.
They almost feared to look, lest
there,
Embodied from the impalpable air,
They might behold the Angel
stand,
Holding the sword in his right
hand.
At last, but in a voice subdued,
Not to disturb their dreamy mood,
Said the Sicilian: " While you
spoke,

Telling your legend marvellous,
Suddenly in my memory woke
The thought of one, now gone from
us,—
An old Abate, meek and mild,
My friend and teacher, when a
child,
Who sometimes in those days of
old
The legend of an Angel told,
Which ran, if I remember, thus."

THE SICILIAN'S TALE

KING ROBERT OF SICILY

Robert of Sicily, brother of Pope
Urbane
And Valmond, Emperor of Alle-
maine,
Apparelled in magnificent attire,
With retinue of many a knight and
squire,
On St. John's eve, at vespers,
proudly sat
And heard the priests chant the
Magnificat.
And as he listened, o'er and o'er
again
Repeated, like a burden or refrain,
He caught the words, " *Deposuit
potentes
De sede, et exaltavit humiles :* "
And slowly lifting up his kingly
head
He to a learned clerk beside him
said,
" What mean these words? " The
clerk made answer meet,
" He has put down the mighty
from their seat,
And has exalted them of low
degree."
Threat King Robert muttered
scornfully,
" 'Tis well that such seditious
words are sung
Only by priests and in the Latin
tongue;

For unto priests and people be it
known,
There is no power can push me
from my throne! "
And leaning back, he yawned and
fell asleep,
Lulled by the chant monotonous
and deep.
When he awoke, it was already
night;
The church was empty, and there
was no light,
Save where the lamps, that glim-
mered few and faint,
Lighted a little space before some
saint.
He started from his seat and gazed
around,
But saw no living thing and heard
no sound.
He groped towards the door, but it
was locked;
He cried aloud, and listened, and
then knocked,
And uttered awful threatenings
and complaints,
And imprecations upon men and
saints.
The sounds re-echoed from the roof
and walls
As if dead priests were laughing in
their stalls!

At length the sexton, hearing from
without
The tumult of the knocking and
the shout,
And thinking thieves were in the
house of prayer,
Came with his lantern, asking,
" Who is there ? "
Half choked with rage, King Robert
fiercely said,
"Open: 'tis I, the King! Art thou
afraid ? "
The frightened sexton, muttering,
with a curse,
" This is some drunken vagabond,
or worse! "

Turned the great key and flung the
portal wide;
A man rushed by him at a single
stride,
Haggard, half naked, without hat
or cloak,
Who neither turned, nor looked at
him, nor spoke,
But leaped into the blackness of
the night,
And vanished like a spectre from
his sight.
Robert of Sicily, brother of Pope
Urbane
And Valmond, Emperor of Alle-
maine,
Despoiled of his magnificent attire,
Bare-headed, breathless, and be-
sprent with mire,
With sense of wrong and outrage
desperate,
Strode on and thundered at the
palace gate;
Rushed through the court-yard,
thrusting in his rage
To right and left each seneschal
and page,
And hurried up the broad and
sounding stair,
His white face ghastly in the
torches' glare.
From hall to hall he passed with
breathless speed;
Voices and cries he heard, but did
not heed,
Until at last he reached the ban-
quet-room,
Blazing with light, and breathing
with perfume.

There on the dais sat another king,
Wearing his robes, his crown, his
signet-ring,
King Robert's self in features, form,
and height,
But all transfigured with angelic
light!
It was an Angel; and his presence
there

With a divine effulgence filled the
air,
An exaltation, piercing the dis-
guise,
Though none the hidden Angel
recognise.

A moment speechless, motionless,
amazed,
The throneless monarch on the
Angel gazed,
Who met his looks of anger and
surprise
With the divine compassion of his
eyes;
Then said, " Who art thou? and
why com'st thou here? "
To which King Robert answered
with a sneer,
" I am the King, and come to
claim my own
From an impostor, who usurps my
throne! "
And suddenly, at these audacious
words,
Up sprang the angry guests, and
drew their swords;
The Angel answered, with un-
ruffled brow,
" Nay, not the King, but the
King's Jester, thou
Henceforth shalt wear the bells and
scalloped cape,
And for thy counsellor shalt lead
an ape;
Thou shalt obey my servants when
they call,
And wait upon my henchmen in
the hall! "

Deaf to King Robert's threats and
cries and prayers,
They thrust him from the hall and
down the stairs;
A group of tittering pages ran be-
fore,
And as they opened wide the fold-
ing-door,
His heart failed, for he heard, with
strange alarms,

The biosterous laughter of the men-
at-arms,
And all the vaulted chamber roar
and ring
With the mock plaudits of " Long
live the King! "

Next morning, waking with the
day's first beam,
He said within himself, " It was a
dream! "
But the straw rustled as he turned
his head,
There were the cap and bells beside
his bed,
Around him rose the bare, dis-
coloured walls,
Close by, the steeds were champ-
ing in their stalls,
And in the corner, a revolting
shape,
Shivering and chattering sat the
wretched ape.
It was no dream; the world he
loved so much
Had turned to dust and ashes at
his touch!

Days came and went; and now re-
turned again
To Sicily the old Saturnian reign;
Under the Angel's governance
benign
The happy island danced with corn
and wine,
And deep within the mountain's
burning breast
Enceladus, the giant, was at rest.

Meanwhile King Robert yielded to
his fate,
Sullen and silent and disconsolate.
Dressed in the motley garb that
Jesters wear,
With looks bewildered and a
vacant stare,
Close shaven above the ears, as
monks are shorn,
By courtiers mocked, by pages
laughed to scorn,
His only friend the ape, his only
food

What others left,—he still was unsubdued.
And when the Angel met him on his way,
And half in earnest, half in jest, would say,
Sternly, though tenderly, that he might feel
The velvet scabbard held a sword of steel,
" Art thou the King ? " the passion of his woe
Burst from him in resistless overflow,
And, lifting high his forehead, he would fling
The haughty answer back, " I am, I am the King ! "

Almost three years were ended; when there came
Ambassadors of great repute and name
From Valmond, Emperor of Allemaine,
Unto King Robert, saying that Pope Urbane
By letter summoned them forthwith to come
On Holy Thursday to his city of Rome.
The Angel with great joy received his guests,
And gave them presents of embroidered vests,
And velvet mantles with rich ermine lined,
And rings and jewels of the rarest kind.
Then he departed with them o'er the sea
Into the lovely land of Italy,
Whose loveliness was more resplendent made
By the mere passing of that cavalcade,
With plumes, and cloaks, and housings, and the stir
Of jewelled bridle and of golden spur.

And lo! among the menials, in mock state,
Upon a piebald steed, with shambling gait,
His cloak of fox-tails flapping in the wind,
The solemn ape demurely perched behind,
King Robert rode, making huge merriment
In all the country towns through which they went.

The Pope received them with great pomp, and blare
Of bannered trumpets, on Saint Peter's square,
Giving his benediction and embrace,
Fervent, and full of apostolic grace.
While with congratulations and with prayers
He entertained the Angel unawares,
Robert, the Jester, bursting through the crowd,
Into their presence rushed, and cried aloud,
" I am the King! Look, and behold in me
Robert, your brother, King of Sicily!
This man, who wears my semblance to your eyes,
Is an impostor in a king's disguise.
Do you not know me? does no voice within
Answer my cry, and say we are akin ? "
The Pope in silence, but with troubled mien,
Gazed at the Angel's countenance serene;
The Emperor, laughing, said, " It is strange sport
To keep a madman for thy Fool at court ! "
And the poor, baffled Jester, in disgrace
Was hustled back among the populace.

In solemn state the Holy Week went by,
And Easter Sunday gleamed upon the sky;
The presence of the Angel, with its light,
Before the sun rose, made the city bright,
And with new fervour filled the hearts of men,
Who felt that Christ indeed had risen again.
Even the Jester, on his bed of straw,
With haggard eyes the unwonted splendour saw,
He felt within a power unfelt before,
And, kneeling humbly on his chamber floor,
He heard the rushing garments of the Lord
Sweep through the silent air, ascending heavenward.

And now the visit ending, and once more
Valmond returning to the Danube's shore,
Homeward the Angel journeyed, and again
The land was made resplendent with his train,
Flashing along the towns of Italy
Unto Salerno, and from there by sea.
And when once more within Palermo's wall,
And, seated on the throne in his great hall,
He heard the Angelus from convent towers,
As if the better world conversed with ours,
He beckoned to King Robert to draw nigher,
And with a gesture bade the rest retire;

And when they were alone, the Angel said,
"Art thou the King?" Then bowing down his head,
King Robert crossed both hands upon his breast,
And meekly answered him: "Thou knowest best!
My sins as scarlet are; let me go hence,
And in some cloister's school of penitence,
Across those stones, that pave the way to heaven,
Walk barefoot, till my guilty soul is shriven!"
The Angel smiled, and from his radiant face
A holy light illumined all the place,
And through the open window, loud and clear,
They heard the monks chant in the chapel near,
Above the stir and tumult of the street:
"He has put down the mighty from their seat,
And has exalted them of low degree!"
And through the chant a second melody
Rose like the throbbing of a single string:
"I am an Angel, and thou art the King!"

King Robert, who was standing near the throne,
Lifted his eyes, and lo! he was alone!
But all apparelled as in days of old,
With ermined mantle and with cloth of gold;
And when his courtiers came, they found him there
Kneeling upon the floor, absorbed in silent prayer.

INTERLUDE

And then the blue-eyed Norseman
    told
A Saga of the days of old.
" There is," said he, " a wondrous
    book
Of Legends in the old Norse tongue,
Of the dead kings of Norroway,—
Legends that once were told or
    sung
In many a smoky fireside nook
Of Iceland, in the ancient day,
By wandering Saga-man or Scald;
Heimskringla is the volume called;
And he who looks may find therein
The story that I now begin."

And in each pause the story made
Upon his violin he played,
As an appropriate interlude,
Fragments of old Norwegian tunes
That bound in one the separate
    runes,
And held the mind in perfect mood,
Entwining and encircling all
The strange and antiquated
    rhymes
With melodies of olden times;
As over some half-ruined wall,
Disjointed and about to fall,
Fresh woodbines climb and inter-
    lace,
And keep the loosened stones in
    place

THE MUSICIAN'S TALE

THE SAGA OF KING OLAF

I.

THE CHALLENGE OF THOR

I am the God Thor,
I am the War God,
I am the Thunderer!
Here in my Northland,
My fastness and fortress,
Reign I for ever!

Here amid icebergs
Rule I the nations;
This is my hammer,
Miölner the mighty;
Giants and sorcerers
Cannot withstand it!

These are the gauntlets
Wherewith I wield it,
And hurl it afar off;
This is my girdle;
Whenever I brace it,
Strength is redoubled!

The light thou beholdest
Stream through the heavens,
In flashes of crimson,
Is but my red beard
Blown by the night-wind,
Affrighting the nations!

Jove is my brother;
Mine eyes are the lightning;
The wheels of my chariot
Roll in the thunder,
The blows of my hammer
Ring in the earthquake!

Force rules the world still,
Has ruled it, shall rule it;
Meekness is weakness,
Strength is triumphant,
Over the whole earth
Still is it Thor's-Day!

Thou art a God too,
O Galilean!
And thus singled-handed
Unto the combat,
Gauntlet or Gospel,
Here I defy thee!

II.

KING OLAF'S RETURN

And King Olaf heard the cry,
Saw the red light in the sky,
    Laid his hand upon his sword,
As he leaned upon the railing,

And his ships went sailing, sailing
Northward into Drontheim fiord.

There he stood as one who dreamed;
And the red light glanced and
gleamed
On the armour that he wore;
And he shouted, as the rifted
Streamers o'er him shook and
shifted,
" I accept thy challenge, Thor!"

To avenge his father slain,
And reconquer realm and reign,
Came the youthful Olaf home,
Through the midnight sailing, sail-
ing,
Listening to the wild wind's wail-
ing,
And the dashing of the foam.

To his thoughts the sacred name
Of his mother Astrid came,
And the tale she oft had told
Of her flight by secret passes
Through the mountains and mo-
rasses,
To the home of Hakon old.

Then strange memories crowded
back
Of Queen Gunhild's wrath and
wrack,
And a hurried flight by sea;
Of grim Vikings, and their rapture
In the sea-fight, and the capture,
And the life of slavery.

How a stranger watched his face
In the Esthonian market-place,
Scanned his features one by one
Saying, " We should know each
other;
I am Sigurd, Astrid's brother,
Thou art Olaf, Astrid's son!"

Then as Queen Allogia's page,
Old in honours, young in age,
Chief of all her men-at-arms;

Till vague whispers, and mysteri-
ous,
Reached King Valdemar, the im-
perious,
Filling him with strange alarms.

Then his cruisings o'er the seas,
Westward to the Hebrides,
And to Scilly's rocky shore;
And the hermit's cavern dismal,
Christ's great name and rites bap-
tismal,
In the ocean's rush and roar.

All these thoughts of love and
strife
Glimmered through his lurid life,
As the stars' intenser light
Through the red flames o'er him
trailing,
As his ships went sailing, sailing,
Northward in the summer night.

Trained for either camp or court,
Skilful in each manly sport,
Young and beautiful and tall;
Art of warfare, craft of chases,
Swimming, skating, snow-shoe
races,
Excellent alike in all.

When at sea, with all his rowers,
He along the bending oars
Outside of his ship could run.
He the Smalsor Horn ascended,
And his shining shield suspended
On its summit, like a sun.

On the ship-rails he could stand,
Wield his sword with either hand,
And at once two javelins throw;
At all feasts where ale was strongest
Sat the merry monarch longest,
First to come and last to go.

Norway never yet had seen
One so beautiful of mien,
One so royal in attire,
When in arms completely fur-
nished,
Harness gold-inlaid and burnished,
Mantle like a flame of fire.

Thus came Olaf to his own,
When upon the night-wind blown
  Passed that cry along the shore;
And he answered, while the rifted
Streamers o'er him shook and
   shifted,
  "I accept thy challenge, Thor!"

III.

THORA OF RIMOL

"Thora of Rimol! hide me! hide
  me!
Danger and shame and death be-
  tide me!
For Olaf the King is hunting me
  down
Through field and forest, through
  thorp and town!"
    Thus cried Jarl Hakon
    To Thora, the fairest of
    women.

"Hakon Jarl! for the love I bear
  thee
Neither shall shame nor death
  come near thee!
But the hiding-place wherein thou
  must lie
Is the cave underneath the swine
  in the sty."
    Thus to Jarl Hakon
    Said Thora, the fairest of women.

So Hakon Jarl and his base thrall
  Karker
Crouched in the cave, than a dun-
  geon darker,
As Olaf came riding, with men in
  mail,
Through the forest roads into Orka-
  dale,
    Demanding Jarl Hakon
    Of Thora, the fairest of
    women.

"Rich and honoured shall be who-
  ever

The head of Hakon Jarl shall dis-
  sever!"
Hakon heard him, and Karker the
  slave,
Through the breathing-holes of
  the darksome cave.
    Alone in her chamber
    Wept Thora, the fairest of
    women.

Said Karker, the crafty, "I will
  not slay thee!
For all the king's gold I will never
  betray thee!"
"Then why dost thou turn so pale,
  O churl,
And then again black as the
  earth?" said the Earl.
    More pale and more faithful
    Was Thora, the fairest of
    women.

From a dream in the night the
  thrall started, saying,
"Round my neck a gold ring King
  Olaf was laying!"
And Hakon answered, "Beware
  of the king!
He will lay round thy neck a blood-
  red ring."
    At the ring on her finger
    Gazed Thora, the fairest of
    women.

At daybreak slept Hakon, with
  sorrows encumbered,
But screamed and drew up his feet
  as he slumbered;
The thrall in the darkness plunged
  with his knife,
And the Earl awakened no more in
  this life.
    But wakeful and weeping
    Sat Thora, the fairest of
    women.

At Nidarholm the priests are all
  singing,
Two ghastly heads on the gibbet
  are swinging;

One is Jarl Hakon's and one is his thrall's.

And the people are shouting from windows and walls;
While alone in her chamber
Swoons Thora, the fairest of women.

IV.

QUEEN SIGRID THE HAUGHTY

Queen Sigrid the Haughty sat proud and aloft
In her chamber, that looked over meadow and croft.
Heart's dearest,
Why dost thou sorrow so?

The floor with tassels of fir was besprent,
Filling the room with their fragrant scent.

She heard the birds sing, she saw the sun shine,
The air of summer was sweeter than wine.

Like a sword without scabbard the bright river lay
Between her own kingdom and Norroway.

But Olaf the King had sued for her hand.
The sword would be sheathed, the river be spanned.

Her maidens were seated around her knee,
Working bright figures in tapestry.

And one was singing the ancient rune
Of Brynhilda's love and the wrath of Gudrun.

And through it, and round it, and over it all
Sounded incessant the waterfall.

The Queen in her hand held a ring of gold,
From the door of Ladé's Temple old.

King Olaf had sent her this wedding gift,
But her thoughts as arrows were keen and swift.

She had given the ring to her goldsmiths twain,
Who smiled, as they handed it back again.

And Sigrid the Queen, in her haughty way,
Said, "Why do you smile, my goldsmiths, say?"

And they answered: "O Queen! if the truth must be told,
The ring is of copper, and not of gold!"

The lightning flashed o'er her forehead and cheek,
She only murmured, she did not speak:

"If in his gifts he can faithless be,
There will be no gold in his love to me."

A footstep was heard on the outer stair,
And in strode King Olaf with royal air.

He kissed the Queen's hand, and he whispered of love,
And swore to be true as the stars are above.

But she smiled with contempt as she answered: "O King,
Will you swear it, as Odin once swore, on the ring?"

And the King: "O speak not of
    Odin to me,
The wife of King Olaf a Christian
    must be."

Looking straight at the King, with
    her level brows,
She said, "I keep true to my faith
    and my vows."

Then the face of King Olaf was
    darkened with gloom,
He rose in his anger and strode
    through the room.

"Why, then, should I care to have
    thee?" he said,—
"A faded old woman, a heathenish
    jade!"

His zeal was stronger than fear or
    love,
And he struck the Queen in the
    face with his glove.

Then forth from the chamber in
    anger he fled,
And the wooden stairway shook
    with his tread.

Queen Sigrid the Haughty said
    under her breath,
"This insult, King Olaf, shall be
    thy death!"
    Heart's dearest,
  Why dost thou sorrow so?

V.

THE SKERRY OF SHRIEKS

Now from all King Olaf's farms
    His men-at-arms
Gathered on the Eve of Easter;
To his house at Angvalds-ness
    Fast they press,
Drinking with the royal feaster.

Loudly through the wide-flung
    door
    Came the roar

Of the sea upon the Skerry;
And its thunder loud and near
    Reached the ear,
Mingling with their voices merry.

"Hark!" said Olaf to his Scald,
    Halfred the Bald,
"Listen to that song, and learn it!
Half my kingdom would I give,
    As I live,
If by such songs you would earn it!

"For of all the runes and rhymes
    Of all times,
Best I like the ocean's dirges,
When the old harper heaves and
    rocks,
    His hoary locks
Flowing and flashing in the
    surges!"

Halfred answered: "I am called
    The Unappalled!
Nothing hinders me or daunts me.
Hearken to me, then, O King,
    While I sing
The great Ocean Song that haunts
    me."

"I will hear your song sublime
    Some other time,"
Says the drowsy monarch, yawn-
    ing,
And retires; each laughing guest
    Applauds the jest;
Then they sleep till day is dawn-
    ing.

Pacing up and down the yard,
    King Olaf's guard
Saw the sea-mist slowly creeping
O'er the sands, and up the hill,
    Gathering still
Round the house where they were
    sleeping.

It was not the fog he saw
    Nor misty flaw,
That above the landscape brooded;

It was Eyvind Kallda's crew
    Of warlocks blue,
With their caps of darkness hooded!

Round and round the house they
      go,
    Weaving slow
Magic circles to encumber
And imprison in their ring
    Olaf the King,
As he helpless lies in slumber.

Then athwart the vapours dun
    The Easter sun
Streamed with one broad track of
    splendour!
In their real forms appeared
    The warlocks weird,
Awful as the witch of Endor.

Blinded by the light that glared,
    They groped and stared
Round about with steps unsteady;
From his window Olaf gazed,
    And, amazed,
"Who are these strange people?"
    said he.

"Eyvind Kallda and his men!"
    Answered then
From the yard a sturdy farmer;
While the men-at-arms apace
    Filled the place,
Busily buckling on their armour.

From the gates they sallied forth,
    South and north,
Scoured the island coast around
    them,
Seizing all the warlock band,
    Foot and hand
On the Skerry's rocks they bound
    them.

And at eve the king again
    Called his train,
And, with all the candles burning,
Silent sat and heard once more
    The sullen roar
Of the ocean tides returning.

Shrieks and cries of wild despair
    Filled the air,
Growing fainter as they listened;
Then the bursting surge alone
    Sounded on;—
Thus the sorcerers were christened!

"Sing, O Scald, your song sub-
    lime,
    Your ocean rhyme,"
Cried King Olaf: "It will cheer
    me!"
Said the Scald, with pallid cheeks,
    "The Skerry of Shrieks
Sings too loud for you to hear me!"

VI.

THE WRAITH OF ODIN

The guests were loud, the ale was
    strong,
King Olaf feasted late and long;
The hoary Scalds together sang;
O'erhead the smoky rafters rang.
    Dead rides Sir Morten of
    Fogelsang.

The door swung wide, with creak
    and din;
A blast of cold night-air came in,
And on the threshold shivering
    stood
A one-eyed guest, with cloak and
    hood.
    Dead rides Sir Morten of
    Fogelsang.

The King exclaimed, "O gray-
    beard pale!
Come warm thee with this cup of
    ale."
The foaming draught the old man
    quaffed,
The noisy guests looked on and
    laughed.
    Dead rides Sir Morten of
    Fogelsang.

Then spake the King: " Be not
    afraid;
Sit here by me." The guest
    obeyed,
And, seated at the table, told
Tales of the sea, and Sagas old.
        Dead rides Sir Morten of
        Fogelsang.

And ever, when the tale was o'er,
The King demanded yet one more;
Till Sigurd the Bishop smiling said,
" 'Tis late, O King, and time for
    bed."
        Dead rides Sir Morten of
        Fogelsang.

The King retired; the stranger
    guest
Followed and entered with the rest;
The lights were out, the pages gone,
But still the garrulous guest spake
    on.
        Dead rides Sir Morten of
        Fogelsang.

As one who from a volume reads,
He spake of heroes and their deeds,
Of lands and cities he had seen,
And stormy gulfs that tossed be-
    tween.
        Dead rides Sir Morten of
        Fogelsang.

Then from his lips in music rolled
The Havamal of Odin old,
With sounds mysterious as the roar
Of billows on a distant shore.
        Dead rides Sir Morten of
        Fogelsang.

" Do we not learn from runes and
    rhymes
Made by the gods in elder times,
And do not still the great Scalds
    teach
That silence better is than speech ? "
        Dead rides Sir Morten of
        Fogelsang.

Smiling at this, the King replied,
" Thy lore is by thy tongue belied;
For never was I so enthralled
Either by Saga-man or Scald."
        Dead rides Sir Morten of
        Fogelsang.

The Bishop said, " Late hours we
    keep!
Night wanes, O King! 'tis time
    for sleep! "
Then slept the King, and when he
    woke
The guest was gone, the morning
    broke.
        Dead rides Sir Morten of
        Fogelsang.

They found the doors securely
    barred,
They found the watch-dog in the
    yard,
There was no footprint in the grass,
And none had seen the stranger
    pass.
        Dead rides Sir Morten of
        Fogelsang.

King Olaf crossed himself and said:
" I know that Odin the Great is
    dead;
Sure is the triumph of our Faith,
The one-eyed stranger was his
    wraith."
        Dead rides Sir Morten of
        Fogelsang.

VII.

IRON-BEARD

Olaf the King, one summer
    morn,
Blew a blast on his bugle-horn,
Sending his signal through the land
    of Drontheim.

And to the Hus-Ting held at
    Mere
Gathered the farmers far and
    near,

With their war weapons ready to
confront him.

Ploughing under the morning
star,
Old Iron-Beard in Yriar
Heard the summons, chuckling
with a low laugh.

He wiped the sweat-drops
from his brow,
Unharnessed his horses from
the plough,
And clattering came on horseback
to King Olaf.

He was the churliest of the
churls;
Little he cared for king or earls;
Bitter as home-brewed ale were his
foaming passions.

Hodden-gray was the garb he
wore,
And by the Hammer of Thor
he swore;
He hated the narrow town, and all
its fashions.

But he loved the freedom of
his farm,
His ale at night by the fireside
warm,
Gudrun his daughter, with her
flaxen tresses.

He loved his horses and his
herds,
The smell of the earth, and the
song of birds,
His well-filled barns, his brook with
its water-cresses.

Huge and cumbersome was his
frame;
His beard, from which he took
his name,
Frosty and fierce, like that of Hy-
mer the Giant.

So at the Hus-Ting he ap-
peared,
The farmer of Yriar, Iron-
Beard,
On horseback, with an attitude
defiant.

And to King Olaf he cried
aloud,
Out of the middle of the crowd,
That tossed about him like a
stormy ocean:

" Such sacrifices shalt thou bring;
To Odin and to Thor, O King,
As other kings have done in their
devotion! "

King Olaf answered: " I com-
mand
This land to be a Christian
land;
Here is my Bishop who the folk
baptises!

" But if you ask me to restore
Your sacrifices, stained with
gore,
Then will I offer human sacrifices!

" Not slaves and peasants
shall they be,
But men of note and high de-
gree,
Such men as Orm of Lyra and Kar
of Gryting! "

Then to their Temple strode
he in,
And loud behind him heard
the din
Of his men-at-arms and the
peasants fiercely fighting.

There in the Temple, carved
in wood,
The image of great Odin stood,
And other gods, with Thor
supreme among them.

King Olaf smote them with
    the blade
Of his huge war-axe, gold in-
    laid,
And downward shattered to the
    pavement flung them.

At the same moment rose
    without,
From the contending crowd, a
    shout,
A mingled sound of triumph and of
    wailing.

And there upon the trampled
    plain
The farmer Iron-Beard lay
    slain,
Midway between the assailed and
    the assailing.

King Olaf from the doorway
    spoke:
" Choose ye between two
    things, my folk,
To be baptised or given up to
    slaughter! "

And seeing their leader stark
    and dead,
The people with a murmur
    said,
" O King, baptise us with thy holy
    water! "

So all the Drontheim land be-
    came
A Christian land in name and
    fame,
In the old gods no more believing
    and trusting.

And as a blood-atonement,
    soon
King Olaf wed the fair Gud-
    run;
And thus in peace ended the Dron-
    theim Hus-Ting!

VIII.

GUDRUN

On King Olaf's bridal night
Shines the moon with tender light,
And across the chamber streams
    Its tide of dreams.

At the fatal midnight hour,
When all evil things have power,
In the glimmer of the moon
    Stands Gudrun.

Close against her heaving breast,
Something in her hand is pressed;
Like an icicle, its sheen
    Is cold and keen.

On the cairn are fixed her eyes
Where her murdered father lies,
And a voice remote and drear
    She seems to hear.

What a bridal night is this!
Cold will be the dagger's kiss;
Laden with the chill of death
    Is its breath.

Like the drifting snow she sweeps
To the couch where Olaf sleeps,
Suddenly he wakes and stirs,
    His eyes meet hers.

" What is that," King Olaf said,
" Gleams so bright above thy
    head ?
Wherefore standest thou so white
    In pale moonlight ? "

" 'Tis the bodkin that I wear
When at night I bind my hair;
It woke me falling on the floor;
    'Tis nothing more."

Forests have ears, and fields have
    eyes;
Often treachery lurking lies
Underneath the fairest hair!
    Gudrun beware! "

Ere the earliest peep of morn
Blew King Olaf's bugle-horn;
And for ever sundered ride
    Bridegroom and bride!

IX.

THANGBRAND THE PRIEST

Short of stature, large of limb,
    Burly face and russet beard,
All the women stared at him,
    When in Iceland he appeared.
        " Look! " they said,
        With nodding head,
" There goes Thangbrand, Olaf's
    Priest."

All the prayers he knew by rote,
    He could preach like Chrysos-
tome,
From the Fathers he could quote,
    He had even been at Rome.
        A learned clerk,
        A man of mark,
Was this Thangbrand, Olaf's Priest.

He was quarrelsome and loud,
    And impatient of control,
Boisterous in the market crowd,
    Boisterous at the wassail-bowl,
        Everywhere
        Would drink and swear,
Swaggering Thangbrand, Olaf's
    Priest.

In his house this malecontent
    Could the King no longer bear,
So to Iceland he was sent
    To convert the heathen there,
        And away
        One summer day
Sailed this Thangbrand, Olaf's
    Priest.

There in Iceland, o'er their books
    Pored the people day and night,
But he did not like their looks,
    Nor the songs they used to write.

    " All this rhyme
    Is waste of time! "
Grumbled Thangbrand, Olaf's
    Priest.

To the alehouse, where he sat,
    Came the Scalds and Saga men;
Is it to be wondered at,
    That they quarrelled now and
then,
        When o'er his beer
        Began to leer
Drunken Thangbrand, Olaf's
    Priest?

All the folk in Altafiord
    Boasted of their island grand;
Saying in a single word,
    " Iceland is the finest land
        That the sun
        Doth shine upon! "
Loud laughed Thangbrand, Olaf's
    Priest.

And he answered: " What's the
    use
Of this bragging up and down,
When three women and one goose
    Make a market in your town! "
        Every Scald
        Satires scrawled
On poor Thangbrand, Olaf's Priest.

Something worse they did than
    that;
    And what vexed him most of all
Was a figure in shovel hat,
    Drawn in charcoal on the wall;
        With words that go
        Sprawling below,
" This is Thangbrand, Olaf's
    Priest."

Hardly knowing what he did,
    Then he smote them might and
main,
Thorvald Veile and Veterlid
    Lay there in the alehouse
slain.

" To-day we are gold,
     To-morrow mould! "
Muttered Thangbrand, Olaf's
     Priest.

Much in fear of axe and rope,
     Back to Norway sailed he then.
" O, King Olaf! little hope
Is there of these Iceland men! "
     Meekly said,
     With bending head,
Pious Thangbrand, Olaf's Priest.

X.

RAUD THE STRONG

" All the old gods are dead,
All the wild warlocks fled;
But the White Christ lives and
     reigns,
And throughout my wide domains
His Gospel shall be spread! "
     On the Evangelists
     Thus swore King Olaf.

But still in dreams of the night
Beheld he the crimson light,
And heard the voice that defied
Him who was crucified,
And challenged him to the fight.
     To Sigurd the Bishop
     King Olaf confessed it.

And Sigurd the Bishop said,
" The old gods are not dead,
For the great Thor still reigns,
And among the Jarls and Thanes
The old witchcraft still is spread."
     Thus to King Olaf
     Said Sigurd the Bishop.

" Far north in the Salten Fiord,
By rapine, fire, and sword,
Lives the Viking, Raud the Strong;
All the Godoe Isles belong
To him and his heathen horde."
     Thus went on speaking
     Sigurd the Bishop.

" A warlock, a wizard is he,
And lord of the wind and the sea;
And whichever way he sails,
He has ever favouring gales,
By his craft in sorcery."
     Here the sign of the cross made
     Devoutly King Olaf.

" With rites that we both abhor,
He worships Odin and Thor;
So it cannot yet be said,
That all the old gods are dead,
And the warlocks are no more,"
     Flushing with anger
     Said Sigurd the Bishop.

Then King Olaf cried aloud:
" I will talk with this mighty Raud,
And along the Salten Fiord
Preach the Gospel with my sword,
Or be brought back in my shroud! "
     So northward from Drontheim
     Sailed King Olaf!

XI.

BISHOP SIGURD AT SALTEN FIORD

Loud the angry wind was wailing
As King Olaf's ships came sailing
Northward out of Drontheim
     haven
     To the mouth of Salten Fiord.

Though the flying sea-spray
     drenches
Fore and aft the rowers' benches,
Not a single heart is craven
     Of the champions there on
     board.

All without the Fiord was quiet,
But within it storm and riot,
Such as on his Viking cruises
     Raud the Strong was wont to
     ride.

And the sea through all its tide-
     ways
Swept the reeling vessels sideways,

As the leaves are swept through
    sluices,
    When the flood-gates open
      wide.

" 'Tis the warlock! 'tis the demon
Raud!" cried Sigurd to the seamen;
" But the Lord is not affrighted
    By the witchcraft of his foes."

To the ship's bow he ascended,
By his choristers attended,
Round him were the tapers lighted,
    And the sacred incense rose.

On the bow stood Bishop Sigurd,
In his robes, as one transfigured,
And the Crucifix he planted
    High amid the rain and mist.

Then with holy water sprinkled
All the ship; the mass-bells tinkled;
Loud the monks around him
    chanted,
    Loud he read the Evangelist.

As into the Fiord they darted,
On each side the water parted;
Down a path like silver molten
    Steadily rowed King Olaf's
    ships;

Steadily burned all night the tapers,
And the White Christ through the
    vapours
Gleamed across the Fiord of Salten,
    As through John's Apoc-
    alypse,—

Till at last they reached Raud's
    dwelling
On the little isle of Gelling;
Not a guard was at the doorway,
    Not a glimmer of light was
    seen.

But at anchor, carved and gilded,
Lay the dragon-ship he builded;
'Twas the grandest ship in Norway,
    With its crest and scales of green.

Up the stairway, softly creeping,
To the loft where Raud was sleep
    ing,
With their fists they burst asunder
    Bolt and bar that held the door.

Drunken with sleep and ale they
    found him,
Dragged him from his bed and
    bound him,
While he stared with stupid won-
    der,
    At the look and garb they wore.

Then King Olaf said: " O Sea-
    King!
Little time have we for speaking,
Choose between the good and evil;
    Be baptised, or thou shalt die!"

But in scorn the heathen scoffer
Answered: " I disdain thine offer;
Neither fear I God nor Devil;
    Thee and thy Gospel I defy!"

Then between his jaws distended,
When his frantic struggles ended,
Through King Olaf's horn an adder,
    Touched by fire, they forced
    to glide.

Sharp his tooth was as an arrow,
As he gnawed through bone and
    marrow;
But without a groan or shudder,
    Raud the Strong blaspheming
    died.

Then baptised they all that region,
Swarthy Lap and fair Norwegian,
Far as swims the salmon, leaping,
    Up the streams of Salten
    Fiord.

In their temples Thor and Odin
Lay in dust and ashes trodden,
As King Olaf, onward sweeping,
    Preached the Gospel with his
    sword.

Then he took the carved and gilded
Dragon-ship that Raud had builded,
And the tiller single-handed,
    Grasping, steered into the main.

Southward sailed the sea-gulls o'er him,
Southward sailed the ship that bore him,
Till at Drontheim haven landed
    Olaf and his crew again.

XII.

KING OLAF'S CHRISTMAS

At Drontheim, Olaf the King
Heard the bells of Yule-tide ring,
    As he sat in his banquet-hall,
Drinking the nut-brown ale,
With his bearded Berserks hale
    And tall.

Three days his Yule-tide feasts
He held with Bishops and Priests,
    And his horn filled up to the brim;
But the ale was never too strong,
Nor the Saga-man's tale too long,
    For him.

O'er his drinking horn, the sign
He made of the cross divine,
    As he drank, and muttered his prayers;
But the Berserks evermore
Made the sign of the Hammer of Thor
    Over theirs.

The gleams of the fire-light dance
Upon helmet and hauberk and lance,
    And laugh in the eyes of the King;
And he cries to Halfred the Scald,
Gray-bearded, wrinkled, and bald,
    "Sing!"

"Sing me a song divine,
With a sword in every line,
    And this shall be thy reward."
And he loosened the belt at his waist,
And in front of the singer placed
    His sword.

"Quern-biter of Hakon the Good,
Wherewith at a stroke he hewed
    The millstone through and through,
And Foot-breadth of Thoralf the Strong,
Were neither so broad nor so long,
    Nor so true."

Then the Scald took his harp and sang,
And loud through the music rang
    The sound of that shining word;
And the harp-strings a clangor made,
As if they were struck with the blade
    Of a sword.

And the Berserks round about
Broke forth into a shout
    That made the rafters ring:
They smote with their fists on the board,
And shouted, "Long live the Sword,
    And the King!"

But the King said, "O my son,
I miss the bright word in one
    Of thy measures and thy rhymes."
And Halfred the Scald replied,
"In another 'twas multiplied,
    Three times."

Then King Olaf raised the hilt
Of iron, cross-shaped and gilt,
    And said, "Do not refuse;

Count well the gain and the loss,
Thor's hammer or Christ's cross:
    Choose! "

And Halfred the Scald said, " This
In the name of the Lord I kiss,
    Who on it was crucified! "
And a shout went round the board,
" In the name of Christ the Lord,
    Who died! "

Then over the waste of snows
The noonday sun uprose,
    Through the driving mists re-
    vealed,
Like the lifting of the Host,
By incense-clouds almost
    Concealed.

On the shining wall a vast
And shadowy cross was cast
    From the hilt of the lifted
    sword,
And in foaming cups of ale
The Berserks drank " Was-hael!
    To the Lord! "

XIII.

THE BUILDING OF THE LONG SERPENT

Thorberg Skafting, master-builder,
    In his ship-yard by the sea,
Whistled, saying, " 'Twould be-
    wilder
Any man but Thorberg Skafting,
    Any man but me! "

Near him lay the Dragon stranded,
    Built of old by Raud the
    Strong,
And King Olaf had commanded
He should build another Dragon,
    Twice as large and long.

Therefore whistled Thorberg
    Skafting,
    As he sat with half-closed eyes,

And his head turned sideways,
    drafting
That new vessel for King Olaf
    Twice the Dragon's size.

Round him busily hewed and
    hammered
    Mallet huge and heavy axe;
Workmen laughed and sang and
    clamoured;
Whirred the wheels, that into rigg-
    ing
    Spun the shining flax!

All this tumult heard the master,—
    It was music to his ear;
Fancy whispered all the faster,
" Men shall hear of Thorberg
    Skafting
    For a hundred year! "

Workmen sweating at the forges
    Fashioned iron bolt and bar,
Like a warlock's midnight orgies
Smoked and bubbled the black
    cauldron
    With the boiling tar.

Did the warlocks mingle in it,
    Thorberg Skafting, any curse?
Could you not be gone a minute
But some mischief must be doing,
    Turning bad to worse?

'Twas an ill wind that came waft-
    ing,
    From his homestead words of
    woe;
To his farm went Thorberg Skaft-
    ing,
Oft repeating to his workmen,
    Build ye thus and so.

After long delays returning
    Came the master back by
    night;
To his ship-yard longing, yearning,
Hurried he, and did not leave it
    Till the morning's light.

" Come and see my ship, my dar-
    ling! "
    On the morrow said the King;
" Finished now from keel to carl-
    ing;
Never yet was seen in Norway
    Such a wondrous thing! "

In the ship-yard, idly talking,
    At the ship the workmen
    stared:
Some one, all their labour baulking,
Down her sides had cut deep gashes
    Not a plank was spared!

" Death be to the evil-doer! "
    With an oath King Olaf spoke;
" But rewards to his pursuer! "
And with wrath his face grew
    redder
    Than his scarlet cloak.

Straight the master builder, smil-
    ing,
    Answered thus the angry King:
" Cease blaspheming and reviling,
Olaf, it was Thorberg Skafting
    Who has done this thing! "

Then he chipped and smoothed
    the planking,
    Till the King, delighted, swore,
With much lauding and much
    thanking,
" Handsomer is now my Dragon
    Than she was before! "

Seventy ells and four extended
    On the grass the vessel's keel;
High above it, gilt and splendid,
Rose the figure-head ferocious
    With its crest of steel.

Then they launched her from the
    tressels,
    In the ship-yard by the sea;
She was the grandest of all vessels,
Never ship was built in Norway
    Half so fine as she!

The Long Serpent was she chris-
    tened,
    'Mid the roar of cheer on cheer!
They who to the Saga listened
Heard the name of Thorberg
    Skafting
    For a hundred year!

XIV.

THE CREW OF THE LONG SERPENT

Safe at anchor in Drontheim bay
King Olaf's fleet assembled lay,
    And, striped with white and blue,
Downward fluttered sail and
    banner,
As alights the screaming lanner;
Lustily cheered, in their wild
    manner,
    The Long Serpent's crew.

Her forecastle man was Ulf the
    Red;
Like a wolf's was his shaggy head,
    His teeth as large and white;
His beard, of gray and russet
    blended,
Round as a swallow's nest de-
    scended;
As standard-bearer he defended
    Olaf's flag in the fight.

Near him Kolbiorn had his place,
Like the King in garb and face,
    So gallant and so hale;
Every cabin-boy and varlet
Wondered at his cloak of scarlet;
Like a river, frozen and star-lit,
    Gleamed his coat of mail.

By the bulkhead, tall and dark,
Stood Thrand Rame of Thelemark,
    A figure gaunt and grand;
On his hairy arm imprinted
Was an anchor, azure-tinted;
Like Thor's hammer, huge and
    dinted
    Was his brawny hand.

Einar Tamberskelver, bare
To the winds his golden hair,
  By the mainmast stood;
Graceful was his form, and slender,
And his eyes were deep and tender
As a woman's, in the splendour
  Of her maidenhood.

In the fore-hold Biorn and Bork
Watched the sailors at their work:
  Heavens! how they swore!
Thirty men they each commanded,
Iron-sinewed, horny-handed,
Shoulders broad, and chests ex-
    panded,
  Tugging at the oar.

These, and many more like these,
With King Olaf sailed the seas,
  Till the waters vast
Filled them with a vague devotion,
With the freedom and the motion,
With the roll and roar of ocean
  And the sounding blast.

When they landed from the fleet,
How they roared through Dron-
    theim's street,
  Boisterous as the gale!
How they laughed and stamped
    and pounded,
Till the tavern roof resounded,
And the host looked on astounded
  As they drank the ale!

Never saw the wild North Sea
Such a gallant company
  Sail its billows blue!
Never, while they cruised and
    quarrelled,
Old King Gorm, or Blue-Tooth
    Harald,
Owned a ship so well apparelled,
  Boasted such a crew!

XV.

A LITTLE BIRD IN THE AIR

A little bird in the air
Is singing of Thyri the fair,
  The sister of Svend the Dane;

And the song of the garrulous bird
In the streets of the town is heard,
  And repeated again and again.
    Hoist up your sails of silk,
    And flee away from each other.

To King Burislaf, it is said,
Was the beautiful Thyri wed,
  And a sorrowful bride went she;
And after a week and a day,
She has fled away and away,
  From his town by the stormy sea.
    Hoist up your sails of silk,
    And flee away from each other.

They say, that through heat and
    through cold,
Through weald, they say, and
    through wold,
  By day and by night, they say,
She has fled; and the gossips report
She has come to King Olaf's court,
  And the town is all in dismay.
    Hoist up your sails of silk,
    And flee away from each other.

It is whispered King Olaf has
    seen,
Has talked with the beautiful
    Queen;
  And they wonder how it will end;
For surely, if here she remain,
It is war with King Svend the
    Dane,
  And King Burislaf the Vend!
    Hoist up your sails of silk,
    And flee away from each other.

O, greatest wonder of all!
It is published in hamlet and
    hall,
  It roars like a flame that is
    fanned!
The King—yes, Olaf the King—
Has wedded her with his ring,
  And Thyri is queen in the
    land!
    Hoist up your sails of silk,
    And flee away from each other.

XVI.

QUEEN THYRI AND THE ANGELICA STALKS

Northward over Drontheim,
Flew the clamorous sea-gulls,
Sang the lark and linnet
   From the meadows green;

Weeping in her chamber,
Lonely and unhappy,
Sat the Drottning Thyri,
   Sat King Olaf's Queen.

In at all the windows
Streamed the pleasant sunshine,
On the roof above her
   Softly cooed the dove;

But the sound she heard not,
Nor the sunshine heeded,
For the thoughts of Thyri
   Were not thoughts of love.

Then King Olaf entered,
Beautiful as morning,
Like the sun at Easter
   Shone his happy face;

In his hand he carried
Angelicas uprooted,
With delicious fragrance
   Filling all the place.

Like a rainy midnight
Sat the Drottning Thyri,
Even the smile of Olaf
   Could not cheer her gloom;

Nor the stalks he gave her
With a gracious gesture,
And with words as pleasant
   As their own perfume.

In her hands he placed them,
And her jewelled fingers
Through the green leaves glistened
   Like the dews of morn;

But she cast them from her,
Haughty and indignant,
On the floor she threw them
   With a look of scorn.

" Richer presents," said she,
" Gave King Harald Gormson
To the Queen, my mother,
   Than such worthless weeds;

" When he ravaged Norway,
Laying waste the kingdom,
Seizing scatt and treasure
   For her royal needs.

" But thou darest not venture
Through the Sound to Vendland,
My domains to rescue
   From King Burislaf;

" Lest King Svend of Denmark,
Forked Beard, my brother,
Scatter all thy vessels
   As the wind the chaff."

Then up sprang King Olaf,
Like a reindeer bounding,
With an oath he answered
   Thus the luckless Queen:

" Never yet did Olaf
Fear King Svend of Denmark;
This right hand shall hale him
   By his forked chin! "

Then he left the chamber,
Thundering through the doorway,
Loud his steps resounded
   Down the outer stair.

Smarting with the insult,
Through the streets of Drontheim
Strode he red and wrathful,
   With his stately air.

All his ships he gathered,
Summoned all his forces,
Making his war levy
   In the region round;

Down the coast of Norway,
Like a flock of sea-gulls,
Sailed the fleet of Olaf
   Through the Danish Sound.

With his own hand fearless,
Steered he the Long Serpent,
Strained the creaking cordage,
   Bent each bloom and gaff;

Till in Vendland landing,
The domains of Thyri
He redeemed and rescued
   From King Burislaf.

Then said Olaf, laughing,
" Not ten yoke of oxen
Have the power to draw us
   Like a woman's hair!

" Now will I confess it,
Better things are jewels
Than angelica stalks are
   For a Queen to wear."

XVII.

KING SVEND OF THE FORKED BEARD

Loudly the sailors cheered
Svend of the Forked Beard,
As with his fleet he steered
   Southward to Vendland;
Where with their courses hauled
All were together called,
Under the Isle of Svald
   Near to the mainland.

After Queen Gunhild's death,
So the old Saga saith,
Plighted King Svend his faith
   To Sigrid the Haughty:
And to avenge his bride,
Soothing her wounded pride,
Over the waters wide
   King Olaf sought he.

Still on her scornful face,
Blushing with deep disgrace,

Bore she the crimson trace
   Of Olaf's gauntlet;
Like a malignant star,
Blazing in heaven afar,
Red shone the angry scar
   Under her frontlet.

Oft to King Svend she spake,
" For thine own honour's sake
Shalt thou swift vengeance take
   On the vile coward! "
Until the King at last,
Gusty and overcast,
Like a tempestuous blast
   Threatened and lowered.

Soon as the Spring appeared,
Svend of the Forked Beard
High his red standard reared,
   Eager for battle;
While every warlike Dane,
Seizing his arms again,
Left all unsown the grain,
   Unhoused the cattle.

Likewise the Swedish King
Summoned in haste a Thing,
Weapons and men to bring
   In aid of Denmark;
Eric the Norseman, too,
As the war-tidings flew,
Sailed with a chosen crew
   From Lapland and Finmark.

So upon Easter day
Sailed the three kings away,
Out of the sheltered bay,
   In the bright season;
With them Earl Sigvald came,
Eager for spoil and fame;
Pity that such a name
   Stooped to such treason!

Safe under Svald at last,
Now were their anchors cast,
Safe from the sea and blast,
   Plotted the three kings;
While, with a base intent,
Southward Earl Sigvald went,

On a foul errand bait,
  Unto the Sea-kings.

Thence to hold on his course,
Unto King Olaf's force,
Lying within the hoarse
  Mouths of Stet-haven;
Him to ensnare and bring,
Unto the Danish king,
Who his dead corse would fling
  Forth to the raven!

XVIII.

KING OLAF AND EARL SIGVALD

On the gray sea-sands
King Olaf stands,
Northward and seaward
He points with his hands.

With eddy and whirl
The sea-tides curl,
Washing the sandals
Of Sigvald the Earl.

The mariners shout,
The ships swing about,
The yards are all hoisted,
The sails flutter out.

The war-horns are played,
The anchors are weighed,
Like moths in the distance
The sails flit and fade.

The sea is like lead,
The harbour lies dead,
As a corse on the sea-shore,
Whose spirit has fled!

On that fatal day,
The histories say,
Seventy vessels
Sailed out of the bay.

But soon scattered wide
O'er the billows they ride,
While Sigvald and Olaf
Sail side by side.

Cried the Earl: "Follow me!
I your pilot will be,
For I know all the channels
Where flows the deep sea!"

So into the strait
Where his foes lie in wait,
Gallant King Olaf
Sails to his fate!

Then the sea-fog veils
The ships and their sails;
Queen Sigrid the Haughty,
Thy vengeance prevails!

XIX.

KING OLAF'S WAR-HORNS

"Strike the sails!" King Olaf said;
Never shall men of mine take flight;
Never away from battle I fled,
Never away from my foes!
  Let God dispose
Of my life in the fight!"

"Sound the horns!" said Olaf the
    King;
And suddenly through the drifting
    brume
The blare of the horns began to
    ring,
Like the terrible trumpet shock
  Of Regnarock,
On the Day of Doom!

Louder and louder the war-horns
    sang
Over the level floor of the flood;
All the sails came down with a
    clang,
And there in the mist overhead
  The sun hung red
As a drop of blood.

Drifting down on the Danish fleet
Three together the ships were
    lashed,
So that neither should turn and re-
    treat;

In the midst, but in front of the
   rest
   The burnished crest
Of the Serpent flashed.

King Olaf stood on the quarter-
   deck,
With bow of ash and arrows of oak,
His gilded shield was without a
   fleck,
His helmet inlaid with gold,
   And in many a fold
Hung his crimson cloak.

On the forecastle Ulf the Red
Watched the lashing of the ships;
" If the Serpent lie so far ahead,
We shall have hard work of it
   here,"
   Said he with a sneer
On his bearded lips.

King Olaf laid an arrow on string,
" Have I a coward on board? "
   said he.
" Shoot it another way, O King! "
Sullenly answered Ulf,
   The old sea-wolf;
" You have need of me! "

In front came Svend, the King of
   the Danes,
Sweeping down with his fifty
   rowers;
To the right, the Swedish king with
   his thanes;
And on board of the Iron Beard
   Earl Eric steered
On the left with his oars.

" These soft Danes and Swedes,"
   said the King,
" At home with their wives had
   better stay,
Than come within reach of my
   Serpent's sting:
But where Eric the Norseman leads
   Heroic deeds
Will be done to-day! "

Then as together the vessels
   crashed,
Eric severed the cables of hide,
With which King Olaf's ships were
   lashed,
And left them to drive and drift
   With the currents swift
Of the outward tide.

Louder the war-horns growl and
   snarl,
Sharper the dragons bite and sting!
Eric the son of Hakon Jarl
A death-drink salt as the sea
   Pledges to thee,
Olaf the King!

XX.

EINAR TAMBERSKELVER

It was Einar Tamberskelver
   Stood beside the mast;
From his yew-bow, tipped with
   silver,
   Flew the arrows fast;
Aimed at Eric unavailin
   As he sat concealed,
Half behind the quarter-railing,
   Half behind his shield.

First an arrow struck the tiller,
   Just above his head;
" Sing, O Eyvind Skaldaspiller,"
   Then Earl Eric said,
" Sing the song of Hakon dying,
   Sing his funeral wail! "
And another arrow flying
   Grazed his coat of mail.

Turning to a Lapland yeoman,
   As the arrow passed,
Said Earl Eric, " Shoot that bow-
   man
   Standing by the mast."
Sooner than the word was spoken
   Flew the yeoman's shaft;
Einar's bow in twain was broken,
   Einar only laughed.

"What was that?" said Olaf,
  standing
    On the quarter-deck.
"Something heard I like the
  stranding
    Of a shattered wreck."
Einar then, the arrow taking
  From the loosened string,
Answered, "That was Norway
  breaking
    From thy hand, O king!"

"Thou art but a poor diviner,"
  Straightway Olaf said;
"Take my bow, and swifter, Einar,
  Let thy shafts be sped."
Of his bows the fairest choosing,
  Reached he from above;
Einar saw the blood-drops oozing
  Through his iron glove.

But the bow was thin and narrow;
  At the first assay,
O'er his head he drew the arrow,
  Flung the bow away;
Said, with hot and angry temper
  Flushing in his cheek,
"Olaf! for so great a Kämper
  Are thy bows too weak!"

Then, with smile of joy defiant
  On his beardless lip,
Scaled he, light and self-reliant,
  Eric's dragon-ship.
Loose his golden locks were flow-
  ing,
  Bright his armour gleamed;
Like Saint Michael overthrowing
  Lucifer he seemed.

XXI.

KING OLAF'S DEATH-DRINK

All day has the battle raged,
All day have the ships engaged,
But not yet is assuaged
  The vengeance of Eric the Earl.

The decks with blood are red,
The arrows of death are sped,
The ships are filled with the dead,
  And the spears the champions
    hurl.

They drift as wrecks on the tide,
The grappling-irons are plied,
The boarders climb up the side,
  The shouts are feeble and few.

Ah! never shall Norway again
See her sailors come back o'er the
    main;
They all lie wounded or slain,
  Or asleep in the billows blue!

On the deck stands Olaf the King,
Around him whistle and sing
The spears that the foemen fling,
  And the stones they hurl with
    their hands.

In the midst of the stones and the
    spears,
Kolbiorn, the marshal, appears,
His shield in the air he uprears,
  By the side of King Olaf he
    stands.

Over the slippery wreck
Of the Long Serpent's deck
Sweeps Eric with hardly a check,
  His lips with anger are pale!

He hews with his axe at the mast,
Till it falls, with the sails overcast,
Like a snow-covered pine in the
    vast
  Dim forests of Orkadale.

Seeking King Olaf then,
He rushes aft with his men,
As a hunter into the den
  Of the bear, when he stands at
    bay.

"Remember Jarl Hakon!" he
    cries;
When lo! on his wondering eyes,

Two kingly figures arise,
  Two Olafs in warlike array!

Then Kolbiorn speaks in the ear
Of King Olaf a word of cheer,
In a whisper that none may hear,
  With a smile on his tremulous
    lip;

Two shields raised high in the air,
Two flashes of golden hair,
Two scarlet meteors' glare,
  And both have leaped from the
    ship.

Earl Eric's men in the boats
Seize Kolbiorn's shield as it floats,
And cry, from their hairy throats,
  "See! it is Olaf the King!"

While far on the opposite side
Floats another shield on the tide,
Like a jewel set in the wide
  Sea-current's eddying ring.

There is told a wonderful tale,
How the King stripped off his mail,
Like leaves of the brown sea-kale,
  As he swam beneath the main;

But the young grew old and gray,
And never, by night or by day,
In his kingdom of Norroway
  Was King Olaf seen again!

XXII.

THE NUN OF NIDAROS

In the convent of Drontheim,
Alone in her chamber
Knelt Astrid the Abbess,
At midnight, adoring,
Beseeching, entreating
The Virgin and Mother.

She heard in the silence
The voice of one speaking,
Without in the darkness.

In gusts of the night-wind
Now louder, now nearer,
Now lost in the distance.

The voice of a stranger
It seemed as she listened,
Of some one who answered,
Beseeching, imploring,
A cry from afar off
She could not distinguish.

The voice of Saint John,
The beloved disciple,
Who wandered and waited
The Master's appearance,
Alone in the darkness,
Unsheltered and friendless.

" It is accepted
The angry defiance,
The challenge of battle!
It is accepted,
But not with the weapons
Of war that thou wieldest!

" Cross against corslet,
Love against hatred,
Peace-cry for war-cry!
Patience is powerful;
He that overcometh
Hath power o'er the nations!

" As torrents in summer,
Half dried in their channels,
Suddenly rise, though the
Sky is still cloudless,
For rain has been falling
Far off at their fountains;

" So hearts that are fainting
Grow full to o'erflowing,
And they that behold it
Marvel, and know not
That God at their fountains
Far off has been raining!

" Stronger than steel
Is the sword of the Spirit;
Swifter than arrows

The light of the truth is,
Greater than anger
Is love, and subdueth!

" Thou art a phantom,
A shape of the sea-mist,
A shape of the brumal
Rain, and the darkness
Fearful and formless;
Day dawns and thou art not!

" The dawn is not distant,
Nor is the night starless;
Love is eternal!
God is still God, and
His faith shall not fail us;
Christ is eternal! "

INTERLUDE

A strain of music closed the tale,
A low, monotonous, funeral wail,
That with its cadence, wild and
sweet,
Made the long Saga more com-
plete.
" Thank God," the Theologian said,
" The reign of violence is dead,
Or dying surely from the world;
While Love triumphant reigns in-
stead,
And in a brighter sky o'erhead
His blessed banners are unfurled.
And most of all thank God for this:
The war and waste of clashing
creeds
Now end in words, and not in
deeds,
And no one suffers loss, or bleeds,
For thoughts that men call heresies.

" I stand without here in the porch,
I hear the bell's melodious din,
I hear the organ peal within,
I hear the prayer, with words that
scorch
Like sparks from an inverted torch
I hear the sermon upon sin,

With threatenings of the last
account.
And all, translated in the air,
Reach me but as our dear Lord's
Prayer,
And as the Sermon on the Mount.

" Must it be Calvin, and not Christ ?
Must it be Athanasian creeds,
Or holy water, books, and beads ?
Must struggling souls remain con-
tent
With councils and decrees of
Trent ?
And can it be enough for these
The Christian Church the year em
balms
With evergreens and boughs of
palms,
And fills the air with litanies ?

" I know that yonder Pharisee
Thanks God that he is not like me;
In my humiliation dressed,
I only stand and beat my breast,
And pray for human charity.

" Not to one church alone, but
seven,
The voice prophetic spake from
heaven;
And unto each the promise came,
Diversified, but still the same;
For him that overcometh are
The new name written on the
stone,
The raiment white, the crown, the
throne,
And I will give him the Morning
Star!

" Ah! to how many Faith has been
No evidence of things unseen,
But a dim shadow, that recasts
The creed of the Phantasiasts,
For whom no Man of Sorrow died,
For whom the Tragedy Divine
Was but a symbol and a sign,
And Christ a phantom crucified!

" For others a diviner creed
Is living in the life they lead.
The passing of their beautiful feet
Blesses the pavement of the street,
And all their looks and words repeat
Old Fuller's saying, wise and sweet,
Not as a vulture, but a dove,
The Holy Ghost came from above.

" And this brings back to me a tale
So sad the hearer well may quail,
And question if such things can be;
Yet in the chronicles of Spain
Down the dark pages runs this stain,
And naught can wash them white again,
So fearful is the tragedy."

THE THEOLOGIAN'S TALE

TORQUEMADA

In the heroic days when Ferdinand
And Isabella ruled the Spanish land,
And Torquemada, with his subtle brain,
Ruled them, as Grand Inquisitor of Spain,
In a great castle near Valladolid,
Moated and high and by fair woodlands hid,
There dwelt, as from the chronicles we learn,
An old Hidalgo proud and taciturn.
Whose name has perished, with his towers of stone,
And all his actions save this one alone;
This one, so terrible, perhaps 'twere best
If it, too, were forgotten with the rest;
Unless, perchance, our eyes can see therein

The martyrdom triumphant o'er the sin;
A double picture, with its gloom and glow,
The splendour overhead, the death below.

This sombre man counted each day as lost
On which his feet no sacred threshold crossed;
And when he chanced the passing Host to meet,
He knelt and prayed devoutly in the street;
Oft he confessed; and with each mutinous thought,
As with wild beasts at Ephesus, he fought,
In deep contrition scourged himself in Lent,
Walked in processions, with his head down bent,
At plays of Corpus Christi oft was seen,
And on Palm Sunday bore his bough of green.
His only pastime was to hunt the boar
Through tangled thickets of the forest hoar,
Or with his jingling mules to hurry down
To some grand bull-fight in the neighbouring town,
Or in the crowd with lighted taper stand,
When Jews were burned, or banished from the land.
Then stirred within him a tumultuous joy;
The demon whose delight is to destroy
Shook him, and shouted with a trumpet tone,
" Kill! kill! and let the Lord find out his own! "

And now, in that old castle in the wood,

His daughters, in the dawn of
womanhood,
Returning from their convent
school, had made
Resplendent with their bloom the
forest shade,
Reminding him of their dead
mother's face,
When first she came into that
gloomy place,—
A memory in his heart as dim and
sweet
As moonlight in a solitary
street,
Where the same rays, that lift the
sea, are thrown
Lovely but powerless upon walls of
stone.

These two fair daughters of a
mother dead
Were all the dream had left him as
it fled.
A joy at first, and then a growing
care,
As if a voice within him cried,
" Beware! "
A vague presentiment of impend-
ing doom,
Like ghostly footsteps in a vacant
room,
Haunted him day and night; a
formless fear
That death to some one of his house
was near,
With dark surmises of a hidden
crime,
Made life itself a death before its
time.
Jealous, suspicious, with no sense
of shame,
A spy upon his daughters he be-
came;
With velvet slippers, noiseless on
the floors,
He glided softly through half-open
doors;
Now in the room, and now upon
the stair,

He stood beside them ere they
were aware;
He listened in the passage when
they talked,
He watched them from the case-
ment when they walked,
He saw the gypsy haunt the river's
side,
He saw the monk among the cork-
trees glide;
And, tortured by the mystery and
the doubt
Of some dark secret, past his find-
ing out,
Baffled he paused; then reassured
again
Pursued the flying phantom of his
brain.
He watched them even when they
knelt in church;
And then, descending lower in his
search,
Questioned the servants, and with
eager eyes
Listened incredulous to their re-
plies;
The gypsy? none had seen her in
the wood!
The monk? a mendicant in search
of food!

At length the awful revelation
came,
Crushing at once his pride of birth
and name,
The hopes his yearning bosom for-
ward cast,
And the ancestral glories of the
past;
All fell together, crumbling in dis-
grace,
A turret rent from battlement to
base.
His daughters talking in the dead
of night
In their own chamber, and with-
out a light,
Listening, as he was wont, he over-
heard,

And learned the dreadful secret,
word by word;
And hurrying from his castle, with
a cry
He raised his hands to the unpity-
ing sky,
Repeating one dread word, till
bush and tree
Caught it, and shuddering
answered, "Heresy!"

Wrapped in his cloak, his hat
drawn o'er his face,
Now hurrying forward, now with
lingering pace,
He walked all night the alleys of
his park,
With one unseen companion in the
dark,
The Demon who within him lay in
wait,
And by his presence turned his love
to hate,
For ever muttering in an under-
tone,
"Kill! kill! and let the Lord find
out his own!"
Upon the morrow, after early Mass,
While yet the dew was glistening
on the grass,
And all the woods were musical
with birds,
The old Hidalgo, uttering fearful
words,
Walked homeward with the Priest,
and in his room
Summoned his trembling daugh-
ters to their doom.
When questioned, with brief
answers they replied,
Nor when accused evaded or
denied;
Expostulations, passionate appeals,
All that the human heart most
fears or feels,
In vain the Priest with earnest
voice essayed,
In vain the father threatened,
wept, and prayed;

Until at last he said, with haughty
mien,
"The Holy Office, then, must in-
tervene!"

And now the Grand Inquisitor of
Spain,
With all the fifty horsemen of his
train,
His awful name resounding, like
the blast
Of funeral trumpets, as he onward
passed,
Came to Valladolid, and there
began
To harry the rich Jews with fire
and ban.
To him the Hidalgo went, and at
the gate
Demanded audience on affairs of
state,
And in a secret chamber stood be-
fore
A venerable graybeard of four-
score,
Dressed in the hood and habit of a
friar;
Out of his eyes flashed a consuming
fire,
And in his hand the mystic horn
he held,
Which poison and all noxious
charms dispelled.
He heard in silence the Hidalgo's
tale,
Then answered in a voice that
made him quail:
"Son of the Church! when Abra-
ham of old
To sacrifice his only son was
told,
He did not pause to parley nor
protest,
But hastened to obey the Lord's
behest.
In him it was accounted righteous-
ness;
The Holy Church expects of thee
no less!"

A sacred frenzy seized the father's
brain,
And Mercy from that hour im-
plored in vain.
Ah! who will e'er believe the
words I say?
His daughters he accused, and the
same day
They both were cast into the dun-
geon's gloom,
That dismal ante-chamber of the
tomb,
Arraigned, condemned, and sen-
tenced to the flame,
The secret torture and the public
shame.

Then to the Grand Inquisitor once
more
The Hidalgo went, more eager than
before,
And said: "When Abraham
offered up his son,
He clave the wood wherewith it
might be done.
By his example taught, let me too
bring
Wood from the forest for my offer-
ing!"
And the deep voice, without a
pause, replied:
"Son of the Church! by faith now
justified,
Complete thy sacrifice, even as
thou wilt;
The Church absolves thy con-
science from all guilt!"

Then this most wretched father
went his way
Into the woods, that round his
castle lay,
Where once his daughters in their
childhood played
With their young mother in the
sun and shade.
Now all the leaves had fallen; the
branches bare
Made a perpetual moaning in the
air,

And screaming from their eyries
overhead
The ravens sailed athwart the sky
of lead.
With his own hands he lopped the
boughs and bound
Fagots, that crackled with fore-
boding sound,
And on his mules, caparisoned and
gay
With bells and tassels, sent them
on their way.

Then with his mind on one dark
purpose bent,
Again to the Inquisitor he went,
And said: "Behold, the fagots I
have brought,
And now, lest my atonement be as
naught,
Grant me one more request, one
last desire,—
With my own hand to light the
funeral fire!"
And Torquemada answered from
his seat,
"Son of the Church! Thine offer-
ing is complete;
Her servants through all ages shall
not cease
To magnify thy deed. Depart in
peace!"

Upon the market-place, builded of
stone
The scaffold rose, whereon Death
claimed his own.
At the four corners, in stern atti-
tude,
Four statues of the Hebrew Pro-
phets stood,
Gazing with calm indifference in
their eyes
Upon this place of human sacri-
fice,
Round which was gathering fast
the eager crowd,
With clamour of voices dissonant
and loud,

And every roof and window was
alive
With restless gazers, swarming like
a hive.

The church-bells tolled, the chant
of monks drew near,
Loud trumpets stammered forth
their notes of fear,
A line of torches smoked along the
street,
There was a stir, a rush, a tramp of
feet,
And, with its banners floating in
the air,
Slowly the long procession crossed
the square,
And, to the statues of the Prophets
bound,
The victims stood, with fagots
piled around.
Then all the air a blast of trumpets
shook,
And louder sang the monks with
bell and book,
And the Hidalgo, lofty, stern, and
proud
Lifted his torch, and, bursting
through the crowd,
Lighted in haste the fagots, and
then fled,
Lest those imploring eyes should
strike him dead!

O pitiless skies! why did your
clouds retain
For peasants' fields their floods of
hoarded rain?
O pitiless earth! why opened no
abyss
To bury in its chasm a crime like
this?

That night, a mingled column of
fire and smoke
From the dark thickets of the
forest broke,
And, glaring o'er the landscape
leagues away,

Made all the fields and hamlets
bright as day.
Wrapped in a sheet of flame the
castle blazed,
And as the villagers in terror gazed,
They saw the figure of that cruel
knight
Lean from a window in the turret's
height,
His ghastly face illumined with the
glare,
His hands upraised above his head
in prayer,
Till the floor sank beneath him,
and he fell
Down the black hollow of that
burning well.

Three centuries and more above
his bones
Have piled the oblivious years like
funeral stones;
His name has perished with him,
and no trace
Remains on earth of his afflicted
race;
But Torquemada's name, with
clouds o'ercast,
Looms in the distant landscape of
the Past,
Like a burnt tower upon a
blackened heath,
Lit by the fires of burning woods
beneath!

INTERLUDE

Thus closed the tale of guilt and
gloom,
That cast upon each listener's face
Its shadow, and for some brief
space
Unbroken silence filled the room.
The Jew was thoughtful and dis-
tressed;
Upon his memory thronged and
pressed
The persecution of his race,

Their wrongs and sufferings and
  disgrace;
His head was sunk upon his breast,
And from his eyes alternate came
Flashes of wrath and tears of
  shame.

The student first the silence broke,
As one who long has lain in wait,
With purpose to retaliate,
And thus he dealt the avenging
  stroke.
" In such a company as this,
A tale so tragic seems amiss,
That by its terrible control
O'ermasters and drags down the
  soul
Into a fathomless abyss.
The Italian Tales that you disdain,
Some merry Night of Straparole,
Or Machiavelli's Belphagor,
Would cheer us and delight us
  more,
Give greater pleasure and less pain
Than your grim tragedies of
  Spain! "

And here the poet raised his hand,
With such entreaty and command,
It stopped discussion at its birth,
And said: " The story I shall tell
Has meaning in it, if not mirth;
Listen, and hear what once befell
The merry birds of Killingworth! "

THE POET'S TALE

THE BIRDS OF KILLINGWORTH

It was the season, when through all
  the land
  The merle and mavis build, and
    building sing
Those lovely lyrics, written by His
  hand,
  Whom Saxon Cædmon calls the
    Blithe-heart King;
When on the boughs the purple
  buds expand,

  The banners of the vanguard of
    the Spring,
And rivulets, rejoicing, rush and
  leap,
  And wave their fluttering signals
    from the steep.

The robin and the blue-bird, piping
  loud,
  Filled all the blossoming or-
    chards with their glee;
The sparrows chirped as if they
  still were proud
  Their race in Holy Writ should
    mentioned be;
And hungry crows assembled in a
  crowd,
  Clamoured their piteous prayer
    incessantly,
Knowing who hears the ravens cry,
  and said:
" Give us, O Lord, this day our
  daily bread! "

Across the Sound the birds of
  passage sailed,
  Speaking some unknown lan-
    guage strange and sweet
Of tropic isle remote, and passing
  hailed
  The village with the cheers of all
    their fleet;
Or quarrelling together, laughed
  and railed
  Like foreign sailors, landed in the
    street
Of seaport town, and with out-
  landish noise
Of oaths and gibberish frightening
  girls and boys.

Thus came the jocund Spring in
  Killingworth,
  In fabulous days, some hundred
    years ago;
And thrifty farmers, as they tilled
  the earth,
  Heard with alarm the cawing of
    the crow,

That mingled with the universal
        mirth,
    Cassandra-like, prognosticating
        woe;
They shook their heads, and
        doomed with dreadful words
To swift destruction the whole race
        of birds.

And a town-meeting was convened
        straightway
    To set a price upon the guilty
        heads
Of these marauders, who, in lieu of
        pay,
    Levied black-mail upon the
        garden beds
And corn-fields, and beheld with-
        out dismay
    The awful scarecrow, with his
        fluttering shreds;
The skeleton that waited at their
        feast,
Whereby their sinful pleasure was
        increased.

Then from his house, a temple
        painted white,
    With fluted columns, and a roof
        of red,
The Squire came forth, august and
        splendid sight!
    Slowly descending, with majes-
        tic tread,
Three flights of steps, nor looking
        left nor right,
    Down the long street he walked,
        as one who said,
" A town that boasts inhabitants
        like me
Can have no lack of good society ! "

The Parson, too, appeared, a man
        austere,
    The instinct of whose nature was
        to kill;
The wrath of God he preached
        from year to year,
    And read, with fervour, Edwards
        on the Will;

His favourite pastime was to slay
        the deer
    In summer on some Adirondac
        hill;
E'en now, while walking down the
        rural lane,
He lopped the wayside lilies with
        his cane.

From the Academy, whose belfry
        crowned
    The hill of Science with its vane
        of brass,
Came the Preceptor, gazing idly
        round,
    Now at the clouds, and now at
        the green grass,
And all absorbed in reveries pro-
        found
    Of fair Almira in the upper class,
Who was, as in a sonnet he had
        said,
As pure as water, and as good as
        bread.

And next the Deacon issued from
        his door,
    In his voluminous neck-cloth,
        white as snow;
A suit of sable bombazine he wore;
    His form was ponderous, and his
        step was slow;
There never was so wise a man be-
        fore;
    He seemed the incarnate " Well,
        I told you so ! "
And to perpetuate his great renown
There was a street named after
        him in town.

These came together in the new
        town-hall,
    With sundry farmers from the
        region round.
The Squire presided, dignified and
        tall,
    His air impressive and his reason-
        ing sound;
Ill fared it with the birds, both
        great and small;

Hardly a friend in all that crowd
they found,
But enemies enough, who every one
Charged them with all the crimes
beneath the sun.

When they had ended, from his
place apart,
Rose the Preceptor, to redress
the wrong,
And, trembling like a steed before
the start,
Looked round bewildered on the
expectant throng;
Then thought of fair Almira, and
took heart
To speak out what was in him,
clear and strong,
Alike regardless of their smile or
frown,
And quite determined not to be
laughed down.

" Plato, anticipating the Reviewers,
From his Republic banished
without pity
The Poets; in this little town of
yours;
You put to death, by means of a
Committee,
The ballad-singers and the Trouba-
dours,
The street-musicians of the
heavenly city,
The birds, who make sweet music
for us all
In our dark hours, as David did for
Saul.

" The thrush that carols at the
dawn of day
From the green steeples of the
piny wood;
The oriole in the elm; the noisy
jay,
Jargoning like a foreigner at his
food;
The blue-bird balanced on some
topmost spray,

Flooding with melody the neigh-
bourhood;
Linnet and meadow-lark, and all
the throng
That dwell in nests, and have the
gift of song.

" You slay them all! and where-
fore? for the gain
Of a scant handful more or less
of wheat,
Or rye, or barley, or some other
grain,
Scratched up at random by in-
dustrious feet,
Searching for worm or weevil after
rain!
Or a few cherries, that are not so
sweet
As are the songs these uninvited
guests
Sing at their feast with comfortable
breasts.

" Do you ne'er think what won-
drous beings these?
Do you ne'er think who made
them, and who taught
The dialect they speak, where
melodies
Alone are the interpreters of
thought?
Whose household words are songs
in many keys,
Sweeter than instrument of man
e'er caught!
Whose habitations in the tree-tops
even
Are half-way houses on the road to
heaven!

" Think, every morning when the
sun peeps through
The dim, leaf-latticed windows
of the grove,
How jubilant the happy birds re-
new
Their old, melodious madrigals
of love!

And when you think of this, re-
member too
'Tis always morning somewhere,
and above
The awakening continents, from
shore to shore,
Somewhere the birds are singing
evermore.

" Think of your woods and or-
chards without birds!
Of empty nests that cling to
boughs and beams
As in an idiot's brain remembered
words
Hang empty 'mid the cobwebs
of his dreams!
Will bleat of flocks or bellowing of
herds
Make up for the lost music, when
your teams
Drag home the stingy harvest, and
no more
The feathered gleaners follow to
your door?

" What! would you rather see the
incessant stir
Of insects in the winrows of
the hay,
And hear the locust and the grass-
hopper
Their melancholy hurdy-gurdies
play?
Is this more pleasant to you than
the whirr
Of meadow-lark, and its sweet
roundelay,
Or twitter of little field-fares, as
you take
Your nooning in the shade of bush
and brake?

" You call them thieves and pil-
lagers; but know
They are the winged wardens of
your farms,
Who from the corn-fields drive the
insidious foe,

And from your harvests keep a
hundred harms;
Even the blackest of them all, the
crow,
Renders good service as your
man-at-arms,
Crushing the beetle in his coat of
mail,
And crying havoc on the slug and
snail.

" How can I teach your children
gentleness,
And mercy to the weak, and re-
verence
For Life, which, in its weakness or
excess,
Is still a gleam of God's omni-
potence,
Or Death, which, seeming darkness,
is no less
The selfsame light, although
averted hence,
When by your laws, your actions,
and your speech,
You contradict the very things I
teach?"

With this he closed; and through
the audience went
A murmur, like the rustle of
dead leaves;
The farmers laughed and nodded,
and some bent
Their yellow heads together like
their sheaves;
Men have no faith in fine-spun
sentiment
Who put their trust in bullocks
and in beeves.
The birds were doomed; and, as
the record shows,
A bounty offered for the heads of
crows.

There was another audience out of
reach,
Who had no voice nor vote in
making laws,

But in the papers read his little
speech,
  And crowned his modest temples
with applause,
They made him conscious, each one
more than each,
  He still was victor, vanquished
in their cause.
Sweetest of all the applause he won
from thee,
O fair Almira at the Academy!

And so the dreadful massacre
began;
  O'er fields and orchards, and o'er
woodland crests,
The ceaseless fusillade of terror ran,
  Dead fell the birds, with blood-
stains on their breasts,
Or wounded crept away from sight
of man,
  While the young died of famine
in their nests;
A slaughter to be told in groans,
not words,
  The very St. Bartholomew of
Birds!

The Summer came, and all the
birds were dead;
  The days were like hot coals;
the very ground
Was burned to ashes; in the or-
chards fed
  Myriads of caterpillars, and
around
The cultivated fields and garden
beds
  Hosts of devouring insects
crawled, and found
No foe to check their march, till
they had made
The land a desert without leaf or
shade.

Devoured by worms, like Herod,
was the town,
  Because, like Herod, it had ruth-
lessly

Slaughtered the Innocents. From
the trees spun down
  The canker-worms upon the
passers by,
Upon each woman's bonnet, shawl,
and gown,
  Who shook them off with just a
little cry;
They were the terror of each
favourite walk,
The endless theme of all the village
talk.

The farmers grew impatient, but a
few
  Confessed their error, and would
not complain,
For after all, the best thing one can
do
  When it is raining, is to let it rain.
Then they repealed the law, al-
though they knew
  It would not call the dead to life
again;
As school-boys, finding their mis-
take too late,
Draw a wet sponge across the ac-
cusing slate.

That year in Killingworth the
Autumn came
  Without the light of his majestic
look,
The wonder of the falling tongues
of flame,
  The illumined pages of his
Doom's-Day book.

A few lost leaves blushed crimson
with their shame,
  And drowned themselves de-
spairing in the brook,
While the wild wind went moaning
everywhere,
Lamenting the dead children of the
air!

But the next Spring a stranger
sight was seen,

A sight that never yet by bard
  was sung,
As great a wonder as it would have
  been
    If some dumb animal had found
    a tongue!
A wagon, overarched with ever-
  green,
    Upon whose boughs were wicker
    cages hung,
All full of singing birds, came down
  the street,
Filling the air with music wild and
  sweet.

From all the country round these
  birds were brought,
    By order of the town, with
    anxious quest,
And, loosened from their wicker
  prisons, sought
    In woods and fields the places
    they loved best,
Singing loud canticles, which many
  thought
    Were satires to the authorities
    addressed,
While others, listening in green
  lanes, averred
Such lovely music never had been
  heard!

But blither still and louder carolled
  they
    Upon the morrow, for they
    seemed to know
It was the fair Almira's wedding-
  day,
    And everywhere, around, above,
    below,
When the Preceptor bore his bride
  away,

Their songs burst forth in joyous
  overflow,
And a new heaven bent over a new
  earth
Amid the sunny farms of Killing-
  worth.

FINALE

The hour was late; the fire burned
  low,
The Landlord's eyes were closed in
  sleep,
And near the story's end a deep,
Sonorous sound at times was heard.
As when the distant bagpipes blow.
At this all laughed; the Landlord
  stirred,
As one awaking from a swound,
And, gazing anxiously around,
Protested that he had not slept,
But only shut his eyes, and kept
His ears attentive to each word.

Then all arose, and said " Good
  Night."
Alone remained the drowsy Squire
To rake the embers of the fire,
And quench the waning parlour
  light;
While from the windows, here and
  there,
The scattered lamps a moment
  gleamed,
And the illumined hostel seemed
The constellation of the Bear,
Downward, athwart the misty air,
Sinking and setting toward the sun
Far off the village clock struck one.

FLOWER-DE-LUCE AND OTHER POEMS

FLOWER-DE-LUCE

Beautiful lily, dwelling by still
    rivers
      Or solitary mere,
Or where the sluggish meadow-
    brook delivers
      Its waters to the weir!

Thou laughest at the mill, the whir
    and worry
      Of spindle and of loom,
And the great wheel that toils amid
    the hurry
      And rushing of the flume.

Born in the purple, born to joy and
    pleasance,
      Thou dost not toil nor spin,
But makest glad and radiant with
    thy presence
      The meadow and the lin.

The wind blows, and uplifts thy
    drooping banner,
      And round thee throng and
      run
The rushes, the green yeomen of
    thy manor,
      The outlaws of the sun.

The burnished dragon-fly is thy
    attendant,
      And tilts against the field,
And down the listed sunbeam rides
    resplendent
      With steel-blue mail and
      shield.

Thou art the Iris, fair among the
    fairest,
      Who, armed with golden rod

And winged with the celestial azure,
    bearest
      The message of some God.

Thou art the Muse, who far from
    crowded cities
      Hauntest the sylvan streams,
Playing on pipes of reed the artless
    ditties
      That come to us as dreams.

O Flower-de-luce, bloom on, and
    let the river
      Linger to kiss thy feet!
O flower of song, bloom on, and
    make for ever
      The world more fair and sweet

PALINGENESIS

I lay upon the headland-height,
    and listened
To the incessant sobbing of the sea
    In caverns under me,
And watched the waves, that tossed
    and fled and glistened
Until the rolling meadows of
    amethyst
    Melted away in mist.

Then suddenly, as one from sleep, I
    started;
For round about me all the sunny
    capes
    Seemed peopled with the
    shapes
Of those whom I had known in
    days departed,
Apparelled in the loveliness which
    gleams
    On faces seen in dreams.

A moment only, and the light and
glory
Faded away, and the disconsolate
shore
   Stood lonely as before;
And the wild-roses of the promon-
tory
Around me shuddered in the wind,
and shed
   Their petals of pale red.

There was an old belief that in the
embers
Of all things their primordial form
exists,
   And cunning alchemists
Could re-create the rose with all its
members
From its own ashes, but without
the bloom,
   Without the lost perfume.

Ah me! What wonder-working,
occult science
Can from the ashes in our hearts
once more
   The rose of youth restore?
What craft of alchemy can bid de-
fiance
To time and change, and for a
single hour
   Renew this phantom-flower?

"Oh, give me back," I cried, "the
vanished splendours,
The breath of morn, and the exul-
tant strife,
   When the swift stream of life
Bounds o'er its rocky channel, and
surrenders
The pond, with all its lilies, for the
leap
   Into the unknown deep!"

And the sea answered, with a
lamentation,
Like some old prophet wailing, and
it said,
   "Alas! thy youth is dead!

It breathes no more, its heart has
no pulsation;
In the dark places with the dead of
old
   It lies for ever cold!"

Then said I, "From its conse-
crated cerements
I will not drag this sacred dust
again,
   Only to give me pain;
But, still remembering all the lost
endearments,
Go on my way, like one who looks
before,
   And turns to weep no more."

Into what land of harvests, what
plantations
Bright with autumnal foliage and
the glow
   Of sunsets burning low;
Beneath what midnight skies, whose
constellations
Light up the spacious avenues
between
   This world and the unseen!

Amid what friendly greetings and
caresses,
What households, though not alien,
yet not mine,
   What bowers of rest divine;
To what temptations in lone wil-
dernesses,
What famine of the heart, what
pain and loss,
   The bearing of what cross!

I do not know; nor will I vainly
question
Those pages of the mystic book
which hold
   The story still untold,
But without rash conjecture or
suggestion
Turn its last leaves in reverence
and good heed,
   Until "The End" I read.

THE BRIDGE OF CLOUD

Burn, O evening hearth, and wake
 Pleasant visions, as of old!
Though the house by winds be
 shaken,
 Safe I keep this room of gold!

Ah, no longer wizard Fancy
 Builds its castles in the air,
Luring me by necromancy
 Up the never-ending stair!

But, instead, it builds me bridges
 Over many a dark ravine,
Where beneath the gusty ridges
 Cataracts dash and roar unseen.

And I cross them, little heeding
 Blast of wind or torrent's roar,
As I follow the receding
 Footsteps that have gone before.

Naught avails the imploring ges-
 ture,
 Naught avails the cry of pain!
When I touch the flying vesture,
 'Tis the gray robe of the rain.

Baffled I return, and, leaning
 O'er the parapets of cloud,
Watch the mist that intervening
 Wraps the valley in its shroud.

And the sounds of life ascending
 Faintly, vaguely, meet the ear,
Murmur of bells and voices blend-
 ing
 With the rush of waters near.

Well I know what there lies hidden
 Every tower and town and farm,
And again the land forbidden
 Reassumes its vanished charm.

Well I know the secret places,
 And the nests in hedge and tree;
At what doors are friendly faces,
 In what hearts a thought of me.

Through the mist and darkness
 sinking,
Blown by wind and beaten by
 shower,
Down I fling the thought I'm
 thinking,
Down I toss this Alpine flower.

CONCORD

[NATHANIEL HAWTHORNE][1]

MAY 23, 1864

How beautiful it was, that one
 bright day
 In the long week of rain!
Though all its splendour could not
 chase away
 The omnipresent pain.

The lovely town was white with
 apple-blooms,
 And the great elms o'erhead
Dark shadows wove on their aërial
 looms
 Shot through with golden thread.

Across the meadows, by the gray
 old manse,
 The historic river flowed:—
I was as one who wanders in a
 trance,
 Unconscious of his road.

The faces of familiar friends seemed
 strange;
 Their voices I could hear,
And yet the words they uttered
 seemed to change
 Their meaning to my ear.

For the one face I looked for was
 not there,
 The one low voice was mute;
Only an unseen presence filled the
 air,
 And baffled my pursuit.

[1] Hawthorne died May 1864 and
was buried on the date given to this
elegy.

Now I look back, and meadow, manse, and stream
  Dimly my thought defines;
I only see—a dream within a dream—
  The hill-top hearsed with pines.

I only hear above his place of rest
  Their tender undertone,
The infinite longings of a troubled breast,
  The voice so like his own.

There in seclusion and remote from men
  The wizard hand lies cold,
Which at its topmost speed let fall the pen,
  And left the tale half told.

Ah! who shall lift that wand of magic power,
  And the lost clue regain?
The unfinished window in Aladdin's tower
  Unfinished must remain!

CHRISTMAS BELLS

I heard the bells on Christmas Day
  Their old, familiar carols play,
    And wild and sweet
    The words repeat
Of peace on earth, good-will to men!

And thought how, as the day had come,
The belfries of all Christendom
    Had rolled along
    The unbroken song
Of peace on earth, good-will to men!

Till, ringing, singing on its way,
The world revolved from night to day,
    A voice, a chime,
    A chant sublime
Of peace on earth, good-will to men!

Then from each black, accursed mouth
The cannon thundered in the South,
    And with the sound
    The carols drowned
Of peace on earth, good-will to men!

It was as if an earthquake rent
The hearth-stones of a continent,
    And made forlorn
    The households born
Of peace on earth, good-will to men!

And in despair I bowed my head;
"There is no peace on earth," I said;
    "For hate is strong,
    And mocks the song
Of peace on earth, good-will to men!"

Then pealed the bells more loud and deep:
"God is not dead; nor doth he sleep!
    The Wrong shall fail,
    The Right prevail,
With peace on earth, good-will to men!"

THE WIND OVER THE CHIMNEY

See, the fire is sinking low,
Dusky red the embers glow,
  While above them still I cower,
While a moment more I linger,
Though the clock, with lifted finger,
  Points beyond the midnight hour.

Sings the blackened log a tune
Learned in some forgotten June
  From a school-boy at his play,
When they both were young together,
Heart of youth and summer weather
  Making all their holiday.

And the night-wind rising, hark!
How above there in the dark,
   In the midnight and the snow,
Ever wilder, fiercer, grander,
Like the trumpets of Iskander,
   All the noisy chimneys blow!

Every quivering tongue of flame
Seems to murmur some great
   name,
   Seems to say to me, " Aspire! "
But the night-wind answers,
   " Hollow
Are the visions that you follow,
   Into darkness sinks your fire! "

Then the flicker of the blaze
Gleams on volumes of old days,
   Written by masters of the art,
Loud through whose majestic
   pages
Rolls the melody of ages,
   Throb the harp-strings of the
      heart.

And again the tongues of flame
Start exulting and exclaim,—
   " These are prophets, bards, and
      seers;
In the horoscope of nations,
Like ascendant constellations,
   They control the coming years."

But the night-wind cries: " De-
   spair!
Those who walk with feet of air
   Leave no long-enduring marks;
At God's forges incandescent
Mighty hammers beat incessant,
   These are but the flying sparks.

" Dust are all the hands that
   wrought;
Books are sepulchres of thought;
   The dead laurels of the dead
Rustle for a moment only,
Like the withered leaves in lonely
   Church-yards at some passing
      tread."

Suddenly the flame sinks down;
Sink the rumours of renown;
   And alone the night-wind drear
Clamours louder, wilder, vaguer,—
" 'Tis the brand of Meleager
   Dying on the hearth-stone here! "

And I answer,—" Though it be,
Why should that discomfort me ?
   No endeavour is in vain;
Its reward is in the doing,
And the rapture of pursuing
   Is the prize the vanquished gain."

THE BELLS OF LYNN

HEARD AT NAHANT

O curfew of the setting sun!   O
   Bells of Lynn!
O requiem of the dying day!   O
   Bells of Lynn!

From the dark belfries of yon cloud-
   cathedral wafted,
Your sounds aerial seem to float, O
   Bells of Lynn!

Borne on the evening wind across
   the crimson twilight,
O'er land and sea they rise and fall,
   O Bells of Lynn!

The fisherman in his boat, far out
   beyond the headland,
Listens, and leisurely rows ashore,
   O Bells of Lynn!

Over the shining sands the wander-
   ing cattle homeward
Follow each other at your call, O
   Bells of Lynn!

The distant lighthouse hears, and
   with his flaming signal
Answers you, passing the watch-
   word on, O Bells of Lynn!

And down the darkening coast run
　the tumultuous surges,
And clap their hands, and shout to
　you, O Bells of Lynn!

Till from the shuddering sea, with
　your wild incantations,
Ye summon up the spectral moon,
　O Bells of Lynn!

And startled at the sight, like the
　weird woman of Endor,
Ye cry aloud, and then are still, O
　Bells of Lynn!

KILLED AT THE FORD

He is dead, the beautiful youth,
The heart of honour, the tongue of
　truth,
He, the life and light of us all,
Whose voice was blithe as a bugle-
　call,
Whom all eyes followed with one
　consent,
The cheer of whose laugh, and
　whose pleasant word,
Hushed all murmurs of discontent.

Only last night, as we rode along,
Down the dark of the mountain
　gap,
To visit the picket-guard at the
　ford,
Little dreaming of any mishap,
He was humming the words of
　some old song:
" Two red roses he had on his cap
And another he bore at the point of
　his sword."

Sudden and swift a whistling ball
Came out of a wood, and the voice
　was still;
Something I heard in the darkness
　fall,
And for a moment my blood grew
　chill;

I spake in a whisper, as he who
　speaks
In a room where some one is lying
　dead;
But he made no answer to what I
　said.
We lifted him up to his saddle
　again,
And through the mire and the mist
　and the rain
Carried him back to the silent camp,
And laid him as if asleep on his bed;
And I saw by the light of the sur-
　geon's lamp
Two white roses upon his cheeks,
And one just over his heart blood-
　red!

And I saw in a vision how far and
　fleet
That fatal bullet went speeding
　forth,
Till it reached a town in the distant
　North,
Till it reached a house in a sunny
　street,
Till it reached a heart that ceased
　to beat
Without a murmur, without a cry;
And a bell was tolled, in that far-
　off town,
For one who had passed from cross
　to crown,
And the neighbours wondered that
　she should die.

GIOTTO'S TOWER

How many lives, made beautiful
　and sweet
　By self-devotion and by self-
　　restraint,—
　Whose pleasure is to run without
　　complaint
　On unknown errands of the
　　Paraclete,—
Wanting the reverence of un-
　shodden feet,

Fail of the nimbus which the
artists paint
Around the shining forehead of
the saint,
And are in their completeness
incomplete!
In the old Tuscan town stands
Giotto's tower,
The lily of Florence blossoming
in stone,—
A vision, a delight, and a de-
sire,—
The builder's perfect and centen-
nial flower,
That in the night of ages bloomed
alone.
But wanting still the glory of
the spire.

TO-MORROW

'Tis late at night, and in the realm
of sleep
My little lambs are folded like
the flocks;
From room to room I hear the
wakeful clocks
Challenge the passing hour, like
guards that keep
Their solitary watch on tower and
steep;
Far off I hear the crowing of the
cocks,
And through the opening door
that time unlocks
Feel the fresh breathing of To-
morrow creep.
To-morrow! the mysterious, un-
known guest,
Who cries to me: " Remember
Barmecide,
And tremble to be happy with
the rest."
And I make answer: " I am satis-
fied;
I dare not ask; I know not what
is best;
God hath already said what shall
betide."

ON TRANSLATING THE DIVINA COMMEDIA

FIRST SONNET

Oft have I seen at some cathedral
door
A labourer, pausing in the dust
and heat,
Lay down his burden, and with
reverent feet
Enter, and cross himself, and on
the floor
Kneel to repeat his paternoster o'er;
Far off the noises of the world
retreat;
The loud vociferations of the
street
Become an undistinguishable
roar.
So, as I enter here from day to day,
And leave my burden at this
minster-gate,
Kneeling in prayer, and not
ashamed to pray,
The tumult of the time disconso-
late
To inarticulate murmurs dies
away,
While the eternal ages watch and
wait.

SECOND SONNET

How strange the sculptures that
adorn these towers;
This crowd of statues, in whose
folded sleeves
Birds build their nests; while
canopied with leaves
Parvis and portal bloom like
trellised bowers,
And the vast minster seems a cross
of flowers!
But fiends and dragons on the
gargoyled eaves
Watch the dead Christ between
the living thieves,

And, underneath, the traitor
  Judas lowers!
Ah! from what agonies of heart
  and brain,
  What exultations trampling on
    despair,
  What tenderness, what tears,
    what hate of wrong,
What passionate outcry of a soul
  in pain,
  Uprose this poem of the earth
    and air,
  This mediæval miracle of song!

THIRD SONNET

I enter, and I see thee in the gloom
  Of the long aisles, O poet satur-
    nine!
  And strive to make my steps
    keep pace with thine.
  The air is filled with some un-
    known perfume;
The congregation of the dead make
  room
  For thee to pass; the votive
    tapers shine;
  Like rooks that haunt Ravenna's
    groves of pine
  The hovering echoes fly from
    tomb to tomb.
From the confessionals I hear arise
  Rehearsals of forgotten tragedies
  And lamentations from the
    crypts below;
And then a voice celestial that
  begins
  With the pathetic words, "Al-
    though your sins
  As scarlet be," and ends with
  "as the snow."

FOURTH SONNET

With snow-white veil and gar-
  ments as of flame,
  She stands before thee, who so
    long ago

Filled thy young heart with
  passion and the woe
From which thy song and all its
  splendours came;
And while with stern rebuke she
  speaks thy name,
  The ice about thy heart melts as
    the snow
  On mountain heights, and in
    swift overflow
  Comes gushing from thy lips in
    sobs of shame.
Thou makest full confession; and
  a gleam,
  As of the dawn on some dark
    forest cast,
  Seems on thy lifted forehead to
    increase;
Lethe and Eunoe—the remem-
  bered dream
  And the forgotten sorrow—
    bring at last
  That perfect pardon which is
    perfect peace.

FIFTH SONNET

I lift mine eyes, and all the win-
  dows blaze
  With forms of Saints and holy
    men who died,
  Here martyred and hereafter
    glorified;
  And the great Rose upon its
    leaves displays
Christ's Triumph, and the angelic
  roundelays,
  With splendour upon splendour
    multiplied;
  And Beatrice again at Dante's
    side
  No more rebukes, but smiles her
    words of praise.
And then the organ sounds, and
  unseen choirs
  Sing the old Latin hymns of
    peace and love
  And benedictions of the Holy
    Ghost;

And the melodious bells among
the spires
O'er all the house-tops and
through heaven above
Proclaim the elevation of the
Host!

SIXTH SONNET

O star of morning and of liberty!
O bringer of the light, whose
splendour shines
Above the darkness of the Apen-
nines,
Forerunner of the day that is to
be!
The voices of the city and the sea,
The voices of the mountains and
the pines,
Repeat thy song, till the familiar
lines
Are footpaths for the thought of
Italy!
Thy fame is blown abroad from all
the heights,
Through all the nations, and a
sound is heard,
As of a mighty wind, and men
devout,
Strangers of Rome, and the new
proselytes,
In their own language hear thy
wondrous word,
And many are amazed and many
doubt.

A BOOK OF SONNETS

NATURE

As a fond mother, when the day
is o'er,
  Leads by the hand her little
  child to bed,
Half willing, half reluctant to be
led,
  And leave his broken playthings
  on the floor,
Still gazing at them through the
open door,
  Nor wholly reassured and com-
  forted
By promises of others in their
stead,
  Which, though more splendid,
  may not please him more;
So Nature deals with us, and takes
away
  Our playthings one by one, and
  by the hand
Leads us to rest so gently, that
we go
Scarce knowing if we wished to go
or stay,
  Being too full of sleep to under-
  stand
  How far the unknown tran-
  scends the what we know.

IN THE CHURCHYARD AT TARRYTOWN

Here lies the gentle humorist,
who died
  In the bright Indian summer
  of his fame!
A simple stone, with but a date
and name,
  Marks the secluded resting-
  place beside

The river that he loved and glori-
fied.
  Here in the autumn of his days
  he came,
  But the dry leaves of life were
  all aflame
With tints that brightened and
were multiplied.
How sweet a life was his; how
sweet a death!
  Living, to wing with mirth the
  weary hours,
  Or with romantic tales the heart
  to cheer;
Dying, to leave a memory like the
breath
  Of summers full of sunshine and
  of showers,
  A grief and gladness in the
  atmosphere.

ELIOT'S OAK

Thou ancient oak! whose myriad
leaves are loud
  With sounds of unintelligible
  speech,
  Sounds as of surges on a shingly
  beach,
  Or multitudinous murmurs of
  a crowd;
With some mysterious gift of
tongues endowed,
  Thou speakest a different
  dialect to each;
To me a language that no man
can teach,
  Of a lost race, long vanished
  like a cloud.
For underneath thy shade, in days
remote,
  Seated like Abraham at eventide

Beneath the oaks of Mamre, the unknown
Apostle of the Indians, Eliot, wrote
His Bible in a language that hath died
And is forgotten, save by thee alone.

THE DESCENT
OF THE MUSES

Nine sisters, beautiful in form and fate,
Came from their convent on the shining heights
Of Pierus, the mountain of delights,
To dwell among the people at its base.
Then seemed the world to change. All time and space
Splendour of cloudless days and starry nights,
And men and manners, and all sounds and sights,
Had a new meaning, a diviner grace.
Proud were these sisters, but were not too proud
To teach in schools of little country towns
Science and song, and all the arts that please;
So that while housewives span, and farmers ploughed,
Their comely daughters, clad in homespun gowns,
Learned the sweet songs of the Pierides.

VENICE

White swan of cities, slumbering in thy nest
So wonderfully built among the reeds
Of the lagoon, that fences thee and feeds,
As sayeth thy old historian and thy guest!
White water-lily, cradled and caressed
By ocean streams, and from the silt and weeds
Lifting thy golden filaments and seeds,
Thy sun-illumined spires, thy crown and crest!
White phantom city, whose untrodden streets
Are rivers, and whose pavements are the shifting
Shadows of palaces and strips of sky;
I wait to see thee vanish like the fleets
Seen in the mirage, or towers of cloud uplifting
In air their unsubstantial masonry.

THE POETS

O ye dead Poets, who are living still
Immortal in your verse, though life be fled,
And ye, O living Poets, who are dead
Though ye are living, if neglect can kill,
Tell me if in the darkest hours of ill,
With drops of anguish falling fast and red
From the sharp crown of thorns upon your head,
Ye were not glad your errand to fulfil?
Yes; for the gift and ministry of Song
Have something in them so divinely sweet,

It can assuage the bitterness
of wrong;
Not in the clamour of the crowded
street,
Not in the shouts and plaudits
of the throng,
But in ourselves, are triumph
and defeat.

PARKER CLEAVELAND

WRITTEN ON REVISITING BRUNS-
WICK IN THE SUMMER OF 1875

Among the many lives that I
have known,
None I remember more serene
and sweet,
More rounded in itself and more
complete,
Than his, who lies beneath this
funeral stone.
These pines, that murmur in low
monotone,
These walks frequented by
scholastic feet,
Were all his world; but in this
calm retreat
For him the Teacher's chair
became a throne.
With fond affection memory loves
to dwell
On the old days, when his
example made
A pastime of the toil of tongue
and pen;
And now amid the groves he
loved so well
That naught could lure him
from their grateful shade,
He sleeps, but wakes elsewhere,
for God hath said, Amen!

THE HARVEST MOON

It is the Harvest Moon! On gilded
vanes
And roofs of villages, on wood-
land crests

And their aerial neighbourhoods
of nests
Deserted, on the curtained
window-panes
Of rooms where children sleep, on
country lanes
And harvest fields, its mystic
splendour rests!
Gone are the birds that were
our summer guests,
With the last sheaves return
the labouring wains!
All things are symbols: the ex-
ternal shows
Of Nature have their image in
the mind,
As flowers and fruits and falling
of the leaves;
The song-birds leave us at the
summer's close,
Only the empty nests are left
behind,
And pipings of the quail among
the sheaves.

TO THE RIVER RHONE

Thou Royal River, born of sun
and shower
In chambers purple with the
Alpine glow,
Wrapped in the spotless ermine
of the snow
And rocked by tempests!—at
the appointed hour
Forth, like a steel-clad horseman
from a tower,
With clang and clink of harness
dost thou go
To meet thy vassal torrents,
that below
Rush to receive thee and obey
thy power.
And now thou movest in tri-
umphal march,
A king among the rivers! On
thy way
A hundred towns await and
welcome thee;

Bridges uplift for thee the stately
    arch,
  Vineyards encircle thee with
    garlands gay,
  And fleets attend thy progress
    to the sea!

THE THREE SILENCES
OF MOLINOS

TO JOHN GREENLEAF WHITTIER

Three Silences there are: the first
    of speech,
  The second of desire, the third
    of thought;
  This is the lore a Spanish monk,
    distraught
  With dreams and visions, was
    the first to teach.
These Silences, commingling each
    with each,
  Made up the perfect Silence,
    that he sought
  And prayed for, and wherein
    at times he caught
  Mysterious sounds from realms
    beyond our reach.
O thou, whose daily life antici-
    pates
  The life to come, and in whose
    thought and word
  The spiritual world preponder-
    ates,
Hermit of Amesbury! thou too
    hast heard
  Voices and melodies from be-
    yond the gates,
  And speakest only when thy
    soul is stirred!

THE TWO RIVERS

I

Slowly the hour-hand of the
    clock moves round;
  So slowly that no human eye
    hath power

To see it move! Slowly in
    shine or shower
  The painted ship above it,
    homeward bound,
Sails, but seems motionless, as if
    aground;
  Yet both arrive at last; and in
    his tower
  The slumbrous watchman wakes
    and strikes the hour,
  A mellow, measured, melan-
    choly sound.
Midnight! the outpost of advan-
    cing day!
  The frontier town and citadel
    of night!
  The watershed of Time, from
    which the streams
Of Yesterday and To-morrow take
    their way,
  One to the land of promise and
    of light,
  One to the land of darkness and
    of dreams!

II

O River of Yesterday, with cur-
    rent swift
  Through chasms descending,
    and soon lost to sight,
  I do not care to follow in their
    flight
  The faded leaves, that on thy
    bosom drift!
O River of To-morrow, I uplift
  Mine eyes, and thee I follow, as
    the night
  Wanes into morning, and the
    dawning light
  Broadens, and all the shadows
    fade and shift!
I follow, follow, where thy waters
    run
  Through unfrequented, unfami-
    liar fields,
  Fragrant with flowers and musi-
    cal with song;
  Still follow, follow; sure to meet
    the sun,

And confident, that what the
  future yields
Will be the right, unless myself
  be wrong.

III

Yet not in vain, O River of Yester-
  day,
  Through chasms of darkness to
    the deep descending,
  I heard thee sobbing in the rain,
    and blending
  Thy voice with other voices far
    away.
I called to thee, and yet thou
  wouldst not stay,
  But turbulent, and with thyself
    contending,
  And torrent-like thy force on
    pebbles spending,
  Thou wouldst not listen to a
    poet's lay.
Thoughts, like a loud and sudden
  rush of wings,
  Regrets and recollections of
    things past,
  With hints and prophecies of
    things to be,
And inspirations, which, could
  they be things,
  And stay with us, and we could
    hold them fast,
  Were our good angels,—these
    I owe to thee.

IV

And thou, O River of To-morrow,
  flowing
  Between thy narrow adaman-
    tine walls,
  But beautiful, and white with
    waterfalls,
  And wreaths of mist, like hands
    the pathway showing;
I hear the trumpets of the morn-
  ing blowing,
  I hear thy mighty voice, that
    calls and calls,

And see, as Ossian saw in
  Morven's halls,
Mysterious phantoms, coming,
  beckoning, going!
It is the mystery of the unknown
  That fascinates us; we are
    children still,
  Wayward and wistful; with one
    hand we cling
To the familiar things we call our
  own,
  And with the other, resolute of
    will,
  Grope in the dark for what the
    day will bring.

BOSTON

St. Botolph's Town!   Hither
  across the plains
  And fens of Lincolnshire, in
    garb austere,
  There came a Saxon monk, and
    founded here
  A Priory, pillaged by maraud-
    ing Danes,
So that thereof no vestige now
  remains;
  Only a name, that, spoken loud
    and clear,
  And echoed in another hemi-
    sphere,
  Survives the sculptured walls
    and painted panes.
St. Botolph's Town!   Far over
  leagues of land
  And leagues of sea looks forth
    its noble tower,
  And far around the chiming
    bells are heard;
So may that sacred name for ever
  stand
  A landmark, and a symbol of
    the power,
  That lies concentred in a single
    word.

ST. JOHN'S, CAMBRIDGE

I stand beneath the tree, whose branches shade
  Thy western window, Chapel of St. John!
  And hear its leaves repeat their benison
  On him, whose hand thy stones memorial laid;
Then I remember one of whom was said
  In the world's darkest hour, "Behold thy son!"
  And see him living still, and wandering on
  And waiting for the advent long delayed.
Not only tongues of the apostles teach
  Lessons of love and light, but these expanding
  And sheltering boughs with all their leaves implore,
And say in language clear as human speech,
  "The peace of God, that passeth understanding,
  Be and abide with you for evermore!"

MOODS

O that a Song would sing itself to me
  Out of the heart of Nature, or the heart
  Of man, the child of Nature, not of Art,
  Fresh as the morning, salt as the salt sea,
With just enough of bitterness to be
  A medicine to this sluggish mood, and start
  The life-blood in my veins, and so impart
  Healing and help in this dull lethargy!
Alas! not always doth the breath of song

Breathe on us. It is like the wind that bloweth
  At its own will, not ours, nor tarries long;
We hear the sound thereof, but no man knoweth
  From whence it comes, so sudden and swift and strong,
  Nor whither in its wayward course it goeth.

WOODSTOCK PARK

Here in a little rustic hermitage
  Alfred the Saxon King, Alfred the Great,
  Postponed the cares of king-craft to translate
  The Consolations of the Roman sage.
Here Geoffrey Chaucer in his ripe old age
  Wrote the unrivalled Tales, which soon or late
  The venturous hand that strives to imitate
  Vanquished must fall on the unfinished page.
Two kings were they, who ruled by right divine,
  And both supreme; one in the realm of Truth,
  One in the realm of Fiction and of Song.
What prince hereditary of their line,
  Uprising in the strength and flush of youth,
  Their glory shall inherit and prolong?

THE FOUR PRINCESSES AT WILNA

A PHOTOGRAPH

Sweet faces, that from pictured casements lean
  As from a castle window, looking down

On some gay pageant passing
  through a town,
Yourselves the fairest figures in
  the scene;
With what a gentle grace, with
  what serene
  Unconsciousness ye wear the
    triple crown
  Of youth and beauty and the
    fair renown
  Of a great name, that ne'er
    hath tarnished been!
From your soft eyes, so innocent
  and sweet,
  Four spirits, sweet and inno-
    cent as they,
  Gaze on the world below, the
    sky above;
Hark! there is some one singing
  in the street;
  "Faith, Hope, and Love! these
    three," he seems to say;
  "These three; and greatest of
    the three is Love."

HOLIDAYS

The holiest of all holidays are
  those
  Kept by ourselves in silence
    and apart;
  The secret anniversaries of the
    heart,
  When the full river of feeling
    overflows;—
The happy days unclouded to
  their close;
  The sudden joys that out of
    darkness start
  As flames from ashes; swift
    desires that dart
  Like swallows singing down
    each wind that blows!
White as the gleam of a receding
  sail,
  White as a cloud that floats and
    fades in air,

White as the whitest lily on a
  stream,
These tender memories are;—a
  Fairy Tale
  Of some enchanted land we
    know not where,
  But lovely as a landscape in a
    dream.

WAPENTAKE

TO ALFRED TENNYSON

Poet! I come to touch thy lance
  with mine;
  Not as a knight, who on the
    listed field
  Of tourney touched his adver-
    sary's shield
  In token of defiance, but in
    sign
Of homage to the mastery, which
  is thine,
  In English song; nor will I keep
    concealed,
  And voiceless as a rivulet frost-
    congealed,
  My admiration for thy verse
    divine.
Not of the howling dervishes of
  song,
  Who craze the brain with their
    delirious dance,
  Art thou, O sweet historian of
    the heart!
Therefore to thee the laurel-
  leaves belong,
  To thee our love and our allegi-
    ance,
  For thy allegiance to the poet's
    art.

THE BROKEN OAR

Once upon Iceland's solitary
  strand
  A poet wandered with his book
    and pen,

Seeking some final word, some
  sweet Amen,
Wherewith to close the volume
  in his hand.
The billows rolled and plunged
  upon the sand,
The circling sea-gulls swept
  beyond his ken,
And from the parting cloud-
  rack now and then
Flashed the red sunset over sea
  and land.

Then by the billows at his feet
  was tossed
A broken oar; and carved there-
  on he read,
"Oft was I weary, when I
  toiled at thee";
And like a man, who findeth what
  was lost,
He wrote the words, then lifted
  up his head,
And flung his useless pen into
  the sea.

KÉRAMOS

1878

Turn, turn, my wheel! Turn
  round and round
Without a pause, without a sound:
  So spins the flying world away!
This clay, well mixed with marl
  and sand,
Follows the motion of my hand;
For some must follow, and some
  command,
  Though all are made of clay!

Thus sang the Potter at his task
Beneath the blossoming hawthorn-
  tree,
While o'er his features, like a mask,
The quilted sunshine and leaf-
  shade
Moved, as the boughs above him
  swayed,
And clothed him, till he seemed
  to be
A figure woven in tapestry,
So sumptuously was he arrayed
In that magnificent attire
Of sable tissue flaked with fire.
Like a magician he appeared,
A conjurer without book or beard;
And while he plied his magic art—
For it was magical to me—
I stood in silence and apart,

And wondered more and more to
  see
That shapeless, lifeless mass of
  clay
Rise up to meet the master's hand,
And now contract and now ex-
  pand,
And even his slightest touch obey;
While ever in a thoughtful mood
He sang his ditty, and at times
Whistled a tune between the
  rhymes,
As a melodious interlude.

Turn, turn, my wheel! All
  things must change
To something new, to something
  strange;
  Nothing that is can pause or
  stay;
The moon will wax, the moon will
  wane,
The mist and cloud will turn to
  rain,
The rain to mist and cloud again,
  To-morrow be to-day.

Thus still the Potter sang, and
  still,
By some unconscious act of will,

The melody and even the words
Were intermingled with my
　　thought,
As bits of coloured thread are
　　caught
And woven into nests of birds.
And thus to regions far remote,
Beyond the ocean's vast expanse,
This wizard in the motley coat
Transported me on wings of song,
And by the northern shores of
　　France
Bore me with restless speed along.

What land is this that seems to be
A mingling of the land and sea?
This land of sluices, dikes, and
　　dunes?
This water-net, that tessellates
The landscape? this unending
　　maze
Of gardens, through whose lat-
　　ticed gates
The imprisoned pinks and tulips
　　gaze;
Where in the long summer after-
　　noons
The sunshine, softened by the
　　haze,
Comes streaming down as through
　　a screen;
Where over the fields and pastures
　　green
The painted ships float high in air,
And over all and everywhere
The sails of windmills sink and
　　soar
Like wings of sea-gulls on the
　　shore?

What land is this?　Yon pretty
　　town
Is Delft, with all its wares dis-
　　played;
The pride, the market-place, the
　　crown
And centre of the Potter's trade.
See! every house and room is
　　bright

With glimmers of reflected light
From plates that on the dresser
　　shine;
Flagons to foam with Flemish
　　beer,
Or sparkle with the Rhenish wine,
And pilgrim flasks with fleur-de-
　　lis,
And ships upon a rolling sea,
And tankards pewter topped, and
　　queer
With comic mask and musketeer!
Each hospitable chimney smiles
A welcome from its painted tiles;
The parlour walls, the chamber
　　floors,
The stairways and the corridors,
The borders of the garden walks,
Are beautiful with fadeless flowers,
That never droop in winds or
　　showers,
And never wither on their stalks.

Turn, turn, my wheel!　All life is
　　brief;
What now is bud will soon be leaf,
　　What now is leaf will soon decay;
The wind blows east, the wind blows
　　west;
The blue eggs in the robin's nest
Will soon have wings and beak and
　　breast,
　　And flutter and fly away.

Now southward through the air I
　　glide,
The song my only pursuivant,
And see across the landscape wide
The blue Charente, upon whose
　　tide
The belfries and the spires of
　　Saintes
Ripple and rock from side to side,
As, when an earthquake rends its
　　walls,
A crumbling city reels and falls.

Who is it in the suburbs here,
This Potter, working with such
　　cheer,

In this mean house, this mean
    attire,
His manly features bronzed with
    fire,
Whose figulines and rustic wares
Scarce find him bread from day to
    day?
This madman, as the people say,
Who breaks his tables and his
    chairs
To feed his furnace fires, nor cares
Who goes unfed if they are fed,
Nor who may live if they are dead?
This alchemist with hollow cheeks
And sunken, searching eyes, who
    seeks,
By mingled earths and ores com-
    bined
With potency of fire, to find
Some new enamel, hard and bright,
His dream, his passion, his delight?

O Palissy! within thy breast
Burned the hot fever of unrest;
Thine was the prophet's vision, thine
The exultation, the divine
Insanity of noble minds,
That never falters nor abates,
But labours and endures and waits,
Till all that it foresees it finds,
Or what it cannot find creates!

*Turn, turn, my wheel! This
    earthen jar*
A touch can make, a touch can mar;
And shall it to the Potter say,
*What makest thou? Thou hast no
    hand?*
As men who think to understand
A world by their Creator planned,
Who wiser is than they.

Still guided by the dreamy song,
As in a trance I float along
Above the Pyrenean chain,
Above the fields and farms of
    Spain,
Above the bright Majorcan isle,

That lends its softened name to
    art,—
A spot, a dot upon the chart,
Whose little towns red-roofed
    with tile,
Are ruby-lustred with the light
Of blazing furnaces by night,
And crowned by day with wreaths
    of smoke.
Then eastward, wafted in my flight
On my enchanter's magic cloak,
I sail across the Tyrrhene Sea
Into the land of Italy,
And o'er the windy Apennines,
Mantled and musical with pines.

The palaces, the princely halls,
The doors of houses and the walls
Of churches and of belfry towers,
Cloister and castle, street and
    mart,
Are garlanded and gay with flowers
That blossom in the fields of art.
Here Gubbio's workshops gleam
    and glow
With brilliant, iridescent dyes,
The dazzling whiteness of the
    snow,
The cobalt blue of summer skies;
And vase and scutcheon, cup and
    plate,
In perfect finish emulate
Faenza, Florence, Pesaro.

Forth from Urbino's gate there
    came
A youth with the angelic name
Of Raphael, in form and face
Himself angelic, and divine
In arts of colour and design.
From him Francesco Xanto
    caught
Something of his transcendent
    grace,
And into fictile fabrics wrought
Suggestions of the mastes's
    thought.
Nor less Maestro Giorgio shines
With madre-perl and golden lines

Of arabesques, and interweaves
His birds and fruits and flowers
      and leaves
About some landscape, shaded
      brown,
With olive tints on rock and town.
Behold this cup within whose bowl,
Upon a ground of deepest blue
With yellow-lustred stars o'erlaid,
Colours of every tint and hue
Mingle in one harmonious whole!
With large blue eyes and steadfast
      gaze,
Her yellow hair in net and braid,
Necklace and earrings all ablaze
With golden lustre o'er the glaze,
A woman's portrait; on the scroll,
Cana, the Beautiful!   A name
Forgotten save for such brief fame
As this memorial can bestow,—
A gift some lover long ago
Gave with his heart to this fair
      dame.

A nobler title to renown
Is thine, O pleasant Tuscan town,
Seated beside the Arno's stream;
For Lucca della Robbia there
Created forms so wondrous fair,
They made thy sovereignty su-
      preme.
These choristers with lips of stone,
Whose music is not heard, but
      seen,
Still chant, as from their organ-
      screen,
Their Maker's praise; nor these
      alone,
But the more fragile forms of clay,
Hardly less beautiful than they,
These saints and angels that adorn
The walls of hospitals, and tell
The story of good deeds so well
That poverty seems less forlorn,
And life more like a holiday.

Here in this old neglected church,
That long eludes the traveller's
      search,

Lies the dead bishop on his tomb;
Earth upon earth he slumbering
      lies,
Life-like and death-like in the
      gloom;
Garlands of fruit and flowers in
      bloom
And foliage deck his resting place;
A shadow in the sightless eyes,
A pallor on the patient face,
Made perfect by the furnace heat;
All earthly passions and desires
Burnt out by purgatorial fires;
Seeming to say, "Our years are
      fleet,
And to the weary death is sweet."

But the most wonderful of all
The ornaments on tomb and wall
That grace the fair Ausonian
      shores
Are those the faithful earth
      restores,
Near some Apulian town con-
      cealed,
In vineyard or in harvest field,—
Vases and urns and bas-reliefs,
Memorials of forgotten griefs,
Or records of heroic deeds
Of demigods and mighty chiefs:
Figures that almost move and
      speak,
And, buried amid mould and
      weeds,
Still in their attitudes attest
The presence of the graceful
      Greek,—
Achilles in his armour dressed,
Alcides with the Cretan bull,
And Aphrodite with her boy,
Or lovely Helena of Troy,
Still living and still beautiful.

Turn, turn, my wheel! 'Tis Na-
      ture's plan
The child should grow into the man,
      The man grow wrinkled, old, and
      gray;
In youth the heart exults and sings,

Keramos# Kéramos

The pulses leap, the feet have wings;
In age the cricket chirps, and brings
The harvest home of day.

And now the winds that south-
ward blow,
And cool the hot Sicilian isle,
Bear me away. I see below
The long line of the Libyan Nile,
Flooding and feeding the parched
land
With annual ebb and overflow,
A fallen palm whose branches lie
Beneath the Abyssinian sky,
Whose roots are in Egyptian
sands.
On either bank huge water-wheels,
Belted with jars and dripping
weeds,
Send forth their melancholy moans,
As if, in their gray mantles hid,
Dead anchorites of the Thebaid
Knelt on the shore and told their
beads,
Beating their breasts with loud
appeals
And penitential tears and groans.

This city, walled and thickly set
With glittering mosque and mina-
ret,
Is Cairo, in whose gay bazaars
The dreaming traveller first in-
hales
The perfume of Arabian gales,
And sees the fabulous earthen jars,
Huge as were those wherein the
maid
Morgiana found the Forty Thieves
Concealed in midnight ambuscade;
And seeing, more than half believes
The fascinating tales that run
Through all the Thousand Nights
and One,
Told by the fair Scheherezade.

More strange and wonderful than
these
Are the Egyptian deities,

Ammon, and Emeth, and the grand
Osiris, holding in his hand
The lotus; Isis, crowned and veiled;
The sacred Ibis, and the Sphinx;
Bracelets with blue enamelled
links;
The Scarabee in emerald mailed,
Or spreading wide his funeral
wings;
Lamps that perchance their night-
watch kept
O'er Cleopatra while she slept,—
All plundered from the tombs of
kings.

Turn, turn, my wheel! The human
race
Of every tongue, of every place,
Caucasian, Coptic, or Malay,
All that inhabit this great earth,
Whatever be their rank or worth,
Are kindred and allied by birth,
And made of the same clay.

O'er desert sands, o'er gulf and
bay,
O'er Ganges and o'er Himalay,
Bird-like I fly, and flying sing,
To flowery kingdoms of Cathay,
And bird-like poise on balanced
wing
Above the town of King-te-tching,
A burning town, or seeming so,—
Three thousand furnaces that glow
Incessantly, and fill the air
With smoke uprising, gyre on gyre,
And painted by the lurid glare,
Of jets and flashes of red fire.

As leaves that in the autumn fall,
Spotted and veined with various
hues,
Are swept along the avenues,
And lie in heaps by hedge and wall,
So from this grove of chimneys
whirled
To all the markets of the world,
These porcelain leaves are wafted
on,—

Light yellow leaves with spots and
    stains
Of violet and of crimson dye,
Or tender azure of a sky
Just washed by gentle April rains,
And beautiful with celadon.

Nor less the coarser household
    wares,—
The willow pattern, that we knew
In childhood, with its bridge of
    blue
Leading to unknown thorough-
    fares;
The solitary man who stares
At the white river flowing through
Its arches, the fantastic trees
And wild perspective of the view;
And intermingled among these
The tiles that in our nurseries
Filled us with wonder and delight,
Or haunted us in dreams at night.

And yonder by Nankin, behold!
The Tower of Porcelain, strange
    and old,
Uplifting to the astonished skies
Its ninefold painted balconies,
With balustrades of twining leaves,
And roofs of tile, beneath whose
    eaves
Hang porcelain bells that all the
    time
Ring with a soft, melodious chime;
While the whole fabric is ablaze
With varied tints, all fused in one
Great mass of colour, like a maze
Of flowers illumined by the sun.

Turn, turn, my wheel!   What is
    begun
At daybreak must at dark be done,
    To-morrow will be another day;
To-morrow the hot furnace flame
Will search the heart and try the
    frame,
And stamp with honour or with
    shame
    These vessels made of clay.

Cradled and rocked in Eastern
    seas,
The islands of the Japanese
Beneath me lie; o'er lake and plain
The stork, the heron, and the crane
Through the clear realms of azure
    drift;
And on the hillside I can see
The villages of Imari,
Whose thronged and flaming
    workshops lift
Their twisted columns of smoke
    on high,
Cloud cloisters that in ruins lie,
With sunshine streaming through
    each rift,
And broken arches of blue sky.

All the bright flowers that fill the
    land,
Ripple of waves on rock or sand,
The snow on Fusiyama's cone,
The midnight heaven so thickly
    sown
With constellations of bright stars,
The leaves that rustle, the reeds
    that make
A whisper by each stream and lake,
The saffron dawn, the sunset red,
Are painted on these lovely jars;
Again the skylark sings, again
The stork, the heron, and the crane
Float through the azure overhead,
The counterfeit and counterpart
Of Nature reproduced in Art.

Art is the child of Nature; yes,
Her darling child, in whom we
    trace
The features of the mother's face,
Her aspect and her attitude,
All her majestic loveliness
Chastened and softened and sub-
    dued
Into a more attractive grace,
And with a human sense imbued.
He is the greatest artist, then,
Whether of pencil or of pen,
Who follows Nature. Never man,

As artist or as artisan,
Pursuing his own fantasies,
Can touch the human heart, or
please,
Or satisfy our nobler needs,
As he who sets his willing feet
In Nature's footprints, light and
fleet,
And follows fearless where she
leads.

Thus mused I on that morn in May,
Wrapped in my visions like the
Seer,
Whose eyes behold not what is
near,
But only what is far away,
When, suddenly sounding peal on
peal,

The church-bell from the neigh-
bouring town
Proclaimed the welcome hour of
noon.
The Potter heard, and stopped his
wheel,
His apron on the grass threw down,
Whistled his quiet little tune,
Not overloud nor overlong,
And ended thus his simple song:

Stop, stop, my wheel! Too soon,
too soon
The noon will be the afternoon,
Too soon to-day be yesterday;
Behind us in our path we cast
The broken potsherds of the past,
And all are ground to dust at last,
And trodden into clay!

ULTIMA THULE

DEDICATION

TO G. W. G.

With favouring winds, o'er sun-
lit seas,
We sailed for the Hesperides,
The land where golden apples
grow;
But that, ah! that was long ago.

How far, since then, the ocean
streams
Have swept us from that land of
dreams,
That land of fiction and of truth,
The lost Atlantis of our youth!

Whither, ah, whither? Are not
these
The tempest-haunted Hebrides,
Where sea-gulls scream, and
breakers roar
And wreck and seaweed line the
shore?

Ultima Thule! Utmost Isle!
Here in thy harbours for a while
We lower our sails; a while we
rest
From the unending, endless quest.

BAYARD TAYLOR

Dead he lay among his books!
The peace of God was in his looks.

As the statues in the gloom
Watch o'er Maximilian's tomb[1];

So those volumes from their
shelves
Watched him, silent as themselves.

Ah! his hand will never more
Turn their storied pages o'er:

Never more his lips repeat
Songs of theirs, however sweet.

[1] In the Hofkirche at Innsbruck.

Let the lifeless body rest!
He is gone, who was its guest;

Gone, as travellers haste to leave
An inn, nor tarry until eve.

Traveller! in what realms afar,
In what planet, in what star,

In what vast, aerial space,
Shines the light upon thy face?

In what gardens of delight
Rest thy weary feet to-night?

Poet! thou, whose latest verse
Was a garland on thy hearse;

Thou hast sung, with organ tone,
In Deukalion's life, thine own;

On the ruins of the Past
Blooms the perfect flower at last.

Friend! but yesterday the bells
Rang for thee their loud farewells;

And to-day they toll for thee,
Lying dead beyond the sea;

Lying dead among thy books,
The peace of God in all thy looks!

THE CHAMBER OVER THE GATE

Is it so far from thee
Thou canst no longer see,
In the Chamber over the Gate,
That old man desolate,
Weeping and wailing sore
For his son who is no more?
    O Absalom, my son!

Is it so long ago
That cry of human woe
From the walled city came,
Calling on his dear name,
That it has died away
In the distance of to-day?
    O Absalom, my son!

There is no far or near,
There is neither there nor here,
There is neither soon nor late,
In that Chamber over the Gate,
Nor any long ago
To that cry of human woe,
    O Absalom, my son!

From the ages that are past
The voice sounds like a blast,
Over seas that wreck and drown,
Over tumult of traffic and town;
And from ages yet to be
Come the echoes back to me,
    O Absalom, my son!

Somewhere at every hour
The watchman on the tower
Looks forth, and sees the fleet
Approach of hurrying feet
Of messengers, that bear
The tidings of despair.
    O Absalom, my son!

He goes forth from the door,
Who shall return no more.
With him our joy departs;
The light goes out in our hearts;
In the Chamber over the Gate
We sit disconsolate.
    O Absalom, my son!

That 'tis a common grief
Bringeth but slight relief;
Ours is the bitterest loss
Ours is the heaviest cross;
And for ever the cry will be
'Would God I had died for thee,
    O Absalom, my son!'

FROM MY ARM-CHAIR

TO THE CHILDREN OF CAMBRIDGE

Who presented to me, on my Seventy-
second Birthday, February 27,
1879, this Chair, made from the
Wood of the Village Blacksmith's
Chestnut Tree.

Am I a king, that I should call my
    own
  This splendid ebon throne?

Or by what reason, or what right
divine,
Can I proclaim it mine?

Only, perhaps, by right divine of
song
It may to me belong;
Only because the spreading chest-
nut tree
Of old was sung by me.

Well I remember it in all its prime,
When in the summer-time
The affluent foliage of its branches
made
A cavern of cool shade.

There, by the blacksmith's forge,
beside the street,
Its blossoms white and sweet
Enticed the bees, until it seemed
alive,
And murmured like a hive.

And when the winds of autumn,
with a shout,
Tossed its great arms about,
The shining chestnuts, bursting
from the sheath,
Dropped to the ground beneath.

And now some fragments of its
branches bare,
Shaped as a stately chair,
Have by my hearthstone found a
home at last,
And whisper of the past.

The Danish king could not in all
his pride
Repel the ocean tide,
But, seated in this chair, I can in
rhyme
Roll back the tide of Time.

I see again, as one in vision sees,
The blossoms and the bees,
And hear the children's voices
shout and call,
And the brown chestnuts fall.

I see the smithy with its fires
aglow,
I hear the bellows blow,
And the shrill hammers on the
anvil beat
The iron white with heat!

And thus, dear children, have ye
made for me
This day a jubilee,
And to my more than three-score
years and ten
Brought back my youth again.

The heart hath its own memory,
like the mind,
And in it are enshrined
The precious keepsakes, into
which is wrought
The giver's loving thought.

Only your love and your remem-
brance could
Give life to this dead wood,
And make these branches, leafless
now so long,
Blossom again in song.

JUGURTHA

How cold are thy baths, Apollo!
Cried the African monarch, the
splendid,
As down to his death in the hollow
Dark dungeons of Rome he de-
scended,
Uncrowned, unthroned, un-
attended;
How cold are thy baths, Apollo!

How cold are thy baths, Apollo!
Cried the Poet, unknown, unbe-
friended,
As the vision, that lured him to
follow,
With the mist and the darkness
blended,
And the dream of his life was
ended;
How cold are thy baths, Apollo!

THE IRON PEN

Made from a fetter of Bonnivard, the Prisoner of Chillon; the handle of wood from the frigate *Constitution*, and bound with a circlet of gold, inset with three precious stones from Siberia, Ceylon, and Maine.

I thought this Pen would arise
From the casket where it lies—
  Of itself would arise and write
My thanks and my surprise.

When you gave it me under the pines,
I dreamed these gems from the mines
  Of Siberia, Ceylon, and Maine
Would glimmer as thoughts in the lines;

That this iron link from the chain
Of Bonnivard might retain
  Some verse of the Poet who sang
Of the prisoner and his pain;

That this wood from the frigate's mast
Might write me a rhyme at last,
  As it used to write on the sky
The song of the sea and the blast.

But motionless as I wait,
Like a Bishop lying in state
  Lies the Pen, with its mitre of gold,
And the jewels inviolate.

Then must I speak, and say
That the light of that summer day
  In the garden under the pines
Shall not fade and pass away.

I shall see you standing there,
Caressed by the fragrant air,
  With the shadow on your face,
And the sunshine on your hair.

I shall hear the sweet low tone
Of a voice before unknown,

Saying, 'This is from me to you—
From me, and to you alone.'

And in words not idle and vain
I shall answer and thank you again
  For the gift, and the grace of the gift,
O beautiful Helen of Maine!

And for ever this gift will be
As a blessing from you to me,
  As a drop of the dew of your youth
On the leaves of an aged tree.

ROBERT BURNS

I see amid the fields of Ayr
A ploughman, who, in foul and fair,
  Sings at his task
So clear, we know not if it is
The laverock's song we hear, or his,
  Nor care to ask.

For him the ploughing of those fields
A more ethereal harvest yields
  Than sheaves of grain;
Songs flush with purple bloom the rye,
The plover's call, the curlew's cry,
  Sing in his brain.

Touched by his hand, the wayside weed
Becomes a flower; the lowliest reed
  Beside the stream
Is clothed with beauty; gorse and grass
And heather, where his footsteps pass,
  The brighter seem.

He sings of love, whose flame illumes
The darkness of lone cottage rooms;

He feels the force,
The treacherous undertow and
stress
Of wayward passions, and no less
The keen remorse.

At moments, wrestling with his
fate,
His voice is harsh, but not with
hate;
The brushwood, hung
Above the tavern door, lets fall
Its bitter leaf, its drop of gall
Upon his tongue.

But still the music of his song
Rises o'er all elate and strong;
Its master-chords
Are Manhood, Freedom, Brother-
hood,
Its discords but an interlude
Between the words.

And then to die so young and leave
Unfinished what he might achieve!
Yet better sure
Is this, than wandering up and
down
An old man in a country town,
Infirm and poor.

For now he haunts his native land
As an immortal youth; his hand
Guides every plough;
He sits beside each ingle-nook,
His voice is in each rushing brook,
Each rustling bough.

His presence haunts this room to-
night,
A form of mingled mist and light
From that far coast.
Welcome beneath this roof of
mine!
Welcome! this vacant chair is
thine,
Dear guest and ghost!

HELEN OF TYRE

What phantom is this that appears
Through the purple mist of the
years,
Itself but a mist like these?
A woman of cloud and of fire;
It is she; it is Helen of Tyre,
The town in the midst of the
seas.

O Tyre! in thy crowded streets
The phantom appears and retreats,
And the Israelites that sell
Thy lilies and lions of brass,
Look up as they see her pass,
And murmur 'Jezebel!'

Then another phantom is seen
At her side, in a gray gabardine,
With beard that floats to his
waist;
It is Simon Magus, the Seer;
He speaks, and she pauses to hear
The words he utters in haste.

He says: 'From this evil fame,
From this life of sorrow and shame,
I will lift thee and make thee
mine;
Thou hast been Queen Candace,
And Helen of Troy, and shalt be
The Intelligence Divine!'

Oh, sweet as the breath of morn,
To the fallen and forlorn
Are whispered words of praise;
For the famished heart believes
The falsehood that tempts and
deceives,
And the promise that betrays.

So she follows from land to land
The wizard's beckoning hand,
As a leaf is blown by the gust,
Till she vanishes into night.
O reader, stoop down and write
With thy finger in the dust.

O town in the midst of the seas,
With thy rafts of cedar trees,
    Thy merchandise and thy ships,
Thou, too, art become as naught,
A phantom, a shadow, a thought,
    A name upon men's lips.

ELEGIAC

Dark is the morning with mist;
    in the narrow mouth of the
    harbour
  Motionless lies the sea, under its
    curtain of cloud;
Dreamily glimmer the sails of
    ships on the distant horizon,
  Like to the towers of a town,
    built on the verge of the sea.

Slowly and stately and still, they
    sail forth into the ocean;
  With them sail my thoughts
    over the limitless deep,
Farther and farther away, borne
    on by unsatisfied longings,
  Unto Hesperian isles, unto Au-
    sonian shores.

Now they have vanished away,
    have disappeared in the ocean;
  Sunk are the towers of the town
    into the depths of the sea!
All have vanished but those that,
    moored in the neighbouring
    roadstead,
  Sailless at anchor ride, looming
    so large in the mist.

Vanished, too, are the thoughts,
    the dim unsatisfied longings;
  Sunk are the turrets of cloud
    into the ocean of dreams;
While in a haven of rest my heart
    is riding at anchor,
  Held by the chains of love, held
    by the anchors of trust!

OLD ST. DAVID'S AT RADNOR

What an image of peace and rest
    Is this little church among its
    graves!
All is so quiet; the troubled breast,
The wounded spirit, the heart op-
    pressed,
    Here may find the repose it
    craves.

See, how the ivy climbs and ex-
    pands
    Over this humble hermitage,
And seems to caress with its little
    hands
The rough, gray stones, as a child
    that stands
    Caressing the wrinkled cheeks of
    age!

You cross the threshold; and dim
    and small
    Is the space that serves for the
    Shepherd's Fold;
The narrow aisle, the bare, white
    wall,
The pews, and the pulpit quaint
    and tall,
    Whisper and say: 'Alas! we are
    old.'

Herbert's chapel at Bemerton
    Hardly more spacious is than
    this;
But Poet and Pastor, blent in one,
Clothed with a splendour, as of the
    sun,
    That lowly and holy edifice.

It is not the wall of stone without
    That makes the building small
    or great,
But the soul's light shining round
    about,
And the faith that overcometh
    doubt,
    And the love that stronger is
    than hate.

Were I a pilgrim in search of
    peace,
Were I a pastor of Holy
    Church,
More than a Bishop's diocese
Should I prize this place of rest,
    and release
    From farther longing and far-
    ther search.

Here would I stay, and let the world
    With its distant thunder roar
    and roll;
Storms do not rend the sail that is
    furled;
Nor like a dead leaf, tossed and
    whirled
    In an eddy of wind, is the an-
    chored soul.

IN THE HARBOUR

BECALMED

Becalmed upon the sea of Thought,
Still unattained the land is sought,
My mind, with loosely-hanging sails,
Lies waiting the auspicious gales.

On either side, behind, before,
The ocean stretches like a floor,—
A level floor of amethyst,
Crowned by a golden dome of mist.

Blow, breath of inspiration, blow!
Shake and uplift this golden glow!
And fill the canvas of the mind
With wafts of thy celestial wind.

Blow, breath of song! until I feel
The straining sail, the lifting keel,
The life of the awakening sea,
Its motion and its mystery!

HERMES TRISMEGISTUS

As Seleucus narrates, Hermes de-
scribes the principles that rank as
wholes in two myriads of books; or,
as we are informed by Manetho, he
perfectly unfolded these principles
in three myriads six thousand five
hundred and twenty-five volumes. . . .
. . . Our ancestors dedicated the in-
ventions of their wisdom to this deity,
inscribing all their own writings with
the names of Hermes.—IAMBLICUS.

STILL through Egypt's desert places
    Flows the lordly Nile;
From its banks the great stone faces
    Gaze with patient smile.

Still the pyramids imperious
    Pierce the cloudless skies,
And the Sphinx stares with mys-
    terious,
    Solemn, stony eyes.

But where are the old Egyptian
    Demi-gods and kings?
Nothing left but an inscription
    Graven on stones and rings.
Where are Helios and Hephaestus,
    Gods of eldest eld?
Where is Hermes Trismegistus,
    Who their secrets held?

Where are now the many hundred
    Thousand books he wrote?
By the Thaumaturgists plundered,
    Lost in lands remote;
In oblivion sunk for ever,
    As when o'er the land
Blows a storm-wind, in the river
    Sinks the scattered sand.

Something unsubstantial, ghostly,
    Seems this Theurgist,
In deep meditation mostly
    Wrapped, as in a mist.
Vague, phantasmal, and unreal
    To our thought he seems,
Walking in a world ideal,
    In a land of dreams.

Was he one, or many, merging
    Name and fame in one,
Like a stream, to which converg-
    ing,
    Many streamlets run?

Till, with gathered power proceed-
ing
    Ampler sweep it takes,
Downward the sweet waters lead-
ing
    From unnumbered lakes.

By the Nile I see him wandering,
    Pausing now and then,
On the mystic union pondering
    Between gods and men;
Half believing, wholly feeling,
    With supreme delight,
How the gods, themselves con-
cealing,
    Lift men to their height.

Or in Thebes, the hundred-gated,
    In the thoroughfare
Breathing, as if consecrated,
    A diviner air;
And amid discordant noises,
    In the jostling throng,
Hearing far, celestial voices
    Of Olympian song.

Who shall call his dreams fallaci-
ous?
    Who has searched or sought
All the unexplored and spacious
    Universe of thought?
Who, in his own skill confiding,
    Shall with rule and line
Mark the border-land dividing
    Human and divine?

Trismegistus! three times great-
est!
    How thy name sublime
Has descended to this latest
    Progeny of time!
Happy they whose written pages
    Perish with their lives,
If amid the crumbling ages
    Still their name survives!

Thine, O priest of Egypt, lately
    Found I in the vast,
Weed - encumbered,   sombre,
stately,

    Graveyard of the Past;
And a presence moved before me
    On that gloomy shore,
As a waft of wind, that o'er me
    Breathed, and was no more.

THE POET'S CALENDAR

JANUARY

I

Janus am I; oldest of potentates;
    Forward I look, and backward,
    and below
I count, as god of avenues and
gates,
    The years that through my
    portals come and go.

II

I block the roads, and drift the
    fields with snow;
    I chase the wild-fowl from the
    frozen fen;
My frosts congeal the rivers in
    their flow,
    My fires light up the hearths
    and hearts of men.

FEBRUARY

I am lustration; and the sea is
    mine!
    I wash the sands and headlands
    with my tide;
My brow is crowned with branches
    of the pine;
    Before my chariot-wheels the
    fishes glide.
By me all things unclean are puri-
    fied,
    By me the souls of men washed
    white again;
E'en the unlovely tombs of those
    who died
    Without a dirge, I cleanse from
    every stain.

MARCH

I Martius am! Once first, and now
  the third!
  To lead the year was my ap-
    pointed place;
A mortal dispossessed me by a
  word,
  And set there Janus with the
    double face.
Hence I make war on all the
  human race;
  I shake the cities with my hur-
    ricanes;
I flood the rivers and their banks
  efface,
  And drown the farms and ham-
    lets with my rains.

APRIL

I open wide the portals of the Spring
  To welcome the procession of
    the flowers,
With their gay banners, and the
  birds that sing
  Their song of songs from their
    aerial towers.
I soften with my sunshine and my
  showers
  The heart of earth; with
    thoughts of love I glide
Into the hearts of men; and with
  the Hours
  Upon the Bull with wreathéd
    horns I ride.

MAY

Hark! The sea-faring wild-fowl
  loud proclaim
  My coming and the swarming
    of the bees.
These are my heralds, and behold!
  my name
  Is written in blossoms on the
    hawthorn-trees.
I tell the mariner when to sail the
  seas;
  I waft o'er all the land from far
    away

The breath and bloom of the Hes-
  perides,
  My birthplace. I am Maia. I
    am May.

JUNE

Mine is the Month of Roses; yes,
  and mine
  The Month of Marriages! All
    pleasant sights
And scents, the fragrance of the
  blossoming vine,
  The foliage of the valleys and
    the heights.
Mine are the longest days, the
  loveliest nights;
  The mower's scythe makes
    music to my ear;
I am the mother of all dear de-
  lights;
  I am the fairest daughter of the
    year.

JULY

My emblem is the Lion, and I
  breathe
  The breath of Libyan deserts
    o'er the land;
My sickle as a sabre I unsheathe,
  And bent before me the pale
    harvests stand.
The lakes and rivers shrink at my
  command,
  And there is thirst and fever in
    the air;
The sky is changed to brass, the
  earth to sand;
  I am the Emperor whose name
    I bear.

AUGUST

The Emperor Octavian, called the
  August,
  I being his favourite, bestowed
    his name
Upon me, and I hold it still in
  trust,
  In memory of him and of his
    fame.

I am the Virgin, and my vestal
flame
    Burns less intensely than the
Lion's rage;
Sheaves are my only garlands, and
I claim
    The golden Harvests as my
heritage.

SEPTEMBER

I bear the Scales, where hang in
equipoise
    The night and day; and when
unto my lips
I put my trumpet, with its stress
and noise
    Fly the white clouds like tat-
tered sails of ships;
The tree-tops lash the air with
sounding whips;
    Southward the clamorous sea-
fowl wing their flight;
The hedges are all red with haws
and hips,
    The Hunter's Moon reigns em-
press of the night.

OCTOBER

My ornaments are fruits; my gar-
ments leaves,
    Woven like cloth of gold, and
crimson dyed;
I do not boast the harvesting of
sheaves,
    O'er orchards and o'er vine-
yards I preside.
Though on the frigid Scorpion I
ride,
    The dreamy air is full, and over-
flows
With tender memories of the sum-
mertide,
    And mingled voices of the doves
and crows.

NOVEMBER

The Centaur, Sagittarius, am I,
    Born of Ixion's and the cloud's
embrace;

With sounding hoofs across the
earth I fly,
    A steed Thessalian with a
human face.
Sharp winds the arrows are with
which I chase
    The leaves, half dead already
with affright;
I shroud myself in gloom; and to
the race
    Of mortals bring nor comfort
nor delight.

DECEMBER

Riding upon the Goat, with snow-
white hair,
    I come, the last of all. This
crown of mine
Is of the holly; in my hand I bear
    The thyrsus, tipped with fra-
grant cones of pine.
I celebrate the birth of the Divine,
    And the return of the Saturnian
reign;—
My songs are carols sung at every
shrine,
    Proclaiming "Peace on earth,
good will to men."

MAD RIVER

IN THE WHITE MOUNTAINS

TRAVELLER

Why dost thou wildly rush and roar,
    Mad River, O Mad River?
Wilt thou not pause and cease to
pour
    Thy hurrying, headlong waters o'er
    This rocky shelf for ever?

What secret trouble stirs thy
breast?
    Why all this fret and flurry?
Dost thou not know that what is
best
In this too restless world is rest
    From over-work and worry?

THE RIVER

What wouldst thou in these moun-
    tains seek,
      O stranger from the city?
Is it perhaps some foolish freak
Of thine, to put the words I speak
      Into a plaintive ditty?

TRAVELLER

Yes; I would learn of thee thy
    song,
      With all its flowing numbers,
And in a voice as fresh and strong
As thine is, sing it all day long,
      And hear it in my slumbers.

THE RIVER

A brooklet nameless and unknown
      Was I at first, resembling
A little child, that all alone
Comes venturing down the stairs
    of stone,
      Irresolute and trembling.

Later, by wayward fancies led,
      For the wide world I panted;
Out of the forest dark and dread
Across the open field I fled,
      Like one pursued and haunted.

I tossed my arms, I sang aloud,
      My voice exultant blending
With thunder from the passing
    cloud,
The wind, the forest bent and
    bowed,
      The rush of rain descending.

I heard the distant ocean call,
      Imploring and entreating;
Drawn onward, o'er this rocky
    wall
I plunged, and the loud waterfall
      Made answer to the greeting.

And now, beset with many ills,
      A toilsome life I follow;
Compelled to carry from the hills
    These logs to the impatient mills
      Below there in the hollow.

Yet something ever cheers and
    charms
      The rudeness of my labours;
Daily I water with these arms
The cattle of a hundred farms,
      And have the birds for neigh-
        bours.

Men call me Mad, and well they
    may,
      When full of rage and trouble,
I burst my banks of sand and clay,
And sweep their wooden bridge
    away,
      Like withered reeds or stubble.

Now go and write thy little rhyme,
      As of thine own creating,
Thou seest the day is past its
    prime;
I can no longer waste my time;
      The mills are tired of waiting.

AUF WIEDERSEHEN

IN MEMORY OF J. T. F.

Until we meet again! That is the
    meaning
Of the familiar words, that men
    repeat
      At parting in the street.
Ah yes, till then! but when death
    intervening
Rends us asunder, with what
    ceaseless pain
      We wait for the Again!

The friends who leave us do not
    feel the sorrow
Of parting as we feel it, who must
    stay
      Lamenting day by day,
And knowing, when we wake upon
    the morrow,

We shall not find in its accustomed
place
  The one beloved face.

It were a double grief, if the de-
parted,
Being released from earth, should
still retain
  A sense of earthly pain;
It were a double grief, if the true-
hearted,
Who loved us here, should on the
farther shore
  Remember us no more.

Believing, in the midst of our
afflictions,
That death is a beginning, not an
end,
  We cry to them, and send
Farewells, that better might be
called predictions,
Being foreshadowings of the
future, thrown
  Into the vast Unknown.

Faith overleaps the confines of our
reason,
And if by faith, as in old times was
said,
  Women received their dead
Raised up to life, then only for a
season
Our partings are, nor shall we wait
in vain
  Until we meet again!

THE CHILDREN'S CRUSADE

[A FRAGMENT]

I

What is this I read in history,
Full of marvel, full of mystery,
  Difficult to understand?
Is it fiction, is it truth?
Children in the flower of youth,
Heart in heart, and hand in hand,

Ignorant of what helps or harms,
Without armour, without arms,
  Journeying to the Holy Land!

Who shall answer or divine?
Never since the world was made
Such a wonderful crusade
  Started forth for Palestine.
Never while the world shall last
Will it reproduce the past;
Never will it see again
Such an army, such a band,
Over mountain, over main,
  Journeying to the Holy Land.

Like a shower of blossoms blown
From the parent trees were they;
Like a flock of birds that fly
Through the unfrequented sky,
Holding nothing as their own,
Passed they into lands unknown,
  Passed to suffer and to die.

O the simple, child-like trust!
O the faith that could believe
What the harnessed, iron-mailed
Knights of Christendom had failed,
By their prowess, to achieve,
They, the children, could and
  must!

Little thought the Hermit, preach-
ing
Holy wars to knight and baron,
That the words dropped in his
teaching,
His entreaty, his beseeching,
Would by children's hands be
gleaned,
And the staff on which he leaned
Blossom like the rod of Aaron.

As a summer wind upheaves
The innumerable leaves
In the bosom of a wood,—
Not as separate leaves, but massed
All together by the blast,—
So for evil or for good
His resistless breath upheaved
All at once the many-leaved,
Many-thoughted multitude.

In the tumult of the air
Rock the boughs with all the nests
Cradled on their tossing crests;
By the fervour of his prayer
Troubled hearts were everywhere
Rocked and tossed in human
    breasts.

For a century at least
His prophetic voice had ceased;
But the air was heated still
By his lurid words and will,
As from fires in far-off woods,
In the autumn of the year,
An unwonted fever broods
In the sultry atmosphere.

II

In Cologne the bells were ringing,
In Cologne the nuns were singing
Hymns and canticles divine;
Loud the monks sang in their stalls,
And the thronging streets were
    loud
With the voices of the crowd;—
Underneath the city walls
Silent flowed the river Rhine.
From the gates, that summer day,
Clad in robes of hodden gray,
With the red cross on the breast,
Azure-eyed and golden-haired,
Forth the young crusaders fared;
While above the band devoted
Consecrated banners floated,
Fluttered many a flag and
    streamer,
And the cross o'er all the rest!
Singing lowly, meekly, slowly,
"Give us, give us back the holy
Sepulchre of the Redeemer!"
On the vast procession pressed,
Youths and maidens. . . .

III

Ah! what master hand shall paint
How they journeyed on their way,
How the days grew long and dreary,
How their little feet grew weary,
How their little hearts grew faint!

Ever swifter day by day
Flowed the homeward river; ever
More and more its whitening cur-
    rent
Broke and scattered into spray,
Till the calmly-flowing river
Changed into a mountain torrent,
Rushing from its glacier green
Down through chasm and black
    ravine.
Like a phœnix in its nest
Burned the red sun in the West,
Sinking in an ashen cloud;
In the East, above the crest
Of the sea-like mountain chain,
Like a phœnix from its shroud,
Came the red sun back again.

Now around them, white with
    snow,
Closed the mountain peaks. Below,
Headlong from the precipice
Down into the dark abyss,
Plunged the cataract, white with
    foam;
And it said, or seemed to say:
"Oh return, while yet you may,
Foolish children, to your home,
There the Holy City is!"

But the dauntless leader said:
"Faint not, though your bleeding
    feet
O'er these slippery paths of sleet
Move but painfully and slowly;
Other feet than yours have bled;
Other tears than yours been shed.
Courage! lose not heart or hope;
On the mountain's southern slope
Lies Jerusalem the Holy!"

As a white rose in its pride,
By the wind in summer-tide
Tossed and loosened from the
    branch,
Showers its petals o'er the ground,
From the distant mountain's side,
Scattering all its snows around,
With mysterious, muffled sound,

Loosened, fell the avalanche.
Voices, echoes far and near,
Roar of winds and waters blending,
Mists uprising, clouds impending,
Filled them with a sense of fear,
Formless, nameless, never ending.

. . . . .

THE CITY AND THE SEA

The panting City cried to the Sea,
"I am faint with heat,—O breathe
  on me!"

And the Sea said, "Lo, I breathe!
  but my breath
To some will be life, to others
  death!"

As to Prometheus, bringing ease
In pain, come the Oceanides,

So to the City, hot with the flame
Of the pitiless sun, the east wind
  came.

It came from the heaving breast
  of the deep,
Silent as dreams are, and sudden
  as sleep.

Life-giving, death-giving, which
  will it be;
O breath of the merciful, merciless
  Sea?

SUNDOWN

The summer sun is sinking low;
Only the tree-tops redden and
  glow;
Only the weathercock on the spire
Of the neighbouring church is a
  flame of fire;
  All is in shadow below.

O beautiful, awful summer day,
What hast thou given, what taken
  away?

Life and death, and love and
  hate,
Homes made happy or desolate,
  Hearts made sad or gay!

On the road of life one mile-stone
  more!
In the book of life one leaf turned
  o'er!
Like a red seal is the setting sun
On the good and the evil men have
  done,—
  Naught can to-day restore!

PRESIDENT GARFIELD

"E VENNI DAL MARTIRIO A
  QUESTA PACE."

These words the Poet heard in
  Paradise,
  Uttered by one who, bravely
    dying here,
  In the true faith was living in
    that sphere
  Where the celestial cross of
    sacrifice
Spread its protecting arms
    athwart the skies;
  And set thereon, like jewels
    crystal clear,
  The souls magnanimous, that
    knew not fear,
  Flashed their effulgence on his
    dazzled eyes.
Ah me! how dark the discipline of
  pain,
  Were not the suffering followed
    by the sense
  Of infinite rest and infinite re-
    lease!
This is our consolation; and again
  A great soul cries to us in our
    suspense,
  "I came from martyrdom unto
    this peace!"

DECORATION DAY

Sleep, comrades, sleep and rest
  On this Field of the Grounded
    Arms,
Where foes no more molest,
  Nor sentry's shot alarms!

Ye have slept on the ground before,
  And started to your feet
At the cannon's sudden roar,
  Or the drum's redoubling beat.

But in this camp of Death
  No sound your slumber breaks;
Here is no fevered breath,
  No wound that bleeds and aches.

All is repose and peace;
  Untrampled lies the sod;
The shouts of battle cease,
  It is the Truce of God!

Rest, comrades, rest and sleep!
  The thoughts of men shall be
As sentinels to keep
  Your rest from danger free.

Your silent tents of green
  We deck with fragrant flowers;
Yours has the suffering been,
  The memory shall be ours.

CHIMES

Sweet chimes! that in the loneli-
  ness of night
  Salute the passing hour, and in
    the dark
  And silent chambers of the
    household mark
  The movements of the myriad
    orbs of light!
Through my closed eyelids, by the
  inner sight,
    I see the constellations in the
    arc
    Of their great circles moving on,
    and hark!

I almost hear them singing in
  their flight.
Better than sleep it is to lie awake
  O'er-canopied by the vast starry
    dome
  Of the immeasurable sky; to
    feel
The slumbering world sink under
  us, and make
  Hardly an eddy,—a mere rush
    of foam
  On the great sea beneath a sink-
    ing keel.

FOUR BY THE CLOCK

Four by the clock! and yet not
  day;
But the great world rolls and
  wheels away,
With its cities on land, and its
  ships at sea,
Into the dawn that is to be!

Only the lamp in the anchored
  bark
Sends its glimmer across the dark,
And the heavy breathing of the sea
Is the only sound that comes to me.

THE FOUR LAKES OF
MADISON

Four limpid lakes,—four Naiades
Or sylvan deities are these,
  In flowing robes of azure dressed;
Four lovely handmaids, that up-
  hold
Their shining mirrors, rimmed
  with gold,
  To the fair city in the West.

By day the coursers of the sun
Drink of these waters as they run
  Their swift diurnal round on
    high;
By night the constellations glow

Far down the hollow deeps below,
  And glimmer in another sky.

Fair lakes, serene and full of light,
Fair town, arrayed in robes of
  white,
    How visionary ye appear!
All like a floating landscape seems
In cloudland or the land of dreams,
    Bathed in a golden atmosphere!

MOONLIGHT

As a pale phantom with a lamp
  Ascends some ruin's haunted
    stair,
So glides the moon along the damp
  Mysterious chambers of the air.

Now hidden in cloud, and now re-
  vealed,
  As if this phantom, full of pain,
Were by the crumbling walls con-
  cealed,
  And at the windows seen again.

Until at last, serene and proud,
  In all the splendour of her light,
She walks the terraces of cloud,
  Supreme as Empress of the
    Night.

I look, but recognize no more
  Objects familiar to my view;
The very pathway to my door
  Is an enchanted avenue.

All things are changed. One mass
  of shade,
  The elm-trees drop their cur-
    tains down;
By palace, park, and colonnade
  I walk as in a foreign town.

The very ground beneath my feet
  Is clothed with a diviner air;
White marble paves the silent
  street
    And glimmers in the empty
    square.

Illusion! Underneath there lies
  The common life of every day;
Only the spirit glorifies
  With its own tints the sober
    gray.

In vain we look, in vain uplift
  Our eyes to heaven, if we are
    blind;
We see but what we have the gift
  Of seeing; what we bring we find.

TO THE AVON

Flow on, sweet river! like his verse
Who lies beneath this sculptured
  hearse;
Nor wait beside the churchyard wall
For him who cannot hear thy call.

Thy playmate once; I see him now
A boy with sunshine on his brow,
And hear in Stratford's quiet street
The patter of his little feet.

I see him by thy shallow edge
Wading knee-deep amid the sedge;
And lost in thought, as if thy stream
Were the swift river of a dream.

He wonders whitherward it flows;
And fain would follow where it goes,
To the wide world, that shall ere-
  long
Be filled with his melodious song.

Flow on, fair stream! That dream
  is o'er;
He stands upon another shore;
A vaster river near him flows,
And still he follows where it goes.

ELEGIAC VERSE

I

Peradventure of old, some bard
  in Ionian Islands,
  Walking alone by the sea, hear-
    ing the wash of the waves,

Learned the secret from them of
the beautiful verse elegiac,
Breathing into his song motion
and sound of the sea.

For as the wave of the sea, up-
heaving in long undulations,
Plunges loud on the sands,
pauses, and turns, and retreats,
So the Hexameter, rising and sing-
ing, with cadence sonorous,
Falls; and in refluent rhythm
back the Pentameter flows.[1]

II

Not in his youth alone, but in age,
may the heart of the poet
Bloom into song, as the gorse
blossoms in autumn and
spring.

III

Not in tenderness wanting, yet
rough are the rhymes of our
poet;
Though it be Jacob's voice,
Esau's, alas! are the hands.

IV

Let us be grateful to writers for
what is left in the inkstand;
When to leave off is an art only
attained by the few.

V

How can the Three be One? you
ask me; I answer by asking,
Hail and snow and rain, are they
not three, and yet one?

VI

By the mirage uplifted the land
floats vague in the ether,
Ships and the shadows of ships
hang in the motionless air;

---

[1] Compare Schiller:
"Im Hexameter steigt des Spring-
quells flüssige Säule;
Im Pentameter drauf fällt sie
melodisch herab."
See also Coleridge's translation.

So by the art of the poet our com-
mon life is uplifted,
So, transfigured, the world floats
in a luminous haze.

VII

Like a French poem is Life; being
only perfect in structure
When with the masculine
rhymes mingled the feminine
are.

VIII

Down from the mountain descends
the brooklet, rejoicing in free-
dom;
Little it dreams of the mill hid
in the valley below;
Glad with the joy of existence, the
child goes singing and laugh-
ing,
Little dreaming what toils lie in
the future concealed.

IX

As the ink from our pen, so flow
our thoughts and our feelings
When we begin to write, how-
ever sluggish before.

X

Like the Kingdom of Heaven, the
Fountain of Youth is within
us;
If we seek it elsewhere, old shall
we grow in the search.

XI

If you would hit the mark, you
must aim a little above it;
Every arrow that flies feels the
attraction of earth.

XII

Wisely the Hebrews admit no
Present tense in their lan-
guage;
While we are speaking the word,
it is already the Past.

XIII

In the twilight of age all things
    seem strange and phantasmal,
As between daylight and dark
    ghost-like the landscape ap-
    pears.

XIV

Great is the art of beginning, but
    greater the art is of ending;
Many a poem is marred by a
    superfluous verse.

A FRAGMENT

Awake! arise! the hour is late!
    Angels are knocking at thy door!
They are in haste and cannot wait,
    And once departed come no
    more.

Awake! arise! the athlete's arm
    Loses its strength by too much
    rest;
The fallow land, the untilled farm,
    Produces only weeds at best.

POSSIBILITIES

Where are the Poets, unto whom
    belong
    The Olympian heights; whose
      singing shafts were sent
Straight to the mark, and not
    from bows half bent,
But with the utmost tension of
    the thong?
Where are the stately argosies of
    song,
    Whose rushing keels made
      music as they went
Sailing in search of some new
    continent,
With all sail set, and steady
    winds and strong?
Perhaps there lives some dreamy
    boy, untaught
    In schools, some graduate of the
    field or street,
Who shall become a master of
    the art,
An admiral sailing the high seas of
    thought,
    Fearless and first and steering
    with his fleet
For lands not yet laid down in
    any chart.

MISCELLANEOUS POEMS

THE GOLDEN SUNSET

The golden sea its mirror spreads
    Beneath the golden skies,
And but a narrow strip between
    Of land and shadow lies.

The cloud-like rocks, the rock-like
    clouds,
    Dissolved in glory float,
And midway of the radiant flood,
    Hangs silently the boat.

The sea is but another sky,
    The sky a sea as well,
And which is earth and which is
    heaven,
    The eye can scarcely tell.

So when for us life's evening hour,
    Soft fading shall descend,
May glory, born of earth and
    heaven,
    The earth and heaven blend.

Flooded with peace the spirits
    float,
  With silent rapture glow,
Till where earth ends and heaven
    begins,
  The soul shall scarcely know.

VIA SOLITARIA

Alone I walk the peopled city,
  Where each seems happy with
    his own;
Oh! friends, I ask not for your
    pity—
      I walk alone.

No more for me yon lake rejoices,
  Though moved by loving airs of
    June;
Oh! birds, your sweet and piping
    voices
      Are out of tune.

In vain for me the elm-tree arches
  Its plumes in many a feathery
    spray;
In vain the evening's starry
    marches
      And sunlit day.

In vain your beauty, Summer
    flowers;
  Ye cannot greet these cordial
    eyes;
They gaze on other fields than ours,
      On other skies.

The gold is rifled from the coffer,
  The blade is stolen from the
    sheath;
Life has but one more boon to
    offer,
      And that is—Death.

Yet well I know the voice of Duty,
  And, therefore, life and health
    must crave,
Though she who gave the world its
    beauty
      Is in her grave.

I live, O lost one! for the living
  Who drew their earliest life from
    thee,
And wait, until with glad thanks-
    giving
      I shall be free.

For life to me is as a station
  Wherein apart a traveller stands,
One absent long from home and
    nation
      In other lands.

And I, as he who stands and listens,
  Amid the twilight's chill and
    gloom,
To hear, approaching in the dis-
    tance,
      The train for home.

For death shall bring another
    mating,
  Beyond the shadows of the tomb,
On yonder shores a bride is waiting
      Until I come.

In yonder field are children playing,
  And there—oh! vision of de-
    light!—
I see the child and mother straying
      In robes of white.

Thou, then, the longing heart that
    breakest,
  Stealing the treasures one by
    one,
I'll call Thee blessed when thou
    makest
      The parted—one.

THE BELLS OF SAN BLAS

What say the Bells of San Blas
To the ships that southward pass
  From the harbour of Mazatlan?
To them it is nothing more
Than the sound of surf on the
    shore,—
  Nothing more to master or man.

But to me, a dreamer of dreams,
To whom what is and what seems
  Are often one and the same,—
The Bells of San Blas to me
Have a strange, wild melody,
  And are something more than a
    name.

For bells are the voice of the
    Church;
They have tones that touch and
    search
  The hearts of young and old;
One sound to all, yet each
Lends a meaning to their speech,
  And the meaning is manifold.

They are a voice of the Past,
Of an age that is fading fast,
  Of a power austere and grand;
When the flag of Spain unfurled
Its folds o'er this western world,
  And the Priest was lord of the
    land.

The chapel that once looked down
On the little seaport town
  Has crumbled into dust;
And on oaken beams below
The bells swing to and fro,
  And are green with mould and
    rust.

"Is, then, the old faith dead,"
They say, "and in its stead
  Is some new faith proclaimed,
That we are forced to remain
Naked to sun and rain,
  Unsheltered and ashamed?

"Once in our tower aloof
We rang over wall and roof
  Our warnings and our com-
    plaints;
And round about us there
The white doves filled the air,
  Like the white souls of the
    saints.

"The saints! Ah, have they grown
Forgetful of their own?
  Are they asleep, or dead,
That open to the sky
Their ruined Missions lie,
  No longer tenanted?

"Oh, bring us back once more
The vanished days of yore,
  When the world with faith was
    filled;
Bring back the fervid zeal,
The hearts of fire and steel,
  The hands that believe and
    build.

"Then from our tower again
We will send over land and main
  Our voices of command,
Like exiled kings who return
To their thrones, and the people
    learn
  That the Priest is lord of the
    land!"

O Bells of San Blas, in vain
Ye call back the Past again!
  The Past is deaf to your prayer:
Out of the shadows of night
The world rolls into light;
  It is daybreak everywhere.

THE SLAVE'S DREAM

Beside the ungathered rice he lay,
  His sickle in his hand;
His breast was bare, his matted
    hair
  Was buried in the sand.
Again, in the mist and shadow of
    sleep,
  He saw his Native Land.

Wide through the landscape of his
  dreams
The lordly Niger flowed;
Beneath the palm-trees on the plain
Once more a king he strode;
And heard the tinkling caravans
  Descend the mountain-road.

He saw once more his dark-eyed
  queen
  Among her children stand;
They clasped his neck, they kissed
  his cheeks,
  They held him by the hand!—
A tear burst from the sleeper's lids
  And fell into the sand.

And then at furious speed he rode
  Along the Niger's bank;
His bridle-reins were golden chains,
  And, with a martial clank,
At each leap he could feel his
  scabbard of steel
  Smiting his stallion's flank.

Before him, like a blood-red flag,
  The bright flamingoes flew;
From morn till night he followed
  their flight,
  O'er plains where the tamarind
  grew,
Till he saw the roofs of Caffre huts,
  And the ocean rose to view.

At night he heard the lion roar,
  And the hyena scream,
And the river-horse, as he crushed
  the reeds
  Beside some hidden stream;
And it passed, like a glorious roll
  of drums,
  Through the triumph of his
  dream.

The forests, with their myriad
  tongues,
  Shouted of liberty;
And the Blast of the Desert cried
  aloud,

With a voice so wild and free,
That he started in his sleep and
  smiled
  At their tempestuous glee.

He did not feel the driver's whip,
  Nor the burning heat of day;
For Death had illumined the Land
  of Sleep,
  And his lifeless body lay
A worn-out fetter, that the soul
  Had broken and thrown away!

THE SLAVE SINGING AT
MIDNIGHT

Loud he sang the psalm of David!
He, a Negro and enslaved,
Sang of Israel's victory,
Sang of Zion, bright and free.

In that hour when night is calmest,
Sang he from the Hebrew Psalmist,
In a voice so sweet and clear
That I could not choose but hear.

Songs of triumph, and ascriptions,
Such as reached the swart Egyp-
  tians,
When upon the Red Sea coast
Perished Pharaoh and his host.

And the voice of his devotion
Filled my soul with strangee mo-
  tion;
For its tones by turns were glad,
Sweetly solemn, wildly sad.

Paul and Silas in their prison
Sang of Christ, the Lord arisen,
And an earthquake's arm of might
Broke their dungeon-gates at night.

But, alas! what holy angel
Brings the Slave this glad evangel?
And what earthquake's arm of
  might
Breaks his dungeon-gates at night?

THE WITNESSES

In Ocean's wide domains,
  Half buried in the sands,
Lie skeletons in chains,
  With shackled feet and hands.

Beyond the fall of dews,
  Deeper than plummet lies,
Float ships, with all their crews,
  No more to sink nor rise.

There the black Slave-ship swims,
  Freighted with human forms,
Whose fettered, fleshless limbs
  Are not the sport of storms.

These are the bones of Slaves;
  They gleam from the abyss;
They cry from yawning waves,
  "We are the Witnesses!"

Within Earth's wide domains
  Are markets for men's lives;
Their necks are galled with chains,
  Their wrists are cramped with
    gyves.

Dead bodies, that the kite
  In deserts makes its prey;
Murders, that with affright
  Scare schoolboys from their
    play!

All evil thoughts and deeds;
  Anger, and lust, and pride;
The foulest, rankest weeds,
  That choke Life's groaning tide!

These are the woes of Slaves;
  They glare from the abyss;
They cry from unknown graves,
  "We are the Witnesses!"

THE WARNING

Beware! The Israelite of old, who
    tore
  The lion in his path,—when,
    poor and blind,
He saw the blessed light of heaven
    no more,
  Shorn of his noble strength and
    forced to grind
In prison, and at last led forth to be
A pander to Philistine revelry,—

Upon the pillars of the temple laid
  His desperate hands, and in its
    overthrow
Destroyed himself, and with him
    those who made
  A cruel mockery of his sightless
    woe;
The poor, blind Slave, the scoff
    and jest of all,
Expired, and thousands perished
    in the fall!

There is a poor, blind Samson in
    this land,
  Shorn of his strength and bound
    in bonds of steel,
Who may, in some grim revel,
    raise his hand,
  And shake the pillars of this
    Commonweal,
Till the vast Temple of our liberties
A shapeless mass of wreck and
    rubbish lies.

MEZZO CAMMIN

*Written at Boppard, on the Rhine, Augus
25, 1842, just before leaving for home.*

Half of my life is gone, and I have
    let
  The years slip from me and have
    not fulfilled
  The aspiration of my youth, to
    build

Some tower of song with lofty
   parapet.
Not indolence, nor pleasure, nor
   the fret
   Of restless passions that would
     not be stilled,
   But sorrow, and a care that
     almost killed,
   Kept me from what I may ac-
     complish yet;
Though, half-way up the hill, I see
   the Past
   Lying beneath me with its sounds
     and sights,—
   A city in the twilight dim and
     vast,
With smoking roofs, soft bells, and
   gleaming lights,—
   And hear above me on the
     autumnal blast
   The cataract of Death far thun-
     dering from the heights.

THE CROSS OF SNOW

In the long, sleepless watches of
   the night,
   A gentle face—the face of one
     long dead—
Looks at me from the wall,
   where round its head
   The night-lamp casts a halo of
     pale light.
Here in this room she died; and
   soul more white
   Never through martyrdom of
     fire was led
   To its repose: nor can in books
     be read
   The legend of a life more
     benedight.
There is a mountain in the distant
   West
   That, sun-defying, in its deep
     ravines
   Displays a cross of snow upon
     its side.

Such is the cross I wear upon my
   breast
   These eighteen years, through
     all the changing scenes
   And seasons, changeless since
     the day she died.

AMALFI

Sweet the memory is to me
Of a land beyond the sea,
Where the waves and mountains
   meet,
Where, amid her mulberry-trees
Sits Amalfi in the heat,
Bathing ever her white feet
In the tideless summer seas.

In the middle of the town,
From its fountains in the hills,
Tumbling through the narrow
   gorge,
The Canneto rushes down,
Turns the great wheels of the mills,
Lifts the hammers of the forge.

'Tis a stairway, not a street,
That ascends the deep ravine,
Where the torrent leaps between
Rocky walls that almost meet.
Toiling up from stair to stair
Peasant girls their burdens bear;
Sunburnt daughters of the soil,
Stately figures tall and straight,
What inexorable fate
Dooms them to this life of toil?

Lord of vineyards and of lands,
Far above the convent stands.
On its terraced walk aloof
Leans a monk with folded hands,
Placid, satisfied, serene,
Looking down upon the scene
Over wall and red tiled roof;

Wondering unto what good end
All this toil and traffic tend,
And why all men cannot be
Free from care and free from pain,
And the sordid love of gain,
And as indolent as he.

Where are now the freighted barks
From the marts of east and west?
Where the knights in iron sarks
Journeying to the Holy Land,
Glove of steel upon the hand,
Cross of crimson on the breast?
Where the pomp of camp and court?
Where the pilgrims with their prayers?
Where the merchants with their wares,
And their gallant brigantines
Sailing safely into port
Chased by corsair Algerines?

Vanished like a fleet of cloud,
Like a passing trumpet-blast,
Are those splendours of the past,
And the commerce and the crowd!
Fathoms deep beneath the seas
Lie the ancient wharves and quays
Swallowed by the engulfing waves;
Silent streets and vacant halls,
Ruined roofs and towers and walls;
Hidden from all mortal eyes
Deep the sunken city lies:
Even cities have their graves!

This is an enchanted land!
Round the headlands far away
Sweeps the blue Salernian bay
With its sickle of white sand:
Further still and furthermost
On the dim-discovered coast
Paestum with its ruins lies,
And its roses all in bloom
Seem to tinge the fatal skies
Of that lonely land of doom.

On his terrace, high in air,
Nothing doth the good monk care
For such worldly themes as these.
From the garden just below
Little puffs of perfume blow,
And a sound is in his ears
Of the murmur of the bees
In the shining chestnut-trees;
Nothing else he heeds or hears.
All the landscape seems to swoon
In the happy afternoon;
Slowly o'er his senses creep
The encroaching waves of sleep,
And he sinks as sank the town,
Unresisting, fathoms down,
Into caverns cool and deep!

Walled about with drifts of snow,
Hearing the fierce north wind blow,
Seeing all the landscape white,
And the river cased in ice,
Comes this memory of delight.
Comes this vision unto me
Of a long-lost Paradise
In the land beyond the sea.

As the ocean surge o'er sand
Bears a swimmer safe to land,
    Kyrat safe his rider bore;
Rattling down the deep abyss
Fragments of the precipice
    Rolled like pebbles on a shore.

Roushan's tasselled cap of red
Trembled not upon his head,
    Careless sat he and upright;
Neither hand nor bridle shook,
Nor his head he turned to look,
    As he galloped out of sight.

Flash of harness in the air,
Seen a moment like the glare
    Of a sword drawn from its sheath;
Thus the phantom horseman passed,
And the shadow that he cast
    Leaped the cataract underneath.

Reyhan the Arab held his breath
While this vision of life and death
    Passed above him. "Allahu!"
Cried he. "In all Koordistan
Lives there not so brave a man
    As this Robber Kurroglou!"

A WRAITH IN THE MIST

"Sir, I should build me a fortification, if I
came to live here."—BOSWELL'S *Johnson*.

On the green little isle of Inch-
        kenneth,
    Who is it that walks by the shore,
So gay with his Highland blue
        bonnet,
    So brave with his targe and
        claymore?

His form is the form of a giant,
    But his face wears an aspect of
        pain;
Can this be the Laird of Inch-
        kenneth?
    Can this be Sir Allan McLean?

Ah, no! It is only the Rambler,
    The Idler, who lives in Bolt
        Court,
And who says, were he Laird of
        Inchkenneth,
    He would wall himself round
        with a fort.

CHAUCER

An old man in a lodge within a
        park;
    The chamber walls depicted all
        around
    With portraitures of huntsman,
        hawk, and hound,
    And the hurt deer. He listen-
        eth to the lark,
Whose song comes with the sun-
        shine through the dark
    Of painted glass in leaden lattice
        bound;

He listeneth and he laugheth at
        the sound,
    Then writeth in a book like any
        clerk.
He is the poet of the dawn, who
        wrote
    The Canterbury Tales, and his
        old age
    Made beautiful with song; and
        as I read
I hear the crowing cock, I hear the
        note
    Of lark and linnet, and from
        every page
    Rise odours of ploughed field or
        flowery mead.

MILTON

I pace the sounding sea-beach and
        behold
    How the voluminous billows
        roll and run,
    Upheaving and subsiding, while
        the sun
    Shines through their sheeted
        emerald far unrolled,
And the ninth wave, slow gather-
        ing fold by fold
    All its loose-flowing garments
        into one,
    Plunges upon the shore, and
        floods the dun
    Pale reach of sands, and changes
        them to gold.
So in majestic cadence rise and fall
    The mighty undulations of thy
        song,
    O sightless bard, England's
        Maeonides!
And ever and anon, high over all
    Uplifted, a ninth wave superb
        and strong,
    Floods all the soul with its
        melodious seas.

THE TIDES

I saw the long line of the vacant
  shore,
  The sea-weed and the shells
    upon the sand,
  And the brown rocks left bare
    on every hand,
  As if the ebbing tide would flow
    no more.
Then heard I, more distinctly than
  before,
  The ocean breathe and its great
    breast expand,
  And hurrying came on the de-
    fenceless land
  The insurgent waters with
    tumultuous roar.

All thought and feeling and desire,
  I said,
  Love, laughter, and the exultant
    joy of song
  Have ebbed from me for ever!
    Suddenly o'er me
They swept again from their deep
  ocean bed,
  And in a tumult of delight, and
    strong
  As youth, and beautiful as
    youth, upbore me.

A NAMELESS GRAVE

"A soldier of the Union mustered
  out,"
  Is the inscription on an un-
    known grave
  At Newport News, beside the
    salt-sea wave,
  Nameless and dateless; sentinel
    or scout
Shot down in skirmish, or disas-
  trous rout
  Of battle, when the loud
    artillery drave
  Its iron wedges through the
    ranks of brave
  And doomed battalions, storm-
    ing the redoubt.

Thou unknown hero sleeping by
  the sea
  In thy forgotten grave! with
    secret shame
  I feel my pulses beat, my fore
    head burn,
When I remember thou hast given
  for me
  All that thou hadst, thy life, thy
    very name,
  And I can give thee nothing in
    return.

THE TIDE RISES, THE
TIDE FALLS

The tide rises, the tide falls,
The twilight darkens, the curlew
  calls;
Along the sea-sands damp and
  brown
The traveller hastens toward the
  town,
  And the tide rises, the tide falls.

Darkness settles on roofs and
  walls,
But the sea in the darkness calls
  and calls;
The little waves, with their soft
  white hands,
Efface the footprints in the sands,
  And the tide rises, the tide falls.

The morning breaks; the steeds in
  their stalls
Stamp and neigh, as the hostler
  calls;
The day returns, but nevermore
Returns the traveller to the shore,
  And the tide rises, the tide falls.

L'ENVOI

Ye voices, that arose
After the Evening's close,
And whispered to my restless
    heart repose!

Go, breathe it in the ear
Of all who doubt and fear,
And say to them, "Be of good
    cheer!"

Ye sounds, so low and calm,
That in the groves of balm
Seemed to me like an angel's
    psalm!

Go, mingle yet once more
With the perpetual roar
Of the pine forest, dark and hoar!

Tongues of the dead, not lost,
But speaking from death's frost,
Like fiery tongues at Pentecost!

Glimmer, as funeral lamps,
Amid the chills and damps
Of the vast plain where Death
    encamps!

EVERYMAN'S LIBRARY: A Selected List

This List covers a selection of volumes available in Everyman's Library. Those volumes marked with a ★ indicate that a paperback edition of this title is also available. Numbers only of hardback editions are given.

BIOGRAPHY

ESSAYS AND CRITICISM

FICTION

2

HISTORY

LEGENDS AND SAGAS

POETRY AND DRAMA